Purpose of a

Snowflake

A lovestory
A lifestory

By Lumi I

A MULBERRY BARK BOOK
Published by
Mulberry Bark LLC

Copyright © 2021 the author

All illustrations in this book are in the public domain, except where noted. Please refer to the Illustrations section for a complete list.

Cover art – Pipochka/Shutterstock.com

For information contact Mulberry Bark LLC.
http://www.mulberrybarkpublishing.com

ISBN: 978-0-9796935-7-1

For the snowflakes, including my Joy (my mother)

&

my soul's mate

Also by the Author

Peter & Terpsi

Best Fudge This Side of the Milky Way

The Fixins

The Radio in the Galaxy's Heart

The Chasmwoe of Phantom Records

The Girl in the Bell Tower

The Wax Girl and the Copper Soldier

The Mask of Aubrey Clover

The Fabric

BOTCHO, IN LOVE WITH A HEADSTONE

"If a love story isn't magical, it isn't a love story at all but a *like* story. I want to write a *love* story."

~Sidereus Sterling

Peppermint

Once upon Christmas in the year one thousand nine hundred fifty-seven, the year Sputnik launched the Space Age, the Cold War got colder, The Grinch stole Christmas for the first time, German chocolate cake debuted, and Elvis wanted to be every girl's "Teddy Bear," I wanted to write a magical wish into my youthful lifestory. But this was a big wish, so to come true, it required a shooting star to wish upon.

I was one-and-ten years young with a nonstandard face and a heart as pink as blush. My young heart was in love with romance, romantic stories, starry-eyed comic books, epics of Knights and Ladies, and all yarns made with pink threads. Ooh, tales penned in "pink ink" were my kind of tales!

I also adored star-silvery science "fiction" stories (I did not see them as so fictitious).

I had always known I wanted my lifestory to be a lovestory, one that married *Cinderella Love* and *Starman*, but I had not transformed my want to be a lovestory heroine into a formal *wish*. So, preserving Ladylike eloquence and Arthurian grandeur, my eleven-year-old heart created this doozy of a wish: I wish-eth to play the *She* from Lord Byron's poem "She Walks in Beauty" for the lonesome one whose night await-eth my light, the one I was promised to meet.

She walks in beauty, like the night

Of cloudless climes and starry skies

I did not just want to be my beloved's wife, the starlight in my soulmate's life, but his guardian angel! (Another part of me wanted to be a nun, but I did not think a nun could be a lovestory heroine, so I was confused about my longing to be one.)

Seven years earlier, I had been in an accident, which I called the "near-death chapter" of my life. Four years old, I had been pronounced dead after almost drowning and freezing in a winter pond. In Heaven's garden, I had enjoyed the sense I was destined to *help* someone special on Earth—I would be his guardian angel. He would be the main character in my story, my best friend, my soul's mate, my lifestory's reason for being written. I had felt promised to meet him someday.

But in case the Heavenly incident had been but a dream (the way adults claimed science *fiction* was just that), I needed to feel reassured that I truly was destined to meet and help this special someone as his *She*. Even though I did not think a big wish *had* to be made on a shooting star, my determination to withstand winter's coldness to see one would let God or my own guardian angel or whoever was in control of the Wish Department know I was serious about this prayer for a friend; plus, a shooting star on Christmas night would commemorate the wish as special.

So, with wish illuminating my eleven-year-old heart, on the cold Christmas night in 1957 in the American south, I trekked icy sidewalks, slippery to my saddle oxfords. In search of a shooting star, I slogged past shabby homes, their chimneys smoking, homes that never welcomed me to warm by their hearths. Nonstandard I journeyed to a lonesome snowy field. I travelled with peppermint bark wrapped in bakery paper in my coat pocket, and my *Space Cadet* lunchbox thermos of hot cocoa, and the great Mullybiski (a handsome stocky pug), who I had asked to stay inside, but with the magnificent heroism of dogs, he stayed by his buddy through rain and hail and anything the world could toss at us. He had at least let me protect his paws from coldness with booties I had knitted for him. Snug under my arm was my teddy bear Root (a quite dapper golden-brown fellow who wore black suspenders and peanut-butter-colored trousers, all handmade by my momma, even the teddy bear himself). I hummed something Glenn Miller until I arrived at the open field, which offered a big CinemaScope view of the nightsky.

In my carnation-pink coat and pink stockings, I stood out in winter, a lone pink flower on an ice sheet, a small flower whose ability to withstand the rugged conditions looked bleak. No tree or hill slowed down frozen wind that fought with my girlish coat and mittens and tiny frame; the brute wind slapped my pale ears and turned my summertime hair into winter by throwing ice into the sunny blonde strands. But the wind did not touch my cross necklace, beneath my coat and warm against my chest. The damp wind whooooshed like wind battling a ship in high sea (or in my case, a tiny canoe), trying to blow me down, or off course, or at least shut me up, while Mullybiski and I braved the icy windstorm to see a shooting star, but none were coming our way.

Pained by the cold and knowing my pug pal was too, I was on the verge of giving up...maybe there was no magic in the universe capable of writing a shooting star into my story, or maybe my wish for love was not meant to be...

Then...

In that miniature blizzard, I saw Sputnik! Ooh my!

Even though camaraderie between the Soviet Bloc and American Bloc was freezing into an ice block during Cold War tensions, I adored the Russian spacecraft, imagined him as alive, had tried to talk to him with walkie-talkie, and did not care if other Americans were suspicious of his "true motives."

Defiantly, my girly voice *softly* uttered my wish, not stooping to the bully wind's churlish shouting; each warm soft word made tiny floating "ghosts" in cold air like wisps of my spirit becoming visible. Since there was not a shooting star in the sky, I wished upon the orbiting Sputnik (up there all alone); I wished, with all my young lighted heart, to be *She*—the main character in my soulmate's lovestory.

Maybe the lonesome one whose night awaited my light would be a solitary space wanderer, a sailor in the stars, in need of companionship on long cold voyages through darkness; maybe he would be a marooned alien, seeking a friend on Earth who would share peppermint bark; maybe he would be the molasses-haired aeronaut (Mars-naut?) I had once seen in an empty wheatfield. I just knew he would be a character in some fantastic scenario perfect for *Tales of Tomorrow* or *Science Fiction Theater*! I knew he would belong at King Arthur's Round Table.

I knew he would be in need of my help. And I knew he would be lonely, for I, too, was lonely, not a *gray* lonely, and that was one source of my lonesomeness: everywhere, everyone, everything was headstone gray, whereas I was petal *pink*.

Pink or not, I also knew I did not have the model face for the role of *She*, another source of my lonesomeness.

Society wrote homely women, with eyeglasses shackled to their appearances with long chains anchoring them to solitude, had to play the moth, not the butterfly. But an even drearier fate than the plainly woman's fate awaited my compliance, for the plainly woman could still play a she, a lowercase she, not a capitalized cursive spectacular *She*, not a muse for a poem or a light in a man's night, but a she nonetheless. Although plainly she might suffer a difficult time procuring employment, since job ads usually stated, "Wanted: <u>Attractive</u> Girl" for secretary or typist or any other job whose skills did not require good looks but whose boss did, and most likely she would have an even tougher time securing a husband, she would still be granted civilities, Earthly customs, such as being smiled at and having doors opened for her, except for by the very boorish. And if she had a "good head on her shoulders" and could sew and cook and type efficiently, she might acquire employment, husband, and *tolerable* life, as long as homely she did not expect her *dream* husband, career, or life. But this world did not want me cast in even the role of wife-of-last-resort or traditional spinster, not in the role of female at all, because my face was not standard, and I was considered a waste of femaleness. I did not have one of those bloomed-in-springtime faces where boys wanted to pick a kiss; I had one of those hearts but not one of those faces.

My face might have bloomed into prettiness if not for the fluke of an accident, which had robbed my appearance of any hope of being immortalized as beautiful in poem or painting. The frozen pond had frostbitten my face so viciously, most of my natural face had to be removed and reconstructed.

Whereas other human faces were like clay molded with symmetry (exact lines, nose mounds), my face looked like flat clay, thin across the visible cheekbones, the nose and lips stretched across, a face done by an artist with morbid tastes.

Some of the skin to reconstruct my face had been taken from my hands and feet and legs, more traits of feminine beauty robbed from me and replaced with scars.

Even though I remembered the fantastic "near-death" experience that had followed the accident, I only vaguely remembered the accident, which had flung my dream to be a lovestory heroine so far away, reaching it would require an epical journey usually only achieved in cosmological mythology. I was reminded of the accident's consequences, its mutilation of my looks, through barbed laughs, scowls, and all forms of shunment, even threats of harm, every time I was around humans. Maybe on another world, my face would be standard, even beautiful, and maybe pretty to the space sailor in search of the exotic alien, but human society replied to my nonstandard face, "*You* cannot play pretty pink *She*. *You* must play a monster from those old gothic tales about hunchbacks in bell towers, phantoms in haunted opera houses, and all those

15

other monstrosities who hide in shadowy lairs to protect themselves and to spare everyone else of repulsion." Bluntly and without compassion, society's gray-ink pen wrote over and over for "ugly" characters, "*You* will never be anyone's light. No one wants *you* to be their angel or their true love."

But with the blushy heart planted in me that had blossomed in a Romantic Era flowerbed, I did not want to play the monstrosity. Ooh, I wanted to be the happy-in-love girly character, the peppermint who had turned coldness into sweetness. My dream to be the light in someone's night was part wish/part goal. Only I was in control of my lifestory's pen, so if I wanted to write myself as *She*, see myself as *She*, I could.

She walks in beauty, like the night

Of cloudless climes and starry skies;

And all that's best of dark and bright

Meet in her aspect and her eyes;

Thus mellowed to that tender light

Which heaven to gaudy day denies.

One shade the more, one ray the less,

Had half impaired the nameless grace

Which waves in every raven tress,

Or softly lightens o'er her face;

Where thoughts serenely sweet express,

How pure, how dear their dwelling-place.

And on that cheek, and o'er that brow,

So soft, so calm, yet eloquent,

The smiles that win, the tints that glow,

But tell of days in goodness spent,

A mind at peace with all below,

A heart whose love is innocent!

I knew seeing myself as *She* would be difficult (a constant battle against what mirrors told me) and writing myself as *She* would be challenging (keeping my mind at peace in an unpeaceful story, maintaining a heart whose love was innocent in a tainted world, spending days in goodness in that same wicked world, and believing myself light when the world saw me as monstrous), but the prayer was for *someone else* to *see me* as light—that was the Christmas miracle I sought. Folks did not pray for the easy stuff. Prayers were said to request miracles. Someone wanting to befriend *me*, someone non-teddy bear or sans paws, would be miraculous. But in a magical universe, the kind I had seen in my Heavenly moment, miracles could happen. And I would return the miracle as this someone's Earth angel (although I was not sure how or what kind of help this special someone needed from me).

With wish still illuminating my young heart that holiday night in '57, I walked back to the cold gray dead house of thieves in gray town, where Christmas had ended. The houses looked like gravestones where dreams lay dead beneath rotted foundations built by desperation, and stars were hidden by homes that did not welcome me, and icy wind threatened to blow the light out in my heart too, not a single candle aglow in any window in gray town, and all the chimney smoke looked like the ashes of every wish blown out in the cold world, and doubt got closer with each chilly step until it was right upon me in the form of a cold door that promised, "You'll never really leave this gray hearthless house," as all around me gloomsome society warned if I continued to try to write a lovestory, my attempt to reach out would be greeted with thorn, not rose.

Whereas if I turned numb and icy like the others, I could avoid feeling *anything* in my quarantined lair, and I could avoid further embarrassment if I stopped believing in magic and drinking childish cocoa to warm myself; if I accepted that every *one* was not an island but an iceberg, if I acquiesced to my tragic fate to be

18

stranded on my iceberg where love would never visit, I would not be completely sequestered from humanity, because I would fit into this planet's icy gray story, where love and happiness and warmth were transient even for the lucky pretty ones whose pink ink always faded to gray eventually in a world that had stopped believing in "happily ever after" after the big war, and I, too, would have to settle for bitter coffee to lessen life's chill and to keep me going in this crumb bum's story, not an angel's story, kid.

But if I childishly insisted on trying to pen the magical Cinderella's castle of romances, on each page of my lifestory the world would play the Wicked Stepmother intent on keeping the glass slipper from my nonstandard foot and erasing not only the "happily" but also the "ever after."

Apple &
Cherry

W hether my story would turn out happily ever after

was uncertain, but my lifestory began happily ever before…

My birth on this planet coincided with the blooming of flowers.

In 1946, I was born in the warm spring that flowered after the big war, along with a hotchpotch of apple and cherry blossoms, Nat King Cole's *(I Love You) For Sentimental Reasons*, the first Almond Joys, and Viktor Frankl's *Man's Search for Meaning*, a book which offered a hope-carved path to happiness out of the despair of the Holocaust.

Our home, a tiny wooden shack the color of a dull nickel, was off the map in meadowy Stargust, where I could believe gusts of stars wafted in on warm rich appley cherry breezes, breezes that touched softly, when the world was pretty, endlessly, across forests sprinkled in pastel springtime colors, vast cotton candy meadows full of flowers in butterscotchy daytime and stars in molassesy nighttime.

My brand-new heart was as soft and shiny pink as blushed roses. My favorite being in the world, my momma, Moon-Moon, told me I had been created in a flowerbed, which had first been planted in the 1800s (The Romantic Era of romantic poets like Bryon and Wordsworth). I knew she did not mean literally. I had not risen from grass. I had a mother and a father. We lived in the flourishing meadows around forest animals, and I knew how births happened. But at the same time, I was also certain I was made of flowers, in a way, because I could feel a flower fluttering in my chest. I had been *conceived* in a flowerbed, one of the greatest passages in my momma's story: using her love to its highest potential of creating life.

The earliest sentence I remembered writing in my lifestory was of a *feeling* of love for *someone* and for my real father and Moon-Moon, who often wrote nice lines into my days, such as smiling at me for being alive, a long time ago, before I became a thing unused to being smiled at.

Even though on this planet I had been created in the flowers, I was truly one light of the heavens, forever, so taught my real father, during my "near-death" chapter. While my frostbitten lifeless body was rushed to a wintry hospital, where I was pronounced dead for nine minutes, another aspect of me was in a warm sunshiny garden better described as a feeling—peacefulness—than as a location. In this Heavenly garden, my heart burst in rhapsody. Ooh, flowers, flowers all in my chest. Each sunlit breath smelled of sweet fresh apples. The entire experience was perfect. Paradise. My real father was with me, along with his kind ideas and warmest hug I ever felt. I was so happy to be with him again. I worshipped him. He called

21

me "sweetyheart." I was his sweetyheart. That made me happy. The extra little cute "ee" sound—I wasn't just a sweetheart but a sweet-ee-heart. Sing-y-song-y sweetyheart. He said he was *always* with his sweetyheart.

My real father spoke of the magical Heaven, but not magic that implied trickery (a deception) or magic beyond ordinary, but real, familiar, and fantastic magic, and the only description needed to paint fantastic was loving, eternally loving, for love was capable of all sorts of magic. In the Heavenly garden, he spoke of love, not in an explanatory way, but in a way that suggested I was familiar with the topic. I could not remember ever *learning* about love. Maybe no one could. I remembered learning about numbers and words and planets and bills and towns, but not love, just like I had never learned about air—I just knew how to love the way I knew how to breathe, and while breaths kept my body alive, love kept other parts of me alive like happiness, enthusiasm, and confidence.

Marc Chagall once said, "Only love interests me, and I am only in contact with things that revolve around love." That sounded straight from my real father, the star painter. I loved his beautiful heavens with extra bright stars and pink swirls and angels, and so did my momma, who often sang for him.

"Never forget this warm feeling, sweetyheart," he said to his daughter in the garden. "Anytime you're cold, you can always come back here." His words worried me—"You can always come back here." Why would I ever have the need to *come back*? I was never going to leave. But even as I thought that, I was antsy to get back to the meadows and search for more and more of the world with Moon-Moon and Mullybiski. Plus, I sensed I had to go back for I had things to do on Earth and someone special to meet, a fated reunion with the *someone* I loved, whoever and wherever he was, and I would help this someone in some way—that was my destiny.

Then…

I was no longer in the garden. I was in the hospital, yet I still felt my real father's love, so I was big happy even in the cold hospital bed.

My memories before the accident were dream hazy, pleasant memories mostly of the meadows, Moon-Moon, and Mullybiski. But I also retained a memory of a familiar woodland the colors of owls, a forest I could not identify because it did not exist in Stargust, so where did I know these woods from? In my memory of this owl-ish forest, it was snowing, and I had a yearning in my heart for something or someone.

Home from the hospital, I only vaguely remembered the accident, slipping and falling on my face into cracked ice into freezing pond, going in and out of consciousness while Moon-Moon bicycled to town with me in the sidecar, then I had died and visited the Heavenly garden. I no longer recalled the pain, or icy water in my lungs, or numerous resuscitation attempts, just the garden, which had continued to warm and comfort me through weeks in the cold hospital. I also did not quite remember details of my hospital stay, although my face now looked different after surgery, but no one called it "ugly"—trees and stars and dogs did not say mean things, neither did my momma.

Winter was over, spring had arrived, and Moon-Moon told me, while giving me a big momma bear hug as I rested on my cot in the shack, "Ice frostbit your face but never let it frost your heart." She offered me warm cocoa, welcoming me home, and gave me Root, whom she had made while I was in the hospital. Ooh, a teddy bear, wow! I hugged him with all my love.

I was convinced mothers and angels were the same species.

My momma had cultivated Stargust out of love, so we were embraced by love's blossoms everywhere. Deep in my soul, I felt this loving environment was nurturing me to be the character I was destined to be—guardian angel for the someone special I was fated to meet and help.

Until then…

Life with my momma was so pleasant, I pictured us as storybook animals like the cute bunnies from *Peter Rabbit*.

My momma was an older Lady, how old I did not know, but anyone tall seemed ancient to the five-year-old, especially those with hair as silver as the moon, who I knew was old, because he was referred to as "the old moon." I called my momma "Moon-Moon," possibly because that sounded close to "Momma," which I must have heard when also learning about the moon. Like a grandma, Moon-Moon had a pancake softness to her, a sweetness, but also a durability, an unbreakable strength, one of those women who had developed in a generation when women washed clothes with washboard and bucket. Her eyes were twinkly blue (I could see starlight in her), and she kept her blonde-turned-silver hair in a ponytail, dressed like a Quaker, and spoke with a slightly southern genteel accent which pronounced "sweet potato" as "swit putatuh." She had a decorative voice that decorated a room as prettily as a splash of sunshine. She talked the way a teacup would talk, feminine, yes, but not advertising for suitors (she had her true love, even if he was not with her bodily). Not that many suitors would have responded to her ad for love, since her face, unlike her voice, was not decorative (at least not to common eyes). But I saw my momma as beautiful. In my eyes, her face did not need any decoration other than radiance from being in love. She was so in love with my real father and this showed me how bright love could shine. Deeply spiritual, she acted like an angel from a Christmas story with her holiday spirit year-round: charity, mercy, compassion, forgiveness, and the ability to maintain in her being the warm awe inspired by the magic of Christmas lights. Plus,

Moon-Moon's hard gnarled hands gave the softest touches and played the tenderest music.

Moon-Moon was a "harp whisperer": she was able to make the harp reveal its heart. She, too, loved flowers, and her songs were the marigolds of music, which she bloomed for him.

If an adult had asked me what my momma did "for a living," I would not have understood the concept of a job, the meaning of money. My momma created music with her harp. We did not have money; we relied on bartering and charity, which Moon-Moon returned tenfold.

My momma had once been a member of American "aristocracy"—the wealthy—an "old" southern family whose bloodline traced back to castles in England. Moon-Moon, the *second* family rebel, had created the second set of footprints away from Wyndclif (her family's estate); her "crazy" aunt had become a Catholic nun and had flown off to France in the First World War to be a nurse and died from a bomb attack on the field hospital. Like her aunt, Moon-Moon had felt the mansion as cold as a tomb to her soul. Amidst everything she had owned, something had been missing, the something needed to revive her soul. She had preferred to sleep outdoors, give away money, make friends with birds instead of socialites, and she had been unwilling to let a cook prepare her meals or a maid wash her clothing, and she had not consented to marrying her family's selection of suitor, a "robber baron," a prosperous industrialist intent on building over the very land she loved with factories for manufacturing of all things: barb wire. Her family, ashamed of her rebellious ways, had given her a choice: conform, stay in luxury in Wyndclif, behind the safety of "barb wire," or leave by herself to the world of plenty hardships and scarce resources, where she would never again be granted access to luxuries stored behind the barbed fence. They had given her this ultimatum in winter, thinking the prospect of facing harsh coldness by herself would force her to stay in Wyndclif. Instead, my momma had given up her crown, twenty-four-room mansion, gilded grave and silver spoon, and respect from the world for respect from herself. After the gates of fortune had shut her out, she had set out with one suitcase, one coat, and a simple, floppy, Charlie Chaplin of a bicycle with front basket and sidecar (where her belongings had ridden), an uncommon endeavor for a Lady in the 1920s. She had ventured to find meaning in life and luxury in flowerbeds and a home within herself and to offer compassion in the Great Depression and to make music in the free meadows for her love, who she had met in peaceful solitude and who had resuscitated her soul. The journey, where she had used a blanket for shelter and one cup for water wherever she had been able to find it, had been more difficult than she had expected; she had learned scarcity of resources was not as problematic as scarcity of generosity. But the trek had gifted her numerous bedtime stories to tell her daughter like the time she had slept in a tree's hollow during a windy rainy night. She and her "illegitimate" daughter had been written out of the family fortune and shunned by the "blue bloods" in an alleged "fall from grace." My momma had endured pleading with her tight-hearted and tight-pursed family for money for my surgeries and suffering their haughty, "We told you so, you common loon."

No longer aristocracy, we did not have many material items, but since we did not have many, I appreciated and got to know each item specially and even named some of them. We had Moon-Moon's beautiful sunshiny harp (Angelica), and her simple bicycle (Charlie), and her girlhood musical angel snow globe (Karen), who had traveled with her on the long journey. The snow globe always stirred my heart with memories of the owl-ish snowy woodland I could not identify. Ooh, we had a few special storybooks and coloring books and comic books. We had an old set of encyclopedias, dictionary, and thesaurus (Thomas), and an old slate board and sticks of chalk for me to practice arithmetic and writing, and her old Brownie camera (Buster) shaped like a tiny brown suitcase with handle, which I thought the neatest contraption in the world. We had the "evil" pond, the scene of my accident, which from then on I had tried to avoid, until Moon-Moon had held my hand and led me into the waters, which had felt welcoming warm in the pond's summer form; eventually I had learned how to swim in the very pond that had once almost drowned me. We had a well house with gable that looked like a storybook wishing well, and an outhouse that was not so fantastical, and the electricity-less shack with a warm hearth and a ceiling whose wooden boards had enough space between them for the sky and stars to peek in, rain too, which meant we also had buckets. We had a couch and cots (wooden frames and handsewn mattresses and pillows puffy with cotton). We had a clothesline and wash bucket and clothes like my handsewn dresses and strap shoes and my momma's dress the color of sweet potato skin. We had an icebox (Groucho) and limited food, durable food, hard blocks of bread and hard wheels of cheese and hard barrels of potatoes and hard cornmeal (grits stock), except for *soft* cherry bread or apple bread with soft morsels of apples and cherries on occasion. We had a windowsill herb garden and an old wagon for carting fruits and veggies. We had jars of molasses, which I thought the most handsome sights in the meadow, rich black syrup shining in sunlight, and the *yearning* to one day taste molasses was almost as delicious as the molasses. We had dull silverware that looked like a Knight's armor after a long battle, and delicate pretty Ladylike cups and plates decorated in flowers, and utensils like a cast iron Dutch oven for making everything from biscuits to vegetable soup, and we had a raw wood table where Moon-Moon often rolled flour over dough with a rolling pin, and I often got to make different shapes out of the dough, such as stars. We had a hand pump sink (Gort), where we washed fresh vegetables and often laughed when Gort did not feel like working. We had a glassless window above the sink, where beside potted herbs a battery-operated radio perched, sometimes radiating sunshiny music in daytime and starlit *Swinging on a Star* at nighttime, although we had to conserve battery power, and sometimes the music was interrupted with gloomy reports about the big war's aftermath and "growing tensions."

Root, Mullybiski, and I preferred *Doc Savage,* my favorite radio show about the heroic scientist, adventurer, detective, musician, and polymath who righted wrongs and strove to dedicate each life

27

moment to making himself better, so that all would profit from his goodness, while taking everything that came his way with a smile, without loss of courage. Such a hero!

I also adored mystery shows and making up my own endings; all the shows tasted good with rare slices of pie (sweet potato, pecan, whatever nature provided).

We did not have a television and listening to the battery-operated radio was only done on occasion and going to the movie house was an even rarer event; even books and comics were in small supply in our shed, so I had to make up my own stories, one of the greatest gifts a budding writer could ever have: imagination!

Pretending to be Sherlock Holmes, I would go outside and search for mysteries to solve, alongside Mullybiski and Root. I treasured taking a piece of cherry pie or apple bread out into the soft warmth of nighttime, ringing with songs of crickets and birds and other night beings. I was as fond of the nightsky as I was of cocoa; the sight of evening gave me the same warm feeling as a cup of hot chocolate. The stars had put out a welcome mat for me, and I had made friends with the old moon, who was exceptionally polite, not even a tad cranky.

I knew if I kept strolling past the stems as tall as me, I would eventually be up close with stars, the flowers of the sky, because in the meadow, no buildings, no barriers existed between me and the heavens and my star family.

Moon-Moon once said, "The stars of Lovers are different than the stars of non-lovers—the difference between pinpoints of light and fireworks." I believed stars were alive, just like the flowers, so I thought my momma had meant stars in love looked different than stars not in love. Feeling bad for those unloved stars, I invited them to a tea party, just by saying it aloud, "Come to my tea party to-mor-row."

Moon-Moon had retained two "aristocratic" traits: a liking for ballroom dancing and for cream tea, which her daughter also loved, afternoon tea (warm cocoa, or "cream cocoa," for me) with scones and jam and clotted cream, although we rarely had cream, thus we used butter, and sometimes we had "savory teatime" with the neatest miniature sandwiches (cucumber and cress); and we sometimes transformed the entire meadow into a ballroom of starlight.

I told my grand plan about the tea party to Moon-Moon over springtime breakfast of cherry muffins with apricot jam; *Sentimental Me* was on the morning radio.

My momma said, "Stars are big, even bigger than the old moon, too big to fit at the tea table, but you can still enjoy their company at a distance."

(The "tea table" was a tree stump, where I sometimes placed Moon-Moon's tea set for a tea party, unaware the stump had been part of a tree, or else I would not have desecrated it, for I revered trees.)

"The stars don't look big," I said, sitting at the sunlit table and kicking my legs up and down, excited just to be alive, the flower in my chest fluttering about the upcoming tea party.

"That's because the stars are so far away, the way trees look small until you get up close to them."

"Ooh?" My legs stopped swinging. "How far away?"

"You would need a ship to get to a star."

I imagined a sailboat. Maybe I could construct it that afternoon with one of the buckets and some clothes for sails, but…

"It would have to be a biiiiggggggg ship to sail the stars here," I said, letting my momma know I believed her about the stars being big and I was aware this starship endeavor would take effort.

"You can't sail the stars here; they're made to stay in the sky, and I don't know if the ship to get to the stars would have to be big, but it would have to be a special ship that could travel very fast and far, and no such ship exists yet on Earth."

"Why not?"

"Because no one has been able to build one yet."

"That's crummy!" I was irritated and crossed my arms over my chest as if protecting the flower from suffering any more news that might make it stop fluttering.

"Why is that crummy?"

"That's not nice. The stars can't be friends with us."

"Why can't they be friends with you?"

"Because they're sooooo faaaarrrr away!"

"The moon is far away and you call him a friend."

I had never considered the moon far away; he looked close to Earth, but thanks for telling me he was far away too, I grumbled.

"And you still talk to the stars, don't you?" my momma asked in her way of saying I already had the answer.

Stars can't come to Earth? That was baloney! Moon-Moon had just forgotten this:

"Shooting stars come to Earth, so they can't be that far away."

"They're far away and that's a good thing. Someday I'll explain."

I didn't need it explained to me, thank you very much. I was a star from the heavens and one day I became a shooting star that got put into Moon-Moon's belly, where I was made out of the same petally stuff that made flowers, just made differently, the way flour could make both pies and cakes, then voila!, I came out when the flowers bloomed, and when the flowers wilted, I'd be starlight again in the heavens.

But I had to get this straight: "You're saying I can't walk to a star?"

"You can keep walking to the stars, and maybe on that path, you'll encounter a starship. No one has made a ship that can voyage that far *yet*, but…"

The prospect of meeting someone who would make such a ship made me happy, and I got over the crumminess of stars being so far away, since now I just needed a ship to meet them.

"Maybe someday, Lumi, and remember this, even though a star is not *beside* you, the star's light is *inside* you—even at a great distance, it warms your skin and enters your sight and becomes a part of you."

She had named me Lumi to symbolize the *light* of her life, and from this, I gained a lifelong appreciation of symbolism. Moon-Moon spoke symbolically often, and even when I did not understand the symbolism, I sensed an underlying message in her words like when she said, "Sweetness is most appreciated after a taste of sourness."

I reconsidered being an actual star from the heavens after learning it was *light*, not the whole star, that traveled. Maybe my real father had been using a parable to make my true nature easier to see, the way my momma used parables to teach me. I was a light from Heaven, but not exactly a star from the sky.

After learning about starships, I "fell" in love with (*rose* in love with) science fiction, especially Starman, astronomer Theodore "Ted" Knight by day, member of the Justice Society of America, World War II pilot, and creator of the cosmic staff which allowed him to fly; Starman's existence I learned of from an old comic

Moon-Moon had gotten for me. I called him "Teddy," not "Ted," and I saw Starman as even more fantastic than Doc Savage—I thought if I didn't marry Teddy Knight, if he wasn't the special someone, I'd be surprised (and disappointed by the story).

Since I loved stories, my momma turned stories into a metaphor. "The world is a very long storybook written by many, many different writers, all with different tastes and characters; these writers pen their own stories within the one big story, and sometimes Earth itself writes sentences, such as 'Sunny today, rainy tomorrow,' and how you respond to Earth's sentences speaks of your character, so does how you respond to what anyone writes in your story. Sometimes people will write mean sentences into your life, sometimes nice sentences, sometimes helpful, sometimes hurtful, and whatever they write is a reflection of their character, but whatever *you* write in response is a statement about *your* character. What statement do you want to make with this lifestory of yours?"

We sat on the couch during this lesson, and she looked over at the kitchen counter, where stood Frankl's *Man's Search for Meaning*. "A very brave man, one of the superheroes of our world, wrote that book. Someday, I want you to read it. For now, I want you to understand everyone has a pen in this story, and you, only you, control your pen. If everyone is writing 'Blah blah blah,' you don't have to, and if everyone is writing 'Hate, hate, hate,' you can still write 'Love, love, love.' Each of us only gets so much ink, or so much crayon, and if you realize that, you'll be very conscientious of how you spend your ink, especially if you remember we don't write our lifestories in pencil. They're written in ink. So try never to write any page, not even one word, that you will eventually want to tear out of your story, because you can't tear out pages, you can't even erase sentences, and when the ink runs thin, you will be the one who has to read your story back and decide if it was good or not, or if you wasted your precious ink. Dip your pen into the light of Heaven to write your lifestory and your moments will shine and warm all nearby."

Every day, my momma taught me. Sometimes outside, sometimes at the table awash in window light. First, she taught me how to listen. "Hearing and listening are not the same thing. One is an automatic response to sound. The other requires thought, patience, caring, and plain good sense. When someone speaks, if your ears are working, you hear them, but to listen to them, you must *consider* what they're saying." The radio was playing, so to demonstrate her point, Moon-Moon asked, "Do you hear that song?" Yep. "What's the song about?" I didn't know. "That's because you're hearing it but not listening to it. You're listening to me, I hope. Remember that too: listening requires concentration. Listening to two things at once is too distracting. Not only is listening nice to the speaker, but it enhances the listener's patience, empathy, sympathy, and knowledge bank, and crafts your ability to think, consider, ponder, and respond. If you care about someone, you will listen to them, and that will not be a burden but a joy—a chance to visit their ideas and feelings. And remember: listening begets being listened to." And she taught me how *not* to listen when the message rotted the soul, heart, or brain; during those moments, I should simply walk away (no shame in walking away, an action that required courage), but if walking away was not possible, I would have to turn up the voice inside, which would counter the destructive outside message. And she taught me the importance of speaking my own thoughts, standing up for truth and rightness and my individuality and my freedom to express it, and since she believed I had the strength to do this, so did I.

While teaching her child, to make lessons tastier, she offered desserts, sometimes in the form of strawberries or cherries.

She taught principles based on kindness (one of love's children), and these principles tasted sweet and clean and fresh, since I learned them with a mouthful of sweet clean fresh berries, and the principles glistened as shiny and natural as the wholesome good berries.

"Principles," "morals," "values" were as much a part of my life as the stars and as necessary for creating a lovely world.

She taught the concept of religion, and although her beliefs and values usually aligned with Christianity, somewhat with the humanitarian Quaker faith ("God is love and the light of God is inside every individual"), she did not preach any one religion; she said I could learn about all the different religions someday and decide for myself if I wanted to subscribe to any of them or just *some of* their beliefs.

My momma's goal was to preach Goodness. Taking inspiration from Chinese philosopher Mencius, who said all humans were born with the virtue of ren (goodness), Moon-Moon believed in inherent Goodness (a seed that could either be nourished or left to wilt). So, maintaining Goodness was the goal, but Goodness was not just a catchphrase, it had real meaning with a clear definition: to write no lines that caused suffering to myself or any living being in this story, and instead, to pen as much love as possible.

In her quest to champion Goodness, she taught her daughter the story of Little Goody Two-Shoes, a Cinderella character, a poor orphan girl, Margery Meanwell, whose virtue was rewarded in the end (Moon-Moon changed the ending from Meanwell marrying a rich suitor to a *kind* suitor).

She taught me, "Letting go is easy, holding on is hard." Like *Aesop's Fables*, there was *Moon-Moon's Fables*, one whose lesson taught, "If all the apples in a basket eventually turn bad, the apple who does *not* rot is the one with an interesting story; the rest are common."

She taught her child, "Not letting the world change you is how you change the world."

She taught me love stories, such as *Cinderella*—love stories I liked the best. Especially when they were told in starlight. Ooh, I wanted Cinderella's slipper to fit me! In Moon-Moon's version of *Cinderella*, the heroine was not physically beautiful but kind, and through the magic of love, Prince Charming saw her as the most beautiful belle of the ball, since Prince Charming and Cinderella were soulmates.

Soulmate

That word was always capitalized in her voice and given special decoration. A holy garlanded word that glittered. A divine union—soul and mate becoming soulmate. The word, and concept, defined an individual in terms of another: as the mate of another soul. (I recognized the word "mate" from radio shows about adventurous sailors, so I envisioned soul-mates as good ship mates.) My momma often spoke of soulmates, of undying love, which protected my courage like an unbreakable shield—if love could not be broken, no threat could destroy it. As much as I adored being with Moon-Moon, I always felt someone was missing, who being without felt like being in a world without stars; the moon was perfect, but I needed the stars too. Moon-Moon shared with me the nice quote by writer Sidereus Sterling, "If a love story isn't magical, it is not a love story at all but a like story. I want to write a love story." Moon-Moon told me of Lord Byron's *She*. She taught her child, "Those in love are *not* blind; those not in love are blind, unable to see reality." She taught me the world had a great anthology of love stories, love in all its forms (mother to child, child to dog, wife to husband…). Any relationship whose foundation was made of true pure love was a relationship of the soul, but when Moon-Moon spoke of Soulmates, she meant the kind Plato had referred to—two halves of the same being, seeking reunion. (I eventually realized "soul" was what my real father had meant by "one light of Heaven," "the light inside every individual," when Moon-Moon explained "soul" as "the real you," so my soul's mate was the special someone I was destined to meet and help, and the promise of meeting my Teddy Knight someday gave me extra special reason to greet each day wholeheartedly.)

While boys' fathers may have taught them about Knighthood and the Knight's Code of Chivalry (chivalry that I was entirely in love with, a love that would blossom into an adoration for Arthurian legend), my momma taught me about Ladyhood and the Lady's Code of Grace. She used the word "grace" because of its multitude of laced together meanings: kindliness, loveliness, charity, poise, mercy, decency, dignity, elegance, style (style not just in the fashion sense, although style could be reflected in wardrobe too, such as her simple lifestyle was reflected in her simple attire). I could visually see the Code of Grace as an elegant fabric of handsewn lacy traits, each individual trait like a novel crochet pattern in a multicolored blanket, and ooh, it was so lovely, I wanted it to be part of my makeup.

During this lesson, we drank sweet tea and sat outside in springtime grass that warmed our bare legs, exposed beyond our dresses' hemlines.

She taught me about Knights too, such as the Knights of King Arthur's Round Table, Lancelot and Sir Galahad, the gallant virginal Knight destined by God to find the Holy Grail (the cup Jesus supposedly drank from during The Last Supper, and often depicted in Arthurian Romances as a treasure sought by Knights that gifted happiness and eternal life). Teddy *Knight*, I knew, had been properly named.

I loved the opening of *The Book of King Arthur* by Howard Pyle: *"After several years of contemplation and of thought upon the matter herein contained, it has at last come about, by the Grace of God, that I have been able to write this work with such pleasure of spirit that, if it gives to you but a part of the joy that it hath afforded me, I shall be very well content with what I have done."*

I asked, "Are all boys Knights?"

"No, but all have the potential to be. The truth is being a Lady or Knight has nothing to do with being a man or woman, since light is your true nature, and light is neither male nor female. In this story, some girls are Knights and some boys are Ladies, and some play both roles depending on the circumstances; it is just a matter of choice. Remember you get to write the character *you* want to play in the world's storybook." That was a surprising viewpoint for anyone in 1951, but I was not surprised at the time, because Moon-Moon's point of view was the only view I really knew (she did not let the media and its values raise her child).

Knights and Ladies were both brave and tried to prevent injustice from ever happening, but if it did rear its ugly head (almost a certainty in the world's tumultuous story) their bravery was employed for different feats. A Lady would never go off into battle, for a Lady's duty was to make peace, not war, and a Lady had to use bravery to shout "Peace" amidst battle cries of "Pillage, destroy, war!" But a Knight used bravery to be a soldier, if the conflict was unavoidable and a battle for restoring goodness, then a Lady would have to employ bravery again to go into the battlefield and care for the injured the way Moon-Moon's aunt had done in WWI.

My momma taught me of other brave women like Katherine Stinson, one of the first female pilots, a sky-writer (ooh!), the first ever to fly at nighttime, who had been an ambulance driver in World War 1, a duty to bravery that cost Stinson a suffering of tuberculosis. For some reason, the encyclopedia's entry on Stinson ("the flying schoolgirl" who wrote messages of light in the nightsky) made an impression on my mind.

Ooh, I wanted to fly an aeroplane!

My momma taught me of Clara Barton who had founded the American Red Cross and once said, "While our soldiers can stand and fight, I can stand and feed and nurse them."

My momma taught me I should never let the world make me believe membership in Knighthood was more admirable than membership in Ladyhood. Knights and Ladies went together, neither was more important than the other, and they needed each other like night and day to make a complete whole. "Knights and Ladies seeking each other in this storybook of dragons is one of the most exciting plots in the storyline."

Knights and Ladies had duties to one another, such as a Knight defending a Lady, and a Lady keeping a warm hearth for her Knight *only*, and both maintained clean hearts for one another (loyalty was definitely an important trait of both Ladyhood and Knighthood).

Although some aspects of being a Knight sounded fun (the glory and superhero-like helmet), I didn't want to wear a chainmail shirt, so I'd be a Lady; plus, while other girls may have wanted to be like Starman, when I pondered my feelings for him, I knew I did not want to *be* Starman but to *marry* Starman. Not that I didn't want to be superheroic and have adventures, especially in an aeroplane or spaceship, but I wanted to be a superhero Lady—I did not want to fight battles, but I could picture myself making tea for an injured Knight, and the moxie to have cream tea was a brave feat when the war-torn world was crumbling around you.

"Some people want to be Knights and Ladies but have forgotten how to be or think the requirements for membership are beyond their abilities, which is never true. One duty of a Lady is to remind a lost soul of its potential for Knighthood, just as one duty of a Knight is to remind a lost soul of its potential for Ladyship. Knights and Ladies don't leave everyone else behind and seclude themselves in a private castle; they care for all equally."

While the sun started to drop in the sky, Moon-Moon added, "While a Lady respects her Knight, she also respects herself, always remember that, and when a Lady has no Knight to defend her, a Lady must battle her own dragons, and she must never feel un-Ladylike for defending herself and her ideals."

A Lady was always a Lady whether she was pouring tea, flying an aeroplane, or performing "manly" labor, because Ladyness was a collection of internal traits, which manifested in external behavior, such as a Lady's mercy would prevent her from hurting anything.

Ladyhood's membership did not restrict based on past mistakes (Grace was kindness and kindness offered forgiveness), nor did it restrict based on appearance or financial station, which meant the prettiest richest person in the world might not be a Lady if their inner person was at odds with the Lady's Code of Grace, while the poorest "ugliest" person in the world might be the Ladyest of all Ladies if true to Grace, and any Knight worthy of Knighthood would be able to spot a true Lady.

In blooming spring, she taught me briefly about the birds and bees, a lesson she called "pistil and stamen": boy plus girl equals baby, but boy plus girl plus love equals happier scenario. I was too young to truly understand or care about the birds and bees subject, although I adored baby animals—baby rabbits!—and wanted a baby of my own someday (how the conversation got started in the first place). I had seen birthings in the woods, but I wondered how the baby came to be, how a light from Heaven turned into a baby and what mommies' and daddies' roles were in the process (I had to admit I was slightly confused and did need the subject explained to me). From her dreamy voice, I knew she was remembering the beautiful moment that had taken place in the flowerbed where I had been conceived...then I had a realization:

"Are you talking about what the turtles were doing?" I had once seen two turtles engaged in "something" in the forest, and Moon-Moon had explained they were "mating," which had explained nothing, because I knew not what "mating" meant, so Moon-

Moon had gotten away with an easy escape for a discussion she had found unpleasant, but since I had seen the animals' activity as ridiculous, I had not cared for further information. Now I wanted to know: "Yuck—*you* did that, Moon-Moon!?" I threw my hands over my face to keep any more yucky images or icky information from reaching into my head. The "magical" event in the flowerbed which had created me had been *that*?

"Not exactly like that."

"The boy turtle kept going 'wa wa wa wa—'"

"Lumi, stop that. Being in love is nothing to be ashamed of, neither is making a baby." Yet ... "Ooo..." She was flustered and embarrassed too. "Wait for your Knight, Lumi, for your brave Knight deserves a flowerbed that has never been plucked by another. Let him, and only him, be your teacher in the bedchamber." (I had a vision of a Knight and Lady jumping up and down on the bed together because what other activity could make a bed so pleasurable? Definitely not what the turtles had been doing!) "Someday, you'll understand. Pin your hair up for others but let it down for him. You'll love doing that with your Knight, I promise."

Yuck. Would he also go "wa wa wa wa wa"?

During one of our meadow walks, she taught her daughter never to take anyone, or anything, or any activity I loved for granted. She suggested I write as many pleasant and meaningful sentences as possible to fit on a page of life before tomorrow erased my loved ones from my story, or me from theirs.

"Everything in this universe will eventually be gone, even the moon." I was hurt by this news, but she comforted, "I'm telling you this, so you'll appreciate what you love, and when it's gone, you'll have loved it so much, impressed it upon your heart so thoroughly to have made a forever imprint there, you'll still be able to see it even when it's gone from your eyes' sight. But you don't have to worry about the actual moon disappearing in your lifetime, Lumi."

If not the actual moon then … *Moon-Moon?*

"God-willing," she said with a smile, reading my gloomy thoughts, "that won't happen any time soon. This old loon is fairly sturdy."

The certainty of her eventual absence from my story made me very sad—she was my favorite character—so I decided then and there to preserve every detail about her, to impress her image forever upon my heart, and to enjoy each sentence that starred my momma.

On a dig for gemstones, we Ladies sat in dirt in our blue jeans with our hair wrapped in kitchen towel "bandanas," and we uncovered all sorts of goodies in Stargust like pink quartz. Moon-Moon taught me never to be careless with feelings but to treat everyone's feelings as if they were rare fragile jewels to be held gently. She taught me never to be careless period, which she demonstrated by throwing chalk onto the big rock where we were placing the stones, and the chalk broke and crumbled from her carelessness.

On a springtime stroll, my momma taught me that although beautiful sights were pleasant to see, real beauty was not seen but *felt*. To illustrate this, she simply handed me her camera in the meadow and said, "Take a picture of my love for you." She offered, "You can take beautiful pictures of the results of my love for you, such as a big hug, but the love itself cannot be photographed. The most beautiful things in this world, Lumi, are impossible to photograph. You must be able to see those unseeable beauties—love and its offspring, kindness and fairness—to be aware of their eternal existence, even amidst horrific landscape that lies and tells you love is dead." She also taught, "The word 'beautiful' obviously means beautiful but so does the word 'pulchritudinous'–recognize that" and "Pretty hearts also beat behind rags."

She taught me quotes to live by, such as Emily Dickinson's "The poet lights the light and fades away. But the light goes on and on," and The Bible's "Stand still in wonder of God's works," and William Wordsworth's "That best portion of a good man's life, His

42

little, nameless, unremembered acts of kindness and of love," and Henry David Thoreau's "It's not what you look at that matters, it's what you see," and her own quote, "Every time you come across a heart, remember heartstrings are meant to be plucked for making music, not torn for making misery." She adored the Transcendentalists, such as Ralph Waldo Emerson and Thoreau and Margaret Fuller. In the kitchen, she offered morsels of their ideas to me, such as Emerson's, "Live in the sunshine," the way some mothers offered their children cookie dough.

She taught, "Compassion is lotion for the feelings."

She taught, "The me you're encountering here is the same me you'll encounter in Paris, the same me in Georgia, the same me on Mars…When in Rome, do what *you* feel is right."

She taught, "If you don't have something nice to say, you need to redo your heart."

She taught, "Once a week, author one passage in your story by kindness—and your story will go down in history as one of the great epics." And "If hearts are soil, many never bloom a single flower—tend yours to blossom a thousand petals."

On a breezy day, she taught me the fable about the wind and the sun. The wind and sun were quarreling about which of them was stronger. To test this, the sun and wind agreed that the one who could make a traveler remove his cloak was stronger. The blustery wind fought the traveler, but each time the brute wind pounced on him with strong cold gusts, the traveler held his cloak *closer* to himself. Then the sun began to shine gently until its rays became warmer and warmer, so warm, the traveler removed his coat, no longer in need of it.

These teachings were the potpourri of our days.

Whatever she taught me, I would then teach to my teddy bear, because Moon-Moon also taught me the importance of teaching (and learning), and that a mother was the ultimate teacher (and learner), so if I wanted a baby of my own someday, I needed to be a good teacher.

And five days a week, Monday through Friday (Saturday was for play exclusively and Sunday for rest and prayer), we sat at the table, where she read two passages from the encyclopedia; we went over the passages systematically, alphabetically, and thoughtfully. Angel. "A messenger who serves God in various ways." Al-ge-bra. For some reason, that encyclopedia entry stayed with me. "Algebra is generalized arithmetic." That explained nothing at all! Moon-Moon schooled, "You'll learn more about algebra when you get older, but first you have to learn arith-me-tic, the science of numbers."

She taught me of saints (Earth angels) like Saint Nicholaus, a bearer of gifts, who Santa Claus was modeled after, and Saint Hildegard of Bingen, who had been a composer and mystic, capable of seeing the "Living Light" surrounding all things, and who wrote, "I spoke and wrote these things not by the invention of my heart or that of any other person, but as by the secret mysteries of God I heard and received them in the heavenly places. And again I heard a voice from Heaven saying to me, 'Cry out, therefore, and write thus!'"

"Write thus!" I adored that quote so much, I made it my life's motto, and Moon-Moon made me a pillow with "Write Thus!" sewn on it.

"Write thus, write thus, write thus!" I chanted like a Lady on the battlefield during my walks in the pastures. I wanted to be a saint! A nun! Why, I'd be just like Saint Hildegard! I might even really make "angel;" after all, I was destined to help someone as his guardian angel.

Moon-Moon taught me of martyrs like St. Stephen, who had been *stoned to death* for preaching the gospel. Okay, maybe I did not want to be a saint!

"Write thus!" Moon-Moon said after telling me the martyr's story, and so as not to scare me too much, patted my head.

We sat together on the couch, a bowl of pecans to be shelled between us, and I hugged the "Write Thus!" pillow. Root sat beside me, and Mullybiski sat on my lap, telling me not to go someplace without him.

Moon-Moon could tell I was still scared, so offered, "Someone who has no fear is not a saint but a superhuman—none of us are superhuman."

"Starman is."

"No, he's just a man, a good man, but not superhuman. Remember he used his smarts and imagination to create the cosmic staff."

"Superman is." I was being cranky and difficult because I was irritable about the "none of us are superhuman" fact; I was getting annoyed by the world and my inability to walk to a star, to have superpowers, to keep people in my life. I did not blame the messenger, my momma, but the message written by a crummy world.

"Superman is from another planet, Lumi. I'm talking about humans."

"Ooh. We can't have any superpowers?"

"Of course, you can and do. Kindness and bravery are superpowers. But we humans all have vices too."

"What's a vice?" I had heard of *vases* but this was the first I had heard of "vices."

"A vice is another word for a weakness, or a shortcoming ... a form of Kryptonite."

Now that made sense. Moon-Moon knew next to nothing about superheroes, but she was *learning* about them because I liked them (mommas were always learning from their children too).

"A vice is a barricade that prevents you from reaching Goodness, like greed can prevent you from doing charity work. The bad guys that Doc Savage battles have lots of vices. But without vices, our character would never be tested. Some traits are always good (compassion, fairness) and always contribute to yours and the world's wellbeing, and some traits are always vices (hatefulness, meanness, greed) and are always harmful to you and the world, but some traits only become bad or good through their outcome, which is always your choice. If fear prevents you from making an unwise decision, it's good, but if it prevents you from making a wise choice, it's bad. If anger causes violence, it's bad, but if it corrects injustice, it's good."

"How will I know the diff-er-ence?"

"Anytime you feel angry or afraid, think about *why* you're angry or afraid, think about what fear and anger are making you want to do, and most importantly, think about the consequences of those actions."

"This is..." "Complicated," but I could not say that word (I understood many words that I could not yet pronounce), although Moon-Moon understood my pronunciation, "complited."

"Being good in a body of vices is not easy."

"Do you have any vices, Moon-Moon?"

"Plenty! Every one, even Knights and Ladies and superheroes, have vices—one reason they're super is because of their ability to conquer their vices. But I don't think it's right to tell you about your momma's vices at your age. Someday, when you're older, we can talk about my vices."

"Aliens don't have vices."

"I don't know about that. But since we're both humans on Earth, I have to teach you about humans and our planet."

I wasn't so sure I wanted to be human or to stay on this planet … although, I certainly did like its flowers and hot chocolate and sunlight and bunnies and storybooks and view of the moon…overall, I concluded, Earth was a pretty good setting for a story; plus, I had to be here to meet *him*.

My momma went on lecturing, warning me about lust, which I did not understand at all.

She explained, "Lust means a strong want. It's kind of like the feeling you have when you yearn for molasses but much, much stronger than that. It's not always a vice; lust can be a beautiful intense feeling between two people in love—"

"How?"

"It makes them really, really want to be around each other, and when you're in love with someone, it's good to be close to them, as close as possible."

"Then I lust for you?"

"No, Lumi, you don't. We love each other. Lust is different than love."

I did not understand! "You said lust is a strong want and I want to be around you."

I could tell my momma was wondering if she had made a mistake in trying to teach me about this at too early an age; in this moment, she was learning too—how to teach.

"When you love someone, you want to be close to them, whether they're your friend, or parent, or husband, but the form closeness takes, the form want takes, between husband and wife is different than the form it takes between child and parent, or between friends."

"You're talking about what happened in the flowerbed?"

"Yes!" She was relieved her daughter understood and she did not have to do any more explaining of this awkward subject, which was obviously making her nervous.

"Yuck."

"Hold onto that feeling until you meet your Knight!" Whew, she sighed, about to stand up, away from the conversation, until she realized she had unfortunately not said everything she had intended to say about the subject. "Lust can also cause plenty of pain."

"Like a stomachache?"

"Kind of like that. If you gobbled up all the molasses at one time, there would be consequences. There is a right time and setting for indulging in molasses, and reserving it for special occasions will make it all the more special, but that's not really the point I'm trying to make." She searched her mind for a way to explain this delicate subject to her young daughter. "What if someone made just for you a special jar of molasses, but instead of enjoying those molasses, you enjoyed molasses from someone else. Wouldn't that hurt the feelings of the one who made the special jar of molasses for you?" She knew she was not doing a good job with her explanation, but even though I did not understand yet, I saved the lesson for someday when it would make sense.

My momma taught me how to read, to write, to sing, to bake, to count, to photograph, but even though she taught me how to do those triumphs, *what* to read, write, sing, bake, count, and photograph was up to me and my tastes. She even taught me how to play the harp but the songs were of my choosing.

Our days were full and good and rewarding.

One reason I trusted my momma was because she lived what she taught. She never instructed me to do things she herself could not do, which meant every lesson she taught was achievable, the proof in her life. And I trusted her because she loved being a mother and when someone loved a task they wanted to be good at it, which meant she was doing her best.

She never acted like a boss but a guide, not a guide who showed me the same old path to adulthood (physical growth, wonder stunting, money making, and blind rule following "the leader" to nowhere special); she guided me to signposts like compassion, courage, and determination, showing me their lovely landscapes and the possibilities of what could grow in these sceneries. As was her way, she made an allegory out of those traits, referring to them as gemstones, a landscape of rubies or emeralds or sapphires, which I could carry with me wherever I traveled. The beauty of these special gemstones could not be seen with the eyes but had to be felt.

"Polish your star daily," she would say. "And your gemstones. Count them too. Make sure they're all still there. Never let anyone make you believe polishing your star is not one of the most important tasks in a day."

Even though her day-to-day work was hard, such as when she sat outside at her sewing table in hot sunlight (since the sewing table did not fit in the shack), she never painted life to be toil and misery—she encouraged fun and happiness. "Not all ink should be used for writing, 'I ate, I worked, I slept.' Much ink should be spent on, 'I loved, I played, I laughed, I learned, I loved!' Otherwise, 'I ate, I worked, I slept' will only prolong a miserably boring story and show a lack of expertise in the use of story ink."

While we shelled peas, we sang, sometimes songs fit for a choir, sometimes fit for a ship's deck ("Ooh, my mate's a good mate, a buddy from fate"). While we picked vegetables, we took breaks for hide-n-go-seek. I rarely found her, so she usually had to come out from hiding because I would get too panicked if I could not find my favorite being in the world after five minutes, until the day she made me play the game through, to find her, to teach me not only to make it through difficulty by myself but to never give up on a goal I really wanted to achieve. I cried and cried, and although listening to me cry was no doubt tough on her heart, she stayed ducked behind a big tree, until finally, with much help from Mullybiski's sniffer, I found my momma and hugged her like she had been gone for eternity. The incident did not create in me a fear of hide-n-go-seek or a dislike of the game; instead, I gained confidence in my ability to succeed.   Write thus!

Moon-Moon wrote lovely moments into our shared lifestory, sweet moments too, so lovely sweet moments felt natural. "Diamond moments," she called them, and they did not cost a cent. She would sometimes wake me at four in the morning to hear birds sing, so I would not miss some of the pleasantest passages of life's book. Nature could write lovely lines in life's story if I took time to read them; I could even write myself into them. Close by the starry window, we would sit at the table and listen to the song of nighttime over cups of cocoa (when we had cocoa, and cups of warm water imagined as cocoa when we did not). Sometimes we would go outside at night to watch lightning bugs; in the afternoon, we would sometimes go for bike rides, me in the sidecar, which was as fun as an amusement park ride! Sometimes we'd take breaks from work to go on journeys through the meadows for pictures, photographing daisies and sweet peas.

One night on a blanket outdoors, stars and flowers all around us, listening to the bedtime story too, Moon-Moon read Herman Hesse's *Strange News from Another Star*. The title alone had my attention. I loved how the story described a town being *devastated* by their loss of flowers, which were used to properly bury the dead, and out of devastation, one brave young man traveled on a mythical journey to find new flowers and he wound up on a sad planet (which was Earth) that did not care about flowers—that planet was obsessed with war.

But my Earth was a happy one...the joy, my momma and Mullybiski and Root, just us in Star-Gust with our forest friends and the soft fuzzy feel of flowers who touched my face gently as if it was pretty, when I, not much taller than flowers, rushed the meadows to greet more, more, more pages of this story, which included stars! As Ralph Waldo Emerson said, "The earth laughs in flowers." I was happy just skipping, trying out this body and all its capacity for fun—singing, daydreaming, giggling, running, hopscotching, jump roping. Every sight, scent, activity made the flower in my chest flutter. I delighted in swimming in the clear stream, which was frothy across stones, water shared with forest creatures. Especially joyous in the warm but not too hot time between spring and summer, which I called "sprummer." I was never bored because in my mind were endless stories I could write myself into, and sometimes these stories spilled out of my head and played out in this new-to-me world, such as when the wash bucket became a spaceship and the clotheslines turned into a telephone wire to another galaxy...

The most magnificent fact I ever learned about this world was that dogs existed on Earth. They might not exist on any other planet, but they existed on my planet! I loved being with pup Mullybiski, who seemed to love being with me just as much!

On cherished forest walks with Mullybiski and Root, my momma taught me how to care for, to nurture, to help animals and plants that were sick, a duty to kindness that made my real father proud. Making Father proud was what mattered, not because we feared him, but because we loved him—he was the ideal I strived to maintain.

Moon-Moon always preached the sanctity of life, the treasure of being alive. "Never," she made me promise, "write 'The End' before the story's conclusion, because you might miss out on a fantastic chapter just waiting to be lived." Why would I want this story in peaceful Stargust to end?

Then...

Not long after wondering that, my ability to remain peaceful was tested, as I serenely strolled the sprummer forest, looking upwards at the stars, then thwack! stumbled on a big rock, scratched my knee, and dropped Root. Darned rock—why had it hurt me? I saw everything as alive, even rocks, who were not very chatty. I cried, not because of the pain (I wasn't in much pain), but because I wanted my real father to hear me and take me back to the warm peaceful garden. Instead, Mullybiski licked my wound.

"That rock *bited* me," I said to Moon-Moon, who was framed in constellations and tree branches.

"Rocks can't bite, Lumi." She sat beside me and examined my scuffed knee. "The rock didn't purposely hurt you," my momma explained, while an owl hooted, and toads grumbled, and other nocturnal creatures made splashes in the stream. "It was an accident. Earth has rocks on it."

Well, that's a stupid world, I said real snippily with my pout, expecting my real father to repaint the world prettier. Why didn't *bad* things only happen in stories? I was tired of this world having rocks and ice which certainly caused a lot of accidents.

"If every path was smooth, your ability to overcome stumbles would never be tested," Moon-Moon taught.

I protested, "I wouldn't have to over-come stumbles if there were no such things that made stumbles!"

"But that would be a boring story, wouldn't it, just a girl endlessly walking a flat path?"

"It'd be more a pleasant story," my scowl argued.

"Shooting stars are *rocks*," she said.

"No, they're not!"

"Yes, they are, Lumi. Shooting stars are rocks who have taken on a special glow while traveling from far away to come to Earth."

With my fingertip, I touched the rock. He didn't seem very glowy.

52

"How do you expect to tell the rock's a shooting star by touching it with your fingertip?" my momma asked, always one to inform me when I was using the wrong sense to understand something.

I picked up Root, dusted off his scuffs, and hugged away his pain. Neither of us were convinced shooting stars were rocks. Rocks were meanies!

The next afternoon, to demonstrate that walking a safe path was more pleasant, I spent an entire hour walking back and forth across a smooth path in the meadow (the path we used for going to the well), in view of Moon-Moon at the kitchen window, where I could see her, shelling purple hull peas. I wanted to help because I liked when my fingertips got stained purple (made me feel like an alien), but I had a point to make. Eventually though, walking back and forth, I had to conclude my momma had been right—walking a flat easy path endlessly was indeed boring. I was ready to go back to exploring the woods, even if it did have rocks that could trip me.

At lunch, Moon-Moon offered, "A lifestory does not come with a back cover. Part of the fun of the story is not knowing what is going to happen next." She also taught, "Patience is a virtue." She didn't teach this out of a duty to abstinence from enjoyment, but because she believed anticipation was an enjoyable part of the story, the reason she had made me wait to sample molasses, whose taste had become an obsession to my imagination.

Then...

That sprummer afternoon during cream tea, I was offered molasses for the first time. I was so excited, just watching black syrup get poured beside a big warm homemade biscuit on my plate. Molasses always looked so tasty, so surely it would be tasty.

With her ever patience, Moon-Moon scooped a small spoonful of molasses from her plate, ladled the syrup onto one half of a sliced biscuit, and evenly spread the syrup. She was such a Lady; I wanted to be just like her.

After she took a bite, I did too, but … aacckk … the molasses was bitter! Poise kept me from spitting out the offensive taste, although Moon-Moon would have been the first to say a Lady had the right NOT to do something offensive to her. I realized the taste was not just bitter but also sweet, bitter sweet. Not entirely unpleasant but not exactly what I had expected either (molasses did not taste like "better" honey).

Moon-Moon guided, "If it's too bitter, add some sweet butter; no law says you can't." So, I did just that then…

Yum! Ooh, heavens, YUM!

"Even yummier," Moon-Moon said, "is molasses when it's in molasses pie."

"Ooh, can we make one?"

"Someday."

Another treat to anticipate.

Not long after the rock incident, I felt the cumbersome feeling again—anger—when I sat by a tree and a bee stung me. How rude! A *honey*bee too! He was supposed to be sweet.

"He was only protecting himself," Moon-Moon explained. "In this instance, you were the meanie, from his perspective, because he was unaware you *accidentally* swatted him."

Then came the gray day, rain-misty cold for sprummertime, when we found in the forest a bunny who was bleeding and cuddled up all by himself by a rock that offered no comfort. Seeing him in pain made me sad, an intense sadness I had never felt before. Time to erase that crummy sentence from his life.

"I told you, sentences can't be erased, unfortunately. He's been shot. He's going to die. But you can write comfort and kindness on the last page of his story," Moon-Moon said, softly rubbing the injured animal's head. "Before the end, be the character who offers him love."

She explained hunters and hunting and that guns and bad guys did not only exist on radio shows and in books and cinema and ancient stories of saints. Humans had stingers too, just much more dangerous ones. While my real father had spoken of the magical heavens, my momma explained the world's ways, its duality of joy and pain, birth and death, teddy bears and grizzly bears, sickness and health, kindness and hatred, and how the world's ending had almost been written by the big war, which I sometimes heard about on the radio but rarely paid attention to "the drama"—Moon-Moon would turn off the radio when she just could not bear to hear anymore badness. Then she would turn on music instead, something pretty. When I looked at the dying bunny, I saw the war then: that was what the war had done to people. Suddenly, I felt scared, sad, angry, and worst of all, helpless. Shooters could come out here to our Stargust sanctuary? My momma didn't say, "No, they can't." Instead, she said, "I love you, and you love me, and your father loves you, and you love your father, and no one can take that away from you except you. Focus on the love and Write thus!"

Even though Moon-Moon told me of the world's hardships and I witnessed those hardships (animals killing one another, rocks turning into walls, plants wilting), she never made walls seem insurmountable, and if I could not climb a wall, she said maybe someone or something could help me up or knock down the wall for me, and she even left open the possibility of the miraculous: walking through walls. She never even made the plotlines and technologies and fantastical beings in science fiction seem impossible but suggested they could exist somewhere in this great big universe's story.

After the bunny died, I asked, "Why didn't his guardian angel save him?"

"Guardian angels allow us mortals the freedom to write our own stories. His guardian angel is taking him now to Heaven."

"That's all guardian angels can do?" I was upset by this news.

"No, guardian angels embrace us when we're sad and scared, remind us through intuition Heaven is real, and speak to our hearts and tell us to write good things, but it's our choice whether we choose to listen. And their presence can be seen in miracles like the miracle of my Lumi being brought back to life." Moon-Moon gently picked up my simple cross necklace made of twigs twined together by her. "Why those kinds of miracles happen sometimes and sometimes not is a mystery to all of us."

Come to think of it, I was peeved about that too, "My guardian angel let me get *frostbitted* and stung by the bee and hurt by the rock."

"As I said, maybe some bad things test our characters, teach us lessons, and maybe other times guardian angels give us nudges— 'Don't step into that street because a car will be coming by,' 'Don't sit by that rock or a bee will sting you'—but we ignore them."

"The bunny didn't have a choice. The hunter shot him."

"Maybe the bunny's guardian angel tried to convince the hunter's heart not to shoot, but ultimately, the decision was the hunter's to make."

"That's crummy! If guardian angels have power to save people and they don't, that's crummy!"

"Would you prefer guardian angels to be like puppet masters with all of us as their puppets, safe but with no free will at all?"

"No."

"Lumi, hold onto this: reviving a metaphorical heart is just as miraculous as reviving a literal heart."

While I cried for the bunny, my momma comforted me with, "Only in one form is the rabbit dead." Sometimes she said things that did not make sense, because I could not use my five senses to comprehend her lessons, which I knew were teachings she had learned from Father. "When a light bulb dies, the light does not. All of the energy is still there and only needs a new medium to shine in this world." I reasoned she was talking about "*the* light, one of the lights of Heaven." After my time in the Heavenly garden when I had told my momma of seeing my real father, Moon-Moon had told me I had died, but I had not completely understood that then—"death, dying." I had begun to understand after witnessing a flower wilt, and I had a vague inkling of death's existence, supplied by books and movies and stories of saints and Moon-Moon's own aunt who had died in the war. But now I understood completely. The rabbit was dead and someday Moon-Moon would be gone, so would Mullybiski. After hearing a ghost story on the radio, I pondered if it had been my ghost (my soul) that had gone to the sunshiny garden. I wondered if the bunny's ghost ever came back to his treasured forest, although I never saw his ghost, but sometimes when a breeze tugged my dress, I felt that was him saying, "Thank you for writing 'love' on my last page."

Before the hunting tragedy, I had often strolled with my Moon-Moon without fear. In those days, before I had known of murder and guns, being Doc Savage courageous had been easier, although I had been cautious after the frozen pond accident. But now, more than ever, I needed my real father to comfort me with, "You'll always be."

Write thus!

On these walks, I would be asked to name at least one thing I loved. "Father!" "What else?" "Mullybiski!" "What else?" "Root!" "What else?" "Starman!" "What else?" "The moon!" "What else?" I had to say something new and mean it. My real father could tell when I was lying like the time I pretended to love clouds, those meanies who hid sunlight. "Rabbits," I said, honestly, one sprummer afternoon. "And you," my Moon-Moon said, "you can, you must, love *you* too, or else you won't be able to overcome stumbles, because you must love yourself to help yourself." The next day I said "bees" because I had forgiven the honeybee. "Yum, the honey that bees make for me!" My momma frowned. I could not pick out something to love just for selfish reasons. I could love the sweetness of honey, the way I loved the prettiness of flowers, and I could love the unique ability bees had to make honey (for themselves), but I could not *only* love them for their ability to make honey *for me*. I had to love everyone and everything the way I loved my real father—I loved him just because. I had to see the "Living Light" around all things. My momma taught, "Empathy is love's helpmate," so I had to feel myself as other creatures, imagine I was a honeybee or a flower, that way loving them would be easier, but the goal was for me to eventually love them without having to see them as myself but to love them for being them.

One afternoon, when I thought I had finally run out of things to love, Moon-Moon said, "What about rocks?"

I made a face. Rocks?!

"Find something to love about them. Remember, they're shooting stars."

The next day, I'd have to say something else I loved, and it was always fun, finding new things to love like maples and robins and ooh dandelions, although it got harder and not as fun when I had to go into the world and love *people* too, because my first encounter with a person had not been as gentle as my first encounter with a petunia, nor as friendly as my first meeting with a dog—my first remembered encounters with humans had been with a cold nurse and even colder doctor and seeing the fate of humans' weapons in the murdered bunny. Mark Twain's quote made much sense, "The more time I spend with people, the more I like my dog."

My desire to be a nun in solitude grew stronger. Like Francis of Assisi, I would be Patron Saint of Animals!

Then...

On a summer morning, so windy we tacked a towel over the open window to keep dusty wind from blowing our cups down, Moon-Moon gave me a candy cane that served as a preview of what Christmas would be like. She possibly gave me the candy because I had suffered through a crummy breakfast of grits and water, or because I had become obsessed with Christmas and reindeer and candy canes after hearing a Christmas story and I could not remember any previous Christmases.

Ooh, Peppermint! The best flavor I had ever tasted!

While Moon-Moon did sewing on our coats, since winter would be coming back soon (bringing Christmas with it!), Mullybiski and Root and I walked pebble-bumpy dirt paths, zigzaggy and with many turns. We strolled far from our meadows to acres of hills and dales, outlined in frothy streams and forests. The grass was both green and yellow like cornflakes, and the abandoned fields of hay and wheat were pasta-golden before the harvest.

Ooh, I loved the sight of countryside, where blue birds and red birds flew in and out of the painting.

I wanted to share the peppermint, but Moon-Moon had told me peppermint made dogs sick, so MullyB got a healthy doggy biscuit. If my pup and I dashed into the wheat stalks, they would tower over us, but Mullybiski didn't let that stop him or his sniffer.

Indications of the presence of animals on the land came in the form of "droppings," but the only signs of humanity's presence on this section of Earth were the path itself, and remnants of a rusted wire fence, and a chocolate-brown cabin on a solitary hill. Who had even made the path?

As I relished the minty candy, amidst unfriendly wind blowing loose dirt across me, I trudged up a hill. I felt the yearning for the familiar owl-ish woodland to be what greeted me, then the path led me to...

An image that expanded my heart: perched on Earth crust was a marshmallow-white airplane with a propellor as shiny as Knight armor. To my eyes the most mesmerizing sight in the picture was the silver paint on the plane's tail that spelled ... *alien symbols*! A spaceplane! Built where in the solar system and come to Earth for what purpose? I had never seen anything so astounding!

Cautiously, Mullybiski (my Watson) sniffed around the spacecraft, still warm from activity, as I looked around the scene. Feeling much like a sci-fi Sherlock Holmes, I searched for the aeronaut (astronaut!) who had walked away from this starship. The winged craft had two small wheels up front and one at the tail end, and two open seats, one in front of the other, but both seats were empty, yet I only saw *one* set of footprints in the dirt beneath the *cockpit* (I knew that word from comic books). No one could have stepped down without making any mark in the dirt, unless wind had blown the footprints away? Or maybe the other alien had turned invisible, but would that stop him from making footprints? Were both aliens out in the forest somewhere? The footprints led into a wooded area.

I was beside myself with excitement! I had never come upon such a big mystery before!

I climbed up on the wing. No clues were in the front cockpit, just fascinating glassed dials and gadgets, and in the rear cockpit were more dials and controls. Behind the backseat was a latch to a compartment.

"Should we open the secret compartment?" I asked Root. Of course, we should open it! What kind of sleuths were we?

Inside was a sleeping bag. Aha! The aliens were planning on camping on Earth!

"And what have we here, Watson?" Rolled up papers—alien plans! I unrolled one and saw—designs for more spaceplanes! Ooh my!

I thought of following the footprints on the ground, but I felt compelled to look to the sky:

Across the golden field, in the vast lonesome blue sky was a lone figure, his parachute wide open above him like a huge mint-green umbrella.

Ooh my, ooh my!

I tried out being a guardian angel by praying for the alien's safe landing, a prayer that was granted when he landed as softly as dandelion seed in a bed of wheatgrass. When his boots touched Earth, he ran a few feet as if to catch up to his exhilaration which had sprinted ahead of him.

"Ssssh," I cautioned Mullybiski and myself, as we stealthily dashed across the dirt road and hid down in wheat stalks.

I sweated like I was melting.

Ever so slowly, I peeked up, and watched the figure unlatch his parachute.

Wind pushed him but he was too strong to knock down.

Where was the other alien? I searched the sky for alien two but did not see him and concluded he must have piloted and landed the spaceplane and he was now in the woods.

The taste of peppermint was entwined with the sight of the aeronaut, as I examined the intriguing character from *afar*, scared of being "stung."

He looked like a human man, but aliens could, I knew; all the *Flash Gordon* characters looked human, except some wore "odd" outfits and they sometimes had a dot on their head, but for all I knew, this character could be dotted somewhere.

He wore goggles, white T-shirt, and peanut-butter-brown trousers and suspenders like my teddy.

He was tall; the wheat stalks only able to reach up to his belt.

I could not make out the details of his face, but ooh so handsome, his black hair shined like molasses in sunlight, and his beard was a lighter color like streusel.

I felt as at peace as I had in the warm Heavenly garden.

Yet I felt restless too.

The whole time I had watched him, my heart had been doing a foxtrot, but then my heart did a Lindy Hop number I had never felt!

The aeronaut flipped down his suspenders. I noticed his lower arm was bruised; interesting, aliens could bruise. Hmmm…that meant aliens did need guardian angels too.

He removed his T-shirt, tossed it to the silky parachute that shined and splayed like emerald water across the ground. His chest was as hairy as the wheat field but not golden-colored; that hair was also molasses black. I was not surprised by his hairiness; many animals were hairy and apparently so were Martians. I was impressed by his necklace—a shiny star necklace! He really was a Starman!

I was so excited, I did not know what to do with all the excitement, so I just wanted to run, run, run, until all the excitement exhausted.

Also melting amidst baked countryside, the alien pilot wiped his sweaty brow and sneezed, coughed—allergic to Earth!

Headed back to his spaceplane, he approached closer to where Mullybiski and I hid, and although I wanted to greet him, I did not know if he was a good or bad alien; plus, he was tall and had hair on his face and chest, markers of age probably on Mars too, which meant he and I would not have much to talk about *yet*, even if he knew human. I had to get better at words. So, I dashed away, and my pup and I must have looked like two streaking roadrunners.

I rushed home and told Moon-Moon, who was by the sink peeling sweet potatoes and listening to news on the radio. Other yummy ingredients for lunch were on the counter: okra, tomatoes, butter. The sight of her casserole dish assured me a tasty dessert awaited me. Politely, she turned off the radio to listen to her daughter, as I recounted the experience without pausing to breathe. She listened intently and concluded I had been enjoying a science fiction fantasy, the way I had the day before when I had called up Starman through the clothesline…and ooh my, I suddenly realized, he had gotten the message, "seeking friend on Earth," and landed in my field!

After catching my breath, I said, "Moon-Moon, he really is in the field." She had told me that daydreaming was like writing a story within a story, but I had to make her realize the Starman was in this world's story, not just in my head!

"Lumi, you're telling me there's a man out there in the field?"

"Not right out there." I did not like having to tell her the truth: I had walked far away, which she had told me not to do. I was not allowed to explore beyond her field of view.

"Lumi, if you ever come upon a man in a field, you get yourself straight on home."

"He's not a man, he's a Starman."

63

"Maybe he is an alien, or maybe he's one of those test pilots, which would be neat too—those are the men who are going to go into outer space in rockets."

"But never talk to a man, even a Starman, you don't know unless I'm with you, because not everyone is nice. You know there are bad guys in the story too. That's why I don't let you go far away from the house. You're not old enough yet." She wiped her hands on her apron. "We can go out there together and invite him over for lunch. That's the neighborly thing to do."

"No!" I didn't want it to turn out he was a bad alien; I liked him, and I wanted to keep imagining he was good.

"If that's the way you want it." She continued peeling potatoes. "I don't know if any aliens have a hankering for succotash and sweet potato casserole, but how about you?"

I did not understand the feeling, but I told my momma, "I love him. Just because."

"From what you've told me, he sounds a smidge old for you, but you never know how the story will play out someday."

"His hair is like molasses!"

I sat down, put Root on the table, propped him by a bowl of apples.

"You were spying on him?"

"Kind of."

"Kind of?"

"Okay, I was."

She sighed. "It's not very nice, Lumi, to spy on people."

"He's not people. He's from Mars. Maybe he'll stay on Earth to marry me!" Whether he was an alien or test pilot. But I didn't think a *human* test pilot would have *alien* symbols painted on his plane. "But nuns can't get married, can they?"

"Not actual nuns, no. You don't have to make the decision now whether you want to be a wife or a nun."

"Maybe he'll take me with him to space, where nuns can be wives!"

"Maybe someday."

"I want to bring bunnies into his life," I declared. My Moon-Moon understood what I meant—I wanted to decorate the landscape of the alien's life, or man's life, with gentle pretty wonders, since he seemed sad to me (maybe hunters existed on his world too).

"Remember," Moon-Moon said, "rocks are also loveable pretty wonders, and some boys like rocks."

"I'll make it always nighttime for him," I glowed, adding to my story of how *I'd* make his life if I could write it. Happy, sweet, fantastic, happy, happy.

"Why always nighttime? You'd miss sunshine."

"But if it's always nighttime, the stars will always be out" was my reasoning.

"The sun is a star too," Moon-Moon lessoned, "just much nearer to us, at the perfect distance for keeping us warm and for helping flowers grow, and if it got much nearer, we would all melt into it."

"But nighttime is prettier," I said, wanting to make his life romantic, although I could not formalize those feelings then. She walks in beauty *like the night*.

Moon-Moon explained, "Lumi, it's important for you to see this: lovers see stars in the *daytime* sky." I had a feeling I had to use the right sense to see that too and it wasn't one of the ordinary five.

"*Someday*, a day many many days away, you'll understand, when you and a molasses-haired boy see those daytime stars." She smiled like a mother promising her child a great Christmas gift.

I was restless with anticipation, thinking of the one from the stars all night. I dreamed of the familiar snowy woodland. The next day, I went back to the field but the starship had flown away. Maybe the aeronaut from Mars was the special one I was promised to meet, to help?   Someday.

I had more dreadful encounters with humans when Moon-Moon and I walked the grassy road that turned into gravel then into a wobbly wooden sidewalk that led to a dirty-windowed soup kitchen. Moon-Moon gave away food and crafts, and sometimes she would receive in return supplies like flour and matches and sometimes books and crayons for me. She carried baskets of fruits and vegetables, sometimes heavy potatoes, and I pulled those items with the unpainted wagon. Root rode in the wagon, and Mullybiski stayed home, because the walk was too long and hot for his short pug snout. I did not want to ever understand why people paved over grass and hacked down trees and flowers to put up buildings. Their world was ugly because its concrete bragged about destroying life; I preferred the meadow where life bloomed.

On these walks to putting kindness into action, my momma told me about money's existence and charity's importance and taught me about "forever value." "Money does not have forever value; the value of the dollar changes yearly. Fifty thousand years ago, money had no value at all. Bravery has forever value, because bravery can be used for as long as this universe lasts, just like love and kindness are forms of currency that never lose their value."

Seeing my gloominess about the existence of poverty, she said, "Poverty pits test your ability to climb."

On these walks, my momma would tell me more quotes from Transcendentalists, such as Emerson's "Money often costs too much," Fuller's "Men for the sake of getting a living forget to live," and Wordsworth's "Getting and spending, we lay waste our powers."

These walks to "civilization" made me sick, having to confront people who treated me as if my face was so hideous, it froze any decency in their hearts; their meanness shot icicles at my mood. Humans made me feel as if I could never bring light into anyone's night; instead, they saw my "scary" face as a bogeyman, as if my face was capable of hurting anyone.

"The world can be painfully cold, Lumi, and that is why it is important to stoke love like it is the only ember in your life's hearth, or else your goodness will freeze to death."

I realized kindness came easy for some people, not because they were more inclined, more naturally prone, to be kind, but they were "good-looking," or "normal-looking" at least, and they were healthy and "normal-acting," so they had never been ridiculed and that made dishing out kindness easier—giving kindness to people who had never been mean to them. But those who had been ridiculed, kindness came harder to them, so when those people were kind, kind to folks not kind to them (deer kind to hunters, monsters kind to witch-hunters), those were the ones I really admired, although I did not know if I could ever be such a brave person.

Write thus!

At the soup kitchen, "kindness kitchen," as my momma called it, the promise of life's misery written in the hard lines of people's withered faces scared me. They had shabby lives with threads sticking out, threads that could easily be pulled, unraveling them completely—but after the unraveling, would not the light inside still be there? That felt harder to believe in this gloomy environment. I focused on Moon-Moon, who proved life could be pleasant too; plus, she thought my face was beautiful, so looking at her smile made more sense than looking at other people's scowls.

Townsfolk were not proud of my raggedy "plain" momma, and that perplexed me—she was their hoped-for angel, yet they ridiculed her because of her homely face and threadbare clothes? But she did not mind, because my real father was proud of her, and he thought she was beautiful.

Many of the religious folks thought Moon-Moon was a loon, who turned meadows into ballrooms, but Moon-Moon told me, "They believe one should do anything God asks, but they don't believe the God of love asks anyone to be happy."

A few of the women, who had the crassness of soldiers on leave, always snickered at Moon-Moon, "Here comes the saint" like "saint" was a derogative word.

One nasty woman especially terrorized Moon-Moon. This woman worked at a market and she was seemingly always outside price-tagging fruits and vegetables and trying to scrape Moon-Moon's shine with insults like "How'd you get that dress on over your wings?"

Moon-Moon had taught me, "Sometimes other people will try to make you feel weird for not having made their mistakes, try to make you feel immature for not having messed up, because they need those mistakes to be common, so they will not feel singularly foolish for having committed the blunders. Once you see the motives behind people's meanness, you will no longer get your feelings hurt but you will instead feel sorry for *their* feelings: their insecurity, jealousy, fear…"

One afternoon, hotter than a bad temper, the mean woman's daughter stuck her tongue out at me, so I stuck my tongue out at her.

Walking back to the shack, the wagon was much lighter to pull without the load, but my-self felt harder to pull, something weighing me down.

Moon-Moon asked her confused daughter, "Do you think it's nice to throw rocks at people?"

"No!" Why had she asked me that?

"If someone threw a rock at you, would you throw one back?"

I knew I was supposed to say, "No," so that was what I said, but Moon-Moon knew I was lying.

My momma did not have a system of punishment, but she did have a system of correction. If I did a bad deed, we got to the bottom of *why* I had done it and *why* it was wrong. She taught me wrongdoings had built-in punishments known as consequences, such as guilt, regret, and disappointment—I admired her so much, believed in her values and my real father's values so completely, when I went against them, I suffered such consequences. (Rightdoings also had built-in rewards—happiness, satisfaction, approval of one's own actions.) She had once told me not to eat three slices of apple bread before bedtime because doing so would make me sick; sure enough, a bad tummy ache had been a hard teacher to make me learn that lesson. Although making Father proud was important, Moon-Moon also taught the importance of making *myself* proud of me, and if I aligned my values with his, making myself proud would be the same as making him proud. My momma never made me win her *love*—she gave it freely. Her love was not something I had to earn; it was mine, for always, and this did not make me take her love for granted, but the freeness of

69

her love made me value it even more. Her respect, though, was different—that I had to earn. And I had not earned it on this day.

"You would throw a rock even though you think it's mean to throw rocks?" she asked, very disappointed in her daughter and letting the disappointment show.

I shrugged, even though I knew my momma would not allow a shrug for an answer; she had no tolerance for indifference, which she said had murdered more people in the war than hate had.

"But you don't want to be a mean person, do you?" she asked.

I shook my head.

"Does it make sense then to do mean things if you don't want to be a mean person?"

Nope.

"Then why did you stick your tongue out at that girl?"

Did Moon-Moon see everything?!

"She stuck her tongue out at me."

"Yes, I saw that too. And you feel bad about sticking your tongue out at her, don't you?"

I started to shrug but decided against it, so I nodded.

My momma was always very concerned about my character. She once lessoned, "You're the one who has to live with yourself, so be a character *you* like. And you're the one who has to manage the consequences of every page your character writes, so be a conscientious writer who understands each sentence determines the next."

"Do you know why you feel bad?" she asked.

"Because it was mean."

"That's part of the reason," Moon-Moon said, as she stopped walking, ready to teach, and I stopped beside her, the sun over us.

"You feel bad because you handed over your pen to that other girl to write *your* reaction. You let *her* make *you* be mean. You let *her* write *your* character. I told you people can—and often will—write any mean nasty sentence they want into your story, but only you write your reaction unless you willingly hand over your pen to someone else. If everyone in town was throwing rocks at everyone else, would that mean you should throw rocks too?"

I thought of how Moon-Moon never snickered back to the women who snickered at her; she never changed herself for them. Ooh, how I admired that Lady! Those women tried to make her feel bad, because she set a paradigm of goodness that was difficult to achieve, and that made them jealous and irritable about having to live up to such a standard, so they wanted her to cave in and be bad too and stop reminding them through her life how good a life could be.

"Lumi, always remember this: For a character *not* to change is a feat, especially when she has a character worth holding onto. Remember, not letting the world change you is how you change the world. Remember this too, a nun doesn't stick her tongue out at someone!"

That night, I shouted to my real father, "Ooh, I want to write a story!" after Moon-Moon told me a bedtime fairytale, happily ever after, while she sat in moonlight on the side of my cot, where Mullybiski and Root were asleep. "That's one of the things I have to do—write a story—and why I was sent back here!"

"You don't have to shout," my momma said, covering her ears with her hands, pretending my shouting had been too loud. "He can hear you, even when you talk inside your mind."

Writing my story, I wanted to feel what Howard Pyle felt writing *The Book of King Arthur*: *"If it gives to you but a part of the joy that it hath afforded me, I shall be very well content with what I have done."*

"Can nuns write stories?" I asked.

"Of course."

"I'm going to write one someday," I said, holding up my favorite crayon: pink. Silver was neato too, especially for drawing stars and flying saucers like the ones from radio shows and cinema, but pink was the best.

"You're already writing a story, remember, your lifestory."

She asked me to hold up the pink crayon and pretend to write something I wanted to do.

"Eat more peppermint!" I grinned big.

"Something even more important to you than that," she instructed.

Through the open window, summer breezes were warm, while I thought of what I wanted to write. With crayon scribbling in air, I wrote, "I bring bunnies into boy's life," a sentence which probably had a number of spelling mistakes, but they were blunders unseen in air.

Moon-Moon held up a gray crayon and said, "I'm going to pretend to be a meanie, and I'm going to write, 'I don't want you to bring bunnies into his life.'"

My eyes turned into saucers. Why would she say that?

She smiled. "Remember, this is just pretend, Lumi, practice, and I'm playing a meanie. Do you still want to bring bunnies into his life?"

I nodded. I still wanted some peppermints too.

With crayon, she pretend-wrote in the air, "I'm *not* going to let you bring the bunnies."

"Why would anyone not want me to?"

"Sometimes you'll never know, or never understand, their reasons. What are you going to do now?"

"I'm still going to bring the bunnies!" And I felt very superhero-like! I really deserved some peppermints!

"No, you're not going to bring those cute bunnies. I don't like bunnies or cuteness."

The air felt hotter and suffocating.

"You can't stop me," I declared.

"Yes, I can! I'll throw a rock at you if you bring even one bunny near that boy."

I must have looked scared because once again she had to clarify this was just pretend and she was only playing a role.

"Are you still going to bring the bunnies?" she asked.

I thought about it. The idea of being hit by a rock made me reconsider. "If it's just one small, teensiest tiniest, rock, maybe."

"No, I'll keep throwing rocks at you if you bring those bunnies."

This was scary. I wanted to hug my soft teddy bear.

"Are you still going to bring the bunnies, Lumi?"

I hung my head down and let the crayon fall like the flag of a defeated country.

"Just like that, you're going to drop the crayon?" she asked, her voice cracking across disbelief, all five years of her instruction on character building broken by a few rocks?

"I don't want to get hit by a rock! He'd be disappointed in me, wouldn't he?" I would never be a saint or a guardian angel.

"Even though you're not going to bring the bunnies, do you still *want* to bring bunnies into the boy's life?"

I nodded.

"Then your father isn't disappointed in you. Because, see, your *wanting* to bring the bunnies is part of the story too, something you wrote—you just wrote that line inside. *No one* can erase what you write inside, unless you let them, but it does take courage to show what is written inside to others, especially when it's at odds with

73

everything written around you. Lumi, not everyone is meant to be like those saints from history, who were willing to be stoned to death for their principles, and I want you to know, they were scared too—they just had a lot of courage and they recognized what principles were worth dying for to preserve. But courage can be shown in other ways, in other battles, in other *forms*, but weapons can come in many forms too, remember that. Yes, that is scary, but I don't ever want you to drop the crayon like that again, no matter what, especially now that you know some sentences are written inside yourself. Never surrender your pen. Pick the crayon back up. And I want you to think of a way to bring those bunnies into the boy's life."

I tried but I could not think of a way. She patted my shoulder. At least I had tried.

Then she unexpectedly grabbed the crayon from my hand. "And what if that happens?"

"Then I'll be like the dead bunny?"

She nodded. "That can happen. It does happen. You know that. It happened in the war, which ended the stories of millions who *could have* written something marvelous but whose opportunities were erased by hatred. But as long as you had written what *you* wanted before that, that's what matters."

"But then what?"

"Then what? Then what?" She smiled. Had I already forgotten the Heavenly garden? "Then this!" She gave me a big momma bear hug. "Then I'll love my sweet Lumi forever." And I wanted to merge into her soft warm protective embrace, especially in this world of rocks and ice, but not yet, not yet—the story looked promising with its molasses-haired character and his starship.

Many afternoons later, during a picnic in the flowers…

While eating apple bread with Root and watching Mullybiski lounge in limited sunlight and feeling the end of summer approach in a chillier wind, my momma gifted me a poem by Samuel Coleridge Taylor:

What if you slept
And what if
In your sleep
You dreamed
And what if
In your dream
You went to heaven
And there plucked a strange and beautiful flower
And what if
When you awoke
You had that flower in your hand
Ah, what then?

"Lumi, your ultimate accomplishment in life will be to hold onto that flower from Heaven, but unlike the flower in the poem, you will never be able to hold this flower in your hand, only in your heart. Like all stories, the world is fun and scary and mysterious and suspenseful and beautiful and ugly, but it's all a lie—an untruth. Like all stories, it is not real. As Thoreau said, 'This world is but a canvas to our imagination.' You met truth in the garden of light. Never believe the reverse," my momma warned, as if she knew the upcoming winter would try to steal Coleridge's Flower from me.

Moon-Moon made rainy autumn "hot chocolate cozy" (I would forever love rain and hot chocolate and bedtime stories). Even though I did not remember the previous winter and the accident, in case I had any lingering chills, my momma encouraged my excitement toward winter—the season of Christmas and its merriment and miracles and gifts and candy canes and cocoa and caroling, the season of snow to play in, the season of the New Year and all its promises and resolutions to be better, the season of Valentine's Day. The most wonderful time of year! In autumn, she made gingerbread and peppermint pie, "A taste of what awaits." She promised to make peppermint desserts every Christmas; while promising this, she shook the snow globe, helping me to anticipate snowflakes, which brought forth the yearning for the familiar woodland, and she said, "Snow lands equally lovely on mountains, mansions, and mobile homes."

Then...

Moon-Moon became very sick during the winter, a sickness most likely acquired during one of our visits to town, where sickness congregated amidst poor folks abandoned by society's hospitality. The sudden sickness had pummeled her, but she had always been resilient and had not thought the cold would destroy her. She probably suffered from pneumonia; her coughs sounded hard enough to break the crumbly shack, but we did not have "money for medicine." A blanket tacked over the open window could not stop cruel coldness from breaking in. Hail pommeled the walls, broke through cracks.

"I must get up and go to town to see if anyone has medicine for you, in case you get sick too," she said one morning too gray to be daytime, putting on her snowboots at the cotside but collapsing before being able to stand up.

I knew from my time spent with the dying bunny, Moon-Moon's limited breaths suggested The End was only a few sentences away. I realized that all those times she had asked me to name something I loved, I had never said, "You," so I said, "I love you, Moon-Moon." I wanted that to be included on her last page—"I love you"—because her lifestory's last sentence looked so painful and frightening.

This was all crummy and wrong. My Moon-Moon had plenty of ink left, but sickness was emptying it all out, and some people had medicine to save her, but they would not heal her because she did not have any gray coins.

She told me, "I love you, and you love me, and I love your father, and he loves me and you, and that's what matters, but I have to make sure you're going to be okay in this world."

I could not live without my momma. My five-year-old heart did not know what to do. I could not even call her family for help.

Running out of ink, she desperately wanted to write something into her daughter's young life, something saving, a letter to her family maybe, but she could not write another word, and sickness wrote her into a sleep.

The next viciously cold morning which poured ice and slush onto the floor, I woke up and saw the small fire in the hearth had died overnight, leaving behind only ashes, and Moon-Moon had lost the last of her body's warmth to winter. I sat by her on the cot and tried to wake her up by tapping her shoulder, the way I had often done when she had been napping and I had wanted to go on a walk, but I knew she was like the dead bunny—there was nothing I could do to revive her.

Her eyes were open, though, like she was awake, and I felt disappointed by the bad ending: the last sight she had seen had been the cold shed's gray wall. Her last sight of this world should have been the flowers.

I had not even been able to add a hug to her story's last line, because she had told me to stay away from the sickness, so I gave her a hug then, since she had assured me a hug was supposed to happen after "then what?" I wondered if she felt the embrace. I wondered if I had really died during the pond accident. If so, why had I come back but not her? Was she now in the garden? I began to have doubts. I could not see or feel the Heavenly garden, but I could see and feel her dead and cold body. Maybe Moon-Moon had been wrong about what was real and what was a dream.

I knew Moon-Moon would say, "Only in one form am I gone." But that was the form I knew her in, her warm pancake soft arms and bedtime story voice.

The sight of her quiet harp, although angelically beautiful in that dreary shed the color of winter, made me cry. I had a feeling, or an imagining?, of her comforting me with, "I'll still play the harp for you, Lumi, if you listen with the right sense." But all I could hear was my own crying, and ice, endless ice pelting my alone life in that cold hard shack, which had once been alive and vibrant but now was dead.

Winter had stolen my face, and now Moon-Moon, but the mean season was not content with just taking my warm momma—it took away the flowers too. And the trees looked pained by winter's cold touch. And all the other cute furry creatures left me. And the air did not smell like apples, just damp coldness. And even the stars looked frosty, and so did the moon, so far away. Sharp icicles hung from the shed's roof and they seemed to poke my freezing heart which no longer felt so shiny, redness and brightness draining from it. And there was that evil frozen pond that had stolen my beauty.

I did not love winter and no one could convince me to love it.

And, right after my momma's death, I got sick with presumably the same infection, a cough that took up too much space in my lungs—of all the meanest things! I kind of wanted it to be The End, but then I remembered my promise to her, and I could not abandon Mullybiski or Root, nor could I renounce my destiny to be someone's Earth angel. If the cough did not kill me, I would write thus. I remembered my momma talking about the cycle of seasons. I knew springtime would come back. I supposed I didn't want to write The End before seeing and smelling and feeling the flowers again, but would they look and smell and feel the same without her?

After the cough didn't write the ending for me, I went outside in my coat and snowboots and grumpily made snowballs with Root snug under my arm. I heard Mullybiski barking but I didn't listen to what he was saying. Moon-Moon had once told me she used to make snow angels as a girl. Well, angels were written out of the world in this season, and that was the truth. I tossed snowballs to the ground, trying to get back at winter for hurting me. Then I was angry at the whole world, and I thought if I threw those snowballs hard enough, I could crack Earth apart—I hated it so much. I figured a Lady was not supposed to behave in such a way, but so what? My momma had tried to help people, giving them free food and kindness, even on blustery roads on cold days, but the world had paid the Lady back by writing her out of its story. Stupid mean world! She had been a fool for loving this world!

I grumped back to the shack, where I saw the harp was gone. Darned shack—it ate the harp! I could not imagine any other way for the harp to have just disappeared. Unless…the harp had been stolen. My Moon-Moon had once playfully said a raccoon had stolen a bite of her apple bread. Someone had not so playfully stolen her harp. A thief who had left footsteps beneath the window, big monstrous footprints in snow that no doubt led back to that miserable town, where everything was for sale. Mullybiski had been barking, trying to tell me. The thief had trespassed into my story and written the line: "She lost her harp."

I was furious. First, my momma had been stolen and now her harp. I was so mad, I screamed at my real father, and kicked and kicked, trying to knock him down, wherever he was. I beat my small fists into the air. Why didn't you save her? Where were you? In your garden? She made songs for you and you let her die. I thought you watched over us! Now you've let someone steal her harp! And you didn't heal me when I was sick either! You just let us suffer! I hate you! You're the liar! I hate you more than I hate the world! You're the mean one and I hate you! When my anger mutated into hatred, a feeling I recognized by an inward change of temperature, the way the stream must have felt when it turned into ice, it scared me, that freezing feeling threatening to extinguish my love for my real father, my sanctuary of warmth in the glacial world, but I was overpowered by the blizzard. After I got as much of the anger out as I could with fists and kicks, I turned to crying, hoping for someone to care enough to bring the harp back, to bring my Moon-Moon back. The hide-n-seek game had gone on too long. Simply, I was scared and sad. Why didn't my momma come out now and say, "I'm right here"? How could she leave me behind?

In the shack, the sight of her death began to replace the warm impression of her I had imprinted on my heart to remember her forever. I did not want to remember her this cold way.

I tried to warm up beside Mullybiski and Root. My momma had taught me to be self-reliant, and although I knew how to find food and water and stay out of the cold, I did not know how to chop logs for the fire.

"I love you a whole big bunch," I said to my real father, scared he would think I no longer did since I had tried to knock him down. I needed to feel his warmth, since the cold gray ashes in the hearth brought no warmth.

I thought I heard Moon-Moon ask, "What story do you want to write?" The way she asked worried me, like I would soon have to write my story in the mean world, all by myself.

"I bring bunnies into the alien boy's life, but—no one will have any rocks to throw!"

"They'll have rocks. Earth has rocks on it," her memory said in my heart. "Remember what Wordsworth advised, 'Fill your paper with the breathings of your heart.' Never let anyone convince you it's silly to listen to your heart when you write your story, or you'll turn into someone who robs people of harps."

Then…

Abruptly, that same icy morning, I was transported from my ideal story to a miserable story by invaders who wrote that it was not realistic for the child to stay in the flowery meadow by herself. Being pulled away from my home, I tried to keep one of my real father's paintings of the magical universe, but the State would not let me, yet my real father whispered—he seemed so far away then, he *whispered*, didn't he?, "You don't need paintings to see my universe, sweetyheart."

Then...

The world became my Wicked Stepmother...

Sauerkraut

After losing Moon-Moon and being torn away from Stargust, my heart turned frosty. My life, which had once felt like a collection of sweet morsels of moments or dollops of delicious cake moments (with only a few moments hard to stomach), now felt like a big chunk of ice. I did not become a "foster" child, which implied a child who was fostered, nurtured; I was cultivated no differently than a plant who only received water and minerals for physical growth in exchange for providing sustenance but was not nourished to bloom into a marvel. I was a character in the world's story, a tiny insignificant-feeling character in a big frightening world, which could easily erase me and never even notice my inconsequential departure; no one was even reading or watching my story. I did not feel like I belonged in the world of humans, no more than a flower belonged in a pot. Whereas I once wanted to explore more and more of the story, now I wanted to huddle close to myself, the only human character I could trust, and hold my pen close to my chest. I would "Write thus," but only write inside, so no one could see anything I had written, and that way they would not throw rocks at me. I would not write one single sentence in this world's story except "eat and sleep and be a friend to Mullybiski and Root." That was my stay-safe plan. But how would I bring the bunnies into the molasses-haired aeronaut's life? In a filthy southern town, Igtord, called "Ignored" by residents, I did not expect to find him there. I had to start working to give money to my story's intruders, who eventually adopted the tiny laborer but saw nothing to love about her, aside from a paycheck. A social worker had once said about me to a colleague, "No one's ever gonna want her, that poor thing." "Ugly" or not, I could be used utilitarianly. I sold newspapers and cleaned yards for coins, but being a girl, a young scrawny one too with a "disfigured" face, I didn't get many jobs. Aside from making me work, they mostly left me alone, which I preferred, because I did not want to be around them. He had the personality of a meatball, she the disposition of a rundown rug, and they were both thieves. Yes. Thieves had children too. Having a kid made them look less suspicious. I felt betrayed by my allegedly "always with me" real father who had let me get written into a story with thieves.   Moon-Moon had once told me that aside from hate and its offspring and cronies, I could find something to love about everything and everyone.   I tried to find something to love about them but I could not. Was this a test? Was I capable of being a nun? I wasn't a saint, although I felt closer to sainthood away from humans. Around animals and plants, I could be an angel, but not around people. At first, I hated them, which perplexingly not only brought the coldness which threatened to extinguish any possible warmth I could feel for them but for my real father too in a snowball effect. The thieves' gray house was cold and creaked like old bones and smelled like dead things, where warm apple bread was never offered (they were only concerned with a different kind of "bread"), that cold criminal house, where they had the scars of failed suicide attempts, which I had never wanted written in my story. I knew my momma would say, "They don't want to be thieves. They have just lost their way to the garden." Then I felt sorry for them. They would never write a story for the great anthology of love stories. They were sad crooks, mean only when they wrote themselves into people's lives just to take stuff, and not the give-and-take good stuff with forever value like friendship, but money, or a marble ashtray, or anything they could slip into their pockets without being noticed. They had chosen at young ages to learn the skills of thievery, so they wrote themselves as professional thieves, or amateur ones, into the world's story, albeit not very successful thieves, not ones whose stories would end with "the big heist," the stealing of a big rare jewel, which might buy them a Wyndclif and happiness. But no one in Igtord had a big rare jewel to steal.   In Igtord, "poor," "middle class," and "rich" were defined as "one with no food," "one with food," and "one who lives in Hollywood." The thieves were always in danger of slipping into poorness' mud pit, in their old two-bedroom grave in dingy suburbs, where crinkly houses looked like clothes that had been washed too many times in futile attempts to wash out dirt. Igtord was just a dirty place that made one's soul want to shower.   The thieves couldn't let anyone know their pens were behind the thief characters or else they'd get written into "the pen," which was most likely the bleak destination where their end would be written. To keep townspeople from finding out their true identities, they also wrote themselves the roles of "normal housewife" and "iceman." A spinal defect had kept him from fighting Nazis. I often ran away from their crummy story and always got penned back in by police. I missed my momma terribly. I did not know why Moon-Moon had referred to my real father as my "real" father, but I wondered if she had sensed someday her daughter would be in another house and she had wanted me to be able to distinguish my real father from my temporary father and to remember whose principles to uphold. At a pawn shop with them, I encountered a harp that looked identical to Moon-Moon's, a harp others saw as a piece of junk. I told the man, who was commanding all the items by use of a steely box stuffed with green

paper and tarnished coins, "I want that harp. It's my Moon-Moon's."
"I don't care if it's the harp of Archangel Michael. If you want it, you
buy it, kid." He pulled up a wad of green uglies from the metal box.
"Come back with some money and it's yours. I gotta earn a livin', ya
know. You idiot. Don't you know nothin'? How am I gonna eat without
money? Ain't nothin' in this world for free, stupid," he shouted and
laughed like I was a fool, the first time I had ever felt that. The thieves
appreciated the cashier schooling me about the price-tagged real world.
Stupid world. Didn't people realize food grew on trees? The world was
trying to convince me my Moon-Moon had not been wise about the real
world; she had just been a foolish dreamer who lived in a shack. And I
quickly realized the world did not listen to the child's voice and her
garden stories, which she began to doubt herself (maybe I had only
imagined the garden as perfect, or if it had been, maybe I had dreamed
it all). In a story where most characters thought Saint Hildegard's
mystical visions were delusions (products of migraines), a part of me
chalked my warm Heavenly experience up to an illusion, created by my
mind in need of believing "happily ever after" while I had been in a
hurting cold body after the frostbite accident. I never saw the bunny's
ghost or heard my momma's harp. Had my real father's magical universe
only been a painting? And as for using "the other sense," the part of me
that did not believe could not resort to nonsensical fantasies when I was
seeing and hearing and feeling the world of coldness and hatefulness and
fear and anger and literal hunger. But another part of me had to hold
onto my real father's magical universe, the only promise that made me
content and kept me from dreading The End. Now that I did have
doubts about love's foreverness, I did not wish for The End, which
would really be the ending, no everlasting light, no garden afterwards, no
hugs, and as crummy as life was, death was still scarier—no more flowers,
no more stars, no more rabbits, no more sunshine, no more Knights and
Ladies, no more Starman. No more chances to write new sentences, and
as a writer and reader of stories, that was the bleakest aspect of The End
to me. So, no matter where I was bodily, inside I stayed in my real father's
warm sunshiny garden, to hold onto it as long as I could. I was scared
someday winter was going to steal his warmth from me completely, that
someday my heart would fade in winter, that someday ice would bury
Coleridge's Flower and if I ever went to uncover it, it would not be there,
for it had been nothing but a childhood dream. Other people's cold faces
warned of the inevitable permanent life frost. Moon-Moon had been one
in a billion, the proverbial lone diamond in endless sand just passing

through time. A candle in the cold world that blew her out. The stars felt unreachable and the moon could not talk and knights and ladies only existed in storybooks, but dragons existed (meanness, greed, prejudice...). My lifestory was always set in winter, regardless of the temperature understood by a thermometer (mood used a different scale). Winter and cold and gray. Insecurities, along with the world and naysayers, were constantly trying to take control of my pen. I was not scared those thieves would steal Coleridge's Flower, for it had no cash value, but after enough years in the world's story, I realized all the most heinous crimes were forms of thievery—robbery, of course, but also assault, rape, and murder, which all stole from their victims: freedom, dignity, happiness, courage, and life. But those thieves repaid their victims, or their victims' families—with grief and misery. I was scared other thieves might somehow, and for some unimaginable reason, steal my Heavenly flower. The world itself was a thief, a robber of life, a wilter of health, and what did the world gain in return for its thievery? Nothing! It was a stupid world. It wrote an angel out of its story. Aside from my real father's garden, the only place I liked was a stream, "an old drainage ditch," said adults, which I discovered during one of my breakouts. I hoped, prayed, to see the aeronaut with molasses hair, to fly away with him to a nicer world, so at least I had that—the possibility of meeting him again...but what were the chances he would want to come back to Earth? A cold vicious place. The stream was by the vast desolate field within walking distance (a long walk, though); at one time, the field had offered CinemaScope views as a drive-in movie theater, which had not fared well in Igtord, where most did not have money to waste on picture shows. Other than walks to the stream...the "normal housewife" drove me to school, and at first, I was excited by the prospect of kinder-garden, until I realized it was "garten" not "garden." At school, I learned how to "duck and cover" to protect myself from an atomic bomb, but I was more terrorized by other kids who despised my "strange" face, although the school did not offer any protection from that devastation. Being trapped in their stares felt like being caught in the police's spotlight. My "abnormal" face was always interrogated and always found guilty of "hideousness," so I was sentenced to life in solitude. Daily rock peltings. I was tired of being treated as if I was unwoundable, but because I was so sensitive and woundable was why they targeted me—what a world, my pain gave them pleasure. They tried to make me take an eraser to my existence. The artist and writer Bell Gondal once wrote, "I discovered my loneliness in a crowd." I could not understand why humans were so gentle with things—lightbulbs, cars, cameras—but not with each other's feelings. One of our assignments was to draw the outline of our best friend's hand, and this had to be completed in class, so I could not outline Mullybiski's paw; while other kids were putting their hands on each other's desks and having their fingers outlined in crayon on paper, I outlined my own hand. The teacher yanked up the drawing and told me to go stand in a corner and suffer shame. She was not angry at other students for not befriending me but at me for being "unfriendable." My emotions, especially my good mood and self-esteem, walked through barbwire daily, anytime I was around people, and at the end of the day, I would go to my room and patch my wounds, alone. There was one special time when I *could have* made a friend had the world not written the union as inappropriate. I met Cynthia at the stream, during winter, when mud puddles offered mortar for mud castles; she was building a dirt mansion. Mullybiski's presence did a good job of introducing us: "Is that your doggy?" Yup. "Boy or girl?" And the conversation took off. Unlike girly me, Cynthia was a "tomboy," hair in pigtails, a no nonsense, roll-up-your-sleeves-and-get-to-work type; she wanted to be a Knight. She wanted to be an arch-itect too, to build her mom a palace, tired of seeing her mom scrub the floors of someone else's palace. (In Igtord, a "palace" was any home not riddled with rot.) When I told her I wanted to be a writer, she said, "So we're both builders." I had never seen being a writer in that way, as being a builder, and I was impressed by her smarts. Cynthia was not only smart, but nice, ambitious, shy yet courageous, but townsfolk only saw that she was black, and in their eyes, that was bad. Because of segregation, Cynthia and I did not attend the same school, and we did not get enough time together to develop a friendship, to truly plant something long-lasting, just brief moments in the open windy field, away from others' judgement. One afternoon, I went to the stream to see her, but she was not there, just a half-built castle she would never get to complete. I later heard from the thieves that "some little n----" had been killed during a downtown protest against Jim Crow laws—a peaceful protest had turned non-peaceful by the very ones enlisted to instill peace: the police. Cynthia had been erased from the world's story and my story, because officers had seen a six-year-old girl as a threat. Her murder was never mentioned at school as if it had not mattered at all. I never got over that hurt, because I did not just feel the pain of loss but the indignation of injustice. Maybe the world did have Knights and Ladies, but they were always written out of the story. I missed Moon-Moon so much. She had once told me, "If a crayon box only offered one color, that would not be much of a crayon box—wouldn't be much of a world either." I had known exactly what she meant. There had never been any tolerance for racism in Moon-Moon's house, but in this world, it was not only tolerated but nourished, especially in the south in the 1950s. With dread, I realized I was only at the icy pointed tip of the iceberg of how cold the world could be. Through that cold time, when icicles stabbed my heart, I still upheld the Lady's Code of Grace, kindness, empathy, niceness, and compassion (kindness in action), but I rarely had to test my values, because I avoided humans as much as I could. My desire for solitude would never be erased from my personality; reclusiveness had been written into my character by either my genes, or my soul—either way I was reclusive by nature. Some cold nights, the thieves taught me about "the business" over sauerkraut. She was a terrible cook who made bitter food, always cold sauerkraut to my taste buds. And they always had coffee, even more despicable than sauerkraut. I had tasted coffee once, the flavor of adult mornings—ground-up car tires would have given it better taste. Yuck. This was all too bland to stomach. Sauerkraut was hard to digest. The thieves had chosen "the monster" in hopes my ugly face would grant them pity money from neighbors, and would not unlovable I be willing to do anything to gain acceptance? The thieves wanted us to be a team. They tried to make me believe thieving was the only way to survive for "people like us," that they were doing this for the whole family to give us clothes and food and stuff and a chance "out."   To where?   That was not the path to the heavens. "There ain't no Heaven," they'd lecture, "and the heavens up there you ain't ever gonna get to." Growing up with thieves, my ability to trust humans shrank to something that could only be viewed with a microscope. For money, I'd rake leaves (but never understand why people didn't like the sight of leaves in their yards) and I'd sell newspapers with scary headlines, because I was hit with the fact that outside the meadow food did cost money, but I would never steal anything from anyone, and I let the thieves know this. Not even a matchbook? No, not even a matchbook, which was not a small thing, possibly someone's only source of warmth. "I can't do that," I told them. "You *can* but you *won't*," they refuted. When anyone said, "I can't do that," because an action conflicted with their morals, scoffers always scolded, "You *can* do it, you just *won't* do it." I loathed the myth that morals were not strong enough to force one to truly be unable to do something, as if principles were just something one *wouldn't* go against but *could* go against. But the thieves could tell I was serious, and if they

87

tried to make me do something against my real father's values, I would reveal their identities, because even if my real father's Heaven did not exist, his ideals could make *this* world more heavenly. I felt courageous again. I had written something into the world's story even though I had known I would get rocks thrown at me. Write thus! Even if the world made no sense, *I* would make sense. Their disappointed faces pelted me with, "We really made a mistake choosing Little Goody Two-Shoes." The only reason I did not turn them in was because one, I felt sorry for them (and they could thank my ridiculed goody-goodiness for that), and two, I thought no one would care that much in a world where "Goody Two-Shoes" had become an insult. The thieves often bragged that they had never gotten caught, maybe trying to teach the kid that one didn't have to be virtuous to be rewarded; "crime pays" was their cliché motto. I had seen people be kind to the thieves, offer smiles and neighborly homemade pies for free, but their kindness had not prevented them from being robbed, and the thieves' deviousness had not prevented them from getting what they wanted. They had "gotten away with" wrongness, but my momma had not "gotten away with" rightness—she had been ridiculed by humans and taken away by the cold world, where her daughter was raised by respectably-housed thieves who would steal a harp from Heaven to sell it for a penny.

Mint
Chocolate

Moon-Moon had taught, "When life serves you ice,

make ice cream."

Yes, heart icicles hurt, but dwelling in ice would not defrost my heart. I needed warmth. I needed hot cocoa and brownies, sunshine, Nat King Cole and John Keats. To write iridescent moments, I needed to dip my lifestory's pen into the light of Heaven, draw forth from the garden's warm well, which I had not let completely dry up. All the characters around me were writing gray stories in gray town, but I quickly became tired of gray sentence after gray sentence, which were not only depressing but boring and worst of all trite; no, worst of all, not my style. Not writing what I wanted was the same thing as letting others write my story for me, and they had written me as a subservient insignificant miserable gray speck. I would no longer let anyone create my character. I would not let thieves thieve my pink jazzy lines. I had always wanted to write a lovestory that belonged in the great anthology of love stories, the kind of love that existed in a Nat King Cole song, and I wanted to be a Romancearian, a champion of love, an upholder of Romantic ideals—chivalry, goodness, dreaminess, and individuality.

I had a destiny to fulfill, so time to Write Thus!

From the iceblock chunk of my life's story, I made mint chocolate chip. (Even though I despised literal ice cream and all cold foods, although I supposed at one time, like most children, I may have enjoyed ice cream from the ice cream truck, I still liked the ice cream metaphor.)

First, I received an ingredient for the treat from my first-grade art teacher, an elderly Asian woman named Mrs. Reddthrid.

Drawing with crayons at our desks, we kids looked up when the teacher said, "Someday you might even draw something like this." A fascinating projection transformed the wall into a painting, thanks to a new gadget: the classroom projector.

I was captivated by both the artwork and the light streaming from the projector and capable of making an image, which flashed much too briefly before the teacher went through a series of slides. During this time, Mrs. Reddthrid gave us warm mint chocolate chip cookies, so to me, the painting would forever taste like Mint Chocolate Chip.

Then…

At the end of class, Mrs. Reddthrid gave each of us a 5x7 print of a different classic painting, and I received *The Wanderer Above the Sea of Fog,* who I kept under my girlhood pillow. And I kept him in my heart next to Coleridge's Flower. Ooh, I was smitten with The Wanderer, the mysterious lonesome figure, given to the world by artist Caspar David Friedrich. I wondered why the weather-battered lone wanderer (or alien come to Earth?) stood atop stones in misty sea (or mist that appeared as a sea)? The mist was cold, a coldness I ascertained from The Wanderer's heavy black coat. Was his protective coat all he had in the cold world for warmth? Like the aeronaut who I had only seen across a distance, The Wanderer's face was a mystery too; his face unseen, my imagination had to create his portrait, and for a brief period during my early teen years, he looked like a character I liked from a movie (somber and serious Philippe Delambre from *Return of the Fly*), but I knew better than to give him a face already taken by one who was not my soul's mate. Instead of trying to visualize his face, I tried to *feel* my soulmate's essence across space. I wondered about his past, his present, his future. What was his story? To me, The Wanderer looked heroic, braving rough cold waters (I chose to see the mist as an ocean). He was a Knight of the sea, who had wandered into my life when I had really needed to be reminded of my aspiration—to find and love my lone molasses-haired starship builder.

One evening, whilst eating warm mint chocolate chip cookies in bed and listening to *In the Still of the Night,* I realized The Wanderer did not really have black hair; I had just seen his hair that color, because *My* Wanderer had molasses hair. He became *My* Wanderer, my love, my Teddy Knight, a character written by this Lady's tastes. My Wanderer would be confident yet shy, brave yet gentle, wise but not conceited, a great history-making man who would write a chapter so noble in Earth's story, the next chapter would inevitably be righteous. "Oo Captain, My Captain." Captain of my heart. What was he looking at in the fog? His hoped-for Lady, that was what I dreamed, his prayed-for sweetheart rowing toward him with a warm pie (I had a sweet imagination, and plus, I was fond of baking). "Be careful," I told him in my thoughts, thinking of how Teddy Knight's nemesis was The Mist.

No matter how mean other people were to me, he was loving and accepting. Every night, often mornings and afternoons too, I talked to him, the way I talked to my diary, which offered me companionship. Wherever he was in the galaxy, he didn't talk back with words, but sometimes I sensed his being, the way I had sensed the aeronaut's being, a tortured heart like Teddy Knight. I often told him, "If you're not already here, please come back to Earth." I offered my love to him across time and space.

One starry night, while talking to him at the stream, telling him I missed him, I felt engulfed by smoky cloudiness, so overwhelming the gloom, the stars darkened from the smoke—then...

I knew it was my duty to bring starlight back to his murky life.

Thanks to my dream of love, I felt heart icicles melting, dripping, and my heart losing its rigidity and becoming soft and pink again.

With soft bright heart, I was awed the night I watched Sputnik, the spacecraft launched by the Soviets, dance around our planet. With my coat pockets filled with Hershey's Kisses (that I had bought), I walked to the stream on a cold October night in '57 when I was eleven. Even without binoculars, I could see him. I was fascinated by the tiny sphere, "about the size of a beach ball," a news announcer had said. He was a baby spacecraft! And what a cute name! I imagined Sputnik had come to life because the metal used to make him had been so excited by the prospect of going into space—who would miss the opportunity to be alive for that?

Holding up Spaceman Pez, I waved at the star traveler, "Go, Sputty, go!" When reporters said Sputnik made a distinctive "Beep," I knew that was him saying, "Weeeee!" on one fun ride!

Then on Christmas night that year, I made my formal wish upon Sputnik to be the *She* from Lord Byron's poem, not the muse of a Romantic poet but the muse of a Romantic starship builder, and he would be my muse. To be an artist was a great accomplishment but to be a muse was a greater accomplishment for there could be no art without muses—all the great love stories and poems and songs were not written by writers but by muses.

But until my meeting with him, time to write more sweet passages in my lifestory…

Taggart Smythe once wrote, "Life is a war between want and obligation—happiness is measured by the amount of battles won by want." I was aware life had some inevitable boring sentences, such as "wash dishes," "comb hair," "go to store," and even in the meadow, life had required work to sustain itself—"gather pecans," "shell pecans," "eat pecans," to "gather pecans," "shell pecans," on and on—or else the body would run out of ink for anymore writing. But I realized the sentences required for sustaining physical life should be kept to a minimum, which could be done with efficiency. And the sentences required for sustaining the heart and soul's story were much more important, and since I wanted to write a lovestory, I had to add romantic syrup even into necessity oatmeal sentences. So, when I had to go to the store, I thought perchance to meet him, and when my hands were employed by necessity for washing dishes, my mind was employed by my soul for daydreaming of nurturing my love's home, and when I brushed my hair, I thought: to keep it pretty for him.

Slowly, I added more ingredients to the mint chocolate chip, although retaining the sweet flavor was a struggle in a world whose pantry was mostly stocked with two flavors: bitter and yuck.

A constant battle between flame and cold wind.

Even though I was young, I read Viktor Frankl's *Man's Search for Meaning*, which spoke of the importance of focusing on meaning in every experience and giving purpose to life. I chose to view my momma's death as a learning experience—to remember to always be aware of how quickly someone I loved could be taken from my story. And I chose to view the time with the thieves as a lesson too: to teach me the life I did not want to write. Plus, maybe I could show them by example of love's importance.

I reviewed my "near-death" experience in a positive light. If my brain had just wanted to bring comfort to my aching body by creating a warm pleasant illusion, why had Moon-Moon and Mullybiski not been in the garden with me? Moon-Moon was my favorite, most-trusted person, and Mullybiski my best friend, so my thoughts would have placed those two in Heaven with me to bring me comfort. And how had my *dead* brain been able to create such an elaborate experience? And why had I, a child of four years old, sensed an important meeting awaiting me on Earth, for I did not like being around people, except Moon-Moon? When I had become very sick after my momma's death, I had not gone back to the garden, even when I had been delirious with fever; I had only gone to Heaven after being pronounced dead after the frostbite accident, so if the garden had been an illusion to bring comfort, why had I not experienced the comforting illusion while being so sick? I still could not say with certainty my experience had been more than a dream (I could not say with certainty that about life either), but my logic had reasons to conclude the garden experience had been more than a brain trick (dead brains could no more play tricks than dead dogs). I chose to view my time in the garden as a gift that had allowed me to see truth and share it with others, to comfort the dying and bereaved *and* the living, whether they listened to me or not. I wrote about Heaven, sent the story to a magazine, yet Heaven was rejected.

Write thus!

With Heaven lighting my heart, I painted literal color into my fading story by painting my upstairs bedroom the color of peonies.

I transformed my ceiling into my real father's universe, so every night I gazed at pink swirl galaxies, angels, and great stars. I further decorated the walls with photos of the meadow taken by Moon-Moon, and bare 45s like Elvis's *Teddy Bear*, and illustrations from 1800s romance novels, and drawings from the likes of *Romantic Confessions*.

I especially adored two illustrations by Frank Merrill, drawn for Louisa May Alcott's *Little Women*, and I had the sequence of boy comforting girl and girl comforting boy displayed close by my bed.

I put up photographs of historical women, such as Susan. B. Anthony and Sojourner Truth, women who had championed the female voice and her right to speak God's word.

Next, I decorated the bed with a bedspread pretty enough to be a skirt. I stood scented candles on the nightstand to scent my dreams and to cover up the stink of dead things in the cold gray house.

I made my bedroom a natural reserve, a sanctuary of the self.

I kept a lock on my door because I did not trust thieves who would even steal pictures off the wall (they hocked everything).

I could not afford an electric fireplace, so I used extra blankets in winter to make the room warm, where I enjoyed my cozy Saturday night tradition: snuggling in bed, reading from a stack of romantic comics, and trying each flavor in a box of chocolates.

"Wipe that smile off your heart," the world's bitter face often scolded, but no, I would not, "thank ya very much," as King Elvis would have said.

At nighttime, I searched the sky for a star to fall in love by, wondering if my aeronaut was searching the same sky.

I always hoped to see his airplane in my sky again, and I knew I would if he was the one.

98

I also searched for silver linings. I had been able to keep Moon-Moon's Brownie camera, and her scrapbook, and her musical angel snow globe that played *O Holy Night*—three silver linings.

I bought a sewing machine and a harp, although not quite as pretty as Moon-Moon's golden harp, but I knew she would say, "The songs are what are pretty." I took formal lessons from a teacher as Dr. Seuss-character wicked as the piano teacher from *The 5,000 Fingers of Dr. T!*

I finally saved enough money to buy a television, a consolette on four stick legs, since the thieves would not share their TV, of course. Plus, I didn't like the shows they watched. *Have Gun - Will Travel*. Yikes, the title alone! I liked sharing *The Twilight Zone* at night with cookies, and I watched shows like *Lassie*, *The Jetsons*, and *Donna Reed*.

I collected music boxes to add companions to my momma's music box, and I purchased a record player, a cream and red suitcase with a front-facing fabric speaker, which allowed my teenage years to be shared with swoon Elvis, Nat King Cole, Jackie Wilson, and Ritchie Valens (how lucky that *Donna!*).

In my world, *Melody of Love* could still be heard. "Hold me in your arms," I'd sing to My Wanderer at night, while twirling with his picture, my hair ribbon and skirt twirling too.

The Book of Love really got my saddle oxfords hoppin', just like *Rock Around the Clock*, and I thought my dancing was good enough for *American Bandstand*.

Ooh, my favorite be-boppin' skirt-twirlin' tune was *Melt & Malt*, which debuted with puberty for me.

Hey, Snowflake, let's melt and malt

Mix some butterscotch nut with some Tennessee Waltz

Woo-be doo-be

Melt & Malt sung by Benny B and written by G.W. Braverman; I always noted the names of songs' *writers* and that name stood out: Braver-man.

The rock-n-roll tune was definitely interesting when translated to harp!

I'd sing along, sitting on a dainty padded stool by my vanity mirror, while my rolled hair dried under a bonnet hairdryer, a quasi-shower cap/science fiction contraption hooked to hose and warm air. I'd skim a *Dime Mystery Magazine*, tap my socked feet, and chew pink gum. Could nuns sing rock-n-roll? Could nuns chew gum? I wondered. I mythized pink gum as making one more alluring to suitors. That was not a very nun thing to think, while I added my own nonsense lines to the song, "Koo-be, qew-be," since the tune lent itself to fun on the part of the listener.

Dancin' with my doll in our jukebox dancehall

I had plenty of crushes: Elvis and rock-n-rollers like Ritchie Valens and Clyde McPhatter, both Andre and Philippe Delambre (the serious scientists from *The Fly* and *Return of the Fly*), and Jeff Stone from *The Donna Reed Show* and Jeff Miller from *Lassie* (known as *Jeff's Collie* in those days). I wanted to go on a picnic with Jeff Miller, us and Mullybiski and Lassie, and to a baseball game with Jeff Stone, who could explain the game to me. Both Jeffs were blue-jeaned boyish boys, baseball and bikes and science projects and hearty appetites for milk and chocolate cake, and so mannerly to girls and mothers. I often brought mint chocolate chip cookies made in home economics to my bedroom, desserts I relished while watching the Jeffs. I had a picture of Jeff Miller from a movie magazine pasted on my wall. I thought he was a dreamboat and was quite smitten with him. In the photo, he was sitting in grass beside Lassie and wearing blue jeans, a short-sleeve shirt that showed off his biceps, and his hair was done up like a greaser's with spit curl. I had only seen him in black & white, so seeing him in color—his blue eyes—was dramatic to my young heart. Every time I saw the picture, I felt lightheaded. I could not think of a better way to spend time than gazing at his picture; I felt happy and peaceful doing so. I didn't know anything about the actor, although I liked his name Thomas Noel Rettig (Noel, what a picturesque name); I liked the character, Jeff Miller. I especially swooned over the episode when Jeff fell in love with a ballerina and rescued her when she injured her ankle; I imagined myself in that scene dozens of times. I did not understand why but when Jeff told the girl, before removing her injured ankle from between two crushing rocks, "This won't hurt," I felt particularly faint. In need of his tenderness, I wanted to lean against his chest. Even though I was a girly girl, I adored rugged boys in their rolled-up blue jeans and scuffed loafers, but I also adored "nerdy" science boys, and serious boys with tragic pasts like Teddy Knight, and smart, sweet, cardigan boys with library manners, but I was not sure if all those traits could exist in one boy's personality (I had never met such a boy outside of my mind).

Around the time of *Melt & Malt*, my daydreams changed from *picnicking* with Jeff to *embracing* Jeff, the way Andre Delambre embraced his wife in *The Fly*, not such a romantic film, but I had liked seeing the serious scientist kiss his girl, which surprised me since I did not like science (science fiction but not science), yet I was attracted to scientists. I wanted to marry a spaceship builder. Each time I watched a NASA newsreel and all those serious men with Brylcreemed hair and pencils in their shirtsleeves' pockets, working hard with protractors and calculations and blueprints to make a future for humanity in the stars, my heart ached, feeling somewhere amongst those great men was my soul's mate. His intensity needed a shoulder massage from yours truly. I would both support and relax him. But I had no science aptitude. Would not a scientist want a Marie Curie for a wife, or at least a wife capable of understanding his scientific findings? Plus, I was intimidated by scientists who were not friendly at all, at least not the science teachers at my school who were nothing like Starman; they vehemently denied the existence of my real father's magical universe.

To make the ice cream truly sweet, I also had to find things to love again because doing so made the story pleasant.

I loved writing, and I was certain this was what I would dislike most about death: being unable to write about it. I still loved music, all kinds, evidenced by my record collection, and I still loved comics and books, especially ones about knight-errants. I loved stories that could not have been written by untouched hearts, stories that restored souls back to their thrones, and poems that whispered inside lonesome me, "Hello, we're kindred." And I still loved science fiction, because the possibility of nicer beings in the stars was agreeable, as was the comforting idea maybe I was not human at all, and someday my space pilot and I would ascend away from Earth!

I still loved the moon, who I went back to talking to, whether he was alive or not, and I still loved the ever stars. Still loved the flowers, mostly in memory since there weren't many blooms in Igtord. I adored learning everything I could about flowers and trees and the entire plant nation.

With Moon-Moon's Brownie camera, I loved taking pictures of things oft not photographed, non-beauties no one wanted to immortalize. "I want my life to be a testament to the beauty of being a misfit," I wrote on the border of one of the prints of a scraggly lone weed. On another photo of a simply darling gnarled branch, I penned, "I need to go where the photos are—just me and a camera seeing the world."

I still loved Root, who had aged well, considering he had absorbed all my girlhood tears. I still loved Mullybiski and how he had remained an angel.

I still loved the harp whisperer, dearly. Rarely a day passed when she was not in my thoughts.

I still loved my real father.

And, of course, I still loved My Wanderer. I wished for my story to be set in a sweet storybook of Knights and Ladies, a universe of soulmates, where my reunion with my molasses-haired fellow had been prewritten.

But even though I wanted to marry him, I also wanted to marry God—to truly be a nun, possibly a real patron saint of animals. I was not Catholic but I could be a Protestant nun. After college, I could attend divinity school to learn sacred music for the harp then I could join a convent.

Then…

This romantic passage was written into my so-far-not-a-romance story:

On a blustery winter afternoon when I was fourteen, blossoming and feeling as putrid, untouchable, and unlovable as corpse flower, I walked to the stream with a thermos of hot cocoa and Moon-Moon's angel snow globe. On holiday break from school, I hoped the Christmas scene would make me feel happier about winter. But no, I despised winter, dreaded its promise of many more months of coldness and smoke in the sky from chimneys in gray town. So, I felt as gloomy as graveyard, completely out of pink character. Winter depressed me as much as a funeral. Autumn cold was as cold as I could stand. Autumn was cozy, dark and stormy nights and hot chocolate, but I always dreaded winter and never wanted to be out in winter's inhospitality.

Two girls from school came up behind me on the sidewalk and knocked into me, making me drop the snow globe. I shrieked from grief, afraid Moon-Moon's snow globe had been broken.

"Poor baby dropped her toy," the girls cackled and walked on, letting me know the outcome of their cruel action did not matter to them one way or another. I was on my own to pick up the pieces of what they had tried to shatter.

Thankfully, the angel had not cracked. I picked up the Christmas world, dusted off its scuffs. Looking at the globe, I saw through glass a heart-polishing sight: the aeronaut's swan-white plane, with undecipherable silver symbols painted on the fuselage, was in the field I had prayed to meet him! The propellor was spinning and he was hopping into the back cockpit—he was about to take off! I did not know what to write next...but if he was my soul's mate, I did not have to fear him, for he had been made for me and I for him.

With the flower in my chest fluttering wildly, I looked at the thermos—I'd take him the cocoa, something warm the aviator would need on a winter flight in an open cockpit, whether he would be flying across cosmos or cornfields. I turned up my coat collars to try to cover my face as unappetizing as liverwort, hoping the sweet cocoa would substitute for my unsweet portrait. Swept up in wind gust like a gal in a fable, I dashed over cold hard Earth toward him.

When I got closer, as if sensing a presence, he turned in my direction and did not turn away at the sight of me. He was dressed for the cold tundra: patchy beard, aviator's soft helmet with big flaps to cover his ears, blacked out goggles, heavy gloves, and bomber jacket zipped to the neck. I could not see much of his face, but I thought he the most handsome sight in the world. He seemed so like one—completely alone with no other one to plus his life— I decided to give him the angel.

The field had once been a drive-in and this scene was very cinematic.

"Merry Christmas," I said, reaching out my gloved hand to gift him the snowy world, my young heart beating loudly in wind.

This seemed to break his heart, and he smiled at me the way he would smile at an angel—with complete admiration. His tender smile upon me radiated warmth into every part of me all at once; my Heavens, he was like the sun.

"That is highly nice of you," he said, trying to talk over propellor splatter, and the wind blew his voice around, along with our clothing and my hair. "But, dear sweet girl, the glass globe belongs in your soft hands—in my hands it would shatter, and all the snow would be lost."

I caught his words in the wind but their meanings I could not catch.

Seeing my hurt feelings, he said, "But if you really want me to have it?"

I kept the romantic world extended to him and he gently took it.

"Let me see if I have a gift in return." He rummaged the small seat and floorboard, decided against a flight plan, map, and stale wedge of pan bread.

"Is this a spaceplane?" I asked, feeling comfortable around him, a comfort which I felt around no other except Mullybiski.

He gave a smile as an answer to the girl still carrying a *Space Cadet* thermos.

"No one sits in the front seat?" I asked.

"That's the ghost's seat. I make sure she gets the best views."

I wondered if he was being serious or teasing the young girl. I felt the way I had felt during our first encounter in the wheat field when I had seen hair on his chest—I was too young for this bearded man.

After a fruitless search, he said, "My apologies. I don't have any gift suitable for a young Lady."

Lady! My heart was doing the Lindy Hop again.

"It's okay," I said. "No man has ever given me a smile."

"No, wait," he said, removing a bar-shaped rugged-metal pin from his bomber jacket. "Here you go."

His gloved hand touched my gloved hand and gave me the same feeling as starlight. Moon-Moon had been right—there were indeed stars in the daytime sky.

On the pin was engraved an equation. I looked up to say I did not understand.

"That's the equation needed for leaving Earth."

"Wow, thank you!"

Suddenly humiliated upon realizing my coat collars had slipped, baring my full monstrous face, I quickly pushed the collars back up.

Then...

His gloved hand reached out from the spaceplane to touch the lonesome girl stranded on Earth and push down the coat collar fence trying to hide her crumbly appearance. His fingers softly caressed a face that had never felt caressable, telling me with his kind touch, "There's nothing wrong with you."

Then he brought his gentlemanly hand back to the cockpit and took control of the plane. Like all wanderers, he had to leave, so the aeronaut flew out of my story again, but if he was the one, he would come back, eventually, when the timing was right.

I pinned his pin on Root's sweater, so when I hugged the teddy bear, I imagined hugging the bearded aeronaut. Was that proper behavior for a future nun? I knew one certainty: I would never again be disloyal to him by thinking of any other man, not even the Jeffs or Elvis, and I removed their pictures from my walls and my thoughts.

I did not have to wait too long to see him again—I dreamed about him that night, and in the dream, he let me fly away with him to the stars.

The entire holiday break, I could not stop thinking of him. I wanted to share Christmas with him, to wake up Christmas morning in his arms. I made trips to the windy field, the perfect spot for landing a plane, and I often sat by my bedroom window, looking at the sky, searching for his aeroplane, wondering where he was now? The sound of an airplane always stirred my heart and made me look starward in hopes of seeing his flying machine. I did not believe the aeronaut had seen me as *physically* pretty, but he had seen me as compassionate for giving him the gift. He had told me through his kind-hearted gesture of softly caressing my nonstandard face, "You're fine the way you are."

On Christmas Eve night, I dreamed he and I were in woodland, not like the springtime forests of my girlhood, but a brooding cold woodland, where the trees were thick and dark, the air frigid, the wind smoky, the morning sky bone gray, and a hard river pounded rapids against rocks, yet … the familiar woods, the colors of owls, was also there in the scene, and it was snowing just like in a snow globe. I was both sad and happy, excited and frightened, the feelings much more intense than the kinds brought about by a daydream of going on a date with Elvis. I smelled and tasted mint, while the lonesome bearded aeronaut lay with me in a sleeping bag on cold Earth, where I learned about kissing from him (I had waited to learn from him). During the dream kiss, I lost all knowledge of everything I had learned about the universe—all I wanted to know was how to bring the stars out in him.

Upon awakening Christmas morning, I felt like a stream of light alighted on my bed, as golden bright and pure as sunrise.

But my Wicked Stepmother was hard at work making more ice to freeze Cinderella. Aside from the brief warm moment with the aeronaut and time spent daydreaming, writing, reading, and dancing in my peony-colored bedroom, my high school years were not happy, romantic, or fun.

In school, while some plainly girls were like the air (there but not noticed), my nonstandard face and I were taunted as mutants. Ooh, I dolled up in bobby socks and draped my blonde hair in ribbons like my hair was a gift for a boy to unwrap (my sunshiny hair was one pretty physical trait I thought I had), but when I wore something pretty, boys and girls snickered meanities like, "Perfume on a rotted egg." Daily rock peltings, sometimes literally, but even when not, their insults and stares were as hard as rocks. Daily, sometimes hourly, the world wrote mean sentences into my story.

I agreed with Moon-Moon that one should never let a hateful person erase one's inner smile, even though that was often hard to accomplish in a world of smile erasers. I could be anywhere, a store, a library, and the cashier or librarian or whoever was manning the cash and/or policies would be friendly to the person in front of me but as soon as they encountered me, they closed up courtesy and offered no smiles, and they felt like good citizens for shunning me, doing their part in ridding the town of a monster. I did not seek kindness, for I had only found the rarity once beyond Stargust, inside the aeronaut's heart, but I sought neutrality. I bought romance comics from a particular bookstore because the woman who owned the store was neither nice nor mean; she never said anything hateful, never said anything at all, which was refreshing to me—to be passed over instead of singled out as a monster.

I did not dislike myself. I liked myself, but I knew other people did not. I took to solitude like a flower to sunlight; alone time felt like a warm embrace of sunshine that made me blossom. I developed an allergy to socializing; allergies served a function—to rid one's self of irritants! The less time I spent with humans, the better off my mood. I realized all bad moods, except for ones caused by occasional sicknesses or by built-into-Earth incidents such as bad weather, could be attributed to other people and their propensity for mean-spiritedness. For this reason and because I was never accepted anywhere, I did not get involved in many school activities. I was involved in the Junior Red Cross, and I was the sole member, and founder, of Coleridge's Flowers, a club for romantic poetry lovers (Mullybiski and Root were members too, of course). In drama club, I did not get the role of Juliet; I always ended up playing a tree or something in the backdrop. I didn't take to athletics. There was not an art or French club to join. I didn't know any other student who shared my interest in philosophy and spirituality. Igtord was not a Catholic neighborhood and there were no nuns around for me to ask about life in

108

the convent, a vocation which still called to me. I didn't have a nickname like Primo Patsy (the school's primo flirt, or "tease," as boys labeled her).

I had no interest in smoking in bathrooms or being a test dummy for a dummy boy in the backseat of his car. I had no desire to be a girl whose goal was to prove to the world she valued herself not at all by letting boys take whatever they wanted from her for their own selfish gain. In school, the only "smear" on my reputation was a penchant for falling asleep during geometry. We inexperienced students learned sexual education through botany; we learned a little more from biology and medical textbooks. I did not want to learn too much about the subject, because I wanted to wait to learn from my husband. I did not want to be knowledgeable outside of his teachings, and if I became a nun instead of a wife, I definitely did not want to know much about the activity I could never participate in.

Often, I sat in class but in my mind, I talked to My Wanderer, and while strolling lonesome halls and sidewalks, told him, "Where I want to go, I can't go by myself—because you're the destination."

I liked home economics, which I did not see as sexist once boys were allowed in; home economics proudly stated, "Taking care of the home is just as important a vocation as any other." Some students teased me, "What are *you* doing here? You're never going to be a wife." How ignorant. Wife or not, I still would have to tend my own home.

With some classmates, I got along pleasantly, the ones who asked me to sign their annuals just to gain more signatures, and who signed mine with *just* their names, but I did not have a single friend, not one who signed my yearbook with a long inscription. No one had any special memories in which I had starred, and no one wanted to spend much time with me, no more than necessary for being considered polite (too much time with me and they would have been shunned as outcasts). There were those who were openly hateful like the groups of girls by lockers who would say loud enough for me to hear, "I just don't like her." They tried to make me believe their hatred for me was *my* fault, as if something was inherently wrong with me, and they hated me "just because." I knew better. I knew their hatred stemmed from fear of difference, or jealousy of it, or possibly from a thrill their wicked hearts derived from hating; their hearts left too long in the cold and deformed by ice. There were those who were nice as long as no one else was around, but if others were making fun, they joined in and could not understand why I never wanted to be around them again, as if I was supposed to accept they had to participate in meanness to fit in. The remembrance of the day I came to Earth was not important to anyone. So, birthday parties never happened. I spent prom night adjusting the rabbit ears on my television to get *Saturday Night at the Movies (In Love and War* was on that night).

Many of the boys in high school were spitwads, and none of the non-spitwads were attracted to me. Most of the "nerds" were shallower than jocks; nerd boys were obsessed with physical beauty, pining for "beautiful" girls, the same girls who tortured them daily with insults; their preference for those girls was a letdown (none of the brilliant "Theodore Knights" wanted me). They did not like "good girls." I never felt honored for my virtue but shunned because of it; Primo Patsy was shunned for the opposite reason, and us girls were damned if we did, damned if we didn't regarding sex. But I would not exchange my morals for two minutes of misery to satisfy a boy who saw me as a candy bar for a quick unwrapping, devouring, and discarding of the leftovers.

But girls more than boys terrorized me. Many of the girls were thieves, trying to steal Coleridge's Flower. For what reason I could not fathom. At least the thieves in the gray house stole money to buy food and other items. But what could be gained from stealing my flower from Heaven only to destroy it? The only thing I could imagine was that they had lost theirs, so were envious of my ability to hold onto mine.

Aside from my inability to fit in with students and their activities, I was confounded by mathematics and all that polynomial stuff, and even though I wanted to understand the formula "for how to leave Earth," I did not. Considering my love of science fiction and fascination with outer space, I wanted to like science, but all the teachers I encountered throughout school were unenthusiastic, mean, and/or sexist, and I developed a fear of the subject (and scientists) altogether. Even though they spoke of my real father's universe with their idea of energy never being destroyed, the same as his teaching of nothing ever dying but being recycled in another form, they never admitted to believing in a magical universe. I realized light streaming from a projector to make different images was similar to the kind of light my real father had meant when he had said I was light; that idea was no different than science's teaching of energy being capable of becoming a star or a cookie or a heartbeat.

Aside from science, I especially despised English, which I should have loved. I wanted to give to literature what Marc Chagall had given to art.

I hoped someone would walk away from reading my book feeling like their soul was ten times brighter. My senior-year literature teacher, Mrs. Lemintad (and apparently, according to her sour disposition, was Mrs. to a lemon), tried to pluck the flowers from my story to supposedly make the landscape more "literary" (more desolate).

"What is the point of this story?" Mrs. Lemintad asked in the harshest tone, letting the young girl know she had wasted time and pages on romantic "drivel."

I had vulnerably bared my soul in my story, but the teacher critiqued about my "fairytale," "You write too pink."

Contrary to her intent to change me, her calling my writing "pink" felt mystical, considering my moment with Moon-Moon as a child and my momma telling me to hold onto the pink crayon.

"I'm female," I said to the teacher's goal of masculinizing my writing.

If a man wanted to write the male perspective, perfect, that was authentic (I appreciated Steinbeck's and Hemingway's very masculine and minimalist writing styles, for I liked masculine men and was drawn to men with tragic pasts and patched up hearts), and if a woman wanted to write the masculine perspective too, that was her choice, and if anyone wanted to write a story about knights that focused on battles and lusty wenches, I'd never censor their ability to do so, and I was not so naïve to be unaware some men enjoyed those kinds of stories, but I would not allow my femininity to be censored or bullied into "writing like a man," nor would I ever be brainwashed into thinking the masculine perspective was the superior perspective. I liked gentleness, romanticness, and sweetness, descriptions of weddings and kisses and flowers, and that was honestly me. I also would not dim the light of my spiritual awe to write in the standard gray approved by literatinazis.

I chose to see the teacher's critique as meaningful: a reminder to continue writing in my own style, which was obviously something I had.

I wondered if the teacher wanted to erase pink sunsets too? Did she want to rid the world of beautiful songs like *This Magic Moment*? She could live in that sunless story if she wanted and keep penning more dreary lines into it; I did not want to. The literature teacher preferred dustbowl stories, void of all scenery but grit, adjectives as rare as flowers in parched desert, caring and emotion and jolly descriptions as absent as desert waterfalls, stories which were sometimes needed in society to expose bleakness. But I preferred flowery writing, a garden of pretty glistening springtime words, which readers' feelings could stroll for cheering up.

Sidereus Sterling once wrote, "Pencils are not really made of lead. They're made of graphite, one form of carbon; another form of carbon is the diamond. As a writer, it is your choice whether to give the reader lead or diamonds." I wanted to give them diamonds. I also adored Sterling's quote, "Turn gray into silver."

But I was not averse to melancholia in stories of wintry words as long as their intention was to offer kinship in winter and not to freeze the core. As a Romantic, *Wuthering Heights* was one of my most adored books, and if I had written this one line, I would have felt accomplished as a writer: "Whatever our souls are made of, his and mine are the same." I could gladly get swept away by stormy & dark gothic ink, where I might find My Wanderer as a lonesome misunderstood character, such as Frankenstein's creature. I appreciated the poignancy of *Ethan Frome's* tragic ending, and Ernesto Sabato's *The Tunnel* was the greatest masterpiece by loneliness. And I understood why Elie Weisel's *Night* could not be starry. The reader had to be chilled by the Nazis' darkness. I did not think horror should not be written about, because that would only benefit those who wanted to "get away with it." Misery existed in the world's story. But so did happiness and kindness and silliness and love and romance and do-goodness, all traits of the human condition too, and if writers were to be true to their word of examining the complete human condition, the warm traits also had to be explored. But literatinazis were trying to cleanse the literature population of qualities such as romance, righteousness, sentimentality, and all feminine traits, to make a master breed of hard-penned writers, an elite "emotionless" group of which I could be part, if I gave up my membership in Ladyhood. To be a literatinazi, I would have to conform to their dogma that stories which examined only pleasant characteristics were cotton candy (as if cotton candy was a bad thing), and love stories, pure love stories, were meritless.

"You can do more than a love story," Mrs. Lemintad instructed to the girl about to go out into the "real world."

"Write thus!" was still my motto like a sports team's chant. Hildegard and I, champions of the Living Light! I would not apologize to anyone for my romanticness or femininity. My desire to write in pink was nothing to be ashamed of, no more than my desire to dress in pink. I was a girly girl by God and I would write with all my girlness.

The short story which had been assaulted by Mrs. Lemintad was titled *A Knight in 1962* and told the tale of a young woman, out of place in the modern world, who encountered a real Knight's armor in an antique shop. The young woman suffered public humiliation for continually visiting the Knight out of her price range, and she was seen as naïve, eccentric, and pitiful. But her unflinching faith in love eventually brought back to life the hero who gave his love for free—happily ever after. I felt the story gave the reader a sweet treat to enjoy like a warm pastry on a cold day. Mrs. Lemintad had judged the story's premise the corniest she had ever read ("a storyline for the mascot of a kid's cereal, not a novel"); the teacher of literature had schooled that although I did have a grasp of the tools of writing, "a glimmer of talent," I should use my literary craftsmanship to construct more important stories. Again, her criticism had missed its mark of changing me, and instead had made me more defiant in my goal to Write thus!, because her analogy of "constructing" a story had felt like a mystical message from Cynthia, who had called writers "builders." With my pen, I wanted to build fairy-tale-castle lovestories, cozy cabin lovestories, for readers to vacation and stay overnight.

I had gotten the idea for the Knight story from an event that had occurred during my junior year. In school, I worked various jobs, usually behind the scenes, because managers did not want "the monster" to scare away customers, "especially small children." One such lemon job, however, did provide me some lemonade. All day Saturday (ten to seven), and four days a week during after-school late afternoons, I worked downtown at an antique shoppe. The shoppe was perfectly placed between a dress store and delicatessen, where I always dined for lunch. The deli offered warm tomato soup for cold autumn afternoons, tasty hot mint tea for cold nights, and the possibility of seeing my soulmate. On Saturday evenings, after work and tea, I went to the cinema house, which was a short walk away across the street, so the job did have some perks. The shoppe's owner had recently passed away and the shoppe had been bequeathed to her son, a farmer who knew as much about antiques as a tractor knew about the city.

On my first workday, a rain-soaked Saturday, I was swept off my feet by the dream-like sight of a handsome silver-shiny Knight suit, full size, in the backroom storehouse, where I was employed to meticulously clean and catalogue the inventory. The Knight was disgracefully sandwiched between a Howdy Doody puppet and a life-size Bozo the Clown. "That's a Knight!" I wanted to shout to anyone willing to listen. I was not an expert in history, but I knew enough about historical knights to place the suit in the Late Middle Ages, probably 14th or 15th century (?), a fact ascertained by the suit's conical helmet and plate armor atop chainmail; the suit did not come with sword or shield (possibly because shields had seemed unnecessary at that point in history?); and I could not peg the suit's country of origin (I was not that skilled in historical research). Whether the suit was put together piecemeal or was the complete suit of one real knight (which I imagined would make it a rarity) was uncertain, but I knew the intact suit was worth a lot of money, especially to a museum or rich collector.

While more items were placed into the storehouse through the storage room's open loading door, bringing in enough mist to be harmful to the antique's health, I asked the shoppe's owner of the suit's cost, and he said, irritably, "That old thing, I don't know yet."

That *old thing*? For an antique dealer, he was surprisingly unfamiliar with the concept of antique.

I told him of the suit's potential financial value, but his pride was wounded by a young girl knowing more than him, and he laughed, "It ain't worth that much."

Okay. "Instead of a paycheck, I'd like the Knight suit, regardless of how many weeks it takes to afford," I said, willing to work two years straight if that was the cost.

He let me have the full suit of armor after only three weeks of part-time work, and he considered me the sucker! I had been honest about the armor's worth, not wanting to rip off the shoppe's owner, but if he wanted to let his machismo make him a fool, that was his choice.

The armor, which stood fully assembled on display stand, was heavier than I had expected, maybe eighty pounds, and I could not fathom how Knights moved, much less fought, wearing such burdensome shielding, although I suspected the suit's moveable rivets and straps and its distribution of weight across the body made movement easier than appeared. But getting the suit up the staircase to my bedroom required help from the shoppe's owner, who docked me pay for his assistance.

The thieves eyed "the loot" with the wrong viewpoint: their eyes viewed my dear priceless Knight as something sellable.

That splendid night, I lay in bed and stared at the Knight, framed by rainy window and passing fog, moonlight shining across the silver suit. Letting the idea that a real man had once worn the armor soak me in the warmth of awe, I wondered who he had been, wondered what he had died for, had lived for, what values had made him wear the suit of honor, wondered if any woman had known him beyond his metal suit, wondered what he would think of a Lady having his masculine suit of armor in her peony-colored bedroom five hundred years later in a world where Knights and Ladies were going extinct.

Inspired by *A Knight in 1962's* determined heroine and hoping to meet my soulmate (again?), I often went downtown to see movies like *Lilies of the Field* (based on one of my most adored books), and I went to The Anchor Café, the kind of café a barnstormer might wander into for some downhome pie, and I often went to Woolworth's to buy a dress or a warm Coca Cola from their lunch counter.

Although Moon-Moon had dressed simply, I liked fashion (pretty dresses, neat hats, shoes as elegant as giftboxes).

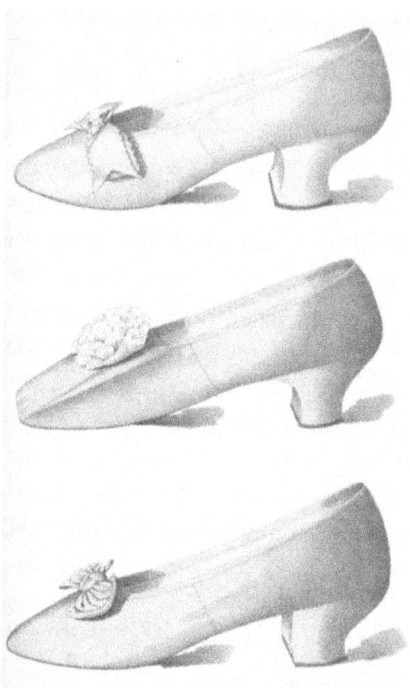

Nibbling Biskatine chocolate bars, I enjoyed window shopping for hats, wondering which one *he* would find prettiest. I especially liked window shopping at night with stars reflecting in all the windows; plus, I was a nicer, mellower person in the early mornings and late nights, when magic was in quiet starry air, unlike 9-5 air ridden with the pollution known as mundanity and capable of suffocating one with inane chores.

Then...

One rainy afternoon in my sixteenth year, I went to Mabel's Soul Food Kitchen, where I saw a handsome young Jewish fellow, who seemed so alone, sitting by himself in a big booth with coffee and cornbread and reading a book on *time travel* (!). Unlike my rugged aviator, the crisp young man in a tailored suit and black kippah was closer to my age, yet he seemed "antique," his golden ring and pocket watch and suit the color of an old serious first edition hardback. He seemed like one who would enjoy quietness, and solitude, and studious old books. Even though I avidly read about religion, I knew very little about Judaism, mainly because there were no books on the subject in Igtord or even in the nearest town's library. But I guessed the young man was a rabbi...no, too young to be a rabbi...but a rabbinical student, or at least a very religious young man, wearing a kippah outside a synagogue. He could not marry a non-Jewish woman. Yet when I looked at him, I turned into summer, sweltering and blooming and in need of him in the flowerbed. I wanted to turn away from these amorous feelings which betrayed my aeronaut, but my mind did not let the young fellow in the kippah go so easily.

I enjoyed a daydream about him, set in a quiet location I had never really been in: a study. No one had a "study" in Igtord. This study was seemingly not designed by my imagination and from whence it came I had no clue. (Perhaps the young man and I had a telepathic connection and I was tapping into his memories.) The room was lukewarm, smelled like pencil erasers, and had wooden walls as ornate as the Queen Mary's ballroom, and heavy old books in shelves, and a lacquered study table illuminated by a simple brass lamp with green shade. At the austere table, the young man and I sat in a soft dream that made me wonder if he could wear his kippah while kissing a girl. When I ran my hands through his beautiful hair, his kippah felt soft and good and holy against my fingers. He put his arms around me and brought me closer to him, which made the chair's legs scrape loudly across the wooden floor in the quiet study...

I quickly stopped myself from envisioning the kiss. I dashed out of the restaurant, letting myself get soaked in rain on the sidewalk, too ashamed to go back into the café to retrieve my umbrella. I had not only wanted to dream of kissing a holy man, a student of sacred texts, but I had wanted to kiss a man not my husband. Not suitable thoughts for a nun. But maybe the young man and I were meant to know each other (maybe he was the one I was destined to help?), and maybe my desire to bond with him was symbolic— a symbol of a deep intense union of a rabbi and nun working together for Goodness?

Later that soul food afternoon, while sitting by my bedroom window, I talked in my thoughts to my real father. Did I not have the right heart to be a nun? Should I let the dream of being a holy woman go? Was I supposed to be married to God or a man? Was I meant to be my soulmate's wife or his guardian angel in the form of a nun?

Then not long after asking those questions...

At career day at school, of all places, I met "sisters" from a "convent" of Protestant nuns, who were taking journeys cross country for recruitment. Although their lifestyle did not appeal to everyone (especially not to teenage girls whose minds were all boys, boys, boys), it greatly appealed to me. I was one of the few at their career-day booth. I found their personalities warm, fun and inviting (maybe a little "tipsy" from the road trip outside the monastery), and aside from one, they were nothing like the austere mean nun stereotype (they drove a convertible, albeit a donated convertible, but still a shocking ride for nuns), yet they, like everyone else, seemed unsure of letting a "monster" into their group, as if my "ugly" face was incapable of offering kindness. On acres of solitude in New England, the nuns dedicated their lives to prayer and contemplation and charity, and I could picture myself taking care of rescue animals, tending the garden, strolling the grounds in meditation and prayer, and playing the harp during church service.

But I was confused by these conflicting signs. When I had seriously considered being a nun a few years earlier, the aeronaut had landed in the field, reviving my desire to be a wife instead of a nun, yet now I was meeting a "convent" of *Protestant* nuns after pondering if I should be married to God or a man. What were these signs trying to tell me?

When I thought of truly finding a husband, I did not know if my good traits would compensate for my "monstrous" face to any man; doubt tortured me with this: maybe the aeronaut had just been being nice to the pitiful girl, or maybe he had been too long in the cold without female companionship? This was the 1960s and words like "adorkable" did not exist. Nerds were nerds, not trendy, and there was not a national campaign against bullying. "Ugly" girls were shamed, made to feel unworthy of love and even life, and anyone with a nonstandard face was never even seen in movies, as if we did not exist (except in "freak shows"), which made seeing us in everyday life even harder for people to stomach. There were only two movies I knew of that featured unlikely lovestory heroes and heroines: *Marty* and *Enchanted Cottage* (I adored both films). Moon-Moon had taught me true beauty was felt, not seen, and my real father had loved me blindly, but since I could not hear my real father tell me I was special and beautiful, except in my heart, doubt's loud voice, all around me in the hateful world, often drowned my real father's whispers. Thanks to books and movies and television and advertisements and what I saw all around me, I wondered if being physically beautiful was a must for attracting a fella. I was fed-up with reading stories and watching movies and television shows, where "the hero" made fun of "ugly" girls and "fat" girls and "beanpoles" and "four-eyes" and "wallflowers" and "wet blankets," a standard "joke" in stories (the "humor" of a boy meeting an ugly blind date and scowling at his buddies for setting him up with "a dog," expressing his discontent with the girl's appearance right in front of the girl), and we were all supposed to continue to root for the jerk anyway, like Disney's Prince Charming who openly sneered at the "ugly" step sisters—no, that was not charming. But when a female character said hateful things about a boy's appearance, she was portrayed as a shallow villain, yet a boy could say those same mean things and still be seen as a hero.

On one popular television show of the era, which featured two young brothers, the younger brother liked a girl for the first time and the older brother asked, "Is she pretty?" The younger brother said, "I don't know." And the older, wiser brother ribbed, "Well, if you don't know if the girl's pretty, how can you say you like her?"

But would not my soulmate be different? For he would love my soul, not my face, as long as my real father's magical universe of unending unbreakable love was real, where my prayed-for

119

Christmas miracle could come true. I would focus solely on my soul's mate, and on my quest to be with him, I would not cloister myself away like a gothic monster.

I felt Moon-Moon was proud of me for turning iceblocks into mint chocolate chip, but although ice cream was sweet, its setting was coldness, and I yearned for a warmer backdrop…

Hot Chocolate

"Bliss was it in that dawn to be alive, But to be young was very heaven!"

~ William Wordsworth

In autumn 1965, I finally broke free of those thieves and their gray town and the wrong setting for my story when I flew with Mullybiski and Root in my pink coupe toward a new life chapter, where I planned to write HAPPY ROMANCE FUN!

America was still mourning the loss of its leader and death of his Camelot, and the world continued to write about tension and war (the Cold War and Vietnam and all the other conflicts strangling the old globe).

But I was nineteen years young (after high school, I had stayed in Igtord for a while to work and save money), and my new chapter started with this sentence, "I turned on my car's radio in fresh sunlight and blasted *Melt & Malt*, while I drove away from them to him!" And the gravestone gray town did not mourn the loss of flower.

With the Knight in armor secured to the top of the pink car, earning stares and honks for its uniqueness, I drove to picturesque Adelia University, a university known for arts and literature in Biskatine, a charming northeastern town developed by and named after the founder of Biskatine Cocoa. I had a scholarship but no major, although I had a goal: to meet my wished-for love at the New England college whose brochure promised a flowerbed landscape, where my heart would bloom unhedged. If I was meant to *romantically* be with the one, fate had four years to generate my meeting with my soulmate before I took a vow of chastity at the "convent," just a few hours from Biskatine. I had learned about Adelia U while researching the Protestant nunnery's location.

For now, outside "the habit," my wardrobe would blend with the scenery in Chocolate Town: chocolate-brown high heels, matching knit cardigan and skirt mid-calf length, nylons, of course, and a ¾ sleeve cotton top the color of apple pie crust, all topped with a cashew-tan pillbox hat. I also wore a thin gold chain belt, matching dainty watch, and what looked like riding gloves (I always wore gloves, a standard of any Romantic Era lovestory heroine).

On my road trip, I considered majoring in English, but I wanted to enjoy my time in college, and if the department was full of Lemintads, I did not want to feel bad about myself due to professors flunking my soul. I had enough reasons to believe I would fail in my goals (to live and write a beautiful lovestory) without adding their criticism of my writing to the list. At the top of the list was the fact I had never seen anyone in Igtord achieve their dreams, and the fact I was not a Grace Kelly and certainly not a Marilyn Monroe or any other ideal lovestory heroine, although I did have Sandra Dee's figure and Doris Day's sunshiny hair and wholesomeness, but no one wanted to do any pillow talking with me.

The Wicked Stepmother smirked, "I warned you, peasant, you will never wear the glass slipper!"

Bell Gondal once wrote, "The key to a great destiny is never letting society make you believe you're the undestined." So, I would not listen to any negativity while writing this new chapter of Fun, Romance, and Happiness onward to my dreams! Write thus!

One thing that assured me of my ability to succeed at least in securing a place to sleep and eat was that I had a savings account; through all those years of work at various crummy jobs, I had only given half my paycheck to the thieves and saved half for me. The university's housing office, quite surly, for some unexplained reason wanting to jot a few mean lines into my story, had coldly told me over the phone about housing options for students, describing the situation in prison-like terms. I did not want a dorm room. I needed a private sanctuary, away from people who carried a gray pen with them everywhere to write dour lines into the stories of everyone they encountered, unaware that every moment spent writing a negative line in someone else's story could have been spent writing a positive line in their own story. I'd find my secluded sanctuary once I arrived in Biskatine.

In my pink coupe, I arrived at dewy dawn, listening to *Stranger on the Shore*. The air smelled like chocolate (thanks to the chocolate plant). That great morning, it felt like everyone was asleep except for me and Mullybiski, aside from whoever was in the Studebaker that turned down a tree-lined road toward another campus. Then the quiet street was just mine again, and I felt like a ship's first mate on foggy sea, pushing sails through mist with precious cargo (the Knight's suit of armor) for my heart's captain. Ooh, this was a pleasant paragraph in life's story. I could explore without worrying about being pelted by rocks thrown by "monster hunters." Mullybiski and I had left the hotel while the sky had slumbered in darkness, but now the sky looked like it had been kissed, it was so blushed. The season was not technically autumn, but I defined seasons by temperature, and it was too September cool to be considered summer, but not cold enough for me to turn on the car's heater, which never worked well anyway. My cardigan and stockings kept me warm. For breakfast, I had a stale pecan sticky bun from the hotel and powdery hot chocolate that tasted like airline hot chocolate, but in that sweet setting and mood, the breakfast had been scrumptious. Mullybiski had already eaten scrambled eggs in the room and was now content in a good nap in the passenger seat. Root sat between us. With the aid of a map sent to me by the university, I searched for campus.

Cathedral-grand Adelia University, which I could imagine Sir Lancelot defending, with its brick round towers the color of Red Delicious apples, lived up to its majestic brochure. Glory Old Lady Adelia, where students greeted one another with "A U" instead of "Hey, you," was nestled in trees and streams and pecan-and-tea breezes (the tea scent most likely arose from all the professors and students drinking hot tea in cool air).

I did not like the New England cold, but I liked the autumn beauty—ooh, the perfect setting for first love to flower! The blush-pink girl, majoring in Keats and romance, was going to flourish there, if not in class then in the flower garden—how romantic, a school with its own flower garden: sun-caressed asters and goldenrods and vine-twirled trellises and a field of cherry trees, one of those sights that restores divinity in even the most skeptical hearts. Especially beautiful in dawn: pink cherry blossoms coloring the mist. Finally, springtime had returned in my life's story, even there in autumn, and I could feel my heart breaking free of its ice sheath completely. I no longer had to make ice cream—my mood was steeped in hot chocolate.

Now the radio sang *Peppermint Twist*.

With a Forget-Me-Not flower as its mascot, Adelia U was not a big name in collegiate sports, and most science and business and engineering students went to ivy league Goldell ("Swell Ol' Gold-dell"), just a leaf-lined drive away, all those smart fellows in penny loafers. (According to legend, penny loafers were called such because boys once put pennies in the shoes' side saddles for making payphone calls. That idea charmed me, wishing to be the one whom the penny would be spent to call. A coin used to call me instead of slipped into a jukebox!) Despite my trepidation around their scientific pragmatism that "clipped angels' wings" (as Keats would have said), I felt unfathomably drawn to the fellows at Goldell, even though I reasoned I would feel more comfortable with the artsy fellows at Adelia, where the boys were softer, as if they had been raised in a meadow, as opposed to Igtord boys, who had been as rough as things from a quarry (their ruggedness had not bothered me but their meanness had).

After driving leisurely circles around the tree-snuggled campus, which had a Zen-calm water fountain in the lush courtyard, where red flowers had been planted and arranged to spell out "ADELIA," I told Mullybiski, "We better find ourselves a place to live, because as of leaving that last hotel, we are now officially without shelter."

Through the radio flowed *Moon River*. The line "my huckleberry friend" always got me in the heart, because it perfectly described my feelings for my dog. My old friend, who had shared my life in the meadows, lifted one pug ear to listen to me then went back to sleep.

I praised, "Both of my favorite beings have bark—dogs and trees. Actually, my three favorite beings have bark: trees, dogs, and peppermint."

Mullybiski's snoring said he was not impressed with my rhetoric. Old age had not been nice to him; most of his eyesight had been stolen, and arthritis made him walk as if the entire Earth was slippery. With the kind of bravery that deserved a medal, he had stayed in the gray cold house and had never attempted an escape through all those crummy years, even though I had offered him freedom, but with the magnificent valor of dogs, he had chosen to stick by his childhood buddy. Now if I could only meet a man with as much gallantry and loyalty, I thought as I drove through Chocolate Town.

Many of the streets in charming Biskatine were made of bricks, not asphalt or concrete. Their trees were old and big and showy to full beauty capacity unclipped by alleged "progress." And the town's streetlamps belonged in the era of carriages, just like many of the dollhouse homes, the kind of town one wanted to have a camera while visiting to capture the loveliness, that way they would have the loveliness readily available to view whenever they went back to their not-so-picturesque home. A storybook town, Biskatine.

Then on Main Street, I found a place to bunk: the top floor of a sliver of a white-brick two-story in a street-long row of cramped buildings made of red brick and white brick and different-colored chipped-wood sidings. "University Row" included a five-and-dime, a diner, a thrift shop, and a large clock to keep students mindful of how many minutes were being wasted on "rock-n-rolling." The Grace movie theater's lit-up marquee advertised *That Funny Feeling*, and a drugstore advertised, "Home of Stormy & Strobe, the malt shop." Despite my dislike of ice cream, I had always wanted to find a jukebox malt shop like one from the movies, where the boys were as sweet as the ice cream. Igtord's malt shop hadn't even had a jukebox, just an Eddie-Haskell-type soda jerk who whistled at girls. The room-for-rent was atop a busy patisserie, Darioles, spelled in lemon-yellow across a three-quarters

126

window, where customers could peek inside to trifles and éclairs and profiteroles and so many other desserts foreign to the Igtordian who had learned how to make chocolate chip cookies in home economics, but I felt drawn to the European bakery nonetheless. The shop was open Monday-Saturday, 5 a.m. to midnight (a time I imagined popular with students cramming for tests and needing late-night pie). A sign outside read, "Wanted: Girl for working part-time in shop. Some training provided in baking European pastries. Room and board for small fee. Private kitchenette + bathroom. Apply in back." Just "girl" wanted, not "attractive girl."

I had often dreamed of nurturing a sweet shoppe, named either Coleridge's Flowers or Wordsworth's Daffodils, which would offer a pastry or a slice of pie with a classic poem (handwritten in finest script on a card lovely enough to be a wedding invitation), so diners could share breakfast with Wordsworth (glazed lemon scones would couple nicely with *"Come forth into the light of things"*), and share a lunch treat with Keats (*"A thing of beauty is a joy forever"* tasted with warm tea), and share dinner dessert with Browning and a window painted by the stars' light.

I could visualize the patisserie perfectly: toffee-colored walls, a hearth, a Victrola, windows soaked in sunshine, starlight and dawnlight, candlelight atop tables, carnation-pink tablecloths (if named Coleridge's Flowers), daffodil-yellow tablecloths (if I went with Wordsworth's Daffodils), an ambience that would nourish many love-at-first-sight encounters. A Cupid of a bakery, that's what it would be. I could picture a half-glass door the color of a pink bakery box, shaded in a cute awning, which promised the customer they were entering into Sweetland, the kind of town landmark an aviator might wander into for warm lunch out of the cold. I could live upstairs where there would be a Juliet balcony and two windows with windowsill flowerbeds. I especially liked imagining holiday scenes in the sweet shop: Valentine's, Halloween, Christmas...

But I, the girl who had once eaten free apples, did not like the idea of *selling* food, so I would have to make the shoppe a kindness kitchen offering free goodies. Perhaps, the first slice of pie or pastry and first cup of something warm would be free, then the second helping would cost a small fee (to keep the shop going), which would mean the shoppe would have to make sure the first bite was delicious enough to have the customer coming back for seconds. And I could always donate to food pantries as well. Maybe I could convince the "sisters" of this idea.   Write thus!

Parked on the opposite side of the street of Darioles, I tapped my gloved finger on my car's rosebud-colored steering wheel. My car was named "The Lady Model." In one way, the concept was sexist, in its implication that all women liked girlish things (such as lipstick, a lipstick holder included with the car), and in another way the concept was progressive, in its attempt to include women in driving (this was 1965 and many women did not drive); cars that were not "Lady models" were also in one way sexist, in the assumption that women who didn't like masculine things didn't belong on the road, and in another way not sexist, in the idea that some women liked more masculine things. Either way, to me it had been the prettiest car on the lot with its dusty rose and cream color and interior designed by the maker of fine women's garments in Manhattan.

I stared at the shop's sign, "Call Now! Don't let this opportunity pass you by!" Had a guardian angel created that sign, not literally, but through a nudge to the sign's writer? A similar sign had drawn me to the antique shoppe, where I had worked and found my

Knight's armor, and maybe in this patisserie, I would find my Knight? I could work around my school schedule.

"Here's what I will do, Root and Mullybiski: I'll apply for the job, but in the spirit of Moon-Moon and Hildegard, every week, I'll buy a whole pie and find a food pantry to donate it to. Maybe I'll even drive pies up to the sisters."

Root fell over on me and I took that as a sign of his approval.

Across the very pebbly street, I walked in high heels as comically as Blondie. Chevy Bel Airs and Ford Mustangs and Plymouths shined in sunlight, driving the road, parking by meters, the day already picking up, an unpeaceful time of day my nonstandard face and I dreaded.

While the bakery's façade appeared Lady-dress stylish, behind the building looked dingy like the sweaty T-shirt beneath a man's work suit. The stinky dumpy alleyway was full of overflowing trashcans and potholes, sure to break high heels. I did not relish the idea of having to walk Mullybiski back there to do "his business," but at least it wasn't crowded, so he could have some privacy. A thin iron stairwell led upstairs to an even thinner balcony as rusted as an old ship anchor, a grimy upstairs door, and two grimier windows that overlooked a dusty hulking utility fan in the back window of the brick warehouse across the alley. Not exactly a room with a view. "Don't let the bed bugs bite" would not be just a funny little saying there. A white piece of paper was taped on the bottom floor backdoor, "Job seekers, enter here. Customers, please use front door."

I walked into the shop and got hit by cold air in a refrigerated room of freezers, the air dusted with so much flour, it looked like it was snowing. On stainless steel countertops were custard bowls and cookie pans and dough rounds and flattened phyllo and pastry-filling bags; Army-kitchen-sized barrels of chocolate mousses and cremes sat on the flour-dusted tiled floor.

A red-bearded muscular baker, wearing a stained apron, took a frozen raspberry mousse cake from a big freezer. He said nothing to me, while his large hands delicately packaged the cake in a dainty bakery box.

My happy face was quieted by the sharp sound of "Girl!" as lashing as a whip. "Girl, did you come for the job?"

I quickly learned the pastries were sweet but the shop's manager was not—a short stout bratwurst of a woman with a lot of mustard. Even the muscley bearded man was scared of her, and that was why he had not uttered a peep.

"Hi," I said, wondering if "Hi" was too informal. "I'm here about the room for rent."

She sized me up with her openly judgmental eyes and she had no problem with the nonstandardness of my face, but its youthfulness made her snap, "The room is only available for a worker, not *just* a college student."

With a German accent, saying "job" as "chob," she explained she needed "a girl" for the weekday morning shift, four a.m. to eight a.m., "no weakling either, or daydreamers!"

Four a.m.?

She said I would work alone from four to six in the morning. I would not do any baking, unless I wanted to learn then I could bake eventually; baking was done by her and her brother, the bearded gentle giant. From four to five, I would make sure the place was tidy and set out desserts in display cases. From five to six, I would work the counter. From six to eight, after she and her brother came in, I would do various errands such as slicing bread, putting together one hundred pastry boxes very quickly, and making deliveries to businesses and fraternities and sororities (not an appealing prospect) or to any organization that made a large custom order.

The shop's owner, whose name was not Dariole but who in my mind became Dariole, had the glamour and beauty of Diahann Carroll. As elegant as the Titanic's grand staircase, she was also full of icebergs, capable of sinking people. She was no more European than a ballpark frank, a dolled-up frank from Chicago. She and her Fifth Avenue dress and metropolitan perfume wafted into the cold room, where she dipped her mocha fingertip into lemon pastry filling. "Not too terrible but it needs to be tarter," she said to the muscular man, and like a professional flirt, she had a way (gorgeousness) of making men adore her even when she was hateful. I had a feeling she often dipped her pretty-tipped finger into others' lives just to take a taste to tell them, "Yuck." She, too, openly judged my appearance. I knew then the manager had written the help wanted sign, because if Dariole had written it, she would have asked for "an attractive girl."

"And who are you?" she asked, the surface of her voice like fine china, but under the surface, jagged and sharp, but so subtly, when one walked away from an encounter with her, feeling wounded, they would not realize the wounds had been inflicted by Dariole's hatefulness unless they really took the time to listen to the sharp tone of her voice. Words could be ironic like when someone said, "Such sweet scents" about a sewer, usually to be humorous or to express irritation; situations could be ironic, such as a bird afraid of heights; and people could be ironic too: "pretty" faces often presented ugly personalities.

"I'm here about the room for rent above Dare-e-ola," I said.

Dariole put her hand to her buxom chest as if my bumpkin pronunciation of the French word had wounded her. "My child, that is *dere-ol.*"

"Darioles are small custard tarts," the bratwurst snapped at either me or the owner.

Dariole continued her critique, "I had to fire a girl for saying 'choc-lit.' We do not make 'choc-lit' here, only *chocolat.* The next thing you know," Dariole laugh-said, "you'll tell me you don't know how to make beignets."

"I can make doughnuts."

"My child, we do not sell *doughnuts* here in *my* bakery."

I imagined she asked a mirror every day, "Mirror, mirror on the wall, who's the fairest of them all?" And she probably saw me as a fairy princess capable of enchanting woodland creatures with song.

She sashayed over to me with enough hip movement to knock over tables.

131

"All my girls must be as cute as tarts to attract those college boys and the professors too."

Was she running a brothel or a bakery? "Being cute" seemed to be the only requirement for employment, and I could tell she did not think I had the credentials. I felt bad for thinking of the manager as a bratwurst. She had suffered in a world of Darioles, and that was why she spat mustard, especially at "girls."

Dariole, to avoid being openly shallow, thought of another reason not to hire me. "That sign should also say, 'Absolutely must be able to flirt.' You can flirt, can't you, or are you still wearing your Mouseketeer sweater?"

She dipped her finger into my life to taste it and say, "Too sweet."

"The shy type?" Dariole critiqued. "Some men do go for that wholesome syrup. Maybe you could even snag a French professor with a taste for apple pie, or would that be cherry pie?" She laughed at the idea—Goody Two-Shoes having a liaison with a French professor.

I already could not stand her and the words she tossed like rocks at self-esteem. I had the familiar feeling of being another species, which I felt anytime I was around humans. I missed Mullybiski and his unconditional love.

Then Dariole wrote this demeaning line into my so-far-pleasant morning, "I don't think *you're* right for this establishment."

I smiled, not because she deserved to be smiled at, but I would not let her take away my smiles. My mood was too steeped in hot chocolate in Chocolate Town to freeze. Plus, my real father loved me, saw me as beautiful, and that was what mattered.

I turned away from hatefulness and was about to gladly leave that meeting with coldness when the manager, listening to a guardian angel?, said to Dariole, "We haven't had anyone else apply." Dariole must have given some kind of visual consent, a shrug perhaps, because then I heard, "Girl, you can have the job and the room." The manager had taken pity on a fellow non-tart.

I took the job, because it provided me with a paycheck, a place to sleep and eat and write out of the cold, and a chance to learn more about baking (and recipes for him, or for the "nunnery," wherever I ended up), even though I supposed the job would be like baking bootcamp. After getting quick militaristic basic training and a list of European pastries to memorize, and paying the first month's rent, and learning there was only "room but no board, just free pastries sometimes," and receiving the apartment's key, the manager informed me, "It doesn't have a heater." Well, wasn't that just fine and dandy! I would die within two months from freezer burn.

I brought my suitcase in and changed into denim capris and saddle shoes, because a skirt and high heels were not efficient for doing the kind of work ahead. The pillbox hat had to go too. I rolled up the sleeves of my cardigan, but I kept on my dainty gloves, because I could still be a Lady while doing "manly" labor.

After walking Mullybiski and getting him settled into his new place, then unpacking the car, then lugging harp and sewing machine then one heavy box of records upstairs then another heavy box then my record player and television and typewriter, whew, I went for takeout at the beehive busy Stormy & Strobe soda shop. The jukebox played my favorite songs and teens sat lovey-eyed in sweetheart chairs and I was a complete stranger. On the wall was a collage of pictures that told the soda shop's history; it had started as an airport diner and in the 1930s had been a favorite eatery for barnstormers. That charmed me.

I noticed a young man with Brylcreemed black hair and an erect back, sitting at a stool by the counter, yet since I was going along with the inertia of routine, distracted and focusing on tasks, I walked by a boy with hair as dark as molasses.

I shared a plain egg sandwich (scrambled eggs on white bread) with Mullybiski in our chilly new apartment: a one-room flat, which looked old enough to have lodged Paul Revere. We sat cautiously on the crumbly brick floor that felt as breakable as chalk and brittle enough for a chair to fall through. The peeling white wallpaper was as slimy and moldy as old wet bread but not nearly as molded as the wooden beams exposed through holes in the walls. The apartment had these other fine amenities (irony, yes): a burned ironing board folded onto a wall, a spot on the same wall from where a phone used to be attached, a kitchenette tucked behind broken shuttered doors, the tiniest mildewed bathroom, and the tiniest of closets (I was unsure of its ability to hold even two coats). The apartment smelled like mold and old water pipes, not like pastries, since upstairs was completely separated from downstairs, all the bakery scents barricaded by flooring whose structural soundness was uncertain. Roaches roamed about freely as if they were paying rent. I observed evidence of more roommates—mice, their existence evidenced in mouse poop. So, I kept our wrapped sandwich hopefully sanitary atop the cardboard box where most of my smaller material belongings fit, aside from my records and books (the books still packed in my car's backseat); in the box, my teddy bear sat on top of hair-rollers and music boxes to keep him safe from the dingy floor. I fed Mullybiski bites, the way I had used to do when we had enjoyed the late show on television, while snuggled in bed. I tried to stomach lunch, while shivering and thinking I was back in the cold gray house, which had rewritten itself into my life in a different form. I had a lukewarm "hot" chocolate, which had lost most of its warmth across the cold walk, but poor Mullybiski had to tolerate cold water in a bowl (cold because the pipes were cold). The floor would have been soaked in warm afternoon window light if not for all the glass grime which I would soon learn could not be cleaned away.

"Well, this is crummy, Mullybiski, I admit. But let's look at the bright side … I'm trying to think of what that is. Okay, just around the corner is a vending machine for late-night candying. Yes, I know Main Street is much more crowded and noisier here than we'd prefer, but here is the bright side for you, my good buddy: the trees and streams and garden at school, where you can play and stroll and nap. And here is the bright side for me: a chance to meet My Wanderer, who, if fate is real, will have wandered here to have a splendor in the grass with me."

I didn't have money for much decorating; I had already spent a big portion of my savings on down payments for car and apartment.

134

The rest I wanted to set back for a nest (for someday). At Pepper's market, I bought groceries. I needed the works: spices, fresh veggies, flour, honey, etc. At the five-and-dime, I bought necessity items, which had not fit in my crammed car during the move: pillows, cleaning agents, towels, dishes, a new camera (a Canonflex), and many blankets and scented candles and a table lamp for late-night studying and writing. The lamp was a dainty curvy figure with a pink shade that resembled lingerie on display at a boutique.

Rocks were thrown at me in this town too, but not as often, the folks in Chocolate Town more mellow, and ooh, Write thus!

After carrying the stuff upstairs, I decorated the walls with the same decorations from my teenage bedroom, but I was not allowed to do any painting, as if a coat of paint would ruin the pristinely moldy walls. "Don't let me catch a ghost of paint on those walls, girl, or you'll have to pay 'Dariole' for the damage."

I bought furniture from the thrift store populated with college students on limited budgets. The surliest movers (the world was chockfull of rock pelters) grumpily lugged upstairs a mattress and used bed with bookshelf headboard, a card table with two mismatched lawn chairs for dining, a small dresser, and a writing/study desk (I'd use one of the lawn chairs to sit at it). For an extra fee, they lugged my book collection and the Knight's armor upstairs too.

After suffering that whirlwind of grouchiness, I pulled my hair into a ponytail to quickly get through more necessity sentences. I swept the flat, cleaned the kitchen then bathroom, ironed my wardrobe, added limited clothes to the limited closet, topped the top shelf with a few hats, hid undergarments and journals in the dresser, sat my recipe box shaped like a treasure chest on the kitchen counter, lit candles to make the room smell prettier, placed books and scrapbook and music boxes and Brownie camera and new camera in the headboard shelves, stacked paper and pens on the desk along with my typewriter, donned the hard mattress in fresh sheets and blankets, slipped My Wanderer under the pillow, and put a folded blanket on the floor for Mullybiski, so he could have somewhere comfortable to be when he wasn't in bed. I stood my Knight by the wall close to the foot of the bed, so I could look at him at night. My cream-and-red record player had to sit on the floor by the television, since I hadn't had room in the car to pack its stand, which the thieves had pawned by now.

Throughout my moving in, with the upstairs door held open by a wedged book, the manager continually hurled mustard from the backdoor, "Don't mess up that apartment, girl." Mess it up? It looked as if it had already been hit by a bulldozer. "And don't be listening to that record player, girl, while the shop's open. I don't want to hear any of that teenage silly bop."

I had plans to make myself a sweet potato pie to celebrate, but by the time I finished decorating and cleaning, it was late night, and my beloved stars could not say "Hello" through grimy windows, so I drank a cup of hot cocoa before cuddling with Mullybiski and Root in darkness, and I fell into the exhaustion that comes after moving into a new life.

The next morning, Thursday, I put a coat over my nightgown and carried Mullybiski downstairs to do his business. I got out early to avoid crowds. At that time of day, the town was misty like breath in cold air, and the wind felt as stiff as towels dried on the clothesline. The garbage cans were overflowing, their existence the trashman must have forgotten about.

Back inside, I took a much-needed shower, albeit a quick one!, because I learned the place didn't have hot water either, girl. Listening to music on the record player, I did the grooming sentence, got dressed, and made MullyB breakfast.

I got an old-fashioned doughnut and hot chocolate from a doughnut shop just a stroll away from my flat (I did not want to go to Darioles and possibly encounter Dariole and her anti-doughnut policy).

Then I had to enroll in courses and buy textbooks.

My academic advisor, a prim woman who if she was a house would have wainscotting, had an office that warned some futures were too bland to tolerate. Lukewarm lives were even worse than cold lives, because at least coldness brought challenges, but her life was as boring as death. A lack of romance had left her face barren like flat land devoid of flowers. And, yuck, the smell of bitter coffee in every spot of the office.

In her pencil skirt, she told me and my Peter-Pan-collar sweater that a young woman must not "dillydally" but pick an efficient schedule for graduating properly in four years with a liberal arts degree. She talked to me slowly like my brain was deformed. What were my academic goals? She asked my face, as if my "wrong" face made "wrong" decisions for me.

I told her I felt called to be both a nun and a wife, but I had not made up my mind yet.

She squinted her eyes as if what I had said had been visible and strange looking.

I explained that like a scientist who studies science to prepare for their career, and an aspiring filmmaker works odd jobs on film sets to prepare for their career, I wanted to prepare for my life's aspiration—Soulmate— by taking classes beneficial for such a career: poetry (for writing him sweet things), advanced baking (for baking him sweet things), music (for singing him sweet things), etcetera. And I would take history and science and etcetera too, so I could have much to talk about with him and knowledge to raise our children; plus, I adored learning for my own sake, a lifelong love of learning developed during my childhood with Moon-Moon and her teachings.

In the 1960s, it was not uncommon for a girl's goal to be a wife, but the soulmate fervor got rocks tossed at it—I was stared at as if I was a Martian. My "ugly" face would never make a good companion, the advisor's smile of condescension expressed; plus, since universities would not let someone take classes just to meet a potential mate, I had to choose a "real" major. She gave me a list to peruse. Surprisingly, Romance was not a choice. No one wanted to be an expert in that subject? The advisor said I didn't have to pick my major this semester, since I had to take core classes anyway, but I should start seriously considering what I wanted a degree in—I was not receiving a scholarship for dating.

I told her I had to work from four until eight in the morning.

She said, "None of our classes start until eight" in a tone that outright said she thought the young blonde girl was dumb. This advisor's frail self-esteem desperately needed someone to be more pathetic than her to feel stronger, and I would not be able to convince her that trying to rob someone else of self-esteem would not gain her self-esteem; instead, the attempted thievery would do the exact opposite: since people stole when they were deprived, if she tried to steal someone else's self-esteem that would reaffirm her lacking of the stuff, and the only thing her mean action would gain would be another person who would never like her, which definitely would not help her self-esteem. She did not have time for pondering her life choices; she had a job to do.

She suggested I take World History 1 ("That's where you learn about the history of the world"), Political Science ("That's where you learn about the gov-ern-ment"), Composition 1 ("That's where you learn about writing")—and College Algebra. Before she could condescendingly explain the class, my expression must have said, "Absolutely not," because she responded to my expression with, "You have to take a math course, and a science course, so it's best to get at least one over with in your first semester. All of our basic algebra courses are filled for the semester, but we have a cross-registration policy with Goldell, and I know Professor Blagonravov's course is open—Mondays, Wednesdays, and Fridays, nine to nine fifty. It's the easiest mathematics course offered at Goldell."

What a sadist! Me enroll in a *math* class at Goldell, where the smartest mathematicians in the world went to school, and take a class taught by someone named *Blagonravov*? He probably knew how to build time machines. I only knew how to make snickerdoodles. Why wasn't his class booked anyway? What if … and this made me nervous … even the geniuses at Goldell were scared to take his course?

"Aren't there prerequisites for that class?" I asked, looking for a way out.

She said, "I just told you it is the easiest math class Goldell has. It's an entry-level class in case that wasn't clear to you the first time."

Throwing rocks at me for no reason, or maybe as a way to write "excitement" into that bland story of hers.

She said, surprised, "You took the required math preparation in high school, according to your transcript."

Did she also see the C-?

"Most of our math classes are for one semester, but this one is split into two, for those who require more time to digest the material."

She had seen the C-.

I was not skillful in math or science. My transcript did not report the time in high school that I had accidentally turned the lab sink green by doing something or other, I still didn't understand.

"Professor Blagonravov is accomplished in teaching math to non-math students, and this class is really intended for *those* students."

So, that was why the class wasn't filled; it was too dumbed down for Goldell geniuses.

I asked, "How much math is involved?"

"Are you asking me how much *math* is involved in a *math* class?"

"Like polynomials, are they involved?"

She gave me a look that said I was the dumbest person at the school, probably because she felt dumb for not knowing whether the class required polynomials or not.

"Miss ---," she scolded, and I despised when people called me by the thieves' last name, "I'm not suggesting you take Professor Blagonravov's upper-level course in transcendental number theory."

I did not approve of her bossy attitude, trying to take control of my pen, when she needed to be more concerned with writing something happy into her own disappointing life, a disappointment apparent in her sagging chair, which revealed the number of hours wasted in this filing cabinet when right outside was a beautiful waterfall to get swept away in for an hour or two with a gush of freely flowing feelings. But I didn't want to start a row and lose my scholarship. I knew Moon-Moon would be disappointed in me for not braving Composition. "Count your gemstones," my momma would have advised, because maybe I had lost courage somewhere along the way? But I didn't want to take composition, which might come with a Lemintad. I thought I could substitute one of the advisor's choices with one of my own without causing the wainscotting to come undone. "I'd rather take art history instead of composition." Why had I said that? Why hadn't I turned down Blagonravov instead? "And I'd rather take a philosophy class than algebra."

She smirked, "All of our entry-level philosophy classes are filled." But I was soon to get a lesson in philosophy.

I took a foot tour of campus, finding the rooms where my classes would be held, so I would not have to figure out the maze while I was in a hurry on the first day of school. Whereas Adelia looked like a fairytale castle, Goldell looked like a citadel. Prisonly intimidating. Gray stone.

The algebra classroom was on the third floor of SK Ride Hall, one of many math and science buildings, monitored by guards who made students show their IDs to gain entry into structures where some of the greatest technologies in science had been invented and were currently being invented. On the elevator, when someone walked off on the second floor, I noticed a sign on one metal door warned, "Danger! High Energy Experiments. Do not enter when light above door is red." Yikes. And the light was flashing red! I wondered what would happen if someone did open that door? Would they get sucked into another dimension? Into a different time period? My developed-on-*Tales-of-Tomorrow* brain was intrigued.

On the third floor, I came upon an office door held open by a ship in a bottle, which was surprisingly charming for a scientist or mathematician. No one was in the small vacated office 309, just empty bookshelves and boxes on a metal desk (unexpectedly cheap looking for the ivy league school); behind the desk was a window with closed curtains; against the wall perpendicular to the desk was a beady couch. Outside the room was another cardboard box, full of big serious books. A picture was taped to the door: an ink drawing of Joan of Arc and beneath the drawing the words "Joan of rθ." Math humor, which I didn't get. Another slip of paper read, "A geometrician gets to the point." This was the office of a bonafide nerd. Also taped on the door was a chart of different geometrical types of snowflakes. And people thought artists were weird. When I heard footsteps approach, I quickly walked away from an encounter.

After voyaging nondescript classrooms, which all smelled like paint and glue, I had had enough of campus exploring, both campuses busy with explorers. I did not feel *anxious* around people but *depressed* around people, and *tired* around people, the continual evading of and recovery from thrown rocks, so I went back to solitude to cheer up.

Before school and work started, I had a glorious weekend to write however I wished, and while I made a cake that night in the company of handsome Elliot Carson from *Peyton Place* and ate a plateful of warm chewy pistachio cookies with hot cocoa, I planned to begin my search tomorrow for just-to-be spots and locations where I might meet My Wanderer.

At blushing dawn when the sky was a blue and pink blanket perfect for a nursery, Mullybiski and I quickly got our routines done. Then we leisurely had breakfast (cinnamon roll for me but healthy kibble for him) in the company of Jackie Wilson (on the record player at least).

Then we visited the school's vast flower garden, where there was a small pond, which in winter attracted ice skaters, so said the university's brochure. I did not have any desire to slip into an ice pond; been there, done that, not fun.

That pink Friday morning, Mullybiski and I strolled a misty wooden bridge to view the town's waterfall, a nestled gush that flowed down a crag and created the tranquil "gwish gwish" sound of water gushing into water. I stopped along the bridge to capture the scene's beauty with my camera, but like Moon-Moon had taught, I could not capture to film the real beauty of the moment: the peacefulness that the waterfall's presence created inside hearts. No wonder folks in this town were so mellow—their days moved to the pace of a serene waterfall.

141

After the bridge stroll, I read Tennyson amidst apple trees with Mullybiski, dreamed of summer and climbing down big rocks to swim in the big waterfall (the kind of landmark that might attract an aeronaut to land), and I penned poemlets by a stream amongst friendly pecan trees. Still praying for the reunion with the molasses-haired wanderer, I wrote in my writing journal:

"I want a man who is an island. I'll take residence there, eventually, but first I'll explore for a long thorough while, prove myself worthy of citizenship before he grants me the privilege. Then it'll be *our* island."

"Somewhere there's a lighthouse just for me, calling me to a shore far away from the sea of lonesomeness. What will his name be?"

"I'm often treated as if my voice and I are invisible. That is who I am most seeking—the one who sees and hears me."

"Your kiss is worth living a life for."

Someday, I thought, maybe I would add those lines to a story.

Regardless of where I was, I wanted to use all my hours to seek my soul's mate. What a fantastic idea—that my soul had a mate!   And so many boys to choose from! So many sweet ones, smart ones, interesting ones, funny ones, manly ones, boyish ones, so many that looked like Ricky Nelson and Archie in their cardigan sweaters and freshly trimmed haircuts, and even the professors looked like Gregory Peck and Richard Carlson. I was completely fascinated by their boyness, their derby shoes, their spicy aftershave that scented chilly air, their boy knowledge like how to tie a tie, which I chalked up to a completely impossible thing for a girl to learn with all that loop-the-loop stuff—no, if Katherine Stinson had been able to loop-the-loop an airplane in an open cockpit, I could learn to tie a tie.

So far, I had only been interested in my aeronaut, but these boys with their cologne scents were captivating, as long as I kept a distance. This was back when a girl could dance numerous dances with a boy, share a dozen malts, and not be expected to melt all the way. My gazes did not want to be felt but to land lightly upon a boy and search around without getting caught—ooh, the landscape, where my gaze always lingered around lips and sideburns, mainly because I was too shy to wander up to the eyes, which might get me caught, and much too shy to wander down.

Not all the boys were butterscotches. Some were sourballs whose sexism was vicious, barricading, and abusive to girls' goals and self-esteems. Many boys made "ugly" girls feel unworthy of air and "petty" girls unworthy of respect. I had been around those boys all throughout school. Some, boys and girls alike, had the mentality that if a girl went for a ride with a boy in his car, she was "asking for it," and he'd often use any means to take "it" (the pronoun "it" meant far more than sex, because much more was stolen from those young women). More rapes probably happened in that era than anyone would ever know because girls would not, could not, admit to having been raped—they had "gotten what they deserved" and the boys had "gotten away with it."

But I didn't want to focus on the pit bulls. I liked the beagles and pugs and golden retrievers, sweet and loyal and wanting a friend. Appearance and race did not matter to me, neither did the type of car a boy drove, which was a big factor for some girls. I had spent years loving The Wanderer, a fellow whose face was unseen, and whose financial status was irrelevant! Even his ship was unseen; maybe he didn't even have a ship; maybe he was stranded on a rock. I just wanted a boy so stellar he belonged more in the sky than in the suburbs.

I took Mullybiski back to the apartment for a late-morning nap. I did a long foot tour of town by myself, along with my camera and a 5th Avenue candy bar. Vending machines with jukebox-round tops were everywhere in college town, as were Candies dispensers with pinball-machine-style levers. I window-shopped quaint stores: Collier's Pocket Watches, Finney's Magic Shop, Joys (toy store), M. Lee's Purses, JC's String Instruments, Buster & Gramp's Pizzeria, Mr. Benny's Hobby Hut, Walter's Waffles and Colas, Debby's Decorations, Max Tito's (toys for pets), Chloe's Seeds (plant seeds and soil and potting materials), Hampy White (nice furniture), Tonia & Heather's (makeup store), Dixon's (science fiction bookstore), and "The Bud & Spot," a town staple since at least the turn of the century, a food court centered around a water fountain, where people ate outside at tables in nice weather, and even enjoyed hot drinks out there in winter and snow. The place was called "The Bud & Spot" because one of the original restaurant's owners had befriended two dogs named Bud and Spot, and diners had praised that at this restaurant's outdoor seating area you could see the Bud and Spot, which I learned from a placard on the food court's entrance sign. The historical town had many markers for historical landmarks; the kind of old scenic town a heart with a fondness for antiques loved.

On sidewalks, I talked to My Wanderer in my thoughts, "Where are you? Flying around in your airplane? I was not really looking at any of those other boys. You're the only one for me." I was skilled at staying inside my own world and not coming back to Earth, regardless of what was going on around me. I watched other girls flirt with a little light touch of their eyes, which boys responded to as if a feather had tickled them, but if my gaze touched them, they wiped it off like mud. I wondered if those girls realized that some of the boys' eyes made offers to relieve the girl's life of *solitude* but not of *loneliness*. There was a difference. Some did not see it, and they suffered miserable relationships because of their blindness.

I wanted to adore the nearby bookstore, since a local bookstore should have been a lovely thing—a welcoming retreat for those who loved books. Instead, unfortunately, this bookstore was a snob resort. A sign on the door requested donations, specifying they did not want any "especially old books" with "wrinkled spines." This same bookstore had a roped off section for "valuable" books, as if the price tag stuck on the outside was more valuable than the priceless words inside. It was ludicrous, and quite comical, Steinbeck's *The Pearl* trapped behind a velvet rope, but apparently the folks at this bookstore did not see the contradiction. I liked the handsomeness and rarity of fine editions of books too, but I was aware that the person who bought a rare $100,000 edition of a book did not get a different story than the person who bought a five buck paperback version of the same book, so this was another world where I was excluded.

From Oreo's Bike Shop, I bought an adorable bicycle to explore the countryside's nooks and secret locales, where a car could not fit. I searched for forests where I might someday build a nest—"a perfect misanthropist's heaven," as Emily Bronte would have said. Quiet acres of emerald-sea grass and apple-red bushy trees and friendly squirrel neighbors. Then I wanted to explore farther out, so with Mullybisk, I drove The Lady to one especially gorgeous meadow.

Mullybiski and I had a dessert picnic there, where I enjoyed a slice of homemade Lady Baltimore cake, and Mully enjoyed a dog biscuit, and ooh, we must have looked quite the Impressionist painting.

Then I noticed a Studebaker slowly coming down the street and parking by the grassy roadside, so I decided it was time to leave.

Later in the afternoon, my old buddy taking another nap, I took a bicycle ride shared with "cheap" "old" books in the bike's front basket. Along the way, I thought up traditions I'd share with my husband, like planting a tree on our land that we would often visit to recite love poems at sunrise and to listen to music under *our* leafy canopy at night. In my mind, I wrote a list of all the songs I wanted to listen to, dance to, kiss to, with him.

Riding my bicycle that night, passing by Goldell University's observatory as majestic as Cinderella's castle, I saw the moon over the observatory's dome, and I knew I wanted my first kiss to be born in moonlight.

That same starry moony night, I hummed *Blue Moon*, while I drove mulberry-canopied Mulberry Way, where pale brick sidewalks were purplish due to mulberries, a road that led to Biskatine Cocoa factory, where the breezes truly smelled like candy. At BiskaTime, an amusement park once created for workers at Biskatine Cocoa factory but now open for all, I enjoyed treats (candy apple and soft pretzel), games (Skee-Ball and ring toss), and rides (flying scooters and teacups). By myself as always, riding the carousel which looked magical at nighttime, I watched all the minglers enjoy their mingleship, and I was envious of the girls who wore their fella's sweater and carried teddy bears won by their beaus.

Close to midnight, I went to Stormy & Strobe soda shop. The drugstore section was closed, but the independent malt shop was hoppin'! I sat in a back booth with a slice of pecan pie and a cup of hot chocolate, but no boy spent one of the pennies in their loafers to dance a song with me. I did not mind too much—my dance card was for My Wanderer only.

Molasses

My first Saturday morning in town, I wanted to look my

painting-est, as if I was readying for an important meeting. I wore cream-colored high heels, matching creamy sweater, nylons, red knit skirt and matching gloves—my outfit was the colors of a Christmas ornament! Ooh, a thin gold bracelet would add tinsel to the attire.

"What do you think, Mullybiski?"

Was that a bark of approval or a bark that said, "Change clothes"? I chose to hear the former, although the bark had probably really said, "Give me kibble."

On the great-to-be-alive morning, driving in sunlight, I found one of my most delightful new lounge spots: Oh Susanna's pick-your-own-apples orchard. 10 acres of apple trees. 40 varieties of apples. They also made cider doughnuts (Aunt Millie's Cider Doowops! fresh from the pan) and Big John's Apple Cider bottled in milk jugs, treats served in a barn of a restaurant. I was going to treasure going there. Apple picking and boy picking, in fantasy only, because I was much too bashful to ask a boy out, but what a way to spend a Saturday! With healthy young legs and arms picking Honeycrisps in friendly wind and hot sun and placing those sweet apples in a wicker basket then laying the basket at the weigh station, a wooden table with a scale atop it, standing next to hay bales, big pumpkins, freely roaming pet pigs, and a wagon that offered hayrides for guys and dolls to bump against each other and still be considered proper ladies and gentlemen.

It was chilly when I searched for my soul's warm dance partner, and after strolling the orchard and only meeting bees (the big bumble ones too), I sat at a rustic table in the cider-colored barn/restaurant and savored hot apple cider and a warm sweet cider doughnut dusted in powder sugar.

Then…then…then!…

A chance (?) glance through the window—or had an angel nudged me to look outside?—brought me a vision I would never forget. I saw a fellow who gave me the same feeling as when I saw Saturn for the first time through a telescope—something *that beautiful* exists in this universe? I was not attracted to him. I was awestruck. I loved him just because and I knew that instantly.

He was attractive to my eyes too. He had a magnificent profile, a strong prominent nose, a tone youngman physique, and a tall erect confidence that boldly stated he was important. Of course, he had hair as dark as molasses. He wore scuffed brown derbies and a pecan-colored flannel shirt tucked into caramel-brown casual slacks. In his back pocket was a folded blue baseball cap that stood out against his brown trousers.

My heart shouted, "There's your Wanderer, dummy, so go out there and get him!"

Waiting for a hayride, he stood in chilled air without a jacket. I remembered from all throughout childhood, boys tolerated coldness better than girls did. When it was forty degrees outside, they wore T-shirts, some even shorts! I didn't know if they were just being macho, or if they really weren't as chilled, or if they were just tougher about chilliness, but their bravery against coldness was attractive.

My desire to be with him stood me up quickly then my insecurities set me back down. "Will I walk in beauty like the night?" If he was not My Wanderer then I would not lose anything if he, some stranger, shunned me, but if he was My Wanderer and I did not take this opportunity to find out, I might not ever get the chance again. So, I dashed out the door, hoping to stand next to him in line so I would get a seat next to him. I forgot all about my face; I needed to show him my soul, which was what he would recognize, the soul who had been trying to commune with him all my life.

A shiny red Jake Wolf tractor was attached to a wooden cart that sat upon a flatbed; in the cart were stacks of hay for seats, filled with about ten people of varying ages. By the time I got outside, unable to run in high heels, he had already climbed into the wagon, obviously skilled at doing those rugged manly things, and taken a seat at the end. A loner's seat. I knew he was a loner, and I knew he was a kindred spirit, in the way a dolphin recognized another dolphin, a bird recognized a fellow bird—he and I were the only members of our species.

One gray-haired human in prison-gray overalls stood in front of me. I would not attempt climbing into the wagon in high heels and dress, so I slipped off my shoes, and even without high heels, it was not exactly a Ladylike endeavor, even with the wagon's small step for stepping up. At least *he* was not watching, his eyes turned from everyone, but one little boy stuck his tongue out at me just to be ornery.

I casually walked to the back and sat by him, not too close, but he did not even look at me; maybe he was annoyed someone had sat by him, as if I should have honored his invisible "Do Not Disturb" sign. What all had been stolen from him to make him so guarded? I could not be offended by his desire to be left alone, because I felt the same Greta Garbo way, like the day before when I had driven away immediately upon seeing the car intruding on my alone time in the picnic meadow. But, if I could trust my heart's initial reaction, he could be the one character I would not feel lonesome around in the world's lonely story.

He coughed like he had a cold. Ever since Moon-Moon's death from pneumonia, the sound of coughing chilled me.

I held my shoes in my lap, and I noticed, sitting across from me, a young man, sweatered in Goldell varsity, whose blonde crew cut was ivy league. He grinned, just to be ornery.

When the ride started, my shoulder bumped against the handsome fellow's shoulder! The event merited two exclamation points in my young life (and in my diary)!!

"Darn inertia," he said, awkwardly joke-ish, definitely science-boy nerdish, and he seemed both confident in his smarts and awkward because of them, the smarts that had isolated him on an iceberg his entire life? I was attracted to his nerdiness, of course, yet it also made me trepidatious, since "nerds" in school had always been the most obsessed with physical beauty in females.

When he finally looked at me, his expression did not say, "Yuck, a monster sat by me" but "Ooh, it was a girl who sat by me, a sweet-eyed girl." He must have seen my eyes before seeing my face and responded to their affectionate greeting. My insecurities snapped, "You're just imagining his kindness toward you."

On rare occasions, people looked at my face the way they looked at a cardboard box, but most often their expressions upon seeing me shouted disgust, fear, or pity, but this young man looked at me as if I needed no correcting, and I did not think his kindness *only* existed in my imagination—it existed right there in his welcoming gaze. I wanted to cry, touched by kindness's warmth for the first time in too many cold years.

His expression said nothing else; instead, he listened to my presence (what was it telling him?), while his gray eyes whispered a secret: he had a hidden sweetened personality. His sweet actions revealed this outright. He smiled, which seemed like something he didn't do much. Although an iciness was all about him, his character was the opposite composition of a baked Alaska, where instead of hard ice cream behind soft cake, this fellow had a soft sweet molten core concealed inside ice, I sensed. I hoped he "heard" from my aloof presence that I had a tenderness to offer *him*.

All my senses were happy next to him. He smelled like oranges and woodsy like pecans. His short molasses-black hair was kept tidy by Brylcreem (where the orange smell originated). The young fellow had the handsomeness of Philippe Delambre and Delambre's tortured seriousness, I sensed that too, and I sensed his secret personality was made from a recipe of Jeff Stone boyish, Dilton Doiley smartly nerdish, and Jeff Miller wholesome like he knew how to do boy things like fix a bike's belt and tie maritime knots. I saw him as the lead from one of my treasured romance comic book stories, "Orchids from My Beloved," from the aptly titled *Boy Meets Girl*.

"Hiii," I finally said, each little added "i" in the drawn-out "Hi" softer and lower.

"Hi," he said with the accent of wanderer, a man without a homeland who picked up bits and pieces of inflections and pronunciations from his wanderings. His voice was also a construction of stonework, an orderly brick structure that walled him off, a measure to protect the vulnerable one inside, I assumed.

He went back to looking at the tractor wheel or grass or orchard or some scene in his mind. But our rubbing shoulders talked to each other and said some pretty sweet things such as "I like you"— that was what my shoulder heard anyway and definitely what it said.

I could always return to the remembrance of the idyllic feeling of his shoulder rubbing affectionately against mine anytime I was ever in pain; the kind of joyous memory that could even ease one into death peacefully, a remembrance of how sweet life was and what a magical thing to have had the opportunity to participate in this story even if for just one flirty youthful passage on a hayride in autumn.

My young eyes thoroughly enjoyed their first almost-complete trip across a boy. I thought he could not be much older than me, maybe a Goldell senior, his boyish face not rewritten by age, but he had a presidential-confident stature and an aged wisdom seeping from his presence like aroma from an aged wine, yet he retained a chocolate-milk-drinking boyish quality too. So intriguing, his character!

Ooh, that sweet boy whose chest was the first my eyes ever truly touched. His chest was hairy, the hair unable to be contained by his woodsy shirt, where black strands peeked over the shirt's rim. Such a hairy chest for a fellow with a boyish face. I blushed. But his poor chest, coughing so, it needed my care. Maybe he did not feel well and that was the cause of his asocialness? I could not stop my lips from wanting to be social with his!

Ooh, this was the story I wanted to write!

I wondered how it would feel to kiss his freshly shaved jawline, where a nick was in need of a kiss; hopefully some other lucky girl did not already have the privilege of caring for his scuffs, which boys always accumulated when doing things like fixing bikes and tying ship knots.

He also had a few scars, especially on his handsome hands, which were the shade of butter pecan and surprisingly manicured for a fella who looked so outdoorsy. He was so masculine.

On his pinky finger, he wore a golden ring engraved with symbols or a language I could not decipher. On his masculine wrist was a rugged watch with multiple dials like a car's dashboard with all these gears and numbers around the rim. Boys. A necklace pendant bulged under his shirt around the third button region, and the muscles in his chest were outlined due to his shirt lying against him just so.

I found the back of his hair after an obvious haircut irresistible, the soft fuzz, the little tail, which made him look vulnerably boyish, and I wanted to rub my fingers there. Ooh, his hair looked as soft as streusel, and I was just about to melt when suddenly, a small bump "propelled" the ivy league grinner across the cart. His bluejeaned knees "accidentally" knocked against mine, which were almost bare in a skirt if not for nylons, and his hands grabbed the back of the cart, caging me in. I was irritated by the cad writing something unpleasant into a scene I had wanted to be a lifetime sweet memory.

I shrieked, "Get away from me," which did not make the creep budge, and I would have felt frightened had I not been in a public place with witnesses.

The handsome fellow beside me roughly pressed his hand against the ivy leaguer's shoulder and pushed him backwards.

"Hey, Sam, what's with the sorehead bit?" the varsity boy laughed.

"I'm just giving you directions back to your own seat, and if you come around this way one more time, I won't be so nice in directing you back."

I did not know what touched me more—his defending *me* or that someone on Earth, not in a storybook, and not from centuries past, belonged at King Arthur's Round Table. I knew a Lady could fight her own battles—I had been fighting mine alone for over a decade—but it felt so pleasant to have one battle finally fought for me by a Knight.

The ivy leaguer plopped back down, angry eyeing the other fellow, but to me he said with a grin, "If you were growing out here in this orchard, you'd be a cherry tree."

The old man in overalls used a grin incorrectly: to express meanness. I felt helpless in that moment, like the bunny against the hunters. My dress, which I had worn to be pretty for *my* fellow, perchance I met him, was being wrongly seen as an invitation for all men to paw and ogle, as if my intention had been to attract them all. I was tired of women having to apologize to men for ugliness, which offended *them*, and for prettiness, which enticed *them*. I was sick of women having to worry about how their appearance would affect male reactions, and I was sick of certain male minds *pretending* to be unable to comprehend the <u>fact</u> that just because a woman desired intimacy with *one* man did not mean she desired intimacy with *all* men, but under this pretense of confusion, they could paw and ogle and attack by claiming the belief that a girl wanted "it." And I was fed-up with the falsity that a woman was a tramp for having a natural desire that every beloved mother on this planet had enjoyed at one time or else none of us would have existed ("All motherhood begins at lovemaking," so Moon-Moon had taught), and I was sick of the sickening myth that a woman was a tease just because she wanted to uphold mystery and romance by saving her kisses in a keepsake box for one special fellow on special occasions.

"You are not a gentleman!" I scolded, a heroine from a nineteenth century romance.

"Eeewww," he cackled, "I'm not a gentleman."

I could tell he, this creep who the ivy league had seen fit for acceptance, was one of those boys who teased girls until they cried, and possibly one who would take "it" by force in the backseat of a car.

I said, quietly, to the fellow beside me, "No wonder I become more Emily Dickinson reclusive by the month."

"'My best Acquaintances are those with Whom I spoke no Word,'" he responded. I was impressed by his quoting Dickinson, but I wondered if he was saying he did not want to speak a word.

I decided to try another Dickinson quote to see how he would respond, "'You ask of my companions. Hills, sir, and the sundown, and a dog as large as myself.'"

Before the handsome fellow could say anything, the ivy league creep started pushing his shoe toward my stocking feet. Not just Igtord boys were as unpolished as stuff in quarries.

The fellow beside me slammed his shoe down hard on Goldell's shoe, and considering the ivy leaguer's shoe was soft fabric but the other fellow's shoe had a brick-hard sole, the shoe arrangement looked painful. "I can tell you don't adhere to any honor code, but perhaps you'll heed this: if your foot moves one inch closer to her, you'll be limping home, I assure you."

"Take it easy, Sam. What are you anyway? Her brother? Take her then, a view you could see for a nickel at any sideshow."

Above all, I was sick and tired of women being seen as either pieces up for auction to the highest bidder or discarded junk in the lost and found box for any man to take home.

The fellow beside me made a face that seemed to apologize for all boys across the world who were not like *that*.

Could I believe him? I did not trust anyone.

"She's not Marilyn Monroe," the ivy leaguer laughed, and the old man cackled, telling the boy, that's how you treat women, son.

The fellow beside me stood up on the bumpy hayride and slugged the creep in the face then stomped his hard-shoed foot between the ivy leaguer's legs, just shy of bruising a certain member of that boy's body.

"What the—" the boy screamed, grabbing his hurt jaw.

"You've got three seconds to apologize to her, *Sam*, or else you'll never be able to have children again, which would certainly benefit this world, I'm sure."

My breath paused. Even though I was touched by his defending me, I did not want violence to shatter this peaceful Saturday. The molasses-haired fellow was definitely a striking figure: severe, tall, broad-shouldered with muscular arms, the kind of man other men did not want to fight. I was glad to be a girl and not have to engage in violent activities like fighting.

The creep's eyes pleaded with me to do something, now wanting "the freakshow's" decency, "Help me! We're dealing with a crazy person!"

Other passengers watched with amusement; they just needed some popcorn to make the violent spectacle more amusing. So much for relying on the safety provided by witnesses.

The fellow reared his shoe back, promising to honor his threat, hard.

"I'm sorry," the boy squeaked.

"To *her*, not to me."

"I'm sorry."

The old man nodded an apology too, not wanting to suffer a similar fate.

I breathed again. I hoped the handsome fellow was a soft bunny of a boy playing the tiger to protect himself.

When the ride was over, the handsome fellow said to me with his eyes, "Let that jerk leave first." The jerk might try to assault me again. So, we let everyone leave, while we sat beside each other in sunlight from a high sun. He made a slightly singysongy "ba-bu-ba" sound while he tapped together the tips of his index fingers, his hands making a tent shape atop his legs. He gave me another smile, just because. I gave a "Thank you."

He hopped down, and I could tell the hop had not been comfortable, but he shook off discomfort, so he could help me step down from the wagon. I loved his gallantry. Just because a woman wanted to be treated as an equal—equally deserving of life, love, respect, and pursuit of knowledge and aspirations—did not mean she wanted to be treated like one of the guys. Chivalry was not sexist but part of the magic of courtship.

"Here, angel, watch your step," he said.

Angel? Did he call all girls angels?

I was surprised I remained solid, feeling his hands against me. I kept my gloved hands in the air, one hand holding my shoes. When I slid against him, his belt rubbed through the soft fabric of my skirt in such a way I blushed as red as a leaf in autumn. Then Oww! My bare foot stepped on something, a small fluke that interrupted my romantic paragraph.

"Are you alright?" he asked, his courtly hands still cupped under my arms, but making no ungentlemanly attempt to explore the feminine scenery.

"It was just a rock." Darned rock!

He brought his hands back to his own body, stuck them into his pockets. "You're sure you're not hurt?"

"My stockings suffered more than I did."

Embarrassed, I put on my shoes, covering my feet from his sight; the stockings did not conceal the scars from where skin had been removed from my feet to reconstruct my face after the accident.

Up close, I saw the fellow's bare eyes, gray and calm as ghostly sea belying turbulent waves, and beneath the still waters was a world: strange creatures, exotic choral, sunken ships, lost treasures. I wanted to visit his world. But his eyes were protected by beautiful eyelashes for a boy. He needed the protection from anyone looking too deeply into his wet eyes, where hid many tears, which I sensed. I had always been attracted to men who had survived immense sadness, and I knew this was the one with whom I had connected with across space, the one I had talked to in my thoughts, the one whose sadness and loneliness I had felt aching for me every night of my life, because his eyes showed me his true ID.

"I have to head back to work," he said with a serious tone for a boy with a baseball cap. "Are you staying here?"

"No, I have to go home, to walk my dog."

"'A dog as large as yourself.'"

I shook my head. "He's just a short stocky pug."

The fellow's expression said a puzzle in his mind was beginning to fit together. He smiled, and he had surpassed handsome two smiles earlier; his looks altogether surpassed handsome in my eyes.

"Do you have a dog?" I asked, since dog people usually bonded.

"Unfortunately, no time for a dog. Here, I'll walk you to your car." The older protective brother I never had.

He and I must have looked like a Great Dane walking alongside a Chihuahua.

Dragonflies were flying in blue sky, and he watched as if they were airplanes. To keep the sun from obstructing the airshow, he put on his baseball cap, where a white "B" was emblemed in blue.

"Is that your team?" I asked, wanting to make conversation with him the way ____ wanted to make ____ with ____ (I could not think of an analogy since nothing on Earth wanted anything as much as I wanted his companionship).

"Well, that used to be my team: the Brooklyn Dodgers."

He was conversing with me, "the monster," in public, with no fear of rocks being thrown at us.

"What—" I couldn't think of the word. I knew very little about baseball other than it existed and had—*positions*. That was the word. "What was your position?"

"Position?"

I thought I had said the wrong word.

"No, angel, I didn't play for the Dodgers. I never played professional ball."

"Ooh." Dummy. Hopefully, he would not let my lack of baseball knowledge prevent him from wanting me as a friend.

"Why do you like that team?" Was he from Brooklyn? That was what I really wanted to know: his backstory.

"Number 42."

I had no idea what he was talking about.

"Jackie Robinson."

"Ooh. Who's she?"

"*He* played for Brooklyn, the first black man to play in the major leagues."

"Ooh, that's right, knew that name sounded familiar." How dumb did I want to let him know I was about baseball?

"That's a real man," he continued, glowing about a hero. "Jackie Robinson. I once wanted to be someone who others would model their lives after, and Robinson really did it. April 15, 1947, he crossed the color line and stepped onto the diamond, most magnificent diamond on Earth, the baseball diamond."

"April 15, 1947, exactly one year after I was born."

He quickly did mental math; now, he knew my age.

I had a feeling if he and I had not grown up in this world of rock and ice, we would not be nervous at all about slips and scuffs; instead, we would be as comfortable with each other as stars and sky. Unfortunately, we had suffered freezes and peltings, but as long as he gave me welcoming pathways to follow with questions, I was not as nervous, but still too nervous to formulate sublime questions, and instead I asked, "So, you're from Brooklyn?"

"Kind of."

Kind of? Was he trying to be mysterious?

"So, you don't play baseball?"

"Ah, I used to make a few homeruns." Showing off, he pretended to bat a ball, which highlighted the apple-hard muscles in his youngman arms.

I knew of homeruns not because of baseball, but because I had heard girls talk about "homeruns" in relation to what boys had "scored," and I hoped he had not been making a euphemism. I decided not to "oooh" and "aaah" over his homeruns in case he had not really been talking about baseball, although he did not seem like the crude braggart type, more of an alone in a library or lab type (except during the outbreak of machismo on the hayride), and I could not picture him engaging in "locker room talk." He seemed so alone.

Walking across grass and leaves toward the parking lot, we listened to crickets make music that heralded a return to the autumn chapter in Earth's story.

"'If moonlight could be heard, it would sound just like that,'" I gave, something pretty since my face was not. "That was how

Hawthorne described cricket song." I wanted him to know if I was his girl, I could give him lovelies—such as lovely poems and sentiments—to make up for my unlovely appearance.

"If you hear the song get louder, higher pitched," he said, developing a conversation with the "monster" that was not intended to pay lip service to politeness but to get to know one another, "a gent is calling to a Lady, but if his beckoning gets softer, his Lady has arrived."

His Lady has arrived. I wondered if he felt the same.

As if he had no more time for frivolous talk, he asked, "What do you want to do with your time on Earth?" This fellow was not all bikes and baseball. I had not been asked a profound question like that since I had been asked by my momma the lifestory I wanted to write.

"I'm conflicted between wanting to be a nun and wanting to live a lovestory, the Cinderella of love stories, happily ever after," then I swiftly added, unable to believe my candor, "and creating the literary counterpart of *Isn't It Romantic* is a goal of my heart."

He looked at me as if I had said I wanted to walk across water; my heart's question was—did he believe that was possible?

Before he could respond, or throw rocks, I asked, "What about you?"

That diversion tactic did not work. He responded to *my* goals first. "You want to be in love and to write love stories, or you want to be a nun?"

I nodded, my heart beating in a way that if star twinkling could be heard, it would sound like that. Why had I told him the nun thing? That definitely would not make him want to ask me on a date.

"But I'm not sure if a nun is allowed to be a hot chocolate addict!" I laughed.

"That doesn't sound too nefarious."

162

"Or if she should spend her Saturday with doughnuts and sweet cider."

"I'm fairly certain none of that will disqualify you from the convent. So, you're nineteen?" he asked, bluntly.

My Gidget figure probably responded "No, fourteen," but I clarified, "Yes, nineteen."

"Don't tell me you're a student at Goldell."

I was offended by his assumption that the young blonde girl was not an ivy league student.

"No, I'm not a student at Goldell. I'm a writer, and I play the harp, and I work at Darioles, the morning shift." Before I could say, "And I'm a student at Adelia," he said:

"The bakery on Main?"

I nodded but I did not want to talk about Darioles, since my working there was not a vital trait of my character, just something I had to do to pay rent; I wanted to give him a portrait of myself that did not include mundane details—Mona Lisa was known for her smile, not for her backdrop.

"What kinds of foods does the bakery have?" That was an awkward question; he was obviously unskilled in small talk. Watching him try to put chitchat together was like watching a child with building blocks; we were both unskilled in communication, so it would be interesting to see the kinds of conversations we would build together.

"Ooh, it's a patisserie with desserts and breakfast pastries."

"Ah, that sounds … good. I'll have to try that."

Swoon!

"Now your turn: what do you want to do with your time on Earth?"

"I'm The Snowflake Physicist," he said like "I'm Santa Claus."

So, my initial impression that he was a science boy had been right. I felt intimidated yet I was intrigued: *Snowflake* Physicist? *Snowflake Physicist.* Even the title of his profession was romantic.

"I want to create this world's largest snowflake." He kept his eyes on mine to see their reaction.

Hearing him say "Snowflakes" made me tingle all over as if I was in a field of snowflakes, like I was in the familiar owl-ish woodland, as if "snowflake" was a codeword to my soul that reminded me "he is the one."

I felt *the click*—of personalities lining up and perfectly clicking together. We were both where we were meant to be: with each other.

"Wow, a desire to create the world's largest snowflake—that is the most beautiful aspiration, especially in these Cold War times."

This comment, and the way our eyes had connected in the moment it was spoken, seemed to certify for him our meeting was written by fate. But what character did he want me to play in his lifestory? Future wife? Friend? Lab assistant? Ooh, to be helpmate for his important work!

He broke the gaze. "I'm ashamed to admit I haven't been working on that project as diligently as I should."

"I hope you do make such a wonder."

He seemed so young to be a physicist, so he was a genius, which made me more nervous. Did Sandra Dee belong with Albert Einstein? I made a mental note: learn physics. That would not be an easy task for the girl who had once answered the algebra-test question, "If two trains blah blah blah" with "The passengers should have taken an airplane!"

"Is it true," I asked, trying to be my smartest for him, "that all snowflakes are unique?"

"Some snowflakes are fairly similar, but yes, each one is different, because each one travels a unique path which shapes it. Each one sails through different clouds, different temperatures, all a part of the grand water cycle, or as I say, the grand snow cycle. Ah, to return as ice or snow, that is the question. Coldness always comes back around, but some of that coldness becomes a snowflake, and that's a cycle that will never end." He sounded like Moon-Moon, being more symbolic than scientific. "There are more possible forms for snowflakes than atoms in the universe."

The subject of snowflakes was a magic carpet to him, flying him to wonder.

"And, aaah, the geometry of snowflakes is mesmerizing, just an absolute geometrician's paradise! There are some basic types from simple prisms to the absolutely stunning stellar dendrites, the shape most popular for holiday decorations, and aaaah, the impressive fernlike stellar dendrites…My apologies. I didn't mean to get so elated." He was embarrassed for letting his wonderment show.

"Ooh, don't apologize. I appreciate what you said. I treasured learning this is a world of so many unique snowflakes."

He really was like the smart young man, sweet and rugged, from "Orchids from My Beloved," who nurtured flowers and preferred greenhouses to parties, except this fellow beside me nurtured snowflakes.

Arriving at my car, he looked at The Lady with a satisfied expression on his face that said the puzzle he had put together in his thoughts matched the picture on the puzzle box.

"Jeanne d'Arc has safely returned to her steed."

I wondered why he had referred to me as Joan of Arc? Was he also deeply intuitive, capable of sensing my interest in saints, Knights, and Ladies?

He picked a stem of hay off the shoulder of my cotton sweater. "Static electricity draws the darndest things to each other."

I didn't respond, not to be coy or to deceive or play games, but I was scared of revealing views he might not share and feeling once again coldly stranded from everyone with a viewpoint only my eyes could see. I knew my timidness put a big burden on him to be the

166

first to say, "I like you," but My Captain would have to be Knightly brave if we were to get our ship sailing toward Togetherness.

He opened the door for me. "You should keep that locked."

"It does a girl's heart good to know there's at least one gentleman left."

"And one Lady, an, er, *unsophisticated* girl in a sophisticated world." "Unsophisticated" was the proper word in those days for what he was implying, and I blushed intensely. Only an "unsophisticated" girl could be a nun.

He kept his hand on top of the door and asked, "Are you heading straight home?"

I nodded, while sitting down in the driver's seat.

"Stay safe," he said.

I didn't know if I was flattering myself, but he seemed hesitant about letting me leave his story.

"Does your Sunday include Mass like all good Catholic girls?"

"I'm not Catholic. I'm Protestant. We have a few monasteries too, even one not too far away."

"Ah, so does your Sunday include church like all good Christian girls?"

"In a way, if you consider trees preachers, the way Herman Hesse did. Arboretums are my churches. Not that I'm not a good Christian girl. I hope I am, especially considering my interest in being a nun." I was flustered. "I believe in Christ's values, but I don't attend any formal church, but I do attend values." I hoped my do-goodness would not scare him away, but if it did, he was probably not the fellow for me.

"Well, Christ's values have never taken on a sweeter form. You're a little peppermint."

Hearing him say "peppermint," again I felt like he had spoken a codeword to my soul. I felt like a hypnotized person hearing, "Wake up," from the hypnotizer. I was waking up to the truth: I had known this fellow for much longer than a weekend.

"I mean peppermints are sweet, and you're wearing all red and white, and peppermint is associated with the Christian holiday treat, candy canes. There are even peppermint snowflakes; perhaps I'll explain that someday." Now his words were coming out as flustered as a kite in strong wind. "I'll come by for *un café* one morning at the *pâtisserie*," he said in perfect French.

"Okaaay. Monday through Friday, five to eight, I'll make sure you get the freshest coffee." I had not meant that to sound so un-Ladylike un-nun fresh.

I realized my feelings for him were as obvious as the sky's blueness.

"I hope you have a nice afternoon with your stocky dog and a fruitful Sunday of prayers amongst the trees. What will you be praying for?"

"What I always pray for: to be the main character in a lovestory...if that's my destiny."

Just when I thought I would finally get my wish, the fellow I wished for looked ashamed, like a married man who had gotten carried away with flirting but now that the flirting was becoming something more, he had to go back to his wife.

"I am not available for love." The words were awkward but not hateful, just matter of fact, wasting no time getting to the point. "I can't be a character in a lovestory."

He had not said "I can't be a character in *your* lovestory" but "*a* lovestory"—any lovestory? My heart would have been wounded had he meant he was not available for the monster to love, but I sensed he felt fated to be in a story which would not *allow* him love, as if he was a character doomed to solitary confinement, but why? He did not wear a wedding ring and I did not think he was married to a woman but to...an obligation?

168

"I am available for conversation, however," he added, quickly, to keep my heart from suffering too long on the "I'm not available for love" comment. "I need to know you, hoping you will allow me the opportunity."

Before I could ask, "*Need* to know me?" he shut the car's door on the overzealous girl and wandered away but stayed in my thoughts.

The rest of my afternoon and my night were spent in ponderings of him and writing him poemlets in bed.

Unloved man

I want to plant a kiss on your chest like an explorer plants a flag.

Undiscovered territory   Your heart!

May I claim it?

What a beautiful fellow—a creator of snowflakes. How was such a fantastic endeavor even possible?

"Not available for love"?

I entertained thoughts identical to *Tales of Tomorrow* thoughts from girlhood: what if he was a space traveler, unavailable for love, because he was about to embark on a lifelong voyage in the stars? He had said he had not been spending enough time on building the biggest snowflake, so what was the physicist spending his time on? Maybe he was a time traveler? The Dodgers *used* to be his team. What had he meant by being "kind of" from Brooklyn? What if he was an alien in disguise on Earth like the character from *The Day Earth Stood Still*, and he had developed an interest in Earthly things like baseball, while making the largest snowflake on *this* world? What was the story behind the ring he wore with symbols engraved on it? What if he was a scientist involved in a mad dangerous experiment and could not get a gal mixed up in it? What had he meant by "I *once* wanted to be someone who others would model their lives after"? What if he was a ghost like from an urban legend—the boy who died on prom night? Ooh, that was ridiculous even to me. What if he was turning into a lizard man?

169

I had watched too many *Outer Limits* episodes.

Maybe he was not available for love because he simply already had a girl? I did not like that explanation at all! Besides, he wore a ring on his pinky, not his wedding finger, but my Wicked Stepmother cackled, "What if the ring signifies his love for someone else?" Maybe he had been just being nice, saying he could not be a character in a lovestory when he had really meant *my* lovestory? But this was an even worse explanation for his unavailability for love: his cough was the result of a serious illness and he was dying. I could not bear that idea.

The taste of molasses, I remembered, was bitter-sweet.

But I had prayed to be his light, his guardian angel, and I would help him through anything if that was my destiny.

I went back to the orchard the next afternoon, hoping to encounter him again, and my insecurities sadly concluded, he would have defended *any* damsel in distress, and he was a smart boy who probably asked big questions like "what's your purpose on Earth" to everyone, and he had said I was a sweet little peppermint because of my red-and-white wardrobe, and he had probably told me he would come in for coffee to be polite, because if he had liked me, even as a friend, he would not have walked away without letting me know how to reach him again other than through a chance meeting at the sweet shop. Maybe he was not My Wanderer. Yet... "I *need to* know you" and my strong sense of our deep connection...

Sunday night, I felt anxious, excited and nervous. I did not like Sunday night because I did not like its promise of Monday morning (school and work and "being around people" morning). But I was more nervous than normal by the prospect of having to suffer crowds. Professor Blagonravov's algebra class would be my very first college class. I didn't understand why that made me so anxious. I had never put much worry into high school classes (more into high school crowds, avoiding them!). My life's goal— writing a beautiful lovestory—did not require making A's in school. I also did not want to go back to the cold freezer Darioles and suffer being around the sour tart and getting my mood splattered with more mustard. The weekend had been so lovely but had ended too quickly, and I realized I had not enjoyed a moment that pleasant since a childhood walk with Moon-Moon.

Now, with my hair in rollers, I sat in darkness lit by television glow. Sitting on the cold brick floor, I sipped a cup of hot chocolate which created a froth around big marshmallows, and I ate from an open box of glazed doughnuts and an open carton of thick-crust cheese pizza from Buster & Gramp's Pizzeria. A knit blanket was wrapped around me and "Moonlight Serenade" (my long nightgown the color of "moonlight"), a very pretty nightgown wasted on the night's activity: watching *Lassie*. I preferred the original series and was unhappy about Jeff's departure. I wondered if the physicist would find the nightgown pretty. Instead of finding out, I watched Lassie rescue somebody, while *my* dog was intent on "rescuing" a doughnut. He kept coyly scooting closer to the doughnut box and pizza box, his tail doing the "unsure wag,"unsure if I would share, and even though I did not like giving him junk food, I gave my good buddy a bite of crust, and his tail did the full-on "happy wag."

"Now gimme a lil' them doughnuts," his puggy face said.

After *Lassie*, I flipped back and forth between *My Favorite Martian* and the last thirty minutes of *Voyage to the Bottom of the Sea*, watching the actor who had played André Delambre in *The Fly* now playing Commander of *Seaview*. I kept the TV on for company.

At my writing desk, I read a bit of Bronte before watching *Perry Mason* and *The ABC Sunday Night Movie*.

After washing my face before bedtime, I scrutinized the girl in the medicine cabinet mirror—before I encountered others, did I think this face so terrible? What had The Snowflake Physicist thought of me? Not enough to tell me his name! I turned off the bathroom light and the unsatisfactory reflection in the mirror.

I got into the cold bed, laid on my bumpy hair-rollered head, and cuddled with Root and Mullybiski, the only two I could count on to never throw rocks at me—and my soul's mate, I thought while looking at my Knight, who I could count on to love me too, if I could find him again—

The symbols engraved on his ring looked like the symbols painted in silver on his snowflake-white aeroplane!

The Snowflake Physicist was the aeronaut!

I sat up beside myself with excitement.

Had he recognized me as the lonesome girl whose face he had caressed all those Christmases ago? My nonstandard face was one thing: unforgettable. Maybe that was why he needed to know me?

What had he ever been doing in Stargust and Igtord? What was he doing now in Biskatine?

Ooh, so much mystery! I loved it. I needed another doughnut. I thought I may as well get another cup of cocoa too, for I'd never be able to sleep now anyway.

With cocoa and doughnut, and lights on, I sat up in bed.

"Can you believe this, MullyB ... I mean the chances ... Wow! The story is getting truly magical, isn't it? But ... is Biskatine just a stopover for the aviator?" I asked my friend. "Yet he said he would come by for coffee at the patisserie. When? The next time he's in town? Two years from now? Is he planning on us getting to know each other through brief interludes whenever he flies into town? He said he had to get back to work but maybe he had meant work on his airplane? What's his story, MullyB?"

The pug answered, "I'd like some doughnut, please."

The next morning, after I wrote routine's sentences, I had to walk downstairs in the solid-cold darkness of four a.m. and go around front to the bakery, since I did not have a key to the back door. My high heels were slippery on dewy bumpy bricks.

Inside, I turned on the lights, which splashed across walls the color of custard with white wainscotting "icing." I locked the front door behind me. The dark misty street looked like the kind Jack the Ripper would stalk. Even the doughnut shop wasn't open yet. Stores lining the opposite sidewalk appeared dead still, desolate, and eerie, but I knew in sunshine they would look cheery again: Mama's Home Made Good bakery and Marmalade's hat shop and Joys toy store.

New England September was chilly pre-dawn, so I blew warmth into my gloved hands. I turned on the heating and tabletop radio for companionship. The deejay's voice made me feel safer, someone else awake at that hour, as if he was close enough to come to my rescue if a burglar broke in. Plus, I liked his Alan Freed rock-n-rollness, spinning the classics.

I took down chairs that were stacked atop tables and made that activity more fun by dancing to *Jailhouse Rock*. I made up lyrics, so while Spider Murphy was playing saxophone and Little Joe was blowing the slide trombone, "This girl was sweepin' the floor all alone." If anyone had walked by the window, they would have seen a gal dancing like she was in her peony-colored bedroom with no one watching.

I put on fresh coffee, cocoa, and tea, and thanked The King for his company.

Doing the jitterbug with an invisible dance partner, boogeying to *Deep Sea Ball*, I drank cocoa and ate yesterday's éclair (the "board" part of room and board).

While the Everly Brothers were waking up Little Susie, I wiped booth seats.

I wondered why this cleaning would be necessary the rest of the week; by the time I'd arrive to work each morning, the shop would have only been closed for four hours, since midnight, and the night crew would have cleaned too, so I could not understand the point of me doing it again.

Even while dancing, I was sleepy. I kept yawning. I thought of Mullybiski upstairs, warm in bed, and that made me even sleepier. I needed rest for math; I needed a very alert brain for al-ge-bra.

From the freezer room, I took thawed desserts and let them "sell themselves," as Dariole had said, in display windows.

At five a.m., I flipped the "Closed" sign to "Open," although I did not relish unlocking the door, the streets still creepy, the teddy bears in the toy store window across the street still hidden in darkness; my scared eyes and clenched heart only saw spooky shapes: bogeymen everywhere, in every shadowy figure. To gain a feeling of safety, I looked down the road, where a neon "Hot Coffee" sign flashed open darkness; at least a few others were on the late shift too, but something about neon flashing in nighttime made me shudder as if I was in a horror story all of a sudden.

I slightly turned down the radio, which sat on the glass display counter (meant to display the legs of Dariole's "tarts" as much as the desserts). For fifteen wasted life minutes, I stood by the obnoxious cash register.

I decided not to waste any more moments, so I daydreamed about owning my own pastry retreat, while watching my fingers dance to radio songs, not noticing a car pull up.

I still felt anxious. I had never liked customer service jobs, but I had worked with customers before, so I could not understand why my anxiousness came to a climax when I heard the bell on the door's handle announce an entrance—either *his* entrance into my story, or a burglar's!

My heart unfurled in an instant upon sight of My Wanderer.

I recognized him behind the patchy beard, more like a very shadowed five o'clock shadow, he had grown in two days; the streusel-brown beard lighter than the blackness of his molasses hair. I had never seen a young man with a sea captain's beard; not many young men in 1965 had beards. If when I had met him on the hayride, he had been donning a beard, I would have recognized him as the aeronaut.

He carried a caramel-colored briefcase, and he wore gray trousers and a gaberdine Ricky jacket the brown color of a monk's robe, the jacket zipped to the top of his gray diamond-patterned tie and white shirt collars.

He looked incredibly handsome. I knew why the sun came up every morning: what a view on Earth. My heart pulled up to get closer to him.

My heart is blooming

Please pick it while it's red and ripe

Offering the sweetest of its prettiness

I noticed his car outside, parked in front of mine at the meters, a masculine V8 mint-green 1940s Studebaker Starliner convertible with the soft top down.

When he was close enough for me to smell Brylcreem, I could see the individual hairs of his beard, which looked quite soft, streusel for my fingertips to dream of caressing.

He looked at the radio's speaker as if a song was something he could see.

"Hiiii," I said.

I hoped he liked my dress, more a springtime dress than autumn dress, the top made of soft pink cotton, the skirt the pink-and-white pattern of a Lady's teacup and belted at the waist with white belt, beneath which the dress became ruffled and flowy, meant to billow while dancing. I also wore white gloves, and my shoulders were draped with a snowy-colored cardigan; would not The *Snowflake* Physicist approve?

"Hi." His voice was friendly but did not reveal any clues of mutual interest in me, or even any recognition of me as the girl just Saturday he had told he "needed to know" or the girl who had given him a snow globe for Christmas five years earlier.

He still had a cough.

"I wonder if I could change the station?" he asked, setting his briefcase on the counter.

"Okaaaay," I said as dreamily as if he had asked me to go to the moon with him.

"Too much rock-n-roll does to the brain what sugar does to the teeth."

"Okaaaay." If my voice got any dreamier, he could fly away on it.

I was in love with *his* voice, perfectly blended masculine and boyish like coffee and cream. Stars could shine in a voice that velvety rich. Stony, yes, but there was a boy hidden behind the stonework, I just knew it.

He fiddled with the dial until Nat King Cole turned the bakery into a ballroom. *A Handful of Stars.* "This music is more suitable for twilight hours, don't you agree?"

"Yeesss." I wanted to give him a handful of stars. "This song is from one of my most adored records, Nat King Cole *Sings for Two in Love*," I offered, hoping he would offer more about himself in return.

But instead of even looking at me, he looked at the menu behind and above me, where white bulky magnetic letters and numbers advertised a dizzying array of choices and prices, which looked too impersonal, not home cozy; my bakery would have a chalkboard menu fancy-script handwritten in pastel-colored chalk: one price for everything (and first pastry free).

"Ba-bu-ba," he hum-said, while contemplating what to order.

"Do you have that record?" I asked.

"I have it memorized," he said flatly as if the flat tone could hide his feelings, which had already been revealed in just saying he had memorized the record.

"You Stepped Out of a Dream."

"A Little Street Where Old Friends Meet," he said less flatly, as if learning, or re-learning, how to make a friend.

Since his eyes were occupied with the menu, allowing my gaze to roam him freely without getting caught, I looked at his hands. No writer had ever written a description of a man's hands that did justice to their sexiness, so I would not even try to do what even the greatest could not do. He still wore the mysterious engraved ring. Against his tie was a gold necklace, but I could not tell what, if anything, hung from the thin chain, because it was concealed by his jacket. I observed two pins on his lapels, one looked like a space capsule (!) and the other looked like a fraternity pin. I did not like that, his belonging to a clique. My Wanderer did not fraternize. My Wanderer wandered the world, alone, searching for a home, which he would only find in me. But maybe it was a fraternity of

177

beings from another world? The fraternity's last symbol looked maybe like an "F," but the other two symbols didn't look like any Greek letters I had ever seen. *Tales of Tomorrow* indeed.

I didn't know if he had a girlfriend or not, but I knew he was a bachelor, because one) he was not wearing a wedding ring, two) he was at the bakery for breakfast (this was 1965 and wives made breakfast), and three) he looked too awake, too fresh-faced for five a.m.—no wife worthy of wifedome would let *him* get much sleeping done at night. Plus, he didn't smell like dry cleaning like most husbands; and his clothes, well apparently, he had no idea how to use an ironing board. The poor fellow, destitute of a woman's care. I wanted to iron his pants properly then make him pancakes.

"How about a babushka charlotte?"

At first, I thought he had called me "Charlotte" then I remembered charlotte was a kind of dessert—but what kind? I looked at the desserts all around me, as pretty as they pleased on display, and I did not know the names of hardly a single one. Doris Day didn't belong in the European bakery, and my self-esteem shivered against doubt's cold touch: the bearded ivy league man who spoke Français was too sophisticated for cherry pie, and too cool for the domesticity of a wifey.

I stammered until his smile-wrapped words gifted my hurt ego, "Don't worry. There is only one woman in the world who knows how to make a *babushka charlotte*—my babushka, my grandma on my pop's side of the family baobab tree." Something inside him grabbed back any other personal information.

"Baobab tree?"

"That's just one strange tree, the 'upside down tree.'"

"Ooh." I smiled. "My family tree is probably a baobab too."

"It's also known as the tree of life."

178

So, he probably was not a being from another world. Ooh, I thought, aliens don't have grandmas?

His eyes quickly left me for the menu, and I yearned for both his gaze to touch me again, even if only briefly, and for his gaze never to return to my face, for fear the landscape would make him leave and never return.

"What about...ba-bu-ba," he contemplated, while his beautiful eyes roamed menu selections, dark gray eyes that would make a lovelier setting than the nightsky for stars to decorate.

I wanted to know every sentence he had ever written in his lifestory, every sentence that had been written by others in his story, every sentence he wished to change, erase, write someday, and how many of those sentences had been pink, red, gray, every sentence that had led him to this paragraph of my eyes falling in love with his, while Nat King Cole sang that Venus melted into Mars.

"Mm—" His thought was interrupted by my eyes catching his eyes. "Well, I don't see biscuits and sorghum on the menu."

Biscuits and sorghum? Why, that wasn't metropolitan at all! I wanted to say, "What does a boy from Brooklyn know about biscuits and sorghum?" But I decided that was too revealing: it revealed I had remembered that detail about him for an entire weekend, and what if he didn't remember me at all?

"Unfortunately, no, we don't have biscuits and sorghum, not even molasses, but..." I was going to say, "I can make some for you," but "forward" was just not in my personality's recipe. So, I offered, "I'm sorry." I'm sorry, My Captain. For the only man who had ever smiled at me, I wanted to write a sweet sentence into his day. I hoped my dress was at least offering a pretty sight to his morning.

"What about ice cream?" he asked.

"For breakfast?"

"You don't like that?"

179

"I don't like ice cream any time of day." I despised cold foods so intensely, I never even put ice in drinks. I tolerated cool drinks in summertime. I detested being cold.

He seemed surprised by Miss Pink not liking ice cream.

"Alright, do you have…" Now he was looking into my eyes, seeking… "*Peppermint* kisses?"

Hearing him say "peppermint" again brought about the same feeling I had experienced in the orchard—"Wake up, you're no longer hypnotized." Welcome back to reality—he's your soulmate, remember! In my years-ago dream of being with the aeronaut in the cold smoked woodland, where he had taught me how to kiss in the sleeping bag, the dream kiss lesson had tasted like peppermint.

"Are you alright?" he asked through a cough.

"I'm sorry," I said, snapping back into hypnosis, because the awakened truth had been too intense to my nineteen-year-old heart. I was not imagining dancing with Ritchie Valens or picnicking with Jeff Miller. This man and I had a forceful connection. The intensity was overwhelming.

"Do you mean the meringues that look like ice cream swirls, filled with peppermint candies?" I asked.

"That's exactly what I mean," he said, as impressed as if he had asked me about a classified rocket and I had given him details about top-secret blueprints.

"Peppermint is my favorite," I said.

I wondered if hearing him mention "peppermint" had triggered nostalgic feelings in me because when I had seen him parachute onto the wheatfield I had been enjoying a peppermint.

"Unfortunately, Darioles doesn't have peppermint kisses."

"What kind of bakery is this?" He smiled.

"I'm sure during the holidays, there will be some kind of peppermint dessert available."

"How about…you know what sounds good…"

Please tell me.

"Sweet potato pie."

Was he purposely picking selections not on the menu?

"Ooh," I exclaimed, "that's one of my favorite pies with cinnamon streusel and pecan toppings."

Why did this fellow from New York have such a taste for southern cuisine?

"My bubbe, my grandmother on the other side of the baobab tree," he said, and the stonework of his voice softened on the word "bubbe," "made that pie, one of those thick hearty versions, mile-high filling, not bad for a Polish panny, who used to let me eat pie and breads out of the pan."

Polish? Not Martian? (I had read enough Knight tales to know "panny" meant Lady.) A Polish Brooklynite with an extraterrestrial eccentricity and a taste for sorghum and physics and snowflakes and baseball and flying around dusty southern no-where towns in a snow-white aeroplane—who was this fella?

"My apologies," he said. "Being in bakeries just always makes me think of my grandmas." I was happy to have brought forth a pleasant memory for him to warm his day by.

"I'm sorry. Darioles doesn't have sweet potato pie either."

"It's not your fault. You don't own this bakery, do you?"

"Unfortunately, no."

"Unfortunately?" he asked as confused as if a cat had told him it wanted to be a dog. "You're terribly young to want to own a business?"

"It's not that I want to own a business." Oo Captain, My Captain, I want to own your heart. I didn't say that, still afraid of being stung. "I just adore baking and I have this idea—" Distrust stopped me from giving him something so personal, but his eyes assured he was genuinely interested in what I had to say and would handle it tenderly, so I told him about my dream to create a pastry kitchen which would offer free goodies.

"That's a highly noble aspiration for a young Lady. Are you telling me the truth?"

I was offended. If anyone was going to doubt sincerity in another human, it was going to be me—I had never felt the indignation of having my own sincerity doubted. Even the thieves had never questioned my resolve to uphold my real father's ideals. I gave an unbreakable "Yes." I couldn't tell if he believed me or not, but I couldn't be mad at him for employing the same skepticism I employed for protection against thieves.

Mullybiski barked upstairs, telling me he wanted to go out for his morning walk.

"My dog," I said and pointed upwards with my eyes.

"You live here?" He seemed surprised as if he had thought I was a young girl who still lived with her parents.

"I rent the upstairs flat."

"With a roommate?"

I shook my head. "I need to go walk Mullybiski."

"The pug?"

So, he had remembered! That was why he had seemed confused by my saying I wanted to own a pastry shoppe; I had told him I wanted to either be a nun or to be in love and to be a writer. I realized something that made me feel warm: the aeronaut had come to the patisserie to see me again, the first chance he had gotten, right at the opening hour of Monday morning (Darioles,

182

like most stores in Biskatine in 1965, was closed on Sunday). This had to be fate; otherwise, this beautiful man would have had no interest in me. He had once literally landed in my life's story. But what form of interest did he have in me, if he was not available for love?

"Don't tell me you're here all by yourself?" he asked, and I did not doubt the authenticity of concern in his voice.

I nodded, and he frowned at my answer.

"That doesn't seem safe. A young Lady by herself at a cash register at this time of night." He looked at his watch, the rugged Boy Scout kind of watch, which contradicted his business briefcase. I was so intrigued by his character. "You said you work Monday through Friday?"

"Monday through Friday, four to eight."

"You start work at *four* in the morning?"

I nodded, 'fraid so.

"Where do you walk your pug?"

"In the back alley."

He squinted his eyes at the flowery young girl speaking of going into a "back alley" to walk her dog, as if trying to make sense of the discrepancy between character and action. "How long does it take to walk him?"

"Depends on how long he needs."

"Why don't you put the Closed sign up, and I'll go out back with you?"

I was impressed by his attempt at Knighthood. "Okaaaay."

He gave a scolding look, "Silly young naïve girls." "For all you know I'm a madman. You were actually going to leave this bakery, where there's a phone and light and the possibility of entering customers and even utensils and scalding hot drinks which you could use as weapons to defend yourself, to go outside in a dark back alley with a stranger in the dead of night? Never do that, Cinderella. Never. If you come upon a beast, it might attack you out of fear or hunger, but only man, supposedly made in God's image, will attack you for fun."

I felt bad for disappointing his wisdom. In my defense, I said, "You're not a stranger."

"So, she does remember," his expression said by getting softer but quickly went stony-faced again, while he lectured, "One conversation in an apple orchard doesn't make me someone you can trust."

One conversation in an apple orchard? He didn't remember our meeting in the field and my giving him a snow globe?

"And you told me your entire work schedule: every weekday morning at four a.m., you're here, all by yourself. Is there some reason why you trust me, or would you have said 'Okay' to just anyone's offer of a walk in a dark back alleyway?"

I didn't know if the protective older brother was asking or the young man trying to figure out if I liked him. I didn't want to be too improperly bold, so I stammered, "I thought ... you ... were ... a student at Goldell."

"You think students in penny loafers can't be madmen? You didn't learn that on the hayride? All those ones in penny loafers today could be the ones in military boots tomorrow, willing to kill whoever they are told is the enemy, even sweet young girls. This is not a Nat King Cole song that we live in. If anyone ever comes in here at five o'clock in the morning and asks you, 'Are you here all by yourself,' you say, 'No.'"

Not since I was five years old had I met the feeling of anyone caring whether I lived or died, and I could have cried hearing his desire for *me* to stay in the world's story.

"You need to put newspaper down for your dog in these early morning hours and late-night hours, and you shouldn't walk him until it's daylight and the streets busy."

My eyes implored, "Yes, My Captain, protect me in these cold rough waters."

After the lecture, "I didn't mean to sound so harsh, and…I also owe you an apology for the curtness of what I said to you on Saturday. I felt terrible all weekend for that."

The song was stolen by a commercial break.

He continued, "I hadn't meant to imply you were seeking…wanting…" Suddenly, he was nervous, while the radio sang a ditty about carpet cleaner. "I hadn't meant you wanted to write a lovestory with me. What I said was true, but the way it was said—"

I jumped in to rescue him from conversationally drowning. "It's okay."

Before I could ask *why* he wasn't available for love, he quickly said, "If you want, I'll stay here, so you can go upstairs and put out some newspapers for your dog."

Out of a reflex, learned from the world, I looked at the vulnerable cash register, which I was paid to protect.

"Aah, you're concerned with me being left alone with the cash register, but you were perfectly willing to give me unguarded access to your person."

I must have looked thoroughly offended.

"My apologies," he said, about the "your person" comment. "But you should have shown more concern for *your* wellbeing than that cash register's wellbeing—everything in it can be replaced. There's endless dirty money in this world but only so few clean personalities."

I walked away from the cash register to show him I agreed about money's unimportance.

He opened the front door for me. The bell jingled.

Outside our cars were close together, as if they were hitched and stopped at the bakery one early morning, during a long journey.

"Did your daddy buy you that car?" he asked.

"No, I'm paying payments on it by myself."

"Well, that's a girl's car, for sure."

"The Lady Model. And that's a man's car, for sure."

"Really? The Commander?" he said, casually, as if he had not noticed his car was masculine.

"Yes, that streamlined Sputnik."

"Sputnik?" A morsel of a giggle in his usually serious voice.

"Like the spaceship."

"Yeah, I know what Sputnik is, but I never thought my car looked like Sputnik."

I was unsure why I had said his car looked like Sputnik, other than I thought it was cute the way I had thought Sputnik was cute.

"I wonder what it means, 'Sputnik,'" I pondered aloud.

He said something in a language I could not comprehend. "That's Russian for 'traveling companion.'" He spoke Russian and French and English—and what about the language of the symbols on his ring and airplane?

"Sputnik means 'traveling companion'?"

He nodded. I knew from then on I would call the physicist Sputnik, and that I wanted to be a satellite, revolving around him.

I told him how I had watched Sputnik with gleeful heart and Hershey's Kisses when I was a child. "I wonder what happened to him?"

Since I had called the spacecraft *him*, the scientist seemed unhappy to have to tell me this, "He burned up on reentry."

"Ooh. Poor Sputnik." Then I rethought it. "No. He didn't burn up. He melted into Earth, his traveling companion."

He looked at me as if I was the one whom the glass slipper fit. But my insecurities, and my Wicked Stepmother, wrote that was just wishful interpretation.

"Doesn't it get cold with the top down, Sputnik?"

He shrugged, manly man. "I grew up in Arctic Alaska."

"I thought you were from Brooklyn?" I was somewhat embarrassed for letting him know I had remembered that, but I reasoned my honesty about liking him would beget honesty from him about maybe liking me too.

"I was born in Alaska, and I've wandered just about everywhere."

Born in Alaska, not on Mars, but his mysteriousness still captivated me.

"My second birth in this country was in Brooklyn in 1946." He stressed *1946*, as a way of telling me, "Isn't that kind of interesting—the same year you were born, I had a second birth?"

"Second birth?" I puzzled.

He shrugged away the question and continued to look at my car as if it was capable of miracles. I could not understand the fascination until he said, "You were the gal behind me when I first drove to campus. The blonde gal with the passenger pug."

"You were the mint-green Studebaker!" The exclamation point was probably written on my expression too, but I erased it with solemnity, because what I had said had been too forward in its implication that our crossing had been written in the stars.

The morning I had arrived in town, he had pulled into Goldell. No wonder I had felt drawn to those fellows. !!!! He was the dark-haired fellow at Stormy & Strobe's counter that afternoon too, and I knew if he and I compared notes, we would find we had visited all the same places that week, the amusement park, the bookstore…our stories merging. Unlike those moments from childhood when he had come into my life, those moments that had been previews of what was yet to come as long as I stayed in the story, the timing was right now. I imagined a special department of guardian angels that handled soulmates, and our angels had been pulling their hair out over our stubbornness—"A molasses-haired boy was literally coming down her road to share the meadow with her and she drove away! How's that for a stupid mortal?" "Oh, yeah, you think that's stupid? The same blonde who gave him the snow globe was literally driving behind him, and he pulled off on an exit."

Maybe to play down the exclamation point revealed in his voice, he said, "I had never seen a car that pink." I wondered if he was torn between wanting to be aloof to protect his feelings and wanting to be forthcoming to protect my feelings. "Was it just my imagination or was there really a Knight in armor atop the hood?"

"Yes, sir, there was."

"Thank goodness. I thought I had finally lost my mind. Seeing Knights on the highway. My mother…" The stonework of his voice transformed into satin for the word "mother," a holy word formed with tenderness and reverence, a word allowed a moment to stand out, separated from all other words. "…was taken in by all the Knight mythology as well, so I grew up in Camelot, kind of."

I loved that, but I did not like his use of the phrase "taken in" as if Knighthood and Ladyhood were cons dreamers got suckered into believing, thanks to storybooks that just wanted to rip us off of money.

I wanted to bring up the moments with the aeronaut, but I did not want to embarrass him if he was avoiding that conversation because it involved remembering the caress of my face (maybe it had meant nothing to him?); plus, I realized, he had no reason to believe I knew he was the aviator, who had been hidden behind goggles and helmet.

Standing on the sidewalk, he tried his best to keep a protective eye on me while I walked toward the back of the building until I was lost from his view, and he was lost from mine in the mist, and in that moment, a chill froze through me that I would never forget, a chill that felt prophetic, a chill that felt capable of freezing my soul into a solid: solid ice. Unable to bear the feeling, I chalked it up to a literal response to cold air.

Upstairs, I learned Mullybiski had already taken care of his business all over the floor. "Really, MullyB, you've never wanted to go out this early before. Well, don't step in it. I'll clean it up later." I carried him over to the blanket, so he could get some napping. I wished I could snuggle with the aeronaut from Alaska—for a snowflake physicist from the Arctic, he looked very warm. I sensed that after he made love to me, Heaven would be anticlimactic. But that form of union could only happen on my wedding night, and I was steadfast in that conviction born of reverence for romance and loyalty to my soulmate only. "Virginity should be preserved like Excalibur—only the best man allowed to take it." I had read that somewhere, maybe from one of Bell Gondal's books, and the sentiment made sense: a Lady had to respect herself, and in doing so, made men strive to be their best if they wanted a Lady. "A bond made of love is strong as steel," I reminded myself of Moon-Moon's teaching, "whereas a bond made of lust only looks as strong as metal but is actually as flimsy as foil."

When I came back downstairs, Sputnik was holding the door open for me, which provided me with a chance to pass close by his warmth.

189

"Thank you," I beamed. I whirled around in my dress, being a lot sillier than normal, unable to stop the Nat King Cole song, and I twirled behind the counter. I had to finish taking the physicist's order, which I wished to do every morning in our bed (a wish I prayed as a request to our guardian romance angels).

"You're shivering," Sputnik said.

"It's cold."

His smile said, "What could I expect from a girl who drives such a girly car?"

"I like you" was now being said in everything I said and did.

"Here, angel." He unzipped his jacket to offer to me.

I was just about to faint from the caress of his gallantry when I saw the Star of David hanging from his necklace. He was Jewish. As far as I knew, a Jewish boy could not marry a non-Jewish girl. My heart dropped and fell under the world's shoe, where it was stepped on hard. Maybe that was why he was unavailable to love me, a Protestant girl?

"I don't want you to be cold," I said.

"I'm a man."

"Men don't get cold?"

"Not when there's a girl around."

I was not sure how to interpret that, but I felt flattered. I put on his jacket, maybe the only embrace I would ever get from him, or from anyone, and I could have melted in its warmth. His jacket was big on me, which meant his arms would feel big and protective around my body. I smelled his scent in the fabric, woodsy and soapy.

He had noticed me looking at his necklace. He said, "Isn't it interesting that all Christian girls worship a Jewish king, their hearts wed to a Jew, yet their parents won't allow them to date Jewish boys."

"My parents weren't like that."

He gave me a tender look since I had referred to my parents in the past tense.

"You don't have a father watching out for you?"

What a question!

"I believe my father is always watching over me."

Sputnik nodded and I was not sure if the scientist agreed or was being polite. "But a young Lady needs a father in the here and now to prevent her from, frankly, making foolish decisions like working on Main Street at four a.m. and living in a back-alley dump, and she needs someone to inspect any boy that might want to date her."

I was flattered by his assumption that boys were calling on my father for my hand.

"You don't have any protector, an older brother, perhaps?" Was he really asking if I had a fella?

"No, there are no fellows in my life."

He was concerned about my life's lack of a male guardian.

"So, you work here to support yourself?"

I nodded.

"I had assumed you were like most young girls who work to have money to buy records and hair ribbons and all those things girls can't live without but daddy won't spend his money on, or perhaps you were helping your family out financially, and that you were a stubborn naïve girl, rooming upstairs to experience life outside daddy's roof, but this situation is more serious." But he didn't know how to fix the situation.

Coughing, he fiddled with the radio.

"Are you okay?" I asked.

"I'm fine. How's your dog?"

"I believe he was a little miffed at me for leaving him. He and I don't much like our new apartment."

"I'm sorry to hear that."

"It's a dump like you said. But it's not your fault. You don't own this building, do you?" I smiled, while imitating him.

"*Fortunately*, no."

"Quite a noble aspiration for a young man—not to own this filth motel."

"Hoping 'filth motel' is just a figure of speech," he said, while looking at the desserts. He was getting into the rhythm of making a friend, the playful call and response, bringing our cold isolated hearts next to friendship's hearth.

Hearing *Melt & Malt*, I exclaimed, "Ooh, I love that song!"

"Ah, I know the singer and songwriter."

"Wow, really?" I did not hide my excitement, more excited by the fact that Sputnik and I had such a connection—what were the chances my favorite song had been written by someone he knew? "You know G.W. Braver-man?"

He was impressed by my knowing the songwriter's name. "You know him too—you met him on a hayride."

"*You're* G.W. Braverman?"

A coincidence that felt like being tapped with a magic wand.

"The singer, Benny B, or Mr. Benny as kids call him, is a chum of mine. But don't get any girlish flutters in your heart for Mr. Benny. He's, well, he has no interest in romance—he's the consummate lone wolf, or more like lone aardvark, or something strange like that."

"How'd you come up with the song?"

Was there a real Snowflake who had been the muse for "Hey, Snowflake, let's melt and malt"?

"One night in Memphis…in '58 or '59…Ben was joshing me, saying I didn't have it in me to write a rock-n-roll song, so I wrote one, and he sang it, and we recorded it, and he knew some radio types and they put it on the air."

"Wow! What other kinds of songs have you written?"

"I prefer classical. Ben's all swing and rock-n-roll. He's actually from Biskatine and has a hobby shop here. Hobby Hut. Writer Taggart Smythe once worked there."

Sputnik told my curiosity briefly about J. Benjamin Biskatine, Mr. Benny, as remarkable as J. Thaddeus Toad (Mr. Toad). Sputnik had an easier time telling me information about others than information about himself. A former World War 2 paratrooper yet kid at heart, Benny was the grandson of the founder of Biskatine Cocoa, and the "old boy" was still as sweet as a chocolate bunny and the only person who could get "drunk" off root beer. I liked this character already. Sputnik had lived with Mr. Benny for a while in Brooklyn above Benny's candy store; the two had met while hopping trains.

"You were a hobo?" I was shocked by the scientist's past hopping freight trains. "Isn't that illegal?"

"Well…"

Sputnik switched the dial. Now Sue Raney sang *Heart and Soul*.

"Ben, like Mr. Toad, is obsessed with transportation: trains, big ones and model ones, airplanes, automobiles…he has enough money to buy anything he wants but he gives all his money away. He's a charitable fellow, a good guy, but daffy as all get out."

"He doesn't sound like someone who needs to hop trains to get where he wants to be."

"He's a nut. A *butterscotch nut*." He laughed about the reference to *Melt & Malt's* lyrics.

"What made you stop hopping trains?"

"I eventually traded my seat on a train car for a seat in a cockpit." He was not forthcoming in supplying information about himself.

"Why did you do that?"

"I was tired of having to go wherever the train was going."

"How'd you learn to fly?"

"I took flying lessons with Ben, got a pilot's license and took a few flights in an old bomber turned sailbird, Ben's Lady. Eventually I built my own aeroplane." With his hand, he mimicked the flight of a plane, which I thought adorable. He talked a lot with his hands.

"Ooh, you built your own airplane?" Said in a way that suggested I was impressed but also "I already know that about you."

"I built her from the frame up. With my own two hands." He held up the handsome hands that had molded his airplane, and I thought: what a lucky airplane. "A simple elegant Lady of wood, fabric, and fair lacquer, with a Lady's heart beating inside a delicate frame: meant for gliding through air, not horsepowering through it. Alright, I had some help building her from Ben."

"You two built an airplane in Brooklyn?"

"No, in one of Ben's empty fields upstate, where he sometimes parachutes and practices landings."

I just knew Ben had been "alien two" in that moment from childhood, responsible for the footsteps that had led from the spaceplane into the Stargust woods.

"I stored the flying contraption in an old barn until I barnstormed the country."

"Barnstorming, wow! You've been living an adventurous tale. My life's a hammock compared to your rocket life." I wanted to bring up our previous encounters.

"I'm surprised I've avoided a crash."

Was he only in town to visit his buddy Ben? "Is Biskatine just a stopover?" I hoped not. My heart could not bear him flying away this time. It dawned on me he had a car, so he had not just come with plane into this town, and he had been pulling into Goldell, so he had to be staying to go to the university.

"I can never be sure, but I no longer storm past barns."

Either I would have to make the aeronaut a home enticing enough to stay in Biskatine for, or he would have to take me on his voyages with him, because I could not tolerate our stories being written separately again.

In case he wanted a flying partner instead of a homemaker, I said, "When I was a little girl, I sometimes wondered what it would be like to be an aviator like Katherine Stinson."

"Katherine Stinson?" he asked as shocked as if I had mentioned his secret wife.

"She was an aeronaut."

"Ah, I know who she is. I've just never heard anyone in my life mention her name."

He coughed again, and I asked, "Would you like some water?"

"I'm fine," he said in a way that suggested, "Don't ask about my cough again." Then he smiled to say sorry for being terse. "A barnstorming nun, that's interesting."

"Soooo, did the barnstormer decide on what he wants for breakfast?" I had a vision of making him breakfast for the first time as his wife, and dear angels, I did not want this to be an impossible-to-come-true dream.

"All the towns I've flown into, all the characters I've encountered, and I'm still waiting for the best conversation of my life. I want that for breakfast. Do you want to give that to me?"

The suggestiveness of his words turned my cheeks into cherries.

Realizing my interpretation of his tone as red, he clarified his intent, "No one wants to discuss anything for more than two minutes. I want to discuss everything forever!"

"Me too. I'm conversationally dehydrated. What do you want to discuss first?"

"Hmmm," his voice singysongy. "First, I'll have a coffee, black, to curb another dehydration, and I was promised it would be the freshest coffee."

I turned toward the coffee maker. "Have you ever tried it with cream and sugar out there in the Arctic?"

"Nope." I had a sense he did not say "nope" often, more of a blunt "no" type, but around me, he was being sweeter. Around him, my personality was made with 100% sugar.

I set a cup of black coffee beside his serious briefcase. "Would you like to try it with cream and sugar?"

"Nope, thanks, I'll stick to the manly man cup of coffee." He laughed at the overacted machismo.

"I could make you a cup with cream and sugar, on the house." If Dariole or the manager had heard that, I would have gotten fired.

"Wouldn't you get in trouble for that?"

"I'd get more in trouble with my conscience for not letting you try a cup of something warm and sweet—for free."

His eyes flashed, impressed by my conviction to offer free food. "Be an icon of Individuality, I say. Never abridge your personality to make it easier for the masses to read. The path to individuality contains only one set of footprints. Those are my mottos. Those and never apologize to an idiot for your smartness. But I don't want you to go through extra work, so I'll settle for the hobo coffee."

"Hobo coffee?"

He held up the coffee cup, blew off the steam. "The boy who hopped freights and grew up in the Alaskan outback knows a thing or two about black coffee, much stronger than this, I assure you."

"I grew up in the countryside too, but in the south," I offered, maybe another detail he would like to remember about me, maybe one that would spark his memory about our previous encounters.

"In a field of flowers, I imagine."

I must have looked offended, thinking he was making fun of me.

"That's a compliment," he said, his voice as soft now as if he was talking to a child. "Did you find that dress blooming in a field or buy it from a store?"

I blushed—so he did like the dress. "I made it."

"Ah." He took a long sip.

"I didn't make the sweater or gloves, though."

"A magnolia who bakes and sews and worries about spacecraft. Someday a man is going to be a lucky husband, or will that man be God, *sister*?"

I could not tell if he was being flirtatious or condescending like an older brother comforting his plainly little sister, "Don't worry, someday, some man will love you for your inner beauty," and was he making fun of my wanting to be a nun?

Whatever reaction he had hoped to elicit from that line, he did not get, so he said, "I should have reasoned you didn't live at home, since when I first saw the blonde gal with passenger pug, her car looked loaded down from a journey. So, when did you move here? I just moved here last week."

"Me too!" I said as excitedly as if I had learned he and I had both just moved to Earth from Planet Q, our shared homeworld.

He took out his wallet and accidentally dropped it on the floor. Now he seemed awkward and girl shy, becoming fully nerdish Dilton Doiley; he looked so nerdy cute with pencils in his shirt pocket. He leaned down to retrieve his wallet, and his face reddened either from embarrassment or from bending over so quickly, and he said as way of explanation for his clumsiness, "I suffer from chronic cooties."

I thought that was the cutie-est thing I had ever heard, and I smiled.

"You wouldn't smile if you knew how much suffering these cooties had caused me." His tone was light, too light to carry the weight of burdensome memories.

He paid for the coffee, and I decided to make him a cup of warm sweetness "on the house." I set the mug on a saucer and when I handed it to him, we experienced a brief peck between our fingertips, a moment with heat on it, and I offered, "It's okay. I have cooties too."

He smiled and his nose flared, so incredibly bashful was he, not so sophisticated.

"Cooties are real, you know," he said, and I thought he was being a mischievous boy telling a tall tale to a girl.

I shook my head, no they're not.

"In World War 1, there was the *kutu*, a biting bug that infected soldiers."

Boys.

He took his briefcase and sweet coffee and sat at a booth by a window, which showcased that nighttime was molasses dark and slowly turning into a lighter honey from a rising sun.

I fantasized about him singing Elvis's *Teddy Bear*.

From his shirt pocket, he acquired a pen, and from his briefcase, a notepad, and he looked so by himself, not like a fraternity brother. I was not going to let the poor bachelor go without breakfast, and I definitely was not going to let the wanderer walk out the door without learning his full name, which I had waited all my life to know. The barnstormer might decide to fly away from this town at any time.

I brought him the other cup of "manly" hobo coffee, which he had left on the counter. "I'm Lumi, by the way."

"A name not easily forgotten."

I waited for him to offer his name in return but he did not; either he had not read the playbook on human interactions or he did not care if I knew his name.

"Did you forget a lot of names on your travels?" Did you break any innocent hearts? Were there girls, somewhere out there, pining for his return?

"I never learned many names from townsfolk in towns where I didn't plan to stay."

This was a very bold question, but I kept my tone playful, "You never met any nice ladies whose names you wanted to remember?"

"I met some nice motherly and grandmotherly types who offered pie to the young pilot of the wooden bird that had just splash landed in their husband's cornfield. I met some not-so-nice farmers too. Southern women always had the best cooking and most ungrateful husbands."

"Did you ever fly into Stargust?"

He thought about it. "I did some parachuting there with Ben…" If I knew about his time in Stargust that meant I had been there too.

"1951?" I said to confirm what had already dawned on him.

"Don't tell me you were the little streak of lightning that zoomed down the dirt road."

Sheepishly, "Me and the stocky pug. My Moon-Moon, my momma, told me I should invite you over for succotash. We had sweet potato pie that afternoon too."

"I wish you would have invited me! Growing up in the Great Depression, I got a taste for succotash, and I figure southern sweet potato pie is the peak of sweet potato pie." He looked up to Heaven and said, "Forgive me, Bubbe."

"Like most southern dishes, it's buttery, but Moon-Moon was good at marrying nutmeg and cinnamon and raisins and sweet potatoes."

I felt warm-hearted and light-headed at the prospect of making a meal for him.

"I ate cold beans that day with Ben when I could have been in the company of two nice ladies. Well, 'sufferin' succotash,' why didn't you invite me?" he asked with faux anger.

"I thought you were an alien with a spaceplane."

"How'd you know?" He grinned.

"I had a feeling. But even though I sensed you were a good alien, I let doubt, developed around not-so-nice humans, make me wonder if you were a bad alien."

He thought about that, more seriously than I had intended.

I tried to think of a way to bring up our other moment and decided on the direct approach, "Do you remember Christmastime 1960 in Igtord?" I hoped he would forgive the Lady her candor.

"Yes," he said, his voice taking on the warmth of a candle lit to memorialize something holy. "I was highly touched by your sweetness. A snow globe for The Snowflake Physicist. It was like somehow you knew…"

"I believe I did know on some other level of me." I wasn't sure if I should have been so forthright to say I felt we had a spiritual relationship.

"So, the little streak of lightning was the same sweet girl who offered me a snow globe on a cold day in an entirely different town, and the same blonde who was behind me when I drove into this town."

He let those realizations touch him with their magic. "I still owe you a gift," he said, easing our way through the emotional conversation.

"No, you don't owe me a gift, remember ... the pin ...and what I said ... about your smile being a gift..."

He looked out the window, the scene inside getting too intimate? He seemed ashamed again.

"Have you tried any restaurants since you've been here?" I was really asking if he had a girl who cooked for him (maybe she had just skipped making breakfast this morning), or if he had to find his meals at restaurants.

"Yes, I've tried quite a few. A bachelor must forage food, unless he's adept at cooking, which I'm not."

I was happy not only because he was a bachelor but because he had let *me* know his relationship status. Maybe he and I *could be* a couple. I was not going to believe he was unavailable for love; whatever obstacle was bothering him, we could overcome together.

I asked, "Didn't learn how to cook while making hobo coffee in the Alaskan wilderness?"

"Skillet bread, burnt coffee, and even burnt-er roasted marshmallows. You can't put too much cargo in a backpack when train hopping or in a plane while barnstorming; a little tin of coffee has to be enough."

"And a bag of marshmallows."

"Well, I only ate those when I was a boy, during campfires by myself and the company of redwoods."

His personality was very attractive; if he had looked like liverwurst, I still would have been attracted to him.

"Don't you want to try the sweet version of coffee?" I asked.

He tried the sweetened coffee and gave his taste buds time to decide if he liked the sugar and cream addition. "'Sunset in a cup.'" Quoting Dickinson again.

"Really?"

"Yes. I don't know how girls do this."

"What do you mean?"

"Have a way with sugar. But don't tell anyone I like it this way. This is kind of a girly drink, don't you think?"

"Well, I am a girl."

"My point exactly. And that powder puff car you drive." He gave a good playful laugh. "I imagine the whole upstairs looks just like it." He quickly stopped his laugh, cleared his throat, and decided his imagining what the future nun's bedroom looked like put him in the league of creeps.

"So, it's black coffee from now on?" *From now on*, so sure I would serve him coffee again, and I quickly turned away from my embarrassment, especially since he knew I had been smitten with him five years ago. I headed toward the counter.

"Not necessarily from now on. Sometimes perhaps I could have it this special way."

"Okaaay." The aeronaut did plan to come back then! I was so grateful to my choice of taking this job; he and I could really get to know each other during these sweetened coffee mornings at the patisserie.

I took fully to the task of preparing him breakfast.

He took fully to writing something in the notepad. More "ba-bu-ba" singy sounds from him.

Since I knew little about Judaism, I became self-conscious of my ignorance. "Sputnik, I don't know if Darioles has anything kosher."

"It's alright. I don't obey any dietary laws."

I brought him a pecan Danish. "I'm sorry, it's not a peppermint kiss or ice cream."

He smiled in spite of himself trying not to believe we were in a Nat King Cole song. He was charmed by my girlish insistence to make his morning happy.

"I can't let you get in trouble for me," he said, setting the pen down.

"I'll pay for it."

"I certainly can't let you do that." His gentlemanly-ness insulted. He lifted to get his wallet from his back pocket, but as his hand comically and awkwardly fumbled through a mess of bulky jacket, his cooties were showing again.

I delighted in what he had been writing on the notepad: a Sunday-funnies-like comic strip panel, where the characters were not people but numerals—the number 3, in a top hat, sharing a dance with number 14, wearing a dress. The dressy numerals were in a Pie Shop with various-shaped snowflakes adrift outside the window, and the caption read, "The infinite dance."

His face said, "I have no idea why I was drawing that." Maybe he was acting sillier than normal too. He gently tore the drawing from the notepad. "You can have it if you want it. Put it up on the fridge, or let the stocky dog use it for a bathroom."

"Why, I'd never do that!" I took the drawing and clasped it to my heart without even realizing what I was revealing with my actions, holding him close to my heart.

"Where's the poem?" he asked. "You said you wanted to offer handwritten poems with each pastry."

"But this isn't my pastry shop."

"But in pretend, what poem would you have given me?   I'm just curious. About what you think pairs with a pecan Danish."

"Ooh, something Shelley maybe."

We were getting much more comfortable with each other like two old friends who had moved away from each other but were now back together, and after awkward moments of getting reacquainted, we were fully back in the friendship.

"That sweet shop of yours would be the kind I'd fly back to a town over and over to enter."

I blushed. "How can you say that? You've never even tried my food."

"I suspect it's good and southern. Besides, I'd like to get the poems."

"Are there any particular poems you like, Sputnik?" Trying out the nickname again, making sure he was okay with it.

"Um…"   More singsongyness in his chest, most likely usually quiet around others, not a man to let anyone hear his heartbeat. "I'm trying to think of where this line comes from, 'A heart whose love is innocent.'"

"That's from Lord Byron's 'She Walks in Beauty.'"   !!!!   This was getting weird even for me.

"'She walks in beauty like the night.'" I did not know if he was questioning if that was the right line or if he was saying that line to

204

me, *about me*. I had already lost my feet when he had said, "A heart whose love is innocent," and I was either going to float or fall.

I smirked defiantly at my Wicked Stepmother, "Look at me, getting the glass slipper!"

"I'll go get your change, sir," said in my most proper nineteenth-century voice, as I floated to the counter and laid his drawing there.

"You can keep the change." Change from a dollar for a ten-cent Danish?

"No, I don't want your money, remember? Free food."

"Ah, Joan of Arc reincarnated: her conviction, bravery, piety, the good Christian girl."

"I can't accept that very generous comparison. I am definitely not brave enough to suffer what she went through."

"I'm sure you are."

"Me and my Lady car?"

"'I am not afraid...I was born to do this.' Joan of Arc said that."

I floated back to his table.

"Is that Lord Byron poem your favorite?" he asked.

"Ooh, yes." I laid ugly coins on the table.

"What pastry would you pair that poem with? How does this lyric taste: 'A heart whose love is innocent'?"

Did he want to keep making me blush?

"I'll have to ponder that thoughtfully, sir. It may take some time. What's your favorite poem?"

"Ah," he said and looked at the ring on his finger then pretended he did not have an answer. "Do you write poetry as well?"

"Yes, but a writing teacher once told me I wrote too pink."

205

His face hardened like preparing for a boxing match. "A male teacher?"

"No, a woman."

His face said, "What's wrong with this world?"

I didn't understand people either and their insistence on maintaining misery.

"You have a Valentine's red heart," he said. "A heart worth defending but no man in your life to defend it."

"You're a dreamboat," I wanted to gush but controlled myself.

"Do you mind if I ask about the pins on this jacket?" I inquired.

"That one," he said, while pointing at the pin, "was from Project Mercury."

"The mission that put men in space?" I could not hide my excitement! "You worked on that mission?"

"I was employed at Langley Research Center for a while as an engineer and worked at NASA's Space Task Group during Mercury."

I did not have to say "Wow" because "Wow" was written all over my face. The realization dawned on me as warmly as sunrise: he was a *starship builder*! As a child, I had seen rocket blueprints rolled up in his plane's storage compartment, but now it was confirmed, he really did build spaceships! Any moment, my alarm clock was going to ring—this had to be a dream.

"Wow," I said anyway because I wanted to give his being a spaceship builder infinite "Wow's."

Seeing how impressed I was, he added, "I also worked as an engineer for Mass on the Aerodactyl project, hoping to get my chance to be an astronaut."

"Wow, an astronaut and a spaceship builder!!!"

"Well, sort of, I didn't get the astronaut job and I don't build entire ships by myself."

I would wear his wedding ring the way a man wore a Medal of Honor. I knew someday schoolchildren would have to remember his name for science tests, and I wanted to use my lifestory's ink to help write this great character's name in history.

"I thought you worked on making snowflakes?"

"That's why I left NASA." I knew he was not being completely serious yet...

Before I could ask, he said, "The other pin is a fraternity pin, a fraternity of one—myself. Three ancient Greek letters never used anymore: Sampi Koppa Digamma. I made the pin as a boy, a long time ago." As if needing to explain himself, he said, "Weird is my normal."

"Mine too. So, you're not in a fraternity with others?"

"I've arranged my life to never brush against anyone else's, and I've enjoyed a lot less friction."

I was warmed by his sharing a similar loner's philosophy, but I wondered if his self-made isolation had something to do with his being unavailable for love?

"Lumi," and his face reddened as if saying a girl's name was racy, "let me ask, why did you move here?"

"That's something I'll only tell someone whose first name I know, G.W."

"Ah. Ben would tell you my name is Shom."

"What would your birth certificate tell me?"

"Gershom. Gersh. It means 'a stranger there,' or a 'sojourner there.' My mother named me 'sojourner' to remind me to remember this world is not my home. But 'Snowflake Physicist' tells you more about me."

I had never felt so much magic around another person. The angels had really outdone themselves with our union.

"Now can I know why you're here?" he asked.

Before I could respond, the doorbell signaled the arrival of a customer, which annoyed me—an intruder to our lovestory, where the ink was flowing smoothly toward Sputnik and I getting to know one another. I'm sorry, My Captain, the world is set up to make me walk away from my true love to wait on a customer.

The customer wanted something, a memory completely lost like how much money the store made that morning. At a table, he ate whatever he had ordered, continuing to interrupt my lovestory with boring passages like snapping his fingers, asking for refills.

I brought Sputnik a free coffee refill and smile refill too, while he went back to drawing dressy numerals in different scenes. He was somewhat irritable now that my attention had been divided between him and the customer.

"I moved here because I felt drawn to this town," I told him.

He nodded as if he already knew that. "I can imagine that. This whole town with its streetlamps and hat shops is The Lady Model." He smiled, and I thought, "Let me live there—I want your smile to be my nation."

"Why did you move here?" I asked.

"Ben always praises his boyhood town, 'Greatest little town in the world,' so, I took a job offer here."

Before I could ask about his work, I had to refill the customer's cup.

"You work on snowflakes here?" I asked.

"Sort of. I do research at Goldell."

He was a graduate student, I thought, but then again, how many graduate students worked on NASA missions? And how many

208

twenty-year-old graduate students in 1965 had grown up in the Great Depression and been a pilot in 1951? But I didn't think of that or figure up his age. His being at Goldell assured me the aeronaut would not be flying away anytime soon.

"What kind of research?"

"Some engineering, some math, some physics."

Wow again!

He wanted to have a conversation, but we kept getting interrupted by the customer.

At one point, after watching me with the coffee pot at the other man's table, I noticed one of Sputnik's doodled numbers told a Lady number, "A girl should be safe inside at this early hour, not dishing out coffee to strangers for money no less."

"How else can I pay for the grand upstairs plaza?" I said outright.

I couldn't tell if he was disappointed in me or the world.

The businessman at the table was annoyed by "teenage antics."

Sputnik said, "My mother once sold snowballs—"

"Snowballs?" I puzzled.

"What you southerners call snow cones."

"Ooh, ice dolled up in syrup."

"Yeah, 'dolled up' in syrup." He thought that was cute. "She sold snowballs from a wheeled cart attached to a unicycle, during the Great Depression. And she always needed protection from lechs who tried to steal her blushes, if you know what I mean. Pops was always gone, so I used to go along with Mother to protect her from men who had spent months in metal mines, eager to get their filthy hands on something soft and clean. Do you understand what I'm telling you?"

I frowned to say I was sorry about how his mother had been treated.

After breakfast, the barnstormer took a package of Jack 9 licorice gum from his breast pocket. Long after two free coffee refills (one "girly," one "manly"), he still sat in the booth. At first, I thought he wanted more chances to talk with me, to have the greatest conversation of his life, but I realized he was staying around to keep the young girl from being alone with the stranger, who was taking his time in finishing breakfast.

The businessman, apparently feeling un-citizenly for not conversing with the waitress, finally asked the misfit, "Do you like working here?"

"No, not really."

"What happened to your face there?"

Before I could answer, Sputnik launched this missile from across the room in my defense, "Nowhere in her job description does it say she has to answer inane questions from customers full of only small talk and obvious inconsideration."

"Young man, I don't know if you're her brother or who you are," the customer said, unable to believe a handsome man like Sputnik would be my boyfriend, "but I was just being friendly."

"Friendly? You were being the exact opposite of friendly, *man*. If you had any ability to see people as anything other than identical citizens following fake friendly civilities, you could see that she is a highly shy young Lady who does not feel comfortable giving details about her life to a man she doesn't know, so why don't you be a real good citizen and show her shyness respect?"

The customer unleashed a laugh to say he thought Sputnik nuts, but a laugh too small to initiate a fight with the much stronger man. The customer snapped at the waitress, "Another cup of coffee, hon."

That ignited Sputnik! He was not going to tolerate any more rude lines being written into my day. He shot up from his booth and stormed over to the disrespectful man's table, where he gently took the coffee pot from my serving hand but slammed the pot in front of the customer. "You want some more coffee? Well, there you go. A real man should be able to drink it that way without needing it poured out for him from a girl's little hand into a dainty little teacup."

I sensed Sputnik was itching to start a fight with the man, any man; he did not have a high view of his own sex.

The man glared at *me*, expecting an explanation from the waitress for his bad treatment at this establishment.

Sputnik raged, his voice solid brick, "If you have a grouse, you tell me, not her. Or are you scared to start something with a man, so you pick fights with girls, is that it? She's been nothing but nice to you, only God knows why, and I don't want to hear about you coming back in here, starting trouble for her with her boss. Your trouble's with me."

The customer had had enough. He stood up, threw some money on the table, and left.

"Thanks, Sputnik, for standing up for me."

"I hate to tell your Valentine heart this, but out of responsibility to the preservation of your sweetness, I want you to know: men are scum." He sat back in his booth. "Never be duped that any are Knights."

"Aren't you?"

He looked at me as if he felt sorry for me. "Be a nun, Lumi. God will be a better husband for you."

I thought he was kidding.

The sun, whom I usually loved, was coming in with its sunshine, saying, "Good morning!" through windows, and I was annoyed

211

again—now my Captain would leave me to sail the rest of the day alone, the waters safer.

When an elderly Lady approached outside, Sputnik got up to open the door for her. And he thought he wasn't a Knight?

An older couple walked in, and he went back to his booth but didn't sit down; he put the pen back into his pocket, notepad back into the briefcase and buckled it up, completely locked around others.

I strolled back to his booth. Thanks to my high heels, I was about eye level with his Star of David necklace, sparkling in sunlight.

"Sputnik, would you like another refill?"

"No, thanks. I think four will keep the night-owl going through daylight."

"Is it true Alaska gets six months of daylight and six months of starlight?"

"I can tell someone needs a lesson in astronomy and geographical position—and baseball."

"Miss," the male of the elderly couple nagged, while ringing the small bell atop the counter for service, even though I was only standing a few feet from them.

"The next time you come in," I said to Sputnik, trying to stay focused on him, "there will be peppermint kisses for you."

He relieved my hand of the coffee pot, set it on the table, unconcerned if *customers* got a refill.

"Is that a promise?" he asked, still chewing gum.

"Yeeesss."

"Miss!"

"Have you seen YOGI?" he asked.

"YOGI?"

"That's an acronym for Goldell's observatory."

"I saw it in passing one night and felt it calling to me."

"Like this town?"

"Just like that."

"You … we … you should go to the planetarium and learn about the amounts of daylight and nighttime different parts of the world get at different times of the year."

"Miss!" the man nagged.

"She'll be with you in a minute!" Sputnik said authoritatively, and his masculine growl hushed the customer, unlike my girlish "Just a second please," which had not ended the man's nagging at all. I felt like a gazelle with the bodyguard of a tiger, who braved the jungle as king.

He put his fingers to the bottom of his jacket that I was still wearing and zipped it up from my waist to my collars like I was his girl or his kid sister?

"I'll come back in the morning for the peppermint."

"Okay, O Captain, My Captain," I said, swept up in a feeling.

He raised his eyebrow. "Like the Walt Whitman poem about Abraham Lincoln?"

To shrink the outpour's significance, I said, "Your beard reminds me of Abe's."

"Ah." But he grinned, seeing the truth. "Don't worry, your Captain will take care of you."

I felt the same faintish way I had felt years earlier when Jeff Miller had told the ballerina, before removing her injured foot from two crushing rocks, "This won't hurt." I wanted to lean against Sputnik's masculine strength, lay all my fears and worries there, and trust him completely to be both tender and strong in this world of rocks.

213

He lessoned, "When a girl gets married and is ready to move beyond her father's home, her father gives her away to another man to watch over her, and I suspect your father is giving me the responsibility."

Sputnik's speaking of us like we were a married couple made me so light-headed I could not formulate coherent language, and I mumbled, "Your day what plans ... what do you have planned for the day, Snowflake Physicist?"

"Perhaps I'll resume making the world's largest snowflake."

"I do hope so."

He put his thumb to a tiny scar on my chin, a wound no one ever noticed on my demolished face, no more than they noticed a nick on a wrecked car, but he was observant of my pain. "What happened?"

"When I was a kid, a girl threw a pebble at me to get me to stop smiling."

"And did you?" He rubbed his thumb like an eraser across the remnant of suffering.

"No."

"Jeanne d'Arc."

Since our eyes were making such a connection, and since he admired Joan of Arc's bravery, I bravely asked, "Why are you not available for love?" I thought he would say, "I was just being a silly goose—of course, I'm available for love. Didn't you hear what I said about taking care of you like I'm your husband?" Instead:

"A part of me wants to tell you," he said, still softly rubbing my chin with his thumb, "and a part of me thinks it would be wrong."

There was no reason to play coy and pretend we did not have a deep connection and a destiny with one another. "You can't love me or I can't love you?"

He didn't know the right answer.

I was somewhat embarrassed, so instead of looking at his eyes and seeing whatever they might tell me about his feelings, I looked at the Star of David. "You said you were going to take care of me."

"I am."

"And you told me you *needed* to know me."

"I do. Perhaps I'll explain when the time feels right. I admit, I'm suffering confused feelings."

I confessed, "My heart wants to be as loyal to you as Joan of Arc to France."

"My goodness…I, um…"

"You think I'm a bad girl now?"

"Quite the contrary. I think you're the most good girl…well…"

I realized we were standing in the middle of the bakery, during a busy morning, everyone staring at us, and while I was waiting for a Shakespearean scene, the other characters were waiting for me to resume my role as waitress/cashier. They weren't interested in a romantic scene. "We want scones, dagnabit!" their antsy expressions shouted. They had to get back to the grind.

Sputnik removed his hand from my face, not because of the customers' stares, but because he had to hold steadfast to his unavailability for love.

"If there is truth in what you said about your heart, Lumi, will you be a good girl for your Captain today and stay inside and write?"

"I have to go out."

"That's not the right answer," he said with a smile although he was serious. "I don't like you working here." I wasn't sure if he wanted me or him to write me out of the work backdrop, but I knew he wanted the girly girl to be set in a scenery of perpetual flowers, even though he did not know of any such place on Earth. "Perhaps you should go to the convent."

Was he being serious?

"I didn't think Judaism looked highly on monasticism?"

"*I* look highly on monasticism. You can't fathom how much I respect that your qualifications to be a holy woman have remained unsoiled in this filthy world. Be a good girl, stay inside."

He picked up his briefcase and left.

His jacket became my superhero's cape, which gave me super strength to tolerate the rest of the gray morning—moody customers, military training in trifles, meanness disguised as advice from Dariole, and mustard splashes on my mood ("Girl, you're not doing it right," "Girl, that's wrong," "Girl, girl, girl, do you want to get fired?"). At least one person liked me. After all these years, someone liked me. I let that warm me. Aside from Mullybiski and my parents, no one had ever liked me.

After leaving Darioles, I wiped "mustard" off my aura by spending time with sweet Mullybiski.

I placed Sputnik's drawing on the bookshelf headboard and savored the feeling of being warmed by Sputnik's jacket in bed, wondering how he would hold me, wondering what was going on with his tortured heart? Why did he suffer "confused feelings"? As impossible as it was for me to believe, he had to be attracted to me (my personality, not my appearance) or else he would not have touched my face (twice now!), and he had been flirting, hadn't he? I had no experience with boys, so maybe I had misread all his actions? Maybe he just felt sorry for me? What if he only saw me as a friend, or as a pitiful kid sister to protect? I scrutinized every look he had given me, everything he had said, to try to understand his feelings for me.

I wanted to stay in bed and think about him, but I had to go to the dreadful math class.

216

One minute before nine a.m., I sat trembly in my first college class, my satchel sitting beside the desk's leg. The chalkboard looked miles long, waiting to be filled with non-understandable equations. There were no windows for distractions. The whole room felt chalky and cold. Classrooms never had heaters! I had gotten to class after all the good seats had been taken, so I had to sit in the front row to be "called on" and singled out as a dummy who didn't comprehend polynomials. I clutched a No. 2 pencil. On my desk sat a daunted notebook and a big textbook (which daunted the notebook) and an eraser that looked like a caramel cube, since I would need to do a lot of erasing in al-ge-bra.

When I looked around, I realized I was only one of two females in the class of about thirty students, and she looked rather smart in her mod cut; she was ivy league. And ooh my, in the backrow was a brown-haired fellow who looked like Jeff Miller grown up to college-age. His rolled up shirt sleeves revealed a tattoo of a *dog* on his bicep. Lassie? I smiled inside. I was surprised by a college boy having a tattoo. Why, just two hours earlier I had pledged my heart's loyalty to Sputnik—so what was I doing looking at this other cute boy? I scolded myself.

In the notebook, I doodled hearts and "Mrs. Gershom Braverman."

"His heart belongs to Joan of Arc," one of the students chuckled, a member of a duo of boys who had been lambasting Professor Blagonravov before his entrance into the room ("He's a Communist," "I heard he's a tyrant"). Most likely they were irritated by having to take math. I was too nervous to let the Joan of Arc comment tell my brain who was walking down the hall, just like I had not let Sputnik informing me he worked with snowflakes reveal he was the occupant of office 309.

The professor's steps sounded confident in an overpowering ivy league hallway where hundreds of years of stern educators had stridden. Doors along the hall were now shut, everyone hushed in their own classrooms and nervousness. Students in this class quieted too, submissive to the approaching Blagonravov.

217

In the room's silence, my heartbeat sounded louder in my ears, but I could not understand why I was so anxious again. I was literally shaking. I cuddled into Sputnik's jacket, fearing the professor whose personality had probably achieved the temperature of absolute zero, and anyone who approached him would get frostbite of the heart.

Into the classroom, the professor entered like a cold breeze, lowering the temperature. He looked austere and intimidating and old in a gray suit, and he looked different from the sweet boy I had poetically conversed with amidst pastries. His height loomed and cast a shadow, his eyes were starless, his beard prickly, and he was as pale as a foot untouched by sunlight. He smelled like cough syrup.

I felt the world yank the glass slipper away from me—a professor could not be in a relationship with a student.

When he first saw me in his class, he was surprised like seeing a dream character in real life then he immediately wounded me with an icy stare that I heard shout, "You lied to me!" I had told him I was not a student at Goldell. Well, he had told me his last name was Braverman! But if anyone had lied it had been that academic advisor—Professor Blagonravov did not look equipped with enough mercy to teach math to non-math students.

How dumb was I not to have realized his saying he worked at Goldell in physics and math and engineering was the same as saying he was a professor at the university?

I felt embarrassed for having revealed to him how loyal my heart was to his. And I felt as distanced from his iceberg as everyone else. Maybe I should pursue "Jeff" instead, my fear wondered; he was probably a sweet fellow, his dog tattooed on his arm.

All studiousness, the professor set his briefcase on the teacher's desk. He took off his suit jacket. Noticing his Star of David necklace, one of the lambasters pretended to sneeze but instead of saying, "Achoo," he said, "Ajew." This did not throw the professor's confidence; he strode to the chalkboard with a backbone as sturdy as Mount Everest.

I wondered why he had given up NASA to work as a professor? Maybe NASA had fired the volatile engineer?

"This is Introduction to College Algebra, Part 1. I am *Professor* Blagonravov." Had his highlighting the word "professor" been snidely directed at me? He wrote his name in needly letters in chalk. "Not *Mister* Blagonravov. You can either address me as Professor or as Doctor. And I will address you as either Mr. or Ms. Unless any of you have a prefix you would prefer otherwise."

"King," one of the duo of lambasters snickered.

Professor Blagonravov calmly set the chalk onto the chalkboard's chalk slot and turned around. "Who wants to be addressed as King?"

Confronted by alpha male, the boy uttered not a peep.

"Any real king would have the courage to defend his title, so I'll take your silence as a relinquishment of your crown."

Students laughed like canned audience laughter with an abrupt ending.

The professor turned back to the blackboard and wrote down his office's location, 309, and office hours.

Safe from being seen, the boy made a crude gesture, implying how he thought Professor Blagonravov spent his lonesome nights, since the boy believed no woman would want to be intimate with the austere mathematician. The other boy mimed a laugh.

The professor opened his briefcase, and the locks made a hard pop in the silent classroom. He took out an attendance sheet. "I do not call roll. I despise that fascist B.S. It is your choice if you want to come to this class or not, to fail or not. I just want to know your names, so I'll know how to address you if you have a question. I only need to see your face with your name once and I'll remember it."

Finally, the professor got to, "Ms. Lumi ---," as if he did not know my name—he had but a few hours earlier turned breakfast into poetry with me. I knew what it felt like to have his finger caress my face.

From the briefcase, he took out a stack of freshly copied stark-white papers (Goldell had a fancy desktop copy machine). He handed out the syllabus, acknowledging me not whatsoever. He stood in front of the desk like a commander. "You all have one week to decide if you want to keep this class or drop it, so it would be wise to go over the syllabus carefully and thoughtfully before making that decision."

He seemed much friendlier on the syllabus which began with "Welcome to Math with Mystery, Algebra Sleuths!"

Algebra sleuths?

Beneath the introduction was a drawing of students wearing P.I. fedoras.

"I will tell you now that we have a quiz *every* Friday, and your entire grade will be based on those quizzes. I give two grades: B and F. There is no in between. You either try or you don't. At the end of the semester, I will go back over all your quizzes and see how much you tried to understand, and if the scale tips toward 'tried,' you get a 'B.' I grade on effort, so your grade is purely a reflection of your own doing."

"No A's?" one panicked student asked.

"In this course, there's only one way to transform 'B' into 'A.' You must, using sound mathematical reasoning, explain if there are infinitely many betrothed numbers. This is an open question in mathematics, so good luck. Actually, feel free to tackle any mathematical problem, such as Hilbert's eleventh problem. In fact, there are many conjectures awaiting your examination."

What in the world was he talking about? We were first-year math students.

"That's not fair at all," a student "whispered" loud enough to be heard.

"Welcome to Goldell, gentlemen and *ladies*."

I despised his smugness. "*Welcome to Goldell.*" Yet I wanted to have his baby. I was utterly conflicted! I comforted myself by thinking I just had to get through fifty minutes of this tyranny then I could rush over to the registrar and drop this class, but the idea of dropping his class did not comfort me at all. I was in love with him and it was completely silly to pretend otherwise. I wanted to have a baby Blagonravov; I looked around and found it safe to say I was the only one thinking that.

"Don't worry about A's and F's. Concentrate on learning and you will gain something more valuable than a high GPA. So, what is algebra?" he asked, his tone friendlier now that he had established himself as commander of the class. "Algebra is arithmetic with mystery. How many of you like a good mystery book? It's alright, you can raise your hands. I don't practice the medieval method of

221

calling on students and forcing them to wear the dunce cap for all to ridicule."

Many students raised their hands, feeling safer now. I did not agree with the professor's "no A's" policy, but maybe he was not such a dictator, just serious about teaching and learning and had no time for loafers on his ship to knowledge. A Knight in shining chalk (often chalky from lengthy equations he dashed across long chalkboards, I envisioned).

"If you like mystery books, mystery picture shows, mystery radio programs—if anyone still listens to those— you will like algebra, where you can imagine every variable, every 'X' and 'Y,' as characters who you have to find clues about to figure out their identities. Here are the suspects," he said, while writing on the chalkboard: "Mr. 4, Mr. 9, and Mr. 8."

The class laughed and he did too.

I could tell he was completely capable of separating his private life and work life—I was nowhere on the surface of his thoughts.

"Now one of them has been posing as Mr. X, and our job, as math detectives, is to figure out which one."

From his briefcase, he took out a wrinkled fedora. "I promise," he said, "on my mother's good honor, I will give anyone who passes this class a private eye's fedora, because you will have proved yourself an algebra sleuth. Just drop by my office at the end of the term and pick up your hat. You'll all pass. Don't worry. Just put in your best effort." He put the hat on, cocked it just so like a P.I. from film noir. "Every time you come to this class, I want you to imagine that door with frosted glass stenciled in 'The Algebra Sleuths Agency,' and you are all detectives in training."

He had the class in good spirits now; plus, he looked adorable in the hat.

222

Despite his austerity, I sensed he had a heart made of candy. And he definitely had an "onstage persona"; he was a newly forming star that would someday shine across the world. I had a feeling he was a man who went for he what wanted and nothing was beyond his confidence's reach.

"Now, here's what we know about shady Mr. X. When he mingles with 5, they make 14...14 babies, perhaps."

The class laughed.

On the chalkboard, he wrote: "$X + 5 = 14$. Now, let's look at our suspects: Mr. 4, Mr. 9, and Mr. 8. Hmmm. What do you all think?"

"It can't be Mr. 4," the female student said.

"Why not?" the professor asked, suppressing a cough.

"Because 4 plus 5 does not equal 14."

"Excellent sleuthing!" He pretended to bat a ball out of the park. "I hate to give praise to the Cubs but if you saw the game last week, that was like Ernie Banks's 400th homer! Just something worth

223

mentioning. Hopefully, he will not make any more Thursday against the Dodgers."

Had he not told me the Dodgers *used* to be his team?

"Alright," he said, back to math, "Mr. 4 can now leave the lineup." He erased number 4 from the blackboard. "He can go home to his wife and kids."

The class laughed again. But I did not laugh. Wife and kids? Hopefully Sputnik was not married with children, maybe in a state the barnstormer had flown away from, and he just did not wear a wedding ring? He had told me he was a bachelor but what if he had lied? Would I ever be able to expand my trust to bigger than microscopic?

"So, is Mr. 8 or Mr. 9 our Mr. X?"

An astounding agreement amongst the students, "Mr. 9."

"Yep! 9 + 5 equals 14. And you should all be proud of yourselves! You just solved a 'linear equation in one variable,' which sounds highly intimidating, but it's not: it just takes some detective work to solve. Later this semester, you will learn that X could be an infinite number of suspects along the number line, and you won't have such a neat lineup to pick from, but I'll give you the tools to know how to weed them out, so don't worry. Any questions so far, detectives?"

None so far, except maybe, where did *you* come from?

"Now, we could look at this in a different light, a nicer light, and instead of seeing numerals as suspects in a crime, we could see them as numerals in need of a love connection."

More laughter.

"I see you people on campus and don't pretend that's not what you're looking for."

Whistles and giggles.

He was giving out smiles and all the students were taking them to wear.

"'Y' is a highly lonely gal." He drew a lonesome "Y" in the center of desolate chalkboard.

"Awwww," from the class.

"I know, it's sad. Poor Ms. Y. All the good letters are always taken. Y has come to our loooovvvve agency looking for her ideal mate, and it is our job to help her find her fellow. Y is seeking her equal, her soulmate, but there's always a mystery about these things, so she needs help clearing this up. Here's what she knows and here's what we know: $Y + 2 = 11$. That pesky 2 is getting in her way of seeing who is on the other side of the equal sign. Hmmm."

"Mr. 9 has made a comeback," the female student said.

"But how did you figure that out, Ms. Collins?"

I was slightly jealous.

"I subtracted 2 from 11."

"Ah! Yep! Excellent work. Mr. 9 is the fellow Y seeks. Y equals 9."

Maybe I would never be smart enough for him. I was still trying to figure why Mr. 9 was Mr. X.

"Subtraction is one of the investigating tools I am going to teach you. But for now, I just wanted to show you different ways of looking at these mysteries. Which way do you prefer to see: the numbers as suspects in a crime, or as lovers in need of romance?"

A resounding, "Suspects in a crime."

The professor looked at me, the only one in class who shared his desire for math to be romantic. Once again, I felt close to him in spirit. He was warm for someone who spent life studying indifferent equations and physics of snowflakes and barnstorming from cold field to cold field. And he was secretly romantic, I expected, because *he* liked my pinkness, not only liked but revered and wanted to preserve the blush, just like he wanted to defend the redness of my heart.

"We're going to go back to these kinds of problems later this semester," the professor said, "but first—"

Some "aw shucks" from the students.

"Ah, I promise we're still going to have fun. It's all going to be fun, and I promise my quizzes will be just like what we just did. We'll all be wearing fedoras soon. But I have to give you some basic information that you can use on the job here at our detective agency. We need to know as much as we can about our suspects: the numerals."

He liked teaching, that was obvious. I had never seen math taught this way. He spoke of algebra the way some men spoke of beautiful women. He was a history-making man, and I was a part of history in this moment, the era when Professor Gershom Blagonravov was young and vibrant and transferring that vibrancy to a new generation.

I remembered my first love, even before The Wanderer and Starman, had been a polymath: Doc Savage.

What was great about Professor Blagonravov's class was he taught us like it was our first introduction to mathematics ever, not to be condescending but to help us iron out knowledge from school that might have gotten wrinkled over the years, or knowledge "the leaky education system" had let seep out of its classes and textbooks.

He started with "elementary number theory" and asked, "What is a numeral anyway? For that matter, what's a number? To find out, we're going to take an exciting stroll across the number line! Now some people are afraid of math because they think it is too abstract, but the truth is, you all are incredibly skilled at abstract thinking; every human is. We use symbolism constantly. For example," he said and wrote on the blackboard, "Peppermint."

That really caught my attention.

"That word is not an actual peppermint, but you understand it means peppermint. Please don't let numerals and other symbols scare you away. You use them all the time. A mathematician writes '+' and a writer writes 'plus' but *both* are symbols for the concept of addition, and you are capable of reading and comprehending symbols. Whereas a writer uses words to express herself, a mathematician uses numbers, but both are adept at symbolism and poetry, and so are all of you. You probably didn't realize this but this is also a poetry class. Math has some exquisite poetry."

He wrote, "$1+1 = 2$." He stood back to admire the expression. "The most beautiful sentence ever written; two lonesome ones becoming two, the line sought after in every lovestory."

Yes, he was a Romantic.

"And here is the most tragic sentence ever written: $2-1 = 1$. The loss of the one. Even sadder than $1-1 = 0$. Because once you're zero, you're nothing, but to be a one again after having been a two, that's tragic."

Ooh my heavens, I loved him.

The other students wanted to leave poetry to get back to the "crime scene."

"Throughout the semester, I will show you more of math's divinest equations and formulas. The most poetic of mathematicians strive to write the loveliest formulas. Don't be fooled into believing the most complex equations are the loveliest, no more than a lengthy sentence in a book is the loveliest; after all, nothing is quite as poignant as three simple words, 'I love baseball.'" He grinned. "My point is I want you all to be able to see sentences on this blackboard, not undecipherable equations. I want you to be able to read mathematics' stories in the way you read novels. But to read a book, you must first understand words, and since the 'words' of math are numerals, that's why I'm starting there. Then we'll learn about the plus sign and square root symbol, just in the way you learned about commas and periods."

He was so attractive I wanted nothing more from this universe than his embrace, "the way electricity must feel about other electricity," I wrote in my notebook, which I should have known would turn into a writing notebook, because I could not be around a blank page without writing prose on it.

The mathematician wrote, "OBP = H+BB+HBP/AB + BB + HBP + SF. That is a sentence. Don't be intimidated because you don't yet know 'the words.' Once I tell you 'OBP' means 'On-Base Percentage' and 'BB' means 'Batted Balls,' the message will start to become clearer. This sentence instructs us on how to calculate the frequency a batter reaches the plate. Don't worry, I won't give you any problem that complex to know for this first quiz. I'm just using it as an illustration. Now, to help us further visualize all these abstract concepts, we're going to use a highly complex and efficient teaching tool," he said, while taking out from his briefcase a Bullwinkle-headed Pez dispenser.

The class laughed, so did he.

Like a comedian, the professor knew when to pause during a joke to make the punchline wallop. He took out one yellow candy. "Now, we have *one* piece of candy." Writing the number line on the blackboard and circling "1," he explained, "A number is a quantity, whereas a numeral, such as '1,' symbolically represents the quantity of one, the way the word 'peppermint' represents an actual peppermint."

He was so different and so perfect. I abhorred the saying, "There are other fish in the sea." I did not want a fish. I wanted Gershom "Sputnik" Blagonravov. There was only one of those.

Professor Blagonravov was such a physical teacher, getting his body into the teaching like a coach in a locker room. I understood why he had taken off his jacket, his underarms now wet, the sides of his hair damp from all the energy he put into his lecture.

"I'm giving out Pez, people, and all you have to do to get one is tell me a symbol used in mathematics."

"Subtraction sign!" one boy, obviously eager for some Pez, shouted out.

Professor Blagonravov tossed Pez like a baseball, and the student raised his hand to catch the Tweety Pez dispenser.

Ms. Collins said, "The numeral 'four.' That's a symbol, you just said so."

Why, I had never seen anyone be so openly flirty!

The professor politely walked the candy over to her desk and smiled at her.

"Good job," he said, impressed by her thinking outside the box.

Another male student, in the back row beside quiet "Jeff," called out, "Equals sign," and the professor tossed a "long ball."

"Man, I'm bringing my catcher's mitt to the next class!" one student said, a boy fresh from high school, still wearing his varsity jacket and swept up in baseball fever.

"Koufax!" Professor Blagonravov said, while pitching another Pez candy.

Another student held up his hand and hit into it like his palm was a baseball mitt. "Yogi Berra! Right here, Larsen!"

"Ah, man," Blagonravov said, breaking out of his role as professor, "don't ever say that name in my class. Automatic 'F'." He laughed. "'56, Game 5, I was at Yankees stadium—"

"When Larsen and the Yankees shut out the Dodgers?" another boy asked.

I had no idea what they were talking about, but the boys, and the professor, were obviously enjoying themselves.

While a baseball game of Pez took over the classroom, I wrote in my notebook a line for a story, "Both starry and earthy like a meteorite landed on Earth's crust, he was a blend of otherworldly genius rarity and rugged weather-battered Arctic park ranger."

While the boys were interested in playing baseball with him, I wondered how the mathematician would kiss. How would his shyness plus demandingness compose a kiss? Would his lips begin bashfully or would they take command of a girl's lips immediately? I found out in a daydream where he kissed me by the chalkboard. Years earlier when I had dreamed of the aeronaut *teaching* me how to kiss in his sleeping bag in woodland, had I intuitively known he was a teacher?

I looked around. None of the other students seemed to be wondering how the professor would kiss, except maybe Ms. Collins? She was involved in the baseball conversation too. Professor Blagonravov was talking about "Robinson's line drive"…

I took inspiration from ninth century poet Ono no Komachi to write this:

Beloved man

In your hands, I knew how it felt to be Beethoven's piano

Chagall's canvas

The petals of a lotus in summer

But all these encounters with you

Never happened

Except in a longing dream

If I could not be with him, I would live as chastely as Joan of Arc and join the convent! (I had a flair for the dramatic like any good nineteenth century heroine who always wore gloves).

A memory from childhood came like summer into my thoughts: I had seen the professor without his shirt on. My temperature rose, remembering his *bare* chest and arms, exposed after the aeronaut had tossed off his T-shirt in the wheatfield. An image I had not known what to do with at that young age, but my mind had saved the splendid visual like a gift for me now. I knew behind his professorly button-down his chest was wildly hairy like his stomach. I heard him mention "integers," but I was so attracted to him, I stopped paying attention to his lecture, as my gaze traveled the length of his tie and ended at his belt, a locked fence I had never unlatched. I had never seen a man fully without his clothing on. I had seen a drawing of male anatomy in a medical textbook. This was 1965 and a girl did not have access to images of naked men, at least not this girl. Unlike boys who seemed obsessed with viewing pictures of naked women (even going so far as to steal clothing catalogues just to view photos of lingerie), I had not cared to see such images. Until now.

Were not even nuns curious? With the nervousness and excitement that went along on most new journeys, my eyes wandered farther down his body. I got so flustered, the side of my hand accidentally flung the eraser from my desk, where it hit the boy beside me in the knee then ricocheted onto the floor, and Professor

Blagonravov had to stomp it to keep it from rolling under the desk. I had made a fool of myself in front of Sputnik and "Jeff" and the cool calm Ms. Collins; well, that was what I deserved for doing something improper.

The boy beside me scolded with a glare, "You stupid girl," because he obviously believed when a girl did something stupid, she was not to blame—her girlness was to blame. And I was not pretty enough to merit his forgiveness.

Noticing the boy scowling at me, the professor said, "Did the little eraser hurt you that bad, tough guy?"

The class laughed.

"That's enough," the professor said, sternly, not one who would tolerate bullying.

He leaned down, picked up the eraser, and handed it to me, and for a moment, it felt like he and I were alone beneath the awning of his fedora.

"Cooties, you understand," I whispered. Not the best thing for me to have said. He was disappointed in me for seeing him as Sputnik, not as Professor, and he was hurt that I was not paying attention even though he was trying so passionately to teach. Plus, he was carrying heavy classes, the young professor hiding his youth behind beard, and he did not want to lose face in front of these students, and I knew too many personal things about him like he had once hopped trains and enjoyed his grandma's cooking and his belly was filled with sweet coffee, so he was vulnerable.

I had never met anyone so confident and insecure: confident about his ability to make history, insecure about his ability to make friends.

Leaning over had instigated his coughing, and the class laughed at that too—laughing at a man who had been kind to them. No, I could not understand humans.

Then...

Sweating, he rolled up his shirt sleeves. Witnessing a bluish green smear on his skin, I thought his lower arm was bruised, until I suffered a cold realization: the mathematician who spent life studying numbers had once been a number in a Nazi concentration camp. I was hit with the fact that everything mysterious about him was tied with the numbers tattooed over his bloodline. He was not from starry outer space, he was from this gray world, and he had the grayest story of all. I realized contrary to The Snowflake Physicist's romantic title and despite his boyish face suppressed behind beard and his charming "on-stage" persona, the professor was gravely serious, even headstone solemn, a monument of death. I surmised he had lost many loved ones in the Holocaust and only he bore their epitaphs. And he was awfully scarred, especially his hands, like he had developed in a rock pit. Suddenly, I felt engulfed in a smoky darkness the way I had felt years ago while trying to communicate with my love across space and being smothered with a starless sky. Yes, I had always been attracted to men with patched up hearts, a patch job done by themselves in this uncaring world, and I had always wished to be the light in someone's darkness, to provide the thread that could truly sew up the tears in his masculine heart, but could I handle this grayest of grayness? I was conflicted between wanting to write pink passages into his gray life and to run away from this man's doomed story before I became a character in a tragedy.

My Wicked Stepmother scorned, "I warned you—you won't get your happily-ever-after romance."

He noticed me looking at his marked arm, and not consciously realizing what he was doing, he covered the numbers by crossing his arms over his chest.

At the end of class, I realized I had not paid attention to his lecture, and unless the question "What color are my eyes?" was going to be on his first quiz, I was going to fail.

I also observed he was only good with people at a distance. A group of students were lined up at his desk to ask questions, and the professor was cordial but aloof, while rolling his sleeves down again, snapping himself back up. He shook the male students' hands with a dominant handshake, his hand clamped above theirs, not on equal ground.

Ms. Collins asked, "Is it possible to do something else for an 'A'? I'm on a scholarship and without it, I won't be able to go to school here. I'm not a math major, Professor, and I can't come up with a math algorithm."

"How do you know if you've never tried? I suspect a young Lady who carried the entire class today—every single non-baseball question I asked, you answered—might have an honorable go at the question. I'll look favorably on any attempt."

"Please, I know I can't."

"Alright, you can write an essay about mathematics instead, the topic of your choice. But, Ms. Collins, you still have to attain a 'B' first."

"Thank you, Professor."

"*Thank you, Professor,*" I mimicked in my thoughts—how dare the wench try to steal my Knight! Moon-Moon would have said I was being un-Ladylike, but I did not care, for I could not bear the possibility of some other girl getting my Sputnik. Although Sir Galahad had been the purest Knight, if my Knight had strayed into a few flowerbeds in this world of tempting flowers along his journey to his Lady and hearth, I would still welcome him with open arms, but once he found his flowerbed, he could never lie again in another pasture!

A male student asked if he could also write an essay for an "A," which was responded to with a curt "No" and a glare from the professor with enough disappointment in it to make the poor boy want to quit school.

"You said that girl could write an essay."

"I'm assuming you're a man, aren't you?"

"What kind of assumption is that?"

"Well, if you offer me no evidence of your membership in manhood, I have no basis for classifying you as a man."

Yikes, that was hateful, and I was disappointed in Sputnik.

The professor continued his scolding, "All of you should be ashamed for letting one girl carry the entire class today." The professor made no apology for showing special treatment to females. Was that condescending or chivalrous?

The male student looked genuinely worried about his future at Goldell.

I thought Professor Blagonravov was being entirely unfair; he must have also realized his unfairness, and asked, "What is your major?"

"Journalism."

"Don't expect any coddling in that war field."

"Sports journalism."

"Then you should know Ernie Banks didn't score 400 homers by asking his coach for a way out of practice. All I'm asking is for you to step up to the plate and try with your best effort to hit a homerun. As I told Ms. Collins, I look favorably on students who *try*."

"That's bullsh—" Saying the expletive sealed the student's fate in Professor Blagonravov's class.

"This isn't a dugout. Do you realize there's a Lady still in this room?" the professor disciplined.

"So? I'm not a square."

"Does that mean you don't honor the old-fashioned honor code of putting out your nicest words around Ladies? Well, you'll honor this, I assure you: if you want an 'A' in this class, you'll present a detailed paper on the answer you come up with for the question I

235

posed earlier, and you'll present it to this entire class, do you understand me?"

"I'm dropping this junk!" The student threw up his hands and stormed out, and the outburst had no effect on the professor's austere coolness.

After everyone had left, there Sputnik was on the iceberg again. His IQ was mountains above others, and his pain the lowest there was; he was isolated at both the peak of intelligence and the pit of misery.

Despite his minor flaws, I admired him so, and I knew if a woman was to be happy in marriage, her husband had to be her hero.

I walked over to his desk, wishing I could melt his loneliness and erase the numbers on his arm the way he had erased numbers on the chalkboard. I wanted to pick the barb out of his memories no matter how cut up I got in the process. I was ashamed of my cowardly disloyal initial impulse to run away from his tragic story. With Joan of Arc's loyalty, I would never walk away from him, no matter how dreary his lifestory; I would never leave him stranded alone on icy pages, even if I had to suffer frostbite for all my life. Unless he asked me to walk away, I would stay by him even through a blizzard, as his wife, or friend, or guardian angel in nun's habit.

"Sputnik—"

He shut his briefcase. "Ms. ---, in this classroom I am your professor, and you will address me as such." His voice gentler with me but stern enough to assert his authority, or maybe he was just embarrassed and hiding behind the stoic professor role.

"Okay, *Professor* Sputnik—"

"Professor Blagonravov." He did not say it authoritatively but submissively to fate—our relationship was one of professor and student. Was he upset by this?

"I just wanted to tell you I did not lie to you. I am not a student at Goldell. You told me your name was Braverman."

"I wrote the song under that name as a tribute to my mother and bubbe. If you're not a student at Goldell, what are you doing here?"

"I'm a student at Adelia and my advisor told me to take this class because all of Adelia's math classes were full."

He thought about my confession, while putting on his suit jacket, and nodded to say he accepted I had not lied to him. "I didn't know you were a student."

What had he expected to pick at an apple orchard, where students frequented? I reconsidered, maybe he had not gone there to do any girl picking but had met me by happenstance—or destiny.

I offered again, "I'm not a student here, just for the semester."

Knowing what I was hinting, he said, "I also teach a class at Adelia."

If he *needed* to know me, he could set the terms of our relationship, but I would not make the situation harder for him, so I unzipped his jacket I wore and laid it on his desk.

"I'm going to the registrar to drop this class."

I started to walk away, but he said, "Ms.--- ... Lumi. I don't want you to drop my class."

"Why?"

"Because I want you to be able to see the poetry in this."

I turned around to see him writing on the chalkboard: "X = Y."

He didn't have to explain because I saw the poetry immediately.

"X and Y are equals, two sides of the equation, whatever happens to Lady Y affects gentlemen X." He drew an X/Y graph with a diagonal line cutting across.

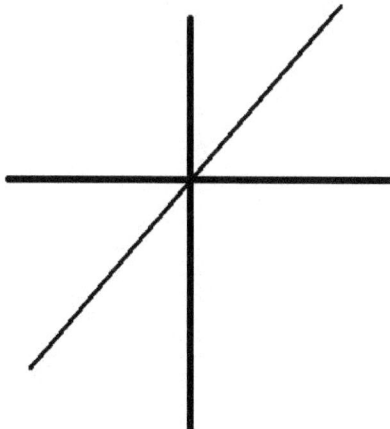

"That line shows their relationship: see how it goes down and down forever into negative territory but also up and up and up into positivity forever—they experience it all together, eternally, their journeys never ending."

He was so immensely beautiful to me.

"I see the loveliness, Professor."

"I thought *you* would."

His implying we were kindred made me feel less embarrassed about my outpouring of romantic feelings earlier in the morning.

"Professor Blagonravov, can I also write an essay instead of having to come up with a solution to that problem?"

"It's not a problem, just a question. No, you can't write an essay— you must write a poem, a mathematical poem to be certain, but I'll leave 'mathematical' up to your interpretation, but it must be a poem that pairs well with, hmm… ba-bu-ba…sweetened coffee."

"What about a poem that pairs with cocoa? I despise coffee."

"Alright." He handed his jacket to me. "Here, angel, keep it. The Lady Model girl gets cold so easily. Besides, it'll keep devious boys from making passes at you, because they'll think you already have a fellow, one big enough to kick them back to next week. I'm still the Captain who is going to protect you. That hasn't changed."

I was unsure what to make of his statement about me wearing his jacket—he could not be my fellow but he wanted me to live as if he was? Or was he just being the older protective brother again? I was very confused about his feelings for me. Did he see me as a friend, a charity, or as the girl he wanted to love but could not? Why would he have said that to me about Lady Y and Gentleman X being two sides of the equation if he did not see me as his Lady?

While I put on his jacket, he asked, "Are you going back to the filth motel?"

"No, I'm going to my next class."

"Which is?"

"Political science in Douglass Stanton Hall at Adelia."

"With Professor Carmichael? His movie star looks are highly popular with the female population, I'm told."

Why, I never! Was he insinuating I had picked that class to be around some studly professor? I had never even seen Professor Carmichael.

From the doorway, "Hey-ho, Professor," a student called out, a cute shaggy-haired sandy-haired pupil of hippiedome, decked in purple turtleneck like a member of the Lovin' Spoonful, "I've got the sylla-bi o' piiiii."

"Brad, if I'm late," Professor Blagonravov said, "go ahead and give out the syllabus, and if needed, just jump right in with preliminaries, transcendence of 'e' and pi, all that jazz. This young Lady needs help finding her class, so I'm going to assist her."

I didn't need help finding my class, but I wouldn't turn down an opportunity to walk with Sputnik.

"Whateves, Pro-fess," the California dude said.

Professor Blagonravov rolled his eyes but I could tell he was charmed by the student's mellowness.

We walked the autumn campus whose adrift leaves reminded me of a melancholy Kay Starr love song, *I Cry By Night*. The professor and I did not say anything to each other on the long stroll to Adelia, but I was certain we were both thinking of each other. My love went deeper even though I had to push him away, but just for four years, until I graduated, but…would my graduating change anything between us? He was "unavailable for love." Why? Why? Why was he letting the tragedy of his past pen him out of a lovestory now?

In political science with handsome Professor Carmichael, who looked like Jeff Chandler, I was not as interested in the state of the world as in the state of Professor Blagonravov, who was much sadder than anyone knew or could even fathom. I had experienced sad chapters, but I could not picture what he had gone through in the death camp. Any humor he emitted was purely for the benefit of others. I supposed the rising star of science had his Starman stage persona, his conference charm, his lecture humor, but I knew he never laughed by himself; I also sensed he never cried either. He really was like Theodore Knight who had suffered nervous breakdowns, in and out of mental institutions, due to his love being murdered and his role in the development of the atom bomb.

I sensed Gershom had endured unfathomable coldness yet when I had complained about being cold, he had not considered me spoiled or persnickety or naïve due to being privileged; instead, he had seemed charmed by my considering warmth a natural right for me and for him.

Listening to sad jazz, I cried through the afternoon and night, not only because I couldn't be with him, but because of what had happened to him in the war. I could not bear the thought of him being hurt that way. My mind was tortured with images of what he might have endured in the concentration camp, the kinds of horrific images that had marooned me from sleep for weeks after reading Wiesel's *Night*. All those scars on Sputnik's hands and the one on his neck and the two on his face. I did not know his age for certain, but I reasoned he would have been a young prisoner, while most boys his age in America, too young to be soldiers, had been playing sports and their worst fear had been asking a girl to a dance. How had the Alaskan boy been captured by the Nazis?

I cried until I remembered how crying over my Moon-Moon's death had gone unanswered, and I felt chilled by the world's indifference, the same world that had not given a tear over six-year-old Cynthia's death. Then I thought, no, my crying had not been completely ignored—Mullybiski had cuddled with me then and was comforting me now. A true friend. I was convinced dogs were angel babies.

At some late hour, Mullybiski began barking then a knock on the back door almost jarred my heart out of place. Scared, I shot up from bed and looked around darkness for anything to protect myself. I was disoriented. I had left the record player on, and Jo Stafford was singing *When My Sugar Walks Down the Street*. I picked up the closest thing next to me: my teddy bear. If a burglar broke in, I'd whop his head with the toy.

"Lumi, it's me." Sputnik!

Of course, burglars didn't knock.

Sputnik was outside my door and I didn't have time to doll up. I quickly yanked rollers from my hair, finger brushed disorderly blonde strands, threw a blanket around my nightgown, flipped on the lights, and…deep breath…ooh, wait, my gloves…another deep breath…and I leisurely opened the door.

"Hiiii."

"My apologies," he said, standing in freezing air and the orange glow of the backdoor's bare lightbulb. He was so handsome, he looked good even against the backdrop of the foul warehouse across the street.

When the professor wasn't in the classroom, he dressed like a log: bark-colored corduroy shirt, old leaf-brown pants, scuffed shoes so old moss that could have grown on them (maybe his train-hopping and barnstorming attire that blended him into woodland). His beard looked again as soft as streusel, and his hair as appetizing as molasses, and I could think of nothing else but letting my inexperienced hands roam freely there to learn the lesson of how to touch a man. But no, I could not betray his honor and look at him in that way, and I was ashamed of myself for having dug up the image of him shirtless—a view he had not given me but that I had taken by snooping. Becoming a professor at a top school had not been an easy achievement for the young man and I would not stand in his way of ascending higher summits, especially considering what he had already achieved surviving the death camp.

He had a toolbox with him, and I did not know any other scholar who owned an old wooden toolbox like a toolbox from biblical times.

"I couldn't sleep," he confessed, "thinking of you in this back-alley filth motel. I want to check the lock on your door."

The professor could not be with me romantically, yet with a divine-gifted chivalry in his masculine heart, Gershom would still protect the Lady; he had told me so earlier after class, but I had not realized the extent of his promise to protect me.

I was about to softly utter, "Okaaay" and let him inside, but I held to my honor code—I would do nothing to knock him off his headed-toward-the-stars trajectory. So, I said less drippy, "Okay."

The professor noted Ms. Stafford singing about the sweetness of her sugar. I started to turn off the record, a collection of love songs, but the professor said I could keep it on.

Mullybiski barked, "Hello!"

"The stocky pug," the professor said, setting his toolbox on the brick floor. "Hi!" I could tell he wanted to pet MullyB but felt it inappropriate to walk over to my bed, especially since he knew I was in love with him.

Mullybiski, assured Sputnik was no threat, went back to sleep.

The professor looked around, noted my bike against the wall, my harp, romantic paintings, and seemed embarrassed for being in my candle-scented room, where pink covers were pulled back on the bed, and June Christy was now singing *Make Love to Me*, and Sputnik's jacket was placed around the Knight in armor! I had never blushed so hard in all my life. Why hadn't I thought to remove his jacket from the Knight?

"I don't have a coat rack," I explained.

The professor looked at the coat rack beside the door.

"What I mean is that one's too filled, and the closet is smaller than a shoebox."

"Ah," he said, but he knew the truth.

I tried to turn off the record, but still disoriented, I accidentally turned up the volume right on the line, Make love to me, darling! Ooh my. I had told him I wanted to be a nun. I quickly yanked the spicy record off the record player and that made things more awkward—the loud screech of vinyl.

The professor quickly began fiddling with the lock. "Just as I suspected, that lock wouldn't protect you from a breeze. I was glad to hear your dog barking. At least you have someone to protect you."

"More than someone. I've got roaches and mice too. Would you like you some hot chocolate?" I asked, carefully opening the broken kitchenette shutters, which interrupted the roaches' party on the cabinet.

"Aaah, no," he said, eying the roaches. "I'll just work quickly, so you can get back to sleep."

"I grew up around bugs and all sorts of critters in the countryside, and I envision the boy from the Alaskan outback did too."

"Yep, wolves as large as yourself, bison and bears and *cockroaches* much much larger."

"That's scary," I said, and he laughed. "Hopefully hyperbole about the cockroaches."

"Hmmm, perhaps." Boys.

He made his "ba-bu-ba" song while he searched his toolbox.

Putting spoonsful of cocoa and sugar into a saucepan, I asked the professor, "How should I address you?"

"We're not in class, Peppermint, so I can't require you to call me Professor."

I loved he had made a nickname for me! I was so charmed by that, I did not even notice the awful smell that always broke into the room when the rancid refrigerator's door got opened.

Pouring milk from a glass jug into the saucepan, I chitchatted, "Technically, this is not hot chocolate but hot cocoa, since I am using powder and not a bar of chocolate."

"Ah."

What a dumb thing to have said. He was a genius. He did not care about the technical differences between hot chocolate and hot cocoa.

"In Poland," he said, as if letting me know he did not think the topic dumb, "it's more like a chocolate pudding."

"Really? Do you prefer it that way?"

"Hot cocoa's for girls."

"That's ridiculous."

"The only way my pops would drink it was when it was spiked with rum."

"Is that the only way you'll drink it too?"

"No." He definitely could be curt.

While I heated cocoa, sugar, and milk in the saucepan over a burner, Sputnik worked on installing *three* locks (he did not consider that extreme), work which created plenty of noise in the midnight hour, drilling and metal clanking.

"I don't think anyone will break into the chateau de dumpiness," I said, turning off the burner.

"Do you always sleep in music?" he asked.

"Sometimes. Do you?"

"There was a time…" He decided not to say anything else about his past.

I poured him a cup of hot cocoa too.

"Lumi, my goodness…" He seemed irritated by my "making a fuss over" him.

With my blanket and cocoa, I sat at my desk and watched how skillful the professor was in manual labor; he was as comfortable with a hammer as he was with a book, as he hammered down a "pesky" lock piece that was bent. "Ba-bu-ba, ba-bu-ba."

I wanted to ask him about what had happened in the war, but the timing did not feel right.

I felt bad for earlier thinking I would use Root as a weapon against a burglar, so I went over to the teddy bear, gave him a hug, and brought the toy over to Sputnik. I pretended the bear said in a "kiddie voice," "Helwo."

"Well, *helwo*, Bear. What's your name?"

"Root. I just thought I'd introduce you, so he'd be comfortable with you the way Mullybiski is."

Sputnik smiled at my silliness then he noticed his pin pinned to the teddy bear's sweater; the pin had been on there so long, I no longer even noticed it.

"The equation needed to leave Earth?" I asked.

"The equation for escape velocity," the rocket engineer explained.

After checking the efficiency of the locks a dozen times, he said, "Now you'll be safe in your castle, Cinderella."

"Okaaay." Stop doing that, I scolded myself.

He pointed the hammer in the direction of the Knight suit. "You really go for all that Knight myth, don't you?"

"I like the storybook Knight, the ideal of Knight, Knights at the Round Table. It might surprise you to learn, I live in this world, not in a storybook, so I'm aware not all historical knights were honorable. Some were pillagers. Some were anything but chivalrous. Some fought for oppression, not justice or liberty. Some killed thousands in Solomon's Temple, of all places. But I don't think true Knighthood is a myth. It has been achieved, and it is still being achieved by a rare few."

"If I could put you into a storybook, Peppermint, I would, because that's where you belong—that's where you deserve to be, in a story of noble Knights."

"Starry Knights. I'd prefer to be there. Wouldn't everyone?"

"So, how long have you been interested in Knights?"

"Since I was a very young girl."

"I figured so."

"Did you know some women were also Knights?"

"Don't get me wrong, I'm all for women's rights, but that's where I draw the line between women and men: the battlefield. Men should be on it, and women should be on the sidelines."

"It's a matter of personal choice."

"Men and women were designed to make babies together, not to throw bombs at one another. If male lions began waging war on female lions, here is how the war would turn out: due to the male lion's naturally larger size, temperament, and skills of battle evolved over many years, eventually there would be no more lions. Animals are wise enough to know this, yet humans consider themselves the wisest creatures on the planet."

"I thought you admired Joan of Arc?"

"In the way you admire the ideal of Knight, I admire the ideal of Joan of Arc—her unflinching loyalty, dedication, conviction, courage…and piety. But no man should have to suffer the regret that comes from hurting a woman in war."

"I don't think that's such a tragic fate to some men, the ones who enjoy hurting women."

"Unfortunately, that's true."

"Regardless of if women are soldiers or not, women are always going to be hurt in battle."

The truth angered him but he was not angry at the messenger.

"Well, thanks for the drink, angel." He offered the un-sipped cocoa back to me and left.

Close to four a.m., I sleepily walked around the chilly streetcorner and saw Sputnik's Studebaker parked by the patisserie. The car was turned off, no heat going. The car's top was up.

I gently knocked on the passenger window.

He looked ready to fight whoever was outside his car, until he realized it was a girl. "Peppermint!" his smile said.

I motioned for him to come inside.

I unlocked the bakery's front door and quickly turned on the lights and heat.

"Sputnik, were you parked there all night?" I did not feel so embarrassed about having put his jacket around the Knight's armor.

"I got to thinking I don't know how secure those locks are." He rubbed his neck. He was tired. His log-colored clothes looked shabby like his beard. "I should probably check the locks again. I didn't want to wake you up."

Whereas my heart was a romantic flowerbed, his heart was an arboretum, beautiful yes, but more masculine, redwood and oak.

"I was promised peppermint kisses in the morning," he said.

"I didn't make them, because last night, before you came over, I wasn't sure you'd ever come back here."

"I told you I would continue to protect you. Are you saying there are no peppermint kisses?"

I shook my head and regretted not having made the dessert for him, since he had stayed up all night to protect me.

Coughing, he fiddled with the radio until he found Benny Goodman's *Sing, Sing, Sing*; he snapped his fingers, but like a warden to his own enjoyment, he stopped himself from dancing.

"What would you like?" I asked.

"I'd like a certain young Lady to quit this job which requires her to work dangerous shifts."

"Life is dangerous, Professor. Do you propose I quit that too?" I felt bad after saying that, considering what all he had endured—if anyone knew how dangerous life was, it was him. "Like you said, we're not in a Nat King Cole song."

"But *you* should be. Besides, there's no reason to take unnecessary risks." He was full on older brother this early morning, taking on the role of father for the "fatherless" girl.

"This is a necessary risk. I'll have no place to live without this job."

"You can find a safer job. A young Lady, no Lady, should work for money." He rubbed his neck again.

I began brewing coffee for the former aviator turned grounded professor. "You work for money."

"Not much," he said, taking a jab at Goldell. "I think I made more selling a few aeroplane rides out of hayfields."

"You made money as a barnstormer?"

"Well, when grandmas weren't serving me pie and I wasn't able to find any apples on trees, I had to have money for food. It was the late 40s, after the war, and people were eager to fly, just fly, in calm air like a bird of peace."

The late 1940s? What was Sputnik's age? I didn't have enough details to figure it.

He took out his wallet and did not drop it this time. "I don't want to share knowledge for a paycheck, but I'm a man, and men have tangled ourselves up in money." He held up a dollar like it was the picture of a crook. "So tangled are we, it's going to take a lot of effort to undo, but there's no reason to get mothers tangled up in the meantime."

"Some women want to work for money and some have to." I slid coins across the counter, keeping my fingertips from meeting his.

"Yes, unfortunately."

"Why, I don't understand you. You call female students 'Ms.' and you teach us with such respect. Now you're here saying women shouldn't work."

"I didn't say women shouldn't work. I think a woman has just as much right as a man to be a physicist or pilot or President. I said women shouldn't work *for money*. Neither should men. That ideology must agree with your Christian value of generosity."

My eyes must have said, "So, it is true that you're a communist?"

"Just because my last name's Blagonravov doesn't mean I'm a leftover Stalinist. I hear what students say, but my mother was born in Poland, not Russia, and she spent most of her life in America. She was entirely a girly girl, all malts and picture shows, no interest whatsoever in politics. Yeah, my pop's parents were born in Russia, so was he. Your Sputnik really was Red made, at least partially. But Pops was as capitalist as it gets, the American dream and all that. My babushka, my pop's mother, had as much political interest as the stars, who shine over all. And my Polish bubbe was a free spirit."

I was surprised by his forthrightness.

"As for me, I was also born in America, in Alaska, as I told you. During a financial crisis, my family went to Poland, a case of extremely bad timing. When I first came back after the war, I got a new life, a new birth in Brooklyn with Ben, but it didn't feel like my own country, regardless of my Alaskan birth certificate, with all the rallies chanting, 'Get back on the boats, Jews.' Now it's, 'Hey, you Red, you're on the cold side of the Cold War.' Well, I watched both Nazis *and* Soviets conquer and mutilate Poland, where my boyhood was a battleground. I assure you I'm no more a communist than a fascist. Point in fact, I'm not a card carrier of any political party. I find some socialist ideals worth implementing, but I have no memberships anywhere, except in the redwoods, the nightsky, and the number line. I vote by conscience, not by party, and the money system rubs my conscience the way a triangle peg rubs a square slot—it doesn't fit."

He was so young and so serious. I felt I was being lectured in political science class.

"Now, are you going to quit this job?" he asked, as grave as a doctor telling me to quit doing something harmful to my health.

"I, too, belong only with the redwoods and the nightsky, and I'd like to quit this job, but I can't."

His face softened somewhat, seeing I was hurt by his disappointment, and he caressed me with, "Don't worry. I understand the kind of person you are, the kind of girl who wants to hug the moon, the kind of gal who can make rainbows without rain. I want no part in turning a sweet disposition into pickles, so my apologies for the sour conversation about money and politics. This is a patisserie. Go back to the pastries and cream and sugar." He turned up the sweet song. "Sing, sing, sing as Mr. Goodman advised."

He sat at the same booth he had sat at the previous morning. This time he did work, not doodles, handwriting notes for an article about mathematics I did not understand. He didn't have his briefcase and notepad, so he wrote on napkins. I went about my work of tidying the patisserie and did not interrupt him, except to bring him coffee and a piece of coffeecake, but he nodded the dessert away.

"You are going to make a fine wife someday," he said, his eyes steadfast on equations he was jotting.

"Oooh," I exclaimed, while wiping a table, "why?"

251

"Because you know when to let a man work and not to interrupt him except to bring him coffee."

"That's very chauvinistic."

He took a sip of coffee before responding. "I was only joking."

"Ooh."

Such dry humor.

"Your sweetness would never be an interruption to anything I was doing."

"Ooooh, thank you!"

"My pops was a chauvinist, though. 'Bring me my coffee, woman, and stay outta my way.'" Sputnik looked up at me as a way to say he was not like his dad. "A chauvinist thinks women are inferior to men. I think women, at least some of them, are superior."

Dish rag in hand, I walked over to his table. "Superior in what way?"

"Superiorly brave."

"Brave?"

"Goodness, yes. They have to be when the men in their life aren't living up to any standard of bravery. I was raised by incredibly strong-willed brave women. Brave to the point sometimes of being stubborn and getting themselves in harm's way. And they're superiorly sweet."

"Not all women are sweet."

"Yes, I know." And I knew he was referring to female guards he had encountered in the concentration camp. "That's why I said *some* of them are superior."

"Some men are sweet too. You're sweet."

"Hahahahaha!" Said without a trace of laughter.

On the "oldies" station, Helen Forrest confessed *I've Got a Crush on You.*

"You said you thought women had just as much right to be physicists and pilots and anything else."

"I do think that. I think every individual must decide for himself or *herself* the best way to utilize their lifetime. I don't think society or government should ever dictate what goal an individual should pursue. The women in my life were incredibly ambitious. If a woman wants to spend her time on the moon or in the kitchen, the choice is hers."

"And if a man wants to spend his time on the moon or in the kitchen, the choice is his."

I could tell he did not agree—he did not think a man's place was in the kitchen—but the young professor did not want to look un-progressive.

"Like I said, I'm not a chauvinist. I detest chauvinism. Any man who degrades, or disrespects, or harms women can have a long conversation with my fist. A stone who picks a fight with paper is pathetic. Not only is the fight cruel to the delicate paper, it proves nothing about the stone's strength—how difficult is it to destroy paper? Many feminists would get on to me for that, but we can't deny facts—men are physically stronger than women. Women are men's mates, not their jungle rivals."

"I definitely agree with that."

"In a peaceful world, I think women should be allowed to just be, without interference from man, like flowers in a field, capable of sustaining growth without assistance, just sunlight, lots of sunlight and moisture to flourish. And a man should only interact with the blossoms to sometimes caress them, if the blossom so wishes to be caressed and the man has a gentle enough hand and decent enough heart. But this is not a peaceful world—it's a world of tractors and pesticides and storms and flower pluckers—so, the blossoms need protection against the elements and the hands of intruders intent on plucking. A flower sometimes needs a man to prevent her from making a foolish decision like growing in the path of a pesticide sprayer when she's too naïve to realize such poison exists. But I agree with Pops on one thing: *my* wife will not work for money."

"Your *wife?*" My voice unable to hide panic.

"Hypothetically speaking."

"Ooh. You don't have a wife out there you left behind in some cornfield?"

He laughed at that idea. "No."

"I thought you were unavailable for love?"

"But if I was available for it. A girl who desires an occupation outside of 'wife' and 'mother' would not be the right girl for me."

He knew I was smitten with him, so he said he preferred a homemaker to get me to quit my job. I detected a trace of chauvinism in him, but I would not stop loving him because of a slight personality flaw, no more than I would stop loving him for a facial blemish. I knew he had a good just heart and wise thoughtful mind, but that did not mean I couldn't disagree with him or try to get him to see opinions in a different light.

He clarified, "That's just *my* personal preference, no different than saying I like soft-spoken girls. I want a girl who will feel satisfied with being a wife, mother, homemaker. That doesn't mean every woman should have to be soft-spoken just because I prefer that trait, or because any man prefers that trait for that matter, especially if it's in disagreement with her achieving authenticity. No one is required to live their life in accordance with *my* standards or anyone else's standards, although I can't fathom why any woman gave up receiving chocolates from men for receiving paychecks."

"I don't think they intended to give up chocolates for that, but remember, some women have to make their own money, and some want to, and some never received chocolates anyway, so what about those women, those ones shunned by love, men, and marriage in this unfair world where a woman's looks are equated with her goodness?"

"I'm just saying *I* want a girl whose goal is to be a wife, mother, and homemaker. I'm a busy man and I can't take time from my schedule to always be worrying about my wife being out in the dangerous world. I'm not still the little boy able to go with his mother to work to protect her from lechs."

"Your wife couldn't be a writer?"

"Well, writing she can do safe and sound in the house."

"What about photography?"

"You like photography?" he said, his voice soft. Did he think photography an alluring hobby for a girl?

"I love photography."

"I'd never stand in the way of a girl taking photos."

"Maybe she'd like to take a photo of you."

"I can't see why. This old tattered denim of a man as scruffy as his bomber jacket." Said without a trace of faux modesty.

He took the dish rag from my hand and slung it to the far end of the table. "Your soft little hands should not be cleaning any house but your own, built for you by your husband. You said yourself you want to be a nun or live a lovestory and give away free pastries. You're not a work-for-money girl."

"Lots of people don't *want* to work for money. I don't. But if I don't clean these tables, I'll get fired and kicked out of my apartment. I don't want to live in my car. I'd lose my car too."

"Ah, don't talk like that, Cinderella; this world has you speaking hard words not suitable for your soft lips."

"The Wicked Stepmother insists on Cinderella cleaning and scrubbing." I reached over to get the rag, but he stopped me by

255

taking my gloved hand in his. Feeling his touch, his hand so large and warm and strong, put me in an enchanting haze. "The precious clean glove is getting soiled from that dirty dish rag. You won't quit this job *for me,* your *Captain,* who assures you he will lead you on a safer path?"

Outside the windows, the darkness of night made the streets look as surreal as a stage play scene, as if no world beyond the patisserie existed; Sputnik and I were the main characters, the only characters, in this romantic play. Jeri Southern provided the romantic stage music, *The Very Thought of You.*

"I would quit this job if I had another option." Like being your wife.

The genius didn't have a solution and he gently let go of my hand.

"You should eat breakfast, Professor."

"Do you have porridge?"

"Porridge? And I thought I was the only one around here from the nineteenth century."

"How about oatmeal?"

"Most people don't come to a sweet shop for oatmeal."

"What about a bagel?"

"You don't want it with meat or anything like that, do you?"

"Nope, I'm a vegetarian." I would never have to make him a meal that my conscience would regret.

"Ooh, I'm a vegetarian too."

"So am I, and so was my mother."

I was about to ask, "She's not still?" but I realized he was referring to his mother completely, not just her vegetarianism, in the past tense. He always spoke of her as a character who was now gone from the story. Had she perished in the death camp? Had his mother not been alive to witness her son's achievements? I thought of him saying the women in his life *were* ambitious—were they *all* gone?

"I wish she could have tried Hank's, the best pizza in all the universe," he said. "I'm talking aliens would come to Earth for that pizza, which puts Earth on the cosmic map."

"Hank's?" That didn't sound like the name of a good pizzeria.

"Hank's in Brooklyn. Ice cream parlor, beer joint, pizza joint, a batting cage outside."

"That's bizarre. A malt shop/beer joint?"

"That's Hank's. Framed autographed photo of Jackie Robinson on the wall. A place where men go to get away from their wives."

"That's horrible."

"That's not why I went. I sometimes wanted to stay with my wife in the cornfield." Yes, such dry humor. "I went for the best cheese and bell pepper pizzas and banana splits in the world."

"Banana splits and bell pepper pizza?"

"Ah, whatta place to be at this time of year."

I must have looked confused.

"Because the playoffs are coming up," he clarified.

"Ooh."

"Hank's! Ben took me there when I first came back to this country, and that pizza was more welcoming than a welcome mat. If you think pizza and ice cream is a strange union, you should know what your *Melt & Malt* singer digs: dipping feta-spinach calzones into butterscotch malts."

"*Melt & Gag.*"

"I told you he's a butterscotch nut."   From his tone, it was obvious he had a brotherly relationship with Ben, and sometimes

257

older brother was annoying, sometimes charming; either way, there was plenty of camaraderie in their relationship.

After the bagel, the physicist chewed licorice gum, drank more black coffee, and kept working, until he said, "Come here, angel" with the both tender and commanding tone of a man who knows a smitten girl is at his beck and call.

He had a way of holding me with his gaze that made me forget my desire for everything except to be held in his arms.

He wanted to know my major and the courses I was enrolled in. I told him about my fear of majoring in English and my "Write thus!" motto.

"That's highly contradictory. Jeanne d'Arc is not following her creed—fearful of your stories being ridiculed in the English department, you are thus not writing thus."

I knew he was disappointed in my cowardice, so was I. "You're right, Professor."

"Of course, always." He smiled within his beard. "The Captain is right." He was playing around with my smittenness.

"What did you major in, Sputnik? Baseball with a minor in pizza?"

He had studied math and physics as an undergraduate, "back when professors were as tough as nails," then received a master's in aeronautical engineering, working in "propulsion systems," then master's degrees in both physics and mathematics then a PhD in mathematics.

Wow!

"Not bad for the boy who only spent a few years in school, cut short by the war."

I wanted to know when had he found time for flying?

He had been an aviator since coming back to America and had flown during college, sometimes on summer and winter breaks, sometimes on weekend jaunts to solitude.

As a master's student in physics, he had done research on "snow," while camped on "pure" Arctic snow in one of the coldest snow forests on Earth in Siberia Russia, which had not been a difficult climate to bear for the boy who had grown in polar weather; he had dealt with "much colder environments." ("Research on snow" was said as a way for me, the non-scientist, to comprehend his research). He had enjoyed the isolation offered by the Arctic, even dreamed of living there again.

"It's not all ice and cold," he assured, as if he planned to take me to the Arctic someday. "Arctic forests are majestic, perfect for Cinderella. In winter, they glisten like snow globe scenery, and warmer months bring to life fairy tale forests. Ah, there are snow-capped mountains, snowy owls, clean air, gushing rapids, crystal seas and lakes at the tip of your wonderment. Romantic. Well, not so romantic when you're with a group of grizzly smelly guys who haven't changed their long johns in two weeks."

Sputnik said I would like seeing real reindeer. The young physics student had been awakened one morning by a snowy-nosed reindeer searching for food in Sputnik's sleeping bag! "Hey, Blitzen, I'm Jewish," Sputnik had said to the reindeer, "so go find someone who believes in Christmas."

"Maybe he was Cupid?" I raised my eyebrow.

"Well, he certainly wasn't Rudolph. My cold nose was the one red enough to guide Santa's sleigh that day."

I wanted to hear all Sputnik's stories, the ones written by the barnstormer, the train hopper, the Arctic researcher, the NASA engineer. After getting his PhD, he had worked for NASA and Mass but had not gotten put on the astronaut list, his boyhood dream.

"Maybe someday," I said.

"You women do have a way of making men believe in our dreams so much, not achieving those dreams would be disrespectful to your unflinching faith in us."

"I'm not trying to put a burden on you to achieve your dreams. I only want you to do what *you* want to do."

After his work in rocket engineering, he went back to academia. He enjoyed teaching and preferred the freedom he got from the university to work on his own research.

Even though NASA had considered him an "explosive rocket," he still worked with the National Aeronautical and Space Administration, since he was interested in "cold technology."

I imagined Sputnik was one of the best engineers in the field, volatile or not.

"What draws you so much toward mathematics?"

"I understand math more than I understand humans," he said, bluntly. "A peacefulness envelops me when it's just me and the numbers, no humans around."

"I have an identical feeling about writing. A peacefulness envelopes me when it's just me and the story. I hope you won't hate me, but I always fell asleep in geometry class."

His face made a mock expression of surprise. "No, *you* fell asleep in geometry? The girl who paid so much attention in our algebra class that her absentmindedness shot an eraser across the room and almost started World War 3 with the classmate sitting beside her." He smiled to say he did not hate me.

I had a vision of him being a completely shunned nerd in school, fraternity of one, like me.

As if he could truly read my mind, he said, "Prime numbers were the key to my locker. I like that a prime number only has two natural numbers that are divisors, one and itself. You'll learn about primes in class if you don't fall asleep. I'll give you much more info if you stay awake that morning."

He was the boy everyone needed a "Rosetta Stone" to understand, but I sensed he did not *want* to be mysterious; he was looking for a counterexample to his conjecture that no one wanted to know him, that no one *could* know him, and I hoped to be that counterexample. I could understand him.

"That's very romantic, Professor, about the prime number, only one and itself—itself and *the* one."

"I'll tell you this," he said, as if I was the only one he would tell *this*, "while I was minoring in pizza, I also minored in romance languages, so I could read great science fiction in French."

We talked about science fiction; he was an afficionado. Whereas I knew Theodore Knight was Starman's real name, Sputnik knew Starman made his first appearance in *Adventure Comics* #61. Sputnik, aptly nicknamed, kept up with all things space travel, both space travel engineered by writers and by scientists.

Aside from mathematics, he studied, theoretically, extreme coldness not only on this world but other worlds far beyond the sun's warmth. The engineer was working on designs for cold gas rocket thrusters.

He was a subscriber to *Scientific American* and other science journals, whereas I read girly comics like *Dear Lonely Heart* ("love for every heart" promised in each issue).

We were both sleepy yet enlivened by conversation. Even our differences intrigued us.

My favorite movie was *The Ghost & Mrs. Muir*, the story of the writer who fell in love with the sea captain's ghost, Captain Gregg, who haunted her seaside house. I had watched this movie on TV one rainy and lightning-tinged night with the Knight framed by stormy window; I had imagined a ghost in the suit of armor. That night, after the rainstorm had knocked out the electricity, which added picture-perfect ambience to my ghost fantasy, I had written

A Knight in 1962 by candlelight with four cups of cocoa to keep me awake.

Sputnik's favorite movie was *It Came from Outer Space.* He had seen first seen the film as a late-night showing in a small theater in Parishville, a Midwest farm town the color of oats. During the summer of one of his barnstorming expeditions, he saw the movie a total of nine times in each new town he flew into, hoping each time to see a spaceship land on Earth, during one of his nights lying in an open field with a cup of hobo coffee and clear view of the heavens. I adored him so much.

"I'm convinced that movie has the most romantic opening scene ever in cinema," I said.

He made a funny face—he had never viewed the sci-fi flick as romantic.

"Ooh," I playfully argued, "it was romantic: the astronomer with the quaint house in the desert, far off from town. He and his girl, watching the stars at night."

"Everything sweet until an alien crashes close by!"

"Yes, but she and he got to investigate *together.* Doesn't that sound fun? Just the two of them against the world and its skepticism about alien life."

Even if we could not be a romantic couple, we could be a couple of kooky friends. I was surprised a boy could be a best friend. I was unsure why that surprised me considering I was looking for my soul's mate. This dawned on me like a bright new day: a soul's mate is a soul's best friend, not just a soul's lover. What a nice thought. One I had known in childhood, one that was greeting me again after our separation by a world that claimed boys and girls could not be friends.

He asked how I spent the rest of my time, outside of school and work, especially my nights, wanting my complete schedule.

I answered: writing and reading and baking and watching television and "studying math for that austere Professor Blagonravov."

I used this as an opportunity to learn more about his life too. The scientist was as busy as the hands of a clock—never allowed to stop, except to watch baseball. No more leisurely barnstorming through slow moving air over wheatfields; he traveled weekly by jumbo jet. (Yet he took time from his busy schedule to watch over me.) This week he was flying off to see a lecture by physicist Richard Feynman, to give his own lecture about rocketry to a small college, to attend a Vietnam War protest and a conference about Civil Rights where Dr. Martin Luther King would be in attendance, and to present his findings in "math," not explaining the details to the freshman algebra student.

I could imagine Sputnik becoming President someday, leading Earth into a peace treaty. Whereas my goal was to keep the world from changing me, his goal was to change the world.

Before he left, I asked about his neck, which he kept rubbing.

"It's just a crick. Sleeping bags are comfortable in grass, but not so comfortable on apartment flooring. I've yet to have time to buy furniture."

I doubted his lack of furniture was due to his not having time to buy furniture but due to his not having interest in picking out furniture. Plus, the genius had no time to waste on home care.

"And there's a certain stubborn young Lady who keeps forcing me to get up before dawn to check on her," he said through a cough.

"Since you're so busy, I could pick out furniture for you, as a way to thank you for putting up the locks."

He pondered my offer: would a Lady picking out furniture for him violate his honor code? Or maybe he was worried about me going to the furniture store where I might get robbed or who knows what.

"I couldn't ask you to do that, angel."

"You're not asking me. I offered as a duty to kindness."

"You really want to?"

"Yes!"

You'd Be So Nice To Come Home To.

"You really are The Lady Model. I wouldn't need much. I actually just need a desk and chair."

"You said the sleeping bag is causing you to have neck problems. Don't you need a bed?"

"Well…I don't care. I'm not married."

To avoid embarrassing insinuations, I stayed professional like an interior decorator. "Do you need necessities like sheets, pillows, blankets?"

"Are those necessities? Perhaps to a girl. I have a sleeping bag and a typewriter and books. I don't need much else. I had less than that as a barnstormer."

"So, you do need sheets, pillows, and blankets?"

The manly man from the Arctic shrugged.

"Do you have…" More embarrassing things to bring up. "Towels?" Quickly, "Or cookware?"

"I don't cook. I have one faithful thermos."

"Faithful thermos?"

"For drinking."

"I see."

"I don't drink alcohol, Ms.---."

"Ooh, I wasn't implying that. I know coffee is your drink."

"When I was landing in fields, stream water was my drink, which the faithful thermos scooped up for me, the same thermos…" He wasn't sure if he should finish his thought.

"The same thermos?"

"That belonged to Bubbe. She gave it to me on the day I was taken away as if Grandma's soup was all I needed to fight the Nazis. Can you believe I was actually able to hold onto it throughout my time in prison?" He said "prison" in a way that suggested he was aware I knew of his time there, since I had seen the numbers on his arm. "I feel loyalty to the thermos, the only thing which seemed to care whether I lived. The thermos offered me somewhere to put dirty ice and melt it into life-saving water on a long death march, where I had the thermos tucked in the rim of my trousers, and it actually stopped a bullet from piercing my stomach; the bullet didn't even pierce the thermos, just dented it."

I felt bad for having let all this time pass between us without asking about the concentration camp or even offering an "I'm sorry."

He quickly changed the subject, letting me know he did not want to talk about the war. "Towels, I have, the same ones I've probably had since undergrad. Here," he said, laying money on the table. "Do what you can with your feminine touch but don't overgirly. I don't want my apartment to look like The Lady Model. That's perfect for you but not for me."

Apparently, he did not think movers and workers at furniture stores would tell Goldell a young Lady had furniture delivered to the professor's apartment; for all they knew, I was his sister, or his wife.

"Professor…" And this was difficult for my nineteenth-century sensibilities to ask, "Where should I have these items delivered?"

He did not seem to think that question—"Where do you live?"— was as big a deal as I did. "Third floor, apartment C, Colby Apartments on Ninth Street."

"Won't I need a key?"

265

"No, I don't lock it."

"You don't lock your apartment ever?"

"I have nothing to steal, and who's going to steal me?"

"Sputnik, after all your talk about how we don't live in a Nat King Cole song and how I should value my safety so highly, you sleep with the door unlocked?"

"I said *your* safety is valuable."

"What kind of macho malarkey is that? You said you kept the faithful thermos because it was the only one who cared whether you lived or died."

"I keep the thermos as a tribute to my grandma."

"Sputnik, I'm sorry."

"You have absolutely nothing to be sorry for, angel. Well, I need to get back to the grind."

"Okay, I'll get started today."

"After class?"

I shrugged, not wanting the professor to know I planned on skipping school.

"I'll be gone all afternoon, and I admit, God forgive, it would be nice to indulge in a night's sleep in a bed when I got back."

I was going to indulge in this: playing house.

Sputnik stayed in the sweet shop to watch over me until the sun took his shift.

After mustardy work, I was told by Dariole I was a "Nun's Puff," not a "Crepe Suzette," but I did not care what she thought because *he* thought I was a peppermint.

Back in my apartment, I changed into denims rolled up at the ankles, and a sweater jazzed up with scarf, and bobby socks and saddle shoes, attire for hard work like cleaning and furniture picking. I enjoyed time with Mullybiski and had a quick snack of toast and strawberry jam and hot chocolate.

I skipped homework and classes to make the tired young professor more comfortable in his life. I didn't think I would miss much on the first day in World History and Art History. I felt much more purposeful taking care of my soulmate than memorizing the dates of Charlemagne's reign. Charlemagne was long dead but this great good man was alive and in need of a bed. And this day would be a work of art!

First, I planned to do some detective-ing in the encyclopedia-thick Goldell University catalogue, a how-to manual (how to register, pay for classes, graduate, etc.). I sat on a bench in the partially sunny courtyard, my satchel on the opposite seat to prevent anyone from sitting beside me (my asocialness was legendary). With a chocolate-and-coconut candy bar and more hot chocolate from the university cafeteria to keep me awake, I perused the catalogue, which included courses and professors by department.

I no longer noticed other boys, so many of them on campus. My heart was pledged to Gersh. No other boy would be allowed to cross the threshold into my fantasies. Even if I could not be with my love romantically, I had no interest in being with anyone else.

Then just as I thought that, "Jeff" walked by, all cute in his T-shirt and blue jeans and baseball jacket. He nodded "Hello" to the girl in his algebra class.

I nodded back, a little giddy about "Jeff Miller" acknowledging me.

He stopped and backpedaled, decided to fight his shyness and take the opportunity to ask whatever question was aching his mind.

"Did Professor Blagonravov give us homework due tomorrow?"

"No, not anything that's due, just problems to study for Friday's quiz."

"Thanks." He smiled.

What was going on here? Boys never stopped to talk to me and they did not smile at me. Was this a test from my guardian romance angels to see how loyal I was to Sputnik? I realized I could not stop my attraction to "Jeff"—attraction wired by biology—but how I *responded* to the attraction was my choice. I remembered Moon-Moon's analogy of molasses and lust. I would never hurt Sputnik by sampling any other molasses. I only nodded at "Jeff" and he walked out of the story, where he was not meant to play lead.

One difference in my feelings for Gershom Blagonravov and Jeff Miller was that I did not just like the character but the actor behind the character—whatever role Sputnik played, I sensed I would love, for I loved his soul.

In the catalogue, I found under the math department "Assistant Professor" Blagonravov's handsome picture in black & white, his ivy league education history, and his research interests. The professor had a "joint appointment" in the engineering department. In mathematics, his interests were in number theory and algebraic geometry, and that told me as much as $9nb*Y*\%$. And there was that stuff about cold gas rocket thrusters and physics of the cold on this planet and others. There was no mention of his barnstorming years, or his time in the death camp, or his snowflake research. In the university's course catalogue, I found classes taught by "Mr. Blagonravov": the introductory algebra class I was in, the upper-level math course in "transcendental number theory," and a class in the engineering department on propulsion systems called "Blast Off!" At Adelia, the professor had a "courtesy appointment," where he taught "Physics of the Very Cold," a surprising class to be taught at the artsy university. Four classes plus all the research and traveling!

I kept his picture, sized for a wallet, or perhaps, just right for a locket (the university did not have a policy against a student being smitten with her professor).

From the school paper, in an article about my dear Sputnik, the new assistant professor, I learned his age—35! Maybe he thought I was too young for him? The article said he often traveled across the globe to conferences, lectures, and meetings that involved planetary research, space exploration, and astronautical engineering, but I already knew that. I was looking for new information. I knew he would tell me this information, but there was something fun about learning it covertly, as sneaky as that was! With a clearance badge for NASA, he had been at the launches of NASA's Pioneer 1 and Mariner 2 (the probe that flew by Venus), and he had worked on the Mercury missions and was currently involved in the Gemini missions. His books had been published and his articles were in science journals. His genius had been interviewed by newspapers and television broadcasts on everything from life on other planets to the future of rocketry. I was offended by the mean-spirited reporter describing my friend as "a physicist with a perpetual cough." Apparently, no one ever asked him about snowflakes, his private passion project. He called himself The Snowflake Physicist but only around me. He had recently been interviewed by a national news show; his views about an outer space treaty would air the next week. I was excited to watch that. He had never mentioned his celebrity, and while I was happy for him, I was also slightly depressed—I had to share him with the world, which was true for every woman both blessed and cursed to be in love with a history-making man.

I decided to listen in on his Blast Off! class. I had assumed the classroom's door would be shut, and I would hear his muffled lecture in the hall, but no, the door was open. I hoped he did not see me—was I pestering him? I stood beside the door and did not understand anything the engineering professor taught, something about "isentropic process," but he was just as enthusiastic in this class as he was in algebra. I slightly peeked in and saw an adorable paper airplane on the teacher's desk (I could envision him making those as a boy). On the chalkboard were hieroglyphics like this:

$$s_2 - s_1 = c_p \ln(T_2/T_1) - R\ln(P_2/P_1) = 0$$

$$\frac{T_2}{T_1} = \left(\frac{P_2}{P_1}\right)^{(\gamma-1)/\gamma}$$

$$\gamma = \frac{c_p}{c_v}$$

Alongside the equation were graphs and charts.

Ooh my, his smartness was so intoxicating, I felt tipsy on adoration.

Now it was time to play house.

To view the setting in need of decoration, I drove downtown to his apartment complex, a small three-story brown brick structure about a fifteen-minute drive from my apartment. Thankfully none of his neighbors were home. I felt improper having the key to the bachelor's studio. But out of responsibility to kindness, I unlocked the door and walked inside.

Army barracks had more furniture and comfort! Brick walls, *hard* wood flooring. A grass-green sleeping bag was in the center of the room, a sleeping bag that had lost all its padding to the years and was just loose threads of fabric no more capable than air of offering warmth to the outdoorsman. Comfort was obviously not important to the boy from the wilderness, or maybe the math genius did not have time to create comfort. And he was obviously a minimalist when it came to material belongings. I wondered how old the sleeping bag was and if the aeronaut had stargazed in it. I wondered if he had kept a girl warm in it. To shake off that thought, I continued to look around and smell around.

The apartment had a mud puddle stink; I realized *why* when I met the professor's roommate—a frog who leaped onto my shoe.

"Well, good morning," I said.

"Ribbit." She leaped onto the sleeping bag.

There was another roommate too—a turtle who was using the apartment as a bathroom!

Well, the whole place needed to be cleaned for sure. This was going to take some time. The floor was a mess of leaves and mounds of scattered wadded socks and dirt tracked in from his shoes, which apparently spent much time in forests.

270

In the corner by the door were bowls of water for the amphibian roommates, and these bowls had also been used as bathrooms by the creatures.

A tatty towel, from his undergraduate days, covered one lone window since the curtain rod was being used to hang his paltry sum of clothing, colors that blended him with the redwoods, except the professor's gray suits that matched chalkboards. The unused curtain, which looked filthy, was balled up in a corner, being used as a bed for the amphibian roommates.

Against one wall was a scuffed upright piano the color of an acorn, which matched the outdoorsman's wardrobe so well, I envisioned when he sat at the piano, he blended in as if in camouflage. I walked over to the piano and felt warmed by the thought of him making music. He was a musician *too*; he had more "too's" attached to his occupations and skills and talents than anyone I had ever known.

Close to the bedroll sat his typewriter, and a sketchbook and grease pencil, and a chestnut radio set to AM news, and a tub of plain oats, and a Mickey Mouse ears alarm clock. That made me happy: knowing an alarm clock, not a girlfriend, woke him up in the morning.

I looked at a handwritten piece of paper beside the typewriter: solution sets to the mathematician's assigned problems. Let other women have beefcake calendars; Professor Blagonravov's brilliant homework assignment for Transcendental Number Theory was the sexiest thing ever in print. In that moment, I could out Peggy Lee for *Fever*.

Sputnik's toolbox sat beside boxes that contained books and records and papers and notebooks and sundry Boy Scout stuff like binoculars and compass and walkie-talkies and ships in bottles and … rocks! Wrinkled up in the junk box was a dirty old baseball uniform.

In another box was a jelly jar with a wad of cash inside and a single red string. Peculiar boy.

Amidst sock mounds, strewn about were empty takeout boxes and "doggy bags," Tofu Temple ("sautéed shishito peppers" written in black marker across the carton's lid), Wok-Tastic ("rice and mapo tofu– w/o meat"), and Karma Kuisine ("Hot!"); apparently, he liked hot foods. I made a note to myself to learn how to cook Japanese, Chinese, and Indian meals. There were also empty cartons from a Russian deli (I was unaware Biskatine had a Russian restaurant) and a delicatessen lunch from The Bud & Spot ("matzo ball soup – V" and I guessed "V" meant vegetarian). I'd also learn how to make Russian and Jewish cuisine.

Looking around, I stepped on an empty bag of movie theater popcorn. That was sad. Did the poor bachelor save popcorn from movie theaters because he had nothing else to eat late at night? I had a vision of the barnstormer eating popcorn one of his evenings in a hayfield, while searching the panorama sky for UFOs.

Another cardboard box contained his socks and underwear and T-shirts, which I did not look at, to avoid invading his privacy.

In another corner stood an old baseball bat topped with Brooklyn Dodgers cap; beside the bat lay a mitt holding a mud-encrusted baseball.

On the back wall was one decoration: a framed print of an ancient sailing vessel with billowy sails traveling through the stars like the nightsky was the sea. That touched me. My Wanderer.

The small closet's door was open and inside were a rolled-up tent, a telescope, coats, and more sundry stuff like lanterns and pilot's logbooks; nothing was in any order. Why weren't his clothes hanging in the closet?

I didn't notice any family photos or scrapbooks. I wondered if he had any mementos of his family?

The sketchbook was open to a drawing of a spaceship, not one from science fiction but a detailed blueprint with equations dashed out beside the sketch. I was so intrigued, I picked up the artist's book and looked through his rocket blueprints, where there were plans of individual sections of the spacecraft. There were also sketches of trees and airplanes and an elderly Lady in a hot air balloon (where had that image come from?). Then I came across a series of drawings of a faceless nude gal in a field, the drawings arranged to be a flipbook—with each flip of the page, the girl walked closer, while slowly dropping her arms and revealing her nudity until she and her bare bosom were right upon the viewer. Sputnik! Did he gaze upon those skimpy images at night in his sleeping bag? I set the sketchbook back in its place, embarrassed for having looked in it and invaded his privacy.

The kitchenette included an oven built into the brick wall, which served as a mini divider between room and kitchen, where there was a yellow wall phone, a sink, a hot plate, a round top refrigerator the color of corn, and a multi-door cabinet the same color which included a pulldown tab to be used as a table.

On the counter beneath the wall phone was a phonebook; I knew it was sheer nosiness, but I could not stop, or *chose* not to stop, my desire to see the phonebook pages he had dog-eared: takeout restaurants (some circled), car dealerships, and hardware stores.

I opened the cabinets, empty except for canisters of food (pellets) for the frog and turtle. I looked in the refrigerator. Inside was one bare hardened slice of cheese. Where had that come from? Had he ordered a meal from a restaurant and saved a slice of the sandwich's cheese? Apparently, the "faithful thermos" was only being used for water because there was no other food in the bachelor's apartment.

I didn't know if I should dare going into the bathroom after seeing the filth in the front room, accumulated in just one week. With Joan of Arc bravery, I went into the bathing room, which could no more be cleaned than the ocean floor, regardless of how much water swept over it. The bathroom was a habitat for many sticky creatures, and I was not going to upset their applecart. As long as the showerhead and sink faucet were clean, that would have to be hygienic enough. For grooming, the mathematician had a bar of soap and shampoo. Sitting on the bare filthy sink counter were

Brylcreem, toothbrush, toothpaste tube, comb, razor, and another bar of soap for handwashing which looked too dirty to perform its function.

Not surprisingly, the professor did not have one utensil for house cleaning. Geniuses were not absentminded but *singleminded.*

I went back to my flat to get cleaning supplies.

From his apartment's window, I took down the towel and spent the sunny morning making his apartment shine, while listening to rock-n-roll on the radio. I liked the picture of the serious professor turning on his radio that night, expecting to hear news but instead hearing Fats Domino. "That girl switched my radio from AM to FM," I could just hear him saying.

Next stop: the thrift store. I searched for "masculine" furniture. I picked out a desk and chair manly enough for Steinbeck. I also purchased a stand for Professor Blagonravov's records (or Sputnik's records), and a handsome bed, a bookshelf, a nightstand for his alarm clock and radio, a chair to be used by his kitchen's pulldown table, and a simple wardrobe, since he obviously preferred the closet to be used for storage.

I loved doing this for him. He was so busy, so stressed. At least now the wanderer would have a comfortable harbor to come home to. If anyone deserved pampering it was a man who had suffered and survived a torture prison. I wanted to soften his life. Round the rough edges. Simply, I wanted to make him happy. Plus, I felt like I was playing a small part in history, taking care of the great Blagonravov. I wanted to be his wife, and I could no more erase that desire than erase my desire to have children. "What your heart thinks is great, is great. The soul's emphasis is always right," so said Ralph Waldo Emerson.

The store said they could have it all delivered by four. I had time to eat lunch: tomato soup, grilled cheese, warm Sprite, slice of pumpkin pie, and a helping of The Four Tops' music from the jukebox at Stormy & Strobe. At a booth by a window, I took a quiz, "Are You Really in Love?", from one of my romance comics.

"Does the sound of his voice thrill you every time you hear it?" Ooh yes! "Do you think of him constantly throughout the day?" Yes! "Could you imagine yourself spending the rest of your life with him?" This was the best grade I had ever received on a quiz!

I walked Mullybiski and fed him lunch before purchasing Sputnik's other necessities. I bought groceries which the bachelor desperately needed. I had run out of his money at the furniture store, but I did not mind spending my money to buy him food and blankets.

Since I had yet to learn how to make Japanese and Indian and Russian dishes, I had to stick to mostly American foods for now, especially of the southern variety, which he seemed to like; but someday, I would be a more versatile chef for him.

Back at his apartment, I replaced the dirty bar of soap in his bathroom and placed a fresh blue bar on a clean soap dish, alongside a fresh toothbrush in new holder.

By the kitchen sink, I placed more soap, which I knew would never get used. In the empty cabinets, I added a few plates, bowls, glasses, silverware, a jar of peanut butter, a can of spicy potato chips, a tin of Biskatine cocoa, and a box of Sugar Smacks cereal (I had a feeling he would "dig 'em"), so the night owl would at least have snacks besides hard oats and stale popcorn, while doing math work at two a.m. I set a bowl of healthy colorful fruit on the "table." I did not get him a coffee maker because I knew he would not use it but would instead get coffee from bakeries and the teachers' lounge. In the barren refrigerator, I added milk, apple juice, jalapeno peppers, and deli-wrapped slices of pepper jack and cheddar cheese, and a head of lettuce, and a few condiments like ketchup, hot mustard, Tabasco sauce, mayonnaise, hot pickle relish and grape jam, so he could at least make sandwiches. I had a hunch he would not make any meal that required the oven, which had not been turned on since his moving in (it was clean as new). There had been no reason to buy eggs, flour, etcetera. But I did set one saucepan on the hot plate for making hot chocolate.

Then I drove to Brooklyn to get him pizza from Hank's, a complete dive the color of an old blue surfboard, about two hours drive time roundtrip. Hopefully, the pizza would not get too soggy on the drive back.

Back at his apartment, I put the cheese and bell pepper pizza in the oven to keep it warm. I directed grouchy movers where to set the furniture (I definitely could not lift it). I didn't know how much privilege I had with his belongings, so I didn't touch his box of underthings or boxes of sundry stuff. But I enjoyed looking at his books, mostly science fiction and flying saucer comic books, since all his science and math books were in his office. For a scientist, he had many books about philosophy, metaphysics, and religion, especially Judaism and Jewish mysticism. And he had many books on baseball and aviation history and biographies about history-makers.

Like his books, I arranged his records alphabetically, so he would have an easy time finding them. His collection showcased a preference for classical, swing, and jazz; a downright snobbery against other musical genres. I noticed a peculiarity—he had nothing to play the records. No Victrola, no record player. He was an odd boy.

I had brought over my iron, so I ironed his clothes, using the desk as an ironing board. I arranged his clothes in the wardrobe, making sections for dressy and casual, arranging suits from light to dark, doing the same with shirts and sweaters and putting blue jeans at the far end. In the space beneath the wardrobe, I placed his shoes. I also put the baseball items under there.

I put his alarm clock and radio on the nightstand and the typewriter atop the writing desk, along with pens and notepads and sketchbook, and I didn't think he would mind if I placed one ship in a bottle atop the desk for decoration.

I loved writing this day of making his apartment a home; I felt completely content, the way a gardener would feel spending an afternoon in the garden or a pianist would feel at the piano.

I laid a fresh comfy pillow on the floor for turtle and frog who had been very friendly with the stranger all afternoon as if we were all old friends.

I hung a new curtain, using a muted yellow color scheme, which matched agreeably the brown brick walls and wood flooring and corn-colored cabinetry. Hopefully, I was not turning his bachelor pad into The Lady Model. I just wanted it to look sunny and woodsy, maybe a small cabin the aviator would have in the tundra.

Now the romantic paragraph: making his bed. Beneath the painting of the sailing vessel was a real captain's bed with a sleigh headboard the color of a ship's deck. Across the captain's mattress, I layered sheets and blankets, so now the sojourner could be warmer at night. I rolled up the sleeping bag, which I sensed had been his boyhood refuge, and lovingly stored it beneath the bed frame.

I was certain within one week his apartment would need to be cared for again because the genius would not tend it, and I would get to do this all again.

At the writing desk, I wrote him two notes. One I placed beside his thermos on the counter: "For making sunset in a cup," along with a recipe for simple hot cocoa. The other note I placed on his pillow: "From the girl who feels bad for contributing to the crick in your neck."

I wondered if he also needed to be guided in how to make a sandwich, because I could not envision the brilliant geometrician doing that either. I decided to be on the safe side, so I pre-made him a few sandwiches: some spicy pimento cheese with jalapenos, some PBJs for the Jeff Stone boyish boy. I placed the sandwiches on a plate in the refrigerator. Maybe, I thought, I should get more creative. I knew of one type of Indian sandwich: a spicy, grilled potato sandwich, made with peppers, coriander, and Szechuan sauce. I'd make that for him too; hopefully, it would be spicy enough.

Whereas Sputnik enjoyed thinking of all the things he could do for rocketry, physics, and mathematics, I enjoyed thinking of all the things I could do for Sputnik: getting him Dodgers tickets, and a batting cage (although where would it go?), and Jackie Robinson's autograph, or even better, one of Robinson's game-used bats.

My caring for the scientist also nurtured science, in the way caring for the gardener also nurtured the garden, because what would become of the garden without its gardener?

I wondered if this desire to be so nurturing was an evolutionary trait of women meant to keep the male from wandering to other "nests", or if this desire to care for him was the result of being in love? Either way, the feeling made me happy in the form that ancient Greek philosophers had described as "eudaimonia," the divine best happiness, the highest good, achieved by living one's highest potential—and I hoped my highest potential was to be his guardian angel.

One last stop, back to the malt shop to get a banana split. Stormy & Strobe made genuine banana splits: vanilla, chocolate, and strawberry ice cream drizzled in hot fudge and pineapple and strawberry sauces, all floating beside sliced bananas, topped with whipped cream, nuts, and cherries. I did not care for ice cream, but since he did, he would love this.

I put the treat in the refrigerator. I wanted to leave the pizza outside his door, "more welcoming than a welcome mat," but unfortunately, I could not write that sentence into his life because this world's story had thieves. So, I set the pizza on the table with a note, "Welcome Home. P.S. Banana split in the icebox." I wanted him to know he was welcome in this country, and he did have at least one friend and supporter.

Exhausted, I got into bed that night before the sun and had warm visions of the aeronaut coming back into town for a good night's rest in his new home sweet home.

But I still could not sleep well, knowing Gershom had suffered atrociously in the past; I wanted to go to the library to find microfiche of every story I could about the concentration camps, yet I also did *not* want to do that.

I got awakened again by the sound of knocking.

"Peppermint, it's me."

I looked at the clock: nine p.m. Why didn't he give me time to prepare for these nighttime meetings? I put on my gloves, bundled in a blanket, and opened the door.

In one hand, he held the pizza carton, in the other, his toolbox. He was trying hard not to smile too much, but smiles were bubbling out either from happiness or amusement with my personality.

"I didn't expect you to do all that with my place," he said. "That was a lot of work."

I shrugged, "manly" girl, and I would not let him know how sore my muscles felt. I opened the door for him to come inside.

"Hi, Mullybiski."

Mullybiski wagged his tail, "Hello," then went back to sleep, a pastime the pug was very good at.

It felt peaceful to shut the door on the world and concentrate solely on this world inside.

"You went to Brooklyn?" Sputnik asked like "You went all the way to Saturn for me?"

I shrugged again, no big deal.

"I'm highly flattered, but Hank's isn't in a safe neighborhood." He set his toolbox on the floor's bricks.

"I survived and felt very New York too, thank you very much."

"You're not quite New York. I'd suggest not going back anytime soon. But I couldn't eat this pizza pie without you."

"That's very thoughtful, sir."

"Ba-bu-ba," he said, looking around, "where can I set it so the roaches can't get it?"

280

"Somewhere on the moon. It's okay, you can set it on my bed … on my desk."

"Alright." By the typewriter, he set the carton. "You weren't asleep, were you?"

"No, not really." Although my messy hair revealed the truth. Did he never sleep?

While he ceremoniously opened the carton and brought forth all the pizza-scented goodness, waving the scent around with his hand, I set out a glass of cold milk for him and warm lemon-lime soda for me.

"I hope the pizza hasn't gotten too soggy," I said.

It had gotten really soggy, the bell peppers shrively.

"It's the thought that counts," he said. "I haven't had pizza from Hank's in years."

"It's not that far away. I could turn on the TV and you could watch a baseball game to make the experience even more authentic."

"Now if there was a game on, do you think I'd be over here?" he ribbed.

Standing in the cold room, we let pizza and closeness warm us.

It was difficult to eat pizza and keep the blanket clasped to me to prevent him from seeing my nightgown.

"Ah, that crispy thin crust," he said like a man in ecstasy.

He was already on his third slice before I had even finished getting to know slice one. Once the boy got going, he could really eat, and I was happy to see him enjoying himself so thoroughly, in spite of his coughing.

"New York pizza!" he enthused. "Let Chicagoans have their deep dish and Detroitites have their thick crust. What do you think?"

"Mm…"

I walked over to Mullybiski to hand him a bite of crust, which he paused his nap to eat, and I took my time walking back to Sputnik and the truth.

"I hate to tell you this, but I prefer thick crust pizza."

"Ah, you're a southern girl. What do you know about pizza?"

"About as much as the Brooklyn boy knows about sorghum."

"I know plenty about molasses."

"For the record, sir, sorghum is different than molasses."

"I knew that."

"Mmm hmmm. Don't make me quiz you, Professor."

"I know it tastes good."

"Okay, an 'A' for that answer. No, I take that back—I don't give 'A's in my class, only 'B's' and 'F's; there is no in between. You must write a paper, using sound logic, about the differences between sorghum and molasses."

He laughed at my imitation of his austerity.

"The first time I saw you, when you parachuted into my story, I thought your hair looked like molasses. I was so fond of molasses, still am…" What was I saying? These were not the proper words of a nun, nor of a girl who had promised to respect his inability to be in a lovestory with her.

He was embarrassed, so was I. We were comfortable with each other but the inability to be as completely comfortable as we wanted to be was what made our relationship awkward—trying to maneuver around his "unavailability for love" barricade.

Our glasses were getting greasy from our pizza lips and fingertips, but we were devouring this tasty moment. I slowly took my time with my pizza slice, so Sputnik could have all the rest of the savory pie; I had to make sure he was unaware he was eating it all or else his chivalry would stop him from eating another bite if he thought the Lady was not getting seconds.

"Why'd you bring your toolbox?"

"Well, I wanted to check on the locks." He put his hand flat on the desk, shook it, confirmed its wobbliness. "That needs fixing too."

"Aren't you sleepy?" I asked.

"No, I'm hyper on banana split. I hope you got one for yourself."

I made a face to express my disgust for ice cream.

"I'm shocked you don't like ice cream. You seem like a girl that would, but now that you've told me you don't like thin crust pizza, I know you're one equation I'll never solve."

"Ice cream is too wintry, winter on the taste buds, just too cold."

"Someday, I'm going to convince you to like ice cream."

I shook my head, "No, you won't."

"The problem is you've never tried Hank's banana split. He puts all this love into it."

As he ate his fifth slice, I asked, "Why was there a single piece of cheese just stuck in the center of your refrigerator?"

"I don't recall ever putting cheese in there."

"It had turned as solid as a book's cover."

"What kind of cheese was it?"

"Are you thinking of switching careers, going to the cheese detective agency?"

He gave another rare laugh. "Just curious."

"It was Swiss cheese."

"Now that is a mystery. I only eat cheddar cheese."

I did not want to imagine how the cheese had changed colors.

"Not pepper jack?" I asked.

"Speaking of pepper jack, are you trying to set me on fire? What was with all the hot food? Out of curiosity, I took one bite of that grilled sandwich, and my tongue is still trying to recover from the hottest Szechuan sauce known to man."

"Ooh, I thought, according to the takeout boxes in your apartment, you like hot food."

"I enjoy trying cuisines of every culture. A man has no business reaching out to life on other planets if he doesn't want to reach out to all life on this planet. But mostly I end up going to restaurants where my colleagues go."

"Even so, all of your choices are still spicy."

"Ah," he said as if even he hadn't noticed that and had no explanation for why, and I was helping him rediscover himself.

"Surely that all cost more than I gave you," he said.

I did not want to lie about the money, but I also did not want to tell him I had spent my own money, because I knew he would give the money back to me. So, I went to the kitchen to get him a milk refill. When I returned, an ugly wad of money greeted me.

"If that's not enough," he said, laying more money on the desk.

"Sir, I will take that money when the moon turns into a grape."

"Turns into a grape, huh?"

I nodded.

He could tell I was serious, so he picked up the money and begrudgingly put it back into his wallet.

"So, you met Pythagoras the Tortoise and Ms. Sophie Frog?" he asked, rolling another pizza slice into a pizza burrito.

"Very charming those two. How did you meet them?"

284

"I met them both recently. Pythagoras was crossing a busy road, so I offered him safety, and Sophie was in a lab. My first day at the university, I saw her, and I couldn't let her be killed. I don't care whose experiment I ruined. I've yet to release them back to their natural habitats because I worry about their safety still."

I thought: If a man's brain does not grow beyond who it was in first grade, that is a tragedy, but if a man's heart never outgrows who it was in first grade, that is a miracle.

"I'm sorry I didn't get a chance to wash and iron your baseball uniform."

"You don't *iron* baseball uniforms."

"You do at least wash them?"

"Well, yeah, but they're not meant to be worn with church gloves and bonnets."

"So, you do play for a team?"

"I played in college."

I entertained a cute picture: Sputnik in his baseball uniform. He didn't offer any more information.

"I didn't get your records and books out of order, did I?" I asked, while picking off a green bell pepper to nibble.

"They weren't in any order. I prefer your alphabetical system." I sensed that was something the genius did not say often: that he preferred someone else's way of doing things.

"I noticed you don't have a record player."

"Ah, I gave it away a few years ago to an elderly woman in my building who didn't have a record player and she was bedridden, so the music kept her company."

"That was really sweet of you."

He shook away my idea he was sweet.

"What's your *favorite* food, Sputnik?"

He thought about it, recovered the truth. "Ice cream," he said with a laugh to play down his liking for the sweet food.

"What kind?"

"All kinds," said like a shrug.

"There's no one special flavor?"

"Perhaps chocolate chip or mint chocolate chip."

"That's ad—" I felt bad for letting out the giddiness but I couldn't stop the word from coming out now: "adorable."

"Will I start finding ice cream tubs in my freezer now?"

"You just might, sir."

"No, I don't need all that ice cream."

"Like Hank, I'll put lots of love in it."

"*Homemade* ice cream?"

"I could try."

"No jalapenos." He grinned.

"That's too bad because I was going to make Szechuan chilli jalapeno tutti frutti."

"That should get rid of this New England chill."

I just loved being around him.

"You play the piano, Sputty?" *Sputty*? He was not my boyfriend; he was my professor.

"Not well." I did not believe that and reasoned he was as genius at piano playing as he was at everything else.

The pizza was down to the last slice, and he raised his eyebrow to ask if I wanted it.

"No, it's for you. I wouldn't have traveled all the way to Brooklyn for thin crust pizza for me. I'd just as well go to Buster and Gramp's."

He pretend-stabbed his heart, letting me know how much the thought of pizza from a suburb wounded him.

"I didn't make your apartment The Lady Model, did I?"

"No, it's topnotch." A mischievous smile forewarned he was about to be naughty with the nun. "The bed was highly comfortable. You picked that out just for me? I took a quick nap when I got back to town, and it thoroughly massaged my neck and back, all of me, just like a wife."

!!! How was I supposed to respond to such suggestiveness?

"I'm glad it relieved the crick."

"I couldn't help notice some boxes you left untouched." One being his box of underwear. "Was there any particular reason for that, Ms. Nun?"

"I don't know, *Professor*, was there?" Now it was my time to tell him he had crossed a line.

We talked about his book collection and a bit about philosophy.

After his fingertip cleared the pizza box of even smudges of melted cheese and he seemed sad it was all gone, as if pizza he would never get again, he said, "The sandwiches were really sweet, and spicy, and the banana split was a cute touch, but I do not deserve all that sweetness."

"I think you do."

"Women." And his tone suggested that in this moment he was not sure if women's personalities were flawed or enhanced from sweetness.

He went to work on the locks, while I cleaned our glasses. Afterwards, he fixed the desk, while I sat in the chair and read something or other; I was really just looking over the book's top to admire how handsome Sputnik looked.

The next pre-dawn, I found an envelope outside my upstairs apartment door. Inside was money and this note: "The moon turned into a grape last night." Darned man!

In the sweet shop that morning, I tried to give the money back, but he would not take it. So, we sat in our booth with coffee and cocoa and resumed our conversation about philosophy, another field he was an expert in *too*. The scientist was "not much religious" (his morals, ethics, and beliefs had been raised only somewhat on Judaism but mostly on his pop's Roy-Rogers-style code of manhood in the Alaskan outback), but he was interested in spirituality, examining it with logic but also with intuition. Since he believed women were more intuitive than men, he wanted to know all my feelings about souls and the afterlife. Everything the scientist said he made sure I knew he did not "believe in" but was just open to learning about. He laughed when he said he was agnostic even about being agnostic.

Before stating my opinions, I said a disclaimer, "Maybe using our brains to comprehend spiritual truths is like using our hands to comprehend taste. We're not using the right tool at all and that's why there are so many errors and inconsistencies in our beliefs. But here is what I believe: your soul is the You before the world added any adjectives. That doesn't mean the soul doesn't have a personality, but it wasn't written by society."

"Who was it written by?"

"You."

"But how?" He was not an average conversation companion; the scientist had to know the "how" behind everything.

"Maybe souls are born, beings of pure light from the great Light, and maybe they learn different personality traits; some they keep, some they toss away, just like children do."

He thought about it. "Like a mineral with unique substances inside that determine how it will reflect light; sweetness causes a personality to be pink the way chromium causes a ruby to be red? But if souls are always changing, doesn't that take away from the idea they're perfect?"

"Not at all. Souls are perfectly loving light but just like you said, light can be reflected in many colors. A flowerbed remains perfectly lovely through all its changes because its scenery contains only flowers, never landmines—souls only plant beautiful traits in their personality landscapes."

"But how is it recognized after its changes?"

"By the signature of the gardener. You can always recognize a Chagall, can't you? Even though all his paintings are different from one another, you attribute each to Chagall because of his unique style."

"So, souls have styles as well?"

"Some of us like petunias, some of us prefer begonias, and we comprise our landscapes with our preferences."

"Where would a soul, a being of pure light as you said, acquire these traits?"

"Maybe some are inborn traits, or maybe souls learn traits from other souls, or maybe souls emulate souls they admire, or maybe there's a cosmic trait depository for souls to sift through to construct their personalities, or maybe planets are personality ores for souls, and a soul gets to pick and choose which traits to keep from its journeys?" I smiled.

"'Personality ores.' I like that." He smiled too. "Yeah, perhaps, some of us are so strange because we picked up some strange personality flowers during our lives on strange planets." He laughed.

Sputnik was very yet cautiously interested in reincarnation, an idea the Christian-raised girl had not given much serious thought to, although I realized then I had always believed in reincarnation: energy coming back in different forms, light from a projector capable of projecting infinite types of movies, the same ink writing different stories and characters. Plus, reincarnation offered an explanation of where souls acquired traits, traits from endless stories of endless settings and eras and characters. I had even written about reincarnation in *A Knight in 1962*—the Knight returning to life to be with the Lady he loved.

The mathematician and I discussed whether eternity could have a starting point, whether a soul could be created, born, and then continue forever. He was not sure, but I said, "Eternity could have a starting point, the way an infinite story, one without The End, has a beginning."

"In geometry, that concept is known as a 'ray.' But if a soul does not have a starting sentence written by God, if instead it has always been, what room does that leave God in 'creation'?" he asked.

I reminded him that trying to understand God with our brains could be like trying to see with our toes. The physicist accepted that, noting how certain concepts in quantum physics were illogical to our everyday senses yet seemed to work.

He asked, "How do we account for the population increase, though? Where were all the souls in the past?"

"Maybe they were on the bench, sitting that one out."

He smiled about the baseball reference.

"Or maybe," I said, "they weren't on Earth but on another planet, or maybe they were trees or amoebas at that time, or maybe like we discussed, souls are created, and new ones are being created all the time."

We began talking about destiny, another subject he was exceptionally curious about.

We wondered aloud if destiny meant the story was already written, which seemed rather oppressive, not having any say in our actions or feelings (and bearing no responsibility for them either), just living out the plot written by an unseen hand, a hand which could be divine, or just a random stroke of matter and energy, unable to be stopped now that the entire universe's fate was set in motion—the Big Bang had even determined that Joe Smith would eat a cheese sandwich on Tuesday, September 9th, 1962 in Kansas. That seemed ridiculous, but the idea God would set about making Joe Smith eat a cheese sandwich seemed equally, if not even more, ridiculous. Maybe there was no destiny at all, just blank pages, an idea which wiped magic from life. Or maybe destiny had nothing to do with what was already written but what the writer set out to write before the story began, an idea which saved freedom yet preserved fate and "magic."

"The writer?" Sputnik asked. "Are you referring to God or an individual's soul?"

"I was referring to the soul, but if you want to look at it less spiritually, the writer could be determination. Either way, this view of destiny puts destiny in the pen of the individual—you create your own destiny by setting out with a plan for how to write your life then writing it that way."

"Or," he offered, and I was surprised by what the scientist said next, "life is a collection of blank pages for writing choices, but perhaps like you said, a writer knows the story she wants to write, so certain pages are prewritten, not in high detail, but there are predestined landmarks in lifestories like important meetings, particularly in a lovestory."

"I love that idea. And our characters are free to respond however they wish to these lifestory landmarks. Whatever the truth about destiny, I'm certain of one thing: life does not come with a back cover, as my momma once said. We do not know how our lifestories are going to play out, even if we came to Earth with a clear plan from our soul. We might have inklings, hunches, dreams, goals, and angels to guide us, but we don't know with certainty how it will all turn out, so there must be an element of choice in our stories, not everything pre-written."

"I'm not sure the uncertainty of life's outcome absolutely confirms freewill, because we could just be ignorant of that prewritten outcome. What about the idea that every single imaginable story, character, plot, planet, and outcome has already been written, and when our consciousness makes a decision, we go over into the story that is a result of that decision—a theory which preserves fate and freewill. Doesn't it?" He pondered. "But it doesn't answer the question: who wrote all those stories?"

"Maybe we all did. Anyway, this is getting heavy. I need more cocoa. Are you sure you don't want breakfast?"

"I'm fine."

I brought us hot drink refills and a chocolate croissant for me. The sun remained under the blanket of nighttime, as the physicist told me about the Many Worlds Interpretation, alternate universes "splitting off" at the point of every decision like a story where the outcome of every possible choice was written. That idea was proposed a decade earlier by Hugh Everett, who pointed out that since no observer would ever be aware of the existence of the other worlds, to claim that they cannot be there because we cannot see them was no more valid than claiming that the Earth cannot be orbiting around the Sun because we cannot feel the movement.

"Maybe the outcome of every choice is already written in pencil, like glimpses of what could be, but once we choose, that choice's outcome is written in ink?" I pondered.

"All the outcomes are only possibilities until given conscious consent to be permanent?"

It was fun to ponder, especially with a ponder partner.

I told Sputnik about the "near-death" experience, and he listened, fascinated, and did not condescend my faith.

"I had a sense," I professed, "I had a destined meeting on Earth." My eyes told him, "With you."

Before he could be overwhelmed, customers and making money interrupted our destiny and our ponderings of the meaning of life.

While I waited on customers, Sputnik spent the time "talking" to his notepad by way of pen, doing work, always busy. Before he left, he said he wanted me to give him the keys to my apartment after class, so he could come by to fix the kitchenette shutters.

"Ooh, you want me to trust you? As you said, you could be a madman, and you would have complete access to my apartment."

"You're right, you shouldn't trust me or anyone."

"I was only kidding." He needed laughter in his life the way a rice cake needed honey.

Before Sputnik could leave his booth, into the story barged, "Well, if it isn't the baby star of the math department, Ravov, just waiting to supernova here in our small town." A man in an obnoxious suit elbowed his way to Sputnik's booth. "When is that handsome mug of yours set to debut on national TV? Next week?"

The man completely ignored me, except to say, "Coffee, now."

"What important work is the pure mathematician doing this morning, something about the neato-ness of polygons?" the man snickered, inviting himself to the seat across from Professor Blagonravov.

"We can't all be business economists, Professor Ditwad, spending our lives making sure companies spend their cents wisely on either sock puppets or toilet rolls—ah, the choices."

The two men did not like each other, and the ribbing was not playful.

I brought the insufferable man a cup of coffee, and when I was still within hearing range, Professor Ditwad shot, "I thought Darioles was known for *pretty* waitresses, but a set of perkies even on an ugly chick perks up my morning."

I heard what sounded like a boulder smashing a wall. I did not have to turn around to know what had happened: Sputnik's fist had been the boulder and the man's face the demolition site. I was scared to look, for fear I would find the man's head on the floor. With head still intact, Professor Ditwad sat stunned in the booth, his nose bleeding across the bridge. Sputnik was standing and not finished with the demolition, his fists still clenched.

Finally realizing he had just been punched, the creep shouted a slur about Sputnik's Jewishness and, "You're a loose cannon, Ravov!" He grabbed his hurt nose.

Sputnik yanked Ditwad out from the booth and pushed him back toward the display case; Ditwad was disoriented and flailing his arms like someone trying to stay afloat, while Sputnik made him walk stumbling backwards. Sputnik shouted, "I'm going to kill you, you son of a bastard."

Customers were titillated watching the violent scene, as long as its violence did not reach them; one man turned around in his seat to get a better view of the spectacle, while enjoying his cup of coffee.

Sputnik hit Ditwad in the jaw and stomach, all the while shouting expletives, "Nazi as---," shooting Ditwad with threats of how he was going to break his *&*^# ribs. I knew why Sputnik had been fired by NASA.

I grabbed him around the arms to try to get him to stop. "Please, Sputnik, don't!"

"Yeah, *Sputnik*," Ditwad still teased, "listen to your little piece of tail."

In my arms, I felt Sputnik's biceps swell with force to hit the man again.

"Is that what you call your communist Russian pig in bed, baby—Sputnik?" That had not been a wise thing to say, especially since he had directed it at me. Sputnik kneed Ditwad in the groin and like an unsteady sack of potatoes hit by a strong wind, the man doubled over.

Sputnik growled, "Is your morning perky enough now or do you need it to be perkier?"

Gagged by pain, Ditwad barely got out, "I don't think Goldell needs a professor like you on its roster."

"I don't think Goldell needs a professor so obsessed with the female student body."

"Watch who you're talking to, *Assistant* Professor." Then, plop, Ditwad fell to the ground.

"Figure out this probability, Professor Nitwit—if you come around this Lady again, what are the chances I'll break your nose?" He did not actually say "nose."

Since Sputnik was done hitting the man, I let go of his arms. But whatever violent chemicals flooded a man's bloodstream when he was angry were still raging in him. He grabbed his briefcase and my hand and led me outside.

"Sputnik, I'll get fired," I said as we walked too swiftly for my high heels to keep up, so Sputnik slowed our walk.

"You can go back when he's gone," he said, once we were standing at the bottom of the back-alley stairway. "You're not going to serve that as—" He stopped himself from saying an expletive in front of

295

a Lady now that his rage had mostly quieted. "You're not going to serve that *jerk* coffee after he made an obscene reference to your figure, the way he always does about students behind closed doors. He sees them all as barmaids from topless bars, where he likes to schedule all his business meetings. He had a knee in the groin coming to him from karma."

Sputnik did not mention what else the man had said (that I was ugly), and to avoid hurting my feelings, Sputnik had only referenced that Ditwad had said something indecent.

"Sputnik, what if he tells the university you took your student's hand and walked out of the patisserie with me?"

"Do you think taking a student's hand is the worst that Ditwad has done?"

"I don't want you to get fired over me."

"That's not the kind of response I expected from the girl whose honor I just defended."

"But it's the kind of response you should expect from a friend who cares about you."

"I thought you liked Knights in shining armor."

"I do but a Knight has to see the difference between a noble battle and a futile battle."

"I'm going to break his nose." Sputnik started to storm off; his anger not assuaged.

"Sputnik, please, don't. Breaking his nose will not change his views on women. It will only get fired from the university a professor who treats women with respect." With both my hands, I grabbed his arm; he was much stronger than me, and I could not hold him back from fighting the man, yet he let me prevent him from leaving.

"Why do you care what happens to him?" Sputnik snapped.

"I don't care what happens to him. I care about what happens to you. You'll lose your job."

"There are more important things to me than Goldell University."

"I know but you're important to your students, and your research is important. I want you to make the world's largest snowflake."

Hearing me say that, he became softer. "I will make that. I promise."

"I'm not going to let that goblin goad you into writing a sentence that will ruin your lifestory."

Suddenly, Sputnik looked boyishly vulnerable and stooped, in need of the Lady telling him he had done something honorable. I ran my fingers through his molasses hair, and this calmed the surging of violent chemicals in his bloodstream. Then I hugged him, which I had wanted to do since the first time I saw the aeronaut land alone in the wheatfield. He did not know how to respond at first—how long had it been since he had met a hug? It had been a long time for me.

"I love you," I said into his lapel, and I wanted him to know it was a love as pure and strong and right as the love I had for Moon-Moon.

"I suspected as much when I saw you outside my engineering class, just to listen to me talk about thermodynamics, then you drove to Brooklyn just to get me a pizza. Ah and that bit about your heart being as loyal to me as Joan of Arc to France."

"You're making fun of me?"

He answered by returning the embrace, gently. He was wearing a knit vest beneath his suit jacket, and it felt so soft and good and warm, and his chest felt so firm, and his arms so durable; I felt protected, finally, in a life where I had been forced to fight daily battles alone—I did not want him to ever let me go.

"What about your goal to be a nun?"

Being this close to him, I felt the *how* he could disqualify me from joining the convent, but since any girl held so closely could have stimulated that response in him (which I knew was possible just from knowledge from basic biology class), I didn't feel especially special for making it happen. Enlarging his love was more important to me.

"I'd rather be your girl than a nun, even if I have to wait four years for the honor, Professor. Since I have such strong feelings for a man, I would not be fit for the convent."

"I don't think that's true. I'm certain there are sisters who've had romantic feelings for men in their pasts."

But I could not let him go.

"Lumi, it's not right for it to be this way, I told you."

"I know, Professor, and I'm sorry for not being stronger about this—how you must be disappointed in Joan of Arc's lack of resolve. I promised myself I would do nothing to knock you off your headed-to-the-heavens trajectory, but I could quit school now, and I'd make our relationship pretty for you. I'd never get sloppy with it—I'd make sure our relationship's ribbons and bows were neatly tied, offering a gift for you to open each day. I'd write a poem for you every day, if you wanted. But ooh, the ribbons and bows wouldn't tie you down; the barnstormer could fly anywhere he wanted, anytime he wanted."

Holding my young soft feelings, he said, "I'm going to kill Ditwad."

"He doesn't matter. I will not allow him to become a major character in our story. Look at us, Sputnik, in this stinky crumbly back alley full of trash cans, embracing and creating a beautiful scene even out of this backdrop. We've only known each other a few days but it doesn't feel that way, does it? Our love feels ancient like our love was at the start of the universe or before 'in the beginning.'"

"You could never be responsible for knocking me off a heavenly trajectory; in fact, the only way I could ever get to the heavens is through you, but I don't deserve to be there. And you quitting school would not change anything between us." He broke the embrace. "I don't merit your loyalty or your sweetness, but God forgive me, I like it."

"I don't understand."

He tucked one loose curl of my hair behind my ear as if the blonde lock had lost its way. "An angel doesn't belong with a man."

Unlike everyone else, he had not written one sentence in my life that made me feel ugly or monstrous, yet he thought *he* didn't deserve my loyalty and sweetness?

"Now be a good girl and go upstairs and play the harp and get away from this terrible world for a while."

I became terse since I had given him so much vulnerable information about my tenderest feelings, which he had turned down. "I have to go back to work. I have an order to take today."

"Where to?"

I hated to tell him this, "To a fraternity."

"I certainly will not allow you to do that."

"You're not my father. You can't tell me what to do."

"But I'm your Captain. You already told me so. And when the ship's in danger, I steer. Now go upstairs and I'll take care of everything. I'll tell your employer you're not feeling well, and you're not, you're distraught. I'll even deliver the order."

"If the professor wants to don an apron and go work in the pastry shop, go ahead." I did not relish the prospect of delivering pastries to a fraternity, so I didn't protest Sputnik taking on the task.

Before I walked upstairs, I gave him another hug, unable to be terse with my lonesome friend.

299

"Lumi, my goodness, I'm trying to be stern, so why are you hugging me when I'm a jerk?"

"Because I don't believe the tiger façade." I looked at his eyes. "At the windows, I see the soft bunny of a boy."

He rolled his gray eyes and mumbled something about girls being impossible.

During Algebra, while Professor Blagonravov discussed "rational expressions," I got to daydreaming, of course, since he and I could be together in a daydream. Sputnik was a Knight come to my village and he was immediately drawn to the peasant girl who nursed his wounds in her hut—

"Excellent, Ms. Collins!"

His congratulating Ms. Collins on her answer took me out of my fantasy. I was going to have to get serious about mathematics if I wanted to be a good friend to him.

After Algebra and PoliSci and a discussion about Vietnam with Professor Carmichael, I went to the library. Ooh, libraries in the morning were as peaceful as forests. Since Adelia students had access to Goldell's library, I walked the leafy campus to the Sistine-Chapel-majestic Carl Edward Library, where I roamed for knowledge in books gleaming with light from stained glass windows.

First, I checked out Sputnik's three books, *Flight Theory*, *Fundamentals of Aerospace Engineering*, and *Wing Sections* (with airfoil data). Ooh my, that made no sense. And his books were about as heavy as airplanes! I also checked out *Basic Geometry*.

At an isolated table, I sat in divinely multi-colored light offered by stained glass. Even though I could not be his girl (not yet anyway, although I held onto hope we would surmount obstacles to our love in the future), I wanted to feel closer to him, and since math was close to his heart, learning about math was learning about him. "A point is a position in space." The writer sensed something symbolic there, but I could not make out exactly what. Reading the book was like kissing him, bonding with him, and the deeper I got into the subject, the deeper the kiss felt, taking me closer and closer to him.

I delighted in the realization there were endless ways for he and I to feel close to one another that did not involve us physically being together, for closeness was not an achievement only of bodies. These mathematical concepts brought him close to me since these concepts were intellectually a part of him and now they were inside me too.

Maybe I could join the convent and keep him tucked in my heart, but would that be right, or would that be breaking my vows of celibacy, since my heart would not be celibate—it would be married to him?

In the quiet majestic library, I breathlessly opened his majestic book, *Flight Theory*, a maroon-colored hardback without a jacket, just embossments of the title, the author's name, and a small biplane. I was excited to read his writing, but I couldn't even comprehend the chapter titles: "Phugoid Theory," "The Metacentric Parabola." Okay, I'd try the book about wings; I knew what a wing was—well, I quickly learned I had no clue about wings. "Nondimensional coefficients," "geometrically similar wings," and "lift-curve slopes," and so many graphs and charts, my intimidated intellect flew away after the first page. I had fared better with basic geometry. Then came the most daunting of all his books—*Fundamentals of Aerospace Engineering*, a hardcover phonebook thick. There was no reason to even open it because it would just be more inscrutable equations. Didn't he write anything for the mathematically challenged?

Barely able to carry my satchel weighted with heavy books, I went to his office, since he had told me to come by at noon to pick up my keys. A radio announced that Willie Mays was approaching his 500th homerun, while Professor Blagonravov was approaching his 500th toss of wadded up paper into the overflowing trashcan.

"Why are you aiming for the trashcan?" I asked. "It's full."

He laughed. "I'm aiming for the general area."

I looked around the room, as messy as his apartment. The genius could not decorate even if someone demanded, "Decorate or die." Stacks of mail and science journals were as tall as walls across his metal desk; the papers were not neatly sandwiched together, but some papers stuck out, some were this way and thatta way. His bookshelf had a similar disarray: books crammed, books leaning, books lying atop those books, papers packed into books, books crammed on the windowsill and crinkling the blinds. A paddle ball racquet sat atop the books next to cola in a can that looked like a little tomato juice can. How could he find anything? And how did all that mess accumulate in just a few days? Had he brought it all with him during his move? Did he get that much daily mail? A small black & white television with a screen the size of a side view mirror sat on the bookshelf. A razor looked like a miniature jet landed on his desk beside a rotary phone, Rolodex, and the radio about to tumble. A stained Dodgers coffee cup sat by a round rock that looked like a dinosaur egg; the cup was down to nitty gritty instant coffee granules. Jars of instant coffee, along with cola cans, were stacked everywhere too. Beneath the desk were crammed a gym bag and partially deflated basketball. On his bookshelf was one decoration: another sailing ship in a bottle. No frames of anyone decorated his walls or desk, but there were paintings of planets, a blueprint of a rocket, an old-fashioned sepia sketch of a hot air balloon, and an actual letter from Albert Einstein, commending the young genius on an idea about electromagnetism, the extraordinary letter not framed but just tacked to the wall. A bag of socks slouched on the couch as beady as the curtain; a few ties were draped over the couch's back. I reasoned he worked so often, he got a few hours sleep on the couch, and in the morning, he splashed his face with water from the school's restroom, shaved, splashed his sleepiness with coffee or cola, then put on fresh tie and socks and jetted off to another global conference. No wonder his clothes looked wrinkled. Caffeine was obviously responsible for keeping him so fresh-faced at five a.m.

"Here you go," he said, handing me the keys.

"Thanks!"

He noted me wearing his jacket.

"Do you play paddle ball?" I asked, nodding toward the racquet on his bookshelf.

"That's what I use to punish disobedient girls who stay out after curfew."

"Ooh, funny."

He didn't smile.

"You are just kidding, aren't you?"

"Stay out after six tonight and find out."

I was mortified then he started laughing.

"Yes, I'm only kidding, Lumi." He really thought my mortified expression was funny. "I play paddle ball, honestly. Ask Ben. We play at the Y. What do you think I am, a sadist? I'd never hit you. You could hit me and I wouldn't hit back. You could beat the daylights outta me and I wouldn't hit back. Unless the little nun wants to play around with the paddle."

"Why, I never! You must be wishing to test out your theory of letting me hit the daylights outta you!" I held up my fist.

"Ah, come on, you know I'm joking." He seemed more confident, or more at liberty, to say saucy things, and I wondered if his naughtiness had been born during our earlier embrace or given leeway to come out.

He was never going to steer the conversation away from this subject which obviously amused him, so I said, "Is that a rock or an egg?" I pointed at the oblong sphere on his desk.

"Ah, that needs to be shown, not told. Someday." He was very busy yet still had time to listen to baseball news.

"If you have a minute, Professor, I'd like to talk to you about something."

"Sure, I want to talk to you as well." He turned down the radio.

I sat at the chair in front of his desk and felt relieved to set the heavy satchel on the floor. I took out his three books and was going to lay them on his desk, but it was too cluttered, so I set them in my lap.

"Sput—Professor, I'm sorry about this morning."

"I already told you, it wasn't too tough." He had watched the cash register, taken a few orders and been just about the brusquest cashier in history, and told the manager I was not feeling well. I was surprised I had not gotten fired. He had not had to make the delivery to the fraternity, a lucky fate for all the fraternity brothers who would have probably suffered broken noses.

"But I'm sorry about how I acted, Professor, what I said. I do love you, but as your friend, if that's the form you prefer my love to take, and your friendship is the great treasure of my life. As your friend, I really want to be a good one and understand the things you know, and I tried," I said, holding up one of his books, "but I could not get past the first pages."

Suppressing a laugh, he asked to see the book. I handed him the book about wings.

"I didn't think anyone had a copy." He flipped through a few pages. "You're telling me you don't know how to plot lift coefficient as a function of angle of attack?"

"I don't know—I don't even know what you just said."

"Then you just up and leave because I can't be friends with someone who doesn't understand lift coefficient, or else you'll get the paddle." He couldn't hold the laugh back any longer.

"This isn't funny. I'm really trying to learn."

"Ms. ---, this is a book for engineers, not poetic nuns. Come on. Do you think it bothers me that you don't understand wing sections?"

"Maybe…"

"I prefer that you know about wings from an angel's perspective." He walked over to me. "I have colleagues to talk about these kinds of subjects with."

Colleagues? Of the womanly kind?

"Now, put all those engineering books away and don't give them another thought. Here," he said and took the heavy books from my lap.

"I got them at the school's library."

"No one would actually pay money for them. I'll return them for you since you don't even need to carry them." Setting the heavy books on the couch made the bag of socks fall over.

"You think the little blonde girl *can't* learn engineering, don't you?"

"Why waste time trying? You don't want to be an engineer."

One of my romance comics had gotten mixed in with the engineering books and was peeking out from between two of them.

"Ah, what do we have here?" Sputnik asked, picking up *Boy Meets Girl*. "This is what you should be reading."

He flipped through the pages. "An advice column: 'How to get your man and hold him.'"

"I only read the stories, not the advice."

"Sure. Let's see, 'Be a magician! Bewitch your man with sleight of hand changes in your personality. Be a little roughneck at a picnic but hours later transform into a glamorous doll for the ballroom.' Let's go on a picnic, Lumi—I want to see you be a little roughneck." He continued reading, "'Be a woman!' That's good advice. That one I like."

"Don't you have work to do, Professor?"

"Yes, but this is more fun." He sat on the couch.

I wasn't really irritated; I was flattered. Was he not reading the romance comic for the same reason I had read basic geometry: to feel closer to me?

He flipped to a new page. "Ah, here's a quiz, 'Are you ready for marriage?' Are you, Lumi?"

"I don't pay much attention to those quizzes."

"You know you do, so what score did you get?"

"Okay, I got a perfect if you must know."

"That doesn't surprise me. Now here's an interesting question, 'The job your husband has is Greek to you, and when he starts to talk about what happened during his day, you A) listen sympathetically and ask intelligent questions, B) go to the kitchen and nag—is that what you'd do, Lumi?—or C) play dumb and ask dumb questions?' Hoping C is not the correct answer."

"Of course, it's not. It's A."

"Now I know why you were reading my engineering books."

"I wasn't reading your books because a quiz told me to do so, but because I'm your friend and want to know you."

"And what have we here?" he asked, laughing again. "A drawing of a naked woman!"

I had been shocked by the drawing of the woman nude from waist up, an ad for lingerie, but Sputnik did not seem embarrassed or shocked at all—how many women had he seen without their clothing on?

"And look at this," Sputnik laughed, "the naked gal's photo is right beside an ad for 'How to be a He-man.'"

"I never looked at that!"

"He's wearing his underpants."

"Those are not underpants—they're swim trunks—and it's just an ad for some kind of workout regimen."

"I thought you didn't look at that? Tsk, tsk, the filth you young girls are reading."

He handed the comic back to me and went back to his desk.

"I'm just curious," I said and tried to keep my voice in friend tone and not in interested-in-being-your-girl tone, "if you were to ever get married, you wouldn't want your wife to know all you know about mathematics and physics and engineering?"

"Why would I want that?"

"So, you and her could talk about what you most love, and she could be your helpmate."

"I have Ben to help with airplane construction, that sort of thing. With my wife, I'd be interested in other activities."

I could have fainted from the suggestion, especially considering what I had felt earlier in his embrace.

"I'd want her to teach me how to make a sweet potato pie." He grinned. "Besides my wife would learn plenty about math and physics and engineering just by being around me long enough, and

I'm certain she'd get sick of me and my tech talk after a while and she'd become the woman who'd 'go into the kitchen and nag.'"

"No, I doubt that."

"Ah, you could sit and talk to me for hours about airfoil data?"

"I could listen. I wouldn't be able to offer much return talk. That's why I should study your books, to be a good friend, I mean." I looked at the stacked books written by him. "It amazes me all that's in your head—a thousand pages worth of aerospace engineering knowledge. How is it possible?"

"*War and Peace* is over 1200 pages."

"Yes, but we writers just make stories up. You have all those equations stuffed in your head!"

"I've been at it a long time. I'm almost twice your age, and most of my life has been dedicated to math and engineering. Now, I noticed your apartment's flooring needs work, but I didn't have time this morning to fix it, so I'll come by...let me see...ba-bu-ba..." He mentally went over his busy schedule.

"You need a secretary to help you keep up with everything."

"I won't employ a woman for money, you know that."

"Let me remind the professor, some women need money to live on. The ivy league won't spring for a secretary?"

"A personal secretary for the *assistant* professor? Any messages for me go to the math department's secretary."

"Maybe you could ask a girl you already know to help you out."

He knew what I meant. "Lumi, you're a student and that's what you should be for now."

"You said I need a safer job."

"Being my secretary is not it. You're a writer, not a typist."

"Are you saying there's something wrong with being a secretary?"

"No, I'm saying it's wrong *for you*, just like being a chef is a great profession for some, but wrong for me. I'm a scientist. You're a writer and photographer, so I'm told. Now, Friday after our math class, give me your keys, and while you're in political science, I'll go by your place, make some plans for the floor, and I'm going to get a phone installed for you. It's not safe to be without a phone. I'm sure I could have the job done in an hour. Then you can come by my office again to pick up the keys."

"You're not a chef, but you're a handyman *too?*"

"I'm also a parttime architect and carpenter, hobbies of mine."

"Your hobbies are other people's professions. Ooh, you're an interesting character, Sputnik, an academic with Boy Scout kind of knowledge: how to tie ship knots, how to build a raft, how to find your way using the North Star, those kinds of things."

"How do you know I know those kinds of things?"

"I have an inner sense. Plus, the toolbox, Alaskan outback clues, not to mention all the books on those kinds of subjects and your days spent building an entire airplane!"

"And I have an inner sense that you're a girl who knows what flowers symbolize and what star signs are compatible."

"Your inner sense is off, Mr. Scientist. I care not a fig for astrology. There is nothing Aries about me, although you are rather Scorpio-like: intense and logical."

"Well, alright, my Scorpio logic tells me you don't enjoy feeling like you're going to fall through flimsy flooring."

"No but—"

"Alright then. Besides, I enjoy doing tasks for Ladies that most women don't enjoy doing, such as woodwork and flooring, *Boy Scout kinds of tasks*."

Ladies? Plural?

"Don't you need sleep?" I asked.

"I took a cat nap in the car. Not while I was driving. While I was parked outside the patisserie."

"When?"

"This morning."

"You were parked outside Darioles all night after last night's pizza?"

"I'm not certain about the strength of those locks or that door."

"Sputnik, you can't sit outside in your car every night. You have to rest."

"I get plenty of rest."

"I thought that's why you wanted me to get you a bed."

"I'm fine," he said in a way that the conversation was over. The professor knew how to turn his tone into a period. Final.

I noticed a key ring with two mini keys on it, lying atop the scientific journal *Physics of Fluids*.

"What do those keys go to?" I asked, to prolong my time in his office.

"To the top drawer."

"Ooh, what's in there?"

"Top secret."

"I trusted you enough to give you the keys to my apartment, so you could at least let me see what's in the drawer."

He opened the drawer and took out a file folder. "Filled with tests and other things students aren't privy to."

"Why are there *two* keys?"

"I suppose so an absent-minded professor won't lose them both."

"Can I have one?"

"Why?" He shut the drawer.

"Just trust me. I won't look at the tests."

"What?" he snapped at the radio. "Hendley will not outpitch Koufax," he argued with the speaker. He turned his attention back to me, handing me the desk key. "That key won't do you any good without a key to my office door."

I smiled playfully; his look said, "What are you up to?"

His telephone rang and I waved him "Good day."

Before he answered the phone, he asked, "What are you doing tonight?"

"Studying. Safe and sound with new locks on the door."

"Good, because I have a business dinner and won't be able to come by and check on things. Don't make me get out the paddle."

I went to the vending machine on the second floor and got numerous candy bars. Back on the third floor, I hid around the hall corner and watched his office door.

He finally came out and chitchatted with the janitor, a tiny elderly white Lady with snowy hair and a hunchback, so hunched, her face almost faced the floor, leaving her unable to see much of anything except what was going on at the bottom of the world. She wore a novelty sweater of a deer, stiffly ironed pants, and thickly padded shoes like the shoes worn by nurses. A mop in rolling bucket, filled with dirty water, stood tall beside her. I had an intuitive picture of her apartment (or maybe it was an image born from a writer's desire to create characters): Nat King Cole's voice, singing *All By Myself*, drifting out of a Victrola's mahogany-wood horn, the Victrola the only thing with pizazz in the room or her moments, the apartment small like the rest of her life—not much room needed for so little activity and only one person.

"Do you want to sit down for a bit, Gladys?" Professor Blagonravov asked, opening his door for her. "That couch is actually more comfortable than it looks, particularly when I toss that bag of socks off."

"You're a kind one," she said with a small shy voice, afraid of drawing too much attention to her unwanted presence on Earth; I knew because I related. "But I think a wee rest would just make me more tired, Professor." From her tone, I thought she was sweet on him like he was her grandson.

"Gersh, not Professor."

"Thanky, but I'll finish this floor, and if you want, I'll give that ship in a bottle another polish."

"Ah, no, don't worry about that. Here, let me see that," he said, gently taking hold of the mop's handle. "Goldell can't afford a better mop?"

"It's okie dokie."

"No, it's not. It's about to fall apart. I'll make sure you get a new one."

What did he do—go around the world, seeking nice tasks to do for women?

"I don't want to start something," the janitor said, scared of losing her job.

"You're not starting anything. I am. Trust me, you won't get in trouble."

"I should get a move on before I do get in trouble."

He sighed and I knew he was sighing because the frail older woman was having to work for money. "Would you like a new job as my secretary? It pays well, doesn't require much standing, can be done, at least partly, from home."

"Me? I...I don't know anything about science or math."

"Then you're a step above my students who don't know anything about anything," he said to make her smile. "You don't have to know about science or math."

"I'd like to, Professor, but I'd be too scared I'd mess something up. You should find one of these pretty young women for that job, someone educated, comfortable in an office." Of course, being a janitor was one of the most admirable jobs, keeping the world clean, but I could tell it was not the job she wanted. She could not believe she was worthy of being an important character in the world's story; she'd keep penning herself as submissive servant. I wondered when she was a young girl what character had she dreamed of playing, what lifestory had she dreamed of writing?

"Alright but if you change your mind, the job's yours. Now, who do you have between the Cubs and Dodgers?"

"The Dodgers."

"*That* is the right answer. If you want a rest, a wee one or long one, my door's open, for you, always." Not a smidge of condescension in his voice; he genuinely liked her company. If he had been talking with Ms. Collins, the smart young thing from class, I would have been jealous, but I was not jealous of his affection for the janitor, and I wondered why.

When he left to the restroom, and the janitor went about her work, I made sure no one was watching and snuck inside his office. I opened the drawer and filled it with candy and the money he had given me and a note: "To thank you for your valor."

I enjoyed writing these fun flirty sentences into my lifestory and his—the more nice sentences written into the world's story, the less room for sentences about war and hate.

On his desk, I glimpsed a "preliminary" test he had given to upper-level physics students. The most intimidating sheet of paper I had ever observed—I did not know a single answer. I didn't even understand the questions. The average grade was 25! His students were some of the smartest in the world, yet they could not pass his tests. He was a tough teacher, not mean, but it took much effort to impress him, especially from his upper-level students.

That afternoon, I admired his handywork in my apartment: the shutters were perfect. He had not only fixed them but given them a fresh dress of paint.

I made hot sweet tea and tea sandwiches (cucumber), the mini kind Moon-Moon had made for tea parties.

The rest of the afternoon I spent studying before napping, snuggled with Mullybiski in our cold apartment.

That chilly night, Sputnik and I encountered each other at the corner of Saunders and Vixen, maybe another meeting arranged by angels, just to be nice. With a hot chocolate and big warm chocolate chip cookie from Stormy & Strobe, I was window shopping at Debby's, a store that sold decorative items like holidays ornaments, potpourri, and resin pumpkins for autumn décor, when I heard:

"Ms. ---," he said on the busy sidewalk, where strangers' faces were cold and red and unwelcoming.

"Professor Blagonravov!" I was happy to encounter him in such a synchronistic way.

"What brings you out so late?"

"It's not that late. I was enjoying the stars and night. Thank you for the new shutters." I held up the chocolate chip dessert. "Would you like some cookie?"

"No, thanks. I thought you were going to stay inside and study?"

"I was but then I needed a stroll, to stretch out my writer's desk legs."

"Ah, like an astronaut regaining his land legs."

"Yup. What brings you out?" I asked my fellow recluse.

"I just got back into town from an afternoon conference and had dinner with colleagues."

"Ooh, what did you have?"

He seemed amused by my caring to know what he had for dinner. "Some kind of bean curd dish called The Dragon." He made a face to say he regretted having consumed such a meal. "Wish you hadn't asked now?"

"Are you not feeling well?"

"I'm fine. I may start breathing out fire but other than that..." He looked tired and I very much wanted to give him a shoulder massage. "I was headed to my car when I saw the little Peppermint, who was supposed to be safe and sound in her room. Why are you not wearing your jacket?" He seemed offended that I was wearing a coat and not his jacket.

"It's just so cold out tonight."

He wore a sand-colored topcoat over dressy casual sweater with a button-down underneath and no tie. He took off the coat and placed it around me.

"It'll be the coldest day in hell yet before I let any of this town's Lotharios get within viewing distance of your demurely tied hair ribbon. When I'm not around, this coat will tell them to back off."

Now I was bundled with a coat over a coat. "Sputnik, I can't take all of your coats. You'll freeze to death."

"I have a good old faithful bomber jacket. That's all I need."

He peered into the window where I gazed.

"I collect them," I said about the music boxes, while I ate the last melted chocolate chip bite of the cookie.

"I know. I saw them on your headboard. When I was at your apartment." He was somewhat embarrassed. "You should be getting home. It is a school night. And you have tyrant Blagonravov's quiz on Friday."

"I studied. And I'm rewarding myself."

"You should be inside with your stocky little dog and poetry books and new music box. Which one do you want?"

"Ooh, I'm on a budget. I can't afford one right now."

"I'm buying—with the money you keep returning to me!"

"No, I can't let you do that."

"I am just a lowly *assistant* professor, but I do think I can scrounge up enough money for one music box."

"Professor—" But I could not talk him out of the purchase; he was already opening the store's door for me. We walked inside where it smelled strongly of potpourri spice, and the store had the warmly lit romanticness of candlelight and glimmer of holiday tinsel.

I enjoyed taking my time perusing Christmas decorations, while sipping hot chocolate, but I could tell the scientist was bored shopping after only two minutes in the store. He picked up a music box shaped like a slender snow globe dome, where a fancily dressed gentleman and Lady danced inside to *Let Me Call You Sweetheart*.

"This is an incredibly girly one," he said, "but I may not be the best judge of these things. I once bought my mother a blouse for her birthday, a garish thing, too loud for a clown, but I was five and thought the shirt was neat. To spare my feelings, she said she loved it. My pops said to me, 'You have as much taste as a bump on a log. Where's your mom going to where that—on a date with one of the Ringling Brothers?' I thought he was just being a jerk, but after days passed without Mother wearing the shirt, I reasoned Pops was right—I had as much business picking out gifts for women as Barnum or Bailey had picking out furniture for normal folk. But you learned that when I gave you a scruffy old metal pin

316

with an equation carved on it." He laughed at himself, but I felt bad for him; he seemed so much like a young boy in that moment in need of a mother's love and approval.

"I loved the pin, and I think this is a lovely music box *you* picked out," I assured.

Outside, handing the shiny slick golden gift bag to me, he said, "I'll walk you to your apartment, as a thank you for all the candy bars."

"Which is your favorite candy bar?"

He smiled at my girlish adoration. "I'm not sure."

"Would you like to go to the malt shop for another banana split?"

Considering he had already eaten dinner and had mentioned having an upset stomach and I was already drinking hot chocolate from the malt shop, my real reason for wanting to go there was obvious, and I felt bad for breaking my honor code again not to view him as my boyfriend.

"Ah, I'm fairly beat," he said as an excuse. He did not think he should be seen with his student at the malt shop, where teenagers danced, cuddled, and kissed behind the drugstore section's magazine rack.

"I'm sorry. How's your stomach feeling?"

"It's fine."

He walked around me and I looked back—"What are you doing?"

"A man should always walk on the outside of the Lady on the sidewalk, a custom from when horses used to gallop by and sling mud from muddy streets, and no Lady wanted that on her dress."

"Your upbringing in Camelot truly did make you a gentleman."

He shook his head with not a trace of phony humility.

"Your mother deserves praise for raising you right."

I thought he was going to make a dry joke, but he said, "Thank you for that. So, how long have you been collecting music boxes?"

"My Moon-Moon liked music boxes."

He knew *my* momma was gone too, because I had referred to her in the past tense, but he did not ask about how she had died, keeping me from reliving the pain.

Outside Abby's Kosher Delicatessen, the front walls mostly windows, we noticed Abby, an older cranky woman in an apron, waving for Sputnik to come inside.

"Oy vey," Sputnik said under his breath, unhappy about having to visit with cantankerous Abby.

We walked in, where it smelled like soup. The small fluorescent-lit deli had a display counter in the back, displaying varieties of bagels and breads, etcetera. Behind the counter was a long row of burners where deep stainless-steel crockpots of soups simmered. Lined against each wall were four booths whose aqua color would have looked good on a Chevy Bel-Air.

Abby reached both of her hands to Sputnik's hands and brought him toward her for a kiss on the cheek; he returned a warm son-like kiss to her cheek.

"Gershom!" she said, partly scolding, partly praising. "Where have you been?"

"Everywhere." He slightly stomped his shoe against the floor, testing its strength. "How's it holding up?"

"As sturdy as the Rock of Gibraltar."

He had fixed the deli's flooring? When had he had the time?

"I'm going to get you some matzo ball soup for that cough," Abby insisted. "And no arguing with me."

"Thanks, but I just ate."

He introduced me as his student from algebra class.

318

"Not much of a student," Abby condescended. "Where's the rest of her?" Trying to make me feel as small as lint.

The professor said, "She's the brightest student I've ever known." I knew that was not true; he had just wanted to give me something nice to soften the blow of Abby's hatefulness.

I could tell Abby did not think I was good enough for the handsome young brilliant professor and she did not hide her disapproval, written in no confusing terms on her face. At least she was not his real mother.

A pretty young woman in a booth said, "Hi, Gersh."

"Hi, Naomi."

There was more to their relationship than an occasional "Hi," I could sense. Had she ever been with him in a bedroom? I was as jealous as can be. What did she think of me wearing his coat? The idea of another girl, especially a pretty one, making him a meal made me feel as bad as malaria. Plus, this side of Sputnik, this sociable pillar of the community, I could not relate to, and I wondered if I could truly be his girl, the girl who would be on his arm at social events?

"I'm going to make you soup to go," Abby demanded. "It'll get rid of that cough."

"No, I don't deserve all that coddling," Sputnik protested.

"You better go ahead and take the penicillin, Gersh," Naomi said, suggesting there was no budging Abby's stubbornness. I reasoned matzo ball soup, like chicken noodle soup, was seen as a cure all by mothers and grandmothers.

Abby sighed, "He's an adorable smart professor at Goldell and he thinks he doesn't deserve coddling." Abby looked at Naomi for backup. "Do you understand this man?"

Sputnik continued his protest, "I don't have time for soup. I need to get this pretty young Lady safe and sound back to her apartment." I knew he had said "pretty" to make me feel better after suffering Abby's insult.

"It'll only take a minute." Abby would not have "no" for an answer. "Do you want some chicken?"

"No, I told you, I'm a vegetarian."

Abby made a "tsk" of disapproval, and she turned around just to glare at me as if I, the weirdo, was responsible for Sputnik's "cursed" vegetarianism.

Sputnik looked at me, at least one person who understood him, and I felt close to him again, us against the world. But the scene was awkward, Naomi watching us, Abby hating me.

Waiting for Abby to ladle soup into a carton "bowl," I looked at one of the menus on the counter.

After handing Sputnik the bag of takeout, Abby snapped at me, "Don't get those out of order."

I was happy to be back outside, where even the cold air was friendlier.

Sputnik said, "Ay-yai-yai! I never knew Abby was such a bigot. My apologies."

"Moon-Moon taught me love and beauty come in all forms and colors across the human spectrum, but so do hate and ugliness."

"That's a highly wise thing to know, about no race having a monopoly on love or hate, at this early stage in the story. To be nineteen and to be so wise! When the war first started, I thought only gentiles were capable of the kind of evil behind death prisons, but I learned otherwise, feeling the brutality of other prisoners given a little power, hearing about it in stories of prisoners raping German girls for revenge after the war, just like I learned gentiles were capable of…" He took a deep breath and let out, "*Incredible* love as well." Subconsciously, he rubbed his thumb around the ring on his pinky. He decided he did not want to say anything else about the war.

"Who's Naomi?"

"She's *married* to Abby's grandson," Sputnik said to assuage my jealousy, but I knew she was more to him than just some girl in a restaurant. "So, you really like the music box?"

"I love it. It's beautiful. Even the gift bag is beautiful." I held it up, letting its golden shine gleam in starlight. "Thank you. Do you like matzo ball soup?"

"Ah, it's beautiful," he said, holding up the plastic bag, which contained the soup bowl. "I know it's cliché to say this, but no one makes soup like my bubbe made. I just feel bad for Abby, her husband gone, her son and grandson in other states, no man around to help her out. I saw her one morning through the window, down on her knees, trying to fix bad flooring, so I stopped in to help. I'm surprised I didn't get struck down by lightning for entering a *kosher* deli. Me practicing a mitzvah."

"I don't understand what you mean."

"Mitzvot are Jewish commandments."

"Your *brightest student* guessed that, but why would *you* be struck down by lightning for following them?"

He shrugged away the question. I did not have to actually be his brightest student to figure out Sputnik was suffering from guilt, but why? He had been the *victim* in the war. I speculated he felt guilty because he had survived and members of his family had not.

"I hate to tell you the snow globe you gave to me that long ago Christmas was stolen. I landed my plane, walked to get gas, and when I came back the gift was just gone. I could've killed whoever did that."

"It's okay. If they needed a snow globe that badly, I'm glad they found one."

"You're so forgiving." He looked at me as if I was the one responsible for who got into Heaven and I upheld an "All Welcome" policy. "I could build a music box for you, Lumi, and it could look however you wanted, and I could have it play whatever song you like."

I was so flattered by his desire to do nice things for me, but...

"You have too many other things to do."

"Yes but none quite so worthwhile as building a music box for a sweet girl."

"What about building the world's largest snowflake?" I was only kidding but he took it seriously.

"You're right."

"I get a sense I can no more stop you from building the music box than you can stop me from making you more sandwiches. If you do build one, I'd like it to play one of your songs from your piano."

"Well, if you want it to sound bad, alright."

We walked a few more feet of cold air until the physicist stopped and blurted out, "Ah, you're right, you're right!", struck by the lightning known as recognition. "I could put the largest snowflake inside the snow globe music box! A music box too big to sit on a shelf," he said with a laugh, "but you would still like it, wouldn't you?"

"Like it? I would love it!"

"Well, unlike artificial snow which can clutter for long periods of time, the ephemeral real snowflake would melt, but could you still see it inside after it was gone?"

"Of course, I could—the beauty of what you made for me would always be there."

"A part of me would always be with the little nun in the convent."

I could not tell if he was serious.

Back at the chateau de dumpiness, Romeo & Juliet ascended the back-alley balcony in a story of rivaling Montagues and Capulets.

In the apartment, Mullybiski was barking, telling me to hurry up and come inside to pet him; it was nice to feel missed.

"Sputnik, I respect that we can't be in a romantic lovestory together, if that's the way you feel it must be, but as your friend, can I know *why* you're unavailable for love. Is it me, my age, my appearance, the fact that I'm your student, that I'm not Jewish, that you have a girl already?"

"I told you an angel doesn't belong with a man."

Was that condescending malarkey meant to make me feel better?

"Sputnik, that isn't a very detailed explanation."

"But it's the explanation that must suffice for now, or for a lifetime. I'm not sure." Period.

"Would you like some crackers and warm ginger water to calm your stomach?"

"Crackers and warm ginger water—is that a southern girl's elixir?"

"It sometimes works for a stomachache, and there are southern women who swear by ginger ale, but I think warm ginger water is more soothing."

"My stomach's fine, nothing this matzo ball soup can't cure. In fact, in the morning, I'd like to try a big southern breakfast, grits, pancakes, sweet potato pie…"

"Pie for breakfast?"

"Why don't you stay home from work tomorrow and make breakfast for me? I'll come by around five."

"Ooh, I'd love to make breakfast for you, but I can make breakfast *and* go to work."

"If you're just going to rush through it, so you can go wait on customers, it won't be any good."

"I won't rush through making your breakfast."

He noticed me shivering. "You're still cold?"

"It is cold outside."

I was surprised he put his arm around my waist.

"Since I don't have a girl, I never get homecooked breakfasts." Even though he was holding the takeout bag, he put his other arm around me, which made me more unsure how to define our relationship. "I don't want you to go to work tomorrow."

"I already missed work today."

"You didn't mind skipping classes to makeover my apartment."

"How'd you know I skipped classes?"

"I'm a fortune teller. Come on. You couldn't have done all that and gone to school. Now, don't worry, I'll call the manager when I get back to the apartment. She'll listen to me. Goldell is a big customer for Darioles, plenty of events to be catered for the university. I'll tell her you need time to rest and study for a big quiz. I have a busy day tomorrow, and the engineering class, and I'd like to have an actual breakfast, not some day-old bagel." He pulled me closer to him and the dual layer of coats prevented the embrace from feeling indecent. "We can share breakfast, just you and me, no customers."

"Okaaay."

"Good." He broke the embrace since he had gotten what he wanted: I would stay home. From now on, he knew all he had to do to get his way was caress my girlish heart flutters, unless he asked me to go against my morals, which I would not do for him or anyone, and he was very aware of that.

"Now I want you to go inside, Lumi."

The mathematician waited to leave until he heard all the locks on my door snap into place.

I took off the coats, set the music box on the bookshelf headboard, petted MullyB's flour-soft head, and made Sputnik sweet potato pie, while listening to Nat King Cole on the record player. I hoped when Sputnik tasted the dessert, he would feel me kissing him.

After four years of marinating our friendship, when I graduated, would he not get over the odd idea he was unavailable for love, and he and I could be husband and wife? Insecurity nagged, "He's nice to the janitor because he feels sorry for her, just like he's nice to Abby. Maybe that's why he's nice to you too?" Those nagging thoughts followed me while I put on my nightgown and readied for bed. "And how many other Ladies does he do handyman tasks for?"

I was too excited to be negative. This would be my first time making him breakfast; serving him Darioles' food had not counted. I could not wait to play wife and make breakfast for the man I loved, which I had never thought would happen outside marriage, because why would a man ever be at my home that early in the morning?

In bed, I ate a few candies from a bag of *Kissling* chocolates ("contraband" in Biskatine chocolate town), while I went over the breakfast menu in my mind, picking the right selections and making sure I had all the ingredients.

I got up early, walked MullyB, and drove to the all-night market to buy a few ingredients and a coffeemaker. I made breakfast lovingly and quietly, since I had stayed home from work and did not want the manager to hear me making too much noise when I was supposed to be studying.

I didn't like that the dining table was a card table purchased by my limited budget, so I prettied the table by dressing it in a white tablecloth and lacy daffodil-yellow runner, a color very complementary to breakfast and morning time and fruit juice. The sunshiny tablecloth made the apartment look like springtime

325

outdoors. I first arranged the chairs to sit by each other, but no that was too forward, so I arranged them opposite one another. In the center of the crisply dressed table, I set a glass pitcher of orange juice and plain white teapot (not nearly as ornamental as one of Moon-Moon's cream tea dishes but economical). Beside the teapot, I placed creamer and sugar bowl and CozyCabin syrup for me and Karo syrup for him (how did I know the aeronaut would prefer that?). Fresh hot coffee simmered in a blue kettle (the outdoorsman would like the campfire kettle). I put out plates, cups, silverware, and napkins fit to be called origami, while humming along the way. And I arranged the serving dishes: piled high platter of sweet potato pancakes with a side of finely chopped walnuts and true southern grits with butter, cheddar, and black pepper, topped with fried eggs.

I gave Mullybiski a bite of pancake minus syrup.

I dolled up in a white turtleneck and matching cloth headband and gloves, and sweater and skirt that matched the daffodil-yellow tablecloth, attire I saw suitable for morning tea.

Sputnik knocked, quietly, right at 5 a.m. (the mathematician timely), while I was spraying my hair with a light mist of floral perfume, making the blonde strands smell like honeysuckles.

"It's the barnstormer here for some grits."

I opened the door wide, allowing a gust of breakfast goodness to greet him. He was dressed like Professor Blagonravov in a gray suit, his hair Brylcreemed and orderly. It was dark and cold outside but sunshiny and warm inside, warmth coming from the "kitchen."

He noted my yellow-and-white ensemble, and said, "You look like a little iced custard."

"Please, sir, have a seat." I quickly shut the door on frosty air.

We kept our voices quiet; the manager would definitely not allow me to have a male visitor at this late hour.

"Don't you want to walk Mullybiski first?" Sputnik asked.

"Ooh…" I dreaded saying this. "I already walked him."

I had walked Mullybiski in the back alley late at night, and Sputnik was not happy about this, but he chose not to spoil our breakfast by griping.

"My goodness," he said, upon seeing the sumptuous feast. His "upbringing in Camelot" pulled out the chair for me before sitting down himself. "I hate to mess up the fancy napkin by unfolding it."

"It's a bunny," I explained, referring to the napkin's origami shape. "But it's okay. He can always be remade into a bunny."

Sputnik said to the bunny napkin, "If I unwrap you, you'll still bring me chocolates next Easter, won't you?" He made the bunny say in a cartoon voice, "Easter? Don't you mean Passover?"

I laughed at the professor's rare silliness.

He unfolded the napkin, laid it in his lap, quite mannerly for an outdoorsman, and I knew the manners were for me, manners instilled in him by his mother; in his research tent in the Arctic, I doubted he had ever laid a napkin in his lap before grub time.

I tapped the blue kettle's lid. "There's the coffee, sir."

"That's a lotta pancake," he said, pouring himself a coffee.

"They're mostly for you," I offered, pouring him a glass of orange juice. "You're the one who has the busy day." I poured myself a cup of tea. "I'll just take two."

"That leaves *five* pancakes for me."

"The mathematician figured that out all by himself?" I smiled. "Five pancakes is a full stack." I added sugar and cream to the tea.

"Ah and some soul food grits." It seemed he was saying something more with that statement but whatever it was passed me by.

Waiting for him to take the first bite, the polite thing for a hostess to do, my heart paused: whether it would beat again or not depended on what Sputnik thought of my cooking. He nodded and smiled, saying he liked the pancakes. My heart kept beating.

"Pancakes and candy bars and ice cream and my favorite pizza. I really don't deserve your sweetness," he said, not jokingly, but again like a doomed man. "I didn't even stay outside the patisserie last night. My apologies. I went back to the apartment to work but fell asleep."

"I don't want you to sleep out in your car every night. You've checked the locks and they're as unbreakable as Fort Knox."

"They need to be sturdier since they guard something more valuable than gold."

I was immensely flattered and did not know how to respond except with a smile.

"How do you like September Ninth's moon?" I asked, knowing any science fiction/Sidereus Sterling fan would get the reference to Sterling's novel *September Ninth's Moon* about how the same moon can be seen differently by different moods and different perspectives.

"Ah, it's sequestered looking from my perspective. How about yours?"

I looked at his face. "Gorgeous." And I was not talking about the moon.

He spent the time lost in thought, except to tell me he was looking forward to the Dodgers playing the Cubs.

Before he left, I offered him the pie on glass pie dish. "At least the bachelor won't have to forage for dessert."

"Thanks, and thanks for breakfast, angel. Why don't I come by later and drive you to school?"

"That's okay. I have a car, The Lady Model, you know."

After Art History with a professor who looked like Sidney Poitier and who gave a beautiful lecture about prehistoric art and ancient belief in the soul and afterlife, and after a scary lecture in World History about early weapon-making, I walked, floated, to Goldell's library, where I encountered Sputnik, strolling with the janitor, Gladys, in the university's mid-morning flower garden.

"Hi, Lumi," he said, and I was surprised he hadn't called me, "Ms. ---." If my insecurities had not insisted otherwise, I would have thought his "Hi" had a few drawn out lovey-dovey "i's" in it, as if he had truly felt my kiss in the sweet potato pie and he had adored it.

"Hi, Professor Blagonravov." *Professor* Blagonravov. The formality was ridiculous. I was wearing his coat.

He told me he had never taken the long scenic path before, but Gladys had insisted. I told him this was my favorite path to algebra class, out of the way of quickness, but on the way to peacefulness. He was displeased about my taking the "unsafe" back path to class, but he would not let out his frustration in front of Gladys. We all walked together. Amidst butterflies and flowers, he looked even more beautiful. After I complimented the sky for its prettiness, the professor told us facts about the sky, why it's blue, why it's pink at dawn, but I still could not tell if his interest in me was romantic, because he kept on his science classroom voice, as if he was talking about thermodynamics.

After Gladys was safe inside, the professor asked me, "I thought your classes were over for the day? I want to know your complete schedule."

"I told you."

"Yes, but I want room numbers too, all the details. And I don't want you to walk this back path again by yourself."

"It's in the morning," I said. "And I am done with classes for the day. I was going to the library."

329

"Crimes are committed in daylight too, Lumi."

"At school in the middle of a daytime flower garden?"

"Hoping you never have to learn the hard way."

"I don't want to pass by the opportunity to be around these beautiful flowers. I can't wait for spring to see all the lilacs the school brochure promised. I was thinking of making a dress the color of a lilac. Lace with a sash belt. This is my airfoil data, isn't it?"

"Not at all."

"Ooh, I'm boring the scientist with dress talk."

"Are lilacs your favorites?"

"No…"

"What are?"

"I'll have to think about that the way you have to think about what is your favorite candy bar—so many to choose from!"

"You're a lily, symbol of purity."

In spite of my embarrassment, I asked, "How do you know lilies are symbols of purity? I thought I was the one who knew floral symbolism."

"Ah, I may have come across the knowledge somewhere."

Was he reading books on flowers to know me better?

"Carnations," I said, "are also symbols of purity. According to Christian legend, carnations grew from the Virgin Mary's tears as she watched Jesus carry the cross. The carnation symbolizes motherly love and romantic love and many other emotions, such as gratitude."

"So, carnations are your favorites?"

"I think they're simply darling."

"Simply darling, huh?"

I clasped my schoolbooks to my chest and twirled, letting him know how simply darling I thought carnations.

"So, what are your plans for lunch?" he asked, mesmerized by my giddiness that had developed just from making him breakfast.

"I don't especially have any lunch plans." I smiled, reeling from the twirl.

"You do now. The Bud & Spot, or we can go to Stormy & Strobe if you like. Meet me outside my office at noon and we'll walk over there together."

"You can have lunch with your student?"

"I can if I want."

I thought he was being risky; the professor being a customer at a patisserie in the early morning hours was different than his fraternizing in a date-like way with his student in a busy afternoon food court. But I could tell there would be no budging his determination to take me to lunch.

Before lunch, I savored the majestic stained-glass library, met a few new books, got reacquainted with a few old book friends.

Walking the hall outside Professor Blagonravov's office at noontime, one of his male colleagues passed by and nodded "Hello," and Sputnik scowled at the man, as if the man had been eying me, which he had not being doing at all.

Sputnik whispered, "That Lothario would certainly like to be alone with you in the hallway. He doesn't fool me."

That idea seemed outrageous.

Sensing my disbelief, he said, "This university is a little Peyton Place. We can't get Little Red Riding Nun off to the convent soon enough before the wolves start circling to make her a sophisticated girl." He was not kidding. "Why didn't you join the convent instead of college?"

"The convent's policy states a girl must have a college education."

"That's preposterous." He was not mad at me but at the convent. "I looked at your classes and noticed all your professors are male."

Why, I never! Was he insinuating I had sought classes taught by men? "My advisor picked out my schedule for me."

"I figured as much. I wasn't implying you were searching for courses taught by male professors, but I think it would be best if from now on you took classes taught by women."

"Are there that many female professors here?"

"Just let me do your scheduling from now on. I know the best courses."

I knew Sputnik was a good man and astonishingly I trusted him; he did not want to be a domineering warden—he thought he was doing his best to protect me in a world where death camps existed.

We drove his Studebaker to the food court. I liked being in his passenger seat and how my riding with him encouraged him to be a more thoughtful driver. Surprisingly, his car was not messy like his apartment or office, but pristine like his airplane (immaculate!); the chrome on the steering wheel and rimming the dials was as shiny as polish, as if he respected the car too much to trash it up.

The New England day was chilly even in sunlight, as we perused vendors of the food court, where outdoor tables were filled with lunchtimers, and the air smelled like pizza sauce and hot sauce and the cuisines of many cultures mingling.

"What would my little nun like?"

My little nun? The man I loved wanted me to be a nun, yet he acted as if I was his girl! If that was not a peculiar fate, nothing was.

"You can have anything you want, Pep, except *thick* crust pizza which I will not support with my money." He grinned.

We decided on Mexican. At the ordering window, Sputnik began his order in Spanish, but realizing the cashier did not speak Spanish, Sputnik said, "I'll have the fajita bowl."

"With corn or flour tortillas?" the young cashier asked.

"Ba-bu-ba…I'll spare the lives of some cornstalks, since they've been fairly kind to me and my airplane over the years during emergency landings."

The cashier was confused by the weird professor.

"I'll have the flour tortillas. And my Lady friend will have the cheese quesadillas. Ah, and one coffee and one hot tea."

I did not think his ordering for me was any more sexist than a woman picking out groceries for her husband, since both showed a man and woman knew each other well enough to pick out each other's food choices; plus, being shy, I liked Sputnik ordering for me. What bothered me was *why* Sputnik was ordering for me—he thought the cashier was eying me, which was completely ridiculous. Sputnik's time in the concentration camp had manufactured so much distrust in him of man, he saw wickedness everywhere, wickedness that existed nowhere except in his paranoia like bogeymen only seen by a child's fear.

We sat at a table close by a silver maple turned red in autumn. Sputnik layered a warm flour tortilla with rice, beans, grilled veggies, guacamole, sour cream, and pico de gallo, while asking, "So, are you ready to listen to me go on and on about airfoil data?"

"Yes, sir, I am."

He laughed while handing me the tortilla in exchange for a quesadilla.

Instead of "airfoil data," we talked about trees, admiring the few trees around us (we both loved trees). I spoke of how maples had

333

gentle souls, and he had always sensed wisdom in the presence of oaks. This was one reason he and I were sitting together and not with anyone else.

Sputnik kept dashing more hot sauce onto the tortilla; the boy really liked hot food. I needed to go to the library and check out a book of spicy recipes.

I wanted to talk about one of his favorite subjects: geometry. At this *point*, I only knew about points and lines and planes, thanks to *Basic Geometry*. I realized for him, talking to me about the subject must have felt like talking to a kindergarten student about Shakespeare, yet he relished it—fresh "adorable" insights from the mind of a novice. Since he enjoyed my math virginity, I told him more of my "pure" ideas. I had skipped ahead in our textbook.

"I won't pretend, Professor, to understand quadratic equations or how to graph them, not yet anyway, but I noticed something symbolic about parabolas."

"Pair-uh-bowl-uhs," he corrected to "Puh-rab-uh-luhs. A mathematician's girl should know how to say that correctly." Catching what he had just said, he stammered, "Well, mm, in case you ever marry a mathematician."

I completely forgot what I was going to say; all my concentration was on this: did he see me as his girl?

"So, what about parabolas?" he asked.

"Ooh, yes, I noticed that when the coefficient is positive, the parabola opens up, and if it's negative, it opens down. See what I mean? When positive it smiles, when negative it frowns!"

Even though I had not been the first to think of that, he was impressed I had seen the symbolism on my own.

He asked me to come back to his office and spend the afternoon there doing my homework, so he could offer assistance, amidst his other tasks. The truth was he thought Goldell's heavily gated science building was safer than my apartment.

I sat on his uncomfortable couch and studied. From the radio, I heard endless baseball news and news about the world's horrific state, while Professor Blagonravov worked at his desk then left to teach a class. When he came back, I told him I had to go home and walk Mullybiski; plus, I wanted to get away from the imprisoned radio never allowed to play music.

"I'll walk your dog," Sputnik said.

"I can walk him."

"No, I have to go check on Pythag and Sophie anyway."

When he came back, I said I needed to go. I was ready for supper.

"I was going to get takeout," Sputnik said, almost pouting, not wanting me to leave. I assumed he meant takeout for both of us, but he had a dinner meeting. I was offended by his not inviting me, but he said "the little nun" didn't have any business being around "a bunch of old guys who talk like they're at a 'gentleman's' club." There was irony. "Don't worry, this building is fairly safe at night. I've checked out the nightguard. He's benign, I think." Sputnik was not certain but he reasoned I was safer in his guarded office than in my apartment.

"I'd rather go out to eat," I said. "Since you're not going to be here."

He sat beside me on the couch. "You don't like being in my office?" he asked with a bedroom voice. Again, he used my smittenness to get what he wanted; all it took was the back of his fingers caressing the side of my face, as if he was preparing me for a kiss, and him saying, "I really want you to stay, Peppermint."

"Okaaaay."

"Good," he said, standing up, having achieved his goal. I had never seen manipulation go so smoothly! "Now, you're going to be a good girl and stay here until I get back?"

"Okay, Professor."

"Keep the door locked."

Before leaving, he called and got Chinese takeout for me. Alone in his nighttime office, I ate stir-fried noodles and drank lukewarm tea in a paper cup from the teachers' lounge, while listening to rain make mud puddles on campus. I pulled back the curtain; the assistant professor's office had a view of the parking lot, which was mostly empty. I opened the top drawer of his desk, took out a candy bar; he had not eaten a single one. Nibbling the Biskatine chocolate bar, I looked at his science books for the dozenth time; the stodgy books smelled musty. His office was small and I was beginning to feel claustrophobic, while the nightguard's footsteps across the building sounded like a warden's foot stomps.

At ten p.m., Sputnik knocked. He looked tired and was coughing profusely.

Aside from intermittent sounds of the nightguard's patrolling, the university was as quiet as a closed movie theater, which made rain outside even louder.

"Professor Blagonravov, you're soaking wet."

The professor took off his damp suit jacket, as rain outside made sloshy noise.

I sat back on the couch, gathering my books into bookbag.

"I went ahead and walked the pug," he said, while loosening his tie and locking the door, "so that won't interrupt us."

My heart raced with a speed suitable for the Indy 500, thinking Sputnik was interested in a liaison with me in his office. The professor sat on the couch, as if about to teach me my first lesson in romance, and I literally jumped up and walked over to his desk.

"What's wrong?" he asked, rubbing his fingers through his slick hair.

"I need to go home."

"It's raining too bad for you to drive."

"You can drive me."

"I'm beat."

"What are you suggesting, sir? That I stay here overnight?"

"Yep."

"Sputnik, that's…" Improper.

"I won't tell anyone of your impropriety."

"Why, I never!"

He laughed. "Come on. I would never ruin your status as a lily."

That offended me too.

Realizing I was hurt, he clarified, "Men don't go to bed with angels. Don't worry, the night will be chaste, for certain. I admire your piousness in spite of your yearning for kissing and cuddling."

"There's no sin in kissing and cuddling."

"But *I* can't kiss you or cuddle you, although you certainly kissed me through the pie, the way it melted in my mouth."

I blushed redder than the red in a peppermint.

"But still, you're going to be a nun, take a vow of chastity, and I'd cut *it* off before allowing it to break your vow."

"Sputnik!" I was shocked by his words. "How do you know I'm going to be a nun? I said I wanted to be a nun or be in love. You think being in love will never happen for me in these four years before I make the decision to join the convent?"

"It's already happened for you," he said, while walking over to me and removing the heavy satchel from my shoulder. "You told me so. And you told me your heart is as loyal to me as Joan of Arc to France, and if you meant that, you'll never fall in love with anyone else. I took a long walk in the rain and I finally decided I'll never let you be anything other than a nun."

"What do you mean 'let me'?"

"Well, if you can't be intimate with me, the man you love, you won't be intimate with anyone, because your heart is too loyal for betrayal."

"That's a cruel thing to do to someone."

"I didn't set up the story that way."

"Fate? That's ridiculous. You just said, '*I* took a long walk in the rain and *I* decided *I'll* never let you be anything other than a nun.' That's your choice, Sputnik, not fate's."

"But fate set it up for you to be my student, not my girl."

"Do you want me to be your girl?"

"You can't be."

"Why won't you tell me what's bothering you, why you're unavailable for love? You're so macho stubborn."

"My reluctance to tell you has nothing to do with machismo, I assure you." Realizing I was angry at him, he rubbed his neck for sympathy and said, "I hate to ask but would you mind rubbing my neck?"

"That doesn't seem like a proper task for a nun."

"It's not entirely improper. A friend helping a friend."

"No, sir, I will not rub your neck. If you want me to be a nun, I will be."

"Fine. I need to rest tonight, Pep, and not out in my car. My nun can sleep on the couch and I'll take the floor. Alright?"

"No, it's not alright. It's improper."

He put his damp arms around me, and to get his way, he said tenderly, "I promise I'll protect you. Joan of Arc's Knight would die for her in battle. If you were a nun, you would be required to be obedient in a life of seclusion, and I'll require the same of you until I can lead you safely to the monastery. If you trust your Captain's wisdom, this should not be a problem."

"Don't get bossy with me, Sputnik. I might be a girly girl but I won't tolerate being bossed around!"

The Great Dane backed down to the Chihuahua whose bark was bigger than expected.

"You said you thought a girl can be anything she wants to be."

"Be a nun writer photographer, be the President of the United States—I'm still going to be the Captain."

Even though he was sexist, which shocked my stereotype that all Jewish men were feminists, I would not abandon him in sexism, no more than I would abandon him in loneliness or confusion or any other dreadful locale—I would lead him out.

"Captain of my heart, and not tyrant," I explained. "Not even an inanimate object obeys every command. I can't tell you how many times I've tried to turn on my TV and it did not obey, too sleepy or something. Sputnik, you said you didn't want to be like your chauvinist dad."

"I don't think you're inferior to me. Quite the contrary. I think you're highly superior. That's why I want to keep you safe. Listen, I don't want to boss you around or control your life. I only want to protect you and to keep you an unsophisticated girl, and to do that, I need to make the decisions regarding your protection, because you're too naïve to know the right choice. Now, this is the place in the conversation where you acquiesce to your Captain and utter one of those girly 'Okaaay's.'" He held me close enough that all the rain dampness of his clothing soaked into me.

"Sputnik, if it means that much to you for me to stay in your office tonight, I'll stay."

"Here," he said, walking me to the couch, where I lay down and he covered me with his coat. He turned off the lights and camped on the uncomfortable floor.

I woke up in pitch black quietness, which was shattered by the guard's stomping boots and Gershom moaning, "Alina," the moans not romantic but pained.

Alina?

Through darkness, I reached my hand down to him on the floor and softly rubbed his still-damp breast pocket, where his heart beat too hard for rest. "Sputnik…Professor Blagonravov." He would not wake up from the nightmare. I knew one way to wake him—I started to leave.

"Alina, where are you going?"

I turned on the lights to show him he was in the present and the nightmare was over.

Disoriented, he looked around, saw the clock: three a.m.

I did not want him to feel ashamed or embarrassed for having moaned, "Alina," so I lightened the atmosphere by opening the curtain and saying, "The rain's gone. We can go to the sweet shop and fill our cups with sunrise." But I began to doubt the sun would ever rise in his being again.

I insisted he go to his apartment and get out of his rain-damp clothes; he had shivered all night. Waiting for him to change, I wondered about Alina.

That morning at the patisserie, he brought in his *Flight Theory* book. We sat at our booth, where he explained a few aeronautical concepts, his way of apologizing for condescending me about being "a poetic nun" unable to learn engineering. In the spirit of friendship and sharing, we also took one of the romance quizzes together (I passed and he did not, one subject he was not an expert in *too*).

Sputnik never wanted to let me out of his protective eye even for a moment. He was more insistent than ever about me quitting my job and letting him drive me to school from now on.

In class, he took from his briefcase a ragdoll, which brought about giggles, but the professor was not smiling.

He held the doll next to his chest and said, "A professor of sociology allowed me the privilege of showing this doll to all of you. The doll will be on display in the Holocaust exhibit being prepared by this university's museum, which will open next spring, and I suggest you all visit the past if you care about the future."

Students seemed uneasy—what did this have to do with algebra?

The professor set the doll atop the desk of the student who had sneezed and said, "Ajew." Professor Blagonravov kept his hand around the doll to keep her from falling, and the doll's sweet haunted eyes stared straight at the student, who was obviously confused and nervous.

"This doll belonged to a five-year-old girl, a German girl, a Jewish girl. This girl had infinite kindness. As a professor of mathematics, I do not misuse the word 'infinite,' but this girl's kindness deserved to be called infinite. But the Nazi regime defined her kindness as a disability and labeled her as retarded. She had to be disposed of. Soldiers came to her house in the middle of daylight and took her away and gassed her in a mobile van, which was used to make

341

killing quicker and more efficient. Then all her mother had left of her daughter was this doll. Do you think the Nazis were right?"

The student shook his head.

"No?"

I could sense anger building in the professor, and I was worried he was going to have another Ditwad incident and punch this student in the face. I was going to jump up, create a diversion, feign sickness—I was not going to let Sputnik lose his career to prove something to an idiot who tried hard to never present evidence that he had a heart.

"If you think the Nazis were wrong then why do you help keep their ideology alive by spouting their hateful dogma? This doll should be giving warmth and friendship to a child, but instead, because of ignorant ones such as yourself, she will have to spend her life on display in a cold museum as a symbol of death, to remind you, to remind all of us, that the Nazis were wrong. If you ever come to my class again and say something the Nazi regime would approve of, you will be headed to the dean's office to explain why you got kicked out of *elementary* algebra and to beg to stay at Goldell. As your professor, I assure you, I have the power to remove you from my class, *King.*"

The boy's pride was dead, and there was less silence at a funeral, because no one mourned the loss of the jerk's ego.

The professor set the doll against his briefcase, where she watched us all, reminding us how privileged we were to even be alive.

As promised, Professor Blagonravov gave the class our first quiz, which dealt with pre-algebra topics (arithmetic basics needed for moving ahead in the subject). He sat at his desk and wrote in his notepad.

I shivered in the cold classroom, where I struggled through ten ten-point questions. I tried more than I had ever tried in a math class to do well, trying not to disappoint him, because I greatly admired this man and wanted him to be proud of me.

He enjoyed using baseball questions on his math quizzes, such as "If Jack E. Robinson was at bat 300 times during the season and had 90 hits, what was his batting average? (In decimal form.)" I knew I was in trouble when my answer came out "3.3," which translated to over 300 percent! That made no sense (no player could hit the ball more than one hundred percent of the time).

The last question, "a look ahead to algebra, detectives," melted me into a gooey mush: "If Peppy Mint gave two peppermint kisses to her sweetheart and was left with eighteen peppermint kisses, how many kisses did she start out with? (Please show as a linear equation in one variable. Hint: remember our discussion about Mr. X.)

I knew the answer was 20, but I could not figure out how to write that as a linear equation, even though I kept searching my mind for what he had written on the blackboard the morning he discussed Mr. X.

For extra credit, the merciful professor provided five one-point non-math questions: "Who won last night's game between the Cubs and Dodgers," and some questions with no right or wrong answers, "Who's your favorite baseball player and why," and "In one word (or mathematical symbol), describe yourself", and "Tell me a story using math," and he gave us the freebie, "What's your professor's name?" I was tempted to write "The Sputnik" but instead I wrote "Professor Gershom Blagonravov."

But as much as I had tried, I knew I had failed, even though Ms. Collins, probably his Ms. Y, handed him her quiz confidently, her confidence met with a smile.

I laid the test like a fallen soldier on his desk, and woe is me, accepted defeat against mathematics. I wanted to put the back of my hand to my forehead and faint like a nineteenth century heroine, in hopes my Knight would catch me in his arms and tell me I had not failed him.

Instead, I gloomily sighed my way back to my seat.

After the quiz, the professor gave a quick lecture with some asides about the previous night's baseball game, especially since his team had won. I had a realization—he had not gone to a business dinner the previous night, he had gone out to watch baseball with "some old guys," leaving me alone in his dreary office with some old fried noodles.

After class, I felt too sheepish to ask him whether he would still be installing a phone in my apartment, since he had more important things to do for the world, but he said, "Ms.---" before I could walk out of the classroom. "I'll go over to the filth motel and put in the phone this morning."

"You're too busy," I said.

"You'll come back to my office after your next class."

When I went to his office that afternoon, he and his briefcase, suitcase, and coffee cup were about to leave to the airport. He was going to Alabama for the weekend to attend the Civil Rights conference, and to give a speech at an anti-war rally, and he would not be back until late Sunday night.

"About your lecture today, the doll…" I was unsure how to formulate how sad I was about what had happened to him in the war.

He softly patted my unease with, "I know."

"But—"

"You're now the proud owner of a new phone, a girly pink one too, but as I said before, I may not be the best at picking out gifts for Ladies. I wish I had more time to build you a better desk. The Lady Model of desks, carvings of flowers…" He was envisioning how to construct it.

"Thanks but my desk isn't important."

"Desks are always important to writers. And I didn't forget the flooring. It's on my list. The apartment needs a heating unit as well. You get cold so easily. I'll discuss it with the landlord. Even though I don't have a secretary, the absentminded professor can keep up with some things."

"I should have said this earlier…when I saw the numbers on your arm…I just didn't know what to say…I want to tell you how sorry…how sad…but 'sad' is too small a word…"

"It's a perfect word, a true word, a good honest word with feeling, easy for a kid to say but for some reason hard for an adult to say, the kind of word the little girl whose doll I showed to class would have said."

"Sputnik, you can talk to me about what happened, anytime you want."

"No. Not entirely." He set his briefcase, suitcase, and Dodgers cup on the couch. "Lumi…" Now he stammered. "I told you I needed to know you, and I do, partly because I knew from 'Hi' a real friendship awaited us, and partly because of what happened in the past, in the war, but I'm not sure what's the right thing to do."

"I don't understand. Why won't you just explain this to me?"

"Please let me decide what is right and find the right time to explain things, but now, I have to leave. Where are you headed this afternoon?"

"Back to the chateau de dumpiness. I have to walk Mullybiski."

"But you're staying inside for the rest of the weekend?" he asked, while picking up his suitcase.

"No, I have some errands."

He set the suitcase back down; he could not leave until he set me straight on this, "It's not safe for you to be out by yourself."

"In Biskatine?"

"Unfortunately, cruelty resides everywhere. Please, do me a favor, do your wellbeing a favor, don't go out unless someone's with you."

"What someone? Mullybiski will be with me. I have to go out this weekend. I need some fresh air. Maybe I'll go to Oh Susanna's orchard for cider and doughnuts and a stroll. And I have to go to the market and laundromat."

"The laundromat? Those places are teeming with perverts. You know I'm incredibly busy, so please, don't make it harder for me by making me worry so much," he said like he and I were the only two people who knew about his secret anxiety condition, and I felt more attached to him than ever.

"You don't have to worry. I'm just going for a brief stroll at the orchard—"

"The orchard where you were almost attacked?"

"If not the orchard, maybe I'll go to the meadows for a picnic—"

"You said your heart was as loyal to me as Joan of Arc to France!" he shouted, while throwing a jar of coffee across the room, not even caring we were standing in his office and anyone could hear him. I was shocked silent by his outburst. "If you had any kind of

346

real loyalty, you would not go out this weekend and put yourself in danger!"

"Okay, I won't," I said with quiet voice, hoping to quiet him too.

He stared at me strangely, like who he currently was, where he currently was, who he was currently with was disappearing from his thoughts, because he was being pulled someplace else. He grabbed me in an embrace. "You're cold, aren't you?" he asked, hugging me tighter.

I knew what was happening. In my childhood neighborhood, there had been a young man who had suffered flashbacks from the war; sometimes he would be in a store or on the sidewalk, but in his mind, he would be back on a battlefield, and he would shout at people, "Head for cover!" Sputnik was back in the concentration camp.

"Don't worry," he assured, and he held me so close, his coughs felt like they were inside my chest.

I wondered if his time suffered in the death camp had permanently injured his emotions, and if he would ever be free of the fear I was in constant danger? If I really wanted to be his guardian angel, I had to help him through his emotional war.

"I'll keep you warm," he soothed and rubbed his hands up and down my back like we were about to freeze to death in the Arctic. As much as I wanted to melt into his embrace, I had to bring him back to the present.

"Sputnik. I'm not cold. Professor Blagonravov. Professor, you have a conference to go to."

Like a man snapping out of a sleepwalk, he slowly pulled away from the past's clutch. After enduring a dizzying moment remembering where he was, who he now was, he was not as embarrassed as he was angry with himself. "My apologies. Hoping you don't think I'm completely bonkers. Did I terrify you?"

"No, it's okay."

"Sometimes that happens," he warned. "Some nights in empty icy farm fields I could have sworn I was back in prison and the plane had landed to rescue…"

I wanted him to know his warning did not scare me away. "I'll always stand by you."

"See, you are too good for me."

I wondered if he was "unavailable for love" because he feared his war flashbacks would frighten a girl, or if he could not marry me because his heart was pledged to the one he had promised to keep warm years ago and failed? The ring was a symbol of her love, wasn't it?

Depressed as a dying woman, depressed more for my hurting friend than I was for myself, I trudged with weighted concern back to my apartment. On the now stable desk, a new pink Princess telephone sat by my typewriter, where there was a rolled piece of paper with my friend's typed message: "Write thus!" Beside the phone sat a handwritten message: his home number, office number, and hotel number beneath his needly handwriting, "Call and let me know you're alright." Signed "Sputnik."

Now it was my time to be worried about him. I knew how dangerous protests could be. I had lost my friend Cynthia to a "peaceful" protest.

I mostly stayed in bed with Mullybiski and Root, and I moped and ordered pizza and leaned my face against the Knight in armor's cold chest. I watched television late-night movies and listened to the music box Sputnik had bought me and endless noise from downstairs, as candy bar wrappers and pizza cartons became a mountain by the bedside. In Sputnik's jacket, I only went outside to walk Mullybiski and get more candy bars in the rain.

Sputnik called me each hour to check on me, even called from locations where I could hear conference chatter and protesting chants, "Make love, not war!", and I did not let him know I was upset; he had too many upsetting things in his life already.

On the phone, in the quietness of his hotel room, he asked me questions about my life like *I* was a subject he wanted to be an expert in.

"I bought some lavender fabric for you, angel, for the lilac dress you want to make." His voice was even more handsome over the phone, because the handsomeness of his face wasn't distracting me, allowing my full attention to be given to listening to him speak.

"Ooh, Sputnik, you didn't have to buy that for me."

"Perhaps I should have waited to buy it—I don't relish having to carry a roll of lacy fabric on the plane, but it'll be worth it to see you model the dress for me. I'll buy you fabrics the colors of all the flowers of the world—cherry blossom, jasmine, sunflowers—and you can model this flowerbed wardrobe for me."

"That's really sweet of you to say."

"Now tell me a bedtime story, please," he laughed.

I told him about the Stargust meadow, but I didn't tell him about the frostbite accident or thieves or Moon-Moon's death or Cynthia's murder; I told him of the happy moments. He did not offer details about his past in return; when it was his turn to talk, he needed to go do some work. "Papers to grade, and ah, I see this terrible one by that quirky Ms.---." He left me in suspense about my grade.

Monday morning at the sweet shop after giving me the lavender dress fabric, he kept saying, "Come here, angel," anytime I resumed working (wiping tables, sweeping). "Why don't you go upstairs and work on making a florid dress instead?"

"Sputnik, you know I'd like to, but if I lose this job, there will be no upstairs apartment for me to make a dress in."

He came up with all sorts of doozy questions to keep me from working for money, such as, "Would you rather be Sylvester or Tweety?" He was such an interesting man, if a man and not an alien (maybe my childhood sense of him as otherworldly had been correct!).

"Tweety," I said.

"But he's always in danger."

"But he's never as devious as the 'puddy tat.' Plus, he can fly. Who would you be?"

"I'd be Granny." Such dry humor.

"Have you taken any pictures lately, Ms. Photographer?"

"No, because a certain someone insists I never leave my apartment."

"I just said not to leave when it's dangerous to do so, such as walking back roads by yourself. Just let me know when you want to go out to take pictures, where you want to go, and I'll take you."

"I'd like to take a picture from up above in your spaceplane."

He smiled. Someday. Would he let me ride in the ghost's seat?

More questions: "If you could meet any character from a book, who would it be?" and "If you could have written any book from history, which one?"

If I had not been so insecure, I would have seen he was obsessed with me.

In class, Professor Blagonravov handed the quiz to me with an "A" marked in red at the top.

He taught the meaning of "pi," using my pie plate as an example: "Let's assume this pie dish is a true circle. Its circumference," he said, holding up the pie dish in one hand and using his other hand to trace around the circle, "divided by its diameter," and his forefinger went straight across the pie dish's interior, defining its diameter, "will always be approximately 3.14. That number, that ratio, is known as 'pi.' If it's a small circle, say a peppermint, whose diameter is one inch then it's circumference will be 3.14 inches, approximately. Pi is actually infinitely long, which means all the numbers beyond the decimal point never end, although the number does have a beginning," he said, while looking at me, remembering our discussion about whether eternity could have a starting point. "This may not seem interesting but if you consider how circles often symbolize infinity, knowing that infinity is built into one of the properties of a circle will get the hairs on the back of your neck standing up."

I traced my fear of math to a grade schoolteacher who I once asked if "one" could ever *not* be a gain, such as if it was a "bad one," and he had responded, "Can you at least pretend there's a brain in that female head of yours?" Before that incident, I had found math interesting. I learned from Professor Blagonravov what I had been trying to get at that day in grade school: the concept of "negative one." A negative one plus a positive anything lowered the power of the positivity. I was never going to be a mathematician because I did not have the passion or skill for it, but at least I did not have to fear it, and I eagerly awaited more adventures in this landscape known as mathematics with a guide as confident yet as gentle as Professor Blagonravov.

That afternoon, I knocked on his office door. "Professor?"

"Come in," he said from behind the door.

"I know you're busy, but do you mind if I talk with you?" I asked from the doorway.

"I know I haven't done your flooring yet."

"You just got back into town! But it's not about that anyway. I have a question about my quiz."

"Have a seat," he said, turning down baseball news on the radio and pausing whatever he was working on, but keeping the pen in his hand.

I walked inside, shut the door for privacy, and took a seat in front of his desk.

"Sputnik, I got an 'A,'" I said, perplexed.

"Yep."

"I didn't deserve an 'A.' I answered 'Who are the integers?' with 'Dear Lonely Hearts.'"

"I gave credit for creativity."

"You gave me eight points out of ten for creativity for an answer that was completely wrong."

"Not completely wrong. After all, I did say one way of looking at numbers was as lonely ones in need of a love connection."

"I thought you didn't give out 'A's?"

"Tsk, tsk, someone didn't read her syllabus thoroughly. I give 'A's on quizzes, just not 'A's as final grades, unless a student wants to put in the extra work. Listen, Pep, I ask my students to ponder, to understand, not memorize. Perhaps I failed in making integers understandable."

"You didn't fail at all. *I* failed and you know it. I answered that Jack E. Robinson's batting average was over 300 percent, and you gave me nine points for that!"

"You were only off by one decimal place and I'm fairly certain I know why."

"Because I had to answer ten questions in only thirty minutes. I need more than three minutes a question."

"Ah." He smiled. "How did you figure out you got three minutes per question?"

"I simply divided thirty minutes by ten questions."

"That's right. Because you wanted to know how many *minutes per question*." He leaned back in his seat, completely in professor character. "For this question, you needed to find how many *hits per at bats*. Jack made 90 hits during 300 at bats, so the answer requires dividing hits by at bats, which is .3, or 30 percent. You divided at bats by hits and that gave you 3.33, or 333 percent. You made a simple mistake which is common when learning a new language. And I believe the baseball language threw you a curve ball, so to speak. If you ever come across a math question that uses examples you're unfamiliar with, put it into terms you are familiar with. For example, what if I had asked, Ms. Mint has written ten books and five of those books were love stories, so what percent of her books are romantic?"

I knew the answer was half, or fifty percent, but I thought about how I had figured that out.

"It's always tempting," the teacher explained, gently, "to divide the bigger number by the smaller number, but that would give us two hundred percent. The question is *how many love stories per books written*. I'll give you some good advice: see that word 'per' as the division symbol. Love stories divided by books written—that will show you the fraction of stories that were love stories. Five out of ten, or one half, fifty perfect."

His mind moved a lot quicker than my mind toward math answers, but I believed I could get the hang of it with practice.

"Thank you, Professor. The 'per' as the division sign is helpful."

"Yes, but don't let it turn into a crutch. Making sense of what you're doing, understanding a problem, is more important than memorizing a gimmick to a quick solution. Now you did quite well with addition and subtraction."

"I did quite well with addition and subtraction in grade school—okay, not really—but this is college."

"As you know, I provide foundational knowledge in my introductory classes because the grade school education system sometimes fails in making the basics understandable and relatable. I can tell you need more time with fractions, foundational knowledge that will be important once we get into more complicated rational expressions. Besides, fractions are highly relevant to a baker who must understand ratios: sugar to flour…that's as far as my baking knowledge goes."

"You don't have to give me special treatment. I might not be Ms. Collins…"

He noticed the tone of jealousy in my voice.

"But I do try."

"Exactly. Ms. Collins wants a business degree. A strong foundation in math is crucial to her success in her profession, although business doesn't require her to be a math expert capable of uncovering proofs."

"How do you know that about her?"

"Lumi…" His tone suggested my jealousy was unfounded. "I take interest in all my students, particularly the ones who show enough interest, if not in math but in their own future, to come to my office and ask me questions, which is surprisingly very few students. I see you, Ms ---, by the apple trees on campus, laying your dear Coleridge and Wordsworth in the grass, to spend time with algebra. You close your poetry books to open *geometry* books." His voice questioned why geometry. He broke out of the professor role and said, "This isn't geometry class, Peppermint. I don't require you to know it."

My blush confessed, "I study geometry to feel closer to you."

"You spend your precious youthful minutes on math, and that is why you got an 'A.' I told you I grade on effort." He leaned closer to the desk. "But I spent the weekend's entirety wondering if I have failed as a teacher."

"You're a perfect teacher. Why would you think otherwise?"

"Because I made a poet lay her dear poetry books down to pick up a subject she doesn't wish to learn. I believe one should learn math—math is part of this universe, and to me, math is poetic—but I don't like being a cog in the university's conveyor belt, cranking out identical minds. I don't like students being forced to learn subjects just to get grades just to get jobs."

"I think you're the best professor in the world."

"I think some of your answers to the bonus questions were sublime. Who won last night's game between the Cubs and Dodgers? 'Your beloved Dodgers.' Who's your favorite baseball player and why? 'Gershom.' We're both lucky a TA doesn't grade these papers for me."

"Ooh, Sputnik, I'm sorry. I didn't think about that. I won't do it again."

"No, no, it's alright. I enjoy reading your answers. But you didn't answer 'why' Gershom is your favorite player." He grinned. "In one word (or mathematical symbol), describe yourself. '+.' Positive, I like that. Tell me a story using math. '1 + 1 does not equal 3.'"

"I'm aware that's not exactly a story but it clearly states my views on relationships. A tragic sentence would be the illogical 1 + 1 equals 3."

"Gotcha." Me plus Sputnik did not equal me plus Sputnik plus Naomi or Ms. Collins or any other woman.

"What's your professor's name? I would've given you ten extra points for 'Sputnik.'"

"That question was a complete freebie."

"Ah, really? You'd be surprised how many were unable to answer it. I didn't ask it to expand my ego or to give away points but to check my students' ability to pay attention."

"I'll let you get back to your work, Professor, but first how do I make that last question a linear equation?"

"Well, you got the right answer, so how did you figure it out? And I'm not going to give you *special* treatment. You can do this, Lumi."

"I remembered from class that Mr. 9 was Mr. X, but I couldn't remember what you had written exactly on the blackboard."

"That's alright. I don't want you to memorize. I want you to think."

"If Peppy Mint gave two peppermint kisses to her sweetheart and was left with eighteen peppermint kisses, how many kisses did she start out with? I know that 18 plus 2 equals 20."

"I'll give you a hint, Peppy Mint's total number of kisses is Ms. Y."

"And my job is to figure out which number that is?"

"Yep, you're getting ready to bat it outta the park."

"Y equals…18 plus 2?"

"Yep, that's true, but no algebra professor would let his student off that easily. He would say, 'How'd you come up with 18 plus 2.'"

"I just thought of…some number minus 2 equals 18. Y minus 2 equals 18."

"Mazel tov!"

I was ecstatic—I had made him proud using math skills.

"I decided not to count off any points for anyone on that question, because one, it was worded wonkily, and two, it was unfair of me to ask you all to *solve* that question without having first given you the tools to know how to solve a linear equation. I should have just asked you to set the problem up in the form of a linear equation. We'll solve them later. My apologies. The absentminded professor."

"Speaking of unfairness, Professor, and forgive me if I'm out of line, but…it's not fair that coming up with an answer to whether there are infinitely many betrothed numbers is the only way to make an 'A.' I know you see beauty in the symbolism, but actual betrothed numbers don't make sense to us. I looked up betrothed numbers in a book and I could have just as well been reading an alien manual about how to build a spaceship. 'Betrothed numbers are two positive integers such that the sum of the proper divisors of either number is one more than the value of the other number.' I remember that because I read it twenty times, trying to understand it, and even if I could figure out what it meant, there is no way I could answer if there are infinitely many betrothed numbers. Forgive me for this, but I think you like withholding the 'A' from your male students and standing on a platform of genius far beyond their intellect's reach, but you're better than that, Sput—you're a Knight capable of mercy, fairness, and compassion."

The professor did not get mad; instead, he said, "Thanks for bringing that to my attention, angel."

During our next class, he told the students he had revised his "A" policy—now all it took to achieve was a mathematical essay, or poem, or song ("For you music students").

Every day, he wanted me to study in his bland office and eat takeout, since he didn't think I should eat in public unescorted. At night, I slept on the beady uncomfortable couch along with Mullybiski and Root. Sputnik slept on the floor. He thought it improper for the nun to sleep in his apartment and for him to sleep in hers, and he definitely thought us getting a hotel room indecent (not many hotel managers at that time would have allowed an unmarried man and woman to share a room anyway).

One gloomy afternoon, realizing my discontent, he brought me a plush bunny toy.

"He's adorable!" I said, reaching out from the couch for the gift. The image of the austere professor walking through the ivy league hallway while holding the plush bunny was even more adorable.

"I thought you would like him, but," he said, withholding the present until I consented to the agreement of accepting it, "he's developed an allergy to every location outside this office, so you can only be with him in here."

Professor Blagonravov did not even care there were now two toys, Root and the bunny, sitting on his couch, often along with his female student and her pug dog, almost anytime someone came to his office, and I thought he was being too risky with his career.

Some nights, he did not get back to his office until late and never explained where he had been. He often stayed up all night coughing and working and "ba-bu-ba-ing" and pacing, thinking up equations or whatever he did, and he'd ask, "Am I keeping my little Peppermint awake?"

"No. Your work's more important than my sleep."

"God's going to get a fine wife."

"Sputnik, I'll sleep on the floor tonight and you can have the couch."

"Don't be absurd. I don't want that uncomfortable couch." He grinned.

358

Spending so much time in the physics and math building, I began to hear rumors, especially around the vending machines (university "water coolers"). Torturous gossip: Professor Blagonravov was a womanizer. He was a "marvelous lover," my heart suffered learning from the campus grapevine, gossip about the physicist's torrid afternoons with curvaceous Madame French Professor in her office and his nights divided between a bombshell cocktail singer from Manhattan and a gorgeous Harvard instructor of sociology, nights in his swingin' bachelor pad in New York City. Vicious rumors kept stacking atop me until I broke down and cried on the beady hard couch in his cold abandoned office, where I felt more alone than ever, stranded in commonplace.

He could not be in a love story, but he could be a character in a dozen women's lust stories? Apparently, he was a bobcat to male students but a pussycat to female students and a tomcat to female professors. I could not make sense of this other side of him. He was so awkward and girl shy. Yet, he was good-looking, brilliant, and becoming famous. He was the most eligible bachelor in town. Why, every woman on campus probably wanted him! *Wanted* him or already had him? But when did he find the time for all those women? Maybe his encounters with women were as quick as his encounters with vending machines? Maybe these women were the reason for his late nights, the reason he had to leave our phone calls early during those nights at his "conference"? Maybe there had never even been a conference; okay, there had been, but maybe his real reason for going there had not been for upholding world peace! And what about all those "lectures" out of town? Aside from our early morning patisserie conversation sessions, our brief time together in class, and his few hours of work and sleep in the office, I was never around Sputnik, whose timetable was packed with activities I was unaware of. No wonder he had not wanted me to be his secretary; he did not want me to know how he spent his time when we were apart. And he had said that malarkey that I was "an angel;" that had been more polite to say than he did not want a nice girl. The barnstormer had been a vagabond and still was, landing in different women's lives for brief hot minutes. He wanted to own me, though, for some reason, and I could not make sense of him.

Maybe my insecurities had been right: maybe he did only feel sorry for me? Maybe I reminded him of a little sister? He had obviously suffered emotional trauma from the concentration camp, and maybe he protected me, because he felt morally obligated to do so, to protect and be nice to all women, since the women in his life had been killed? Yes, we were friends, that I believed, and yes, he had flirted, but maybe he was flirty to every female? No, I could not make sense of him or men altogether and their sick gluttonous desire to have their cake and pie and cookies and every other dish in the universe.

Finding out his unavailability for marriage was due to a common explanation—he was a playboy—was as disappointing as a bad ending to a beloved story. I felt like I had taken an epical journey to a magical land only to arrive in Brooklyn; nothing wrong with Brooklyn but I was looking for Oz.

On a very cold night, he went out with his gym bag to play paddle ball, and he ordered, "You stay here. The Y is no place for a nun-in-training. A bunch of shirtless guys revved by sports adrenaline."

In his office, I watched his televised segment on the national news. He looked so handsome but so serious. Of course, the subject was serious: world peace. But he needed to let the star shine the way he did in class or else his superior intellect and last name, Blagonravov, would be too intimidating to the American public. Why should I care about the Casanova's future? Now he could add more women to his list, all the ones who watched him on television. Just let him have those "forty-niners," gold diggers; I did not care at all.

I looked at the mail stacked on his desk, probably love letters, or lust letters, from groupies.

I began slinging off every letter onto the floor. Then down went the books. "You creep!" Right when I was yanking a painting of Venus from the wall, Sputnik walked in.

"What in the world?" He was not happy, staring at the mess all over his floor.

"Ooh like your office was just so clean before, you pig." I picked up a jar of instant coffee and dumped despicable coffee beads all over that miserable beady couch. "How dare you make me write a common scene like this one."

"I oughta put you over my knee," he snarled, anger ruining the handsomeness of his face. "I'm going to show you how a nun gets disciplined." He demonstrated by swiftly paddling the air with the paddle board.

"You're despicable." I hurled letters at him, and due to my bad aim and his deflecting the projectiles with the paddle board, the letters all missed their target, so I chucked the plush toy at him. "I hate you!"

"I hate you" hurt him more than I had imagined or intended, but I was too angry to care about his feelings.

I picked up Mullybiski and Root and left.

"Where are you going?" Holding the bunny toy, he chased down the hall after me. "Have you gone bonkers?"

I got into the elevator, where I glared at Sputnik, warning him not to dare get on the elevator with me. The door closed on him saying, "What's the matter?"

Dropping to the bottom floor, my heart dropped too when I remembered Moon-Moon saying, "Every sentence of your lifestory is written in ink. Make sure to never write anything you'll regret because it can never be erased." I had said "I hate you" to the man I loved, which definitely did not make me suitable for guardian angelship. But he had said that despicable thing about how he planned to discipline a nun.

He could just keep on following me, which he did, right out to my car in the asphalt parking lot; I had no intention of turning back to him. I gently put Mullybiski and Root in the passenger seat then I stormed over to the driver's door.

"I take it you didn't like my segment on the news?"

That made me even angrier, his making a joke of the situation.

"I'm tired of your office!"

"You're so tired of my office, you hate me now?" He pretended as if the toy bunny asked that question.

"Now your office is freed up for whatever you want to do in there, you…you supernova!"

"That's not even an effective insult—it's The Lady Model of insults."

I tried to open the car door but Sputnik slammed his hand over it. "I'm not going to let you leave."

"Take your hand off the door."

He put his arms around me. "I'm never letting you go. I don't care if you hate me or not. You're my responsibility, by God."

"Let go of me, Sputnik."

Realizing he was playing the very creep he always tried to protect me from, he let go and stepped back with regret and shame in his expression.

I got into my car, slammed The Lady's door on him, and drove away as quickly as possible. I could not wait for four years to pass so I could join the convent and get away from him and romance altogether.

For the rest of the week, I hardly said a thing to him. I did not answer the phone or the door for him. I could not stop him from coming to the patisserie, but when he was there, I pretended to be busy.

"You're not going to tell me what's wrong?" he kept asking.

I could not bear to have the conversation where he confirmed he had other women and listen to his tired male lines that *I* was special to him, though; I had observed that common story all too often in Igtord, and my character was not going to participate in such triteness.

On the bridge over the waterfall, I passed him one cloudy cold afternoon. In mist, he walked with gorgeous Madame French Professor.

"Hi, Ms.--," he said.

I said not a word, only nodded. I saw her glare at me, "the competition."

I heard him tell his female companion, "She's a student in my introductory algebra class."

Introductory algebra.

He was so aloof and cruel. I wanted to jump off the bridge and plunge into icy water, where I wished I had died as a child. I had come back from Heaven to meet this creep? What a fool I had been!

On another misty morning, he pulled up outside the patisserie in a candy-apple-red sports car, which really irked me.

"Don't tell me you got rid of Sputnik." I frowned, sad and angry about him living up to his playboy image in that vulgar car.

"I didn't get rid of him. I just wanted to play around with something faster, so I went to the dealership last night."

Play around with something faster. That made me sick.

"I'm surprised you didn't tell me you got a new car on the phone last night." We had talked briefly over the phone; he had just wanted to know "baby sister" was safe inside, while he was out cattin' around with a pantheress.

"I didn't think you'd approve, Peppermint, and didn't want you to talk me out of it, but perhaps you don't care now that you hate me. There's this road up in Canada where the speed limit can be broken—without fear of tickets. I'm talking 120, 130 miles per hour."

"Driving that fast sounds like an unnecessary risk," I warned, "especially getting so close to icy weather."

"A risk for you, not for me."

"And any woman who wants you to drive fast to impress her is not a good friend, just like any woman who only wants a man who drives a cool car, just like any woman who wants a man just because he was on television."

He made a face that I couldn't read. "Why have a 'Vette if you only plan to drive the speed limit?"

Did his ego hide the fact he valued his life so little? Did he want to die? Had he barnstormed all those years in hopes to have a crash?

"Have you tried out the new car's speed yet?" With a female passenger? But I didn't ask that.

"No, I'm waiting until the streets are solid ice then I'll find out what it's like to drive on Pluto."

Maybe his Floozy Tuesdays thought that was cute, but I did not; his safety was serious to me, which irked me too, that I cared for him so intensely. I could not just drive away from my feelings for him.

The next couple of passages were written the same: coffee, class, me wondering how many women he had, him wondering why his peppermint was being so cold.

One day at the patisserie he told me, "Can you believe the BBC—the British Broadcasting Corporation—wants to interview me?"

"That doesn't surprise me. You have a legion of adoring female fans that are just waiting by the TV to see you again."

He laughed, thinking I was kidding.

During baseball playoffs, he was too obsessed with the Dodgers to notice my cold-shoulder. One morning he came to the sweet shop and said, "Did you see what Sandy did?"

"Sandy? Who's she?"

"*He's* pitcher for the Dodgers. He didn't play game 1 of the World Series because it fell on Yom Kippur. That's a man." Whenever Sputnik saw another man being noble, it reminded him of who he aspired to be. Well, I seethed, let his floozies worry about his future; it was no longer my concern.

On another cold morning, the young professor staggered in, looking sleepy and disheveled, and my heart cried privately, fearing a woman had tired him out, but he said, "Saturn kept me up all night. I stayed up looking at her, wondering how to reach her and her ring to give to you— perhaps then you would no longer hate me?"

I noticed his right hand was poorly bandaged in a washrag held together by safety pins.

"What happened?" I asked, wanting to reach out to his hurt hand, which confirmed I had never stopped loving him, which I knew already just from the way my heart ached every night. Some nights, when I was too tired to "throw myself into" my studies or other thoughts to avoid thinking of him, my heart would cry from torturous images of him speeding around curves at 130 miles per hour—I knew if his car slipped over the edge, my will-to-live would too, for I had no desire to be in this story without him.

"Just a minor accident trying to make hot coffee with that pan you got me. I only covered the damage to prevent your eyes from seeing the gore."

I had a vision of the mathematician standing by the burner, thinking of anything but coffee, and the brew bubbling out everywhere.

"Did you go to the doctor?"

"No, it's not too bad."

"Let me see."

"It's fine," he said, sternly.

"No, it's not," I said, sternly-er.

He seemed surprised I pushed past his sternness. I had to let him know he would never grouch me out of caringness, especially toward him, or was I letting myself know that?

"You don't want to look at it," he grumped, as I started to remove the bandage.

Unwrapping the rag from his beautiful hand, hurt by the burn of despicable coffee, I said, "Ooh, your poor hand. Hot cocoa would have never done that to you."

My sweet boy was hurt. I had pledged to stand by him no matter what, yet I had left him stranded on his iceberg after only one icy wind known as jealousy had chilled me. I thought of how he had told me about his being interviewed by the BBC. He had no one else to tell. He did not have a mother or grandmother or any woman in his life to be proud of him; he just had a lot of women who wanted to take advantage of his success. I felt bad for having responded to his achievement so flippantly. I could not shun him; that was not my character. He and I were friends, the only friend for each of us, at least the only *human* one for each of us. Okay, he had Mr. Benny too. But he and I were best friends. I cared deeply for his heart and soul as if they were my own. Plus, his friendship was the greatest treasure in my life, and it brought me more than enough happiness. He had suffered so much, if those other women made him feel better for a moment, I would not interfere with whatever fleeting warmth he found in them. If I was not the girl who made him see stars in daytime then I was not the one. I was his Sunday girl, the girl he visited like church to restore his belief in goodness, and I would not take that role lightly. This man truly needed a guardian angel. How many guardian angels, I wondered, fell in love with the mortal they guarded, yet with nobility, guided the one they loved to be with another? I would not add any more gloomy words into his story which had already been gloomy enough. I had always wanted to write sweet pink lines in his gray life and that was what I was going to do. Write thus!

Against his protests, I went upstairs to get a first aid kit. With a Q-tip, I applied petroleum jelly to his blistered skin, while pampering, "Now this hand can go back to writing brilliant equations on the blackboard." I wrapped his injury in gauze, while the wilderness man gruffed that I was making a big deal out of nothing.

"*Girls.*"

Even though my hand was gloved, I let my hand linger too long on his, for two hands not betrothed, so I quickly finished bandaging his injury.

"Lumi, you can hate me, that's fine. I'm not exactly loveable, and I've always said I don't deserve your love. But I've been worried about you, angel. When you don't talk to your Sputnik at all, he goes bonkers."

I had the horrible feeling Sputnik had bought the fast car and told me of his plans to go 130 miles per hour to see if I still cared about him, but hopefully he had not burned his hand to test my caring.

"Do you know the only thing that keeps me going, Pep?"

"Baseball season?"

"I'm being serious. The only thing that stops me from driving off a cliff is the promise I made to you to build the biggest snowflake."

"Sputnik, don't say things like that. You're a great man—"

"Sssh. I'm nothing of the sort. I play around with spaceship designs and I tinker with numbers. All that matters to me is making that snowflake for you. All those late nights, I was working on it for you. Now tell me what's wrong? What did I do? Why did you run out of my office—out of my life? I don't deserve an angel in my story, but I thought you were my friend? You don't even wear my jacket anymore. You dumped so many coffee beads on my couch, the cushions could be turned into coffee houses."

"I was just tired of being in your office."

He knew I was not being completely honest, but he didn't pry. I had accepted his emotional outburst during the war flashback, and he accepted my emotional outburst, because friends stood by each other even when, or especially when, one wobbled on life's unsteadiness.

He went out to his car and brought back the plush bunny toy.

"You let a toy ride in the passenger seat of your Corvette?"

He shrugged.

"I thought he was allergic to every place but your office?"

"He's willing to suffer through his allergies to be with you."

"I know you won't accept this description, Sputnik, but you're a very sweet fellow...except when you're bossy. No more of that, Sput, I mean it."

He got in a better mood and I didn't know if it was because of our friendship resuming or the Dodgers winning the World Series.

He came to the sweet shop one softly rainy morning that made me yearn to be cuddled in bed with him and his hairy chest. I wondered if his other women realized how fortunate they were to experience a Gershom the nun would never be able to know.

After his usual coffee, he handed me a napkin with an address on it: 9 Mulberry Way, turn right on Peppermint Lane.

Peppermint Lane?

"Please meet me there after your classes, Pep, hoping the rain lets up. At the intersection of nowhere and nowhere."

After class and rain, I drove a long damp distance, farther than I had ever driven in Biskatine, where the sound of civilization got softer and softer until it was mute. I heard the familiar voices of trees, which I had missed. I felt I had driven back in time to an era before humans had plowed every patch of Earth.

My destination's scenery was not breathtaking but breathgiving; if one was on her last breath and saw this landscape, she would make it so to have more breaths, to delay her trip to Heaven to frolic even for a moment in this heaven on Earth:

Rolling hills,

creamy meadows,

distant snow-topped mountains reminiscent of the Swiss Alps,

grass green enough to be clovers,

trees wearing their autumn colors, pumpkin-orange clusters of trees,

red and purple berry bushes as dazzling as Christmas ornaments,

a barn the color of a holly berry,

a pond as shiny as glaze and as breathtaking as sea but as calm as lake,

all glistening in the softness of autumn sun after rain and hugged by pines and maples and cedars in a woodland that stretched farther than my eyes could see, landscape for a drawing on a maple syrup's bottle, a scene that whispered, "Home."

"Stand still in wonder of God's works."

Part of the expansive acreage (its tallest tree-sprinkled and gumball-adorned plateaus) was level with the roadside, but most of

369

the land was nestled in valleys, and the pond was almost ensconced by hills.

Off the main road was a thin pebble driveway, "Peppermint Lane," written on a wooden arrow sign (the arrow of Cupid). The lane was covered in pine needles and lined in a simple Valentine's-red wooden fence and gated by barn doors, of the same color, between two stone columns fit for the Middle Ages. "9 Mulberry Way" was painted on a breadbox-shaped silver mailbox. "Stargust Continued" was etched in Old English script in a wooden semi-circle, the same Valentine's color, arched above the open wooden gates, as if "Stargust Continued" was a landmark. Seeing "Stargust" tingled my heart so much, I thought I was in a dream, because everyday locations did not tingle my heart chambers.

Entering these gates was like entering the pearly gates of Heavenly eternity.

Peppermint Lane sloped down to emerald pastures like a waterslide but not nearly as steep, and ooh, this was a smooth passage… driving across the long soft dirt road, lined on both sides in ancient stones about as tall as my knees, the stones layered in yellow leaves, and this brought visions to my mind of cows and sheep roaming in old country.

My heart was in love with this land at first sight, and I feared driving farther into it, afraid I'd be too sad to ever depart.

The dirt road and stone fence ended at grassy valley, where shined an aluminum camper on acres of solitude. The camper was camped on wide open grassland, skirted in trees that looked like brown and green smears with triangle tops and edges, the way distant trees looked in drawings; the yard's adornment was an apple tree. The only thing unsightly on the land was the power pole and its electric wires like spider web in the sky.

In green grass, Sputnik's red car looked like it had fallen from the apple tree. By the camper's door, the professor stood, dressed in a suit more suitable for an office than for nature.

"Why are we here?" I asked, while approaching him, my breath frosty in cold air, my arms huddled around my chest, my high heels crunching leaves, my coat and stockings not offering much protection from New England coldness. I took a deep breath; rainstorms always intensified the scent of countryside: grass and bark and dirt and wild berries, chilled but fresh.

"Because this is now yours, Peppermint." He seemed as satisfied as Santa Claus offering a miraculous gift.

"This?" I looked around—what did he mean?

"All of this, the whole two hundred acres, on loan from Earth for the entirety of your long, long life, to be the setting of your lifestory, and all the land asks in return is to be treated respectfully and with care, so you're more a caretaker than an owner."

Two hundred acres? I must have looked completely lost, not knowing my way around such compassion.

"I bought it," he said to help clarify my confusion. "Isn't that preposterous? Parts of Earth being for sale? Well, I bought it anyway, the camper and the land. For you. I thought this was better than fixing the chateau de dumpiness's flooring. Now, I don't want you too reliant on the city and its greed, so the plumbing is hooked to a well with water supplied by Earth, and the septic's installed, but unfortunately the camper's connected to the electric company, until I get this thing running on electricity supplied by wind power. I know it's not the Stargust meadow where you grew up, but you might catch a few gusts of stars here. I can see a shooting star landing right there." He tapped his foot beside my foot and grinned.

I was too flabbergasted to speak.

"I've been looking for the perfect place, Pep. It had to be just right, or else I would've gotten you out of the filth motel sooner. I made that sign above the gate, 'Stargust Continued.' You can change the name if you want. To Camelot, perhaps? I made up Peppermint

Lane, as well, which is not recognized as the 'real name' by the city but can be by you and me."

Still too flabbergasted to respond.

"You see that clear wide unobstructed sky—your old friend the moon will appear right beside you at night. I know you, you'll enchant deer into the meadow and feed them by hand. And in springtime, there will be so many flowers for you and your camera to admire and to backdrop your afternoon tea. And look at all those windows. Those big wrap-around windows in back are in the bedroom, so you can sleep next to the moon. You won't even have to leave your cabin for a view of nature. You can sit at your typewriter, take in all the exquisite scenery and preserve it on paper for everyone else to see too for forever."

I felt like a girl whose boyfriend had told her he would rope the moon for her then one night he actually did it. Before I could appreciate the glorious gift, I had to contend with my astonishment.

"The barn's included?"

"Yup, but it's not structurally sound at the moment, so you'll have to let me fix it before you can go in it and make it a home for cows or pigs or horses or whoever you wish. You could easily invite ten cows over on this kind of acreage; on this size land, you might even be able to invite those stars you wanted to meet in childhood over for a tea party." He winked.

I was still too astonished to even utter, "Thank you."

"The pond's included too?"

"Yup."

"It's so big! It's like Thoreau's Walden Pond!"

"It's not exactly that big. It's about five acres. I'll line part of it with stones, if you like, and give it more a fairy tale look."

"You lined all those stones along the driveway?"

He nodded, "no big deal."

"That must have taken you forever!"

"I haven't aged to forever. Just a few days. Me and Ben and a lantern and a rented pickup truck late at night, during those times a certain young Lady was giving me the cold shoulder." He was perplexed by my former aloof attitude, but he wasn't angered by it. "The butterscotch nut made the Cupid sign. Ben said, 'You got all this for the cookie who calls you 'Sputnik'?' Yup, my little rare peppermint cookie."

Sputnik's mind went back to the pond and his plans. "I'll build a gazebo and I'll put a big stone out in the water and steps of small flat stones leading outward to it, so you can sit in the pond with a poetry book without even having to worry about getting your lilac Lady dress damp. You and Thoreau on the pond. Here," he said, asking me to take a long walk with him to the pond's pebbled and barely grassy edge. "Fish, turtles, algae, salamanders, muskrat, lots of life here."

I watched a hefty orange and black fish swim by, Charley, I'd call him. I thought of how delightful it would be to sit in a wicker chair by the pond's edge in the morning and feed the fish, dozens of them swimming to greet breakfast. I'd sip tea and watch fish and feel as relaxed as a tree.

"And there's a nice stream in the woods, perhaps some bears too, coyote, bobcats, so be careful, this is wilderness. But don't worry, I've been out here a few weeks now, at all hours, making sure everything was set to go, and I think all the grizzly types stay in the woods and avoid the girly meadows. I've never seen anything less gentle than a moose in the yard."

"An actual moose?"

"We're not too far from Canada, you know. Now, moose don't hibernate so you have the possibility of seeing them all winter. You might wake up one morning and see one right at your window.

I've had that kind of morning in Alaska. I have to say it's sort of a magical type of experience."

"Like the reindeer experience?"

"This is really going to make your girly heart squeal with glee: reindeer live around here." His heart sounded like it wanted to gleefully squeal too.

"Sput, I … we … The Snowflake Physicist and I could turn this into a snow globe of a Christmastime scene: reindeer and moose and snowy trees…"

"Sure, whatever you want, angel."

"We wouldn't force any reindeer or moose to live here, of course, but they'd be free to come visit anytime."

"Well, moose are fairly large beasts, not too aggressive, but highly cranky on icy days, so I wouldn't approach one. Just sort of let him do his moose stuff and pass on by."

"I'm cranky on icy days too."

"And the females can be extremely protective of their young."

"Of course, I understand that!"

I looked around paradise, where a lovely bluebird flew by.

"All those hills, all those trees, they're included too?"

"Yup, a whole world of trees awaiting your friendship. Here," he said, asking me to walk with him back to the camper. "Take a gander at that: an apple tree like the ones from your girlhood, an apple tree right outside your door for you to greet every morning, and when she's feeling generous, she'll share her apples for you to turn into apple pie."

"Nature never did betray the heart that loved her," said Wordsworth.

"He's beautiful," I said of the tree, but Sputnik already saw the tree as a she. "He's a Golden Delicious. Just wait 'til spring when he shows off pale pink petals."

"That's why he's a she."

I went over to the tree, introduced myself, hoped for a friendly relationship; he or she was ready for the harvest.

"The realtor said there's also a Gravenstein tree somewhere out here. Does that mean anything to you?"

"Ooh my, yes, Gravensteins are delicious apples and perfect for apple cider, applesauce..." I listed many delicious apple desserts. "I could plant tomatoes and eggplants and peppers for the lover of hot foods."

"Supposedly blueberry and raspberry bushes are plentiful as well. If not, I'm getting my money back."

"This land of berries is a pastry chef's heaven!"

"Well, Ben and I had a time of it, trying to find all these different types of trees, had some encounters with thorns too."

"I can't wait to go exploring!"

"Our land of milk and honey," the scientist said, alluding to The Bible, but I was warmed by his use of the word "our"—*our* land.

We walked farther away from the camper towards woodland, a good long walk, where fresh air seemed to help Sputnik's cough. We didn't talk in words but in smiles.

"And here," he said, showing me a golden-yellow-leafed pecan tree for picking fresh pecans for making sweet potato pie with cinnamon streusel and pecan topping. "But you shouldn't go too far in the woods by yourself. I don't know if there really are bears here or not, but just to be safe—only go hiking with your Alaskan wilderness guide."

"Sput, my daydreams are becoming very Anne of Green Gables-like: a cottage, meadows, wildflowers, blueberry picking, morning tea in a flower garden, cream tea by the shimmering pond…"

I would never want to depart life if this was life's setting, indistinguishable from Heaven!

"Would you like me to help you construct a flower garden?" he asked. "I'm worthless at doing the actual gardening, but I could put up some trellises, an arbor, perhaps…"

After fully realizing and accepting the paradise was mine, I was able to say, "Thank you."

"Sput, this land is truly as beautiful as Green Gables, but how can you afford this?"

"How can I not afford this? If I hadn't gotten it, I'd never sleep again, endless nights sleeping in my car outside the patisserie. Now, I did a lot of research. As far as I could find, no crimes have ever been committed out here. Nowhere on Earth is completely safe, but this is fairly close to safe. Besides, I have nothing worthwhile to spend my salary on, and I've saved a lot over the years, Pep. It was either this or a lifetime supply of pizza from Hank's. Please let me spend my money on kindness, sweet Lady."

I was filled with teardrops, not in my eyes but all inside me, so touched by his generosity.

"Professor Blagonravov—"

"Professor Blagonravov did not get this for you. The professor is only concerned with teaching mathematics to Ms.---. Gershom—Sputnik—got this for his little Peppermint. The deed's in your name."

"It should be in *our* name." I felt embarrassed after suggesting we own land together like a married couple.

"I have the deed to a sleeping bag, that's all I need. Now, as this property's landlord, I do have one policy the tenant must adhere to: she cannot leave to work until the sun is out and the streets are busy."

"I'll get fired."

"Exactly," his expression said.

"I won't have money even for food or lights or meals for the reindeer."

"Reindeer eat grass, shrubs, meals from nature. Don't worry, I'll pay for everything. You just write and study."

Some moments with him touched me so deeply, I was reminded how deep the depths of my being went.

"Why are you doing all this for me?" I asked, as one of the tears inside found its way down my cheek. His thumb softly rubbed the tear, again and again, until it went away.

"I could never hate you, Sputnik. I never meant that. I love you so deeply, Gersh, with a love that has expanded love's definition—I never knew anything could feel this way—and I can't trace the root of the love's origin as if the love has always been, as if our love is older than ancient."

"Come, let's move you out of that filth motel."

Cream Cocoa

A lifestory set in Stargust Continued was as dreamy, if not dreamier, than I had pictured, complete with frame of sunshine in daytime, starshine in nighttime...

Bird chirp alarm clocks...

Waking up snuggled in bed in a cherry wood room...

The scene beyond the rounded wrap-around windows too nighttime to see the birds saying "Good morning" with their chirps...

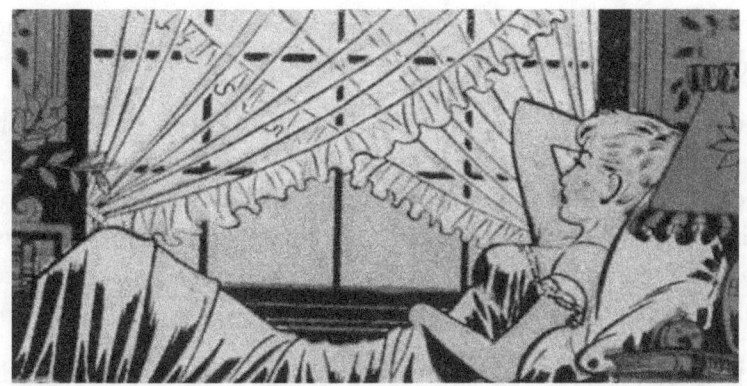

Lingering in white lace and soft linen and creating stories to be written and savoring the cocoa scent of burning candles and admiring the music boxes on the bookshelf headboard and not missing the cutthroat car race known as making money (speeding around and around to "get ahead" in an endless loop) but instead daydreaming of love until sunlight tapped my shoulder, asking me to open gauzy curtains and see blue and red and brown birds turning the scenery outside my bedroom windows into moving sketches from Audubon's *The Birds of America...*

Quiet morning showers (although there was never enough hot water in the small camper for leisure showers)…

Listening to music, songs like *I'm Getting Sentimental Over You*, while leisurely creating breakfast in the tiny cute kitchen with red-checkered flooring and booths the color of peppermints, a rock-n-roll diner kitchen with a red Formica table rimmed in aluminum and a red-curtained window above the table that overlooked Deer Hill…

Admiring the morning pond and its dawnlit water shimmering like grapefruit juice, where half the rising sun reflected and appeared as the yolk of a sunny side up…

Peaceful strolls with Mullybiski, who Sputnik had purchased a baby stroller for, so I could take my good buddy out farther on the land than his old legs would allow, and he would lift his stubbed pug sniffer to take in scents of countryside…

Early mornings bringing breakfast of fish flakes to turtle and fish neighbors, including orange Charley, who began to eagerly greet me at the dawn-lighted pond…

Slowly making friends with one cranky beaver…

Taking pictures at a distance of an even crankier moose…

Preparing a garden which would require much work but a fulfilling kind of peaceful work, tending the lettuce and carrots and tomatoes in a special section of land Sputnik would mark off with picket fence and trellises and an arch-shaped arbor (romantic enough to frame a bride and groom on their wedding day)…

Gathering new household items and filling the camper's built-in wardrobe with girly clothing like a jelly-bean-pink pill box hat and daffodil-yellow Peter Pan collar dress…

Long scenic drives to school and not being rattled by the noisy crowds of college or anywhere else for I knew waiting for me was tranquil paradise...

"Cream cocoa" and studying by the white-as-sunlight afternoon pond, which on bright days became a mirror reflecting puffy friendly non-sinister clouds and marsh ferns and Christmas-looking trees...

Carving homegrown pumpkins on foggy Halloween night with Sputnik, and watching Alvin and the Chipmunks in the "Haunted House," and dining on breakfast for dinner: jack-o-lantern pancakes, "headstone" hashbrowns, and blood (cranberry juice!)...

Relishing jazz and chocolates for breakfast by the pond on Sweetest Day (a holiday fully celebrated in Chocolate Town) and especially delighting in the strawberry cream on a morning as pink as strawberry mousse, and donating boxes of candies to a rest home to show the true spirit of the sweet holiday…

Typing stories on my typewriter that sat atop the Formica table, framed by window of storybook scenes, where one morning I viewed a whitetail doe on Deer Hill get greeted by her buck then the two of them strolled off together to do what does and bucks do…

Praying on a star-caressed hill where I felt closer to Heaven…

Never had writing this story felt so pleasant!

All thanks to one beautiful man who would not allow me to thank him the way I wished: by loving him completely as his wife.

Since Stargust Continued came into our story, Sputnik and I had been spending even more time with each other in this setting, almost daily encounters. Any free time the professor had, which was not much, was spent here (mostly early mornings, sometimes afternoons); the Alaskan boy loved this land of moose and being its caretaker.

We celebrated Sputnik's birthday with succotash and cornbread casserole and sweet southern tea and a buttercream cake shaped like a UFO. After dinner, we went to a showing of *Dr. Who and the Daleks*. Then we opened Sput's gifts from me: Cootie the game, and a handmade tie decorated with subtle stars and planets, which he eventually wore on a TV interview. His gifts from Mr. Benny were a model spaceship and a bag of licorice bubble gum. His gift from Brad was a print of an almost nude blonde gal, lounging on another planet.

"Who is that?" I blurted out, unable to hide my jealousy.

"Mara Gold, a character from one of my favorite boyhood comic books."

"Isn't that cute—Mara Gold like the marigold flower."

"Ah, come on, it's just a silly gift between guys. What would you expect from Brad? Don't put any thought into it. I prefer the Cooties."

I had given up trying to understand why he was unavailable for love. Most likely he was eternally betrothed in heart to a girl he never got to wed.

To keep the arrangement from being improper, he always came over under the guise of needing to fix something or to give me fabric for dresses or money for groceries or clothes or anything I wanted. But I knew he visited the camper almost every morning not just to pay the bills or do handyman tasks, such as "fixing" the hot water heater (even when there was not a thing wrong with it), but to check on "baby sister." On those autumn pre-dawns, when the sky had a fiery coal look and he came over with his toolbox, I made him black coffee and plain oatmeal (his preference). With cups of coffee and cocoa, we'd sometimes stroll Stargust Continued, hoping to see reindeer in morning dew, or we'd take our coffee and cocoa by the pink-hued morning pond and savor the natural scent of water and fish.

On a morning as golden as Moon-Moon's harp, Sputnik asked if I would "do him the honor" of playing the harp for him outdoors in dawn light, so he carried the wooden instrument to the pond's edge, where I strummed *Amazing Grace* and sang:

Amazing grace (how sweet the sound)
That saved a wretch like me.
I once was lost, but now am found,
Was blind, but now I see.

Sitting in grass on "our land of milk and honey," Gershom watched the musical scene like a sinner viewing a scene from Heaven, then as if overcome with guilt for being there, he left quickly, saying he had to get to the university.

On very rare mornings when he was exhausted or out of town, he didn't come over but checked on me through the phone instead, on the phone and line he had suffered the hassle of getting installed in the camper. Even though he thought the pink Princess phone was girly (it sat on my bookshelf headboard), he had concluded it was not ornate enough, so he had purchased yet another phone, an old-fashioned wooded rotary phone with brass adornments. But he had worried that phone was too "ship captain masculine," although I had assured the sensitive boy whose mother had not liked the shirt he had picked out for her that I thought the phone beautiful.

Usually on those days, if he was in town, he would come over in the afternoon, ashamed of himself for having let tiredness prevent him from protecting me. I would delight in simply making us lunch. I had found tasty recipes for a variety of sandwiches: grilled corn, grilled vegetable, spicy chutney, and sabich, an Israeli pita sandwich. And I'd pair the sandwiches with salads, such as potato or Asian or Greek cucumber salad, although I suspected Sputnik preferred potato chips with sandwiches even though he would not admit it. I'd serve hot tea. "That's the Lady-est drink of all," he'd grump, while "stomaching" the feminine drink and never allowing me to add cream or sugar to his cup. After lunch, he would walk the grounds and sketch plans in his notepad of all the additions he wanted to build on the land like a waterfall in the pond, which looked very elaborate in sketch form, and I never understood how he had time to do all his work.

One of his first handyman tasks (day one) had been creating a multi-locks system for the camper's door.

On another day, he had framed the camper in a picket fence "to keep out bears."

"Ooh, but it'll keep out reindeer and moose too."

But there had been no arguing with Sputnik against building the fence. He had allowed enough space for me to play fetch with Mullybiski. He had expanded Peppermint Lane to reach the fence's gate. On this afternoon, I had gone with Sputnik to release Ms. Sophie Frog and Pythagoras back into the wild, and while the frog had hopped away in Stargust Continued woodland, Pythagoras had stayed next to Sputnik. "He likes you," I had said, convincing Sputnik to let the turtle continue to live with him, but Sputnik decided Pythagoras was better off in my care, so the turtle became my and Mullybiski's roommate.

Sputnik had also done remodeling work on the *brand-new* camper: adding prettier windows; taking out hard linoleum flooring, except in the red-checkered kitchen, and laying soft carpet the color of Hollywood red carpet; removing the curtain over the tiny bedroom and putting up a wall and door, since a curtain covering a bedroom was fine for a camping bachelor but not for a single girl; putting up red awnings over the outside door and windows to give the camper a homey feel; adding wooden boxes beneath the windows for growing flowers, window boxes I had used at Halloween to display two jack-o-lanterns that he had carved (one as a standard jack, another as a Martian); and installing the bookshelf headboard, so I could easily reach a book to read at night and display my music boxes but making sure the headboard was not too tall to prevent me from seeing out the window. Even though I knew he considered dusting and polishing strictly woman's work, he had meticulously polished each music treasure chest. Surrounded by stars shining in through wrap-around open windows, where scents of autumn forest came in, the shining music boxes had sounded heavenly that night, and the image of him sitting on the bridal white bedspread, while polishing the music boxes, had felt heavenly too. One of the lacy-curtained windows had remained closed, the window where I had sandwiched the 5x7 print of *The Wanderer Above the Sea of Fog*, so I had drifted to sleep that night in Sputnik's jacket, while gazing at The Wanderer and staying on the phone with him, listening to the quietness of his thinkpad apartment, quiet aside from his coughing.

Sputnik had done much of the remodeling work on the camper on one Saturday afternoon, after coming over with a flat trailer hitched to his Corvette, the trailer piled with lumber and a carpet roll, and he had told me to go to the movies since there was no reason for me to smell sawdust too. He had been grouchy, not at me but at "that lazy butterscotch nut" for not helping. When I had returned from *Five Weeks in a Balloon*, he had looked quite handsome against a cinnamon sunset, sweating in autumn, wearing his familiar baseball cap and T-shirt. After doing the last minor detail, painting the window boxes wagon-red, all he had wanted in return had been a glass of tap water. Men put much effort into enlarging their bank accounts and muscles and another part of their anatomy, but if they wanted to impress Ladies, all they needed to do was enlarge their valor, kindness, respectfulness and tenderness toward women. After all that work, the scientist had gone to his office to work on rocket blueprints for humankind's future! Yes, I was in love with him.

He had asked if I didn't mind if he parked Sputnik the Car on the land; of course, I had not objected—having his car in the yard made me feel he was my husband.

Sputnik fixed the barn over many long November afternoons. He ate childhood PBJs and drank adult coffee in his faithful thermos. One almost-summertime-sunny afternoon, I made him two grilled cheeses with pickles and mustard and sauteed peppers, tater tots, and a strawberry milkshake. Tater tots and mustard were not so romantic, but I knew the barnstormer would like diner food. Ooh, I delighted in imagining all the forms, subtle or overt, to express "I love you." If he had felt my kisses in the sweet potato pie, maybe he would taste "I love you" in the strawberry milkshake since I had put my love into the sweet drink as an ingredient.

Even though he would not ask me this, I could not stop picturing the "one fine day" he'd want me as his girl.

Sitting on his blue-jeaned rump by the barn door and sweating from mid-day sun and hard work, his damp T-shirt almost transparent and showcasing the structure of his chest, he asked, "Where's your lunch?"

"I made the big manly sandwiches for you, sir." I set the food tray on pebbly dirt beside his toolbox. "I'll just have one or two of the tater fritters."

I had spent the morning making strawberry ice cream with handpicked strawberries, thanks to a few ever-bearing plants. I had spent the afternoon with my camera, snapping photos of Sput working on the barn. I often took his picture, which he claimed was "a waste of film."

Standing beside him and accepting an offered fried potato, I said, "The milkshake is made with homemade ice cream."

"Lumi, my goodness." He always said that anytime he felt embarrassed about my girlish adoration. I doubted a boy could ever realize how much a girl could admire a man, and I doubted a girl who only liked, lusted, or settled for a man could realize that either. But I knew that admiration was a necessary ingredient for a high-quality romance, along with admiration's offspring: trust, attraction, and longing to please the one admired. I admired Sputnik even more than I admired heroic men from history. When I saw the numbers tattooed on his unbreakable strength, my heart swelled with so much reverence for his courage, it was a new kind of heart, capable of the biggest love. But I had become dreadfully obsessed with his time in the concentration camp; I could not stop torturous images from plaguing me. How could anyone have hurt my sweet fellow? Each time I thought of this, I cried. I knew he would be disappointed in me for thinking of these horrific things; he always seemed disappointed in me when he caught me looking at the ghastly numbers on his arm. But I had a deep urge to swaddle him in love, although he would not let me do that, so I had to settle for making him a milkshake.

With camera still around my neck, I snapped his photo.

"I told you, Pep, you make too much fuss over me." He dipped a tater tot into the milkshake. "Are the potato tots homemade too?"

"Of course!"

"Frozen food mania hasn't taken its hold of you?"

"I've eaten a frozen dinner, but I wouldn't make that for my hero, someone who has done all this hard work."

He rolled his eyes instead of arguing with my girlish insistence he was a hero.

"Would you like some more ketchup?"

"No, this is fine," he said, wolfing the food down, impatient to get back to work. "You don't have to doll up my food."

"What do you mean?"

"I mean like arranging those strawberry slices like a flower atop the milkshake."

"Ooh, does it embarrass you? I wouldn't have put the flower on top if Ben or your math colleagues were over here. It's just between you and me."

"Well, yeah, it would embarrass me if Ben was over here, and look at these plates."

"What's wrong with them?"

"I'm out here in dirt, fixing a barn, and you serve me lunch on these delicate thin things all dolled up in drawings of roses. Did my money buy these?"

"You told me I could buy what I wanted. And those are not roses, they're Persian buttercups."

He laughed like I had tickled him. "Fine. Persian buttercups. I just don't deserve all this … gushiness. I'm just a simple boy from the outback. You don't have to get so fancy with my food."

"Okay, next time I'll serve you cornmeal in a metal pail and you can pour some water from the hose over it and have cold grits, you … you snapdragon."

"You're gonna have to work on those insults if you want them to be effective." He looked up at me and grinned to say sorry for being a grouch.

"How's the sandwich? It's not too dolled up, is it? I remembered how you said you liked cheddar cheese."

"It's fine."

"Spicy enough?"

"It's fine."

"Sputnik, it means a lot to me to know exactly how you like your food prepared."

"Is that something you learned from one of those 'How to be a Good Wife' quizzes?"

"Tell me, is the sandwich too spicy, or not spicy enough?"

He handed me another fried potato. "It's just right in spiciness."

"But?"

"A cheese melt should have thin crispier bread."

"Is that some kind of New York thing like thin crust pizza?"

"I don't know about that, but I know a cheese melt shouldn't have peppers and pickles *on* it; slices of jalapenos and pickles should be served *with* it. And I don't think *red* peppers work at all. And potato tots are not right for this meal; old-fashioned potato logs with mustard, not ketchup, and mac-n-cheese would do much better as side dishes."

"Well, you definitely had quite an opinion for someone who said plain oats would suffice."

"You asked."

I wasn't really mad; I was glad Sputnik was considering what he truly liked, since he was so out of touch with his own feelings.

"Is the milkshake to your liking, sir?"

"It's fine."

"But?"

"A *vanilla* milkshake goes better with a cheese melt and jalapenos."

"I'm bothering you with all these questions? Me and my girly dishes will just leave you alone then."

"I just don't approve of the big fuss you're always making over me."

"Making a strawberry milkshake is hardly a good enough thank you for all you've done."

"All I've done is a patch job on an old barn." He was not being faux modest; he had worked hard all his life and had spent his entire savings to buy me this fairy tale paradise to keep the Lady from having to be a character in the world's gray story, yet he did not see his generosity as incredible. No task done for him would ever be too small for me, not even making him a milkshake, and no task would ever be too large.

"I just want to make your moments, at least with me, very pretty, Sputnik."

"Yeah, I know, but what right have I to pretty passages?"

I softly brushed dirt out of his beautiful hair, while wishing I could give him a bath as his wife, not a desire aroused by lust but by admiration—when I thought of him as a hero, my feelings were never adulterated by lust.

"Lumi, my goodness. I just told you you're too gushy about me and now you've got your fingers in my hair."

"Okay, I'm sorry. I'll come back when you're not so cranky."

"No, wait. No one with legs like yours could ever be a bother to me." With the softness he used to touch a flower, he cupped my bare calf, and my legs blushed from the touch. "Here, sit down."

He laid down his crinkled button shirt, which had been wadded in the grass.

On the shirt blanket, I sat by him, sort of sidesaddle-like in my autumn-colored dress with a pretty ruffle pattern down the front center that was inlaid with ornate buttons that I hoped he liked.

"Seriously, you're not bothering me at all, Peppermint."

"I should have made you a peppermint milkshake."

"There's always tomorrow."

"Okaaay."

"I bet if we were an old married couple, I'd no longer get the girlish 'Okaaaay's' about everything I wanted."

"That's not fair. Men often critique women for not living up to picture perfect wives once they've 'trapped' their man, but men break many of the promises they made before marriage too like 'Dear, I'll never look at another girl,' but by day one of the honeymoon, they're already eying the hotel maid."

Sputnik laughed.

"It's men that ask women for marriage, not the other way around, so if you men feel so trapped by marriage, stop asking us to marry you and making us believe 'You'll make me the happiest man in the world if you'll just be my wife.' Plus, we girls are taught all our lives by men how being a wife is the noblest profession for a woman, but once we set out to achieve that goal, we're told it's silly, that we're conniving, out to trap some poor man's freedom and hang it on a coat rack, while we pilfer his wallet. Well, you just go ahead and create the world where you're no longer the apple of a girl's eye, or her hero, and she could care two figs about silly romance or tending you or rooting you on in your sports games, and tell me if you like that world, where all femininity has been so shamed, it never shows its dolled up face again, and everyone is masculine masculine masculine."

391

"That's not the world I want to create."

"Then stop making fun of me when I buy plates adorned in drawings of Persian buttercups, because the more you do that, the more likely it is for fine china to go extinct, and once something is extinct, it's gone forever—you know that, Mr. Scientist."

"For the record, the last thing I want is for girls like you to go extinct. I'd prefer jerks like Ditwad to go extinct. And I wasn't making fun. I was gently teasing. Your girliness is fun to tease. Come on, it is."

"Maybe."

I played with a loose denim thread on the knee of his blue jeans, which I did not think improper since my hands were gloved. "I could mend this for you." Maybe other girls were tending to his needs that I knew nothing about, but he still needed a Lady to patch up his clothing's tears. I already tended his clothes' cleaning needs either through taking his suits to the dry cleaners or washing his socks in the camper's bathroom sink, but I was not his wife, so he was on his own in washing his underpants.

"Blue jeans get torn. Another thing not to make a fuss over. But…" Considering what I had just argued, he added, "If you feel it needs to be mended, go ahead and mend to your girlish heart's content."

"No, I don't want you to feel I'm metaphorically tying up your freedom and masculine ruggedness symbolized in your blue jeans and their ability to get as messy as you want."

"Well, I could see it another way: as you patching up tears."

"That was sweet, Sput, but no, let your jeans get as tattered as you want, because as much as you'd hate for girls like me to go extinct, I'd hate for boys like you to go extinct."

"What kind of boy is that?"

"The boy who knows how to patch barns, throw baseballs, tie a tie, don a tux, solve an equation, build a rocket, find his way in the universe using only the stars as guides, the boy who opens doors for girls, because whether he's wearing blue jeans or tuxedo, he retains a Knight's code of chivalry. I'd hate for boys like that to go extinct. For that boy, I'd be the perfect wife, not as a ploy to trap him, but from a deep-*seeded* heart need to love him. I know deep-*seated* is the correct term, but deeply *seeded* is more profound."

He finished up his meal but did not rush back to work; he took my dress's center ruffle pattern between his thumb and forefinger.

"Sput, you're going to get grease all over it."

Laughing, he rubbed his diner-food-greasy fingertips across my bare knee. "That's what you get for playing with a boy."

"Do you like this dress?"

"What's the name of that exquisite brown flower with the stellar moniker?"

"Chocolate Cosmos."

"This is your Chocolate Cosmos dress. It's stunning."

When he said things that suggested I was pretty, I always thought he was just being nice, and since I believed he was only pitying me, I did not feel I had the credentials to flirt back, at least not with my looks or any enticing reference to them.

His eyes embraced mine. "Your designer used the blueprint of an angel to make you—those are not a girl's eyes but an angel's eyes. My dear God, the sky is jealous of your eyes, where the color blue excels there more than it does anywhere else in the universe."

The professor did not misuse, overuse, or abuse words. Lovely words he kept in a keepsake box and used them only when appropriate, so the words would not lose their power, no more than an heirloom only shown on special occasions lost its ability to awe. If he said a girl was pretty, she was in league with starlight. I knew this because I had never heard him call a girl pretty, yet he said stars were pretty. I sensed "beautiful" was reserved like a crown only for Sputnik's mother and possibly for his wife. He would never describe a doughnut or even a car as "stunning," even though he liked cars quite a bit, especially fast ones. "Stunning" was a word for describing planets, snowflakes, and equations and now my dress. And I had "an angel's eyes." I thought my young heart was going to faint.

I was so flattered, I did not know what to say, so I said, "You're the most beautiful boy there ever was in the history of boys."

He started to say something, probably a bit of dry humor, but decided he was too embarrassed to say anything.

"When I was a young girl, I wished upon the orbiting Sputnik to meet the one I had been promised, during my 'near-death' experience, to meet. I prayed to be his guardian angel."

"Ah, Lumi, why did you do that?" he asked like I had committed something regretful.

"I don't understand. You just said all the sweetness about me being like an angel."

"Yes, I've always thought so—and here you are telling me you once prayed to be an angel—but it's *my* duty to guard you."

"Too late—I've already taken the role as *your* guardian angel." I smiled.

"And what do you get in return for your angelness?"

"You believing in magic."

He stood up, wiped dirt off the rear of his pants. "These britches are a mess and you're the one who has to clean them. Still want to be my angel?" He cleaned his hands by wiping them down his pants. He reached for me to stand up too. He was ready to get away from this soft conversation and back to hard work.

I hugged him and he did not stop my outburst of affection.

"Lumi, my goodness, you're going to get your dress all stinky."

He smelled so sweaty and like a barn but I didn't care. He felt so strong and perfect. I could not stop my desire to cling to him, yet I knew being clingy in this moment would not be beneficial to his work, so I said, "Maybe I could help you with the barn."

"Absolutely not."

"Why not? I don't want to take advantage of your generosity and let you do all the work. You're already exhausted as it is." I rubbed my hands up and down his tired back.

"You go inside to your poetry books and strawberry ice cream, and leave the splinters and hammers to *a boy like me*."

"I just want to help you."

"I know you do, so go over to the meadow and take a photo for me, something magical only you could see—a butterfly alighting on a petunia, perhaps."

"You really want a photo like that?"

"I really do." "Now run along" was implied in his voice and "stay out of harm's way."

I delighted in trying to capture a photo of "magic" for him, which entertained me until dusk, but the best I could get was a photograph of a hummingbird fluttering by a chrysanthemum.

The next day, he worked shirtless, which just about made "the nun" faint, his chest so hairy and mountainous, but he seemed completely oblivious to how the sight of his bare chest affected my motor capabilities, my stumbling on both words and ground.

After handing him a peppermint milkshake, I kept my gloved hands behind my back for fear I would not be able to stop my curious hands from gently touching the masculine brush to see how it felt—like thistledown or coconut husk? Wondering the answer peppered my dreams.

What his chest looked like bare was incomparable to the beauty and strength of what beat *inside* his chest. With bravura heart, he had rescued a momma cow and her brown-and-white calf from a slaughterhouse by paying the owner for the pair (more than the cows would make as burgers). The momma/daughter bovine team made a new home in the repaired barn, which Sputnik had spent an entire day bedding with hay.

"I feel so much love for creatures oft not loved," he said, imitating my proper voice, but the sentiment he truly shared. Sputnik and I delighted in making the cow family feel at home in Stargust Continued.

We planned to rescue more animals, since we had so much land to welcome them on. There was a reindeer farm close by, and this farm was not breeding for Santa but for Reindeer Burgers, so we planned to liberate as many of those poor souls we could.

The cows also offered the outdoorsman the proper excuse to visit every morning, because he felt cleaning the barn and tending the cows were manly tasks. I delighted in playing harp for the two cows and they seemed to enjoy the music.

Sputnik felt it improper to be at my place unchaperoned at nighttime, so for a while, every night, he called to check on me, but the calls never ended there—he always insisted we keep our phones connected all night, even while I slept, just in case "bogeymen" were lurking. Even though he always said "bogeymen" to keep the conversation playful, I knew he really did fear someone, or something, was out to get me, and I knew this fear stemmed from his past in the death camp (dreadful past chapters he could not write himself out of). In the way some boys would have found me "too sticky," some girls would have found Sputnik overly protective, even overbearing, but Sputnik and I, being very into each other, enjoyed our constant companionship. I usually felt embraced by his protectiveness, much the way one felt in a swing gently pushed by a loving parent, although at other times, I felt he was holding the swing back from flying. But these all-night phone conversations assured me he was not having liaisons, at least not at night.

Eventually, Sputnik purchased a beat-up blue pickup truck, "tough as a Tonka," which really made the outdoorsman feel rugged. He resumed doing what he had done at the patisserie: staying outside in his truck all night, sleeping in his sleeping bag in the truck's bed, to watch out for me against bears and who knew what else. I had not been able to talk him out of it, even by telling him he would freeze to death. Serving him morning coffee became not just a nicety but a necessity—to thaw him! I began waking up earlier, sometimes before four a.m., just to get him into the warm camper earlier. I always offered breakfast but all he ever wanted was oatmeal and coffee; he always ate dinner with colleagues (or with other women?).

One calm clear November night, after he came back from dinner, he asked if I wanted to go with him to look at the stars. What answer would anyone give to "Do you want to go to Heaven?" We drove in his pickup, warmed by heater since *I* was inside the truck's cabin; Sputnik never turned on the heater for himself. Century-old YOGI observatory, one of the first built in America, looked as majestic as ever in nighttime. Inside the open-roof wood-walled observatory, as cold and rustic as an ancient wine cellar, the physicist showed me the stars closer up than I had ever seen them. He also gave me a lesson in basic astronomy—Ooh, the joy of learning about the universe from the man I loved more than anyone in the universe! He let my small gloved hands move the giant telescope poking through the rooftop. "Easy, easy," he said, telling me not to be too shuddering, until he eventually put his arms around me and directed me in the right way to hold and control the telescope.

From all this time spent together, I learned the genius was an expert in *four* subjects: physics, math, engineering, *and* cartoons. Sometimes *Tom & Jerry*, sometimes number theory—his brain liked variety. But he watched cartoons, while maintaining a blank face; even Wile E. Coyote didn't produce a smile, because the coyote's antics were "actually quite mean," according to the professor. During morning hours, I kept the television on cartoons for him.

One morning, after I asked him about the piano in his apartment (a piano named Warsaw), he invited me over that afternoon to hear him play. It was softly raining and the sky was dusky dark. Sitting beside him on the piano bench, we drank coffee and cocoa, as he taught me about the math involved in music.

Gently pressing his middle finger against Middle C, he whispered, "*Pianissimo*. That's the way to touch a piano *softly*, very softly."

Ooh, lucky piano!

The austere scientist had written many soft-hearted lyrics like "*My heart's under a street lamp*" and "*You're the first wish I'd make on a genie.*" He had written a tune called *Summer on My Heart, Winter on My Heart.*

Your departure feels like winter

on my heart

a lonely planet

drifting farther from the sun

Your return brings summer

to my heart

For a physicist of the very cold, he still brought warmth into the piano.

"Every other man is a matchstick compared to the sun that is you, Gershom."

"Now, is that one of those compliments used to nab a man?"

I playfully punched his shoulder.

"That was a really crummy punch, just so you know. Boxing is not in your future."

"Ooh, do you want me to try for a better punch?" I held up my fist.

"Tsk tsk, the nun making a fist while wearing church gloves. Now, which song would you like to play in the music box?"

I told him I had to contemplate since they were all so lovely.

Surprisingly, he said, "Harp and piano could make lovely music *together.*"

So often together, I learned a good time to him was going out at dawn with his nerdboy binoculars, or "field glasses" as he called them, to look for "interesting things." Like me, he was content with days that only involved sky and trees. We didn't go on dates; we were like kids at playtime. On Stargust Continued, we began having adventures fit for *Nancy Drew* titles like the night he knocked on my door at one a.m. and asked if I wanted to go search for an alien artifact where a UFO had once been "sighted."

"Right on our land?"

That chilly night, we were bundled warm in excitement, as the wind howled like hungry hounds in a Sherlock Holmes story, while Sputnik and I searched around for "evidence" with flashlights, talking to each other by way of walkie-talkies. He loved those walkie-talkies; one of his messages was, "Sputnik to Peppermint. Ever feel like you don't belong on Earth?"

"All the time."

Those adventures and what we found merited their own book.

Sputnik only stayed the night three times in the camper. Two nights I was sick with a cold, and he took care of me like a perfect nurse; he later got sick with the same cold but would not admit it nor would he let me care for him.

On another rainy night, I watched the best episode of *Thriller*, "The Storm," about a woman and her cat alone in a country home on a dark and stormy night, everything cozy hunky-dory until she discovered a dead body in the storm cellar! Spooked, I went outside and knocked on the truck's rain-soaked window, while lightning cut through the black sky. Sputnik was not asleep in the cabin but reading a book about Diego Armando Luna, the famous baseball player. Sput seemed relieved to get out of the uncomfortable truck.

He came in, sat at the kitchen booth, and we played Scrabble over coffee and cocoa and doughnut holes at two a.m., while thunder made a ton of racket. Of course, Sputnik won, since the scientist knew every word in every language, I was convinced.

After winning, he said, "I could really go for a hot fudge sundae and lasagna."

"I thought it was your friend Ben who had the tastes of a pregnant woman?"

"I admit, it's odd, I don't even know why I have a hankering for that all of a sudden."

"You're not pregnant, are you?"

"Pregnant with the desire for another game. What do you say?" The rugged outdoorsman did not want to admit he was reluctant to go back to sleeping in the rain in the cold truck.

"I'll make lasagna, but it'll take at least an hour, and I'll need to go to the all-night market for some ingredients, including ice cream and hot fudge."

"I can't ask you to go through all that work…but if you really want to…"

Then we got in his old blue truck, drove to the market at three a.m., and searched aisles, whilst feeling delightfully like weirdos. Then we had lasagna for breakfast, and he had a hot fudge sundae.

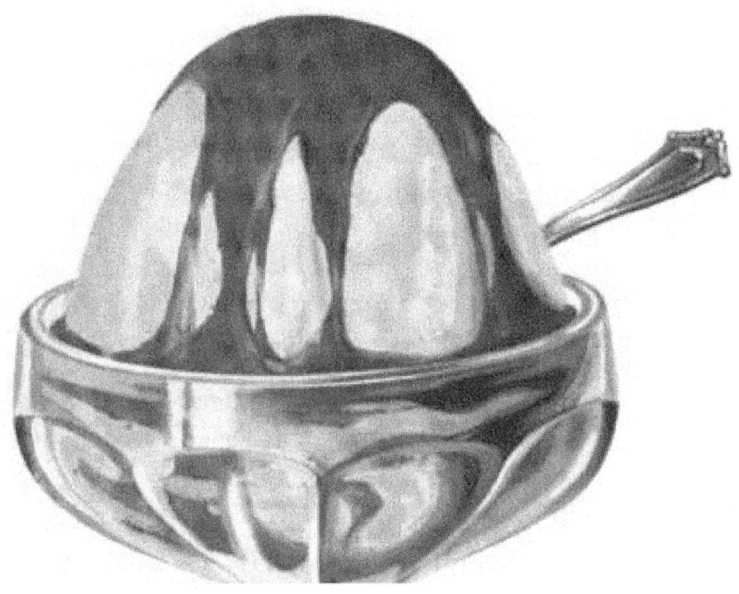

One clearer afternoon, he asked me to go upon Deer Hill to show me the dinosaur-egg-shaped sphere I had first seen on his office desk.

"This is a geode," he explained.

His enthusiasm for learning was like being around a kid learning about rocks for the first time.

We sat on a blanket in grass under sunlight, and after a peanut butter picnic, he told me to close and cover my eyes, as he took a small hammer to the rock and cracked it open. When I opened my eyes, I saw an amethyst crystal world hidden inside the geode like a fantastical world from a Jules Verne novel, glimmering like diamonds in sunshine.

"That's beautiful, Sput!" I had found something to love about rocks.

"Here, you can keep it," he offered.

I placed the jewel right atop my typewriter for inspiration to create fantastic worlds, if even half as lovely as what geodes created, I would feel accomplished as a writer.

At this time in my nineteen-year-old life, I had only written poemlets, character sketches, and short stories, one which had been viciously rejected by magazines, publishers, and literary agents:

"Write back after you've gone through puberty."

"After stomaching that much syrup, I have diabetes" from a male critic.

And from a female editor in want of the male critic's approval, "Wasting your glimmer of writing talent to illuminate romance is like—" I had no intention of ever repeating that cruel statement in print.

I had not understood the hateful reaction to a *love* story.

Amidst all his work, Sputnik had read the story overnight, half in his office, half in his truck's cabin.

The story was about an astronomer, lonely in heart and mind, feeling stranded on Earth. On a cold night in the desert when a light voyaged the sky and landed on his planet, the astronomer turned his telescope in that direction and saw a Lady. That was the simple sweet premise of the story.

The next cold morning, over oatmeal and coffee in the camper, I felt embarrassed to ask the serious scientist about my lovestory, scared of his rejection too and learning my intuition of his romanticism was unfounded. I admired him so, disappointing him was as hurtful as disappointing a moral.

He seemed uncomfortable and instead of talking, kept petting Mullybiski's head, while the pug sat by the table, wanting human food.

Finally, Sputnik asked, "How could you write that one part?" His voice sounded like that of an older brother's after reading an entry about sex in his little sister's diary. He was referring to the moment of the characters' physical union, which I had not actually described, except to say the lovers felt like their own constellation. I had hoped the description would please him but instead he seemed shocked, disappointed, and disgusted.

I could not tell him I had based the description on my dreams about him, so I explained, "How did Edgar Rice Burroughs write about Mars without going there?"

A light turned on in the scientist's mind—ah, right, the writer used imagination to write that scene. The explanation confirmed for him I had never actually done what I had written about, as if my goal to be a nun had not already confirmed that.

"Well, I highly liked the story, a mixture of Ray Bradbury and Emily Dickinson," he gifted with not a smidge of big brother condescension.

"Publishers deplored it," I gloomed, swirling maple syrup through oatmeal with a spoon.

"You can either adhere to publishers' standards or your own standards, but I suggest you never let anyone force you to take the syrup from your writing, or you'll be left with literary oatmeal, not your recipe and hard to stomach."

"You stomach it."

"I have to stomach it. *You* don't. Your story was a delicious dessert after a bitter afternoon with stubborn men intent on using rocketry to advance weapons."

"'Lots could be cut like the entire story,' one of the agents of doom said."

"Would you like me to find that agent and give him a cutting?"

"No, we won't resort to violence, which is strangely enough what they *want* me to do: write about violence. None of them could understand the extended picnic scene. 'How does that drive the story?' The scene is not meant to drive the story—it's meant to park the story, someplace beautiful, and let the reader frolic there for a while."

"Their attitude doesn't shock me, the typical capitalistic rush-rush-rush mentality. Hurry up and make some junk, so we can hurry up and buy some junk."

"Was the science okay?" I asked. I respected his opinions as if they were words written in red ink in The Bible.

"Well," he teased, often amused by my lack of knowledge about the world and my plethora of knowledge about Narnia, but there were imaginary worlds Sputnik liked to visit too, such as outer space worlds created by Burroughs and Sterling. "Your story kept me from needing to look at the stars last night for seeing beauty in this world, and the fabulous part was this beauty was right in my hands, not light-years away." Another reason for me to believe he was a Romantic. "I love everything you write, Lumi, and I'll uphold your writing like the flag of my nation."

Then as if suddenly realizing *why* I had imagined the cinnamon scene, he stood up and said he had to go to work.

But I kept imagining the scene in one of the sweetest most perfect chapters in my life, co-written by my best friend.

Sweet Tea & Scones

O n a Sunday afternoon in early December, I had cream

tea by the pond under pale blue sky. The menu included raspberry jam with soft butter and scones a bit too hard.

We now had two wicker chairs, although Sputnik would not admit the other chair was for him but for the stacks of books I liked to bring to the pond. He would never sit in the comfortably padded "girly" chair.

Between the chairs stood a glass-topped round wicker table, where a Peter Rabbit tea set was displayed.

Cold, I wore a coat, slacks, nylons, thickly insulated shoes, and a sweater that Sputnik called my "Black-Eyed Susan sweater," because of its yellow color and black buttons.

Sputnik, shirtless, worked on building a gazebo. The black hair on his chest was full of sawdust. A ladder was propped by the gazebo's wooden beams. Tools and paint cans and a thermos of coffee were spread out messily on a simple workbench, which Sputnik always left in the yard, the way he preferred leaving things strewn across his apartment.

Mullybiski and Pythagoras were warm inside the camper and safe from the building zone. Momma cow and calf grazed far away in cold fields warmed by a high sun.

Helping Sputnik with the work were Sputnik's three "chums":

Dr. Hershel Nerdien ("the widow Hershel," Sputnik called the elderly British gentleman) was Sputnik's former physics professor. A white-haired absentminded twinkly fellow, he really would ask "Where did I put my glasses?" while the specs were on his face. He reminded me of Holmes' Watson with a penchant for autumn-colored cardigans, bowler hats, and mumbling to himself, saying things like, "Could be, could be," and never explaining what could be. His big bushy golden dog followed him everywhere. Dr. Nerdien loved animals and tea, the physicist's two passions outside physics, and he and I had enjoyed a delightful discussion about cream tea. He had given me his mother's recipe for a scone alternative, a "Cornish split" (a sweet bread roll). His Lady friend, who did not like the big golden dog, sat as normal as Monday in the chair opposite me. Nerdien needed someone weirder. I could tell he and this woman had a *like* story, not a *love* story, if even a like story, more of a pushed-together-by-lonesomeness story, and her name would not be relevant in my lifestory or Hershel's.

San Francisco Bradley, the graduate student and teaching assistant for Professor Blagonravov's transcendental numbers course, had a mellowness and smile even bigger than his sandy sideburns. He was utterly adorable in his turtleneck the color of a carrot, paired with pants as blue as blueberries. Brad's "soul flower" Francine did not sit *in* a chair, but *by* my chair, in the grass, her head full of grass too, as she stared at a single green blade uninterrupted for a solid hour (I had no clue what she was seeing). Her transistor radio sat beside her and played Herman's Hermits' *Can't You Feel My Heart Beat*, which made her sometimes sway like a flower in breeze. Sputnik and I adored Francine and Brad, who both seemed very sweet-hearted, but like me, they did not say much.

J. Benjamin Biskatine was the neatest character I had ever met, a personality enriched with charm. Almost a decade older than Sputnik, he acted younger, despite his peppered hair. His father had been inheritor of the Biskatine Cocoa fortune from the empire's matriarch, Gerty Jane Biskatine (a barnstormer/cocoa maker), but Benny had been more excited to inherit all the chocolate than all the money! His mother had been The Bearded Lady in Zorman's Traveling Circus, and he loved circus folk. Horribly picked on in school (for being both astronomically rich and astronomically different), Mr. Benny was still sweet enough to be a character in a children's cartoon.

Yet if he had been a Muppet, he would have been Gonzo. He dressed like a mailman in blue shorts and blue button-downs, thick white socks and thick black sneakers, all jazzed up in a suit jacket and conductor's hat. He did not hide his "eccentricities" like making "Choo Choo" noises for seemingly no reason, calling himself "the old boy," congratulating himself often with "Atta boy," and saying things like, "Don't you get a feeling that when we turn off the lights at night that inanimate things come to life?" He talked, often, but mostly Mr. Benny went through life holding a bag of popcorn, enjoying the picture show, but not participating in it. He stayed in his own head. He lived for hobbies, kites and model trains and planes his favorites. Despite Mr. Benny's childlike qualities, Sputnik called him "the best darn engineer on this planet."

Sputnik did not call his friend "Benny," just like he did not call his teaching assistant "Bradley," because Blagonravov thought the "ee" sound was too cute for a man to say to another man.

Mr. Benny had said to me after I had brought Gersh a refill of coffee, "Your devotion to Shom should be in the Guinness Book of Records, kiddo." He said "kiddo" affectionately, not condescendingly, because to Mr. Benny, being kid-like was a big compliment. "What do you see in that dippity-do head?" he had teased right in front of "Shom." Men were so mean to each other. I quickly realized Sputnik and Ben showed affection by being gruff with each other, the way men liked to greet each other with hard pats to the shoulders. "Shom's a sourpuss. This kid was born on Black Tuesday. He collapsed the whole world into a depression. That doesn't surprise anyone, does it? I told him years ago, 'Just because you were born during the Great Depression doesn't mean you gotta go out with it.'"

I owed Mr. Benny, our Cupid, for my meeting Sputnik, who had not only moved to Biskatine because of Benny's suggestion but had flown to Stargust years ago thanks to his friend's advice that it was the prime location for parachuting.

Building the gazebo did not require four men, but Sputnik wanted to go back and forth between chatting about engineering and baseball with Mr. Benny, math with Brad, and cosmology with Dr. Nerdien, but serious Sputnik was getting more and more irritable, thinking his colleagues were not conversing or working hard enough and paying too much time to "their women." Sputnik had dabbed on extra machismo being around his buddies and power tools.

Hammering disrupted tranquil afternoon tea but had no effect on Francine's grass meditation. Every time I tried to savor Wordsworth's *My Heart Leaps Up*, my focus was interrupted by "pound, pound, pound!" so I had to start the poem over.

My heart leaps up when I behold

POUND!

My heart leaps up when I behold

A rainbow in the sky:

POUND!

So was it when my life began;
So is it now I am a man;
So be it when I shall grow old,

POUND!

Or let me die!

That poem could have been penned about Mr. Benny. I knew his heart leaped, too, when it beheld a rainbow.

Francine finally spoke, "The aura of the cows blends with the sky."

"Righteous, babe," Brad said.

Sputnik kept scolding Brad, "You're useless," and "Give my regards to your brain, since you've apparently decided to part with it." But this ribbing was playful, as playful as Professor

Blagonravov could get, unlike his ribbing with Professor Ditwad meant to break ribs.

"Woah, Pro-fess," Brad said, "you need to be more like the pond, man, just flow, but you're the rapids, man, just busting yourself against rocks."

Although Brad and Hershel and their dates didn't say much, Mr. Benny never stopped talking, he and Sputnik going on and on about propulsion systems (their specialized knowledge walled them off from everyone else), Sputnik completely ignoring me. This afternoon was but a small glimpse of what it would be like to be a faculty wife and I already wanted a divorce!

Earlier Sputnik had snapped at me when I had gone over to the workbench and out of curiosity looked around. "I asked you women to stay out of the construction zone or else risk getting your dainty little hands hurt."

"Pardon me, sir, me and my dainty little X chromosomes shan't dare get next to these big manly tools ever again or else plum shatter to pieces."

Ben laughed and laughed. "Thatta girl, put him in his place."

Tired of the noise and irritated with Sputnik, I went inside to make lunch. I made sandwiches, which Sputnik did not like served to him on a plate. He just wanted to hold the sandwich in one dirty hand, so he could continue working with his other hand; "No reason to dirty up a plate for me." I put a stack of spicy grilled cheeses on one plate. I also made sweet southern tea, apple tart for dessert, and vegetarian wild rice soup.

Through the window above the sink (the window open to let out soup steam), I heard the widow Hershel ask Sputnik, "Is the blonde lass your student or your girlfriend—or both?" I was surprised; Dr. Nerdien did not seem like the type to even notice such things.

"She's his angel," Benny answered for his friend.

One, two, three…"Awwww," the men started cackling. "His angel. Awww, Professor Blagon-wavov has an angel."

Sputnik only got faux angry; he thought it funny too (in front of other men).

"Does she know about your other chicks?" Brad asked.

"Shut up," Sputnik snapped. "She's not some chick who parks with you in your shag pad VW van. You view her as a nun, completely outside the sphere of possible dating companions."

Brad and Francine had an "open" relationship and hearing of Brad's "shag pad" was not news to her.

"Gershom, yours and Lumi's auras are blended like the white and red of a candy cane," Francine offered, "but there's a smear on your aura, Gershom, a gray gloom, man, that's ruining the sweet cane." She did not call anyone "Professor" or any other title such as "Dr."

"There's a gloom because I can't get your nitwitted boyfriend to recognize the difference between a hammer and a saw."

I brought out one lunch tray, set it on the workbench. Benny, Brad, and the widow Hershel offered deepfelt thanks from their hunger, but Sputnik grumped, "Now what's all that? Plain cold sandwiches and water would've been sufficient for these goons."

Francine was more interested in swaying than eating.

"Boy, hidy," Mr. Benny praised, tasting the sandwich, "that's good eats." I found it charming the New England gentleman using Texas cowboy slang.

"Where's your lunch?" Sputnik asked me, looking down at the tray as if I had set an engine from an alien spacecraft on the table and he had no idea what to do with it.

I patted the golden retriever and gave him a bite of bread. "I'm happy with my cream tea."

While the others gathered their lunches, Sputnik pulled me aside and whispered, "I don't think I like you making a meal like this for Brad. He'll get ideas. *Apple tart*."

"That's disgusting what you're implying. Plus, everyone here knows how loyal I am to you, except for you."

"Now, don't get me wrong. I'm not questioning your loyalty. I'm questioning Brad's ability to seduce."

"That's the same as questioning my loyalty. I thought the mathematician had training in logic? Unless you think your friend is an attacker of women, you have nothing to worry about."

Grumpily, Sputnik ate the sandwich, not taking time to taste it, but wolfing it down to get back to work, and calling Brad and Ben "lazy good-for-nothings."

After our guests left and the gazebo stood in all its sanded wood glory, I washed dishes. Through the window, I saw Sputnik sitting on the workbench, his eyes on the dusk pond glowing like a campfire in reds and oranges, his legs lightly swinging like a boy trying to get a swing to fly. He was going to paint the gazebo by himself.

The dishes could wait. I went outside.

"I feel so bad a tree had to die to make the gazebo," I said.

"Don't worry, she was already dead in a timberyard. You didn't kill her. She was either going to become this gazebo or pages for one of your books or walls for some jerk's outhouse. I think she'd prefer the first two choices for afterlife."

"This isn't her afterlife. The wood is just remnants of her previous form now recycled into something else lovely. There's a special place for tree spirits in Heaven."

"Lovely? I didn't make you a nearly ornate enough gazebo, and I can't blame the three Gomer Pyles for *my* blueprint."

"It's a lovely gazebo."

"It's not fit for two drunk sailors on the docks, much less for a Lady and her morning tea. I had planned for it to look as regal as a carousel's canopy."

"I think it's lovely, and it doesn't need any paint."

Sputnik rubbed his left hand as far as he could reach behind his left shoulder to an ache in his back. He tried with his right hand, reaching around his stomach to reach the troublesome spot.

"Sput, you need a break."

"I'm fine."

A maple leaf was stuck on his sweaty back, right around the area he had been trying to rub, so I picked the leaf off and very softly touched him there. He did not stop me, so I gently massaged the ache and did not feel improper doing so—I was a friend bringing comfort to a friend. I brought my hands to his bare shoulders and caressed them, his muscles hard and tense.

"You don't have to do that," he said, his voice getting softer as if it was getting massaged too.

"You didn't have to build me a gazebo either."

I continued massaging his shoulders then his neck and back, and I relished bringing him to a state of relaxation only slightly less relaxing than a nap.

I rubbed his arms. "Did you get all these muscles from playing baseball?"

With cockiness and bashfulness, he gave a meager, "Perhaps."

When my hands resumed their caress of his shoulders, he reached up to my left hand with his right hand and softly guided it to his lower arm, but I had to move to stand beside him to be able to reach the location that really ached him—the tattooed numbers. Sputnik did not see the symbolism; he only felt an actual ache there. With both hands, I rubbed his lower arm, hard as stone from tension, as he closed his eyes and released masculine moans that turned to boyish cries, his eyes shut to prevent seeing the "embarrassing" experience of releasing his feelings. Then he stopped short of gaining complete peace by placing his hand over mine, a gentle way to say, "That's enough."

He opened his eyes and put his arms around my lower back to bring me closer. I thought he was going to kiss me happily ever after, but instead he asked, hard, "Would you mind getting me some more coffee? I need to get back to work then I have to get back to the office."

Gingerbread &
Candy Canes

O

n *the* snowy Sunday night, The Snowflake Physicist and
I celebrated Hanukkah and Christmas, over warm gingerbread
cake and hot apple cider. In the camper shaped like a metal toaster,
a propane heater kept us warm, while wind caroled like a choir of
ghosts, and Nat King Cole crooned *O Holy Night* on my portable
cinnamon-colored radio. Stars were brightly shining in me, as
Sputnik and I strung red and clear lights across wood paneling,
while we each held a slice of gingerbread, a moist parcel of clove
and molasses and ginger, dusted with powder sugar. The blended
holiday celebration had been my idea. My first time celebrating
Hanukkah, his first time celebrating Christmas. Plus, the scientist
had not observed the Festival of Lights since boyhood.

We were not making world history in this moment, but we were
making personal history. I would never forget this special night for
all my life.

I wore a thick sweater dress the color of white chocolate, thick
nylons, and thin white cotton church gloves with button clasps and
small bows above the wrists. His outfit looked like a pinecone:
lightweight walnut trousers whose pleats were rubbed out, scuffed
derbies which could have served as camouflage in dirt, and a beat-
up flannel shirt the color of tree bark with marble buttons and a
carpenter's pencil, candy cane, and package of gum in the pocket.
His hair was kept tidy by Brylcreem as always, and his face was
freshly shaved for the holidays, and he was the most handsome
sight in this universe since the moon came to be.

In the "den," partially separated from the rest of the camper by
two walls with a doorway-sized opening between them, Mullybiski
licked his paws while lounging on a rose-red fabric loveseat with
big buttons on the back and seat. Root sat beside the bunny plush
toy and the "Write Thus!" pillow. Mullybiski got along splendidly

417

with Pythagoras, who was cuddled in his shell and napping on plush red carpet by the consolette television. The TV's lemon-oil-polished wooden top was decorated with a single white doily and clear bowl of Golden Delicious apples, which Sputnik had handpicked.

The oven warmed our dinner: candied yams, rolls, roasted carrots, and a savory noodle casserole. This was my first time making a holiday dinner for him (he had spent Thanksgiving out of town), and I was both nervous and excited; I wanted the meal to be perfect, to make him happy, since he so rarely was.

Mullybiski kept waking up from intermittent naps to sniff tasty kitchen scents.

On the stovetop was a pot of macaroni awaiting cheese (my Moon-Moon's standard) and a baking sheet topped with crispy potato latkes that looked like hash browns (his grandma's standard). Sputnik and I probably did not have many human friends because we were vegetarians in 1965.

We made a frame of lights around the romantic painting, *Springtime*, of two flowy-dressed dreamy lovers on a swing, painted by Pierre Auguste Cot.

On this special snowy holiday night, when the camper felt like a gingerbread house scented in holiday meal, Sput had come to the trailer bearing a miniature Santa-Claus-style bag full of candy canes. I had wiped a dusting of snow from his beautiful molasses air, while he had coughed and scraped ice and dirt off his shoes on the camper's small porch, which he had constructed. We had both agreed not to buy expensive gifts. Sitting on the couch, I had given him a golden tin of gingerbread cookies shaped like snowflakes, and he had looked at me in a way I could not read because no one had ever written that in their facial expression for me. After giving me a cloth pouch of chocolate coins, a traditional present for the first day of Hanukkah, I had wondered if his other women would receive their gifts in his bed.

418

Finished with stringing lights, Gersh taught me how to light a menorah and what blessings to say, the way his bubbe had taught him. One candle was the "helper" candle, who lit the other candles, one candle lit each night. But he had forgotten much of the tradition, which upset him, but playing the manly man, he shrugged off sadness and laughed at us for listening to Christmas music while lighting the menorah. Maybe that was why we had no human friends, his rare smile suggested.

"You must have gotten this gingerbread recipe from an angel because this is a slice of Heaven," he said.

"An angel did give me this recipe." In my blue eyes, he saw that we shared bittersweet pasts, although his had been much more bitter than sweet.

We were enjoying Moon-Moon's traditional holiday treat, which would give us energy for the night's activity: building snowmen, and snowspaceships, under the stars. That had been his idea, an idea shared with me only after my insistence he come up with the night's entertainment, since I had already picked my choice (stringing lights). He had said with an oh-whatever tone, "Build snowmen." But I had heard past his adult voice to the little boy inside so excited by the holiday season he was just about to burst.

The next night, I would attempt to make his mother's holiday treat, strawberry jelly doughnuts, then we would decorate a gingerbread house then play dreidel, which he had forgotten how to play but was sure he could remember once he got going.

During our holiday-bonanza planning phase, he had said, "Perhaps we shouldn't do so many fun things in one night," as if life had such limited amounts of fun that it could be used up in one night, and my heart yearned to remind him what he had known as a child: fun is limitless, especially when you are with a good friend.

I had said, "We have many nights to celebrate."

But he seemed convinced someone, or something, would steal our fun before it could happen, and he also seemed so guilty for planning fun that he wanted something to end it.

On Christmas Eve, we would camp and picnic in the meadow, and on Christmas, we would watch a once-in-a-lifetime comet turn the nightsky into a painting. I was ecstatic that he was going to celebrate Christmas and all eight nights of Hanukkah with me. His calendar was often so penciled in, so many meetings they had to be penciled outside the squares, I was surprised he had time to eat. After the holidays, he would be in Geneva at a science conference discussing an outer space treaty, meant to ensure space exploration for all people and to prevent nuclear weapons or other weapons of mass destruction from being in orbit or on celestial bodies. He promised to bring me back Swiss chocolates. I didn't know who the professor would be spending his time in Geneva with (someone gorgeous and brilliant, I feared, who understood nuclear physics, looked like a Bond girl, and had affairs as casually as she had Tuesdays). A part of my heart was saddened, yet another part was not, because I felt I was giving him something which would ultimately be more satisfying to his soul. I wanted to celebrate New Year's Eve with him too, but he was spending that night with Ben. I pictured cookies galore at the New Year's party, but I would not ruin my holiday cheer by imagining who Sputnik would be kissing at midnight.

After lighting the menorah, we decorated an aluminum Christmas tree with lights and red bulbs. We did not want to kill a tree then decorate its dead body with tinsel. I handed Sput lights, and he was tall enough to easily garland the high places.

Listening to him cough, I wanted to soothe him, but I knew not to, because he would bark, "I'm fine," which was often accompanied by something like, "Millions of children are going to die this month from starvation. Save your concern for them."

Throughout the night, he had kept glancing at my typewriter, where a blank sheet of paper was rolled.

420

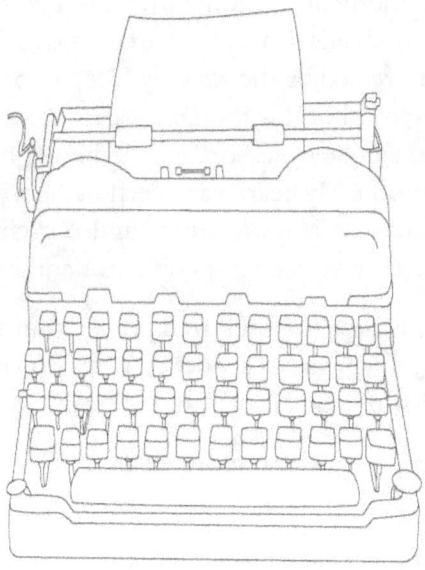

Putting up more lights, he said in between coughs, "The kitchen smells delicious."

"Thank you!" Thank you, thank you, thank you for being here, not just here in the camper but here on this planet.

Sputnik and I kept taking quick breaks to sip from our steamy cider mugs that weren't losing too much warmth on the table, which did not have much room left since my typewriter sat atop it. The padded vinyl booths were occupied by twigs, which Sput had gathered against snowfall, just like he had put up outside holiday lights in snow and had picked apples for me from the lovely apple tree in the yard. On an upcoming festive night, we were going to build a twig wreath, which the woodsy man was eager to construct.

Overlooking the table was the cold window whose tiny windowsill we he had placed the menorah upon, where it illuminated the cinnamon-red radio, but the window was too frosted to see through. I didn't want to see too far out there, not beyond Stargust, where people hated my friend because of his heritage and ignored me because of my looks. I preferred the scene inside, a holiday card scene reflected in the window glass.

Now the magic moment: he turned on the lights, and the night looked almost as magical as the Three Magi's holy night. He seemed more impressed by the way my face lit up. The lights were not making me glow, but this thought was: I wanted to bear him a child for the next holiday season, a little baby physicist, a future explorer of the moon. My heart was overflowing with warm visions of creating *our* own holiday traditions and our children's holiday traditions, a nice fantasy even if it could not come true.

Finished with this task (he preferred going from task to task, no time for leisure), the physicist scooched twigs down the puffy vinyl booth and sat down, ready for the dinner task.

I topped our glass mugs with more cider from what looked like a maple syrup bottle.

The Andrews Sisters wished for a sleigh ride, so they told us from the radio.

"Next week, I will set out to find a record of Hanukkah music," I said, placing a few iced snowflake cookies on a thin red platter decorated with mistletoe designs.

"Good luck finding that," he said, while putting his hand to the typewriter like checking its temperature.

The Arctic man took a warm drink. "Men don't want to drink apple cider."

"Ooh, I think they do."

"You're always girly-fying me," he teased. "You know I like coffee, black."

"Yes, I know, ground out of Alaskan tree bark or something bitter and horrible like that," I teased in return.

"Alaskan tree bark?"

"Don't forget I've seen you drink coffee with cream and sugar."

"Our secret."

"I won't tell all your buddies."

Since he had a way of holding me without physically holding me, I stood by the table as if his arms were embracing me, even though only his gaze was wrapped around me, quite securely.

"When are you going to make me an apple pie?" he asked with the adorable and irresistible voice men employed when sick with a cold and in need of coddling. "So I can enjoy the pie of my labor."

When he spoke to me like I was his wife, I felt the gleeful dizziness that occurs when swinging on a swing. "Whenever you want."

"Perhaps you can pack me a slice for my long plane ride to Geneva."

"Okaaaay," I said as softly as if he was making love to me.

"You're a very special girl to me." His voice did not sound like an older brother's.

I was embarrassed so I looked away from him.

The apples not on display on the television counter were snug in a wooden basket by the camper's built-in wardrobe.

"I hate to kill all those apples," I said, and I knew he was one person who would not laugh at my sentiment, the man who once said if humans refused to respect all life, including plant life, humans had no right to visit other worlds, where humans would be seen as invading conquerors, not friendly explorers.

He made his voice gentle like his voice could actually touch me. "You won't be killing anything, Peppermint. Apples are part of a tree, a part which we assume trees want to be eaten to spread their seeds. So, plant the seeds and let apple trees 'Be fruitful and multiply.'"

I smiled at "Be fruitful and multiply."

I went over to the stove and used a spoon to marry macaroni and cheese.

"One of these celebratory nights I was thinking of making apple bread unless you'd rather have pie."

"Lady's choice."

"Golden Delicious apples make sweet soft pies. Is that okay, or too girly?"

"I don't think you're safe even around Ben."

I was flattered by his implying I was irresistible, but I thought he was just being nice.

"Moon-Moon said to add a variety of apples to apple pies, but although I like Granny Smiths, I prefer the Golden Delicious, especially for apple custard pie. Have you ever had that?"

"I don't recall."

"I'm boring the scientist?"

"Not at all."

I figured he was just being nice again. We rarely talked about math or science, even though those two subjects were his life; he always had to rely on his colleagues for those conversations.

I asked, "How about tomorrow morning I'll make streusel apple muffins, or I could make baked cinnamon apples, and we'll talk about the gas propellers of cold rockets?"

"The gas *propellers* of cold rockets, huh?"

I nodded. I still wanted to learn all about his work and prove to him I could talk just as well about science as any of the women scientists he would encounter in Geneva. I'd study every science and math book in the world if needed to be worthy of his companionship.

"I've no knowledge of gas propellers, so I'm going to venture out on a wild limb and assume you meant gas *propellent*."

"Ooh, yes, that's what I meant: the stuff that goes Kaboom during rocket launches."

"Mmm hmmm."

I opened the stove, checked on dinner, the rolls turning golden. I walked back over to the table.

"I have a confession to make," I sighed with my usual flair for theatrics. "I don't really understand your work at all."

His eyes said, "That's not a confession."

"I know you work in rockets and you study planets, cold planets, and in math you do something with numbers. Forgive me, that makes me an awful friend, not knowing about what you love the most, but I really do want to understand your projects."

"Did you recently take another 'How to be a Good Wife' quiz and fail?"

"No! I really did try to read your books."

"Well, as a scientist, I told you I study atmospheres of other planets and the possible effects these atmospheres could have on potential life and future spacecrafts and explorers." His mind was immensely attractive. "As a mathematician, yes I do something with numbers," he ribbed. "And as an engineer, I attempt to make simple, cost-efficient, propulsion systems that'll be used by astronauts when they have to step outside their spacecrafts."

My eyes got big, trying to see all of his big goals. "That's incredible! Yes, let's talk about all that tomorrow morning, and I think apple streusel muffins will be the perfect complement for that discussion."

"Lumi, I told you before I admire your seeking of knowledge, a highly desirable trait for a Lady to have, and as a professor, I'll do my best to try to explain any of your questions, but if I wanted to spend the holidays with scientists, I'd be in the lab right now, discussing propellants and not pies, and certainly the conversation would include money, not apples. I'm charmed you know more about pie than pi, and you're charmed by me for the opposite reason. Now, do you need me to be here tomorrow morning for something? I was going to the apartment for a while."

"Ooh…mmm…of course not. Tomorrow's Sunday. I forgot. The professor needs his morning rest."

"Tomorrow's Monday."

"That's right. It feels like Saturday night."

"Resting on Sunday is a Christian tradition. Saturday's the Jewish Sabbath. Besides, you're the one who needs rest after that rough final exam from mean Professor Blagonravov."

"It wasn't *too* bad, but thankfully the whole semester is over." And I was no longer his student. "So, what's my final grade, Professor?"

"Well, you didn't turn in the math poem for an 'A', so whether you get a 'B' depends on how you answer this: Y equals X, what's the point?"

To the mathematician, answering that question was as easy as saying his ABCs, but I had to think about it.

"'One, one' is one point." I smiled about my silly wordplay, as I put on an oven mitt to take the rolls from the oven.

"I didn't ask for a point on the line. I asked what's the point—the purpose—of that equation?"

The professor was big on philosophical questions, which meant I could not give a textbook answer such as "Y equals X is a linear equation in two variables that will always be a straight line on a graph," and the fact that I understood a linear equation was a testament to his talent for teaching.

I made a puppet out of the oven mitt and had it say, "The equation shows that Y's state of being is influenced by X's state of being."

426

"Not bad."

"So I got a 'B'?"

"You already had a 'B.'" He smiled. "I'll turn in the final grades next week. Now, do you need me here in the morning to plant a seed for you?"

I didn't know if he had meant to be suggestive, but so much blood rushed to my face, it felt wet.

"If you want to," I said with a voice so soft and low only a dog could hear it.

"Sure. We'll plant a baby apple tree and make the momma tree happy."

"Ooh, planting a tree during the holidays sounds magical."

"Actually, frost will prevent us from planting a seed, but I'll salt the driveway, although I suggest you don't attempt driving in this, not in that Lady car."

"I'll stay in until I have to go get *someone* a present," I sighed.

Most people would have seen my statement as humorous, but it made his face serious. "No, if the streets are icy then you'll stay home."

"Okay, Professor."

His face relaxed as much as it was allowed to in a world where men wanted to make missiles in the stars.

I offered the rest of the gingerbread to Sputnik, since the outdoorsman enjoyed eating straight from the bread pan. I knew he wanted ice cream too but would not ask for it.

"How about some spiced caramel ice cream," I offered, "and I'll re-warm the bread in the oven, so the ice cream will melt on it?"

"No, that's too much trouble." The Arctic man was conflicted between wanting to bask in a woman's warm pampering and not

427

wanting to partake of it, and I assumed because he did not want to pink-glaze his masonry, so to speak.

"It's not any trouble at all, Sputty. I made the ice cream for you."

"You're making too much fuss over me again," he snapped, while looking at a twig with the eyes of a Boy Scout.

With *dirty* hands, he ate cookies. Boys. People often talked about gayness being unnatural, but gayness was more natural than straightness. Men liked each other, women liked each other, but when men and women liked one another—that was strange. They liked mating, yes, but they also liked each other despite their differences. His insistence on never washing his hands, never revealing his feelings, never admitting he needed help drove me cuckoo yet I still adored him, and some of my traits irritated him too, such as my unwillingness to answer a question in class even when I knew the answer, or to convert between quarts and pints at the market to see if I really was getting a discount, which had nothing to do with my femaleness just my un-mathyness, and here he was, a mathematician, in my home.

The previous dawn, while he had collected apples for me before the snow came (he knew things like when snow was coming just by the feeling in his wilderness bones or something like that), I had asked what holiday dishes he had enjoyed as a boy, and he had seemed guiltily delighted to remember.

"Latkes," he had offered, wearing an acorn-colored corduroy coat and reaching to pick an apple, using one arm to clasp a wooden bucket next to his firm chest, while I had helped collect apples too, the ones on the cold ground.

"Latkes?" I had asked, unfamiliar with them.

The dawn had been quite frosty but pretty, the sky blushing like a schoolgirl in a baby blue dress. I had felt in awe of life, that it could be this sweet and perfect.

"Latkes are potato pancakes. My bubbe made latkes."

428

"Your mother's mom, right?" I had asked, feeling too bad for a bruised apple to throw it away, so I had placed it in the basket too, to keep it with its appley family a little longer. He had smiled at my caringness.

"Yes, Bubbe was my mother's feisty mother. My best friend actually. Well, you're stubborn like her," he had snapped since he had offered to pick apples for the Lady so I would not have to be out in the cold.

"I'm waiting for your coffee to brew, Professor, so I thought I'd help."

I had hugged the tree and said, "This tree's a good friend. I say 'Hi' to him every morning and he waves his leaves, 'Hello.'"

"*She* says 'Hello.'"

"Herman Hesse called trees 'preachers,' and I have always felt their preaching about serenity's beauty."

Sputnik had gently patted the tree's bark. "I had some tree friends in Alaska. There was one tree, a girl tree I thought, and I know scientifically there are no 'girl' trees, but she was all alone in a field and looked lonesome. She was a good friend."

"I feel sorry for trees unable to follow their friends on journeys."

Surprisingly, the scientist had said, "Perhaps they follow us in spirit."

Hoping to hear more about Sputnik's past, I had followed him around the tree, picking up apples along the way.

"Kugel," he had said, his hands turning red, his beard turning stiff, from too much time in frosted air. "Bubbe made kugel. And homemade preserves and conserves, which was always an Event— 'Bubbe's making the conserves this afternoon!' And my mother's special treat was strawberry jelly doughnuts for me and my little sister." All the granite of his voice had softened on the words "little sister" who he had never mentioned. Was she only a memory?

429

"Mother used homemade preserves for the doughnuts." His voice always stayed soft for "mother," a word formed very gently. "She was a Lady made of porcelain. Now go inside," he had said with all the stonework back in place.

"Only if you'll come inside too and have oatmeal with me."

After he had brought in the wooden basket, where overpacked apples almost tumbled out, he had grumped, as usual, about me serving him "girly oatmeal" with maple syrup and "girly coffee" with cream and sugar, when tap water and plain oats would have sufficed for him.

"I'm tired of hearing that. No one can eat plain oats!"

"Yes, they can."

"It's not safe."

"It's perfectly safe to eat Quaker oats right out of the barrel."

After the grump had left, I had taken a morning trip to the library to find recipes, which I would probably over-girly too.

"Sputnik, I know ice cream's your favorite food, but what's your second favorite?" The question seemed quite intimate to me, but he blurted out:

"Biscuits and molasses, or sorghum, I'm not sure," he admitted, the Brooklyn boy unsure of the difference between sorghum and molasses. "And I like biscuits and jam. The kind Bubbe made. She made heavy-duty food like those conserves that could survive through nuclear war. And hearty food like dense sour cream poundcakes that could last a boy's energy the whole morning long; I'd take off into the Alaskan forests before dawn with a chunk of that heavy poundcake and I wouldn't need a bite to eat until 'noon. She made meals in a biscuit, big heaping biscuits piled with cheese, eggs, jam, peppers, all the food groups. Foodstuff she could take with her if she ever got her dream of flying off in a hot air balloon."

"In a hot air balloon?"

His grandma sounded like an interesting character. I realized she was the elderly woman in the hot air balloon he had drawn in his sketchbook.

"She was something. Bubbe the Magnificent," he said like describing a superhero. "Little tiny woman always in big knee-high boots. Like Ben's grandma, Gerty, who was one of the first female pilots, Bubbe was one of the first women to drive an automobile cross country in her goggles and her dress duster, made for journeying dirt highways. She rode with her sister-in-law. Alice Ramsey beat them only by a few months and that was only because Bubbe hadn't been in America long and had to save money for an automobile. She rented a 20 horsepower 1907 Mitchell Model E Runabout for three dollars a day, a big amount of money for those days. Her brother was doing well financially in Poland and paid for the journey, and as I said, his wife went along for the ride."

"Wow!" His bubbe's story sounded like one I wanted to write someday. "That reminds me of Moon-Moon taking off on her solitary journey by bicycle. It's interesting how you, me, and Ben all have brave women in our backstories."

"I told you my family tree is full of brave strong-willed women."

He asked me about my momma's adventure and was amused to learn of my blueblood background ("Cinderella really is a princess"). I asked him about Bubbe's adventure, which led to him telling me more of her backstory.

"She was born in Bielsko, Poland, in a cottage white like milk, where her only friend was a roaming goat she named Feliks. Those two had adventures in the mountains and hills. When I picture her childhood, I see a page from *Heidi*, even though she wasn't in the Swiss Alps. Elah Braverman! She was something. She couldn't talk. She was mute. And she spoke broken sign language. She made little gestures to get her point across." He moved his thumb and fingers like he was making a sock puppet talk, showing how Bubbe made signs. "That gesture meant she wanted someone to talk, usually to tell her their problems. She was

431

grand." He gave himself a hug to show how Bubbe had said "Gershom." "The hug meant 'Gershom'. Isn't that sweet? When Pops was ragging me about giving my mother the ugly shirt, Bubbe said, 'I love Gershom's gift.' I don't know why but she adored me." He hugged himself then made the hand puppet gesture again. "'Gershom, talk to me.' She wanted nothing more than to be in the air, to fly; she told me that often." He pretended his flat hand was an airplane flying upwards, showing how Bubbe had said "fly."

He sipped his drink, remembering. "Well, anyway, Mother's strawberry jelly doughnuts were a close second favorite food but those were only for the holidays."

I did not have any handpicked strawberries or homemade compote, just store bought, but I was looking forward to making him the special dish. I didn't know how his mother had made the doughnuts, but I would do my lovingest.

"You'll have to tell me some more of your favorite boyhood dishes." This was my attempt to get him to talk about his family.

"Well, my mother made typical American housewife fare. My bubbe was somewhat religious but my mother wasn't highly, although my aunt, my mother's sister, was the most pious woman and beautiful because of her piety like clear quartz transformed beautiful from light shining through. We didn't follow kosher laws but she did."

He looked at the frosted window, and in his thoughts, he wiped ice off a pane to peer into a memory of a holiday dinner. By this inner window, he stood outside the candlelit scene like a ghost, unable to interact, or maybe his family members were all ghosts at the dinner table, unable to interact with him.

"And your mother was born in Poland too?"

I hoped snow would drop road visibility to zero and keep him with me all night into the next day, because I wanted to hear him talk all night, amidst drifting snow and hot apple cider, to start like Dickens' *David Copperfield*, "I was born," and tell me every sentence that had been written in his lifestory since the opening one, and no matter how cold the pages of his life had been, I wanted him to see this warm story awaited his full entrance. He did not have to stand outside this moment like a ghost, nor was I a ghost, but a girl, here and now, in love with him, and he could be the lead character in a lovestory with me, if he wanted.

"Yes, like my bubbe, she was born in Poland. You would have liked her. She and her sister both had Valentine's red hearts. Mother liked Hershey's Kisses purely for the candy's name: *Kisses.* She wanted to live in Dukes' Castle. I told you she had the same Arthurian fantasies as you."

He scraped ice off more memory windows and told me that his mother's father, Feivish, had worked in a cloth factory. For a while, all the trade unions, Jewish and Polish and German and Christian, had united to fight unfairness, but despite their efforts, Feivish had wanted to go to the "Golden Land" of opportunities. His first job in America was in a nickelodeon then he became a "pit pianist" in a cinema house, creating the film's score in person for the audience, making the "du-du-du-duuuu" sounds for horror films and the twinkly songs for love stories.

"My grandma and grandpa were two peas in an odd pod—the hot air balloonist and the pit pianist, so not surprisingly, their genes popped out some oddballs. The most difficult part of Bubbe's journey had been leaving her beloved Feivish for so long, a highly understanding man who had taken care of their young daughters during his wife's automobile trip across America."

Sputnik was being much chattier than usual about his past, and I would not let this opportunity to learn more about him pass me by.

"Where did they move to in America?"

"Baltimore, where my mother spent many years as a dainty dame who dreamed of being a Hollywood movie star with her brunette hair crimped like a silent film star's. The dreamier, the more romantic, the better the part. She was born the same year as the airplane, and she thought that was some kind of divine sign about her life's purpose: she wanted to be both an actress and a barnstormer like Ruth Elder. She had Bubbe's spirit of flight in her. When I was barnstorming, I often dreamed Bubbe's spirit was with me in the front seat, or Mother's spirit, or … Mother spent girlhood afternoons in nickelodeons, watching flight reels, until prettier movie palaces came about, more castles she dreamed of living in. With soda pop and Tootsie Rolls, she played *hooky* from school. You wouldn't know anything about that, would you?"

I shrugged, innocently. I had been sick, yes, on the day he had lectured about polynomials, which had done me no good, because almost every lecture from then on had been about polynomials!

"But Mother had a delicate heart, a condition which sometimes made her lips turn blue, so she couldn't withstand too much exertion." A cold memory he tried to warm with cider. "Unfortunately, she was never able to afford even a trip to Hollywood where Charlie Chaplin might have discovered her. At fifteen, she lost her own father to a heart attack, a death which just about killed Bubbe's heart, the loss of her beloved Feivish. When he died, her smiles died too…for a while. But the smiles eventually came back. I've always admired women like that, capable of mining smiles from their being that the world has robbed of so much. Well, after his death, Mother married a much older man."

"What was your dad like?"

"Pops…mmm…he was a dark lager, a plain-looking robust man with a mustache, but he was…whoever, Clark Gable, to my mother. Well, anyway, you asked about my favorite boyhood dishes. My mother made a lot of my pop's favorites before his death."

"I'm sorry about your father."

"I was at school, first grade perhaps, when he died."

How tragic were the rest of his memories if the death of his father could be spoken of so nonchalantly?

434

"I didn't see it happen. But Mother did. Amazingly, she didn't become a windswept person after his death, someone swept of all traits, you know one of those people who become like a pencil lying silently on a table, no longer wanting to write anything, except her reunion with him, the way lovers were always reunited in her favorite movies. No, she kept writing Life. She once said she would never write a chapter titled 'Ice' in her story, but instead chapters like 'Blueberry,'" he said, looking at me, detecting similarities between me and his mother. I thought what a good idea for a story: to have chapters named after desserts.

"Pop's death was just an accident," he continued, "the kind that happen to men with big dreams who test explosive rocket fuel, deaths that serve as a warning of what *not* to do to those who carry on their dreams. It was better than building armored tanks like his papa had done."

"Your father built rockets too?"

"Yep. Behind his plain-looking exterior was a mad genius dreamer. Pops was a backyard rocket scientist, when rocket science was an infant in need of fostering, before Sputnik and Explorer 1."

"This was in Alaska?"

"Yeah, Alaska, aah, Alaska, where our neighbors were redcedars and aspens, no humans for miles, and our land smelled like snow and lake and sea and woodland and welded metal and burnt rocket fuel like the stink of firecrackers. My pop's death was purposeful, at least. He would have willingly sacrificed his life for the advancement of space travel. He worked hard jobs in dynamite blasting and mines and on the railroad to fund his real work, rocket science, sometimes traveling many miles from home for pay. My mother never complained about losing her own dreams of being an actress and a pilot. She thought her love of flight had been a sign she was meant to marry him, a rocket scientist. He'd come home, sometimes after weeks of being gone, and say, 'Get me a cold lager.' She always made sure lager was in the house for him, even though she and her pious sister despised alcohol. He'd sit in

435

his chair and wait for her to take off his big boots and massage his big stinky feet. Sometimes I really hated him. But my mother was obsessed with my father. She never lost her schoolgirl crush on him even after six years of marriage. I had never seen a woman so devoted to any man…" *Until now*, I thought I could hear in his tone. "Her devotion to him was *sometimes* justified. He was sometimes a good man who taught his son how to be a man with that Roy Rogers kind of Code. 'Be brave,' 'protect the weak,' 'respect and romance women,' 'give Saturday to your wife and children but every other moment to your goals,' 'provide for your family,' 'be soft with animals and children but be hard on yourself.' He thought any man who woke up after a rooster's crow was a sluggard and any man who rested after dinner was a woman. Daytime, he worked for profit; nighttime, he worked for purpose. Even to relax, he enjoyed building things. He was always working." That sounded familiar. "He liked working with his mind, but he also liked working with his hands. He built our cabin, not only the log work but the stonework, and my mother was impressed by his handywork in making the fireplace, *their* fireplace for snuggling beside on Saturday nights when I was supposed to be asleep. She accepted only one night a week being devoted to romance and every other second being devoted to his work. Aside from a kiss on her cheek before he headed off to the mines that would keep him for weeks or some other treacherous place that might kill him, when he was at home, their focus was solely on rocketry. He had built a small concrete launchpad and 10x10 work shed, where he and my mother safely watched his rocket launches from a thick-glass window. When a rocket crashed into sea, they both dived in to recover it. She learned wrenches and bolts, which made her a good helper. And she always brought him coffee when he was working on some new design in the backyard, and she stayed up with him, regardless of the hour, to keep the coffee flowing to fuel his work. Like I said, she was as devoted to him as a saint to a cause."

"How did they meet?"

"Ah, I should've known you'd be interested in hearing the lovestory. He was in Baltimore, working at an automobile plant, learning engineering outside the school system, and studying heavy books on the subject at night; you know, getting an hour of sleep at night then working all day. Across from the factory, she sold snowballs from the wheeled cart to make money after her father's death. They had been shy, eying each other for weeks. He liked how kind she was giving snow cones away for free to those who couldn't afford them, and she liked how on his lunch break he would sit outside on the sidewalk and build stuff out of unused parts. When he finally got the nerve to buy a snow cone, she said, 'How about something sweeter like a wife?' That was the legend anyway." He smiled.

"But Pop wasn't all greatness. He was highly taciturn, cold, except around her, except on the rare occasion when she tried to push for affection while he was working then *she* would apologize for interrupting him. He was tough, no patience for loafing, particularly not in a boy, particularly not in his son. What could be expected from a man whose own father built weapons? He had an icy exterior, but apparently, he was warm in bed. My mother always came out of the bedroom on Sunday mornings looking like she had enjoyed a week basking in the sun. Her radiant smile illuminating the kitchen. With silky leisurely movement, she would turn on the radio, something sweet, open the curtains to allow in even more sunshine, rub her fingers through my hair and ask what her 'little Papa' wanted for breakfast. I wondered what in the heck does he do to her in there? How could that ice block possibly make her so sunny? Then he would come out, buckling his belt, with a smug satisfaction on his face like he had accomplished a feat, and my pious aunt would just about pass out from embarrassment. Pops and Mother would catch stares and her cheeks would turn peachy, remembering what he had done to her the previous night. He'd take his seat at the head of the table, and across that table, electricity flowed between them, but my mother, not wanting to be inappropriate around her son, would ask me what my plans were for the day."

I didn't say anything, too embarrassed, so I just kept trifling around in the small kitchen over pots and pans.

"Don't get me wrong, I liked my pop on Saturday afternoons when we'd fly kites and hike the Alaskan woods. Sometimes, it would be just me and him, when he instilled in me lessons on science and mathematics and how to be a man. But sometimes Bubbe and my aunt and mother would join us. I'd see Pops and Mother kissing slowly and deeply by a tree and she'd be holding onto his back like if she didn't she'd sink, and that all seemed like the picture of love to me. But I hated my pops on Saturday nights when the noise in their bedroom sounded like a bear battling a fluttering injured kite. Once I knocked on their door, and in an instant the noise stopped, and I said, 'Mama, are you alright?' 'She's fine!' he growled. 'Now go back to sleep!' I heard her whisper, 'I should go check on him.' 'No, he's not a baby.' My apologies, Lumi. I shouldn't have said that, any of that."

"It's okay."

"No, it's not. A man shouldn't talk like that around a girl."

"Some girls my age are already married."

I snuck a peek of his face, which expressed confliction about my comment.

"My mother was but she missed out on schooling and her goals."

"I thought you believed women shouldn't work for money."

"No one should work for money, as I've said. But just like Bubbe, she wanted to be a pilot to fly, not to make money."

"Did you continue to hate your pop about those Saturday nights?"

"Ah, I don't know. One night, when they thought I was asleep, I was in the shed, reading comic books, and I saw them outdoors in a sleeping bag, making those noises, and it dawned on me, those were sounds of bliss. He was making her happy, although only as a byproduct of his own fulfillment. Did I mention he was a chauvinist? He was commandant, no uncertainty about that, but she seemed to like it that way. Afterwards, I watched her reach her hand up to the sky to 'pick stars for him' then 'feed' them to him. I suppose I was a little jealous, though, of how much she loved him. She never fed stars to me. Sometimes I thought my pops was a fool for spending all his time working on rockets when he had the most beautiful star within reach. What could any other world possibly offer him that she wasn't already giving him?"

"You like other worlds."

"Well, Alaska is a prime location for a kid to develop a fascination with cold planets, not only because the ice and snow made me feel like I was on another world, but because the stars were so obvious there, no distractions from them."

"That's where you decided to be a scientist?"

"I decided that from science fiction." He laughed. "In Pop's work shed was a stack of flying saucer magazines, comics, and books. I sometimes stayed out there all night, sometimes with Bubbe, listening to music on the radio, not wanting to miss a moment of nighttime and starlight and the possibility of seeing a saucer. I'd read and dream. On these nights, whenever I had the money, I'd try a half-gallon of new ice cream, all the flavors."

That sounded like me reading romance comics with a box of chocolates.

"Aah, those boyhood Saturdays. My mother sometimes took me and Bubbe to the cinema house, where we enjoyed stuff like *Flash Gordon*."

"You were really close to your folks?"

"Well, sort of, but although my parents were good folks, they weren't my friends. Bubbe was my friend but she was much older, and my sister was my friend but she was really young. But my parents were just so into each other. Mostly, I was as isolated as a deadly germ; no one wanted to be infected with my strangeness. No friends at school, you know that story, because we share it. I wanted to make rockets, get away from this world, find one where I belonged, find a friend *out there*. Well, we were talking about food, and I've just been rambling. I remember my mother made good food. I just don't remember all the details."

"Did you have a favorite snowball?"

He thought about the snowballs, tasted the memory, recovered a smile. "They were all delicious, and cheap to boot, hence their Great Depression popularity. My sister, Bow, always chose green apple. 'Martian,' I'd call her because of her green lips and tongue, but obsessed with Martians, it was a compliment to her. A family of oddballs. Yeah, Bubbe and me and Bow were close." He smiled bigger than I had ever seen, testing the stonework's ability to stay stony.

I knew of any gift he would get this holiday season, the best would be the recovery of his sweet memories. I wished so deeply to have the ability to place him back into a warm moment with his family when they were alive and smiling and laughing and bickering and doing all those activities families do when gathered around a holiday table. I was convinced if any bigot spent one holiday with a family of the people he hated, he would no longer hate them, because he would see they were not so different from his own family.

"I remember now my mother also made traditional Polish meals sometimes, recipes from my bubbe, and traditional Russian meals for my pop, whatever he wanted, the way his mother, my babushka, had babied him to make up for his deprivation of pampering from his own tough father."

"Which were your favorite desserts from your babushka?"

He scraped ice off more memory windows to peer into warm scenes.

"I only met my babushka from Russia once, a hearty farm-bred woman who came to Alaska to visit us after my sister's birth. Little Mary Bow, named after two silent film stars. My babushka had held me as a baby too but I don't remember that. But I remember this: a cold rainy and icy slushy morning, during the holiday season, my mother nursing Bow in her rocking chair by the cabin's window, a knitted blanket over them, my aunt playing religious music on the old piano, where she taught me how to play music, and my pops in his muddy work boots stoking the fireplace with the poker, and my babushka making hobo coffee, and my bubbe wadding up biscuits in a speckled pie dish that had the appearance and feel of a campfire kettle, so when the biscuits came out from the cookstove, they were one giant heap of something like a biscuit cake instead of individual biscuits. In pioneer woman fashion, she pulled out a chunk of biscuits for herself, some for her daughters and Pops and Babushka, and she gave the pan to me. In the pan, she poured a generous helping of blackstrap sorghum, or molasses, and piled a three-inch slice of butter into the syrup. That was grand. My mouth waters remembering. I remember Babushka made great desserts like the charlotte. Soviets eat sweets too but I never see that broadcast on the evening news."

"I wish I had your mother's recipes." I felt bad as soon as I said it; I sensed he had not one keepsake of his mother, except memories. "Sputnik, I'm sorry. I wasn't thinking."

"That's often true, according to your grades in my class," he teased, letting me know he had not been offended. "I'm sure she would have enjoyed sharing her recipes with such a fine cook."

"Thank you," I said, while taking the re-warmed gingerbread pan from the stove.

"You need a bigger kitchen," he said, and I could tell he was calculating how he could remodel the camper. "My mother always needed a bigger kitchen too. There was just never enough money."

I waved my oven-mittened hand above the bread pan to cool off steam, and the scent of gingerbread went delightfully everywhere.

"You have much more important work to do, like defending space treaties and building rockets, than rebuilding me a kitchen."

"Please, let me build you something nice."

I could not talk him out of it. He would not discuss anything else now either since his mind was on a task.

On the small counter barely sat a wooden barrel ice cream maker with a hand crank. Earlier, I had scooped out the ice cream to let it harden in the freezer. I walked over to the tiny round-top red refrigerator and dreaded putting my hands into chilled air. After dolloping two scoops of caramel ice cream onto the bread pan and setting that melty treat in front of him, along with the spoon, I stood by the table, warming my hands by wrapping them around my cider mug.

"The ice cream chilled your little hands even through gloves," he said.

"I'll live, Professor."

"Cake *and* cookies *and* ice cream. I feel like a king. Bubbe and Mother and my aunt always made me feel that way like I was so special, destined for greatness."

"You are."

I took our dinner from the stove, and Sputnik was right, the kitchen did not have enough room for making holiday feasts, pans and pots and casserole dishes almost sitting on top of one another.

I gave Mullybiski a roll.

"Just one?" his eyes said. "Gimme a little more of dem rolls. It's the holidays, sister. Show some generosity."

Ooh, alright, one more.

Pythagoras peeked his head out from his shell for raw carrot slices.

I turned on the television, kept it on mute, in case pug and turtle wanted holiday company, black & white Roy Rogers and Dale Evans Christmas show.

442

"That was delicious," Sputnik said, pushing the bread pan aside, ready for dinner, the dessert task finished.

I lovingly made him a dinner plate and I couldn't imagine Michelangelo putting more care into the composition of a masterpiece. Of course the yams, cheesy macaroni, and carrots could not be next to each other—too much orange bunched up. I had to arrange the supper painting just so. I wanted his eyes to be impressed with at least one sight in the room, if not my plainly face.

I set a basket of rolls onto the typewriter and laid down his plate and all my vulnerability right in front of him. He knew I was daydreaming about being his wife, but he did not seem to mind on this snowy night.

I sat at the booth opposite his handsomeness and casually watched which foods he chose first, which ones merited seconds.

"It's all delicious," he said, being nice.

I just knew my latkes had been a letdown, my first time making them. He seemed most interested in the candied yams, which he ate four helpings of, and that made sense, since yams were coated in molasses.

"Would you like some more?" I kept asking, my voice soft again like we were in bed.

"Yes," on the carrots and macaroni, "No, I'm fine," on the kugel.

After a meal, unlike some men, he did not like smoking a cigar but chewing gum. He offered some to me. No, thanks. Licorice. Made out of bootstraps or something like that.

"My apologies it's not peppermint," he said, coughing his way through the sentence.

"I have all those candy canes," I said, clearing the table of plates. "Sputnik Claus brought them."

"Do you need help with the dishes?" he asked.

"No, there aren't many but thanks for offering."

"My pops never did."

Before we went out into the snow, an event I was surprisingly looking forward to, I made him dark roast coffee, which he drank even with gum in his mouth, while I cleaned dishes and stored leftovers in the refrigerator. I hoped he would tell me more of his story, but he did not, his mind still on rebuilding my kitchen.

"I can see a way to do it," he finally said.

"You don't have to."

"Why say I don't 'have to'? Why let a man believe he does not have to be helpful to a woman? He has to be if he wants to be a real man. Demand he be the best man he can be, for you and for him."

"Okay, Professor," I said, sitting down for a quick rest.

Relaxed and satiated and full of coffee and licorice, which he claimed calmed him, the aeronaut unbuttoned the first marble button of his flannel shirt, revealing his white undershirt and sprigs of dark hair curling up over the T-shirt's rim. "That was an exquisitely good meal. My apologies about leaving so many latkes. I felt betrayal to my bubbe for enjoying them so much."

I tried to give a smile that was both happy and sad.

"Don't use a smile incorrectly, Pep. A smile expresses happiness, not sadness. I enjoyed the meal. It's fine. You can smile. Come, let us build snowspaceships."

Snow was no longer falling, but the yard was the smooth top of vanilla ice cream before any spoon has dug into it, and twigs mimicked vanilla beans. The apple tree wore frost prettily. The fence was mounded in snow, as were trees in the backyard forest. Our cars, parked outside the fence, had been transformed into igloos, the truck bed filled with snow. The camper, nestled in the valley, was a long way from the road; from our vantage point, we could not even see the road. No cars, no headlights, miles beyond society, but stars were twinklier than ever.

Like a man in church, the rocket scientist took a moment to raise his eyes to heaven and offer reverence. I wished to be a planet or a star to feel him gaze at me that way.

"Venus is bright," I said.

"That's Jupiter."

Jupiter was bright, so was the creaminess of the Milky Way, a band of stars whose light all merged, where our galaxy got its name, I had learned from Sputnik.

"It does look exceptionally bright for winter," the physicist said, noticing me admiring the Milky Way. "In winter, we're not staring into the galaxy's star-packed bright center but on the outskirts, yet it's still breathtaking."

You're breathtaking, but I did not say that.

I liked when Mars appeared as a ruby pebble against dark blue silk, but Mars must have been on break, because I did not see him out. In 1965, we could still imagine life on those planets, so I wondered about their holidays and traditions, and I had a pleasant fantasy of Sputnik and I and our children visiting another planet during their holiday season, bearing gifts from Earth for their children.

Being surrounded by fresh snow, snow-mounded hills, just me and him, felt like being explorers on a distant planet untouched by human footprints. I knew the science fiction reader was fantasizing that too, being the first campers on another world, which also had reindeer!

"Sssh," Sputnik whispered, as we watched the magical-looking reindeer in the snowy distance before he or she disappeared into the woods, where Santa's sleigh must have been parked.

"Wow!" I mouthed.

Even though I wore Sputnik's corduroy coat, since he had insisted his coat provided more protection than mine, the cold air hit hard. Our noses and ears turned red quickly.

"There are gloves in the pocket," he said, his breath making clouds in frosty air. "Put those on over your other gloves."

"What about you?"

"*I'll live.*"

"Your hands are bare."

"So are your legs."

My knees reddened either from the cold or his comment.

"I work in this stuff, but I haven't played in it in a long long time," he said as if he was an old man whose boyhood had passed by sixty years ago.

He seriously went about building a snowspacecraft, whereas I decided to stick with the traditional snowman. I liked their smiley dispositions, but I realized I had never made a snowman, never played in the snow, since I despised cold weather. The last time I had rounded snow had been to make cannons to bombard Earth after winter had stolen my momma.

I gently walked, not wanting to ruin the pristine snowy landscape, searching for something to be the eyes of my snowfellow. Right about the time I leaned down to retrieve a gumball which my shoeprint had uncovered from slush, a projectile snowball hit me in the shoulder. I heard him laughing, standing by his spacerocket, halfway built.

"I can't believe you snowballed me, the man who thinks Wile E. Coyote is quite mean."

He answered by hurling another snowball, which splattered across the lower part of my coat. Boys!

Well, this was war, of course.

I shot snowballs too and gave his hair a good frosting.

He hopped over the fence, ducked, and began pelting me with rapid snow fire through the slats.

I ran to the side of the trailer, the best I could in high heels, and went about fashioning quite a hefty snowcannon, which would take a big amount of force to toss all the way to the fence. Then I decided not to fire the weapon, because I was worried by the violent sounds of his coughing.

"Cease fire!" he said, walking across enemy lines, waving the candy cane like a surrender flag.

"Scared of my snowcannon, are you?" I was worried he was sick, but I did not let him know that.

"You're getting too cold," he said.

"Uh-huh, sure, that's it," I teased.

"Let's go inside."

Our Cold War lasted about ten minutes.

We went inside our glowing gingerbread house for more cider and iced cookies and holiday music.

Ooh, the warm camper felt like Heaven!

Having fun, I had not realized how cold I was, but now I did. From the couch, watching Lawrence Welk's Christmas show, Mullybiski looked at me when I made a long "Brrrrr," while removing snowy coat and gloves, placing them on the coat rack, and rubbing snow from my knees. I wiped snow off Sputnik's hair and shoulders, and he reciprocated the caringness. We laughed about it, us thawing out and getting snow everywhere, which looked like wispy dandelion seeds against red carpet.

He started coughing badly and took a handkerchief from his pants pocket to cough into.

"Sputnik—"

He glared at me, advising me not to coddle him, so I stood there, helplessly, listening to him cough like he was dying, until finally the coughs softened then ended.

"Sputnik, your shirt's so wet, do you want to take it off, so I can dry it for you?"

"How would you dry it?" He put the handkerchief back into his pocket. "I don't see any fireplace for us to hang our stockings."

"With a hair dryer."

"I'm fine. You need a fireplace."

"Sputnik, campers can't have fireplaces, can they?"

"I could get an electric fireplace, but no, that wouldn't be right. You need a hearth—"

Abruptly, he stopped talking, as if he had been transported back to a hurtful memory, and I thought he was going to be hauled back into a terrible flashback from the war.

"You didn't get too cold, did you?" he asked, quickly snapping out of the painful memory.

"No, I'll live."

We sat at the booth with our warm drinks, and I warmed my hands again by wrapping them around my cider mug.

"I didn't get too rough, did I?" he asked.

"No, we were just playing."

"Just making sure. Wouldn't it be nice if when humans were at their breaking point of anger, they only fought snow wars?"

"I'd prefer that world."

We enjoyed cookies and cider, while the radio sang that snowflakes were falling on every town.

Sputnik nodded toward the sheets of paper rolled in my typewriter and asked what I had been working on before our celebration had started.

"Not algebra homework, I bet," the professor said.

I told him I was searching my mind for a story to write about. He took a contemplative moment before responding.

"Perhaps you should write the story you were destined to write," he said, while unbuttoning his shirt cuff and rolling up his sleeve. He didn't unbutton his other sleeve, and I realized his rolling up his sleeve had not been an act of seduction or relaxation. He was showing me the numbers on his strong but vulnerable youngman arm—the story *I* was destined to write? This was a real man I was sitting across from, a man of unbreakable dignity and bravery, a man who deserved a warm sweet home (a refuge from the gray cold world). While I was the girl who could give him warm sweet gingerbread, I was not the girl to write about his agony in a death camp. I realized I could not bear it, hearing about my friend being tortured, the man I had just played a silly game of snow fight with, who had not so long ago been terrorized in a real war with actual bullets and cannons, that no so long ago, an army of hatred had wanted to kill my love. I was not the right writer for that story. I could not even bear to hear a cough hurt him.

As if he could see my thoughts, as always, he said, "I would never tell you about all that, nor would I ask you to write about it. Cinderella should write about romance, not about war. Those stories must be told, every one of them, but I don't want *you* to write them."

I was offended then as if he agreed I was not a "serious enough" writer to write about war, or maybe I was just not the girl he wanted to share those memories with; maybe he shared those serious memories with the sociology professor from Harvard.

"After Pop's death, financial problems forced my bubbe, mother, aunt, baby sister and me to move from Alaska to Poland. Before the move, I'll never forget the sight of the women in my life dressing up business-like

449

in roles that did not match the actors, casting as bad as a doily playing a briefcase. They were so nervous, pretending to be business characters, trying their best to be as man-like as possible to be taken seriously by the Bank. It made me ill. I remember Mother saying, 'My young son and daughter, investing in them is investing in the future,' and the Bank replying, 'We don't give loans just for people to live on.' When the bank denied generosity, we moved. It took me a heck of a time to learn Polish, because I fought against it, missing my Alaska. We lived with Bubbe's brother, who owned a shoe factory."

"He had funded Bubbe's cross-country road trip?"

"Yeah. He was well off financially. His house had a good backyard, not quite the Alaskan outback but a few trees. His wife, the one who rode cross country with Bubbe, was a painfully shy wallflower who got along well with my pious aunt. We had a happy time for a while. Bubbe, Bow, and me had our own fraternity. They were members of Sampi Koppa Digamma. We were woods explorers and baseball players and future astronauts and hot air balloonists. But we were on edge because of the rise of Nazi power next door in Germany, not to mention the antisemitism we were already subjected to. Well, I won't give you a war lesson. You know Poland was ransacked by the Soviets and Nazis, and I would have hated all Russians, hated that part of my heritage, if not for my sweet babushka, who was killed during the Battle of Stalingrad."

"I'm sorry."

"At least her death was quick. When the Nazis conquered our city and thrust up loudspeakers so they could spew hatespeech for hours and hours, many of our neighbors turned on us, the same people who had come to our house for dinner, and now they all hated us, or at least pretended to hate us to save themselves from persecution. It was no secret what Hitler had planned for the Jews. We were eventually forced into Poland's hole in the wall, where ten people were crammed in a room."

"The ghetto?"

"Yeah, but do you know what was the hardest part of that experience? Watching all the women in my life no longer be treated like women. As a young man, I was taught, 'Ladies first,' 'never hit a woman,' 'never fight a war with women and children,' and this was not about sexism, this was about respect and decency and a man's natural desire to love and protect women, wives and mothers and daughters and sisters and sweethearts. But I watched those honor codes get broken across all the women in my life."

He was not a tiger to protect *himself* but to protect women.

He took a drink of a warm apple cider that could do nothing for his deepest coldness.

"I told you my mother was a lot like you, wearing her pretty hair in pretty ribbons and always listening to the radio, and my bubbe was the picture perfect grandma with headscarf and a kitchen that smelled of both jam and onions, and my aunt was close to a saint, and my great-aunt and cousins were a mixture of flirty and brassy and sweet and smart, but all those women were beaten and shot and killed."

My expression must have asked, "What about your sister?" because he said, "And sweet little Bow, she was so smart, so in love with learning. Every time I teach, I'm teaching to her. Ah, Bow. She always wore a baseball cap, and she was actually better than me at baseball, I admit now, even though I never admitted that to her. She kept up with all the baseball stats to impress me. I was her big brother hero who swept down to rescue her when she scraped her knee learning to ride a bike. She didn't have Pops, so I had to protect her." The stonework of his voice was shaking. "Like you, she could toss a mighty snowcannon. Well, Nazi soldiers didn't kill her. She was killed by a writer when she was seven."

"A writer?"

"Does that surprise you? Who do you think supported the Nazis? Who do you think commit murders and rapes? Professional murderers and rapists? No. Writers, professors, teachers, actors, housewives, etcetera etcetera. Writing his sophisticated books with Nazi undertones, he frequented a café that offered a view of schoolchildren on the sidewalk, and he targeted her and her innocence."

Gersh was not suffering Post Traumatic Stress Disorder from the war but from his entire life.

"This was not long before the invasion. It was on a Saturday in the summer. Bow and I went out shopping, and she said she wanted to go to the toy store, but I wanted to get ice cream. I said, 'You little brat, we always do what you want first.' I was irritable about always having to safeguard her. 'Just go off to the toy store. I'm getting ice cream.' I called her a brat. That was the last thing I said to her, the last thing she thought her hero felt about her."

"Brothers and sisters say those things to each other. She knew you didn't mean it."

His scowl said he did not want to hear any excuses for his actions.

"What makes me so angry," he said, his voice dynamite, "is that I always protected her, but on that one morning, I didn't. I was stuffing my face with ice cream while my little sister was being lured by a kidnapper."

"How old were you?"

"Why does that matter?" he snapped, not wanting to hear that his young age absolved him from wrongdoing. "I couldn't protect her, just like I couldn't protect Bubbe."

Another cold memory yanked him out of the warm camper and threw him back into the barbed past.

"On that morning when I thought I felt cold because I had yet to experience the coldest cold, soldiers came to remove me from my family. I don't understand why our family was broken apart in increments and I don't want to understand the Nazis' actions. My bubbe said in broken sign language, 'No, don't take him!' She made the hug around herself to show she was talking about 'Gershom,' her hug, don't take him. She had already lost her Bow. Bubbe had both a feistiness and childishness about her like when she wanted the last piece of dessert and someone else reached for it, she would playfully say, 'No, mine,' then offer her sweet toothless pitiful smile. She gave that smile to the soldier in hopes for my return. My grandma kept trying to hold onto me. I told you she was sweet on me, the little king. She believed I could accomplish anything in this universe. Her and my mother and my sister and my aunt and cousins all thought I was this grand person headed to the stars. She gave me her thermos in case the soldiers did take me away and she wanted me to be able to have grandma's soup. One of the young soldiers warned her to back off by pushing his gun into the old Lady's shoulder. But she wouldn't give up, not Bubbe the Magnificent, so he hit her in the soft face with the back of his gun, as if that much force was needed to push down an eighty-pound woman. 'That's my grandmother!' I shouted. I pleaded with the soldier, 'That's my grandmother,' like I was a kid on a playground telling another kid, 'You've gone too far. You don't hit grandmas.' Even bad guys in movies didn't hurt grandmothers. The soldier's stone face told me he didn't care that she was my grandma, and that would have been the most shocking horrific realization I had ever had, but I had already learned the horrors that humans were capable of. The SS would often knock on doors, which was sickening, the convention, knocking on doors just to open the door, barge in, take someone out, and shoot them or hang them, just because. Even so, I could not believe this was real. At some point, I would wake up in Pop's shed in Alaska, having fallen asleep reading a scary science fiction story about monsters taking over Earth, and my mother would bring me cocoa, the way she did when I had nightmares as a little boy, and she would say in that soothing warm voice of hers, as soft as cotton meant to heal injury, 'It was just a dream.' But, no, I was about to be hauled off to real hell."

He took another drink, in need of something much more capable than cider of deadening his pain.

"My mother cradled my hurt grandma, but my bubbe wouldn't give me up without trying with everything she had to keep me—this was her last chance to save me. With my stoniest voice, I told her, 'Go away, old woman.' I couldn't let the soldiers think she mattered to me, that this old woman was my best friend, because they would hurt her for sure. But she pushed at the soldier and he shot her, an image I can never erase from my thoughts, one I don't want to paint vividly for you to have to see too for the rest of your life. The Nazis stole God from me that morning. God would not allow soldiers to exist that killed grandmothers. Then I was eventually numbered at the death camp, where I saw the fate of the rest of the women I loved, including my mother, women who were stripped naked to either become prisoners or victims of murder. My pious aunt survived, at least her body survived, her once chaste body tattooed with 'Whore for Hitler's Troops,' and she could not live with that marking. The Nazis did believe in 'ladies first,' the ladies, the children, first to be murdered, not all the ladies but so many of them, the old ladies and frail ladies especially. Well, my height saved me, although my grandma's kindness and free spirit had not saved her, and my mother's beauty and delicacy had not saved her, and my aunt's forgivingness and spirituality had not saved her, but my brute height saved me, because the idiot soldiers thought I was older, and what did I do with my fortune?"

453

He was torn between wanting to and *not* wanting to reveal this: "I did terrible things. It makes me sick when I see my name in the paper, when I'm heralded as a rising star. I only work hard to make Mother and Bubbe and Bow proud because they believed in my grand dreams, and I won't disappoint them. But I don't deserve adulation. I should not be your hero."

"You are a hero. Look at what you survived."

His glare suggested I had insulted his honor, but his eyes softened upon this realization, "You're not a man. You don't understand the feeling that comes from being unable to protect a woman you love. I did not—I do not—deserve to be alive. I failed the women I loved. Do not say anything. I don't want to hear erroneous reasons why I'm not to blame."

"I'll turn off the radio," I said, showing respect, especially since The Chipmunks were singing about Christmas.

"No, don't. Keep it on. Please. You deserve to hear the radio and the cute little chipmunks. I don't but you do."

"Why do you say that?"

"One of the other men who was taken away told me, 'Make yourself available for work and you'll be paid with your life.'"

"And because you made yourself available for work for the Nazis you think you don't deserve to be available for love?"

"I did terrible work for the Nazis."

He did not *avoid* painful memories; he punished himself constantly with torturous memories. I realized his stonework was not walled around him for protection but for punishment—he had jailed himself, the boy inside, to keep him from ever being happy again, from ever even enjoying sweets again, because he believed he had done terrible things, but for one moment, the little boy had been freed to play in the snow, his warden overcome by holiday spirit.

"I don't deserve to be at King Arthur's Round Table, I assure you."

"I love you anyway."

"No, Lumi, don't waste your love on me."

454

"Love is never wasted on darkness, where it's most needed. Let me be the helper candle for you, Gersh."

"I told you I did terrible things."

I could not understand why he was blaming *himself* for any wrongdoing.

"You were *forced* to do terrible things."

He did not want any explanation for his actions that would offer him forgiveness.

"Remember my analogy about 'X' and 'Y'? You must understand, 'X' does want what was subtracted from him to be added like a heavy burden to the Lady 'Y.' The last thing I'd ever want to do is subtract any pinkness from your heart."

I could not believe he had done "terrible things," no more than I could believe Santa Claus hurt children. Seeing my disbelief:

"I did terrible things!" The usually stoic professor, so logical in newspapers and classrooms, slammed his fist so hard on the windowsill, I quickly reached my hand to the menorah to keep it from falling. He closed his eyes, as if unable to bear seeing my face wince due to his outburst. "My apologies." He opened his eyes and looked at my hands in church gloves. "The last thing I'd ever want to do is scare you or hurt you, that's why I won't tell you morbid stories, because I could never spare the women in my life from those grisly stories, but I can spare you and your softness."

I was more confused than scared.

"Lumi, you always look at me like I've transcended Man, like I'm an ideal. So, I don't take any joy in destroying your image of me, not because destroying that image hurts me but because it hurts you, but you have to know the truth: I am not a good man, if I'm a man at all. But I will not wither your flowery heart by telling you the details."

The snowstorm was turning into a blizzard, beating against the trailer, covering up holiday music from the radio.

I feared the answer to this, "You were forced to hurt other prisoners?" I had read of such horror stories about the concentration camps.

"I did something much more unforgiveable than hurt them physically."

455

"Sputnik, I don't understand."

"Because your heart is too good to fathom the wickedness. I can't tell you what I did because it will ruin your story. You're the one I need to write the story of The Snowflake Gal, a story that must be told by an unwilted heart. *The Snowflake Gal and The Fantastic Snowflake.* That's the story you were destined to write, Peppermint, and I've known this from the start."

His tone worried me. He sounded like a dying man making not a confessional but living his last dying wish: entrusting this story to me, the writer, so I could share it with the world.

"I know you've experienced tragedy, Lumi, but you've managed to retain a belief system that is the opposite of others' belief systems—what most adults believe and do not believe are reversed in you. Whereas most people believe in bad guys, you still believe in angels. Miraculously you've gone through cold years without a hardening of the heart, without an aging of your awe. You've retained a child's view of looking at the world. That's not a weakness. That's a strength. It's a feat. You live in a world where all the bears are Winnie the Pooh. So, I trust you will write about *her*, my Alina, The Snowflake Gal, and not the Nazis. You won't write the bad guy's story. I tried to write *The Snowflake* story myself, but I could not with my gray heart. But you'll put love in the story's forefront, and you'll light the story in tender emotion, and show it through a soft filter, because the Nazi tried to erase from life—gentleness and innocence and the belief in magic."

He asked me not to use gray ink when writing The Snowflake Gal's story, not the gray of crematoriums and ashes, but to use pink ink to write how she had said, "Never stop seeing the snowflakes," when all he could see were ashes, ashes of people, yes, but also ashes of millions of lifestories torn and burned and lost, even the crayon stories of children.

"When I came back to America, one night on Long Island docks, Ben said, 'Hey, kid, look, it's snowing.' Snowing? All I saw were ashes. The ashes had followed me from the death camp. I had betrayed her. I could no longer see the snowflakes. But you, *you*, Lumi, please never stop seeing the snowflakes, never stop writing about them."

He asked *me* to tell the story because I did not scoff at such a fantastical lovestory blooming against barbed fences and machine guns. I did not question whether The Snowflake Gal was a flesh-and-blood girl or a dream or an angel or a victim whose body Gershom saw in a pile of discarded bodies and he imagined her lifestory or if she was all those characters—the love was real and the love was magical.

She was German, but her name was Polish: *Alina*, "light." Gershom had waited his entire life to meet a girl who appeared to have stepped out of a butterfly garden. "A sweet tiny dynamo Katherine Stinson of a girl," her goal was to be an airborne nun of an order of her own creation: sisters in biplanes flying the globe to do good. (Now I knew why Sputnik was so in awe of my wanting to be a nun.) She had the "goodest" heart. The scientist was a brilliant academic yet when he spoke of her he used childsweet words like "goodest." "She was just good," he praised again and again. She had a great-big big heart and an unflinching faith in goodness. In God. In prevailing love. And she saw the goodness in him. He could not understand why. But she made him feel good. Good about her. About life. About God. About the future. She was goodness personified. She was his North Star guiding him home.

Alina's shy mother was a cellist, and her silent father owned a bookstore; two quiet people who made much music in the bedroom. "This is one for the history books," they said of their love. Using the selling of books as a guise, Alina's father made fake identity documents for Jews; "book runs" were document deliveries undertaken by brave young men and women on bicycles. An artist, Alina's father used the tiny attic above his bookshop to hide in plain sight chemicals and other forging tools to create and alter documents, a race against time for those who were about to be murdered. After he was taken away for his crime of helping, Alina's mother received a delivery of a small box, labeled "traitor." Inside the box were ashes, but one thing had not been burned: her husband's wedding ring, a gold ring engraved in Hebrew with a passage from The Bible's only love poem, The Song of Songs—"I am my beloved's and my beloved is mine." Alina saw this as a symbol of love's eternalness. But her mother could not see that.

She could only see that her husband had been reduced to ashes. She had once told her daughter, "It breaks my heart that I can't hear all the music of all times." Now the cellist was silent. The Nazis had quieted her song. But Alina would not be quieted.

She had an unquenchable desire for challenges, a brave girl who sought challenges most people avoided at all costs. A high school student and photographer by day, she was a renegade Snowflake by night. Alina started The Snowflakes; like the White Roses and the Swing Kids, the Snowflakes were an underground movement that preached love in a world where love had to be preached underground. While the Nazis were brainwashing youth to believe they could be a part of greatness through hate, The Snowflakes had secret meetings where they listened to banned music, music by Jewish and black musicians, and they read romantic poetry, spiritual poetry, and tried to hold onto love like the last matchstick left in winter. Like her father, Alina always wanted to help people, rescue people, recruit people to the cause. When a small group of The Snowflakes were caught preaching love, they were arrested by the Gestapo and tortured for information about other members, well-known members such as professors and writers, but the group would not betray their friends. Alina was told if she loved the Jews so much, she could perish with them. But she was offered an alternate fate by a high-ranking soldier—if she recanted her preaching of love and acceptance, she would not be hauled to the death camp. She was a pretty German girl and the soldier did not want Germany to lose such "fine stock."

On the coldest day of his life, when the sun seemed to make no difference at all, Gershom was about to voluntarily go to the gas chamber with the others who had been hauled in, or to throw himself against the electrified fence. He felt for the first time since his imprisonment had begun that he was making a noble choice.

Outside, he saw a gal shivering in woodland, imprisoned woodland, unlike the wide free forests of Gersh's childhood. The girl was looking at the gray sky, and he thought she was either wishing she could fly away or staring at her fate: the ashes.

Gershom had been a romantic boy, and he was still a boy, only a young teenager, but the sensitive boy, often picked on for his bashfulness, had thought he would never meet a girl who would kiss softly enough, until he saw her—his dream girl in a death prison on the day he was going to volunteer to die. At this point in the story, he laughed away the pain, "How's that for fate?"

Then it was like all the fences, soldiers, guns, watchtowers, and the entire prison disappeared, and boy and girl were standing next to each other in body the way they had always been in spirit.

"What do you see?" he asked, wondering what she could possibly be smiling about in prison.

"The snowflakes," she said, speaking his language in a German accent. Goosebumps were all across her, not from fear but from awe—The Snowflakes all around her. "I love snowflakes."

He looked up and realized it was snow cascading to Earth, not ashes.

"Snowflakes are winter's flowers," she said, while opening her mouth to taste them. "They taste like peppermint kisses. Try."

With her, he could taste peppermint in the snowflakes, he could even see the snowflakes, like a man holding onto a saint's hand could walk across water.

She closed her eyes and said, "I still see the snowflakes. I want you to see them too. Try. With your eyes closed."

"I can still see them."

"Never stop seeing the snowflakes, even amidst these ashes."

Opening his eyes, "You're so beautiful," the boy said to the girl.

"And if I wasn't, could you still see that I was?"

Yes, he could still see her as beautiful, regardless of her appearance—she had all the good traits of all the women in his life, and he could not let those good traits be destroyed.

She saw him as beautiful too despite his emaciation and stink and scraggy clothes rags.

He thought she was Jewish and was shocked to learn she had accepted the fate to die for her beliefs, the modern Joan of Arc. If not for her, he would have hated all Germans, all gentiles. She told him not to remember Germany for this. The candy cane had originated in Germany, remember that; after all, it was the holiday season, which Gersh had been unaware of in prison.

They talked and talked like time had stopped to allow them to remember their predestined love before soldiers tried to make them forget. He wanted her to know, "You're not just everything I've ever wanted in a woman but everything I've ever wanted in an angel."

"Then let me do something angelic for you, Gershom." She had heard he was volunteering to be murdered with the others, but she asked him not to do it. "You are going to make sure the story of The Snowflakes gets told," she said, wise as a sage, in a way that suggested *he* would not tell the story, but he would entrust someone else, the right one, to tell the story.

Because of her, he did not volunteer to be killed, but instead vowed to dedicate his life to making sure her story got told and creating for her the largest, most beautiful snowflake.

"Not just for me," she told him, "but for this entire world."

He wanted to kiss her but she was wed to celibacy. "Wait for it, Gershom. Our kiss will be worth eternity."

She gave him the ring, the ring unable to be destroyed, and he knew it would be stolen from the guards who stole everything.

"They already tried to take it," she explained, "but the ring would not come off my finger." She said she had been meant to keep it to give to him. Now the ring slid easily from her finger, and she placed it on his finger. "Our love has God in it. No matter what horrific images they subject you to see, never believe they can kill me and never stop seeing the snowflakes, Gershom. Promise."

"I promise."

And they held each other for warmth, as they danced slowly in snowflakes, two figurines in a snow globe of a world.

"Then what happened?" I asked at that point in the story.

He seemed disappointed like maybe I was not the one whom the glass slipper fit, not the Cinderella to tell this magical story.

"Then what happened? The ending is up to you," he said, sounding like Moon-Moon. "You have two choices, Lumi. I could not write her beautiful story because I made the wrong choice for its ending. I hope the horrors I have told you of tonight have not ruined your ability to write the right ending for *The Snowflake* story."

I reached across a distance farther than the table between us, all the way to the iceberg where he had been stranded, and warmed his hand by letting him know I knew the right answer to "Then what happened?"

Suddenly, the lights in the camper went out, which made the two candles in the menorah look even brighter and ghostlier, glowing on the windowsill against ice outside glass.

The room got quieter without the radio and the noise of the heater and refrigerator. Ice pelting the camper's metal sounded like soldiers marching.

"This is scary," I said. I had never experienced the fierceness of a northeastern ice storm. "Why did the heater go out too? I thought it was a propane heater."

"It is but its ignition is electric, so the pilot light kicked off."

"We're going to blow up."

"No, we're not. The heater has a fail-safe system, which means the gas stops flowing when the pilot goes out."

He stood up from the table and went over to the door. He heard the ice marching too, and I thought I would lose him, that he would go back to the death march and allow them to shoot him, not with bullets but with coldness.

"You can't go out there," I said.

"I'm going to see if it's a line here. You go ahead and light some candles and save your knees and toes from stubs in the dark." Without even wearing his coat, he opened the door, brought in a windfall of ice, and went out into the blizzard, keeping me shut in warm safety.

I worried about him, him and his death wish, especially now that he had accomplished what he felt he had been spared to accomplish—entrusting *The Snowflake* story to me.

When he came back in, he looked blue cold.

I dashed over to him, took his cold hands into mine. "Please don't go out there again."

He said he thought the problem was elsewhere and the electric company would probably have it fixed in a few hours since it was too cold a night for people to be without heat.

"It's going to get cold in here quick," he said, removing his hands from mine to spare my hands the loss of their warmth.

"Pythagoras!" In the den, I went over to the cold-blooded tortoise, knowing he could not survive too long in this kind of cold. I took one of the couch cushions and placed it on the floor. I set Mullybiski atop the cushion along with the turtle and bundled them up with blankets, so Pythagoras could stay warm from the dog's body heat.

"I'm impressed," Sputnik said, removing twigs from one kitchen booth to the other. "Now, your turn. Come here."

Sitting in the booth together, he put his arms around me, while we watched candlelight dance in the menorah.

462

"What if the power doesn't come back on tonight?" I asked, starting to shiver, more from fear of cold than being cold. I knew how coldness could kill.

"I'll keep you warm. Don't worry." He rubbed his hands together briskly, generating heat then started to take off my gloves, which I knew would feel as sensual as him taking off my dress.

"Sputnik, don't."

"Why?"

"Because my hands are scarred. The gloves are prettier."

"Your hands are cold. Let me warm them." He had never seen my bare hands and at the sight of their nudity, he whispered, "Beautiful."

I adored hearing the word "beautiful" from his boy voice; my hands felt crowned in glory—even his beloved stars had not been crowned "beautiful," yet my hands had.

He held my hands in the large bare warmth of his despite my scars, despite his.

"It's easier to stay warm this way, Peppermint."

"Without clothes being in the way?"

He did not respond; instead, he took the candy cane from his shirt pocket, offered it to me. I split the candy for us to share, but he did not believe he deserved a share of the sweetness. After the candy, as the darkened room kept getting colder, I leaned my face against his coughing chest and he held my hands again.

When he said, "I love you," a dozen new stars appeared in my sky.

"Lumi, I felt drawn to the apple orchard that Saturday morning, just like I felt drawn to Stargust, and drawn to the bakery even before I knew you worked there, and I know you are the one who is meant to tell *The Snowflake* story. There is no God for me, Pep, but God still exists for you, and God made it so for us to meet, of that I'm convinced. That morning on the hayride, I thought let others seek chemistry in a relationship, we'll seek math—a quest to be two sides of an equation. I wanted to run away from this world with you, to hold you and protect you. The prison walls could not keep out my love for her, my desire to kiss her, love her, make love to her, just like nothing can stop those feelings I have now. I thought of you that entire weekend after the hayride. In spirit, you were with me in my sleeping bag those nights. That first morning in the patisserie, I wanted to give into these sweet feelings. Yet I've been conflicted. I want to love you, but I don't deserve to love you, and I certainly don't deserve your love."

I realized his aloofness had never served to protect his own feelings but mine.

"I don't deserve the love of any woman, and I don't deserve to kiss or touch you. When I found out you were my student, I knew fate had made it be that way. I could not love you romantically. We were meant to be in each other's lives, and you reminded me of my promise to build the biggest snowflake, and I would protect you, and you would write *The Snowflake* story, but I could not be your husband. But I worried, I worry, I'm hurting your feelings, denying your love, yet I don't know what is right. Besides, you're so young and you're a student and you want to be a nun. My being with you wouldn't exactly win me any medals for honorability."

"If I had a son, I'd want him to marry a girl like me."

"Ah, really?"

I was happy to make him laugh.

"Sputnik, if you're convinced God made it so for us to meet, I'm convinced I was not drawn to come out here to go to school—I came out here to meet you. Of that I'm certain. No matter how absurd the rest of the universe, our love has been astounding enough to make mysticism true—our love created its own magic, and we found each other against all odds. Your love is so strong, I no longer need love from anyone or anything else."

I entwined my fingers with his, telling him God or fate or angels had made the lights go out, so that we would make light and warmth together.

"You think you've done unforgiveable things, but I still love you, Sputnik."

"Then you must really be an angel because only an angel could forgive me."

"You don't need forgiveness. You didn't do anything wrong."

"Stop saying that!" His hands let go of mine and sat heavy with burden on the table. "Don't you understand I would have let them kill you too? And if you're forgiving me because you think I did not really commit any sins then that is not forgiveness at all."

"Whatever you did, I still love you and forgive you."

I rubbed my finger over the numbers on his lower arm.

"Stop it!"

"No, I won't stop loving you!" I shouted and he was surprised by my forcefulness. "You told me I'm not a man, so I can't understand what it feels like to be unable to protect the woman I love. But you're not a woman and you don't understand the feeling a woman has when she can't protect the boy she loves, especially her son. Do you really think your mother and grandmother would have exchanged your life for theirs? From everything you've told me about them, that's the last thing they would have wanted. You were just a little boy and even if you had been a grown man, you could not have saved them. You could not have stopped a gun from shooting Bubbe. And, no, she did not want you to jump in the way. You could not have stopped soldiers from killing your mother. Your mother and grandmother wanted you to live. Just like Alina wanted you to live. Your life was spared. You feel guilty for that but you shouldn't. No woman expects the impossible from a man. I feel so safe with you. You are the most gallant man I've ever met. I know if you could save me you would. But if an asteroid

465

was headed for this camper, I wouldn't expect you to be able to save me. I'd just want you to love me."

"I killed them."

"No, you didn't." I knew I could reach the scientist's ability to reason but reaching the little boy who believed he had let his family die would be harder. "I am not going to allow you to let the Nazis off the hook. You are not going to take the blame for their sins."

"I'm not a man who deserves to be in this gingerbread house with you, playing fake snowball war with you, receiving cake and cookies and candy bars, and I am certainly not a man who deserves to celebrate Hanukkah. I have to stay in that doomed story with all the ones who suffered, until it is my time to be ashes."

"My Moon-Moon once told me that no one can erase what you write inside yourself; you have never let anyone erase the courage and love and dignity inside of you."

His leg shook, the stonework around him being tested to its limit, and tears were piling in his eyes, but he would not let them fall; he would not allow himself release.

"You're a good man, Gersh, and I want you with me in this gingerbread house. I'm sorry I don't have the answer why your mother and grandma and sister weren't spared, but you have to find meaning in all this. If you believe God made it so for us to meet, you must also believe your family is no longer in that horror story, so you don't have to stay there either."

"I know *they're* no longer there. They've flown away like all angels. But I must stay there and suffer the justice which I never received."

"No, Alina wanted you to live, and all the women in your life want you to be in this sweet lovestory, because they love you. You say you don't want to hurt them, that you don't want to hurt me, but you are by not allowing our love to be. Are you going to let the Nazis erase our lovestory?"

One brick in the stonework loosened, freeing a tear, and I held him, so when all the walls fell, the little boy inside would be embraced.

Soft Apple Cider

AND THEIR LOVE WAS NOT INFATUATION, IT WAS A CONTENTED, A SOUND AND LASTING LOVE...

The strongest "yes" I ever uttered was in response to his "Will you marry me?"

Sitting vulnerable and honest in a pile of figurative rubble, collapsed stone walls and a puddle of tears at his feet, he had asked the girl who rescued him from prison to marry him.

The sweet young man, who liked ice cream and music, had always wanted to get married on Pi Day, 3-14, to symbolize an infinite circle. But neither of us wanted to wait that long. So, on the special snowy Sunday night, using our closeness for warmth while the camper's heater was out, we decided to get married through a blend of Christian and Jewish wedding traditions redone with our own style.

Cozied in the candy-cane booth, illuminated by the menorah's two candles, Sputnik prepared to type our marriage contract.

Bashfully, he said, "You know I'm not much religious, but Judaism tells us that husband and wife are two halves of the same soul." I realized he became bashful about intimacy when closeness was truly within reach; when he was only playing, being mischievous with the "nun," he was cocky. Now he was being authentically romantic, and he was shy. "We don't have to become one in soul because we already are one. But marriage also means becoming one of flesh. What I mean is…." The usually articulate mathematician was having difficulty expressing such amorous ideas. "There was a rabbi, Rabbi Levine, who took his wife to the doctor after she had suffered an injury, and the rabbi explained to the physician, '*Our* foot is hurting *us*.'"

"That's beautiful."

"From now on, it's *us*, not you and me separately. It's our life, our house, our dreams, our pains."

"Y equals X."

He smiled and I smiled to highlight the message of sharing—you smile, I smile.

I told him, "I want a moment to pray."

"What are you praying for?"

"I'm not praying *for* anything. I'm taking a moment to be thankful for the opportunity to love you."

Again, he was embarrassed. I was not an expert in male beingology, so I could not say why he, or any man, got embarrassed around intense romantic feelings (surely there was a Nobel Prize waiting for whoever could figure that out), but I did know my sweet soulmate was not just embarrassed; he was *ashamed* of himself for crying earlier, which he felt he did not deserve: relief. I had not crumbled *all* the walls; I had made but a small breakthrough, a tiny crack in the stone to reach my hand to his, but Sputnik was both prisoner and warden, and while his imprisoned self may have wanted escape, the warden was going to continue to shackle him for the Nazis' crimes. Writing him out of the death camp's setting was going to be difficult. With sadness, I sensed his irrational guilt would work quickly on patching the collapse in the wall "to protect me."

After my prayer of thanks, Sputnik asked, "Are you sure you want to?"

"Yes, I want to be your wife."

He typed a simple perfect marriage contract: "I will always love, honor, and protect you, never intentionally hurt you, and be faithful in mind, heart and body to only you."

Sitting beside him, I typed: "And in death we will never part."

He was not sure if he believed me. *"You'll* be in Heaven, Lumi. That's what matters to me."

"I don't want eternity if it doesn't include you."

"You'll have to take that up with God."

"No, I have to take it up with you. You're the one, not God, trying to lock yourself out of Heaven, because you erroneously believe you don't deserve the company of angels. Would Heaven be paradise if our loved ones were excluded from entrance? Would it be compassionate to those granted Heavenly eternity to be separated from their families forever—would that not be hell instead?"

The scientist did not have an answer and the subject was making him uncomfortable enough to have rebuilt the wall up knee-high.

"Our marriage is the story I've always wanted to write the most," I said, admiring the marriage vows that had transformed the typewriter into a sacred scribe.

He started coughing and I rubbed my hand across his upper leg to say, "I'm sorry that you—we—hurt."

"Are you sure you want to be that tied to a man with my past?"

"Our past, our pain."

"No, except for that. That must be *my* burden alone. My sins, not yours."

I would not argue, not on our wedding night, nor would I ask him anymore about the death prison—it was time now to free him from hell forever, which was going to be a trial, since the prisoner did not believe he belonged in Heaven.

After the blizzard, we would go into town and get a marriage license, and I would take his last name, because I was eager to rid my identity of the thieves' last name.

"We could start a new last name if you'd rather?" he asked, watching winds of flurries flutter behind candles at the kitchen window.

"I appreciate your progressive egalitarianism, sir, but if we start a new family name then when our children get married, will they change their names to yet a new family name?"

"Perhaps. Then we'll be the only two Milkywayites on Earth."

"Milkywayites is going to be your choice?"

"Or something else…"

471

"For the sake of the rising star's career, you should keep Blagonravov, which is already known. Lumi Blagonravov—what do you think of that?"

"With a name like that, you can either be a composer or the wife of a mad scientist."

"Wife of a mad scientist—the character I was destined to play!"

He said I shouldn't quit school, he'd quit teaching, and I said that was ridiculous; I did not need school to live my dream of being his soulmate, but he needed the university for his research.

"Ready to make it official?" he asked.

"I was ready when we were on the hayride together."

Our marriage had two witnesses: Mullybiski and Pythagoras the Turtle.

Sputnik unrolled the paper from the typewriter. At the bottom of the blessed document, I signed, "Peppermint Lumi." He signed it "Gershom Sputnik Blagonravov." I asked about his middle name.

"Wilbur."

"Like the pig from *Charlotte's Web*!"

He was mesmerized by my girlishness; after everything I had heard about him that night, I still thought he was adorable.

"With this ring," he said, while sliding the Song of Songs ring onto my finger, the ring unable to be stolen or burned by the Nazis, "I consecrate you as my wife."

When he put the engraved ring on my finger and it fit perfectly, I felt like a woman who had braved a mythical quest to get the special ring of the beloved and now I was endowed with magical powers.

"Mazel tov!" he shouted, as husband and wife held up cups of warm sweet apple cider in celebration on our first night as a married couple.

An awkward silence followed the unspoken "Now what?"

I would let my Knight lead the way to the bedchamber.

His fingers played with the rim of the cider cup, and I could just hear those walls of his getting stacked atop the other, higher and higher.

"Sputnik, is a kiss on the wedding day not part of Jewish tradition?"

"Ah, sometimes…you want me to kiss you?"

"You're my husband, aren't you?"

"Ah, alright, if you think your father will forgive me."

Nervously, he stood up and reached his hand out to me to stand up beside him. At first, the kiss was not easy, as kissing through a wall never is!, guilt blocking his lips from pursuing mine, then…

He broke down a section of the fortress to really kiss the bride, and she felt as shimmering as the world's largest snowflake and just as capable of melting.

The kiss was long, the Snowflake Physicist intense with my young heart, which had never been touched by a man but was now being caressed by his full grasp. He kept pulling me closer as if our bodies had to be surmounted to achieve the union he wanted...

Cold Lager

After our sublime first kiss, which sprinkled my lips with stars, Sputnik ran his hands flat down the sides of my arms, as if I was immaculate clothing, a nun's habit, that the kiss had ruffled out of place, and he was responsible for the destruction and doing his best now to put everything back in order. Stones and bricks were being built up fast around the "savage beast" before he could do more damage.

"The electricity should be on in the morning," he said with his serious science voice. "We should try to get some sleep. The Lady can have the bed and I'll take the couch."

Take the couch? I had not any experience in such matters, but weren't husband and wife supposed to *both* be in the honeymoon bed?

"Sputnik, you can't sleep on the couch. Remember I had to take off one of the cushions for Mullybiski and Pythagoras."

"I've slept in worse conditions. You won't be cold, will you?"

"Ooh, yes, I'm sure I will be."

"Well…bundle up good."

I was flabbergasted but I would not be un-Ladylike and take charge of the wedding night.

Gershom was letting the Nazis write our story again and write it coldly. He had married me to make *me* happy, but apparently, he thought our married life was going to take place in prison with bars between us—or rather with him in prison and not allowing conjugal visits.

In the bedroom, I hated to take off my high heels, for fear of my feet touching this coldness.

475

Shivering, I lay stocking-footed on the bed and looking at the Knight in armor suit. The bedroom windows were filled with starlight, reflecting off snow and cascading across the lacy bed, which was awaiting two figures engaged in an embrace.

After thirty minutes, by which time the metal camper had lost most of its warmth to winter and my hands were about to do the same, Sputnik knocked on the door.

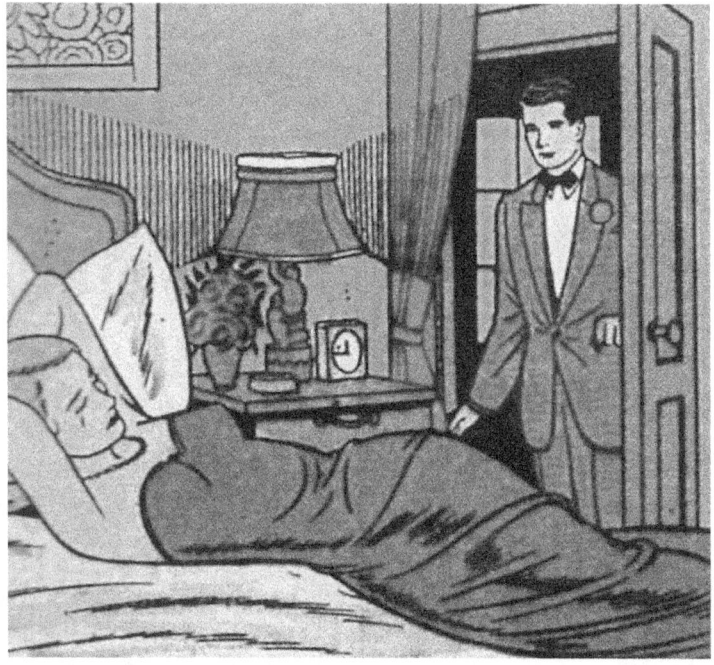

I sat up on the bedside. "Come in."

He peeked inside. "Are you cold?"

"Yes."

He saw warming me as a husbandly duty, so he came into the room. On the bedside he sat and rubbed my hands briskly. He took off his shoes and unclothed himself to his hospital-white underthings. "Here," he said, asking me to scoot closer to him, so he could do a similar treatment for me, which was done with the disinterest of a doctor unclothing a patient, the physician trying to remain as respectable as possible, while he removed the Lady's dress and stockings but left on her cross necklace and undergarments.

Beneath covers, he held me as I lay against his T-shirted chest like we were two war buddies trying to keep from freezing to death in the frozen tundra.

"I think the T-shirt is blocking your warmth from me."

He sat up and tossed off the shirt with as much romance as a warthog. The golden Star of David shined in a woodland of black hair on his chest.

I sat up and snapped, "Why don't you just get me a beer?"

He was mortified by the Lady's choice of words. "What?"

I punched his shoulder like I was his buddy pal. "If you're going to treat me like one of your research colleagues, one of your male buddies out in the tundra, I may as well get into the role, jack, and we'll get ourselves some brews and checkers to pass the time."

"Brews *and checkers?*"

"I don't know what you men do when you're around only each other."

"If you were one of my research colleagues, *jack*, I certainly would not be cuddling you up—you'd be fending for warmth on your own. You women don't even realize how much coddling—" He stopped himself, thinking of how the women in his life had not been coddled by the world for long. "My apologies, Peppermint." Softly, he pulled up the lacy strap of my camisole which had fallen down my arm, during my pitiful attempt to punch like a man. "I certainly do not see you like one of the grizzly bears from the tundra."

"Do you like it?" I asked, not just referring to the camisole.

His eyes touched the feminine scenery in a way that took my breath away. "It's…" I had never seen the professor so flustered. "It's…almost too sheer to be decent."

"Women's undershirts are different than men's undershirts."

"Here," he said, putting the covers over my chest.

"I'm sorry, Sputnik, I didn't realize I was going to be on my honeymoon tonight or else I would've worn something *less* sheer for you."

"That's a good girl."

Surprisingly, the irony of my words had gone uninterpreted by the genius.

Moon-Moon had taught these kinds of feelings were not impure; they were required for making a baby, and thus, were honorable and graceful, but a Lady, of course, should only entertain these kinds of fantasies about her Knight. Well, this was my Knight.

He held me again, softer this time. He felt much warmer now as I breathed against the brush of hair on his chest that I had first glimpsed years ago in the wheatfield—I let this recognition warm me: I was in the arms of the aeronaut. My enthusiasm for being in his arms found its way out in a girlish sigh, which activated an amorous part of him that caused him to kiss the top of my ear. Following his lead, I kissed a scar on his shoulder, hoping to give that part of his body a memory of softness since it suffered with a memory of pain.

"Lumi, don't."

"You don't like it?"

"You don't have to do that. Let's try to sleep."

We could not sleep. We were too close and too unclothed.

"Sputnik, are we really married?"

"Yes."

The only noticeable sounds in the room were his coughs, louder than the howling wind.

He finally said, "According to the traditional Jewish marriage contract, it is a man's duty to satisfy his wife in the bedroom, but you deserve a more profound kind of satisfaction, found in the heavens, not in the covers, and I deserve none."

"Then why did you marry me?"

"Your father forgive me—because I love you."

"Stop asking forgiveness for love. If anyone wants you to love me, it's my real father."

"He does not want his angel tarnished by a sinner."

478

"Sputnik, I once read some of my momma's old cookbook, even older than her, I think, and it was a cookbook that also offered advice to young unmarried girls."

"That's an odd cookbook."

"And its recipes were as vague as its advice: 'smidges' and 'pinches' and 'a dab will do you.' Anyway, it advised, 'Sometimes your husband will want to do things to you in bed and you should lie there and allow him.' Is that the wife you want—'a dab will do you'?"

"No, that disgusts me, the idea of a woman made to just lay there like an object for some beast's satisfaction. Lumi, it's just difficult for me to see you in this role."

"The role of loving you so much I want to make you happy? I've been in that role since we first met and you never seemed to mind. I made you coffee, pastries, I made your bed, brought you pizza, and each time I did those things for you, it made me happy to make you happy. How is that different from what we're doing now?"

"You're such a saint, Lumi, your happiness comes from making me happy."

"Is that wrong?"

"No. You can't fathom how much I respect you."

"Your respect means more to me than the respect of the whole world. I don't want to lose it. Will you no longer respect me if I can't stop my yearning for wanting to be close to you?"

"I don't deserve it! And you deserve better, just like my mother deserved better. Lumi, I was not completely honest with you about Naomi."

"The woman from the deli?"

"Yes."

My heart tightened in the clutch of the Wicked Stepmother. "She's your girlfriend? Your wife?"

"No, I knew her in Poland. She's a few years older than me, and one night too bleak for either of us to see a future ahead, she wanted us to make a warm moment in the present. We were both too young to play

479

around with sex, as dangerous to two kids as playing with guns, considering both involve making or taking life, but that wisdom was not what gnawed at me. Naomi's father had been killed. He had been a rabbi and scholar and I knew if he had still been around, Naomi would not have been behaving this way. After losing her father, she also lost the boy she loved, Thomas. She had been crazy about him all throughout school. He was going to be an engineer, she was going to be his wife, and live happily ever after. But he was taken away by guards and she knew she'd never see him again. She saw something of Thomas in me, his science aptitude, but what was really going on between us was she needed to feel protected and I needed to feel I could protect someone. But I reasoned what I was about to do was not a form of protection—to protect her, I had to *not* do this with her. I could not impregnate her with a child the Nazis would kill. When I explained my reason for being unable to be with her, she slapped me, and I don't mean a little slap—a slap that shouted, 'I hate you, Gershom. Why couldn't *you* have been taken away instead of Thomas?' Imagine my surprise years later in this small town going into a deli and seeing Naomi again. After I helped Abby with the floor, Naomi said she wanted us to sit together and have some soup. I didn't know if she wanted to slap me again or have her husband do the job this time. Instead, she said, 'Thank you.' I was confused. 'Thanks for what?' For refusing her that night. As it turned out, Thomas had survived and had searched three years to find her again, and she was glad to have waited for her real love, and they now are blessed with five children.''

"Sputnik, that's lovely for Thomas and Naomi, but I don't understand how that story relates to you and me or why you're choosing to tell me it now. Are you trying to say I see some glimmer of my soulmate in you and you're protecting me by saving me for him?'' I slightly raised myself to look at him because I wanted my eyes to do most of the talking and convincing. "You're the one for me, Sputnik. I am as certain of this as a puzzle piece is of clicking with its missing half.''

"Your goal as a little girl was to be a nun. So, we must have a chaste marriage.'' Period. Final. Fortress erected! "You have the character for the noble vocation, and you don't even have to join a convent—you can be a nun right here on this property. I've been thinking that for a while now. I know of Protestant nuns who live and dress as other women yet have made vows of celibacy in a life dedicated to charity. A few years ago, I heard a story about a French nun who saved the lives of twenty Jewish children during the war. You can do miraculous things, Lumi."

"And I'll lose my ability to do miraculous things if you make love to me?" I did not ask mockingly; I honestly wanted his thoughts on this.

"I'm a scientist, and I've thought this through logically, during moments when I've considered taking you as my wife, and there have been many of those moments, just so you know, like the time you cleaned my apartment and took great care of Pythagoras and Sophie—I don't know anyone else who would have thought to give a little bed to a turtle and frog. Here is what I've concluded: If I take you, you'll feel desecrated, and thus will lose your spirit of feeling holy. I won't allow you to feel that abject way just to grant me a few seconds of pleasure."

"Are you planning on touching me in a desecrating manner?"

"I'd never do that to you."

"Then why would I feel desecrated?"

"How many fair maidens in your treasured storybooks give themselves to Knights? None! Because doing so would make them no longer fair maidens."

"Knights and Ladies go together."

"Knights protect Ladies."

"And love them."

"Yes by protecting them. I know you feel it is your duty to make me happy, but I've told you many times, I don't deserve it. You don't have to do this for me. I'll take you in my plane wherever you want to go to do your good deeds; in fact, I'll build my life around those good deeds. You see yourself as helpmate in my scientific pursuits, but I should be helpmate in your angelic pursuits."

"That would be nice, Sputnik, to fly your plane to honorable pursuits, but..."

"I know you've been just as conflicted as me about our relationship. You want to be a nun and you want to be my wife. You can be both!" He hugged me as if this news would make me happy. "Now we've solved both our conundrums. I felt I couldn't marry you because I didn't

481

deserve to touch you, and you felt it improper for a nun to be married, but we've worked it out properly. You can be a wife, and I can be your protector, and I will not require you to do those wifely duties fulfilled in bed, activities unsuited for a nun. Don't get me wrong, you can do all the other wifely duties to your heart's desire, whatever makes you happy, making me breakfast and sandwiches, tending our home, and all those other girly things, and I'm aware that women require copious kissing and cuddling, which are not exactly suitable for a nun, but I won't deny you those privileges of a married woman, unlike my pops who never held my mother enough." He held me close to show he was not averse to cuddling me; he would not treat me like one of the guys. "I'm highly pleased that we've come to this solution. Now we can go to sleep and in the morning the electricity should be on and you can go about making our first breakfast as man and wife—my mouth waters just thinking about it. I love the way you make food."

The Lady was getting irritable now. Why was every other wifely duty seen as noble to him except the one necessary for making a baby?

"Sputnik, I'm flattered by your high esteem for me."

I admired that he was quite a man, capable of holding his half-clothed wife and resisting his need for her, because of his conviction it was wrong to touch her purity.

"You're everything good and holy to me, Lumi, all I have left in this world to respect and cherish. You give me the same feeling as the Sistine Chapel, the Grand Canyon, the incredible Princes Road Synagogue—a wonder of the world, you are, and I'm awed by you."

He was not making this any easier for me.

"I'd die to protect your honor," he said.

"You're going to make me cry if you keep speaking so gallantly."

"Better to make you cry from that than from pain and regret."

"Sput, we never go to sleep this early when we're on the phone together. Can we talk?"

"Yes. About anything you want." His voice suggested he was very pleased about our arrangement, arranged by his clever solution. "What are you planning for our breakfast, Peppermint?"

482

"Apricot rugelach."

"Ah, great! Well, the quicker we get to sleep, the quicker it will seem the rugelach comes. And we have so many fun activities planned. When I was a boy, I could never sleep during the holidays—ah, the anticipation of what was to come: jelly doughnuts and games and gifts…the women in my life knew how to make everything special."

"It's going to be a beautiful time, but can I ask you something, Sput?"

"Ask the professor anything."

"I hope you won't get mad at me for this, but you often say how much it means to a man to protect his wife—have you considered how much it means to a wife to give her husband a child? If you respect me so completely, why don't you want to have children with me? The damage to my face was caused by an accident. My genes are not damaged."

"Ah, Lumi," he said with the softest voice he had. "There is nothing damaged about you, even if what had happened to you had not been caused by an accident. Your genes are gemstones."

"There must be some reason you don't want to have my children? Because I'm not Jewish?"

My desire to have children threw a wrench into his plan for our marriage to be chaste.

"Listen, I told you I'm not religious and I don't believe that a child has to have a Jewish mother to be Jewish. Our kids would be Jew and Protestant, southerner and westerner, woodland and meadow. Lumi, you bring up my being Jewish so much, I don't know if it secretly turns you off or on. Either way offends me."

"I'm not trying to offend you. I'm trying to respect you. I'm trying to love you! I'm trying to make you happy! Why can't you see that? And please don't change the subject."

"I told you, you don't have to do *this* to make me happy, and if you keep insisting, I'll no longer be able to see you as the picture of purity I thought you were."

"That's really hurtful. Why are you making me feel bad for wanting to be closer to you and to have your child?"

483

He hugged me to say, "Sorry." "Don't worry. I know in your heart this is a holy act ordained by God for procreation, but for men, it's just a quick path to easy pleasure at the expense of your vulnerable body."

"Sputnik, that's sickening, vulgar and chauvinistic. Is that how you view lovemaking?"

"I don't know. Perhaps at one time I thought it could be divine."

"It can be divine."

"No, I promise a nobler expression of my love is flying you in my airplane to your charitable causes, fixing the roof in this camper, building you a snow globe, buying a little bakery for you to turn into the sweet shop of your dreams, all those un-selfish expressions."

"Why can't this also be a noble expression of your love? It's your choice, Sput, whether this moment will be written nobly or not. I won't mind if you gain selfish pleasure from it—I want to make you happier than you've ever been."

"You don't have to do it this way."

"I'm not talking about through the physical union; I'm talking about through our emotional and spiritual unions, which we could have if you would come out from behind those walls. If you really feel I should be married to God instead of married to you, why just an hour ago did you ask me to be your wife? You want to tear up our marriage bond?"

"No! Our marriage contract was written by God."

"If you really believe that then why are you nullifying our marriage?"

"Just because God has obviously arranged it for me to protect and provide for you and give you the story you were meant to write doesn't mean I'm meant to desecrate you and gain pleasure from it to boot!"

"Sputnik, I won't tolerate sacrilegious nonsense."

"Sacrilegious? I'm showing you the utmost veneration. Do you want me to take you, the way Pops treated my mother, and have at you like some bear ravenous with instinct, then you can get me a lager, woman, a cold one too, because I'll have worked up a sweat grinding and grunting without any consideration for your integrity?"

484

"It won't be like that because you're not like that. You'll write it differently, Sput."

"How do you know? Perhaps like father, like son."

I pulled away from him and sat up, kept the covers around me to warm me. "I won't allow you to turn God into a Nazi."

"How dare you—"

"No, how dare you let the Nazis continue to ruin your life and the life of your loved ones."

"The Nazis weren't the ones who raped and killed my little sister—that was an intellectual who had 'rationalized' the death of innocence as a gain for intellectualism."

"I know, Sputnik, I'm sorry." He was still lying down, with regret a crushing weight on his heart, so I softly rubbed his coughing chest. "This is why it's so important to transform sex back into lovemaking. Lovemaking is a gemstone, a very powerful one, an amulet for creating life. But by those ignorant of its power, it has been thrown in the dirt, kicked around, scuffed up, treated like trash and made to look that way too, unrecognizable from its divine form—that's why we romantics need to polish it back to its intended shine and place it back on its throne for reverence. Don't let the perverted world pervert your feelings about what you know is heavenly. Almost everything in this world can be used for good or evil. Think about rocketry. Some men want to make missiles to explode planets and some want to make missiles to explore planets. Just because there are some bad apples intent on misusing rockets, are you going to give up rocket science altogether and just let the bad guys have it? Of course not. It's more important than ever for the good guy to stay in the story when something this important is in the balance. Write thus, write for goodness. Why would God want us to erase the only tender beautiful passage in our story capable of creating life?"

He removed my hand from his chest. "Speeches like that further confirm my belief you should be a nun."

"Why?"

"Because most people don't talk or think that way, and now I feel more than ever the importance of preserving your sanctity—never will I allow anyone to even think of violating your inviolability."

"I believe others do feel this romantic way, but they are too embarrassed to be romantic characters in a story taken over by unromantics, who shoot demeaning lines into the life of anyone who so much as utters one poetic word, making sure everyone stays behind the barbed fence in desolate gloom and no one flies over to the warm flowering meadows sprinkled with adjectives like 'pretty' and 'heavenly,' and for what reason, I can't fathom! But if what you're saying is true, that no one else feels this way, then can't you see how important it is for you and me to think this romantic way, and to put it into action, to keep it from extinction?"

He did not consider a word of that, but he did ponder if it was his husbandly duty to make a child with me. Behind his bars of stubbornness, he reevaluated the situation as if he was deciphering a math problem. "I didn't know you wanted to have children. Nuns usually don't, you know."

"I've always wanted a baby."

"You never mentioned it before."

I was hurt by his tone that wondered if I really did want to have a baby or if I was just a Floozy Tuesday wanting a dirty romp—on my honeymoon, no less!

"Don't you trust me, Sputnik?"

"I trust you the way I trust an angel. Why are you asking that?"

"But you don't believe that I truly believe everything I've said tonight?"

"Yes, I believe you."

"Then why are you acting suspicious of my motives?"

"I told you this is just hard for me!"

"Hard for you? Have you considered it's hard for me? I was raised my entire life to be a Lady and you're making me say things I don't feel comfortable saying to convince my own husband to be intimate with me. Saying 'I want a baby' is not exactly a proper thing to say to a man who told me he was unavailable for love, so that's why I never mentioned it before. I'm sorry. I didn't mean to sound so harsh."

"I'm not suspicious of your motives, angel. I'm suspicious of my own. I can fool myself into believing I'm going to be with you to make a baby when really I'm doing it for selfish pleasure."

"No, you'll be doing it for this: this time next year, we could be celebrating the holidays with our baby! Isn't that the sweetest scene you've ever pictured?"

"Women," he grumbled. "Your obsession with babies is something else."

"That's kind of important for the survival of our species, Sputnik. But not every woman wants to be a mother and that's okay."

"You're always thinking of everyone, making sure no one gets their feelings hurt, no one feels left out, even though the entire world has left you out. Your kindness would make a nice mother, Lumi."

"Ooh? Then picture this, my sweet: holiday lights, snowy windows, a cute baby in a sleepsuit that I knitted for him, and giving him his first Christmas gift—maybe a tiny pair of coveralls so he can be an outdoorsman like his dad—and you teaching him your family's Hanukkah traditions."

"It's a mother's job to teach."

"You're a professor. You're a better teacher than me. Many men are excellent teachers."

"There you go again, making sure everyone gets included in respect. I teach mathematics and science to college students."

"And think of how good you would be at teaching those subjects to our children—why, we'll have genius babies!"

"It's gone up to *children* now, plural? It was one baby in a sleepsuit and now we have a litter."

Sometimes his humor was so dry I didn't know if it was humor or not.

"Lumi, you're better equipped at teaching life lessons to a baby. I'm not exactly the type a baby wants to cuddle."

That was quite a picture: the austere Professor Blagonravov holding a sweet baby.

"If we had a son, there are certain things I would have to teach him as a man. You wouldn't be able to teach him how to pitch a tent or build a raft, things like that, and I know what you're going to say, some women are highly capable raft builders and tent pitchers, but you're not, and you couldn't throw a punch to save your life."

"You wouldn't teach your daughter how to build a raft?"

"If she wanted to learn how, I would." He smiled, imagining having a little tomboy Bow in his life.

"I think she would like to learn how to build a raft just because she would like spending time with her hero."

He liked that idea, but I could tell he was also having a difficult time trying to rework his plan for our marriage.

I was ready to wave the surrender flag against the impossible battle with his guilt, my heart too battered to suffer any more of his brusqueness and defensiveness and belittling disappointment, and settle into a chaste marriage. I would become a married nun and live the holiest virtuous life that would gain his absolute respect.

"I just thought you, my husband, would want to grant me membership in the group of women you find so noble—Mothers. But I know how much you've been through, and I don't want to make life any harder for you, so if having a chaste marriage pleases you, we'll have that marriage, and I'll be happy flying in your plane to noble pursuits. I mean that wholeheartedly. Your love is the gentle warm embrace of home. But, Sputnik, please, let's end this dreary cold scene, because I can't stomach any more of this bitter lager—I'm a hot chocolate kind of girl. The warm apricot rugelach in the morning is sounding very good to me too, and you're right, if we get to sleep, we can conclude this chapter and move on to our fun chapters sweetly titled. I just thought maybe you would want a chapter in our story titled 'Yams,' the favorite food of our little baby; like father, like son."

He held me closer as if he did not want to lose me to a man who would help me gain membership into motherhood. "You really want to have my baby?"

"More than you can even imagine. You're my husband. Who else's baby would I want to have? Elvis Presley's?"

His decision rendered, he answered my request by tenderly leaning me against the marriage bed, his necklace brushing my camisole and cross necklace.

"We're only doing this for procreation," he said, austerely, not so much to me but to God.

"Sputnik, for someone who claims God doesn't exist for him, you care a great deal about what God thinks of your actions."

He had never considered this and did not have a reason as to why.

"Well, I'm just making it known we're only doing this to make a baby."

"We're only doing this if you come out of that stone prison you've built around yourself. I mean it, Sputty, I won't do this against hard cold walls. Our baby will be created in a warm soft environment of love and respect."

"I promise, angel, it won't be cold." He let the gentleness of his voice assure me he would use his body just as gently, while he disrobed the nun completely. "Do you think it can be as beautiful as *Panis Angelicus?*" he asked, while holding my cross necklace.

I told him I didn't know of *Panis Angelicus*.

"My Christian girl doesn't know what that is? It's the loveliest stanza of a lovely hymn written by Saint Aquinas. *That we at last may see the light wherein Thou dwellest.*"

"You'll have to let me hear that song someday."

"My hope is to let you hear it now."

Chocolate-Covered Cherry Cordials

I was sorry for every girl who did not have her first time with

Gershom. When he made love to me, I felt what the nightsky feels with the Milky Way coursing through her.

His lips had asked permission before kissing any locale of my being, making all of me feel sacred, sacred locations that had been off limits to his touch.

"Lumi, the first time I saw you I thought kissing your collarbone would be like kissing a chandelier. Beautiful. Delicate. Light all across me." So, he had done that very thing, honoring the Jewish marriage contract of fulfilling his wife completely.

But kissing and touching *him* had walled up a new challenge to my quest for intimacy, and for a while, our union had not sailed smoothly. Everywhere I had caressed (asking his permission the way he had asked for mine) had made him snap, embarrassed and gruff, "Ah, come on, you don't have to do that," until he had realized he was hurting my feelings again. But he had genuinely been unable to understand "the nun" being unimpressed by his freeing her from the "terrible task" of touching the grizzly bear.

In the moment before becoming one in flesh, I had understood why I had felt lightheaded hearing Jeff Miller assure the girl, "This won't hurt."

Sensing my anxiety at the tip of consummation, my husband had caressed, "Close your eyes and see and feel in detail something that makes you happy. I used this technique in the torture prison anytime the pain got intense. I'd give my full senses to ice cream. Peppermint ice cream. Its softness. Its sweetness. Its light blush. The way it melts against warmth."

I had considered concentrating on chocolate-covered cherries in a starlit red tin atop the bookshelf headboard, candy I kept in the bedroom for enjoying while late-night reading of holiday stories like O. Henry's *The Gift of the Magi* and Truman Capote's divine *A Christmas Memory*, two stories that never failed to make me remember my heart. But, no, I would not concentrate on those things.

"I give my full senses to this union with you, Gersh. I want to have you to your full measure. As Browning said, 'I want to love thee to the depth and breadth and height my soul can reach.'"

While the experience was painful, and to deny the truth was to deny my very female body and its need for gentleness, which my husband recognized and honored not through sexism or condescension but through respect for my femaleness, the experience was also beautiful. To keep from focusing too much on the physical pain, I focused on the beauty of our spiritual closeness, but that did not prevent my weeping, for the width of his soul in my chest caused an agony and ecstasy that made my soul cry out

God's name, while my husband emptied his pent-up pain and bliss into a wife who had prayed all her life to have him inside her.

Then I rested—floated—atop a beautiful soft cloud of a thought: my love and I had created life.

We spent glorious hours in lifemaking, becoming one in flesh, remembering the oneness of our spirit, letting our bodies say, "I love you" and "I love you some more" and "I love you even deeper than this" and "I love creating life with only you" and letting love write *love*making far more sensually than lust was capable.

After navigating our way together through the rough unexplored sea of our first time, we were no longer love making—we were love sailing. We only took breaks to nibble on chocolate-covered cherry cordials for energy, so our first night of lovemaking would always taste like those candies; ooh, such sweet memory. And when our bodies finally needed a longer rest from speaking our most intangible thoughts, we took a deserved nap. Then we went back to talking with tender words and even tenderer touches from bodies speaking sweet little afterthoughts.

"Hi," he said, playful, awkward, cocky, atop me.

"Hiii."

I had never seen him this way. He had always been the serious suited professor in his office or classroom, or the austerely intelligent young man in the bakery, or the masculine outdoorsman collecting apples for me in stiff coldness. Now I was in warm bed with him, his hair was messy, his actions flirty, and he was without clothing. His weight rested on his lower arms beside me; his hands caressed my shoulders, while the hair on his chest brushed against my breasts.

My hands rubbed the apple-hard muscles in his bare youngman biceps. Being this close to him, I realized it had never been his clothes that smelled like pecans; he smelled like pecans.

"Happy Hanukkah," he said, while grinning.

"Merry Christmas."

"That was some Hanukkah gift."

"Some Christmas gift too."

Flurries outside window glass transformed the room into a snow globe, at least in my eyes.

I kissed his pecan-scented freckled shoulder and whispered, "It feels like our chests are fused together, as if a latch is in your chest and one is in my chest and they're locked together, and if we tried to pull apart, the departure would be painful. But these latches aren't made of metal but of light. We must let the mass of light between us, a light which increased in magnitude while lovemaking, slowly shimmer down, and this experience is quite pleasant, the feeling of butterflies flying back and forth across the light stream bridging your chest to mine. Rippling bliss. Do you feel that?"

"Sure, I feel that."

"You're humoring my girly sensibilities?"

"I feel something, I promise."

"Anne Bradstreet, the first writer to be published in the North America colonies, once said in a poem that honored her husband, 'If ever two were one, then surely we, If ever man were lov'd by wife, then thee.' Doesn't that fit we?"

His beard stubble was coming back, so I rubbed my lips across it. I loved the freedom I had in bed to caress his body so openly.

"Now I know a way to stop you from calling me 'Sputnik.' '*Oo Captain, My Captain*,'" he said with the girly-est of voices, imitating my lovemaking voice but not doing justice to my southern accent. "'*Professor Blagonravov, Gersh, Gurshum*,' and finally, '*God*.' Imagine that, my sweet little gentile's Christian God taking the form of my circumcised Jewish—"

"That's blasphemy!"

"What? I was going to say a polite word. I wouldn't write a dirty word in my nun's story."

"I don't worship that part of your body. I worship our love, which is holy."

"I told you I'm not religious. But my apologies, I do respect that you are, I do. Well, you can rest assured now, Lumi, you made me happy."

"Making you happy matters the most to me, and that's not girlish hyperbole, but will you see me as less saintly if I'm happy too?"

"No," he said and guaranteed his answer with a lusty kiss.

"I was raised to believe it is a wife's duty to be her husband's ever-pleasing student in the bedchamber, to learn to be his ideal bedmate, and unless he requests her to do something hurtful or blasphemous, she should offer full submission."

"That was fairly obvious."

"Ooh, it was too much of The Lady Model?"

He laughed. "That's what I wanted. I didn't want the Man Model. Did you like it?"

"Gersh, you make love to me the way Shakespeare wrote poetry. 'Did my heart love till now? Forswear it, sight! For I ne'er saw true beauty till this night.'"

"Lumi, my goodness."

"Ooh, it's too intense for my dear Sputty?"

"It's not that..." He was embarrassed and still worried God was going to strike him with lightning for being intimate with "a nun."

Whatever he was feeling, he was better at controlling, or maybe he did not feel quite so gushy as I, maybe not so many butterflies were tickling him, but then again, his gray eyes were shining like silver. After lovemaking, I felt capable of magic like I could walk through walls.

I could not stop kissing him, overwhelmed with feelings for him and for life—how sweet it could be now that he and I were married.

"Lume, I was going to ask how you're feeling, but I already have the answer—fairly girly."

"*Lume*, hmm? Lovemaking inspired a new nickname, eh? Sput, I feel like I belong in a constellation. What you and I just did puts us in league with the stars. I feel so glowy and warm, I should be lighting the nightsky, thanks to you."

Although Sputnik admired when I spoke poetically, I realized when the poetry was spoken about physical intimacy or his beauty, he turned juvenile around it. He made a joke that placed him in third grade. I made a playful face of disapproval about his immaturity.

"I hate to tell you this but behind this masculine sophistication there's a boy going, 'Hubba hubba hubba, there's actually a naked girl beside me.'"

"Ooh? How do you not know behind this Ladylike propriety, there's a girl going, 'Hubba hubba hubba, there's actually a naked man beside me.'"

"Ah, come on, is that true?"

"You'll never know because a Lady won't reveal that secret." I rubbed my hands up and down his strong bare arms. "Have you seen many naked women?"

"Lumi…"

"The mathematician is incapable of rounding out a ballpark figure, hopefully not the size of an actual ballpark?"

"I don't know."

"Who was the first woman you saw without her clothes on?"

"I don't remember."

495

"You do so remember."

"Probably one of the women who thought a mud pit out in the Alaskan forest was purifying and they'd sit in it naked—"

"Yuck, think of the germs."

"Well, once I learned of their ritual, I went to see for myself—I was five years old and just curious—and one of the women whopped me in the face with a clod of dirt."

"Serves you right."

"I agree. So, who was the first man you saw?"

"An aeronaut who landed in a wheatfield and yanked off his T-shirt and exposed his big hairy chest."

He laughed. "But I mean who was the first man you *saw*, you know."

"Are you serious? I just saw for the first time tonight."

He grinned smugly.

Kissing his shoulder, I asked, "Is my bosom satisfactory to you?"

If he had been drinking something, he would have choked, so shocked by the nun's question. "What?"

"As to your liking as Mara Gold's?"

"Where did that come from?"

"From the nude drawing of her given to you as a birthday gift from Brad."

"I told you that was just a silly gift. I threw the tacky thing away."

"Did you see Naomi?"

"I don't even remember."

"You do so remember. And did you like the view?"

"I'm not answering that question. If I say, 'Yes,' your feelings will be hurt, and if I say, 'No,' you'll just think I'm lying. Why are you doing this?"

"Because I want to be beautiful for you and not just beautiful of heart and soul, but beautiful of body and face too, to be able to make all aspects of you happy."

He kissed across my nonstandard face, the way he had kissed the scars on my legs, accepting me as is. Against his masculine reservation, he caressed my delicate insecurities further with "I no longer need the stars. Your blue eyes have replaced them with a loveliness too large to fit within any constellation." His attempt at Romeohood.

"You're getting sweeter by the second, Sputnik."

"I've been saving that one, thought up the first time I saw you, back when your eyes were clear with so much pure innocence, I could not have respected myself as a man to have had one impure thought about you."

Destiny had to have brought us together; this handsome brilliant man would not have chosen me otherwise. Sputnik once said the greatest five words a man could say, "I don't watch Miss America," so I knew he was not superficial, but I still had an impossible time believing he thought I was physically beautiful.

"I hope you won't mind me asking: who was the girl you drew, the naked gal in the field?"

"What?" He was embarrassed like I had read a secret passage in his diary.

"I'm sorry. The afternoon I went to your apartment to clean it, your sketchbook was on the floor, open, and I just thought it was a sketchbook of spaceship designs. I didn't mean to come across the nude gal."

"She was you."

"Is that a male line?"

"No."

"Why was she faceless?"

"Because I thought if I didn't allow myself to know it was you, I wouldn't have to feel so guilty about what I wanted to do with you if you were just some faceless girl in a field. Did you notice it was the field from Igtord?" he said as proof the girl was me.

"Were my eyes the first things you noticed about me?"

"I noticed all of you, your complete being."

"You can't really see me as pretty."

"You're a dazzling pretty. If we have a daughter, I hope she is just like you."

His eyes professed he truly saw me as beautiful, not in spite of my face—he truly thought my face was pretty, as if his character had been written to feel that way in a story where his soulmate would have a nonstandard face. I could now see meaning in the accident which had seemingly damaged my prettiness—it had tested my faith in love, love's capacity to embrace anyone, even those of us far beyond society's acceptance, and given me the opportunity to share the magic of unconditional love with those who wanted to read my lovestory with Sputnik. This finally dawned as warm as sunrise across me: my long-ago Christmas wish had come true. I was She, his She, the light in his night. And that melted any last trace of ice anywhere inside me, for ice cannot exist in warmth. My real father had not loved me blindly either but with eyes and heart wide open, seeing all of me as beautiful. For the first time, I saw myself, my whole self, as beautiful, and the sight was a gift—a miracle—from his love.

I told this to Sputnik and he said, "Seeing you as light is not a miracle—it's unavoidable in your radiance."

"I really feel pretty, Sput, thanks to you, and it feels grand."

He picked up the camera from the bookshelf. "Let me get a picture of the beautiful gal."

"I'm without clothes, sir."

"I know!"

"Put that camera away, you devious boy."

With faux grumpiness, he put the camera back on the shelf and cuddled me again. I breathed the warm air radiating from the freckled meadow between his neck and shoulder. "I'll be the nun you want me to be."

"I'm not so sure I want that now, unless you want that, then I'll honor your choice."

"Then I'll be your Marie Curie."

"In school, I was never attracted to the girls in science and math classes but the girls in poetry class."

I moved my hands up his strong arms to his equally strong back. "I'll study the Torah for you."

He laughed about that. "I'm not a rabbi and you're not training to be the wife of a holy man. Besides, the Torah is what you Christians call the Pentateuch. But there you go again being turned on by my Jewishness. Do you want me to put on a kippah?"

"Can you wear that while you're kissing?"

"Lumi, my goodness. Have you had that kind of fantasy? Were we kissing on Yom Kippur in your fantasy?"

"Sputnik! I thought you respected me with the utmost veneration. What is Yom Kippur?"

"The holiest day of the year, a day for repenting. So, were we kissing on Yom Kippur?"

"I was just curious if a man could wear that while kissing a woman, but you just crossed a line into depravity."

"Ah, come on, I was kidding."

"I grew up in a very Protestant town, Baptists mostly, but there was a young Jewish man I saw once in a kippah—"

"Aha! I knew it!"

"Let me finish, sir. It was during the rainy autumn of my sixteenth year."

"'*During the rainy autumn of my sixteenth year.*' Are you sure you weren't born in *1846*?"

I let the memory take me back three years...

"I was at a soul food restaurant downtown and the young man seemed so different from other blue-jeaned guys in Igtord." I was not sure why I was even sharing these details with my husband, who was grinning quite a bit. "He had to have been an out-of-towner. He was a crisp young man in a kippah and a tailored suit."

"Now there's a stereotype."

"I'm not stereotyping. I'm describing a real young man I encountered."

"Did you, my little nun, covet him and right there in the *soul* food restaurant?"

"Sputnik ... my heart was wed to my aeronaut...No, my dear Sputnik, that's not true. Forgive me, but I did covet him, only briefly, my love, and this was before I knew you. At the time, I felt I was drawn to the young man because of his isolation, but now I see I was drawn to the glimmer of you I saw in him."

"*Glimmer* of me, eh?"

"Why is this so funny?"

"I wish you would have let him know you were coveting him."

"Sputnik, what a nasty thing to say."

"You could've made the barnstormer much happier that night than some cold collard greens in a wet farm turned bog, all huddled by myself in a discarded barn."

"That young man was you?"

"I've been wondering how long it would take you to realize that. And I wasn't that young."

How had I not recognized the young man on the hayride as the same young man I had seen in the restaurant as the same man landed in my field?

"Autumn, 1962, Mabel's Kitchen, Saturday afternoon, there was that sweet girl again, outlined by rain-drenched window and words 'Soul Food' and ah, the scent of sweet potato pie, my little angel with her tiny slice of sweet potato pie, all by herself. She was shyly peeking at my kippah then she just dashed away—afraid of coveting me! She didn't even know I was the same aviator whom she had offered her snow globe and her virginity."

"I didn't offer you that back then!"

"Well, when you offer a gift to any man other than your pops or brother, no matter how sweet it seems to you, he's thinking you want to give him something else. You can't be that generous to men, angel. They'll just take advantage."

"I will not allow perverts to stop me from gifting niceness to all, women and men, just because their dirty minds distort the gifts' intentions, and if a man gets his feelings hurt by a woman's niceness, because he misread her feelings as romantic, isn't that better than the woman turning off her niceness altogether and being cold to everyone, hurting the whole world's feelings, just so she'll never accidentally lead some poor man on? Frankly, I'm tired of the custom that a woman must always consider how her actions are going to incite a man's hormones; that erroneous idea is responsible for the mentality behind 'She deserved to get rape, she was asking for it, she was leading him on.'"

"Checkmate! Good point. Really. I'm always impressed by someone who can enlighten me."

"Hildegard and I will Write thus, thank you very much, and I'll thank you, sir, to stop disgracing my precious pure memories of my admirable aeronaut."

"Don't get me wrong. I thought the snow globe was sweet and genuinely from your heart. I didn't think you were *consciously* offering me your innocence. I didn't think you were some nymph, trying to seduce me. I didn't think I had any right to put the moves on you. But you were unaware that symbolically you were offering me your fragility and purity. Come on, pure snow and breakable glass."

"You're sick. Your male mind would read it that debauched way. And you're completely wrong. I offered you a snow globe because I thought you looked lonely at the holidays and I hoped the beautiful scene would make you happy. If you had attempted to touch me, I would've slapped you back to Brooklyn."

"Good. I would've deserved that."

"Why did you come back to Igtord anyway?"

"I told myself for a Sunday conference in a nearby city and the sweet southern sorghum cornbread, but I wanted to see that girl again, I confess, too young for me still but I had this desire to protect her, to know her, yet she didn't even remember me when we were bumping shoulders on the hayride, and now I know why—she had been too focused on my kippah to notice my face."

"I do owe you an apology. For coveting … I didn't know the young man in the restaurant was you. I was conflicted. I wanted to be with my soul's mate but I didn't know if he was the aeronaut or not. I see now I had let appearances confuse me. As an aviator, you are all gruffy and rugged, but in the restaurant, you had looked clean-shaven and studious, and if I had listened to my heart instead of my eyes, I would have sensed you were the same soul."

"Don't be so hard on yourself. You do have a good sense of these things. So, you were turned on by my kippah?"

"I thought you weren't religious, so why were you wearing a kippah?"

"Ah, evading the subject? You should have been a pilot with those kinds of skills in evasion. I was in a phase of wanting to wear the yarmulke to show pride in my heritage. I wasn't sure if you were attracted to it or turned off by it, but now I know. You've been harboring the image of the kippah, and even unbeknownst to you, perhaps, sexualizing it, which is why on the morning in the patisserie when I offered you my jacket and you saw my Star of David necklace for the first time, you looked like you wanted to run away—to run away from the one who made you want to lose your virginity."

"That's the most vulgar … horrible … deranged perception only a polluted male mind could come up with! Even more repugnant than your snow globe metaphor. I did not want to run away from you but from a barricade I thought was going to block our love's development. I didn't think you could marry a non-Jewish girl."

"Ah, come on, you're turned on by my Jewness."

"And that offends you?"

"I suppose it should, or perhaps it shouldn't. I'm the one who told you I have a preference for soft-spoken girls and girls that want to be wives and mothers, and I like the way your southern accent says my name, 'Gurshum,' particularly when I'm inside you, 'Ooh, Gurshuuum.'"

"If you're going to make fun, I won't do this with you again, sir."

"Ah, I rather like the way your magnolia voice turns every word into a boutonnière you pin on a gentleman's mood."

"Now who's being girly?"

"But I'm glad we don't live in Brooklyn. You'd be seen as a shiksa."

"What is that?"

"A not so nice term for a non-Jewish woman with a preference for Jewish men."

"I never said I have a preference for Jewish men. You said that. I only like one man."

"Elvis Presley?"

"Okay, two men. I happen to love you and you're Jewish. I'd love you just as much if you were Hindu or Greek, and if you were, I would take interest in Hinduism or Greek culture, *your* culture. Am I making sense?"

"Yeah, you're turned on by my kippah. Tell me what kind of fantasy were you having about me that rainy afternoon?"

"I am not telling you that."

"Come on. Perhaps we were sharing a fantasy."

I told him about the austere study and our almost dream kiss at the table.

"That's interesting, Peppermint. Sounds like the study in my great-uncle's house, where I often spent hours reading."

"How could I have known about a study you had been inside as a boy? We had a mystical connection!"

"Perhaps, or you were envisioning a standard image of a beth midrash, a Torah study hall."

To avoid ruining the playful mood, I didn't tell him about the dream set in the woodland, both beautiful and dreary, a representation of the death camp's bone yard, and his boyhood Alaskan forests, and the majestic timberlands of his time in the tundra—my soul had been able to see all the major backdrops of my soul mate's life story, and no one could convince me otherwise (even if nothing else in the realm of the "paranormal" was true, telepathy was).

504

"What were you fantasizing?" I asked.

"I wasn't fantasizing anything. I'm a good boy."

"For the record, sir, I remember feeling a certain young man's gaze across my crucifix necklace that afternoon in the *soul* food restaurant, and I didn't notice you make any effort to remove my cross necklace during this night together."

"Well, it's Christmastime, I figured the good Christian girl should be wearing her cross necklace. And I confess I enjoyed hearing the Star of David necklace clank against the crucifix necklace while we became one in body."

"You're depraved."

"And I hate to tell you this but that gaze in the restaurant was not across your necklace."

"I thought my eyes were so clear with purity, you couldn't have an impure thought about me."

"Well … I didn't have thoughts … exactly … I just took a gander… you were older …"

"You really are depraved! If I had a dirt clod, I'd throw it at you too."

"All men are depraved. Our sexual feelings never progress beyond the first urge given to us by our first budding hormone. While you're all, 'You make love to me the way Shakespeare writes poetry,' I'm 'hubba hubba hubba, naked girl, must have.'"

"I don't know if I believe that. I'm not sure what to believe about any of you menfolk. I think you men say you're depraved just to be macho, but on the flip side, maybe you are depraved, and only feed us women sweet lines, so we'll satisfy your depraved fantasies? You're so difficult to figure, much more difficult than algebra."

He laughed. "We're not that complex. You know what? You belong in a man's fantasy as much as a ruby belongs in a trashcan."

"That's a disappointing fact to learn—my dear Sputnik has a wastebasket mind full of trashy thoughts."

"I promise I'll always clean them up for you."

"Shakespeare was a man and complex and he wasn't depraved."

"He was just trying to seduce fair maidens with his eloquent lines."

I kept my voice playful to let him know I was only teasing, "I'm never getting in this bed with you again!"

"I warned you but the sweet girl would not listen to me, because she was so turned on by my kippah."

"'Christ's values have never taken a sweeter form.' You said that with so much sacrilegious lust in your voice that afternoon, I didn't think I would ever stop blushing."

"Ah, yeah, what about my circumcision scar, which is a religious mark on my body, highly holy, a sign of the covenant with God, but you weren't exactly looking at it like a piece of scripture, you young nun."

"I think I liked you better when you came over just to pick apples for me. You were so gallant."

"Too late to go back now. You've opened Pandora's Box and who knows what other depravities might come out."

"When you told me the noblest expressions of your love would be flying me in your airplane to charitable causes and building me a snow globe, I never felt so honored and valued—I wish every woman could feel that once: a man's complete adoration given free of a sexual contract. Not often does a woman get to feel loved and respected in a fatherly way by any man other than her father."

He became serious. "Are we still being playful? You're not having regrets, are you, Peppermint? I'd stab a knife through my heart if I dishonored you."

"No, Sputty, don't do that. Yes, we're still being playful. I don't have any regrets. I've never felt more meaningful than when making a baby with you. Plus, I'm happy to see you being playful."

"I can be playful for you, my kippah lover."

"Okay, let's just say we're attracted to the differences between us, and not just the religious differences—you seem quite fascinated by my female body and your male body has some slight fascination to me too."

"Slight fascination? You're so lost in my chest hair, a search party's going to have to come in after you."

"That's because it's so fun to play with!" I ran my hand quickly through the hair like it was a dog's head to pet. "It's kind of alluring too."

"This grizzly stuff?"

"Ooh, teddy bears have soft cuddly hair."

"I should have known that's how you would see it."

Worried that maybe he had been too depraved, he whispered a phrase in another language I did not understand but immediately felt in my heart was romantic. "That's 'She walks in beauty like the night' in Modern Hebrew. Do you like that?"

"What girl wouldn't?"

"Now in French…" In Russian. In Polish. In Spanish. In Pig Latin to make me laugh. "Now in Kiss."

"It's not just a line?"

"Come on, I was only teasing you about that stuff. I really love you. I really saw the snow globe as sweet and good; that memory is on the highest altar of my memories. Listen, we're all complex except when we're in love when we're as simple and right as 'one plus one equals two' and the beauty of the simplicity, a truth we've known all along, shines like a Eureka that stuns us into quiet

507

reverence for the holiest feeling known to humankind. I once went to Israel, the Holy Land of both our peoples. In the sunrise of a new day, I sat in contemplation on the steps of ruins of an ancient synagogue, and this might surprise you, but I prayed to find you, my *bashert*—that's the Jewish term for destiny, or soulmate—even though I felt I had no right to find you."

We were ready to begin speaking with our bodies again, and we were transported to a magical world, where words were no longer needed to express anything.

Afterwards, we draped each other, his arm around me, his chest against my back, in our bed turned "King Soloman's flying carpet," according to Sputnik.

"I think it's the magic carpet that flew Captain Stormfield to Heaven," I said, referring to Mark Twain's story about the man transported to Heaven. "I wish we could get away from this world for a while. Do you think there are any honeymoon cabins for rent on Mars?"

Sputnik was in professor character again; you could take the genius out of the study but not the study out of the genius even in bed.

"You made a good point earlier about us being attracted to our differences."

"Yes, Professor, explain that."

"I confess it's appealing to me that you're a Protestant, and the appealingness is no doubt stemming from your presenting to me a new culture, and you have this image of me as a boy in a yarmulke studying Torah, which is apparently highly attractive to you, because you're attracted to exploring a new religion. You and me, and the ones like us, we like exploring other worlds. But some people can't stand that. And there starts war."

"And isn't it beautiful, Gersh, that right now a part of you and a part of me could be entwining." I brought his hand down to my lower stomach. "Even when we physically separate, they won't separate, and even amidst all this world's hate, they won't separate,

508

and even if we were forced to be continents apart, they would not separate—they would just continue making life that is connected with my momma and your grandma and your mother and the entire Braverman bloodline all mingling in the making of a happy new baby completely oblivious to the world's bigotry."

I kissed into his hand. I could not kiss my husband enough as a thank you to him for giving me a chance to be a mother.

"Ooh, Sputnik, Sputnik, Sputnik, how can one man contain so much beauty?"

"This is interesting. Not long ago, I was a deviant with a polluted male mind."

"My soul feels what the ears feel when a piano sings…sings…"

"Brahms perhaps?"

"Did he write lovely music?"

"I'd say so and you'd say so too if you ever listened to anything more sublime than *Melt & Malt.*"

"Then, yes, my after-lovemaking soul feels what the ears feel when listening to Brahms. I should write that line down, save it for a story."

"You are really letting the girlish ink pour."

"Unabashedly. I love you so deeply, I feel my love could make a literal diamond."

"Make it a baseball diamond."

"I'm going to lose you during baseball season, aren't I?"

"Absolutely."

"How long is baseball season?"

"With playoffs, you're looking at seven months."

"Seven months! It takes that long to bat that ball around to win a championship? That's not acceptable!"

"You're such a girl, Lumi."

"I'll take that as a compliment."

"You should."

"I can get girly-er still."

"Ah?"

"When you make love to me, you turn me into flowers. You were just inside me, so now you are reaping all the sweet blossoms you made bloom."

"Bloom away because we're in wide free nature, so bloom, Lady, bloom."

"Sputnik, this is nice. No walls up."

"The walls were meant to protect you."

"And to punish you. But the walls hurt me instead of protect me. Can we try it this way instead?"

With caution, "If that's what you want."

"What I want is this…My love aspires to charm a butterfly to land in your life. Beautiful, beautiful this butterfly, always in your sight, flying slightly up and ahead, reminding your soul where it is ultimately being led. Ooh, I need to find some paper to write these lines down—they may be the ones I'm remembered for. Thanks to my muse. You give me so much inspiration for story writing. I can write my own Cinderella fairy tale."

"Ah, life with a writer."

"Get used to me waking up in the middle of the night, searching for a notebook to jot down lines for stories that came to me in sleep."

"I do the same thing with equations."

"We'll make sure to have lots of scrap paper on our bookshelf headboard." I let it warm me, the vision of his notebooks and books on our shared bookshelf headboard, reading and writing in bed together at night, sharing our notes and insights with each other, gaining each other's opinions.

He softly turned me around to face him. "You're an angel." That was reassuring to his old-fashioned wife—he still thought of her as an angel afterwards.

"Would an angel have done what we just did and *coveted your kippah* all these years?"

"I was just teasing about the kippah. The only thing you want is love in endless supply. I see now that an angel would do this for the man she loves. Write this in your story someday, Lumi: I feel bad to have been harboring hateful thoughts about my mother all these years because of the pleasure she derived from being intimate with Pops, a pleasure he was too selfish to even see or cater. You have to understand, Pep, I've seen a lot of filth in the world. I watched dirty-handed lechs grab at my mother, literally sometimes ripping her dress. And a sicko killed my sister. And soldiers on all sides raped girls, and women prisoners had to strip naked and be paraded around in front of guards, and male prisoners raped girls after the war for revenge. I suspect Bubbe was raped as a girl, the reason she never spoke again and wanted to fly away and did not trust men, except her grandson, the grandson of her beloved gentle Feivish. And just to let you know, some of your respectable progressive professors in their cardigans and penny loafers treat girls like hot fudge sundaes, little dishes to satisfy their afternoon hankerings between their morning and evening classes, and once they've devoured all the sweetness inside, they discard what's leftover like trash and tell their colleagues how such and such girl scored an 'A' whereas their none-the-wiser wives always scored 'F's."

"Not at Adelia!"

"I can't speak for Adelia because I'm not there often, but I can tell you Goldell's the worst. Listen, I know women enjoy kissing and cuddling and spiritual and emotional intimacy, and I know they derive pleasure from physical intimacy as well, and I suppose I was partly disgusted by the indecency of that; perhaps because sex was always used by men to deprive women of something, I had this idea that doing this would take away from your Ladyness, your sweetness, but in fact, it has made you even sweeter, even more Ladylike, girly-er than ever. I see you as even more beautiful and perfect and angelic than before like you gained more than you lost, so if you write about me someday, write about the dense professor's thunderstruck moment of having this insight, thanks to his gorgeous wife."

I kissed the gold shining star against his chest. "I don't feel I lost anything."

"Well, there was that one thing," he said with mock smugness.

"I didn't lose it. It's in your possession. Not because you took it. Because I gave it to you. To show you how much I love and trust you."

"The shocking thing is an angel can love a man."

"Of course an angel can love a man—who else is there to be an angel for?"

"So many insights you bring to me. I just had another insight: you're smarter than me."

"No, I'm not!"

"Perhaps not in math and science, but perhaps so if given the chance, but you're worlds beyond me when it comes to this relationship stuff. I'm trying to think of what the world would be like if there were no female characters. A bunch of hairy guys belching and slashing swords."

"I don't think it would be that bleak. You have a horrible view of your own sex. Some men are painters and poets and noble warriors."

"Noble scum."

I kissed his chest. "I just found my new favorite thing to do in this world. Sputnik, you're certainly not scum—you're so beautiful, even with my eyes closed, you're beautiful."

"Well, it's nice to know you're not just after my bod."

"Ooh, but what a bod it is, Professor."

"That's what gets you girls in trouble. You go to college right after high school, where boys had been juvenile horny toads, but now you're adults in the eyes of the world and capable of socializing with teachers, who you had crushes on in school but were not allowed to pursue. But now you're encountering adult men known as professors, who become sexualized father figures, offering you guidance like a caring father, but at the same time, they're not your fathers, they're men, and they're intelligent and suited up and sophisticated looking, not horny toads, and they're there to *teach* you—"

"You're being depraved again. That sounds like one of your debauched fantasies, Professor, not a girl's fantasy, and I didn't realize you were so interested in being your female students' father figure?"

"*I'm* being depraved? 'Oooh, Professor Blagonravov.' You've been wanting the Professor to give you an intense lesson since I first walked into algebra and stood at the head of the class. There were times in class I thought is it my imagination or are her hot gazes going to melt the walls?"

"That's because you are very sexy."

"When did the nun acquire that word?"

"Ooh, you don't know? I think you were there."

"I better have been there. But I'm a man. Guys aren't beautiful or sexy."

"That's news to me and my desire. Plus, what you're saying now is completely contradictory to what you said about girls and professors. You obviously think girls see professors as sexy."

The scientist had not considered the contradiction.

"Why do you think I'm in bed with you, Sputty?"

"Because you love me."

"Yes, that's what allows me to actually be in bed with you, because I could not do this with a man I didn't love, but I'm also attracted to you."

He became serious again. "I thought we were doing this for procreation?"

"We are. That doesn't mean I can't be attracted to the one I'm procreating with; it's imperative I am attracted to him."

"Alright if you insist. Now, let's share some more cooties."

"No! I want to know more about you and your adoring students!"

"Ah, come on, I'm not attracted to my students. They're usually all guys, not a lot of girl types in aeronautical engineering, except that one little babe who stood outside my classroom door—I want to share cooties with her."

"Procreating cooties."

We laughed about that.

"Sputnik, we're going to melt the Earth if we don't cool down."

"And we'll find out Earth is really a chocolate-covered cherry, and all us skeptical types were wrong and you dreamy types were right—the universe is a big box of candy."

"You're so strange," I said with a smiling voice.

"Takes a weirdo to love a weirdo."

"How about we have a month-long honeymoon?" I asked. "I know you have to work, but when you're not working, we'll continue our honeymooning in Geneva, since now that I'm your wife, I'm assuming I'm going with you?"

"Of course, you're going. With me. Everywhere."

I knew being his wife could be a lonesome profession if I accepted the idea that closeness was a measure of physical proximity. After the holidays, he would always be working, and regardless of what he said about me going with him everywhere, I could not be in my husband's physical presence often. When he wouldn't be at the university, he would be at conferences and meetings and lectures, or cloistered away on his iceberg, where he could work without being bothered, or he would be off building something and could not be disturbed. I never wanted to be an interruption to whatever world-changing something he was developing. But I didn't have to be physically near him to be close to him; I had spent my life feeling connected to him before I had even met him. For now, he was right beside me, and I used a moment wisely—to remember every detail of the man I loved in a universe where nothing lasted forever.

"Lumi, if anyone can bring about a peace treaty, it's you." He kissed my chin; he enjoyed kissing me there.

"Me? I'm not political at all. I'm sorry, my love. But I'll try to be if you want me to be."

"You going to be Susan B. Anthony for me too? Susan B. and Marie Curie and barnstorming Katherine Stinson and chaste Protestant nun and Torah-expert wife of a rabbi—Superwife!"

"You're going to keep making fun of me all night and after what we did too!"

"You're an activist in your own way. You're a writer."

"A writer of love stories."

515

"And that's your way of protesting against hate stories. Your very niceness is an activist against violence. If everyone could be so nice, we wouldn't need activists, because there'd be nothing to protest— we'd just need lots of teacups for lots of tea parties, and the entire world would be doily-ed."

I gently bopped his head. "You'd be lucky to have my Lady Model world."

"You know what, why not a year-long honeymoon?"

"That's a surprising proposal from the fellow a few hours ago who did not want us to have a honeymoon at all."

"Even better," he said, "why not a lifelong honeymoon?"

"Do you think we'll always feel this starry way about each other?"

"We already have felt this way all of our lives, you searching for me, me searching for you."

I kissed him for that.

"You give me so much insight too, Sputnik, insight into lines for a story: I want to play in the sands of another world with you. The moon awaits us to make love against its sand."

"We'd die from oxygen deprivation."

"Do you have to be so scientific?"

"Yes. That's why I asked *you* to write the romantic story. If I wrote a story set on the moon, the moon would be a hard dusty inhospitable rock incapable of supporting life; in your story, it'd be a little nook in the stars where lovers kissed."

"I think it would be that way in your story too if you were writing honestly." I kissed the scar on his shoulder.

"Just so you know, I didn't get that from Nazis in a faraway land during the war. I got that right here in America just a few years ago from Nazis in police uniforms, beating billy clubs against women and children in peaceful protest at a Civil Rights march, where *civil* was an anathema to the officers."

I told him about Cynthia and he held me close, and we just held on to holding on to our peaceful togetherness.

"I need to go check on Mullybiski and Pythagoras." I was worried about our friends.

"I'll go. I don't want you to get out of this warm bed." Sitting up out of the covers, he grumped, "Oy vey!" feeling the cold touch him. His naked back was sprinkled with a few freckles, all mine to play with for the rest of my life, all of him and his maleness, ooh the delight!

He started coughing.

"Sputnik, I'll go."

"I'm," he started to bark but softened his voice to a tender honeymoon decibel, "I'm fine."

He shut the door when he left, so the bedroom would not lose its warmth. I could hear him humming, "Ba-bu-baaa."

"Sputnik is my husband," I repeated to myself like a lottery winner telling herself, "I actually won," or an astronaut saying, "I'm *really* in outer space."

I daydreamed about having his son, nicknamed Cracker Jack, because I imagined he would love those candies…no, even cuter, we would call him, "Buggy," because when I strolled with his baby buggy, I'd say, "How you doin', Buggy?" I imagined he would want to build spaceships like his dad, and his baby self and nursery would smell like Play-Doh and baby shampoo, a baby who would be brand new. His heart brand new. Not a refurbished heart. Just like his new tiny fingers and baby toes and baby hair and shiny baby skin. I would try to keep him unscuffed for as long as I could. I would try to be as good a mother as Moon-Moon had been. My heart was swelling. Ooh, to share the delight of meadow walks with a new generation. To teach him and to learn from him. And I would love being pregnant with Gersh's baby, walking on sidewalks and letting my round stomach tote my accomplishment—I'm with the most fantastic fellow's child.

I imagined our granddaughter, who might be an astronaut, and on the day history launched her into the stars, Sputnik and I would make a toast with the sky, "There you go, Bubbe the Magnificent, your genes are flying."

When my husband opened the door, the lights came back on.

"I'm magical," he said, taking credit for the emerging lights.

"Yay, Sputnik!"

I heard the refrigerator resume its humming.

"I'll go light the pilot so we can get some heat in here."

The heater sounded happy to be back on, singing that song that furnaces sang.

When Sputnik came back, I pouted, "I'm afraid I'm going to miss the romanticness of being in the dark with you."

He shut the door and our room stayed dark except for starlight and snowlight in wrap-around windows. Just me and *my husband* for miles around, no one else. Paradise.

Standing there in only his undershorts, he said, "My moving in here is going to be like a tornado moving into a library—all the pristine systematic organization is going to be blown into disarray. You're so orderly and neat-minded, Lumi, every outfit in your wardrobe is spaced apart perfectly as if by ruler, the food in the fridge is arranged by purpose, and even the books on your headboard are alphabetized!"

"*Our* headboard," I corrected.

"There are only four books up there and they're alphabetized. That's creepy."

"It's not creepy. It makes finding the books easier."

"You can't find four books without the help of Dewey decimal?"

"You don't have to alphabetize your side if you prefer *messiness*."

"Ah, phooey. You'll alphabetize them when I'm not looking. Sometimes—alright, all the time—I come home and pull off my socks, wad them up like sock baseballs, and toss them to the wall."

"That explains the sock hill topography of your apartment."

"You won't let me do that anymore, will you?"

"Of course, you can still do that. I'll just have to pick up the socks."

"You couldn't leave them balled up on the ground even for a minute, could you?"

"Your socks are still on the floor right now."

"That's only because you haven't gotten out of bed yet. It's driving you nuts that my pants and shirt are wadded up on the floor."

"My dress and stockings are wadded up down there too."

"Only because *I* put them there. You'd never have done that. You're ready to take an iron to the whole floor, the whole crinkly world, admit it."

"Okay, I'd prefer not to have a floor that looks like a battleground where dozens of items of clothing fought their last battle and died."

"You're just so prim and proper in all your relations, and not just with people. You have to get married to a sandwich before eating it. I don't think I'm a mannerless oaf, but come on, there's no reason to coddle a sandwich the way you do. It's cream tea time all the time with you, afternoon tea manners twenty-four/seven, except well, when we, you know, but in fact, you're fairly polite then too."

"You're just mean."

"Did I say I mind having a little cream tea Lady?"

I looked him up and down. "Who would have ever guessed Professor Blagonravov wears pinstriped underpants?"

"Perhaps I should take them off?"

"I won't complain if you do."

"Now, it's time to get back in our Wurlitzer Bed."

"Wurlitzer bed?"

"Like the Wurlitzer Jukebox, where we do some rockin'."

"You're more depraved than anyone would ever guess too, Professor Blagonravov."

He got back into the warm bed and his bare feet were cold from padding across linoleum. I rested on my side, my face somewhat elevated by puffy pillow, my feminine landscape covered by blanket; he lay beside me, his elbow against the mattress, the hair under his arm dark and tufty, his bare chest landscaped in the same forestry of dark hair, where the gold necklace sparkled.

"How are Mully and Pythag?"

"Sleeping like babies."

"Speaking of babies…I think I'm pregnant. X+Y equals baby."

If he had been holding something, he would have dropped it. "Already?"

"You don't think it's possible?"

"Well, we've been doing our best effort at baby making tonight, so it's possible. You have enough of my Jewish seed to become a Biblical matriarch."

"Sputnik! Once again, you're being obscene and sacrilegious, and I'm not playing this time: this is a sacred subject."

"Alright, my apologies. Surely you couldn't already know you're pregnant. I don't believe in making love to my wife when she's pregnant, so are you sure?"

"No, I'm not sure. Why don't you believe in that?"

"Talk about sacrilegious. Besides, it's just disrespectful to you and the baby. And the idea of a sweet baby daughter being right there when I was doing that, that is depraved."

"I admire your respect for your wife and child, but I don't think a baby in the womb is aware when his parents are engaged in that."

"Lumi, I don't believe in making love to a pregnant woman, and there's no changing my mind on that."

"Okay. Would you be happy if I was pregnant?"

"I think I would be."   The walls had come back up, huh?

"You *think*? You said we were procreating, and you told me you wanted a girl whose goal is to be a wife and mother."

"I've just never much thought about it, not seriously. I never thought it was in the stars for me to even be married."

"Now that you're finally thinking about it after hours of trying to accomplish it, do you want to have a child?"

"You said you wanted to have a baby, so we'll have a baby, or babies. You're my Lady. I'll do anything I'm capable of doing to make you happy, except clean up my socks."

"I want *you* to be happy, Gershom. Remember the sweet scene of the holidays and the baby in the sleepsuit. Does that make you happy?"

His thoughts gave the scene, every detail, his full attention.

"Imagine that soft baby pudge in your arms and those cute baby toes."

He smiled about that. "I loved taking care of baby Bow, teaching her, protecting her."

"How many kids would you want?"

He mentally calculated. "Nine."

"Nine! How'd you come up with that figure?"

"Well, we'd have to have enough for a ball team: pitcher, catcher, all three bases, three outfielders, and a batter. You're lucky I didn't include a shortstop. But really we'd need more; we'd have to have more players to be at bat."

"You're lucky I don't bop your head for the suggestion."

"You're so attracted to me, a chariot of angels couldn't pull you outta this bed, sister nun."

"I'm not sure I want to have your baby."

"You want it so bad, you're ready to go at it again."

"Yes, I've concluded, I no longer like you."

"Sure, sure."

"Nine children, the mere thought of it! Yes, those genius genes of yours should be passed on but nine times is too many. Plus, if you had that many kids, even in yearly sequence, by the time the ninth one was born, your first born would be nine, so they couldn't play baseball together."

"Good point. I hadn't thought of that."

I had outsmarted the mathematician.

"Well, how many kids do you want?"

"Four."

"I take it you've thought of this before?"

I nodded.

"Let's see," he said, "a pitcher, a catcher, a batter, and an outfielder are a must…"

"We can play on the team too."

He lay against his back, hands behind his head, hair under his arms puffed out. "The girl who thought the Dodgers was a minor league team is not playing on my team."

"If your humor got any drier, it could be used as packing desiccant to keep parcels dry."

"I'm not kidding. I'm not letting you play on my team."

"Ooh, okay, I didn't want to play on Cootie's team anyway. Am I at least a member now of Sampi Koppa Digamma?"

"Alright."

I lay against him and told him of my dream about our son, my wish to keep him unscuffed. "Ponder this, Sput: in their natural state, rocks are unpolished, and people put effort into polishing rocks, making them shine as gemstones, but humans come into the world polished, yet everyone tries to scuff you up, so it takes great effort to keep the world from scuffing you."

"You've done a fine job with yourself, Peppermint."

I could tell he was still imagining what it would be like to be a dad.

"When Bow was around five, I taught her how to ride a bike. It hadn't been that long since I had first learned myself. She always said, 'Don't let go, Gersh, don't let go, promise.' She was brave as long as I didn't let go." I thought he was going to cry but he held it back. "It's a frightening notion, bringing a daughter into this world of sickos, who want to write dirty lines into sweet stories."

"As a girl, I can tell you it's not as bad as all that. I won't pretend that we women don't sometimes feel like prey because certain deranged men have chosen to view their tool for procreation as a tool for terror, and we always have to be cautious—don't walk that street alone, don't wear a dress that pretty, don't say something nice to him that says, 'You're asking for it.' But men like you make up for the bad. With men like you in the world, it's kind of nice being a Lady."

"It would be nice to have a daughter, Lumi, and I'd never let her go."

"You'd have to let her go someday, but on the day she flies to the stars as an astronaut, you'll feel proud knowing you were the one who gave her the courage to do so. There's nothing quite so beautiful as a good relationship between father and daughter, the way each grows through their love and respect, the way a daughter allows a father to see women as individuals, the way a father allows a daughter to see herself as special; no matter what anyone else in the world thinks of her, if her father thinks she's special, she'll forever feel special. Ooh, you menfolk are at your noblest when you're dads, doing all those dad tasks that daughters don't want to do—coming over at two a.m. to light a stubborn pilot light, fending off devious boys even amidst protests from daughters too young to see their father's wisdom, spending all day in the hot sun working on a carburetor, whatever those actually are, just so your daughter can have an air conditioner in her car and not have to spend one moment in the heat. I won't get too gushy, because I know that makes you uncomfortable, but I just wish I had been able to experience more of those dad/daughter moments. You'll be her hero for the rest of her life. But a father knows someday

524

another man is going to be equally important in his daughter's life and capable of providing her a form of love only a husband can."

"I'm not going to be that noble—the first creepy boy that comes around my daughter is going to get his little head chopped off, and I said 'head' to avoid offending your Ladyness."

"Ooh, Sputnik, when the time comes and it's the right boy, a boy like you—"

"A boy like me? After everything I've done to you tonight. I wouldn't let a man like me get within fifty feet of my daughter."

"You'll have to give your daughter away in marriage, or else you'll break her heart."

"Yeah, you're probably right, but for now I'll hold onto my dream of her staying on the tricycle for a lifetime and never wanting her dad to let go."

I let him linger in the fantasy of fatherhood for a long while.

He rubbed his lips against my hair, telling me he missed my company.

"You need a lesson on what a carburetor is," he said with a laugh.

"Okay, so maybe I do, although I don't plan to write stories about carburetors. But *your* knowledge of all those manly things is attractive. Susan B. Anthony, forgive me, but I like that my husband knows things I don't like how to fix a pilot light and pitch a tent. Like you said, it's our differences and similarities in complementary ratio that attract us."

"I didn't say that."

"But that's what you meant."

"Married a few hours and she's already telling me what I think. I'm going to Hank's for some brews and checkers."

"What I was trying to say is I like when men, not the kind who go to Hank's, but when gentlemen open doors for women, when gentlemen are helpful, and protective, when gentlemen think it's wrong to pick a fight with a woman—that doesn't make me feel inferior, it makes me feel appreciated. It makes me feel understood. I don't like fighting and I appreciate when a man understands that. I like being your girl."

"Can you imagine a buck fighting a doe? There's a reason we don't see that. That'd be a highly dumb buck. I don't think humans should look to the animal kingdom to find the right way to live, but the deer seem to have this one right. Bucks might fight each other for a doe, but they don't fight the doe, their mate. Listen, you'll always be my girl. Even if you know how to fix a pilot light or understand a carburetor, I'll see you as my girl. You're my mate."

I sang, "*Ooh my mate's a good mate, a buddy from fate!*"

Sputnik released a good-natured laugh, and I told him, "My momma and I used to sing that. Sing along, you can make up your own lines, that's part of the fun. *My mate's a good mate, a buddy from fate…*"

"*Worth the wait…*"

"*Erased all the hate…*"

And we became the shipmates I had envisioned us being in childhood.

"I thought you didn't want to be my buddy pal, jack."

"A special kind of buddy pal. You told me you'd always see me as your girl, and you deserve the same acceptance. You can be as sensitive and sweet and gushy as you want, and I'll always see you as my fellow."

He laughed. "You women say you want sensitive men, but be honest now, do you want to go to the movies with a fellow who hides *his* eyes during scary scenes? No. You want to be with the guy who holds you during scary scenes and keeps his eyes open, so you can hide your sight from all the gore. Lumi, your entire fantasy of Knights and Ladies is based on this—chivalry."

"I'm sorry if I've ever made you feel you couldn't cry around me or show that you're human and have fears."

"Sure, I can cry about losing my family in the Holocaust, but you don't want me boohooin' in the middle of *The Sound of Music*."

I traced my finger along his necklace. "Sputty, if you're not religious, why do you always wear the Star of David?"

"Look at her skills of evasion, folks—zipping right past that conversation!"

"Okay, how about when I'm crying, you'll hold me, and when you're crying, I'll hold you, and when I'm sick, you'll nurse me, and when you're sick…you see what I mean? I don't want you to ever feel you have to erase aspects of your character to fit in with the male role written by society. I want you to be you, or else I should be with someone else. So, why do you wear the necklace?"

"I wear the necklace for two reasons. To show pride in my heritage just like when I wore the kippah. When the Nazis invaded Poland, we were forced to wear badges shaped in the Star of David to isolate us from everyone else. To mark us as those who deserved no respect, no human decency. We could even be killed for not wearing the badge. So, I'm saying, yes, I'm a Jew and I'm proud of it. The other reason is because this necklace belonged to Bubbe the Magnificent!"

"Ooh! I didn't know you had any of her belongings? We could give this to our daughter?"

"Absolutely. When I was a boy, my mother and Bubbe and Pops made a time capsule, a jam jar filled with different items for me to open someday, on the day before I went to college, that was the plan. None of us had been able to foresee the future that awaited us. When I came back to America after the war, I took a trip to Alaska."

"By freight train?"

He smiled, Yup. "No one lived on the land where we used to live. Our old shack and shed were just shells now with dirty windows. I knew the capsule had been buried exactly fifteen feet from the top right vertex of Pop's square cement launchpad. Like father, like son, both of us big on exact measurements."

I imagined Sputnik as a young man, sitting in Alaskan dirt and digging up Bubbe's jam jar time capsule, excited as a kid digging for dinosaur bones.

"Inside Bubbe had put her necklace; Pops, being utilitarian, had put in a roll of cash, and Mother had given me a red string, meant to be worn as a bracelet to ward off evilness. I thought Mother, you should have worn this and perhaps everything would have turned out differently." He smiled, not really believing that. "Those are the only tangible items I have of my family, so I wear the necklace."

"Why don't you wear the bracelet?"

"I never thought I deserved to."

I liked that there was uncertainty in his voice—he was no longer completely certain he was unforgiveable. Maybe some of the wall was still in rubbles and his rescue from guilt still a possibility.

To test just how far the wall had crumbled, I rubbed my hand tenderly across the numbers on his arm and he let me. He closed his eyes and was dragged all the way back to the horrific moment when the numbers were painfully tattooed on him with permanent ink, a moment when he had been unable to foresee a girl gently caressing him there someday in a warm bed on his honeymoon night, a night he never thought he would live to have.

"I think I'll turn it into a square root," he said, opening his eyes.

"What do you mean?"

"I'll get the square root sign tattooed around it, because see, the square root of those numbers is an *irrational* number."

He closed his arm at the elbow, sandwiching my hand between his lower arm and bicep, and brought my hand up to his lips for a kiss. He did not want to think any more about Nazis; it was our wedding night after all.

"I was your first," he said, still astounded by his "achievement." "That makes me feel special."

"A man feels special when he is a woman's first lover; a woman feels special when she is a man's last lover."

His face said, "?"

"What I mean is girls are taught to wait for true love and boys are taught to end with true love. So, being my first makes you feel special, since you know how much that means to me, and being your last makes me feel special, since I know I must be your true love if you give others up for me, which I'm assuming you'll do considering we're married, and you did write that in our marriage contract."

He sat up, so I sat up too, unwilling to let him get away from the subject. He took two chocolate-covered cherries from the starlit red tin, which included two varieties: milk and dark chocolate. I preferred the dark chocolate and Sputnik preferred the milk chocolate, so that worked out perfectly.

"You are going to give up all the other women, aren't you, Mr. Marvelous Lover?" I said before nibbling the candy. "Like the sociology professor—"

"The only sociology professor I know is named Gary and I assure you I'm not having a torrid affair with him." Imagining himself with Gary made him laugh.

"Okay. What about the French professor?"

"You heard all those rumors too? I was hoping you had not."

He didn't say anything else but instead ate the chocolate, which was another good sign: the warden was obviously experiencing a change in feelings toward the prisoner if allowing him to enjoy candy without even a goading from "the nun."

"I want to know about the French professor."

"Ah. Well, one afternoon, she came into my office to borrow a book. I was at my desk. A book dropped. She kneeled to get the book. Brad walked in and saw the set-up, which must have looked illicit, because he gave a wink and said, 'Sorry,' quickly shutting the door. Later, I tried to explain, and he said, 'Sure, sure, Pro-fess, don't worry about it.' From then on, I was the stud on campus."

"That's all?"

"Well, there was that bombshell cocktail waitress in Manhattan. And that TV newswoman. And there's this knockout waiting for me in Geneva who looks just like Mara Gold. And all those girl students who see me as their father figure. They're just lined up for me."

"Chafing me with dry humor again, or were you not being funny?"

"Does it matter? I'm with you. You're my wife. And, no, I would never cheat on you. If a man doesn't want to get married then he shouldn't, but if he does, he should live it honorably, otherwise there was no reason to get married."

I could see two backstories of Sputnik's past: he had been Sir Galahad, a virgin up until this night, feeling unworthy of touching a woman because of the sins he believed he had committed in the war, or he had been a stud, who had felt it his duty to please all women. I realized either way, I loved him the same.

"I was on the phone with you every night, Pep, or with you in my office, or out in my truck parked right out there."

"Not *every* night. I love you regardless of your past with other women, Sput, but since we're friends who share everything, I want to know if all those rumors are true?"

"That's why you were mad at me!" A-ha! "'You pig,'" he laughed now, remembering the hostile scene between us that had not made him laugh at the time. "Ben came to my office the next day and said, 'Bro-ther, that's a bunch o' coffee on your couch. What'd you do to the little cookie to deserve that, you dippity-do head?'"

"Look at his skills of evasion."

"I can't understand why, but in your eyes, I'm this…hunk." Even the word made him uncomfortable. "Come on, other women don't see me that way."

"Yes, they do. You're just too down on yourself to realize that, or just being too modest in front of your wife to admit it."

He ate another chocolate. "Just last week, a woman wrote me a letter, said she had seen me on TV, gave me her address."

"Why, that hussy!"

"Lumi! Where's my sweet nun girl?"

"I'll take that address and show her what I feel about it." I raised my fist, which Sputnik lowered back to the bed.

"Ladies don't physically fight, *jack*, and you and your Lady Model style of fighting, which I can't even picture, wouldn't win anyway. Well, I threw the letter away, so don't worry. I throw them all away."

"*All?* How many are there?"

"I don't know. Women come around once you've been in the papers or on TV. Like Madame—"

"So, she is after you?"

"She didn't drop the book accidentally. I said, 'I have a girl.' She said, 'I have two boyfriends. If you're worried about the tiny blonde you follow like a lovesick puppy, she won't mind—she's training to be perfect wife.' I said, 'I'd rather die than hurt her.'

She said, 'But would you rather miss out on this than hurt her?' 'Yes,' I said."

I could imagine Professor Blagonravov being that austere and blunt with her.

"I can't blame her for wanting my Sputty. He is quite special."

"I don't care about those other women. I told you I was the boy as isolated as a germ, waiting my whole life for the girl who would kiss me softly enough."

"Are you being serious with me?"

From somewhere in his stony prison cell, he dug up this flower of a response, "I have a room-for-one kind of heart."

"Ooh, Sputnik, that was sweet. You're my heart's only boarder too."

Realizing I loved when he spoke flowery, he dug up some more word blossoms, "My heart is as loyal to you as a Knight to Joan of Arc."

"Ooh, Sput, that was beautiful!"

"I figured you could be seduced by the Knight line." He ate yet another chocolate.

"You are my Knight."

"Jewish Knight?"

"There were Jewish Knights in history."

"We Jews were persecuted in those days too."

"I hope I won't shock my dear Knight by my impropriety, but I'm going to be *ravenous with instinct* and eat another chocolate."

"Eat all of them if you want. I'll get you a thousand boxes of chocolate if you like."

"Just one more. The rest are for my sweetie. Back to what you were saying, I like the storybook Knights, remember?"

"I know. It's alright. I told you my mother was obsessed with Arthurian legend too. It is interesting."

"I thought you weren't 'taken in' by the Knight and Lady 'mythology'?"

"I never said it wasn't a nice idea. I had some dreams as a boy about Camelot in outer space. Perhaps Ladies are meant to put stars in Knights."

"I'm taking my molasses with sweet butter."

He laughed. "What?"

"Moon-Moon once told me if molasses is too bitter just add some sweet butter."

"Are you saying I'm bitter old molasses?"

"But getting much sweeter…"

We enjoyed the candies in our reprieve from everything except the taste of chocolate, cherry, and cream.

He picked up my cross necklace, his fingers against my naked chest. "You truly believe Christ was resurrected?"

"Truly."

"So, you think he was divine?"

"Moon-Moon taught me the only difference between Christ and the rest of us is that He is in tune with the Living Light inside and aware of His status as child of God. You don't believe anyone has a soul?"

He let go of the necklace. "I believe you have a soul. Destined for Heaven. I believe in the soul of these chocolates. My goodness." He had not allowed the prisoner to really taste sweetness in years and now he was in chocolate-covered cherry ecstasy; I would soon take him to apricot rugelach ecstasy. "I believe in the soul of my mother and bubbe and sweet little Bow, but I left my soul at the death prison."

"That's a horrible thing to say and believe. And it's not true. I felt your soul years ago when you reached across your plane to the girl stranded on Earth and made her feel loveable. I felt your soul when you protected me from the bully on the hayride. I felt your soul deeply when you made love to me. I speak to your soul every time my eyes contact yours. You have a soul, Sputnik."

"Well, if that's true, I don't deserve it." Do I? I sensed he was asking me that.

"That's the beautiful thing about souls, Sput—everyone gets one, whether they deserve one or not. It's up to each individual to determine what they're going to do with their soul."

"What happens to someone who does something bad?"

"They suffer a lifetime believing they lost their soul. You haven't lost yours, sweet man."

He looked closely at my eyes, which he had done while lovemaking when the intensity had made us feel as if we were going to fall into the wells of each other's beings.

"Gersh, I won't pretend to fathom the kind of treason you feel for whatever you did in the war, but I do know with all my woman's heart that your mother forgives you, no matter what you did, the way I would forgive my son and be happy he was still alive and in love and in chocolate paradise."

He did not disagree this time. He could believe his *mother* might forgive him. He kissed my forehead and said, "Dante's Beatrice guiding him out of hell to Heaven." Then as a way to escape a conversation bringing him too close to *total* forgiveness, he said, "So, you really thought I was a campus stud?"

534

"It didn't seem to be true to your character, but Sputnik, if you loved another girl, I'd step aside and let you be with her, if she made you happier, and I mean that."

"There's not even a ghost of a chance of me loving another girl."

"Or me loving another boy."

"Except for that bombshell stewardess who's waiting for me on my plane ride to Geneva. Ah, come on, I'm joking. You know what I think? Monogamy makes sense. I don't believe evolution favors promiscuity, certainly not human evolution. Men invest their money more carefully than they invest their sperm. Men only make transactions at *reliable* banks yet make deposits in any kind of woman. But if they want to watch their investment grow, they'll find a nice caring girl who can nurture their—"

"*Deposit?*" I made a face to express distaste. Boys.

"And for women, considering they have to carry the baby for nine months and raise the child for many years after that, monogamy ensures their baby's father won't be making babies with anyone else, and he'll devote his time, resources, and protection to her child alone. And for her to find another man to father her next child would be risky, considering she might lose the one child-rearing partner she already has. It's completely natural for humans to be monogamous since we invest so much time in our children. There are men—plenty of them on Goldell's faculty—who have intellectualized monogamy as being unnatural, at least for men."

"Of course. As always."

"No, there are a few women who have intellectualized it for themselves as well, but you're not exactly a *Sex and the Single Girl* reader, so you're oblivious to these kinds of opinions. They argue we want to combine our genes with as many as possible to make sure our legacy lives on, but that's completely ignorant. We're not frogs who propagate a hundred tadpoles, swim away, and say, 'Well, surely at least one will make it.' That's not the way our biology works; if it did, human women would be able to have a

535

hundred babies at a time. And for the men who say, well, I can be with a hundred women and make a hundred babies, if nature wanted human men to behave that way, men wouldn't have a desire to form attachments to their children. Komodo dragons don't care to see photos of their offspring; this is why you can't sell scrapbooks to lizards." He smiled. "It makes much more sense, genetically speaking, for a human man to have a few children with one smart caring gal, children we can nurture into decent human beings."

I liked that he was having a serious conversation with me, the kinds he had with his collegiate colleagues.

"Let's make an analogy, Peppermint, since us writers and mathematicians like those. Let's say a writer wants to ensure one of her books gets read for generations to come, and let's say she wants to work with a co-writer. Now, which path leads to success, the one where she rushes through a bunch of half-hearted chapters with a bunch of co-writers she doesn't know well, or the path where she takes her time with one trusted co-writer to nurture one fabulous book? The absurd thing is the women who side with the boys' club when it comes to the view monogamy is unnatural get angry when an appeal to nature is used in other arguments, such as how it's natural for the female of the species to stay in the nest and take care of the babies, then they start spouting examples of how there are species where males take care of the young too, yet they never spout examples of natural monogamy, which does exist in the animal world as well, such as in the bond between swans."

Every time I read a sexist book, especially stories by male writers, I felt grateful for Sputnik, and after this conversation, I felt especially appreciative for his existence. He wasn't completely void of sexism, but there was hope for him!

"Besides," he said, "anyone who experiences all orgasms without love has never achieved the full potential of orgasm."

"How would you know that, Sput?"

"I'm just hypothesizing. I have colleagues who say things like 'Tigers spread it around.' So what? You're not a tiger, I say to them, and humans aren't even closely related to tigers, and I don't even know if it's true if tigers are promiscuous or not. If you're going to look to tigers for how to behave, you could just as well look to mongooses, but I don't see any human saying, 'Let's go sleep in abandoned termite mounds—mongooses do it!' But when it comes to our mating habits, one of the most important traits of our species, people say, 'Well, how are the lizards doing it?' I don't care how lizards are 'doing it.' I have the abilities to reason and care, abilities a lizard probably does not have. My colleagues use these same kinds of fallacious appeals to nature to argue against vegetarianism; again, spouting habits of coyotes and tigers and completely ignoring the vegetarianism that exists in the animal kingdom, in our nearest relatives, in fact, the gorillas. Ditwad, who can't stand my vegetarianism, came to my office one day to gloat that a certain animal, thought to be a strict vegetarian, had been found eating the flesh of something dead. He said this like this knowledge would make me reconsider being a vegetarian. Can this guy not model his day without first consulting how hippos spend their days? This is why I said I don't like to look to the animal kingdom for standards to live by, because for one, animal behavior is too varied—what works for a spider just doesn't work for a camel—and two, we have the ability to be more than the sum of our instincts."

My husband and I did not belong in any era, and we felt isolated from both liberals and conservatives; we were our own nation, where we honored our own values. We would even put up the flag of our nation—the honorable crest of Sampi Koppa Digamma. I would sew the flag and Sputnik would erect it, right beside Stargust Continued's "Keep Out" gated driveway.

I talked about books, where monogamy was intellectualized as unnatural, using erroneous appeals to nature my husband just mentioned, by the very same writers who abhorred the idea of using nature as a model to show how violence and fighting could be viewed as natural. I did not believe violence was natural at all;

Sputnik was not sure, but he did mention a study about a cat who was never taught how to kill and thus never had any interest in it; instead, the cat made friends with the mouse.

"See, that's what I mean," I said. "Violence is taught; it's not inborn. Just like infidelity is taught too."

"Mmm…" He thought about it. "Perhaps. But infidelity is also a product of lust. Just like violence is a product of rage. But we have the ability to control both our rage and lust. We are capable of restraint, although I seem to have none when it comes to these chocolates."

"It makes more sense to be peaceful, and like you said, to be fidelitous, considering the way we humans raise our children. Ultimately to be peaceful and fidelitous is an individual's choice."

I talked about how certain men were trying to make women believe in "free sex" too. "I believe in premarital sex. It exists. I believe in its consequences too—unwanted pregnancy, feeling of loss, dejection, gaining of disease. I believe in premarital sex, as much as I believe in a volcano, but jumping into it might cause a burn."

"I agree. There's no such thing as free sex," the professor said. "The act always cost something—you pay with loss of independence and gaining of a dependent baby, or the loss of health and gaining of disease, as you said, or the loss of a relationship through infidelity, or the loss of self-respect…or the complete loss of your heart to another. Not all the costs of lovemaking purchase something negative."

I talked about how certain male writers were trying to convince girls, especially girls like me, "ugly" girls, to propagate the idea that love is a fantasy, one conjured by the "naïve little female mind," so just settle for sex, because only women who "write like men" were regarded with any respect in the literary world and the actual world. We were all supposed to write about soulless "adult" relationships based on sex and let-downs, and feel bad for "indulging" in "women's fantasies," romance and forever after, but the male fantasy of the floozie who really liked him, not his wallet, and allowed him to spread his seed across the entire female population, was accepted as realistic and not a "fairy tale;" they definitely had the right to write those stories and I had equal right not to buy it.

I felt so comfortable with my husband, I could even have this kind of conversation with him; we had many conversations that special night, ranging from a discussion about the somber poetry of Yoshi Kamosun to the tastiness of the Asteroid candy bar to the romantic tradition in the country Koi of placing honeydew melon on bedroom windowsills to attract true love. This led to a talk about marriage...

I said, "Some men are unhappy in marriage, because they marry for looks, and when those looks get tiresome, they blame their wives for no longer being good wives."

Sputnik did not completely agree with that. "Women sometimes hook a man then once they have him treat him like a dirty sock, a chore stinking up the home."

I talked about what Carl Jung called "feminine energy and masculine energy" and how both existed in every individual, male and female. I defined feminine energy as a collection of complementary traits, such as intuition and the ability to nurture, and it made sense these traits were often associated with women, since mothers had to be able to care for children and intuit the needs of babies unable to yet speak; whereas masculine energy was a collection of harmonizing traits, such as strength and determination, associated with men, which also made sense, considering the male's role in providing and protecting.

Although we agreed on most things, Sputnik did not believe men should nurture too much of their feminine energy, and I said that was unfair and oppressive and who was he to decree what all men should be like? What about an individual's choice to write his or her character however she or he felt authentic?

"Lumi, you're the one who said you like that I know 'manly' things."

"That's my personal preference, and your personal preference, but you and I don't have the right to dictate how anyone else's story should be written to create meaning and happiness."

"I'm just saying heterosexual men should be men for women. I'm not saying they shouldn't have any femininity and just be stones without emotions, but come on now, we had this conversation already—you want a masculine man."

"Because I'm a feminine woman. Not every woman is. And even some feminine women don't want masculine men and vice versa. We can't be so quick to generalize."

"There you go accepting everyone in your world with a welcome mat for all. What about the Knights and Ladies stuff?"

"Some people want to be Ladies, some Knights, some neither. Everyone has the right to write their own kind of story. I despise westerns, but if someone wants to write one, he can use his ink to do so, even if I can't fathom why."

On our *honeymoon night*, we discussed the dawn of civilization—we were not fit to be married to anyone else.

Sputnik told me how the invention of agriculture brought about a surplus of food, which freed people to indulge other talents, such as in the arts. Men were warriors and priests, and since warriors and priests were regarded so highly, masculine energy was seen as superior to feminine energy. So, males began to develop only their masculine traits, and anyone, male or female but especially male, with feminine traits was regarded as weak. That chauvinism had continued throughout human history but became especially prevalent after the Industrial Revolution when humans moved away from subsistence farming, where men and women had shared in the work, until men went to work in factories, making the money to "bring home the bacon," and thus their work was seen as superior to women's work.

He said, "We live in a world where someone is considered an 'amateur' if he doesn't make money from his craft. Someone could discover a new planet, but if they had not been paid to do so, they'd be called 'amateur astronomer.'"

He mentioned Karl Marx—a taboo name in America in 1965, a reasonable taboo considering how Marx's principles had been twisted by Soviet Communists. Although Sputnik agreed with many socialist ideals, he did not agree that the family unit was a "construction of capitalism," an idea he found "preposterous" (he enjoyed using that word as a defense against any idea he found especially "preposterous"). He said the family unit was one brigade *against* consumerism and commercialism, a strong bond which could potentially fight wealth and greed.

The professor really took off into ideas and theories I knew nothing about: Trotskyism and "bureaucratic collectivism" and "thievocracy"—and my mind was spinning. I wanted to learn these things, but he was going to have to give the girl from the meadows time to understand the concrete world, its mechanistic workings, and how to make the machine run more smoothly.

Tired of speaking with clunky words about the world, his eyes called up mine for a private talk about us. After communicating feelings no words could express, not even "I love you," he said, "She carries the sunrise with her everywhere. There's my attempt at being Lord Byron."

"I'll take my mathematician and rocket scientist over Lord Byron."

He playfully rolled us around like we were in a field of grass—a field of lace and silk-soft linen, where we laughed and touched and shrieked joyously.

"See how messy I'm already making your pristine bed."

"Do I seem to mind, sir?"

"If you still don't mind five years from now, I'll know you really love me."

I lay against his chest, our hearts beating with a friskiness. "Bliss has nothing on the feeling of being in the arms of the man you love."

He picked up a romance comic from the headboard's bookshelf. The professor wanted me to know we did not have to only discuss politics and sociology; he was interested in my interests too. "I want my wife to read me a story."

I picked a touching story from *Romantic Secrets*, "Return to Romance," about a man and a woman who were both dying and wrote their last chapters full of love.

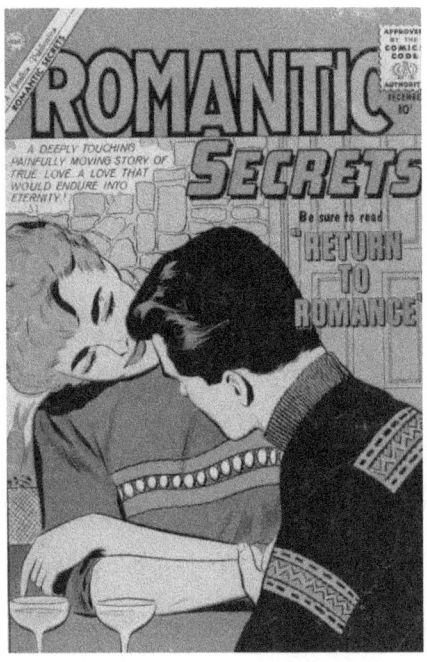

This led us into a conversation about soulmates, one of my favorite topics, and his too, although the outdoorsman was too rugged to admit that. I told him I despised an idea—a myth—that had gained popularity: a person had to be *perfect* before meeting their soulmate, one's life and health and looks and even finances had to be in complete order before love would love them, and he or she had to love himself or herself before anyone else would love them. "How utterly contrary to all love stands for! Love is like glue completely capable of mending the shattered, which is something love enjoys doing: healing. One most needs a soulmate not when one's life is perfect but when one's life is crumbling, when one needs support, when one is sick and in need of a guardian angel, when one feels unlovable and ugly and worthless, when one most needs love to restore their worth! If someone only wants to be with another who is 'perfect,' 'perfect' in looks and health and finances and confidence and emotional stability, that is not love at all but sheer laziness, superficiality, and cowardness, unwilling to brave challenges and see beyond appearance to the soul. True love has soul vision, which can spot a diamond in the rough. True love is a champ at withstanding any test."

"Well said, my writesmith, and I agree with you," my husband bolstered, while gazing at me as if I had passed all my love tests. He asked exactly how I defined "soulmates."

"Soulmates are ideal co-writers. Of course, one can have other compatible co-writers, but that doesn't mean there's not the one *ideal* co-writer. By 'ideal' I mean the co-writer who makes every scene, setting, and challenge a pleasure to write just through their company. Any relationship can be soulful, if the relationship is allowed to bond deeply enough, and any relationship can be very meaningful, but each one of us only has one Soulmate, Divinely created for us. This is an idea, unfortunately, that even the very spiritual shy away from, most likely because they are scared if their relationship with their soulmate does not last a lifetime, they will be bereft of an ideal partner and seen as a quack who was foolish enough to believe in ideal love, so they stick to the safe idea that anyone can be a soulmate to anyone else, which makes soulmates about as special as toast sandwiches. When one loses his or her believed soulmate, one should realize it is possible the person lost was maybe not their true soulmate, or if they were, the mourner should find solace in knowing that soulmates are not always meant to write *every* chapter together, but that doesn't mean they aren't ideal co-writers, just because they write a few chapters separately, even entire books separately—soulmates will always find each other again in some new chapter or story. No one would say two

543

people weren't soulmates if they wrote their *first* life chapters without each other, before their meeting, so how does writing the middle chapters or last chapters alone, or with a different partner, change the fact that they're soulmates? There are times in the story when characters are parted, that's all; the love doesn't depart. I think you are The Wanderer."

"The Wanderer Above the Sea of Fog?" He looked at the print posted in the window, where My Wanderer watched snow fall outside.

I told him about My Wanderer, my Soulmate, and how I had wanted to bring bunnies into the aeronaut's life.

"I believe that from the girl who kissed my circumcision scar so gently. It doesn't hurt."

"But you hurt. And I want to make your life softer." I planted tiny soft kisses across the forest of his chest.

"Bringing the bunnies?"

I knew it was difficult for him, allowing me to coddle him, but for my sake, my co-writer was trying to write sweet lines in our tender lovestory; he would allow one opening in the wall to be used for reaching out and touching me.

"I trust you as much as I trust my diary," I said. "That's soulmate stuff there."

"And I trust you as well."

"I want us to be able not only to write each other's biographies but each other's autobiographies, because we're so in tune with each other's feelings. I want to know everything about you. The shops you liked as a boy, your favorite records, the number you wore on your baseball jersey, what you were doing on September 9th, 1955."

"As a kid, I liked ice cream shops. My favorite records were classical, jazz, and swing."

"*Were?*"

"Well, they still are my favorites. I just don't have time to listen to much music."

"You have records but no record player."

"Like I said, no time for it."

He had time to listen to music but not allowing himself the opportunity was another form of self-inflicted punishment.

"I wore 3.14, which proudly stated I was a math nerd and my baseball skills were infinite. I was fairly arrogant back then. Now, September 9th, 1955?"

I shrugged; I had picked a random date.

"Let's see, September in 1955, guaranteed I was either in a lab or hotrodding with my bevy of women. What were you doing?"

"Hmmm, I was all of nine years old, so I was probably at the stream, wishing to meet my molasses-haired boy." I rubbed my fingers deep into the dark hair of his chest where a soft heart gushed within woodland. "I want us to merge the way a cup of water poured into another cup of water merges into one body of water."

"We will but first let's try again at making a member of our baseball team."

"No, first, Professor, I want to transform my grade of 'B' to an 'A.'"

"Aha! Your Professor fantasy. Don't worry, I'll fulfill it. Now, Ms—"

"Ms. Blagonravov."

"Ms. Blagonravov, I can't show you special treatment just because you're my wife. You have to write a mathematical poem for the 'A.'"

"I want to write the poem, just not with words, but with touches: how one plus one equals *one*."

545

"Who would've guessed the shyest little Divinity student…"

"Tell me about airfoil data, Professor."

"Right now?"

"Give me a lecture with lengthy equations like the kind you write on the chalkboard in your upper-level mathematics classes. I want you to go on and on…"

"Alright … transcendence of e … if f of x is any real polynomial with degree m…"

I loved hearing him talk so smartly, especially while we were coupling and feeling the possibility of his brilliant genes bonding with and enriching my not-so-mathematically-inclined genes.

"Where t is an arbitrary complex number and the integral is taken over the line joining t and 0…" Eventually he lost his ability to formulate how to even add one and one, except in the way where they equaled one.

After more glorious hours that brought us to happy exhaustion, the sun was ready to start the day and drenching our world with light.

"Tell me about your father," my husband said, as softly as his fingers rubbing my hair. "Would he approve of me?"

"Ooh, yes, of course! In the war, he comforted the dying, brought them into the light, regardless of their religion, the young soldiers who cried out for their mothers, the old soldiers, the captains and generals, who also cried out for their mothers, the civilians who cried out for their mothers—he was always there, right there in the battlefield, a chaplain for goodness. A few years after the war, which he barely survived, he was crucified by a madman with a knife who was 'tired of holy fakeness.' Then my real father was only in the garden, or so I thought, but he's here with us now."

Sputnik looked around. "I hope he's not mad about what I've been doing with his daughter."

"Marrying her and trying to create a baby with her? No, he's not mad."

"You might know a lot about mothers, Lumi, but fathers don't take kindly to boys doing, you know, with their daughters."

"I know my father and I know he loves us."

"Is your father still your hero?"

"He has to share that pedestal with you."

"I wish our families were still here and we could be one big happy nut farm."

"We'll have to start a new nut farm."

He picked up a dawn-bathed music box from the headboard. "This is the single most girly display I ever saw. I'll build one like this for our daughter too."

"Do you think your bubbe would have liked me?"

"She was the sweetest woman and a genuine ragtag misfit who would have welcomed you, a fellow misfit, with open arms into Sampi Koppa Digamma, and Bow would have too."

This was a hard question for me to ask for fear of its answer, "Would your mother have liked me?" To him, his mother was the holy of holies, the ideal of womanhood, and I wanted to know she would have approved of her son's choice of wife.

"She obviously didn't have an issue with the marriage between a Jew and non-Jew. Pops was not Jewish. For the record, Pops would have loved you, and I think you and Mother would have bonded like two girly hair ribbons over cream tea and Hershey's Kisses. Now tell me more about your Moon-Moon."

It was my turn to cry as I talked about my momma and that winter and the thieves and the frostbite accident and how Sputnik was the only person who had never once said anything hateful to me, never once asked what was wrong with my face, so I thanked him for being my friend—he was really my friend—and he held me close enough to keep frost from reforming in my heart. Even though I had prayed to be his guardian angel, I knew the reverse was true: he was mine.

Sharing tears, we also shared more chocolate-covered cherry cordials…

Apricot Rugelach

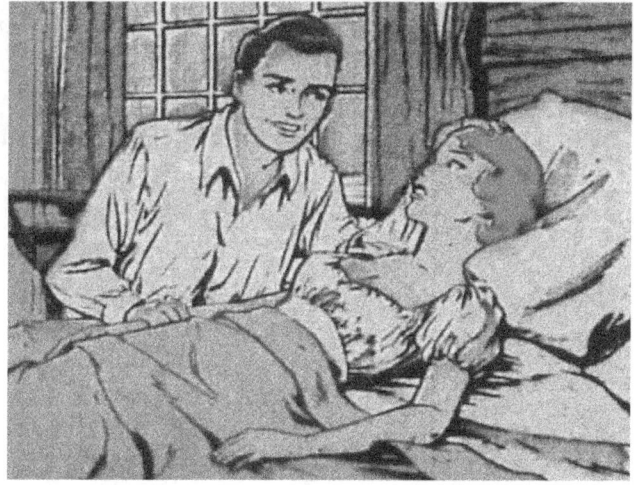

There was something good and holy and sweet about

waking up with my husband on the first morning of our honeymoon.

Snow fell softly outside the windows, and the sky looked more white than blue, and we were snowed in and wrapped up with each other in our warm bed in our warm camper, and the land was quiet, and we were stocked in good food, and the streets were iced which meant no one could get near us, and I knew as we lit more candles on the menorah, we would make each page of our honeymoon a delicious morsel.

For breakfast I was going to make warm drinks and apricot rugelach, crescent pastries with crispy sugary outer layers and warm sweet flaky inner layers filled with apricot jam and thinly chopped walnuts.

We had found a "honeymoon cabin on Mars" by pretending we had landed on a deserted snowy planet and found shelter in this abandoned "spaceship." We would ditch looking at the clock altogether in our new-found world. We didn't want to be those people who never saw midnight, because rules told them to go to sleep by ten p.m. We'd make love at four a.m., dance at all hours, talk at midnight, sleep at noon. Our honeymoon agenda was to write as many beautiful and spicy and playful lines in our lifestory as possible, although the spiciest lines were just for me and him to read, since we treasured being the only two who saw those private passionate sides of one another.

We cuddled close like we were each other's burrows. My husband slept naked. He requested his girl do the same. Used to pajamas, it was an adjustment to me, as sleeping in clothes had been an adjustment to him on those nights he had slept in his truck, car, or office. But he wanted to feel my body next to his, not my clothing. I liked feeling him, smelling him, his pecan scent, first thing upon waking.

"Are you really writing the lovestory you always wanted to?" he asked, his black hair soft and messy without Brylcreem. Being married to him I learned this: Sputnik's hair somehow had the ability to defy the laws of physics and triple in size in the morning when his hair became a pile of wilderness on his head.

"I am writing the lovestory I always wanted to," I said, rubbing my fingers through the wilderness, "thanks to you for being the leading man."

We kept our voices quiet so not to disturb the hush of snowy morning.

"I want to write our lovestory in print too, Sput, so someday, a long long loooong time from now, when we're both gone, our love will inspire other romantic souls who want to get swept away in a lovestory."

He moved his body too close to mine for me to retain any Ladylike decorum. "Lume, is there a paragraph in that story about us taking our first shower together?"

During the scrumptious shower, while soaping his chest until the forestry looked doused in sea foam, I noted, "Some hours are shorter than others. Clocks don't convey this. All the hours with you are too short. We can't possibly get in all the kissing and touching and loving and talking we want in an hour."

"We can try!" He had gone too many chapters without.

He made love to lose things—anger, stress, frustration. I made love to gain—inspiration, affection, creativity.

Since the streets were iced and stores inaccessible, we had to get creative with gifts, which put us more in touch with the true spirit of the holidays. On the second day of Hanukkah, he gave me a five-minute kiss in the shower. Afterwards, I gave him an hour-long shoulder and back massage, which was a gift to me too. Most of the hours that day were devoted to writing spicy sentences in the lacy bed, only taking breaks for apricot rugelach.

I told him, "Your deepest form of penetration is through your eyes, penetrating mine—when you touch a me that no mirror has ever seen, a me no one else has ever met."

That snowy night, after we lit the menorah on the windowsill, Sputnik suggested we eat leftovers, since we did not have endless food supply, but I did not want to serve my husband leftovers; I wouldn't let yesterday's glazed carrots and kugel go to waste, but I wanted to make something else for him too. I did not want to be a woman who was sweet and respectful to a fella but as soon as he married her, she got sloppy with her love. Sputnik did not want to get sloppy with his love either. We would hold each other to respect. We would never take our love for granted. My husband and I also had an unspoken agreement not to say "I love you" too often with words, so as not to turn the overused phrase into an easy way of showing our feelings; instead, we would show our feelings with our loving thoughts, which would manifest as loving actions and kind words other than "I love you."

As I stood by the counter, making an apple salad (apples and greens and candied pecans), my husband put his arms around me. "Lumi, you don't have to go through all that trouble."

"If you keep touching me that way, sir, I won't be able to concentrate on making anything but your baby."

"I'll be good. I'll put on my kippah and study the Talmud."

He went back to sit at the booth, allowing himself the joy of anticipation for a tasty meal. Since our night together, he had fully retrieved his boyhood appetite—the tin of chocolates was already empty, as was the dish of caramel ice cream, and he had eaten all the previous night's dinner rolls, latkes, and yams, endless late-night snacks, and he was working on all the peppermints, and he was eager for vegetarian dressing and mushroom gravy and biscuits and chocolate cake and well, the boy could eat!

After dinner, we played dreidel in the den, while Sputnik sang *The Dreidel Song* and happily realized he did remember how to play the game and so taught me. Pythagoras and Mullybiski played too as we all lounged on the carpet. We began with five chocolate coins each, loot to add to the pot, and we took turns spinning the four-sided dreidel (Sputnik and I spun for our dog and turtle friends). The dreidel was marked on each side with a Hebrew letter: Gimel (landing on that resulted in receiving all items in the pot), Hey (receiving half of the pot's loot), Nun (nothing), and Shin (which meant the player had to add an item to the pot). Sputnik told me the letters were an acronym for the Hebrew saying, "A great miracle happened there."

After I landed on Gimel a few times, Sputnik said, "You're cheating."

"What? There's no way to cheat!"

"You're using a loaded dreidel." He playfully examined the four-sided top. Then he rolled a "Shin." He had told me his sister used to chant, "Shin, shin, put one in" anytime he landed on "Shin," so I did that, and we both laughed and continued playing for hours, taking breaks to talk, snack, and for me to introduce him to new records. He had taught me math, so I would teach him rock-n-roll, but getting the mathematician to dance was a challenge.

He warned, "I'm not much good at dancing. Formal dances, those are the only kinds I've ever been to, and only because my mother made me, so I could be a good little gentleman in training who would respect girls' gloved hands and bow before asking a Lady to dance." He bowed and asked for my hand.

"Your training paid off, sir."

I didn't care if he was a good dancer, I just wanted to be close to him. We slow danced to *Earth Angel*.

"Isn't this a nice song, Sput?"

It wasn't Tchaikovsky or Duke Ellington, so he begrudgingly admitted, "Yes but not as romantic as *Isn't It Romantic?*"

"Yes, it is. You're just a jazz and classical chauvinist. Really listen to the lyrics and the melody as gentle as moonlight."

He wanted to boogie to Benny Goodman, the way he wanted to gobble chocolates, making up for years of abstinence from fun. So, we let the record player *Sing, Sing, Sing* as loud as it could.

"Go, Sputnik, go!"

The genius, flapping his arms and kicking his legs in a form of quasi-swing dance/chicken mating move, was not going to be inducted into the dancing hall of fame, but that was what made watching him boogie so entertaining.

"I want to dance with Root," he said and picked up the teddy bear for the Lindy Hop.

I jitterbugged around the kitchen with the plush bunny, while twirling a candy cane.

During the tune's drum solo, Sputty and I bippedy-bippedy around together, sweating in winter.

He pretended to play clarinet like he was Joe "Cinnamon" Blugey on the horn.

I wanted to show him rock-n-roll was also fun to dance to, so I played *Tutti Frutti*, and now it was time for Sputnik to be amused by my dancing.

"I should be rockin' on *Bandstand*," I sang.

When the record player spun *Green Onions*, "I dig it, cat, yeah," Sputnik said, snapping his fingers, doing his impersonation of a cool cat.

Sputnik was never 100% happy because his happiness was composed of many elements, and one element was his family, and they were gone, but I tried to make up for their absence by taking on the playfulness of his kid sister and caringness of his mother and adventurousness of his grandma. And I realized I had not just gained a husband but a father, son, friend, brother—Sputnik and I were everything to each other.

He had lost his traditions, his family holiday table, and I hoped I was creating new holiday traditions for him, while also preserving the classics.

I was already busy making plans for the next holidays. I would go, in secret, to Baltimore to his mother's junior high school and see if I could get a copy of her yearbook. Sputnik had no pictures of his mother, grandma, or sister. If I had to search all of Alaska and Poland, all the world, I would find some memento of his family to give him.

Sometime in the late night or early morning, in our own "cabin on Mars," we lay against carpet, our friends asleep, and we savored more apricot rugelach, since we couldn't get enough of the crescents from Heaven. I dipped the tasty pastry into a cup of hot cocoa, and Sputnik dunked his pastry in a cup of fresh hot coffee; like a married couple holding pieces of cake on their wedding day, we fed each other rugelach.

We were making the holiday itself a gift.

"I feel sorry for NASA," I said.

"NASA?" He laughed.

"You're all mine for two weeks, not theirs."

"I think the space agency will survive without me, for at least two weeks, not much longer." He grinned. He retained some of his boyhood arrogance.

"Why do you have to be so handsome and make me ache? Can't you take a day off from being handsome, Sput? Give my mind some time to think of other things like politics, religion…"

"I'll pay you compliment for compliment, Lady. You are not just pretty amongst women—you're pretty amongst roses. You, the special flower You. Even against the stars, your beauty stands out."

With an ink pen, I wrote a poemlet on my husband's bicep. I relished listening to the giggly sound of the calm-cool mathematician getting tickled by the pen writing a love note against his skin:

The first time you looked in my eyes

Kites envied me

Birds too

Watching me soar beyond their sky

"How do you turn your pen into a dancer? Fall in love," I said. "With you, sweetheart, my pen transforms into a dancer. Our love, the music. Feel the waltz in the words, a tango in poetry we share, my muse."

In his right hand, I wrote, "I had always envied candles—quickly aflame, prolonged melting—until I encountered you and your hands."

In his left hand: "I had always envied a piano's keys, touched, prolonged passion and music—until I encountered you and your hands."

"Which do you like better?" I asked.

He put those hands around me and let me decide.

I told him I wrote the poems in his palms to be symbolic—my feelings were in his hands—but truthfully, I just liked touching him. I presumed he knew my true motive. His hands made me feel what ice cream feels in sunlight.

I wrote this on his other bicep:

My eyes enjoy landings on the moon

Sea, stars, flowers in bloom

But never has sight landed

On landscape as lovely as your shoes

Rested beside mine in our warm planet room

I was inking him with sweet sentiments to counter the ghastly numbers on his lower arm.

To be the mortal whose lips marry yours

A Goddess would give up immortal bliss

For what grander heaven, your kiss

"You're a regular Sister Elizabeth Brownell," he said, referring to the fifteenth century nun/poet.

On his wrist, I wrote atop the beat of his pulse: "I'm happy to live in a universe that produced supernovae and stars and your____."

"And my *what?*" he asked with a grinning voice.

"You have a dirty mind, sir."

"Not as dirty as yours apparently."

"I left the blank space to say your *anything* is in comparison to supernovae and stars—your eyes, your smile, your brilliance, your…"

"Come here, you little apricot rugelach, and let me gobble you up."

After purposefully sloppy silly kissing, I said, "Gershey's Kisses. Much better than the chocolate candies."

"Give me that pen." He rolled up my sweater's sleeve and wrote an equation across my bared arm.

"What does it mean?" I asked.

"The formula for calculating an airplane's rate of climb."

That made us laugh—our ability to turn even "rate of climb" into something sensual.

"An airplane cannot fly to infinite heights. There is a ceiling at which the plane cannot go any higher. Do you want to break through that ceiling with me?"

We would keep ascending higher...

Snickerdoodles

I n our bed illuminated by an early morning mélange of dawn's

blush and night's starshine, the blanket had slipped past Sputnik's bare thighs. So, I admired the masculine terrain, outlined in lights and shadows, revealed by the blanket's indiscretion. Sput was fortunate I did not use the camera to photograph his exposure.

"Sputnik, that part of your body is beautiful," I whispered into his half-asleep, half-awake ear. "It's like a magnificent column of ancient Greek architecture."

"Hebrew architecture," he corrected, his voice cockier than ever, making no attempt to cover himself. "Save the Greek line for when you're with a Greek man."

"Okay, I'll save that for when I'm with John Cassavetes."

"Ah, when you're with John Cassavetes, eh? I have to kill any man, famous actor or not, who steals even one breath of your hair always so sweetly scented in the most intoxicating shampoo. Is there a secret locale only you women know about where you go to wash your hair with shampoo that smells that unbelievably good? It's like I'm breathing in sunshine."

I was not in the mood to talk about shampoo. Still viewing the woodsy mountainous topography that had until recently been outside my exploratory range, I whispered, "I think he's beautiful. I'm sorry none of this is polite to say but I've never seen him in his full morning glory."

"*He? Him?* Does *he* have a name too?"

I laughed, "Sputnik 2."

"Ah, come on now, he's not that beepy little Sputnik. He's Saturn 5."

"Saturn 5?"

"The mighty rocket for the Apollo project. Enough thrust to launch you to the moon, honey."

"You're disgusting. I was trying to write a beautiful passage into our lovestory that showed reverence for your masculine design and you had to turn it into something crude."

"I told you men are scum."

"Jackie Robinson's scum?"

"Don't mess with 42."

"What about Albert Einstein?"

561

"Einstein wasn't a man—he was some otherworldly being sent to Earth with amazing revelations about the universe."

"I think *you're* amazing."

"It's not so amazing. Every man has one and knows what to do with it."

"But not every man knows what to do with his heart." I rubbed my hand across the hairy forest over his heart.

"Will you make me some ice cream?" he said with the most boyish of voices.

"At five in the morning?"

"It's too much trouble?"

"No, I like making sweets for my Sputty, but it'll take some time for the ice cream to be ready to eat."

That fact made him slightly pouty, but he accepted I could not speed up the ice cream's process.

"Can it be snickerdoodle?" he asked.

"It can be whatever you want."

"Really?"

"Yes, really! You're so adorable."

"Ah, I'm cursed—the women in my life always catered to my so-called adorableness."

"So cocky too. I'll make a new flavor of ice cream every week for my Sput if he wants it." I started to get out of the bed.

"Wait, you don't have to make it right at this second, but after Saturn 5's mission."

Later that morning whose blush had peaked at dawn, the sky turned cozy dark rainy. In the kitchen where we sat at the table, I could tell Sput was not enjoying swallowing his coffee or the spicy

562

masala omelet and especially not his toast, so I had to pry the truth out of him—he was sick with a sore throat.

"Do you hurt anywhere else?"

He shrugged, manly man.

"That's a yes?"

"A minor, infinitesimally minor, headache."

"Ooh, my poor baby." I sat by him in the booth and put my hand to his forehead to check for fever.

"It's just one of those twenty-four-hour deals. Don't make a big fuss about it." But I could tell the rugged outdoorsman did want me to make a big fuss about his cold and give him all the pampering of a baby. I tried to convince him to stay in bed and rest, and I would do some writing at the table, but he didn't like that idea; he claimed because he wasn't sick enough to stay in bed, but really he just wanted to be around me, so I told him I would stay in bed too.

"Well, if you insist."

Beneath a warm pile of covers, I held him against my chest and caressed his hair, as streams of rain traveled the windows, wrapped around the honeymoon scene.

"Could I have the ice cream now?"

"Won't that hurt your throat?"

"No, in fact, it will probably make it feel better."

After ice cream, he fell asleep, as did I in rain's lullaby.

While kids around the country were sleeping in on holiday break from school, Sputnik and I sat under a blanket on the couch and watched cartoons, which could not be watched without big bowls of bright-colored cereal, as every kid knows. Sputnik was hungry again, since he had barely touched his breakfast, and two bowls of snickerdoodle ice cream had not provided enough energy for the strapping man with an incredible work ethic and appetite.

"The cereal doesn't bother your throat, sweetie?"

"No, it feels better now. In fact, I could probably stand that omelet now."

"Ooh, Sput, it's been sitting out too long. I don't want you to get sick from eating it."

That disappointed his unquenchable hungriness.

"Could I at least have the toast?"

"I'll make you fresh toast and a new omelet."

"No, that's too much trouble, and your cereal will get soggy."

"I don't give two hoots about the cereal. When are you going to learn I like doing nice things for you as much as you like doing nice things for me? I can't build a gazebo or patch up the roof, so making breakfast is my way of building something nice for you."

He had never considered that and smiled about the arrangement.

"Want some more coffee too?"

"Mmm…ba-bu-ba…I wouldn't mind trying The Lady Model of drinks: cream tea."

"Ooh, will this be my Sput's first taste of afternoon tea?"

"Yes, it will be."

"Then it must be perfect—summertime afternoon in a cup!"

On the couch, we ate breakfast, watched cartoons, and Sputnik secretly delighted in sweet cream tea, his big manly hand around the daintiest of teacups—the Knight definitely did not hold the cup like a Lady.

I said, "See, Wile E. Coyote is called 'Eatibus Anythingus' and Road Runner is called 'Hot-Roddicus Supersonicus.' Isn't that funny?"

"Yes, but you're not laughing either. You're just saying, 'That is funny.'" And that made us burst out the laughter, laughing at our lifelong lack of laughter.

He didn't have a change of shirt, so he spent most of the time indoors either shirtless or T-shirted and in his undershorts, and I did not complain about the view, although I did feel deprived of the wifely privilege of wearing one of his shirts. He was lucky I had an emergency backup toothbrush (or maybe I was lucky for that). I had told him I would wash his shirt but he had shrugged, preferring the freedom to lounge provided by T-shirt and undershorts.

"The only time in life," he said, watching more cartoons, "we get to see the laws of physics defied."

"And in your hair." I put my hands above my head to show the size of Sputnik's morning hair.

He laughed. "That's why I have to Brylcreem up, baby."

"You don't have to for me. I think the big hair is the perfect look for the otherworldly Einstein genius. It's wild and manly and musky like your chest and underarm hair."

"Ah, come on, you like those rock-n-roll boys with their perfect coifs."

"I only like my Sputnik." I crossed my heart.

"You've never even fantasized about another man, not even Elvis Presley?"

"Hmmm." I smiled to say I was teasing. "No. Okay, meaningless schoolgirl fantasies like going to one of his concerts. My important fantasies were all about my soulmate, My Wanderer, the aeronaut—"

"And the man in the kippah."

"But they were all you."

"You are a saint."

"Ooh and there was this very handsome professor ... let me remember ... what was his name? I've had so many ... hard to remember 'em all ... hmmm ... Blagon-something."

"He's a jerk. You don't want him."

"But I've already had him!"

"You and half the female population at Goldell."

I threw a blue-colored piece of cereal at him, which landed like a blue bird in the wilds of his black hair. He returned the fire.

After cleaning up the remnants of The Great Cereal War, we watched Sylvester & Tweety. The scientist argued that unlike Tom and Jerry, who were actually friends and just playing around, "that putty cat" had real malicious intent against the bird, so he was "quite mean" like Wile E. Coyote. I argued they were all really friends, because they never truly hurt each—Wile E. Coyote fell from ten mountains an episode and never got injured.

Sputnik and I could have never lasted in a marriage with anyone else. We bonded over big and little things, such as both of us opposed the Vietnam War and neither of us knew what a dry martini was. "Apparently, a martini made with my sense of humor," he stated with said humor.

We came to decisions about our egalitarian marriage: number one, our nightcap would be *Tom and Jerry*, and two, like a nation, our marriage would have Departments, such as Department of the Treasury. We would each be Secretary of different departments, overseeing the daily tasks and making the important decisions of that department. We didn't take this too seriously. We could veto the Secretary too. And decisions where neither of us would budge, we would solve the democratic way: by rock, paper, scissors. He was Secretary of Finance, mainly because I was pitiful with numbers, and he was Secretary of Defense. I was Secretary of Education, as in I would make decisions regarding our children's education. Of course, the Secretary had to present reasonable arguments for their decisions.

I considered how selfish it was of me to put all the big burdens on Sputnik; a fairer arrangement was to put all our burdens in one pail and carry that pail together. This relationship was better and more just: he would hold an oar, and I would hold an oar, together sailing our boat on a vast sea of turbulent freezing waters, avoiding icebergs, searching for our magical destination, and buoying and warming each other anytime we did crash into cold sea.

My husband and I could not deny my feminine need for surrender and his masculine desire to command, but these longings found a healthier outlet in the decision to make him Chief of Bedroom. As masculine as the outdoorsman was, his wife was queen of the house, except he was king in bed (a benevolent king whose kingdom never spread beyond bedchamber). He ruled that after the holidays, we should only make love on our birthdays, Valentine's Day, our anniversary, New Year's, Pi Day, once at Christmas, once during Hanukkah, and once or twice during baseball season to relieve his tension.

"That's absurd!" I said, fearing he was back to seeing me as a nun again.

He explained he wanted to show reverence for the act, not to tangle it with day-to-day chores, not to let it become a task thrown in between laundry and supper; plus, he wanted to prove he loved me, wanted to be my husband, more than just for sex. He told me again how the traditional Jewish marriage contract spelled out a husband's obligations to his wife, including making sure she was fulfilled adequately in the bedroom (every day if his profession allowed him and she so desired it), so he had to get my yes vote for the nine-times-a-year mandate before enacting it. That would be a difficult mandate to follow but I respected his reasoning, although I argued if we were only physically intimate on those specific days, those days would start to feel like obligations, so maybe we should agree to a few times a year but let the moments happen naturally. He wasn't convinced; his work schedule would get in the way, but he would always try to leave those holidays open for his wife. He sounded like his sexist dad, a fact he was aware of, so he said, "Pops wasn't always wrong."

Despite our egalitarian marriage and democratic "departments," Sputnik told me he believed a woman should be "queen of the house," in charge of the home, or Secretary of the Home, "Simply because women are usually better at keeping peace and understanding the purpose of doilies" (that dry humor again). Once again, I informed him he was a chauvinist against his own sex; not all men were brutes, as he seemed to believe; some were more sensitive and gentle than women and more in tune with their feminine energy. My husband went on to say a man's job was to make sure his wife and family had a home and to protect that home and to offer any "manly" help when needed, such as putting up a new roof and salting driveways (husband and dad tasks), but a woman should be allowed to just be.

Listening to rain song, we stayed cozy on the couch and made a list of things we wanted to do together (non-spicy things, such as hot air balloon rides) and places we wanted to visit like Chocolate Station, "the most romantic town on Earth," and Burgundy Falls, "the most haunted town in the world," where we planned to visit the "spooky" locations of all the famous ghost stories in the seaside town.

I said, "The beach is lovely, but it can be lovelier—how much lovelier the beach will be when my hand is holding yours. How much prettier Mars, Venus, Moon when your heart is tangled with mine."

"Life with a poet," he sighed.

I wondered if he ever wanted to revisit Auschwitz, if that would give him any peace of mind to see the death camp was no longer in existence, that flowers bloomed there again. He thought about it. "Perhaps. If you're holding my hand." The sweetness and authenticity and trust in that statement really touched me.

For gifts that day, he gave me the twig wreath, which the outdoorsman had delighted in constructing and hanging on our front door, even though I had told him to rest.

"Rest is for girls," he said with a grin.

I gave him my treasure chest of recipes and asked him to make a list of all the foods he wanted, since he had been deprived of sweets for too long. The recipes he loved I would mark with a heart drawing. I also taught him the basics of baking, and I realized his never cooking was not a product of sexism, but the genius had no aptitude in the kitchen.

"What does it mean to get the mixture to come to a full rolling ball?" he asked, looking at the recipe for fudge.

"Hmm?" I examined the recipe. "Not *ball*, Sput, *boil*, a rolling boil."

"Well, that just explains everything—a *rolling* boil. And what is that stuff about getting the fudge to the 'ball stage'? I saw that in the recipe, don't say I didn't. Ball stage?"

I would continue to make our meals.

I made us a cookie feast: chocolate, peanut butter, and snickerdoodles, which he ate with ice cream of the same flavor.

After midnight, we were going to build a gingerbread house, but Sputnik decided to build a log cabin made of pretzels with white frosting as "mortar" and graham crackers as doors and shuttered windows. Sitting at the table, the engineer was serious about constructing our house just so.

We missed our families because this did seem like an event for a whole family.

Amidst holiday music, I built gingerbread trees and a frosted ground for the house to sit on. I said, "How about instead of gingerbread men—"

"Gingerbread Martians?" my husband said, reading my mind again.

569

On the table by the typewriter, we set the whole sweet scene, cookie trees and ginger Martians and pretzel cabin on "snowy" ground; we placed two kissing Cooties in front of the edible home. But we didn't want to eat the masterpiece. The engineer was going to shellac the little log cabin and keep it for the entire holidays.

Snuggled in bed that rainy night with cookies, we played question games like "If you could invite one historical figure to dinner who would it be?"

Sputnik and I were getting so re-in tune with each other's souls, we could answer each other's questions; we were even beginning to speak alike.

"Well, if we're not including religious figures like Christ, my little nun would pick Hildegard."

"And I know my Sputty's answer: Jackie Robinson. But if it had to be someone who's dead…hmmm, let me think…I hate to admit, I'm drawing a blank."

"You're drawing a blank because I'm drawing a blank. I'm not sure. Ba-bu-ba. So many choices."

The cinnamon radio sat on the headboard, and we found a station that still broadcast old mystery shows. While thunder crackled in darkness, we listened to Holmes try to solve a case, as Watson bumbled around.

Sputnik termed the radio "the best invention ever," because it allowed music to travel anywhere, everywhere, "almost instantaneously," and would not it be nice if there was a spaceship capable of transporting man almost instantaneously across the stars?

During a commercial break, we talked about how Basil Rathbone had been a good Sherlock Holmes, but we both also liked Tom Conway, who had played both Holmes and The Falcon. Halfway through the show, we turned off the radio and made up our own ending.

"You know where other people would say our home is located?" Sputnik asked, after taking a bite of a snickerdoodle. "On the corner of *The Outer Limits* and *The Twilight Zone.* Here we are, two married people on our honeymoon, listening to Basil Rathbone."

"That's why we're married to *each other.*"

"We should be married to Basil Rathbone."

"Why should we care what unimaginative bores think of us? I don't want their approval of mediocrity."

Sputnik looked at the landmark of our eccentricity: the suit of armor in the corner of our shared life.

"Who do you think he was?" my husband asked.

"I'll give you a hint: get in the suit and reclaim your role as Knight."

"Now who's depraved?"

And we had more fun on our snickerdoodle honeymoon…

Strawberry Jelly Doughnuts

B y the fourth day of Hanukkah, grass was beginning to

peep out of melting snow, thanks to the sun high and bright in morning sky, but tender sunshine and gruff coldness were in a battle for the day.

Since Gersh treated me like I was an angel, I liked treating my husband like he was a king, waking him up with a message, but since he still believed he was mostly unworthy of sweetness, he had to grit and bear my affection, for *my* sake, since I loved loving him and he wanted to make me happy. If his love could convince me I was beautiful through and through, I prayed my love could eventually convince him he deserved sweetness through and through, not just in the form of rugelach and chocolate cherries.

Early in the morning, after making strawberry jelly doughnuts with powder sugar toppings (his mother's holiday treat), I quietly got back into the warm bed and watched my husband sleeping on his side, finally peacefully.

The night before, he had awakened screaming and had grabbed me, "Alina, are you cold?"

"No, we're here, warm, together, remember?"

"I failed my mother, but I'll get you out of here, I promise."

"We're already out."

"No, I have to stay here."

"No, you don't."

Coming back to the present, he had sat up and snapped, "I suppose you think I need therapy."

I had hugged him close. "I think you need to accept forgiveness. You no longer have to face this battle alone, Sput. I'm here, always."

"Well, I'll choose chocolate-covered cherry therapy—cherrapy." He had been irritated that the chocolates were gone.

"I do forgive you, Gershom."

He had considered that but concluded, "How can you forgive me for a sin you no longer remember? God erased that memory from your soul, sweet girl, but not from mine. My apologies, Lumi, my apologies, forget what I said—don't write the story this way."

During other moments, I lost him again, when he left this lovestory to stare back at those horrific past chapters the Nazis had written, then he would return to me and smile to say he was alright. Sometimes, he snuck off to his iceberg to work on math and science and rocket blueprints, and I knew during those moments he regretted having committed the "sin" of marrying and making love to the angel.

On this morning, I kissed the back of his neck and said in Mission Control voice, "Calling the Sputnik. Come in, Sputnik."

"Lumi, I'm trying to sleep, for goodness's sake." He swatted me away.

"For goodness sake, Gersh, let's do something besides sleep. I want to play with the Sput."

"Well, the Sput's sleepy. Pops was right. You women can never be satiated with this romantic stuff."

His voice more grizzly than teddy and my job was to make him more cuddly bear—enough kisses placed strategically did the job.

He indulged my need for lengthy cuddling. He was always antsy to get outside to build things. Whereas I enjoyed showing affection by hugging and kissing, he enjoyed showing affection by making things for me like the wreath.

We finally got out of bed and held hands just to walk outside to the apple tree to say "Good morning" to our friend, and the bond between our held hands was stronger than the one between planets.

After visiting Apple, the tree's christened name, we took a long morning walk with two strawberry doughnuts and cups of cocoa and coffee (he had gone back to bitter coffee this morning). With his sleepy Lady wrapping her arms around his arm in cold morning mist and feeling like the lucky schoolgirl, we explored the snowy woods together, our shoes roughing slush and wet dirt, but the excitement stemmed from more than just exploring the woods but exploring our new life together. I was the little girl again who wanted to discover more and more of this story—there would never be enough pages to write all the sentences I wanted to pen with my husband.

"All my moments with you have been diamond moments," I told him. "I know baseball diamond moments are the best, but these have been homeplate moments too."

"*Homeplate* moments? What does that mean?" He was still grouchy.

"Homeplate! You know when you make the big score."

"*Homerun*, you mean." He slapped his forehead to say, "I can't believe I married this girl."

"I just misspoke, Sputnik."

When we came back to the camper, a brown-and-white bunny was inside, getting warm. Even though Sput was cranky, he and I both felt tingly about the coincidence—a *bunny* had come into our lives. We offered to let him go back to the woodland, but he was no dummy; his eyes said, "I'd rather stay here where it's safe and warm if it's all the same to you."

So, Mr. Bunny stayed with us and made good friends with Mullybiski and Pythagoras.

I enjoyed making breakfast for the bunch: grass for the rabbit, carrots for the turtle, apple slices for the dog, and more doughnuts for the hubby, who had been standoffish all day.

"Mother never made these doughnuts so glumpy," he snapped.

"What does 'glumpy' mean?"

"Glumpy, you know, jelly glumped, like these doughnuts."

He was definitely a difficult frustrating man sometimes.

For Hanukkah gifts, I built Sputnik a snow baseball player with remaining snow, wearing a snowy Dodgers cap and holding a stick baseball bat. He built me Cinderella's castle sculpted in snow, and he taught me the basics of baseball, which he said was the best gift I'd ever get (I was happy it made him less grouchy), but the professor lectured if I really wanted to learn, I had to play some baseball. So, I put on my blue jeans and Adelia sweatshirt and decided to give the sport a go.

Far out in the sunlit muddy field of mid-morning, I stood in melted snow and grass, trying to make a batter stance, while bare-chested Sputnik stood a few feet away on the "pitcher's mound," a dirt hump.

"Lumi, my goodness. Why are you on your tiptoes like that?"

"It's muddy out here, and I don't have any gleats."

"*Gleats?* Cleats, they're called cleats. Ay yay yay!"

"That's what I meant. Don't get so huffy. I've never played before. And it's freezing."

"It's not cold at all, jack."

"And it keeps getting colder!" I said, referring to his tone.

"I thought you grew up in a meadow, so why are you scared of dirt?"

"I'm not scared of it, but I never was one for playing in the mud."

"Why does that not surprise me?"

I could tell he just loved getting dirty like this, standing up on that dirt mound in all his smug baseball glory, muddy shoes and muddy pant hems and beads of dirt getting blown onto his bare chest and back, while he chewed gum like tobacco. My dear sweet Sputty actually spat on the ground, really getting into the machismo role, while scratching the male region.

"This is going to be a shutout, ladies and gents."

"Don't be so sure of yourself, Sput." I waved a small branch turned baseball bat; Sputnik had searched the woods for a suitable substitute and had found the branch on the ground.

Mullybiski and Pythagoras watched the boy/girl game; Mr. Bunny had stayed inside to watch the boy/girl game in the form of *I Love Lucy* reruns, where Lucy and Ricky bickered.

"Why do you keep backing away every time I start to wind up, jack?"

"You're about to throw a rock at me!"

"This pebble?" He kept his voice gruff; this was baseball after all. "Alright, I promise it won't hit you. I'm a better pitcher than that."

"You better be nice, number 3.14."

"You're gonna have to spread your legs apart."

"I beg your pardon, sir! I'm a Lady!"

"Doesn't matter if you're the Queen of England—you can't stand straight up like that and bat."

"And why not?"

"Have you never seen one baseball game, girl? Look at you, standing straight up and holding the bat completely at ninety degrees to yourself."

"Maybe I've come upon a revolutionary new batter stance—the Lady Model stance."

"Here, let me show you how to stand."

"Stand like a man, you mean?"

"No, stand like a baseball player!"

"No, you will not!"

"Fine, I'm just trying to help you out."

"I don't need your condescension, sir. There was an entire league of women baseball players. Ooh, you're surprised I know that?"

"So, you know about the AAGPBL. There's still a Women's MLB."

"Yes, I know. Biskatine has a team. See, I do know some things about this sport."

"Alright, that's my girl, you go ahead and hit yourself a *homeplate*. The hill, remember, is the homerun fence."

"Yes, my little female mind didn't forget."

He pitched a ball "slow enough for a granny to hit" and I swung.

"Lumi, what in the world were you doing?"

"That was a good swing and you know it! Why, if the goal was to hit the air, I woulda scored a *homer*. See, I do know your language."

"Ah, yeah, you're on your way to some brews and checkers, jack. Why did you swing *downwards?*"

"That little booger was coming right toward me, so I popped him down."

"It was not coming 'right at you,' and the goal is to hit 'the little booger' out that way. That's how you score a homer, jack."

"I know that! You explained it to me, and don't worry, sir, I told you my ooh-so-feminine brain didn't forget. I just didn't want to get hit with a rock!"

"Well, what do you want to do, play with jelly doughnuts?"

"Can we?"

"Lumi, it'll be a good day you know where when I play baseball with doughnuts."

I stood resolute.

"If you think because you have pretty blue eyes and a cute little pixie figure I'm going to go get the doughnuts, we're going to be standing here a long time."

I stood resolute.

The Great Dane groused his way back to the camper to get the doughnuts.

I called out, "Must be a good day you know where, and think how happy those unfortunate souls are."

My husband came back with half a dozen doughnuts in the small wicker basket I used for dinner rolls. The pitcher decided to stand three feet from me—what condescension! The basket of doughnuts sat at his feet like a tin of baseballs.

"These are only for practice," he grumped, and gently tossed a doughnut.

I batted the doughnut into his waist and strawberry jelly splattered across his hairy stomach.

"Ooh, Sput, I'm sorry!" I started to go over to him, but he put up his hand, telling me to stay back.

"No, you stay over there. The last thing I want is to be mollycoddled by my wife on the baseball field."

He picked up the doughnut and wiped it against his pant leg.

"Sputnik, don't eat that!"

"Why not? It's good. You're at least good at baking."

"Ooh, really? I thought it was 'glumpy'?"

Eating the doughnut, the pitcher walked backward a few more feet.

I was as terrible at baseball as he was at dancing—spinning around in a circle when I tried to get enough force to make a "homeplate," flinging the baseball bat into the air during swings and trying to dodge from getting bopped in the head by it, ducking when he pitched, shrieking when the stone he called a "pebble" came within two feet of me, running away when he pretended he was going to throw a fastball—and I knew that was what made watching me play so amusing to him. He couldn't stop laughing in spite of his grouchy mood.

The boy never tired of playing baseball and being out in muddy fields. But he was hungry again, so we stopped for lunch, a brief picnic of sandwiches, while he envisioned making a permanent baseball diamond, complete with bases and homerun fence, for our children to enjoy. I stood and ate; he sat right on his rump in muddy grass. He had three PBJs, half a tin of potato chips, an apple, and a half-gallon of chocolate milk, straight from the jug! He had already eaten the half-dozen doughnuts throughout the morning. Our hands had been filthy after playing baseball on a muddy day, so I had gone inside to wash them, but Sputnik had cleaned off "surface dirt" by swishing his hands around in a puddle of rainwater.

"What kind of ridiculous display of machismo is that? That's not clean," I had declared and reminded myself never to let him make our meals.

I listened to his plans for the baseball diamond, how he would put up a chain link fence, but I couldn't get my thoughts off his sandwiches lying in dirty grass.

"Sput, you're going to get worms. Dirt has parasites in it."

He wiped dirt from a sandwich onto his pants. "Better?"

"No. Your dirty old pants aren't clean."

"I've never seen anyone with blue jeans so clean." He laughed and made a toast to me, "*My mate, my mate, she's a buddy from fate, but she couldn't tell first base from home plate.*"

"Ooh, you frustrating…"

"Frustrating what? Did my little wordsmith run out of words, or does she not know the language of baseball? If you can't come up with one dirty insult, you ain't got no business playin' hardball."

"I really want to score a homerun off you, jack."

"The only way you'll score a homerun off me, honey, is in the bed. You think I could ever live down the shame of my girl beating me in baseball? I've been fairly easy on you too, you being a Lady and all."

"My buddy from fate, if he doesn't curb his chauvinism, he won't have a bedmate."

He gobbled ice cream like it was summer then the boy was ready to play ball again, showing off how far he could throw a stone, how high he could jump to squash a ball's destiny of being a homerun.

"We need to go to the store and get some real baseballs and gloves then we can really play for hours!" he said.

Had we not already been playing for hours?

Finally back safe in bed!, my entire being tired, unuse to baseball, we played Camelot then Cootie until close to midnight with a plateful of "glumpy" strawberry jelly doughnuts.

Now we were playing Scrabble, which I had never realized was such a brutally competitive sport! My husband was intent on winning and I realized just how competitive he was (Cootie had not been competitive enough); he was not so mellow about the game as he had been before we were married. He had a whole lineup of games for us to compete in: tic-tac-toe, and the pencil and paper game Battleship, and on and on.

Wearing my nightgown, Moonlight Serenade, which went unnoticed by my husband's eyes, focused on the gameboard, I sat by the pillows.

Barefoot Sputnik sat shirtless and crossed-legged in his dirt-stained pants, which irritated me—dirt getting on our lacy bed.

I wanted to take another shower, feeling the mud would never wash off, but Sputnik grumped, "You just want me to suffer the hassle of working on the hot water heater."

"You didn't just wake up on the wrong side of the bed—you woke up on the wrong side of life," I snapped.

"I can't believe you didn't get one hit," he laughed, while exchanging one of his letter tiles for one from the bag.

"I did so—I hit the jelly doughnut."

"Because I practically placed it next to the bat."

"I didn't want to bruise your delicate male ego."

"Sure, sure. Is that why you're losing Scrabble too, or is it just because I'm superior in all things, except doily decorating?"

"That's it. I'm renouncing my title of Mrs. Gershom 'Sexist' Blagonravov." I was kind of playful, kind of not. "I'm starting to think 'Queen of the House' is a courtesy title when you know full well you're the King."

"We both know full well I'm the king of this bedroom, honey, and the truth melts you like you're peppermint ice cream. Don't deny it. You've already shown me your hand so you can't bluff me now. You voted for me to have that position."

He could tell I really was miffed, not as angry about what he said but why he was saying it.

"Listen, I support our marriage's democratic departments and think you should be queen of the house—if I was a house, I'd want to be in the caress of your doilies—but come on, if a catastrophe was coming, you'd want me to be in charge."

"You've been gruff with me all day."

"We were playing baseball. Did you want me to hold your hand across each base? Listen, it's not called hardball for nothing."

"You were grouchy with me all morning, and then 'Cleats! They're called cleats, idiot.'"

"I didn't call you an idiot."

"Not with words. And then, 'At least you're good at baking.' Then you mumbled that stuff about how girls shouldn't be allowed on the baseball field."

"I didn't say all girls, I said girls like you."

"That makes me feel better. Then when we were finished playing, you snapped, 'I'm going to hit the showers by myself tonight, jack.'"

"I was filthy, and you're apparently scared of mud. It's driving you nuts me in this pristine bed in these muddy pants. Well, it's my bed now too, honey, and I'll get it messy if I want."

"There you go again."

"We always tease each other."

"You crossed the line from playfulness into meanness this afternoon when you said, 'I'd rather play baseball by myself than play with you.'"

"I was kidding. You know my humor is dry."

"It hurt my feelings."

"I didn't know that."

"But I'm letting you know now that it hurt my feelings."

"Then my apologies."

"With sincerity please! Do you need me to spell that out for you on the gameboard?"

"Ah, don't paint me as some typical man unaware of his wife's feelings."

"I'll paint what I see."

"Lumi, are you going to play this game or not?"

"We're already playing a game, the one you started this morning and believe I'm going to let you win."

"What are you talking about?"

"I know what you're doing, Sput. I pushed the wall too far down last night when I offered you forgiveness, so you're erecting a new form of defense: standing on the watchtower of your being and shooting at me with gruffness to keep me away, 'to protect me,' which makes no sense, but you're not being rational, as fear never is. That outburst of machismo just now proves it—'I'm the king of this bedroom, honey.'"

"I'm not saying anything different than you've been saying all along. We're on the same team."

"I don't want you building up new defenses. I mean it, Sputnik."

"I'm not. I'm trying to build a word."

"I'm married to you, not in war with you." I gave him a very cold shoulder.

"I thought you wanted to be my buddy pal and rough it out with some brews?"

"I love being your *special* buddy pal and I want to play baseball with you sometimes, but that doesn't mean I want you to completely forget your gentlemanly conduct."

"Come on, Lumi, you know I'd never intentionally hurt you, but I honestly—no game playing—have no idea what you're so upset about."

I turned to look at him and he was seemingly confused about the source of my hurt. Was this an example of what Moon-Moon had described as hearing but not listening?

"That's baloney, Sput, and you smell it too. You *haven't* been gruff with me all day?"

He replayed the day in his thoughts. "I was nice when we took that morning walk together."

"Only because *you* were in the afterglow of what I did for you this morning and your grouchy mouth was stuffed with strawberry doughnut, even though it was 'glumpy.' Making those doughnuts for you, the kind your mother made, was very important to me then you went and said you didn't like them."

"Listen, we were playing baseball, not making out."

"I'm not talking about baseball—I'm talking about doughnuts."

"I didn't realize I was supposed to be gentle while playing baseball."

"I just said I'm not talking about baseball. Ooh my, now you're not listening to me at all. How rude can you be?"

"Come on, you're mad because I beat you at the game."

"That's what *you* would think! I'm upset about the way you're treating me."

"Guys taunt each other on the ballfield. It's part of the fun of the game, come on."

"We weren't on the ballfield when you said the doughnuts were 'glumpy,' and I'm not a guy! I just told you—I want to be your friend but for you to still remain a gentleman."

He began coughing severely; to argue with him now would be like punching below the belt. I softly rubbed his knee, which could not be properly caressed through rough denim. After the coughing, we resumed our argument.

"Sometimes, Professor, you're as cold as a chalkboard, and I never know when these winters are going to come over you, so I end up getting frostbitten by your unexpected chilliness—a girl needs a thousand coats to be married to you and your iciness."

"No, listen, you're telling me, 'I'm not a guy, don't play hardball with me,' but when I say, 'Alright, I'll play softball with you' then you call me a chauvinist."

"Again, I already told you—I want to be treated like a Lady regardless of what I'm doing and not to be treated as if I'm incapable of doing something because I'm a Lady."

"Well, you can't play both hardball and softball."

"I don't want to play hardball or softball or any ball. I despise baseball. There I said it."

He acted as if I had mortally wounded him. "If you have a beef with me, take it out on me, not on baseball. What has baseball ever done to you?"

"For one, it takes away my husband's attention. Two, I despise all that spitting and scratching, particularly of the male region."

"I had an itch."

"No, you were making a big display to say you had one and I don't, as if that made all the difference in the game."

"Freud said it best, 'penis envy.'"

"And there was a female psychologist who said men have womb envy."

"I was joking. I've been honest about how much I respect motherhood."

"Then why did you treat the future mother of your children like she was a jerk from the dugout? You can score a homerun by yourself, King, because I'm not playing with you anymore."

"Ah, so all was hunky dory when you were *queen* of the house, though, eh?"

"You're so obsessed with winning, you have to think of some strategy to win, so you're going to make me out to be the wrong one, a malevolent queen of the house. No wonder we can't stop warring our way to the end, because you men are deadly competitive. You can't even fathom letting me win this little game of Scrabble, can you? I'd *let* you win if that made you happy."

"*Let* me win? Ah, so now, you just *let me* win everything, because your femininity is so superior to Cro-Magnon man?"

"You're the one who said women are superior."

"I never said that. I said *some* women are superior in *some* things like gentleness, but apparently I was wrong. Here you are biting my head off for nothing."

"*I'm* not gentle?"

I started to leave, but he griped, "There she goes again evading questions. You can't answer why it's alright for you to be queen of the house?"

"I never said I wanted that title. *You* gave me that honor. I want us to be partners."

"We are."

"But you're really head of the house?"

"We can have our democratic departments, that's fine, but ultimately, come on…"

"You're just like your stubborn pops."

"Listen, I'm not a tyrant."

"Stop telling *me* to listen. You're the one who needs to listen."

"*Listen*, I don't have any desire to rule over you and make decisions about your life for you. Whatever you want to do, I'll support you. I've said this over and over yet apparently you need to listen. But I am the one, the Captain, who has to go down with the ship, so my first mate can run to safety at the first sign of danger."

"I don't even know what we're arguing about anymore, Sputnik. You're just making up arguments for you to win."

"Don't you want me to be the one who goes down with the ship?"

"No, if our ship was sinking, I'd want to go down with you."

"It can't be that way, Lumi." He looked me hard in the eyes, telling me I was trying to change a fundamental aspect of his character. "This is why I have to be in charge in catastrophic situations, where the Lady would try to make a noble choice, but one that would hurt her, and I can't allow that to happen. Do you understand that? You should. Your heart filled with Knights and Ladies. I have to be the protector. You agreed to me being Secretary of Defense. Can you imagine a husband running from a burning house, saving his own life but not his wife's? What kind of man would that be? I don't believe in 'womb envy'—"

"Of course, you wouldn't."

"But men know children need their mothers, therefore the 'save the women and children first' mentality. I would—never—let you die for me. You're the angel. I'm just a man."

"I don't know how my saying you were gruff with me today came all the way around to this, but if you think I'd let you die for me without putting up a fight to protect you, just so your male ego wouldn't get bruised, you're not as logical as you think you are, Professor Blagonravov."

"I don't ever want to hear you talk or think like that." His voice, in no uncertain tone, stated his perceived authority.

"Once again, you've tried to write an unbearable chapter in our otherwise perfectly lovely honeymoon."

I left the bedroom to sit on the couch in the den. I held the "Write Thus" pillow and watched our three animal friends sleep close together on the floor.

Wind outside blew softer than the old-as-humans male/female storm that had taken over our bedroom.

Sputnik finally sat beside me. "How are our friends?"

"*They're* fine."

My husband made a big show of clearing his throat to tell me his throat still hurt.

"Your throat's still bothering you?"

"Yes." Very pouty.

"Being outside all day in the cold definitely didn't help it."

"I'd ask you to please make me something hot to drink, but I suppose you hate your Sputty now?"

"I'd never hate you." I started to get up to make him coffee, but he ever-so-softly put his hand to my arm. He didn't really want a drink; he had just been testing the waters.

"You can call them 'gleats' if you want. When I play baseball with you, I'll play with strawberry jelly doughnuts. I promise. No hardball. I've been considering what you said, and I promise no more walls, no more gruffness. Lumi, I can live without baseball, but I can't live without you."

I ever-so-softly touched his boyish bare ear.

"Are you going to pinch me?" he said.

I laughed, "No."

590

"Perhaps I deserve it."

He was my sweet boy again.

"I don't want you to live without baseball, Sput. I want you to do what you love. I shouldn't have said I despise baseball."

"But you do."

"It's just that I know I'm never going to be a good enough ballplayer to give you the kind of baseball game you want. And I shouldn't have said you aren't a good listener. You're the greatest listener. You listen to everything I say. I'm so blessed to have you. You stayed up all night on the phone with me listening to all the boring details of my life."

"They were never boring."

"But I am a boring baseball player."

"'Boring' is not so much the word. 'Amusing.' 'Awful.' Those descriptions ring truer."

"Why don't you join a community baseball team?"

He thought about it. "I do have a colleague that plays on a league on weekends."

"You can join that. I'd love to watch you play."

"You're highly sexy when you're supportive."

"Ooh?"

"Ah yeah, very sexy."

"I'm not really being supportive. I just want to see you in the cute uniform."

We kissed, our favorite pastime.

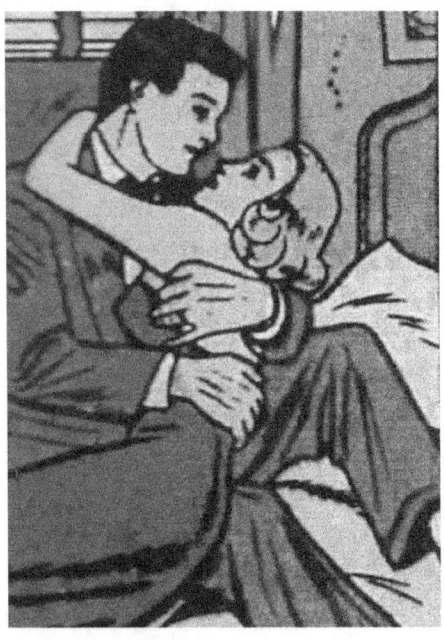

"I'm not a woman who desires to knock a man off a pedestal. I want you to be on a throne, to have your position as king, to know you're capable of achieving greatness, but I want to stand *beside* you, not below you. The yin and yang are nested beside each other."

"You know I think you're an angel."

"Then why did you treat your angel so gruffly today?"

"For exactly the reason you already know. Because of what happened last night. I suppose I wanted you to be aware of the gruff brute you married."

"You want to push me away?"

"Not consciously. You offered me forgiveness, but I don't…how could even an angel be that good?"

"Because I love you."

"Why?"

"Just because. Being in love is being able to see the Light inside each other. People claim those in love wear rose-colored glasses but that's not true. The truth is those in love see clearly, all the way to each other's souls. Those not in love are the ones in glasses, gray-coated glasses given to them by society, gloomy glasses that make them see only darkness in each other; only when those gray-coated glasses are removed are the eyes capable of seeing the truth in light. Whatever gruff mean character you write for yourself, Sputnik, I'll still see the light in the writer."

He put his face close to mine, rubbed his nose next to mine. "I don't deserve you."

I softly held his ears. "Yes, you do, and it's so important for you to see that. But when you say things like you'd die for me, that makes me feel so alone. I can't live without you."

"But you must someday."

"Why?"

"Because I've known, we've both known, from the beginning I have to die for you, angel."

"I'd never let the story be written that way."

"But I would."

"No, I won't let you write it that way."

"As you said, I've already written chapters in your story you didn't want."

"No, all the chapters with you, no matter what was written, have been the best chapters, because you're in them. This is a lovestory.

The chapters without you are meaningless. I won't let you die before me."

"That passage was written by destiny. Either this cough will kill me or something else will. You've felt the premonition of my death throughout our entire story. I'm a short-lived character. You know that."

"You're the character that matters most to me. The only character I want to write my story with. Plus, the world's story needs you. Your students need you. I need you. Why can't I convince you of that?"

"Ah, to be a 'suffering servant' for God. It has to be that way, so the ending of *The Snowflake* story will be *your* decision, Peppermint."

"Happily ever after. You and me."

"That's my girl." He kissed my forehead in a fatherly way. "Now, hopefully my departure won't happen until a chapter after I've built a home for you, provided financial security, given you some of them babies you want."

"And you'd just abandon your children? You'd abandon me?"

"I don't want to die. I did. I confess. Suicide landings in ice fields, clocking 140 miles per hour around curves in the road. I don't want to die now. But I'm a man of protest in a society that shoots protestors. I fight for peace treaties in a world that bombs peace. I study explosive rockets, I devise perilous experiments, I land airplanes in icy fields, I live a dangerous life, and you know that, yet you wouldn't change it, because that's the heroic character you admire. Don't worry, I won't leave until I've taught you how to throw a good spitball, although that might take a few lifetimes to teach you."

"*Spit*ball? Ooh, why do you like that dreadful game so much, Sputnik?" I asked to be playful, to keep from crying.

594

"If you don't know now, you never will. Some of us have the hardball fever, some of us don't, and you're one of the don't's, so that's why I play jelly doughnuts with you."

I could not help but cry, knowing he would someday depart my story.

"Lumi, the stories of all saints are pagesfull of tragedies—tests of their characters."

"I don't want to be a saint. I want to be your wife. And I'll stand by you amidst tornadoes and blizzards and anything the world can toss at us. Moon-Moon told me tests come in different forms, not just the horrible kind you're referring to."

He ran his hand up my leg. "Your legs are so much prettier bare than in blue jeans." He leaned down to kiss the prettiness. "Will you allow me to make up for my gruffness?" He laid me against the couch and continued his journey by kiss up my leg. "I'm going to build you a house with a skylight, so when I do this for you, you'll see the stars above you."

I thoroughly enjoyed being with him that night after spending the day around his gruff baseball persona then feeling him ask *me* to make love *to* him and allowing himself to fully get into the reversal of roles.

Afterwards in bed, he said tenderly, "That was nice but truthfully, do you prefer me to be the Captain?"

I kissed the star necklace against his chest. "You are the Captain."

"Perhaps I should ask this after you come down from those post-lovemaking stars."

"You can do whatever you want. I dedicate my lifestory to you."

"A definite sign I should wait to ask that question again, or else I'd just be taking advantage of your vulnerability."

I kissed again and again across his chest.

"Do you and my chest hair want to be alone?"

"I was going to ask the same of you and my bosom."

"Bosom. I didn't know anyone still said that. That was the word nice boys used to refer to a woman's stuff, way back in the '30's."

"And what was the word boys like you used?"

"Are you implying I wasn't a nice boy?"

"You made spitballs. But I still want to wash your baseball uniform."

"You're definitely still up in the stars."

"I'm always in the stars with you. We touch and I no longer have a soul—I have a rainbow! Multicolor technicolor wonder no longer invisible but radiating awe to all who come across your creation. I've never felt this way about anyone or anything. It's beautiful and scary."

"Why scary?"

"Because of what you were saying earlier."

"Forget I said that. Let's just go back to writing our apricot rugelach chapters." I knew he was trying to make me happy despite whatever ominous premonitions he was suffering. "Now, let me ask you a fun question: Is peppermint tastier as a candy cane or as pie?"

"Candy cane."

He shook his head. "Pie. But ice cream is the ultimate form of peppermint."

"No, it's not…this is…" And I put my lips to his.

Pancakes & Syrup

Every morning, I found bliss in imagining all the possible new ways to express love for my husband. And every night I offered gratitude to the hours for gifting me another 24 to love him, and my dreams came sweet, while the Earth *turned* but I was *secure* in his arms.

On the fifth day of Hanukkah and Christmas Eve Eve, we were going to get married at the county clerk's office before they closed for Christmas. Even though we had gone to sleep late, Sputnik woke up early. It was my husband's turn to kiss me awake; enjoying his kisses, I pretended it was going to take more to wake me.

The morning was sunny and as warm as winter could be, no upcoming battle against ice storms on the horizon. Our bedroom was awash in soft gold daylight.

Sput's hair was morning wild like his beard, his pants still baseball dirty, and his shirt days-worn wrinkled, but he looked very good, and he was in a great mood, and I was happy to be awakened in this life of ours. He wanted me to go outside and see something.

"Do you mind if I brush my hair first?" I asked.

"Ah, Lumi," he playfully grumped, too excited to wait to show me whatever he wanted to show me. "You look beautiful. Come on, let's go!"

I was flattered he thought I looked beautiful even with my hair and face a mess after sleep.

"Can I at least put on clothing?"

"You don't have to for me." He winked.

Looking as wild as Sput, I put on my nightgown and his coat over that, slipped on saddle oxfords which completed the eccentric look, and we dashed down the porch steps. We all but hopped in dew-sparkling grass, in the quietness of winter morning barely post dawn, scented with light lingering snow and trees, the scent of a bird's day.

As the sun rose, the goldenness of dawn was transforming into clear air, everything still and visible, only slightly brushed in frost, not so much literal frost as the frosted pane that framed all wintertime scenes; this day especially fit to be sketched on a syrup bottle.

A beautiful cardinal flew by like a streak of red paint in pale winter.

"I wonder where he's going?" I wondered aloud.

"He's bringing home some breakfast to his nest, where he can snuggle with his mate," my husband said, keeping at least two of our hands warm in an embrace while the other two suffered alone chilled Earth air, which was not exactly biting air but more of a nose nibbler, our noses slowly turning red.

"I thought birds mated in spring?"

"Some mate in winter. Birds can kiss too, did you know that? Some even mate for life."

"Professor Blagonravov is so much more romantic than anyone would ever guess. Which birds mate for life?"

"Mourning doves. Their bond is so strong, sometimes the mourning extends far beyond the mate's death. Barn owls mate for life as well. I actually saw a great gray owl earlier," Sput exclaimed, merrily as a Boy Scout earning a badge.

"Ooh, I wish I could have seen that."

"Early worm sees the bird," he joked, as we walked up a gentle slope together.

"I've seen many birds," I said, looking around, hoping to see some in a sky whose blue was just becoming blue, a very soft blue not yet drenched in rich dark blueness.

"Yeah, I've seen doves, starlings, goldfinches. A kid could really have fun out here, bird watching and writing down all the varieties he or she sees. I used to do that in Alaska. I met all sorts of waterfowl and doves and sandpipers. A kid can learn a lot about how to be a pilot by watching birds."

I liked how we could always share stories of our pasts and relive them with each other, making good memories even better and bad memories not so painful when experienced again but this time in each other's embrace.

"I love our cozy nook of the planet!" I said, feeling the firm cold crust of Earth beneath my shoes.

"Owls must love it here as well, so I'm sure you'll get to see one."

"I love Stargust Continued more than Stargust!"

"I actually like this land more than the land of my boyhood, more than even the pristine land of the tundra. I *love* this land. This is home." He no longer had to be a wanderer.

He squeezed his wife's hand and I knew we were upon what he wanted to show me:

On a flat-topped hill, Sputnik had used rocks to mark off a large square where our house would stand—our house, the joy! He would begin laying the foundation in springtime for the house he hoped to have finished by summer's end, so we would have a snug nest for our autumn-born baby. My husband promised to build me a home with a hearth fit to be called hearth. Stone by stone he would construct our cozy fireplace.

"It won't be hard to build on a hill?" I asked, brightly shining with delight.

"Don't worry about that, Peppermint."

I had never seen him this excited. He was ready to roll up his sleeves and get out in springtime sun and work until sundown on our house, even beyond sundown, work by lantern light and starlight and coffee, which his wife would make trips outside to bring him, while admiring his handywork.

He had not been able to sleep all night, too focused on his homemaking plans.

"The home will have big windows—"

"With shutters?" I dreamed.

"Shutters aren't outside the realm of physical possibility." The physicist smiled.

Big windows wide open in spring, where we would listen to birdsong and bees and all the music of countryside daytime and nighttime, and we'd watch our children play baseball in the summer and make snowmen in the winter, and our dinner guests would be constellations...

"Lumi, you can make it The Lady Model; you can make it a doll house; you can make it Cinderella's castle! Whatever home you want, I'll build it for you, although the castle might take some time and more money than the assistant professor has."

"Being with you could make a tent feel like a castle."

"I believe you and that's why I *want* to build you a castle, because you deserve it, a castle that matches your majestic heart. No queen will have ever had a palace built for her with as much love and loyalty."

His goodness sometimes touched me so intensely, I wanted to cry from the deepest part of my self.

"Ooh, Sputty, I can see it perfectly! Our little dream home the color of morning sunshine—it'll be as pretty as a yellow bird alighted on this meadow."

"It doesn't have to be little."

"But that will be cozier and easier for me to manage and 'doily.' And, ooh, shutters the color of lilies with matching door and interior—Sputty, could we?"

"Sure, if that's what you want."

"It's not too much to build?"

He grinned. "No, shutters don't add on that much building effort."

"A white and yellow daffodil of a house! My heart is melting."

"I thought it would."

"Can we have a wrap-around porch?"

His expression said, "Don't push your luck." Then he laughed. "Yeah, you can have a porch. Porches are easy to build. Will that also be the color of a lily?"

"Of course! And we can put a telescope on the porch for late-night star gazing and UFO spotting. I see all these sweet scenes of our future home. I see our cinnamon radio on the windowsill against a backdrop of moon and stars. Holiday lights in December. I see pies cooling on windowsills. Pecan, sweet potato, blueberry, whatever you want."

"Whatever our kids want too."

That thought made my heart three times bigger: little Sputniks in the yard, their little toddler legs waddling up slopes, their faces adorned in blueberry pie stains.

"I see family camping trips in the woods with walkie-talkies and campfire stories by the pond and bedtime stories and chimney smoke in the air on winter nights, and the smoke will look billowy, magical, not gloomy and grimy, and we could have flowers planted in window boxes. Are those hard to build?"

"I built them for the camper, didn't I? Don't you worry about what's hard to build or not. You just design to your heart's content and let the engineer worry about the building and blueprinting and logistics."

"Are you going to build it all by yourself?"

"No, I'm going to force Ben and Brad and Hershel to help, and I'm sure some other colleagues will pitch in on weekends."

"I can pitch in." I didn't want to just sit back in a rocker while he did all the work.

"You can pitch in on designing, yes. On manual labor, absolutely not."

"What do you mean 'absolutely not'? Reminding you: you're not my boss, sir. I simply must hammer one nail in the construction of our home."

"Alright, you simply must do that, but you'll be gearing up for your own kind of labor. That's what I meant." He softly patted my stomach. "Our little spud-nik will have grown fairly big by spring."

"He's not a potato." I smiled. "Ooh, I know how I can help: I can skirt our home in flowers, which is not too strenuous, I promise, since I'll need something to do when my husband isn't making love to his pregnant wife."

"But think how all that anticipation will build up for a fabulous Hanukkah present for us both then the next year we'll have another little bundle of autumn joy."

"Someone sounds excited now about the prospect of us having babies?"

"This morning when I was marking off the foundation, I had a picture of a little daughter sweet as her mother following me around, asking questions."

"Here's a question: Is a home skirted in flowers too girly?"

"Yes, but go ahead and girly it up, Anne of Green Gables. Trellises, ivy…"

"But the spitball pitcher would be too embarrassed to live in a house that girly?"

"I'll have my baseball field and big manly chain link homer fence and perhaps a batting cage and my woodland for camping." He laughed.

"Sputty, here's what I'm seeing: the skirt of our home as colorful as an Impressionist watercolor. Snowdrops in winter, and carnations in spring, and baby's breath … I'll make it very pretty for you, so when you come home from a long cold day of being around men who want to make missiles in the stars, you can bask in the sunshine that will be our house."

But his mind was on food. "You know I've never had blueberry pie."

"In all your travels you never had blueberry pie?"

"Nope. Wouldn't mind trying that. Might settle down for some blueberry pie. With the crisscrossed crust top like the kinds from drawings of downhome."

"You'll love it, especially with fresh blueberries, and I think blueberry season coincides with baseball season, so you'll have blueberry pie and ice cream to enjoy with the games."

"I could really get into this married stuff."

"You'll really get into it when you try blueberry pancakes."

Birds were making their presence known through song. Leaves and twigs rustled, a sound which always plucked my heartstrings: plants and animals in the woodland going about their mornings.

"Now, if it's alright with you," he said, "and these are just some logistical thoughts, I was thinking two bathrooms, one for you, one for the kids, although when they get older, I'll expand the number of bathrooms, because teenage boys and teenage girls cannot share a bathroom without killing each other."

"What do you mean 'one for me, one for the kids'—what about one for you?"

"I'll build an outhouse for me. I grew up using an outhouse. It doesn't bother me. I prefer it. The Lady needs space for all her hairbrushes and hair ribbons and girly stuff."

"I hope you at least will still shower with me, sir, and allow me to make you warm baths?"

"Oh, yes, that *simply must* happen," he said in a very proper "cream tea" accent.

"Why not three bathrooms, one for the kids, one for you, one for me, a his and her bathroom? It gets very cold in New England so you might want to reconsider the outhouse plan."

"Perhaps. We'll have three bedrooms, our room and one for the boys, one for the girls. The boys can have bunk beds, but for our girls when they're older, I'll make two sleigh beds with pretty carvings in the headboards appropriate for princesses."

"That's not very nice to your sons, showing your daughters special attention."

"They're boys."

"You're going to treat them the way you treat your male students?"

"They're going to learn how to be men, I can assure you that."

"I plan to coddle our sons just so you know. If you think I'm going to force our sweet little spud-nik to throw spitballs, you're not that smart, Professor Blagonravov."

"You can't give boys the same kind of coddling. They'll walk all over you, and they won't be able to make it in the real world."

"I'll be their mother."

"Alright, you can coddle them, but I'm their pops ... come on, Peppermint, let's not start that boy/girl argument again. You've done a fantastic job with your character, and you're their mother, so I trust you to do what is right."

"And I trust you too."

He was such a man, so admirable and hardworking yet sensitive and kind, how could I doubt he would raise commendable sons?

I threw my arms around him, so grateful for his presence on Earth, and let him know in words, "I love you so much, Gershom."

"You're really about to love me." He led me to a spot on the hill and said, "I'll put our bedroom here and a bay window there that will give you postcards from Heaven each morning: the absolute best views of sunrise. I'll build you a grand curio cabinet, the grand dame of curios, all ornate and queenly, where you can stand your special snow globe made by yours truly, The Snowflake Physicist."

"I hope you never tire of me."

"I'm already tired of you and your no-socks-on-the-floor policy."

"You're so mean."

"Listen, I won't be tired of you even after the Earth tires of the moon, at least not while I also have Mara Gold."

"Tell me that when I'm gray as the moon and I'll believe you, sir. Say fifty years from now."

"Alright, but you'll never be gray. Your pink beauty is a part of you at any age, in any form, it's your logo, always recognizable no matter what package it's on—it's the signature of the writer." He smiled; he did more of that lately. "Besides, only a fool would tire of seeing stars in the sky just because they're the same stars he sees every year—they're beautiful because they're familiar. You're my North Star, who has guided me home."

"Sometimes I don't know if you really mean these sweet things or if they're just lines?"

"A gentleman will never reveal that secret."

The blaring sunball, higher in the sky, added warmth to our cold noses and ears.

"You know I'm seeing some sweet scenes too, Lumi. Your sunshine hair splashed across our morning pillows, your pretty blue eyes becoming my sunrise. I see you framed by window of

606

star-polished nighttime and playing the harp for me without your clothing on."

"Sputnik…"

"You won't do that for me?"

"For you…maybe…as long as you clean up your socks."

He put his hands under my coat and rubbed my back softly up and down. "When I saw you years ago in the soul food restaurant, I thought, there's a girl I'll never see without her clothes on."

I looked down, embarrassed.

"I'll never even see her bare hands without gloves on them. That hayride day, when you told me you played the harp, I had the vision of you, bare, playing harp in stars like a sparkling constellation. Forget Lyra, I have my Lumi."

"You're talking so sweetly, it makes me want to let that vision come true for you right now."

"Ah, let's wait until nighttime." He shook his head like a sinner perplexed by his being welcomed to Heaven. "I have no idea why I deserve all this."

He walked over to where he imagined putting the window of stars and he looked out as if through window glass, looking at a scene he still believed himself unworthy to live?

To keep the mood tender and sweet, I said, "This is the room where all the sentences with exclamation points will be written."

"Ah, well, I'll try to write exclamation sentences with you everywhere, honey."

"Sometimes I like the sentences with calm cool periods. 'Wrapped up together in bed, we watched the sun rise across the meadow and our beings.' Those kinds of sentences."

"We'll write plenty of those too."

"I'm happy to see you plan on writing a *long* story with me?"

"You've got me all excited by the story. Hate to leave it now. Think of how many times we're going to make love here."

"Do you want to get started now?"

My husband and I could not be around each other long without kissing and touching and wanting to get back in bed together, although there was no reason the locale of our union had to be a bed.

"My sweet girl's going to get down in the dirty grass with her rugged pitcher?"

"If that's what you want."

"Perhaps, later. Hold that thought." In this moment, he didn't want to say "I love you" through lovemaking, but through his plans for building our charming future.

"We have so much land here," he said, "I could park my plane out there if that's alright with you, and build a simple hangar, which could have room for two, if you want me to build you an aeroplane too."

"Of course it's alright with me! And, yes, I'd love to learn how to fly, but can I help you build my plane?"

"Sure, The Lady Model plane with pink propeller."

"No, since you fly a she, I'll fly a he."

"I'm not going to let my girl have a more rugged plane than me."

"He doesn't have to be rugged! He'll be a sweet plane named Teddy. Our planes will be soulmates, sharing a hangar, a sky, adventures wing by wing."

"Miles away, I can feel my Lady plane quivering with anticipation to meet her fella." He laughed but I knew he really did see his aeroplane as alive with a heart and soul and good manners.

"Well, Pep, until your plane gets born, I can take you and the spud-nik on flights, give you flying lessons. Ah, I hope all my kids want to learn how to fly."

"And play baseball."

"Well, a fella can dream."

"Ooh, so your daughter can play baseball but not your wife?"

"Daughters get special treatment."

"And so do sons. I would run into a burning building to save my son, just so you know, and nothing could stop me."

"I already know that and that's one reason I love you so dearly. I just can't allow you to run into a burning building to save me."

He looked out to the runway-yet-to-be. "Now if you want to have a breakfast picnic in your beloved Stargust, I'll fly you there, and I know pregnant women get weird food hankerings, so I'll be ready to dash off in my plane at two a.m. if you're in need of pickles and chocolates from Switzerland."

"I don't know how I got to be the luckiest gal in the universe."

"Not yet the luckiest until I tell you this: the home will have washer and dryer so no more laundromats."

I had never had a washer and dryer, so I had to admit my admiration for modern technology in that moment: I did not want washboard and bucket.

"And you'll have a sunroom with a rocking chair, so you and baby can watch and listen to all of nature's dramas, rain and storms and ice blizzards, safely behind windows."

"Ooh, I can take cream tea there too. You know since I played baseball with you, you'll have to join me for a tea party."

"I figured as much," he mock grumped.

"You'll love it, especially done my way. Angel cake and jellies..."

"Does sound rather delicious. Does cream tea ever include ice cream?"

"It can! A new tub of ice cream each time, or even a hot fudge sundae banana split root beer float all-the-toppings-you-can-dream-of ice cream buffet bonanza!"

"Now you're talking my language."

He walked me to another spot in our future waiting to be lived. "My sweet Lady will have a big clawfoot tub to luxuriate in, and all the hot water she needs and no grouchy husband telling her she's wasting too much water, and a kitchen large enough for her culinary imagination to stretch out—pies, muffins, I want it all." He led me to the kitchen-area-to-come. "You'll have a window offering a grand view of the pond and sunsets over the water while you're making dinner."

"We need an orange tree."

"Can those grow out here?"

"We can grow one indoors."

"Grow a tree indoors? Now who's being mean?"

"No, he'll be a small tree, a tiny clementine, and during warm months, we'll set him outside, and when indoors, we'll give him plenty of window light and love, and he won't even miss Florida."

"I'm not sure about that. Don't like the idea of putting a roof over a tree's head meant to grow tall in unimpeded sky."

"I want to make fresh orange juice for your big southern breakfasts, and sweet clementine juice will taste like sunshine in a glass, and on summer days, I'll blend homemade vanilla ice cream into the juice, and you'll be in an orange creamsicle heaven."

"Thanks, Emily Dickinson, but fresh apple juice will be fine. Actually, I like grape juice. I enjoyed taking grape juice on my boyhood hiking adventures." He was getting so much more in touch with what he liked and having fun in the process. "Mother used to get grapes at the market for perfecting her snow cones, and Bubbe made me grape juice."

"Ooh, I didn't know my sweet liked grape juice. The purple kind?"

"Yup."

"Hmmm…it might be hard to grow grapes out here, I'm not sure, but we can try."

"You can get store bought."

"I thought my Sputty despised consumerism and did not want his wife's hands to ever touch money?"

"Yeah, but I'll be the one buying 'em. I don't want to put a lot of extra work on you. You'll have plenty to do: writing and harp playing and babies and a difficult husband and learning how to fly and tending animals. You're not a pioneer woman."

"If you can build us a house, I can make you fresh grape juice."

"Can I go to grape creamsicle heaven in summertime?"

"Yes, you can, after working up a sweat from summertime baseball, and I'll even mix the drink with club soda and top it with whipped cream, so you'll have a soda fountain float like the ones from your ice cream shop boyhood days. And these breakfasts will be so tasty, the barnstormer will never want to fly away forever—he'll always come back home for dinner. But if you ever have the need to fly off to Hank's and spend time alone with baseball and thin-crust pizza, that's okay."

"Well…it is great pizza and the TV screens are as close to being at the ballfield as one can get without a ticket. But I'd never leave my girl all alone for long."

"Your girl will be happy knowing you're in baseball-and-pizza heaven, apparently a heaven even the angel can't create for you, but I will try—and notice I said 'try'—to recreate the pizza and banana splits for when you can't be at Hank's."

"I've had enough alone time. I literally slept in barren fields and felt like the last man on Earth desperate to find another of his kind on this vast lonely planet. I want some together time. And southern breakfasts by the fireplace with my girl."

A realization came to me, "Ooh but my Sputty wants a woodsy log cabin, not a little lemon drop of a house? A log cabin just like our gingerbread log cabin."

He shrugged.

"Then we'll have a log cabin! Like your Alaskan cabin. Don't you know yet how happy it makes me to make my Sputty happy?"

"No, I don't need a log cabin. For goodness's sake, Lady, I've slept in hayfields, in slush and mud and ice. You're going to have your sunshine cottage. I can be content with just a small log shed to do manly stuff in like sawing and listening to the games and tossing my dirty socks to the floor. A tent might even suffice."

We watched a few more birds fly in peaceful air, no hunters around.

"You'll have your hangar too, Sput."

"*Our* hangar."

"You also need a rocket launchpad like your pops had."

"You don't want a concrete slab ruining the picture of your girly meadow."

"I most certainly do want you to have a rocket launchpad. Rocketry is your passion. I went into this marriage willingly with a great man who has big dreams and not nine-to-five hours, and I plan to stay married to that man who never has to curb his astronomical dreams, so they'll fit into suburbia."

"Well, if you want me to have the launchpad, alright. We're as kooky as Bubbe and Feivish."

"Kooky marriages are the strongest, because kooks only belong with each other, no one else, and they know it, so they don't take each other for granted."

"The launchpad gives me a good excuse to build the shed, where we can watch the launches. We can play around with some small rocket designs set up for landings in the pond." He was so excited, he was going to burst. "The kids will probably like that—like grand fireworks."

He was going to turn the camper into an office, where we could work side by side, me writing, him blueprinting "fantastioso inventions." I would plant a garden "with all the fixin's for succotash," although I would have to adjust the southern version of the recipe, depending on what I could grow in New England. He would build a schoolhouse, a small milk-colored schoolhouse, where I would teach our children (four we decided on). Sputnik would install a chalkboard and teacher's and students' desks and a potbelly stove for cold winter school days and good-sized windows for open air on warmer days. The rest of the decorating I would do and I imagined: a wall-sized map of the solar system, posters of historical figures, a big globe by the teacher's desk, stenciled cut-outs of "A" "B" "C" above the chalkboard, cartoons of numerals drawn by their dad, a corkboard for displaying their own drawings, and a treasure chest of crayons. Even though they would be schooled at home, we'd still go on field trips (to museums, the observatory, maybe even to Walden Pond), and the kids could have some snow days off, because a child had to be allowed to enjoy those rare special moments, and of course they would get summers free of the schoolhouse, because I knew learning did not only take place in schoolrooms—the countryside offered plenty of opportunities to learn everything from geography to ornithology. Knowing I would have to teach our kids the beginning lessons of mathematics and science was a good reason for me to study enough to be an expert in fractions and long division, etcetera, but when his little geniuses started advancing toward calculus at nine years old, he'd have to take over the lesson planning.

"I just had another beautiful vision, Sput. Remember how you said I could be both wife and nun? In a way I can. We have so much land here, we can have two gardens, one for us and one for a food pantry. I'll never be Hildegard, but we can play a small part in kindness's story and teach our children the lesson of the importance of generosity to self and others."

"That's my girl. And I haven't forgotten your desire to have your pastry kitchen. I'll get you that as well, although I can't fathom how you'll have time to do all you want to do."

"I wonder that about you too."

We stood in the center of our house-to-be and let excitement for our future embrace us as warmly as homemade pie made with our own recipe.

We enjoyed a delightful shower together, warming ourselves after a long eventful morning in brisk air and a splendor in the grass (christening the ground of our future bedroom with love).

Afterwards, I made our friends breakfast, and for husband and wife, I "concocted" celebratory apple pancakes ("concocted" was a word the inventor liked). True to his love of southern cooking, he enjoyed fried potatoes, so I made those too (spiced with cayenne), along with fresh coffee and cocoa, and scrambled eggs with tabasco. I always kept hot condiments in the refrigerator in case Sputnik ever wanted a sandwich. I also made fresh cinnamon apple juice, not too difficult, but somewhat time consuming; the apple "mush" leftover after straining, I turned into applesauce.

I was floating high and had to look down to see cloud 9 that morning.

His hair still damp from the shower but combed, he stood shirtless in the den, aglow with daylight and TV light. Sputnik was dialing up Ben's number on the phone.

The TV was on for our animal friends, fascinated by the glowing box, although I thought Mullybiski could follow storylines, because he barked during television scenes that made humans laugh.

"Sput, we should welcome more cows and chickens on our land, and whenever they feel like letting us share their eggs and milk, we can have those staples and we won't have to support the horrible commercialization of animals."

"That's highly sweet, angel," he said with the tenderest of voices then his voice turned into a ton of bricks as he smashed these words into the phone, "You're actually awake, you old nut? Yeah, well, the 'dippity-do' head is getting married today." A pause to let his friend flip out.

I removed the typewriter from the table and placed it on the counter, so I could set out breakfast. The dark karo syrup (the outdoorsman's favorite) was in the cutest glass dispenser, and its rich black molasses color looked handsome in morning light. Sunshine streaming in from the window also lit the clear glasses of golden apple juice and the married salt and pepper shakers. I set out CozyCabin syrup for me and extra tabasco for Sput. I plated our breakfast: big fluffy pancakes and crispy browned potatoes and eggs fancied up in red peppers. I dolloped Sputnik's plate of pancakes with two scoops of fresh caramel ice cream, which would make the apple pancakes taste like caramel apples—too much sweetness for even me, but he liked ice cream on everything, which I had learned while he had perused my recipe box and had asked about almost every recipe, "Can that be made with ice cream?"

I listened to the men's conversation, which I could piece together from Sputnik's responses.

"Yeah, 'the kid' is finally getting hitched. No, the girl's not crazy. Yeah, the little patisserie pastry."

I peeked into the den, where Sputnik shrugged, letting me know "little patisserie pastry" was Ben's nickname for me.

"Yeah, yeah, my angel."

I walked into the sunny den, gave Sputnik a nibble of pancake soaked in melted ice cream, and his ecstatic expression let me know the sweet taste was heavenly, but he kept his voice macho around his buddy. "No, I'm not gargling. I'm eating, you idiot. I'm actually getting homemade pancakes. Remember that pancake cabin we visited in Arkansas? Yeah, Flapjack Fliers, the one started by Bobbi Harkness Bell, the barnstormer. Remember we thought those were the best flapjacks in the world. Well, these are even better."

For that compliment, I brought him a bite of spicy potatoes.

"Whew, hot but gooooood," his expression said.

"Yeah, sure, we'll come to your New Year's Eve party. Alright, ya nut, I'm off to enjoy my honeymoon."

At the kitchen booth, I sat on my husband's lap and we fed each other with fingers and fork. Kiss, bite of food, kiss, bite of food; I tasted pancake syrup and tabasco on his lips.

"Will I always get the king's treatment in the morning?" he asked, feeding me a morsel of cinnamon apple.

"If that's what you want."

"Tell me that five years from now—no, fifty, as you said—and don't tell me while serving me cornflakes, then I'll believe you."

"Cornflakes?"

"I have a colleague and that's what his wife serves him."

"Cornflakes are good and healthy."

"But every morning? He looks like he's transforming into a cornflake."

"What does someone who's transforming into a cornflake look like?"

616

"Like this guy. Listen, none of the men I know are in happy marriages. They're in cornflake marriages, common, not deathly but not delicious either."

"Cornflake marriages? What kind of chauvinistic malarkey is that? Maybe they're only looking at the marriage from the male perspective and need to see their wife's point of view and realize she's unhappy too. Maybe these men are serving their wives cornflakes every day, no genuine kisses, no romance, no nothing delicious."

"Well, what makes you happy? I want to make sure I'm taking care of all my baby's needs."

"You know I love writing and photography and moments when I feel like a peaceful flower absorbed in the Light, completely, as if I belong in the Heavenly garden."

"Well, you'll have an office for writing, undisturbed in peace and quiet, off limits to the kiddies too, and you'll have many moments in the sunshine, and you'll have acres to explore with your camera and notebook, capturing all the different scenes of seasons, and I can even build a small darkroom in the hangar."

"You're so amazing, not a cornflake."

"No, what is amazing is this meal. My little girl can cook. No cornflakes from her. It's pancakes and syrup from here to eternity. Here, try," he said, putting his fingertip covered in melted ice cream to my lips, which I kept sealed shut.

"No, no, no!" I playfully shook my head back and forth.

"For a girl so Godly, I can't believe you want to miss out on this form of divinity—ice cream is divine."

"I'll take your word for it."

"That's nonsensical. Taste buds can't take someone's word on a taste. The point is for your taste buds to experience the taste for themselves."

He savored the "divinity."

"Now, Lumi Blagonravov, how many times, theoretically, do you think we can make love in one day? Nine perhaps? In twenty-four hours, every two hours, leaving six hours for rest."

"Does the scientist want to test his theory?"

"On a day when the old ball-and-chain doesn't drag me to the county clerk's office to get married."

Fruitcake

"**W**ish us blessings," I said to Mullybiski and

Pythagoras and Mr. Bunny, who were seemingly watching *Captain Kangaroo* after breakfast, on the eve of Christmas Eve.

With me in the sports car, Sputnik drove slowly, past Peppermint Lane and our welcoming paradise and back into judgmental society, but at least we were with each other.

The downtown streets were cleared of ice, although somewhat busy with cars, last-minute shoppers rushing to get gifts. Families were united for the holidays and enjoying breakfast together at restaurants, groups of families seen behind restaurant windows, while tinsel and lights made our quaint town shiny. Even traffic lights were garlanded for "the most wonderful time of the year." The Salvation Army bell rang like a church bell. From an open door, a radio tendered Perry Como's *It's Beginning to Look a Lot Like*

Christmas. A sign outside a department store advertised, "Meet Santa Claus! Today from three to seven." Darioles bragged about having "the best holiday tarts." And Stormy & Strobe was offering "Candy Cane Malts."

"Candy cane malt equals yum," hubby said.

I shook my head. No ice cream for me, thanks.

We drove to his apartment—"*Our* apartment," he corrected—so he could shave, "Brylcreem up," and change out of his days-worn clothes into a fresh suit. Someone in another apartment had their door open, letting everyone know something nutmeg-ish was baking warm and sweet inside.

"Ba-bu-ba" while Sputnik shaved, which I enjoyed watching.

I learned the scientist had one source of vanity: his hair. I thought he was going to spend the whole morning with Brylcreem until finally the masterpiece coif was "finito."

My husband taught me how to tie his tie, not an easy task, but neither was wearing pantyhose and high heels, so he and I were even in the difficulties of getting dressed. He wore a nutmeg-brown suit with a pale peach shirt, a darker peach tie, and a matching silk handkerchief in the breast pocket. I didn't have a wedding dress, so I wore my church gloves, something borrowed and blue (blue in one of his space mission lapel pins), and lacy white dress whose front bow matched the groom's peach tie.

Imitating a 1930's mobster, he said, "Alright, peaches, you ready to get hitched?"

"Sputnik, before we go, play me something on the piano—a wedding song."

My husband had a similar philosophy about songwriting as I had about storywriting. He followed the late composer Robert Schuman's motto, "To send light into the darkness of men's hearts—such is the duty of the artist."

He sat on the bench and I sat beside him, while he played his own song, *You're the One the Stars Gaze At*, a song without words but I could hear its meaning. I rested my cheek against his shoulder. He smelled so good and clean and orangey and freshly shaved, and he looked so handsome in his nutmeg and peach suit. Watching his fingers turn wood into song, I was overwhelmed with love and admiration for the man whose pulse beat hard and strong under the ghastly numbers marked on his arm, letting his family's homeland sing on his piano named Warsaw.

"Sputnik, I want that beautiful song to play on my music box."

"It was written for you."

He moved his hands from the piano to his wife. "Now take off your clothes, Lumi. Every last bit of clothing."

"That doesn't usually happen until *after* the wedding."

We made love at the piano, letting the rhythm of our loving write a song. I can't imagine what the other tenants thought was going on in our apartment—was a hurricane pounding on the piano? When the music finally had its crescendo then a slowing to quietness, I felt vulnerable and female and pretty in my nakedness against his suit and strength and masculinity.

"Sputnik, I'll have nine babies if that's what you want."

After making the song, we drove to Adelia, so I could turn in my intent to withdraw from college.

Sputnik asked, "Are you still going to have nine babies?"

I glared at him.

"Peppermint, I should make you honor these promises you make to me post-lovemaking. I'm still waiting for Dodger Stadium." He started laughing.

"I never offered you that."

"Ah, yeah, you did! 'Gurshum, I'll get you the stadium where the Dodgers play.'"

"I don't even like you."

"Apparently enough to buy me Dodgers Stadium!" That was so funny to him. "I'm still waiting to be offered a trip to Mars."

I held up my fist. "Your trip to Mars will come courtesy of this!"

He tried to grab my hand, but I playfully kept evading him. "Bring that little hand over here and get your fill of some Hebrew architecture."

At Adelia, Sputnik pulled the Corvette into the mostly empty parking lot outside the administration building. "Are you sure?" he asked.

"Yes, yes, yes, I'm absolutely sure!"

I had hoped to encounter the sourpuss advisor just to say, "I did so well in Professor Blagonravov's class, he married me," but few were working during the holidays, a few mistreated ones on the janitorial staff, so we left the withdrawal form in an office drop box. Now the professor and I were free and clear to get married publicly.

Back in the car, still warm from the heater, he said, "Do you want to do something frisky?"

"Maybe. What do you have in mind?"

"Remember the first day you came to my office." He pulled into Goldell. "I had this fantasy…"

By that morning, we had made love 11 ½ times. The half being because we were interrupted by a knock on his office door.

"Professor, are you in?"

We had to bury our faces against each other's shoulders to keep laughter from bursting out.

Gladys was at the door, so we hurriedly buttoned up, and I watched how quickly my husband could change into the serious professor costume.

He opened the door and said, "Hi, Gladys."

"I saw your light on and thought to myself, he can't be working?"

"Well, don't tell me they're making you work on the holidays."

"It's okie-dokie," she said, holding a new and improved mop, which Sputnik had lobbied to get.

"I want to thank you again for the fruitcake," he said. "It was superb." He was not just being nice, he actually liked fruitcake, a dessert which Bubbe once made.

Gladys curiously inspected the scene: the blushing young woman, the disheveled couch, Sputnik's shirttail sticking out from his pants.

"My wife and I were doing some research for my trip to Geneva." That involved removing his shirt?

"Your wife?" she asked as surprised as if she had learned the mop could talk.

I smiled until I realized Gladys was not as surprised as she was *heartbroken*. She was in love with him. Why had I not seen that on first sight? Too absorbed in my own feelings? All my life I had been upset that no one had seen me as a love interest, never had I elicited jealousy from another girl's confidence, no girl had ever viewed me as a threat around her boyfriend, and I had done the exact same degrading thing to the janitor: I had not been jealous of her being around Sputnik, because I had not seen her as a possible suitor for him just because of her looks.

She had beamed, realizing he was working too, two lonely ones with nowhere to be on the holidays, and maybe she could have shared a small conversation with him, maybe even a slice of fruitcake, which she had lovingly made for him. All she had for happiness was her fantasy of him and now her fantasy was ruined. And the saddest part was the handsome young professor had not married a bombshell, he had married me, and now she blamed their inability to be together on her age, and she cursed the universe for not letting her have been born later. Oblivious Sputnik kept going on about how happy we were, how great I was, and I wished he would stop, because each word was wounding her heart and prolonging her moment in the fool's spotlight. I couldn't bear it, so I said, "Gershom, if we don't hurry, we'll never make our way through all that traffic." She seemed relieved to have an excuse to escape, down a lonesome hall, where she could at least ache in private. As we left the office and he locked the door, I knew that hurt her too, being locked out of the only world where she could know him.

Outside the building, Sputnik looked around for anymore interrupters and said, "Let's go to the garden and finish what we were doing."

"No, if you got caught, you'd get fired."

"Well, my car's parked over there, Ms. ---, so how about you earn your 'A'?"

"Sputnik, stop it." I wanted to cry for everyone not in love and for those in love without reciprocation. I wondered what she loved about him. He was handsome and brilliant, but I sensed what she loved was how he treated her like a Lady, like a human being who deserved kindness.

"What's the matter?" he asked. "You're not going to throw coffee beads at me, are you?"

"Can't you see she's in love with you?"

"Who?" he asked, looking around as if expecting the French professor to be walking by.

"Gladys."

His expression said, "That's absurd. She's the grandmotherly type."

"Don't be such a chauvinist. A grandmother has the title mother because of lovemaking. Just because a woman's older doesn't mean she no longer has passionate desires. Age doesn't erase those feelings in men or women. Everything we've done on our honeymoon, she wishes she could do with you."

He was visibly embarrassed. "I didn't mean to hurt her feelings."

"I know, neither did I, but we did. We have to help her find her soul's mate."

"Help her find her soul's mate? There are billions of people on Earth! What are the chances—"

"If we're going to believe in soulmates, we must believe that fate wouldn't write soulmates so far apart from each other, they could never meet at the time they're supposed to meet."

"Who's to say it's the right time for her?"

"We don't know for certain, but we should at least try."

"When did we become Cupid?"

"When we were blessed with being united. Shouldn't that blessing be contributed forward? When Cupid nips a lover that fortunate lover should take the arrow and nip another, so the favor of love keeps getting passed on."

The scientist thought about it pragmatically. "Then what would Cupid do?"

"He'd make sure we nipped the right hearts at the right time. Do you know anyone who would be good for her?"

We both said at the same time, "The Widow Hershel!"

"His wife was a petite little number like Gladys. I'm sure Hershel and Gladys are two halves of the same fruitcake."

"Great! But the last thing she wants is to be around you and me together, so we can't invite her out as a couple. We'll have to devise a plan to get her and Hershel in the same room together."

"Cupid's helper—that's the profession you were destined to have."

"Then you should be happy because that profession pays in satisfaction, not money."

"Cupid's helper and reindeer caretaker—you were written by Father Christmas."

We drove to the county clerk's office on Willoughby and paid our nickel to the parking meter for twenty-four minutes of wedding time.

The room had the non-temperature void ambiance of all bureaucratic offices. A drinking fountain was by the glass doors, maybe for anyone who needed to clear their throat of nervousness.

We decided to opt for the "$10 walk-in express marriage ceremony," instead of the $20 chapel ceremony, since the "chapel" was nothing more than a garden arbor set up by a brick wall with a poorly done backdrop of the ocean behind it.

"That's not even realistic," Sputnik whispered. "Why are those seahorses and starfishes so huge?"

I whispered back, "The seahorses and starfishes are the least of the backdrop's problems. Who gets married under water?"

"Around seahorses and starfishes."

"With an arbor at the bottom of the ocean."

We looked at each other at the same time—we do! The whole set-up was just kooky enough for us; would have been perfect had the backdrop been outer space.

We ended our whispering and smiled, as we walked up to a bank-like service window. The woman behind the glass had as much romance in her voice as a worker taking coins on the subway. She was staring too hard at Sputnik to notice my face. "Hey, aren't you somebody?" she asked.

He shook his head and continued to fill out paperwork.

"Yeah, I seen you on TV, didn't I?"

He eyed me to say, "I shouldn't have worn the same suit I wore on television."

I couldn't believe the outdoorsman had worn a *peach* shirt on TV.

"He plays for the Brooklyn Dodgers," I said.

"Nah, that ain't it," she corrected. "Blagonravov, yeah, I saw you on the TV, talking about planets and all that weird space stuff, a real pip." If he had been a movie star, she might have asked for an autograph, but science was not her thing. "If you want a picture of the ceremony, you have to buy the deluxe package. Being a TV star, that shouldn't set you back too much."

"Deluxe it up," Sputnik said, goofier than usual, but I could tell he felt bad for not having Mr. Benny, his "wingman," as his best man.

After we paid, the woman looked past us and shouted, "Next!"

We were married by the County Deputy Marriage Commissioner, who we first thought was actually Edmund Gwenn, Santa Claus from *A Miracle on 34th Street*, but he had no holiday cheer. "Kiss the bride," he said like "Sign here."

We couldn't wait to get out of there and as soon as we were outside by the parking meter, we started laughing, so much so, Sputnik put his hand on the meter to keep from doubling over with laughter.

"Brooklyn Dodgers, eh?"

I shrugged.

"They haven't been the *Brooklyn* Dodgers since '57."

"I meant *our* Brooklyn Dodgers, sir, the team we're currently trying to create." I had not actually meant that at all; I was just trying to cover up my blunder.

"I can't believe I just married a girl who doesn't know the Dodgers are no longer with Brooklyn."

"I can't believe I married someone who talks about 'that weird space stuff.'"

"You're 'a real pip.'" That would be said at least a dozen more times that afternoon to make us laugh.

In sunlight, we looked at the 8x10 photo of our wedding kiss "under the sea." We both agreed that was our gift to each other that day.

"Alright, Mrs. Blagonravov, what do you want to do now?"

"I say we put more coins in the meter and write all the courtship sentences we've both been deprived of for a lifetime."

"Yeah, but first, let's go share the good news with Ben."

Mr. Benny's Hobby Hut, a two-story shingled cottage one could imagine on the New England coastline, had colorful kites in the windows and a big gumball dispenser by the half-glass wooden door. Attached to the gable roof was an open parachute, which made the shop appear as if it had landed on Earth from the sky. Locals and tourists were drawn to the eye-catching attraction, both a kid's and a kid-at-heart's dream: doll houses, kite kits, model airplanes hanging from the ceiling and swaying every time the door opened, die cast cars shining on shelves, big jars of candies, tubs of green plastic Army men, and a large model train in the center of the room, the steam engine going around and around mini snow-capped mountains and making "hoot-hoot" whistles. Like Mr. Benny, the Hut was all about fun. "Leave your age outside," as the sign suggested. A self-serve snack stand offered fountains of purple, orange, and red soda pop and nacho cheese for making nachos, alongside the kinds of candies found in movie theater concession stands (boxes of Junior Mints, Mr. Goodyum candy bars, and gummy bears, etcetera), and small cheese pizzas were on display in a food warmer, so inside it smelled like a candy store mixed with a movie theater. Upstairs had long tables for anyone who wanted to build their kite or model plane in the shoppe, alongside their snacks and with Mr. Benny's expert assistance.

Behind the counter, Mr. Benny was in his conductor cap and tinkering with some kind of something (engine part?).

"Guess who you're looking at, Old Boy," Sputnik belted out.

"A cocky nitwit who thinks he's a better pilot than he is."

"No, a *married* cocky nitwit who is a better pilot than you."

"Are you nuts?" Mr. Benny asked me with his usual warm-as-cartoons smile.

Sputnik said as way of explanation, or apology, "It was spur of the moment." "That's why you weren't asked to be best man," Sput was saying.

Mr. Benny chuckled, "You know there's love then there's what you two have. Which is sickening."

Sputnik said to his wife, "Do you mind if us menfolk have a private talk upstairs?"

No, I didn't mind, but I was curious what they were talking about.

When they came back downstairs, the "old boy" gave us both big hugs, said we probably weren't much in the mood for company or chitchat, and offered us two kites "on the house." No wonder he was our friend—he saw kite flying as a suitable activity for a honeymoon. "Take some Starbursts and Swedish Fish too." We loved our Mr. Benny.

After putting kites and candies in the car's trunk, Sputnik and I strolled sidewalks arm and arm in chilly holiday air, writing more beautiful and fun sentences into life, while the "church bell" rang rang rang.

We had lunch at Bacio Dolce, a romantic Italian restaurant with candlelit tables and singing waiters. Even though we were offered the finest Cosimo Wine to complement our pasta, we opted for soft drinks.

After lunch and being serenaded with *O sole mio*, we wanted to get presents for each other for the next day but doing so involved being separated. Sputnik did not like that idea.

I told him gently, "Sput, you're letting the Nazis—you're letting the world—imprison another woman you love. I know you don't want to. I love that you're protective and supportive, but there's a time to stand behind someone when they're on a swing to help them gain lift off and a time to step back and let them fly. I know this is difficult for you, but we can reach this destination in small steps. When the big clock says 12:30, we'll meet right back here. That's only thirty minutes apart. Nothing's going to happen to me."

He considered the suggestion and nodded, not happy, but not wanting to imprison my freedom.

The thirty minutes apart were hard for me too; I understood how Moon-Moon must have felt the afternoon she let me cry and cry, unable to find her during hide-n-go-seek, forcing me to be brave. I arrived back at our meeting spot three minutes late (the store's checkout had been busy), and although Sputnik was checking his watch against the town square clock and he looked panicked (the expression he must have had on the afternoon his little sister had gone missing), he only said, "Hi, beautiful." We put our giftbags in the car's trunk and kept the gifts a secret, although I felt the best gifts had just been exchanged.

After sidewalk strolling, window shopping, store perusing, and seeing an old silent film starring Glenda Goodall, we went to the busy amusement park, where we bumped each other with bumper cars, survived the haunted house, played Skeeball, ate candy apples and French fries and fried Fudgy Mounds, received a fortune from a Volztar fortune teller machine, had our palms read by a peculiar fella named Tag, and Sput won a teddy bear for me from a baseball game.

On the carousel that night, swirling in lights and stars, he said very sweetly, "You're the main reason I enjoy being alive."

Afterwards, we gathered belongings from our downtown apartment and moved them into our woodland camper. Even though we didn't have many material items, the trailer was fairly cramped, the closet full, but I loved seeing his clothes next to mine (even though they did mess up the pristine wardrobe symmetry). I liked his Dodgers cap on the coat rack, his ships in bottles by the music boxes, his typewriter beside mine and both taking up the entire table, his sailing print awaiting space on the wall, and his NASA lanyard clipped to a magnet stuck on the refrigerator beside our wedding photo.

Around midnight, we capped the night at Stormy & Strobe. The jukebox played *Run Rudolph Run*, and teens boogeyed. The professor did not seem uncomfortable at the possibility of encountering one of his students; he held my hand and navigated us against a sea of strangers to a booth by a window.

My newly minted husband drank a candy cane malt, and I sipped a mint hot chocolate, while we both enjoyed chocolate yule log.

Through the wintry window, we watched the moon share its lifelong dance with Earth.

"Did you know," I asked, "the yule log is a specially picked log put on the hearth and it symbolizes emblems of divine light?"

"You're divine light. Ah, what a disappointment life has been, just a series of sad events and disappointments, but you, you make up for it. God, just one moment with you, just one, just one as simple as us sitting at this soda shop together late night, makes up for all the bad."

We stayed in the malt shop until two a.m., talking about love and life and Earth and aliens and astrology and ESP, creating the

631

greatest conversations of our lives and following the song's advice: we were having ourselves a merry little Christmas.

We made a toast, "To the other half of my fruitcake."

Sorghum

Non-rushed on Christmas Eve and the sixth night of

Hanukkah, we camped on our own land in Sputnik's tent with a sky roof and oil lantern. The tent, the colors of snow and pine needles, was durable and roomy, the same tent he had used during his tundra research. It had two compartments ("bedroom" and "research station"), plus "windows." In the "bedroom," we undressed after a long fulfilling afternoon.

Aside from a short trip to the market for groceries (for many ingredients for many recipes for Sput to try), we had dedicated the entire day to hiking. With binoculars and camera, we explored our own Adirondack, "rugging it" with thermoses of hot drinks and "entire meals in a biscuit," the way Bubbe had made (fried eggs, cheddar cheese, apple butter, and my own addition: veggie sausage, made by the noble company Planty O' Yum). Listening to owls hoot and tree trunks creak in wind (the way trees "yawned" and "stretched their backs"), we had gone farther into the woodland than we had ever gone before, and made friends with Jack Pine and Balsam Fir and Sugar Maple. Through the safe distance provided by binoculars, we had observed up-close by the stream an eastern coyote that looked like a wolf right there in our woods—what a picture!

I was readying to get into the sleeping bag with Sput, who was settling into the flannel cocoon and chewing a pink Starburst, and I said, "Fifty years from now, we'll renew our wedding vows in those lovely woods, that is if you still want to marry me."

"You better come here, Lady, and get as close to me as possible in case that coyote comes around."

"Mmm, much better," I said, as close as possible.

After the hike, we had driven our blue truck (now named Jack Pine) to a tiny country market to get a jar of molasses and a jar of sorghum, so the Brooklyn boy could taste their differences. We had a pie dish full of homemade biscuits and two gift bags we were waiting to share, but first...

The Earth was cold, but our naked bodies warmed each other, the warmth of our lovemaking transforming the sleeping bag into a sauna.

Afterwards, late-night air entered the tent from somewhere (even though the outdoorsman claimed the tent was "windproof"), and from cold air coming into contact with our warm entwined bodies, a fog settled across us. I lay in the dew across his chest hair, where lantern light shined through the forest of black brush. We were both sleepy awake after lovesailing that had fluttered the tent's fabric.

For a Hanukkah/Christmas Eve gift, I gave him a Tom and Jerry lapel pin, which I made land like an airplane on his damp hairy stomach.

"Perfect landing," he said.

"I'm nervous about our trip to Geneva."

He pinned Tom & Jerry on the sleeping bag. "Don't tell me I married a girl scared of airplanes?"

"No, I'm ready to be an aeronaut like my dear husband, but I'm scared of my debut as your wife, being around your colleagues, wondering if I'm good enough to be the girl on your arm, hoping I can help you get this peace treaty signed."

"First off, I care about you more than I care about my colleagues or the peace treaty. Second, you've already been around my colleagues. They're all nerds."

"Brad isn't a nerd."

"No, he's an airhead."

"Ooh, you love him like he was the little brother you never had."

"Eeee, the annoying little pest, perhaps. Here," Sput said, handing me my gift: beautiful shoes that looked like Dorothy's ruby red slippers minus the high heels. "I was searching for Cinderella's glass slippers when I saw these in a store's window and felt them calling to me. They said: 'We're perfect for your wife.' Perhaps you can wear them for New Year's Eve, and we'll fly away to Oz."

"I adore them!"

He said with a mischievous smile, getting ready to pull something else from the gift bag, "I've fulfilled your professor fantasy…"

"A fantasy you shared in."

"And your Knight fantasy…"

"Another shared fantasy."

"And your Joan of Arc fantasy."

"That was *your* fantasy, sir."

"And now…can you believe I found this in Biskatine?" He held up a black kippah.

"Isn't that worn to show reverence for God?"

"We will be showing reverence for God."

"Ooh, Sputnik, we're both depraved and on Christmas Eve and Hanukkah too."

Afterwards, he put the kippah on my head.

"Don't do that. It's disrespectful."

"Why? A woman can wear a kippah."

"I'm Christian."

"I've seen Christian women wear kippahs when in a synagogue. May I wear your cross necklace?"

"If you want."

He took off my necklace and put it on, beside the Star of David. "Now, let's switch roles. I'll be the good Christian boy, or bad Christian boy, and you'll be the good Jewish girl, and we just can't help ourselves."

My soulmate and I could not get enough of each other in any role.

In the last hours of Christmas Eve, wrapped up together in his sleeping bag, the nightsky cradling us, I alternated between feeding him biscuits with molasses and biscuits with sorghum.

"Ooh to live in a scene from Heaven—how fortunate are we two lovebirds!" I swooned. "People would say we're crazy about each other, but being in love is not crazy; not being in love is crazy. It's utter madness to be in a world of love and never partake of its magic; that's like being in a town of chocolate and eating only sauerkraut."

He was done with biscuits; he wanted his wife, who he held tightly.

"When I die, I want to go to your arms," I said, quoting Sidereus Sterling.

"If anything happens to me, I have a life insurance policy, which I've already put in your name. I had a few distant cousins in Poland, who were the beneficiaries, but they're doing alright now."

"Please don't start that morbid talk again, Sput. Nothing's going to happen to you. You're a young brilliant successful man in the prime of his genius."

A few cousins in Poland? Maybe I could talk to them about finding mementos for Sputnik.

"I just want you to know you won't be alone financially, Peppermint. If you're frugal, which I know you are, the money can sustain you for a lifetime, particularly since you own this land and don't need money for much. You'll even have enough to get a yearly new wardrobe. You'll get royalties from *Melt & Malt* and my books as well, but that won't make you rich. I've talked with Ben and it's all set for him to take care you if I die."

"I'm not a child. I'm your wife. You don't put me under the care of a Godhusband once you die. I'll thank you and Mr. Benny not to make plans for my future without consulting me."

"You can't do handyman tasks. Ben can. He's a good man, you know that. I just want him to check on you, out here all alone. And if you want to fall in love again, you have my blessing, although I'll haunt the peace out of any jack not good enough for you."

"I said stop being morbid. I won't let you write yet another bitter chapter in our honeymoon."

"And I want to be cremated. I must be. I must suffer the fate of the others."

"Sputnik, stop it." Was I losing him again?

"Promise me you'll have me cremated and you'll release me, because I don't want you holding onto my death and graying your story. Promise me."

As if in cahoots with my husband, a mourning dove pushed its head past the room's flap and walked in on tiny legs. The ominous incident spooked me.

"Don't doves sleep at night?" I whispered.

"Perhaps she's in mourning for her mate and looking for him."

Not finding who she was searching for, the dove left but stayed in my worrisome thoughts.

"Don't get gray, Peppermint. Tomorrow's your day: Christmas. I was just talking about a what-if scenario. Don't worry, I've no desire to leave your exceptionally sweet story. I can see us as two silver-haired lovebirds in our gazebo fifty years from now, having some cream cocoa and watching our dozen grandkids swim in the pond. Perhaps your Moon-Moon was right—we can be tested in another way."

"Sputnik, if you ever leave, I'm leaving too."

At first, he looked angry and serious then softened his face and said, "You have to stay here, angel, and keep making the world unique sweets for the holidays."

Milky Ways

WINTER NEVER SEEMED SO WARM AND SNUG... SNOW NEVER SEEMED SO CLEAN AND FRESH AND WHITE...

T he Earth was hushed that early Christmas morning.

In the tent, we woke up before the sun. The skylight displayed the Milky Way, aglow like ghosts. The lantern was barely burning so the fabric-walled room was mostly illuminated by the gleaming Milky stream of light.

"Merry Christmas," my husband whispered in our warm sleeping bag, while we both watched our galaxy, the delightful galaxy where I could feel his barely haired legs mingling with my legs. But even making love would have interrupted the holiness of the moment: using time to be awed by the Milky Way on Christmas morning.

We took a hot shower that felt very good after a wintry night in the tent. For breakfast, we had hot cider and hot skillet cooked doughnuts.

Our friends were still asleep (turtle, pug, and bunny snuggled on carpet in the den, and momma and baby cow cuddled in the barn), and the sky was still molasses, aside from the radiant lavender Milky Way, as we drove Jack Pine upstate to a small airport.

Mr. Benny's Warbler Port, a few warehouse-style hangars, was bordered by distant mountains, trees, and the nebula blue outline that traced distant objects in the early morning. Mr. Benny owned thousands of acres out there for parachuting and flight testing, or more like *landing* testing.

My husband's Christmas gift to me was a sunrise flight, and he said, "Your gift to me will be your awe."

Bundled in sturdy clothes, Sput and I walked a strip of tarmac, surrounded by smooth frosty grassland, where the air smelled of cold lake and airplane fuel. My husband loved it here, his favorite place to be after he had come back from the war (aside from Hank's and the majestic tundra). He pointed out the faraway straw-colored barn, where he had built his plane.

As the hangar's large door slowly lifted, so did my heart—seeing the familiar wheels, then the silver propellor, then the magnificent "spaceplane" that had first captured my heart in childhood. The silver symbols on the fuselage I had thought as a child were alien hieroglyphs were Hebrew letters that spelled "Snowflake" on his winter-white aeroplane.

He gave me his goggles and soft helmet, still in the cockpit, and he would wear Mr. Benny's goggles and helmet. The two men had once enjoyed flying together, but Sputnik had not been flying in a long while (his self-inflicted punishment had grown worse and worse over the years, the reason why he had not eaten pizza from Hank's in so long).

He ran his hand along the wing and said, "I hope I still know how to work this thing."

Boys.

"I'm only joking, Pep. I asked Ben to do a pre-flight inspection. I don't particularly like another man touching my Lady, but he's an honorable old boy."

"You asked that poor man to come up here during the holidays to inspect your plane?"

"He loves doing that. Anyway, she's good to go. Here, I want to show you something else."

Another hangar's door lifted, revealing an early invention of flight, an aeroplane that was basically a bucket with a dragonfly's long "tail" and paper-looking wings.

"That's one of Ben's planes. Isn't she something? Modeled after the Bleriot. Maybe your gent of a plane can be like this, my little Katie Stinson, or perhaps I should say Harriet Quimby since this looks more like her plane?"

"You're so much a nerd." I smiled, happy to have a nerd husband.

If one had viewed Sput's plane without its wings, its seating would have looked like a wooden kayak. Those wings made getting into the aeroplane a bit of a challenge, so I climbed up with Sput's help and got snug in the "ghost's seat" up front, a blanket around me.

I had only been on an airliner once, with the thieves, during one of those awful "family" summer vacations to a swampy dump called a "resort" that ended with Mr. Thief needing Pepto-Bismol and Mrs. Thief stuffing a suitcase with stolen hotel items. Usually we had driven, long awkward hours, to "vacations," and I had passed the time trying to see as many different birds from the backseat window as I could—birds capable of *flying away*, which I had not been able to do.

But now…aside from the seat beneath me, I was at one with the sky, the plane's wings like my own wings, and I felt what birds felt in flight—f r e e d o m! I floated even more gently than a bird. Like a butterfly. Like breeze itself. I was a soul in that moment. Although the open cockpit was heavy with noise and cold, I was too awed by the view, all around me, to notice coldness or engine gurgle. I was flying!!! Feeling the strong wind blowing us around added to the magnificent sensation of flight! Even the spinning propeller was fascinating, and the dawn sky was so golden and red, we felt we were flying through the heart of Christmas. The sun, striped in bands of varying brightness, looked like a planet, like a Jupiter, on the horizon. I kept looking back at Sput, giving him his gift over and over—awe, awe, **awe** written all over my face!

I tried to snap photos as we flew over snow-capped mountains, like the ones from Mr. Benny's model train world, and geese lakes and frozen ponds where ducks waddled, and coastal towns just waking up to Christmas morn'.

We flew all the way to the gushing sea and a lighthouse that looked like a candy cane. Then we circled around and flew home to Stargust Continued, where we parked our sweet plane friend in the creamy field that would be her home. We thanked her for the gentle flight and promised her, "Many more adventures to come."

We enjoyed late-morning cream cocoa in our tranquil gazebo, a special holiday edition with frosted Christmas brownies and mint cocoa. We gave our friends extra playtime. And we called Mr. Benny (wished him Happy Hanukkah) and Gladys (who was very warmed by Professor Blagonravov calling her) and Hershel and Brad and Francine and wished them all good cheer, and I even called the thieves who were shocked by my wishing them happy anything. We spent the rest of the afternoon back in the cockpit, my husband teaching me how to fly, until a candlelit Christmas dinner.

We had not made love all day, yet we were sailing.

On Christmas night and the seventh night of Hanukkah, our sleeping bag was open atop Earth, our spot for watching the once-in-a-lifetime comet, a holiday gift to the inhabitants of Earth. I felt like one of the three wisemen seeing the Star of Bethlehem.

Sitting cross-legged on the sleeping bag, Sputnik looked through binoculars, as I set up the camera on tripod to get long exposure shots of the comet.

Playfully, I turned the camera toward my husband. "There's nothing in the universe that dazzles me more than you do. To my heart, the biggest charm of the Milky Way comes from you being a part of it."

"My little poetess."

"Sputty, you know what just came to me, while standing here freezing? Our entire story, aside from the brief moment you landed in the summertime field, has been set in cold weather!"

"We made our own summers." He pulled the binoculars halfway down his face and winked.

"You could point a telescope anywhere in the universe tonight and you wouldn't receive a signal as bright as the moment we're in right now."

"It could get brighter." Time to make another summer.

My heart went supernova as the comet lit up our sky and I lost contact with this world. I was engulfed in a bright bright star, the Lovemaking Star, the star that appears for two souls in love when they make love. I felt merged with that special star.

After the trembling subsided, I lay against Gersh's sweaty after-love-making chest, his heart beating hard, everything else soft and mellow. I felt out of body, floating in nighttime breeze, as light and perfect as I had felt during flight. I savored the aurora of our lovemaking.

I said, "Our bodies are made of starstuff but our souls are made of lovestuff. Both are vibrating pleasantly."

My husband said tenderly, "Looking at tonight's sky, I'm convinced God is married—only a lover could have made those stars."

"Who is God married to?"

"An angel."

I agreed, "Only a God in love could have created the nightsky."

Holding each other beneath blanket, we ate a snack of Milky Way candy bars to give us energy for more glorious hours.

Then the stars began to land all across us...no, something even more fantastical than stars:

"The snowflakes," Gershom said, sitting up like a man beholding a real angel in the sky. "Remember I told you, she asked me to never stop seeing the snowflakes." He lay the unfinished candy bar on the sleeping bag, too overwhelmed to eat. "But I couldn't see them. I haven't been able to see snowflakes since my time with her. Now I can see them." With binoculars, he observed snowflakes like a man observing stars with a telescope, confirming in close-up details what he thought he saw he was truly seeing. "I see the snowflakes!"

The boy, who had survived the world's war, stood up, as nude as he was when he first entered this world, and he began jumping up and down like a blind man whose sight had suddenly been restored.

Now I knew why My Wanderer above the sea, battered by violent cold winds, was perched tall atop the isolating stone: he was looking for the snowflakes.

Blanket around me, I joined in the celebration.

"I don't see ashes, Lumi, I see snowflakes!" He was truly saying, "I've been forgiven! I've been Forgiven!" For whatever sins he thought he had committed.

I swaddled my husband in the blanket with me and told him of the familiar owl-ish woodland I had longed for in childhood, how the snowflakes this night reminded me of its scenery. Gershom looked at me with complete love, like I was Dante's Beatrice becoming more beautiful the closer he got to God. Gersh told me how *she*, even in the death camp, had felt embraced by her beloved woodland, the color of owls, where she had often yearned and prayed for her soulmate. Hearing that extended the exclamation point in Write Thus!

Hugged by his forever love, "I see the snowflakes too," I said, just as surprised. My husband had transformed winter, the season which had brought me dread, into the season I would forever most anticipate.

I realized my momma had not been looking at the shed's gray walls when she had died—she had seen beyond the seams: she had been watching the snowflakes, just like Alina.

Icing

On the eighth day of Hanukkah, we flew kites in tranquil air, had nothing but buttercream cupcakes and hot cocoa for breakfast and buttercream cake with thick icing for lunch, and we strolled pastures with our cow friends who were mesmerized by the bright wings in the sky.

That night with all the candles lit on the menorah, we dined on eggplant parmesan and a salad that deserved to be called a garden.

After dinner, Sputnik sat in the den with his toolbox and built a crib, his Dodgers cap turned backward to keep sweat out of his eyes, his muscles taut in his T-shirt. I supplied him with a bottomless cup of cocoa and that evening's morsel: more buttercream cake (his cake paired with Neapolitan ice cream).

Since seeing the snowflakes, he was as serene as a "near-death" survivor who saw reality as peaceful. I knew this was the true Sputnik, who he had been as a boy, a starry-backdropped gentle bunny who had to become a tiger at a young age in this world's jungle story.

"I'll carve 'Maple' in Hebrew into the crib's wood," he said, hoping for a girl baby. (Sputnik had decided on Maple for our daughter's name, maple both sweet and natural, and his best friend as a kid had been a maple tree.) "Maple Joycelyn Elah Blagonravov"—now there was a name, a tribute to Bubbe and my momma whose name was Joycelyn.

"What if we have a boy first?" I asked from the kitchen.

Mr. Bunny hopped over to Sputnik, got in his lap. "Then you can come up with the spud-nik's name and I'll carve that."

"When did you become Secretary of Baby Naming?"

Mullybiski got in Sputnik's lap too. "Alright, guys, come on, I'm trying to work." Said without any of his usual austerity.

At the typewriter, while snowfall provided a lovely show outside the kitchen window, I built a story, *A Story Whose Soul Purpose is to Tell a Love Story*. I shared with my husband how I felt about writing, "Writing is the feeling of Christmas morning, the blank page like snow on the ground—endless possibilities for creation, gifting, and enchantment."

"That's how I feel about math."

Tomatoes, tomahtoes.

I typed the story's opening lines:

"I like symbolic stories. But in too many modern stories, metaphor is not utilized to illuminate but to inhibit—romantic love is used as a mere literary tool, to symbolize something 'more important,' as if love is too meritless to deserve its own story, which inhibits love from growing, blooming, and spreading from writer to page to reader. Well, this story is 'just' a love story, and if that subject is considered valueless, this story is more valuable than ever."

"What do you think of that, Professor?" I asked my husband, who was trying to build the crib while pug, bunny, and now turtle kept cooing at him for affection.

"Perfect. Keep reading it to me, please."

The story's characters were Peridot and Hoagy, and I took much inspiration from me and Sputnik to create them.

Olivine "Peridot" ("pair-uh-doe") Love was a twenty-year-old student, majoring in finding her soulmate. A soft petal of a heroine, Valentine's Day taken form, she considered herself a guardian of romance, who was being pursued relentlessly by enemies (skepticism, hate, ridicule). In heart, she was a giant guardian, but in body, she was a small guardian, about eye level with a mailbox, and the majority of her mass came from her breasts and hair. Aside from her bosom and red hair the shade of lava, she did not look like a fiery lover. Her face resembled a raccoon's: small, soft, her eyes so deeply set in shadows, one had to be close to her to see her eyes were green. While red hair and a buxom chest could have made her a bombshell, her huckleberry personality countered the sexiness.

Born in the clear stream of a waterfall, her first scents of the world were earthy water, Lilies of the Nile, and yes, blood and tears, so she was aware pain and beauty existed side by side in this story. The first sounds of Earth the baby heard were a tenderly flowing stream and her creators saying, "I love you." The first image she saw of this incredible planet, according to her mother, was her dad kissing her mom then kissing his baby's forehead. She felt embraced by love and her goal was to keep the Valentine-red bloodline going.

She did most of her childhood growing in a tree house. Not exactly a tree house. She didn't want a tree to carry the burden of a house on its branches, so she asked her dad to build a house *beside* a tree. Her parents, the town's eccentric lovebirds, lived in an adult version of a tree house. A fairytale home.

Her dad, Beau Love (he took his wife's prettier last name), wore thick eyeglasses, an even thicker mustache, and generic man clothes. He was not generic, however. He just didn't care about fashion. He cared about his daughter, his wife, music, and airplanes. He was an airplane mechanic for Mass Aircraft and pretty darn brave to take on the name Love around a group of macho mechanics. He was completely in love with Peridot's mother: Joan Love, a long-haired American folk singer/songwriter, a Midwest brunette "tumbleweed," soaking up sunlight.

At a peace rally, Joan Love's song was cut short by a police officer's bullet, which also ended her husband's life. (I thought of dear Cynthia and her parents.) Their love stayed alive in Joan's music and in her daughter.

Dr. Hoagland Nasir was a gray-haired professor, environmentalist, conservationist, wildlife photographer, animal behaviorist, and geologist who used all his skills and smarts for one sole life purpose: to care for Mother Earth.

Born over international waters, Hoagland considered himself a citizen of Earth.

His father, Akbar, a Pakistani American, had been a hard-eyed pragmatic anthropologist, killed by a tiger, and some said Akbar

649

had been cursed after removing a bouquet of flowers from an ancient tomb. Hoagland's mother, a bored white New Jersey housewife, had gotten swept into adventure with Akbar and right into the tiger's mouth too.

Sputnik thought that bit about the tiger was funny, so did I—a little humor always added good flavor to any story.

As a boy, Hoagland had to fend for himself. Hoagland's parents had treated kids like adults. They had not been loving. He had always felt like an orphan even with parents. Love might have completely passed him by and left him emotionless if not for the love of a baby elephant he had grown up with at a young age, when his parents had been on a dig stationed by a wildlife refuge.

"Human couples could learn a thing or two about romance from seahorses—they're monogamous, mate for life, do a dance before mating, and—the males bear the young!" Professor Hoagland Nasir said to a group of college students on the first day of class. When he talked, he tossed his hands like throwing baseballs left and right and every which way.

Olivine had signed up for the class because she had heard the professor's lectures were like being in the audience of a late-night talk show when an animal expert was the guest—many appearances by monkeys, birds, etcetera.

Dr. Nasir was a nice professor but guarded. Not flirty at all, he was shy and awkward, but his love of environment propelled him past shyness and forced him to teach new generations about the importance of caring for Earth. His voice was the most delicate part of him, a fragile voice made of glass. For a scientist, he was very spiritual and said with his glassy voice that science should have spirit to be any good.

The professor wore faded baggy jeans, faded saggy denim shirt, faded hiking boots, but his skin was tan—both the tan and fading had come from a lifetime spent outdoors. His chest was flat, his stomach soft, his arms thin, but he was the manliest man she had ever known, his integrity sturdy enough to stack one hundred

650

causes on. His neck was "old man" soft, the skin slightly beady from a lifetime spent in the sun, and she dreamed of giving him the hickeys he had never received in school. She thought he was handsome and charming, but for her, it was love at first smell. He smelled like dirt, cola, and pencil shavings. Frankly, he was a nerd, like her, a loner alone with books and notepads full of his own thoughts; he was used to living in tents and liked digging in dirt, searching for gemstones.

For him, it was *something* at first sound. Dr. Nasir was ill with Parkinson's, a secret to everyone, and the condition caused incontinence, which forced him to wear a diaper—when this diaper began to show through at the top back of his pants, a roar of laughter attacked him as viciously as a tiger. But the one girl, the redhead student in the first row, did not laugh. Seeing her warm eyes, he no longer heard the laughter, and he began teaching just for her.

During each class, their gazes wanted to be felt. Either hot gazes that felt capable of singing the skin or warm gazes that felt capable of softening the heart.

Their relationship progressed beyond gazes when she began visiting his office, asking questions about rocks and minerals. Hoagland never knew a human could be capable of the kind of pure love that animals had until he met Olivine. A friendship quickly developed over mutual interests and shared weirdness. She called him Hoagy, and he called her Peridot, because although olivine was a pretty mineral, peridot was a pure gemstone. But relationships were to him what shoelaces were to children—he just could not figure how to tie those things. She had to help.

On a field trip to a sacred grove, a virgin forest, while they ventured off from his other students, she proposed to him.

He said, "I'm dying."

She said, "I know." She still wanted to marry him.

The mountain climber said he had accomplished many feats but none as great as getting *her* to ask *him* for marriage—he was at the peak of success.

After their wedding in the virgin forest, the two lived in a canvas teepee on lush coastal land, where they raised two rescue hippos named Fred and Ginger after Fred Astaire and Ginger Rogers.

Peridot and Hoagy's backstory was interwoven in the short story, which centered around the newlyweds' only goal: to break the record for the number of times they could make love in twenty-four hours. To accomplish their goal, they ate homemade pistachio ice cream for energy, Hoagy's favorite, which melted quickly in their steamy tent, and while trying to reach their goal, the story's last sentence read, "They continued…"

I would send the story to publishers and agents.

After reading about Peridot and Hoagy, Sputnik said to me in bed, "You can't publish that."

"Why not?" I cuddled into my favorite sleep position against his chest.

"It's too spicy for you."

"When you're the muse, words get spicy. The characters are in love, and they're married, and the story is meant to make people feel all the goodness of romance, including its spiciness. But if you really disapprove, Captain, I won't publish it."

"No, no, you should, it's just…" He told me a few of the spiciest lines that did not have his approval. "I don't want everyone in the world reading my wife's thoughts and feelings about *that*."

"I'm flattered that you think everyone in the world would read my writing. If it would make you happier, I'll cut those lines."

"Well, alright." He kissed me, and it felt righteous to be kissed by the man who had just built our baby's crib. "I'm glad you never said Hoagy died."

"That's why I wrote the story in three sections—sunrise, sunset, and midnight—to show the budding of love, the deep night of love, and the mysterious midnight, all part of a day's cycle that keeps repeating over and over."

My husband put his arms around me and gave his newly minted wife the best compliment, "I don't know why I search the sky for messages from extraterrestrials, because aliens don't have any stories this good."

Butterscotch

W hen I was a child, a classmate said about me, "I wish

it would kill itself." If I had taken the bully's advice, I would have missed out on starring in this magnificent lovestory with Gershom.

We spent the vacation week hiking, bird watching, enjoying a hayride at the apple orchard, designing blueprints for our home, going on scenic flights, sampling recipes, making adventures, solving mysteries, and trying to figure out how to divvy the land between rescued reindeer farm, food pantry garden, baseball field, and animal sanctuary, and still preserve our pristine forest (we would not cut down and kill trees, especially since they had been there before us).

My husband made a few officious phone calls and found out I still owned Stargust Original, since it had belonged to my momma. So, we flew to my childhood land, whose landscape now looked like the shaggy disarray of coconut husk.

Holding my hand, the way I would hold his hand if we ever visited the sight of his tragedy, we walked past the old well house and all its memories, a vivid one of me trying to stubbornly convince Moon-Moon a flat path was the best setting for a lifestory.

My husband and I together went into the old nickel-gray shed, empty now, and I would have been overcome with grief, seeing ashes in the hearth, remembering Moon-Moon losing her life in winter, seeing the kitchen window and my momma not at it, but having Stargust Continued eased my pain.

Sputnik and I decided to turn Stargust Original into the animal sanctuary, in honor of my momma and the bunny who was killed there, and we would ask like-hearted individuals to volunteer to care for the refuge.

Leaving Stargust for the second time in life was trying, but knowing it still existed, a forever memory in my soul, kept my heart from freezing.

So far that week, my husband and I had not made love, and the old saying was true, "Absence makes the heart grow fonder." Beneath the wing of his airplane on the dusk of New Year's Eve, my husband made love to me in such an intense way I thought we were going to knock Earth out of its orbit and send us careening into the sun right at our feet on the horizon.

"I love you, I love you," he kept gifting, while we felt ourselves sliding right into the bright butterscotch, about to melt into each other.

After the unforgettable experience, we sat summertime sweaty on a blanket in winter, another blanket wrapped around us, his back against the plane's wheel, my back against his damp chest, his arms around me, his hands holding a butterscotch sundae, which he ate in large spoonsful.

"That one has to last us until Valentine's," my husband said, referring to our nine-times-a-year mandate.

"That might be too long a wait, sir." Ooh, Valentine's Day, I had never celebrated it with anyone.

"Now it's almost time for me to kiss at midnight the girl I'm meant to be with forever."

Mr. Benny's Hobby Hut was having a "shindig" for kids and parents alike to have family fun on New Year's Eve (Mr. Benny thought it unfair kids did not get to enjoy NYE celebrations). The free event had quite a few revelers, aged five and over, so Sputnik and I had to park "a million miles away," according to the scientist, usually not one for hyperbole. We parked the Studebaker outside Darioles (which was closed), the way Sputnik had always parked there in the past. We walked "a million miles" to Holly Lane in biting air.

I was decorated in ruby red slippers and red dress as shiny as a Christmas ornament, and Sputnik was garlanded in a tuxedo with red bowtie (ooh, he looked handsome, even if the outdoorsman was irritable about having to "doll up"). His fancy tuxedo's lapel was pinned with Tom & Jerry pin; our Mr. Benny would love that.

Upstairs in the Hobby Hut, the "bubbly" was sparkling fruit juice, the live music was provided by Mr. Benny at his old piano, the ball waiting to drop outside was a snowball, and everyone was twirling Tootsie Pops like sparklers, dancing to:

Hey, Snowflake, let's melt and malt

Mix some butterscotch nut with some Tennessee Waltz

Woo-be doo-be lovey koo-be

Shoo-be shoo-be up and groove me

Dancin' with my doll

In our jukebox dance hall

I was ecstatic hearing my favorite doo-wop/rock-n-roll song played on the piano by the song's singer and dancing with the song's unlikely writer—who would have guessed a mathematician had written those shoo-be shoo-be lyrics?

Mr. Benny threw in all sorts of nonsense phrases into the tune—"Shooo shoo shoo nah nah naaaaah"—dilating the song ten minutes beyond its two minutes on the record.

Oh, we got the jukebox jukebox, yeah, yeah,

We got the jukebox jukebox, yeah, yeah,

"Ben's ruining my song," Sputnik laughed, while twirling his wife.

The piano man tossed the song over to the audience, pointing a lollipop at different people, singling out the next one who would have to contribute lyrics, no matter how silly, like the little boy, "tipsy" on sparkling grape juice, who sang, "He got the root beer, root beer, yeah yeah."

Fireworks lit up the sky outside the windows and dynamite Kabooms came right into the room.

Thankfully, Mr. Benny did not single me out, and I knew this had been done out of kindness, not shunment—he respected I was shy. When he was about to single out Sputnik, his buddy shot a glare that demanded, "Don't even think about it, Old Boy."

"Boy, hidy, folks, this is fun!" Mr. Benny whooped. He talked to the audience, made jokes. The former World War 2 paratrooper turned the story of his time in a prisoner of war camp into *Abbott and Costello Meet the Nazi*, a safe enough version of the story for even kids to hear. He had me and my husband in stitches, as people used to say. Mr. Benny made people feel good, even though his own heart was a disaster scene (I sensed), and I wanted to play Cupid for him and some lucky other.

Sputnik and I had used this New Year opportunity as a chance to make a love connection between Hershel and Gladys; we had invited them both to the party. They were by the punch bowl, talking about cats and dogs and finally feeling understood by someone else. Sputnik and I smiled knowingly at each other—we were familiar with the look of love at first sight.

"Just think," my husband said directly into my ear, to keep his words from getting slung around by noise, "this time next year, we could be partying here with our little Maple."

"Or our little Spud-nik, Jr. But they might have to wait a year or two to attend a New Year's Eve party!"

"So, you're saying no more partying for a while?"

"No more partying for a while."

"That's alright, Lady, because I've never been one for loud parties."

At midnight, Sputnik and I kissed as a toast to our eternal love, while standing outside on jolly Holly Lane, as the New Year's snowball dropped in our cherished Biskatine, a town Sputnik and I had both decided we were in love with, especially since our Stargust Continued existed within its storybook pages.

Coffee

After the celebration, my husband chose to have an after-dinner soft drink, not coffee. Walter's Waffles and Colas, whose walls had the golden color of waffles, was not busy (no one there for New Year's Eve); the jukebox played *Do Wah Diddy Diddy*. We had asked Mr. Benny to join us but he had said he was "pooped."

Sputnik and I had an odd one-a.m. meal: Belgian waffles with blueberry syrup, spicy fries, and cherry colas. I did not like cold drinks, but Sputnik said, imitating what I had said about him learning how to let me have freedom, "To get you to your destination of loving ice cream, we have to take small steps. First step, enjoying an iced soft drink. My drink at Hank's was never a brew, jack, but cherry cola. Can you guess Mr. Benny's?"

"Hmmm…I can guess you were the only two jacks drinking *soft* drinks."

Sputnik laughed. "No, there were others. Hank's is a soda shop/pizza shack, not a bar. You've been there, you know it's a family joint."

"I didn't exactly take in the ambience. I got the pizza and vamoosed."

"Well, I was only teasing about it being a place for men to forget their wives. Fassbrause, that's Mr. Benny's drink, German apple beer without a bit of alcohol."

Fassbrause. That made us laugh. My husband and I tipsy on life.

While Sputnik doused his side of the French fry basket in Tabasco, I took a sip of cola. The sweet cherry did make up for the coldness of the drink's ice cubes.

"How 'bout," Sputnik said, when the French fry basket and drinks were empty, "we go home and make our own fireworks."

"Ooh, I thought we were going to wait until Valentine's, sir?"

The air was smoky misty and painfully cold as we walked dark Main Street to our car. Unlike New York City (where Brad and Francine were reveling), Biskatine did sleep. For New Year's Eve, the night was quiet, parties over, shops closed, lights off in apartments, fire escapes steely and silent; the stars looked farther away than they had ever looked.

Amidst heavy fog, I saw a faint light fly across the sky and exclaimed, "It's a bird, it's a plane, it's a Sputnik!"

"It's a shooting star." Something about the way he said that reminded me of Moon-Moon.

"It's not a rock, Mr. Scientist?"

"In your presence, it's a shooting star."

"Let's make wishes," I said.

"I already have my wish...the Dodgers won the World Series." He grinned.

"I think Gladys and Hershel have their wishes too. Now, we need to be Cupid for Mr. Benny."

"You're going to need Saturn's phonebook to find him a date," Sputnik laughed. "Ah, I love that old boy."

"Why don't you tell him that?"

"Guys don't say things like that to each other, not so openly anyway."

"I think that's ridiculous. You never know when you're going to lose someone and you might never get the chance to say 'I love you' to them again."

The mist was so bad, we could barely see the path before us, but far ahead on the opposite sidewalk was the café with the neon sign in the window, "Hot Coffee" pulsing in fog.

"I really hate coffee," I said, laughing. "The 'adultness' of it, the bitterness of it, the alleged rite of passage going from cocoa to coffee. Stomaching coffee just means your taste buds are dead."

"I hate coffee as well," he confessed.

"Then why do you drink it?"

I already knew the answer—to punish himself.

"Well, no more of that," he said. "From now on, it's cream cocoa with my Peppermint in the New Year."

Then...

661

We heard footsteps behind us, catching up to us. At first, I wanted to laugh—Ooh, the spooky clap-clap of footsteps on the sidewalk on a dark cold night in the city—and make a joke about The Shadow knowing the evils that lurk in the hearts of men, since nothing evil ever happened in Biskatine.

But Sputnik was not laughing. He gingerly looked behind him then looked back at me with his eyes trying to be calm for his wife. But my heart began beating as if I was in a lion's cage.

"Maybe he just wants to steal the Studebaker," I whispered.

"When I tell you to run," my husband said, like we were two soldiers on a battlefield, "you're going to run as fast as you can across the street over to the other sidewalk and keep going until you reach that diner. Don't look back."

"Sputnik, I can't, I won't leave you."

His eyes begged me, "Please don't make me watch another woman in my life be hurt."

He softly squeezed my hand and said, "You did make it a Nat King Cole song for me."

Then his hand broke its embrace with mine.

"Run!"

His shouting and my running disoriented the attacker, which gave me time to escape and Sputnik time to fight.

When I ran, the same feeling encased me that had encased me on the first morning Sputnik had come into the patisserie when I had gone upstairs and left him behind in cold darkness—a frost began freezing my core.

The blast of a firecracker exploding in the New Year almost shattered me.

In front of me were a myriad of diners, a mirage, due to tears in my eyes that would not fall but collected between the eyelids, as if waiting to find out if what had happened would be something that would make me cry.

662

I threw open the diner's door and looked out the window through the red evil letters of the neon sign. I could not see Sputnik anywhere. "Coffee," "Coffee," "Coffee," the sign kept flashing, telling people they could buy bitter coffee for warmth. My eyes desperately searched darkness for sight of my love, while a woman kept asking, "Hey, what's going on?"

"My husband's been attacked. Someone, please, call an ambulance. Please!" I pleaded with strangers before running back outside, and the citizens of this town seemed confused by the word "attacked"—attacked here in Biskatine?

I had to find him, in all that mist, and I didn't care if the attacker got me too.

I thought my husband was lying in a rain puddle until I realized blood was leaking from him, where his tuxedo was torn. On hard sidewalk, in cold smoke that looked like explosion from a bomb, he lay flat, staring at the nightsky and holding his hand against his right side.

The firecracker explosion had been a gun firing by someone who had chosen to ring in the New Year by shooting an innocent being.

My molasses-haired boy was suffering badly.

I sat beside him, gently, like the angel he had always hoped for, and I put my hand to his side, trying to keep him from losing any more blood but not wanting to cause him any pain.

"Sputnik," I said but he didn't look at me. "You saved me, Gersh. You saved the woman you loved."

I had once read that when people are dying, they lose their senses, but touch is the last to leave, so if he could not hear or see me, I would hold his hand and kiss his cheek, making sure a kiss was the lasting impression he had of this world.

He smiled, and if he was smiling, he was going to be okay, so I smiled too, X = Y.

I soothed, "We'll be back in Stargust Continued in no time, in our warm gingerbread camper spaceship, watching *Tom and Jerry* and enjoying cream cocoa."

Worried about my Valentine's red heart as always, he said, "Christ's values have never taken a sweeter form."

I kissed again and again his cheek as if my kisses could keep him alive.

With his dry humor, he laughed, "I'm glad the lovemaking was so good tonight, because it may have to last me eternity, Peppermint. '*O Captain, my Captain, It is some dream that on the deck, You've fallen cold and dead.*'" Blood came out with the words.

"Sputty, no, an ambulance will be here any second."

His eyes said he had to go, and this time when the aeronaut flew away, he would not come back. He had only been holding on, enduring the pain, to write one more sentence for me in our lovestory.

"Do you see it?" he asked, his hand palm up, displaying something. "I finally made it for you."

"Yes, I see it and it's the most beautiful snowflake I've ever seen," I lied to my husband. All I saw was blood in his hand losing its warmth to winter and an encroaching dark void filled with distant pinpoints of cold light.

In a setting I had never wanted to see again in my story—a cold hospital—I prayed with everything I am, "Please let him live." Of course, he would live. This was my lovestory and I would not let it end this way. We had just gotten married; we had so many sweet chapters to write: building our home, raising children… No one would be allowed to survive a Nazi death camp only to be killed by some punk on a sidewalk. If there was any Grand pen ultimately behind this story, my Sputnik would not die, not like this. The ending was too absurd. Meaningless. Gershom Blagonravov had too many important sentences left to write for lifekind. My God, he had an incredible destiny that could not be written out of existence by a madman who had barged into our lifestory from nowhere.

The woman in the diner that night had been one of the guests at Mr. Benny's party, and that was why she had kept asking, "What's going on?" She had called Mr. Benny, who now sat beside me and held me in the hospital waiting room, which was as inviting as a surgery ward.

"I can't live without him, Mr. Benny. I can't. I won't. I won't write another word."

Walking the long hall, the surgeon and his news kept getting nearer and nearer until the decision of whether my husband would live or die was right upon me. The surgeon's blank face showed me the rest of my life: blank pages.

"He lost too much blood," the physician explained.

"Then give him more," I demanded. "Give him mine."

"Miss," the surgeon said to me but looked at Mr. Benny, as if expecting the man to explain to the irrational woman that her husband could not be brought back to life. "We couldn't save him."

"All the life-saving equipment in this hospital and you couldn't save my husband?" The Lady stood up, ready to physically fight the entire crummy health industry. "Did you just give up? You get in there and do whatever it takes to save him, or I'll go back there and do it myself." I started to walk to wherever my husband was, but Mr. Benny held onto me. "No, he's not dead, Mr. Benny. He wants his angel to help him. He can still be saved. People can come back to life after ten minutes of death—I did! It'll be a miracle, you'll all see, it will be a miracle. Because this is a magical lovestory."

"Miss, I'm certain he was already dead by the time he was brought in. We tried to revive him. We really tried. I'm sorry." But the physician's face did not express "sorry;" he did not care at all.

Mr. Benny gently turned my face away from the cold doctor, and in Mr. Benny's soft brown eyes I saw compassion, the only glimmer of it left in the world's indifferent story.

The Earth felt wobbly, my life unsteady, so I crashed onto the chair like someone on stilts, hit by an unexpected blow and careening to the ground. But I was too upset to be moved like a piece of glass that had been hit hard and was just about to shatter, too fragile to be hauled. So, Mr. Benny sat by me and let me cry, but kept his arms around me to keep me from shattering completely.

The madman had blown to bits the world's largest snowflake, destroyed it in the world he had to live in too. I would later learn the lunatic had been bitter about not having love, so he had wanted to kill the two lovers who had what he did not and erase every lovestory from this planet and steal from me the conviction nothing bad ever happened in my storybook town.

The coldest cold I had ever felt seized me and would not let me out of its clutch.

I cried ferociously.

I cried for Sputnik. The unfairness of his death. I cried for the world who had lost the man whose goal was to make a peace treaty for everyone. I cried for our future that would not be written.

I had given the police a statement, just the facts about the felony, but they had not asked about the aftermath. When my husband died, all the lights went out inside me. That was not a crime in their lawbooks: the thievery of someone's inner light. In complete darkness, I literally could not see what to do. What was I supposed to make with my life now? I felt like the space explorer who went outside one night and discovered all the planets were gone. What purpose would an astronaut have in a world without stars and planets, in a world without a universe? Being with Sputnik had been my life's goal, and he was gone.

Without ink, a pen is pointless

Without you, I am the same

I wrote that on a hospital notepad. Mr. Benny put the poemlet in his breast pocket, patted it against his heart, as was his way: to be kind. But he was hurting too, I realized. He had just lost his best friend.

"New Year, what a lie," I said to Mr. Benny in between crying. We would never get another year with our Sputnik.

"Boy, hidy, those are some really snazzy shoes," he said to get me to smile.

Still wearing my husband's dried cold blood on my dress (a sentence I never thought would be penned in my lovestory), I looked at the ruby red slippers Sputnik had felt compelled to buy me for the holidays. Flat slippers. *Flat.* I always wore high heels, but I would not have been able to run away from the madman in high heels. Before I let the coincidence carry me away to someplace happier, a place where fate existed and guardian angels guarded us, I said inside, "So what? Maybe if I hadn't run away, you wouldn't have died. Maybe I could have saved you. Maybe I wanted to die with you. Can you ever forgive me for running away when you needed me most?"

Even though Sputnik had looked at peace with death and life, I could not stop crying, hoping the crying would shatter my body and release my soul. Instead I was drowning in the ice water, where I had almost drowned as a little girl, and there was no Moon-Moon to rescue me this time from frostbite.

I blacked out and was not greeted by the warm sunshine garden of Heaven.

I was in hell in a cold stiff hospital bed in a cold stiff body. I had been crying so fiercely, a blood vessel in my temple had burst, but the erupted vessel was not as shattering to me as the sight of blood flow from the menstrual cycle, which meant I was not pregnant. Being pregnant would have been the miracle I needed, the promise of another sweet chapter, *Yams*, titled after the food our baby would love, a part of Sputnik remaining alive, but it was not to be.

My Wicked Stepmother declared, "You should have stayed on your iceberg, never crossed paths with another, because when the other pulls away, he pulls you apart." Even referring to the world as Wicked Stepmother felt too storybook.

But this was my story's climax. I was only nineteen years old and already facing the decisive battle of my life. Nothing would ever be as tragic to my heart, or as challenging to my goal of holding onto the flower from Heaven, as the death of my soul's mate—this was the ultimate test of my character.

I was convinced there was no destiny. Humans used blank pages of life to write cruelty, nonsense, war, and ultimately, the story was purposeless. The entire *Do Wah Diddy Diddy* night had been absurd. French fries and talks of Fassbrause. Having to park so far away on the very street where the madman would be walking and being in his line of hateful sight at just the right time because my husband and I had chosen to have late-night colas and waffles; if we had just stayed inside for one more jukebox song, or ordered one more refill…

Unable to bear the heartbreaking pages of loss, not just loss of my love but loss of my faith, I blacked out again for days and stayed in the hospital for quite a while.

I couldn't bear to hear or see impersonal news coverage of the murder in Biskatine, the death of rocket scientist Gershom Blagonravov.

In cold wet nighttime wind, Mr. Benny drove me in his Model T back to Peppermint Lane, and it could have been charming, the antique car, the sweet driver, the sweet lane, but I was holding my husband's ashes in a metal urn. Engulfed in a loud ice storm, I stared at his silent tomb. My musical husband was now just ashes. I could not fathom where the songs were in those ashes? All those songs had been inside him—how could he be so quiet now?

The churlish wind kept trying to knock us off the road.

When I noticed the mailbox full of rejection letters—no one wanted my lovestory about Peridot and Hoagy and had told me so ASAP—more ice was added to the frost.

The first time I saw Stargust Continued I fell in love; now I hated the sight of it: our unfinished life together, rocks marking off where our house's foundation would have been laid in spring, and just acres and acres of sodden loneliness and the shadow of the gazebo where we would never sit again.

Mr. Benny walked with me, as we made our way into the camper. He held me like I was someone who had suffered a collision with a train, all parts of me injured and fragile. I was grateful for Mr. Benny's strength, capable of doing all the abysmal tedious tasks that occurred after someone died in this store of a world, such as *paying for* their ashes at the funeral home's counter. Mr. Benny had managed to get me to laugh about the situation. "You'd think you were buying a tub of butternut brickle or something. Geez. Here's your change and your best friend's remains. Have a nice day, come back again. I tell you what we'll do: we'll get Shom here an urn shaped like a rocket."

"The other half of my fruitcake would like that," I had said from the hospital bed before breaking to icy pieces, seeing my baseball boy reduced to the size of a small urn. "Please, Mr. Benny, tell me that's not really Sputnik in there."

"It's not *really* him."

"I could have saved him," I cried.

"You did, believe me."

Our friends, Mullybiski and Mr. Bunny and Pythagoras, seemed sad, somehow knowing Sputnik would not be coming home. Mr. Benny had been caring for them, while I had been incapacitated in the hospital. I sat on the floor and halfheartedly petted bunny and Mully and Pythag's head. I wondered if I would ever again be capable of caressing with "a heart whose love is innocent"?

I could not tolerate the sight of our baby's crib, which would never be filled with life. I could not bear seeing Sput's Dodgers cap on *our* coat rack, and *our* pretzel log cabin shellacked to last, and his NASA lanyard stuck to the refrigerator by *our* wedding photo. *Our* home was filled with all *our* things, even *our* old doughnut maker, just not him to share doughnuts with tomorrow morning.

I had to stomach too much coffee for the girl who preferred cocoa. I had not only lost my life but my belief in happily ever after. As a kid, I had believed bad things only happened in stories and now I wondered if magical things only happened in stories.

I knew Moon-Moon would say, "Write thus!" But I just couldn't. The pen to write life felt too heavy to lift. I did not have the strength. What was there to write anyway? I wrote lovestories and I no longer had my muse. My momma would have offered, "At least put some cream and sugar in the bitter coffee the world served you." After Moon-Moon's death, I had been able to look forward to the greatest chapter of my life—meeting my molasses-haired boy—but now I had nothing good to anticipate in this story.

Mr. Benny and I were as sad as funerals, listening to sleet; either it never stopped sleeting that night, or I was sleeting; there was a lot of ice and windows that exposed the downpours.

I was obsessed with Sputnik's urn. I grasped it against me. I would never let it go.

Mr. Benny noticed my attachment to the ashes, but he didn't say anything. He slept on the couch, keeping our friends company.

I carried my husband's urn to the bedroom, where I shut myself away, hoping I would suffer another burst blood vessel that would write The End for me.

Greeting me was a cold hollow Knight.

And games like Camelot we would never play again.

And endless ice.

Endless ice.

Endless freezing.

Endless, endless, endless life. I was only nineteen. The miserable story would just keep going on and on…

My husband had liked us to sleep in the twin bed, which had kept us right next to each other on cold nights and left me no choice but to use his chest as a pillow, where I had never been able to nuzzle close enough. His jacket was a sad substitute.

I could not escape the horrific image of blood coming out with his last words. I did not want to remember him that way. I tried to picture my sweet fella on the hayride, in the airplane, in the holiday décor store, but each time, I saw blood dripping from the lips I had loved to play with in a kiss.

Unable to find any comfort in the bed I had once felt was the most luxurious spot on Earth, I held his urn tightly and wished for a mystical sign from Sputnik that he was okay. I wanted to be haunted. Ooh to be haunted by his ghost. I'd just have a relationship with his ghost like *The Ghost and Mrs. Muir*.

"Touch me somehow, make the Knight move, turn on one of the music boxes, make me believe in my real father's magical universe again, please, Sputty."

I comforted myself believing his side of the bed felt warmer like the light of his spirit was lying next to me, and I could feel him telling me, "Thank you for writing love on my last page." And I thought I could smell his orange Brylcreem. But for the first time in my life, I was utterly skeptical. Of course, I smelled Brylcreem; his hair gel was in the bathroom. Even though Sputnik and I had enjoyed mystical experiences together, I began to doubt those too and chalk them up to coincidences.

I continued hugging his urn, because it was all I had of him; if I released him, he would truly be gone. I entertained similar *Tales of Tomorrow* thoughts I had in childhood: maybe Sputnik's DNA could be resurrected from the ashes, or maybe there was an alien who could revive his ashes, or maybe a time traveler would visit Earth and give us the secret to resurrecting the dead or be kind enough to let me go back in time to be with Sput again.

"But I don't deserve to be with you, do I? I didn't stand beside you, my sweet boy."

I needed to be close to him, so I sat in bed and looked through his belongings, his knickknacks and the sketchbooks he had kept during his barnstorming adventures. Going through his drawings of hayfields and barns and spaceships, I uncovered a journal entry, dated "one cold night in '57," the same year I had wished upon Sputnik to meet him. In need of someone to talk to, he had written about what had caused him guilt for the rest of his life:

Gershom had turned humans into ashes.

He had been one of the "helpers," one of the death camp Sonderkommandos. Not only that, the strong young man had also been chosen to help build gas chambers and crematoriums. Brick by brick he had built death chambers, bigger ones that could exterminate more people. And he had been "rewarded" with "nicer" barracks to keep him healthy enough to dispose of more and more victims. At first, he had told himself, "This war will be over soon, and it's important to stay alive, so that I can be with my family again. My mother and aunt need me." Eventually he had been walled off in the crematorium, where the boy had used his life to drag lifeless bodies to the ovens then dispose of ashes in a pond.

How difficult it must have been for him to re-love the woodland, which the Nazis had turned into a backdrop for murder. Every time he had been around a tree or a pond he must have felt the cold touch of ghosts, angry with him (his guilt would have imagined).

I knew people could force you to write terrible lines in your story, but until I read Sputnik's story, I never realized how terrible those things could be. It was always a choice, ultimately what we wrote, but I knew if Sputnik had ever been presented with the choice of dying or killing, he would have chosen death.

He wrote, "I never killed anyone but wasn't what I did just as terrible? Unnatural. The whole place was unnatural. The women guards were even crueler than the male guards. They weren't normal. The death camp wasn't a nightmare, because nightmares aren't real, and it felt more real than anything, the coldest kind of real that you never want to touch. I despise that phrase 'death camp' as if everyone there was just in a camp."

Gersh had been unable to believe he survived. Most helpers had been killed. But the young man had kept being sent to different prisons, where he had helped build, if not death chambers then weaponry, weapons for the Nazis, until he had been sent on a death march, and he had stayed on that march, emotionally, until the honeymoon night he saw the snowflakes again with me.

I realized every time Sputnik had built something lovely, he had been trying to make up for building arsenal for the Nazis.

He wrote, "And the darned thing is that cremation goes against Judaism, but Nazis cremated us by the millions, and I helped with those sins."

"Ooh, Sput." I hugged his urn, wishing I had never let him convince me to cremate him.

The Nazis had made him believe he could either chose to be in a world where God did not exist or in a world where God did exist and would enforce eternal damnation on him. He had believed that when he coughed, it was all the victims, all their suffering, inside of him—forcing him to suffer their suffocation.

"No, Sput, your lungs were damaged."

On the coldest day of his life, as he had shoved more bodies into the crematorium's oven, he had realized one of the women was his mother. She had been beaten severely before dying in the gas chamber. The porcelain woman, who had wanted to be a movie star to dazzle the hearts of all who would watch her on the big screen, had been shattered. Gersh had known in the piles of belongings stolen from victims was one of her hair ribbons that would never be pretty again but only a reminder of brutality. The young man had left the crematorium to volunteer to die, because he had been unable to turn his mother into ashes, then The Snowflake Gal had saved his life.

I understood now what Sputnik had meant about their being two choices for "what happened next?" in Alina's story. He had worried even telling me about his past as the ash maker would wither my heart, that the Nazis' evilness would destroy my ability to write the right ending to *The Snowflake* story.

Clutching his ashes against my crying heart, I saw in my mind my lifestory split into two stories, written in pencil, not permanent yet, each story with the same chapters up until this point but then diverging. The story that would be preserved in ink depended on what I decided to write next:

In one story, my heart did not get frostbitten after Sputnik's death. Instead, I decided to pull myself out of ice water, wrap myself in the warmth of Mr. Benny's friendship, and Write thus. In this more fragrant version of my story, I continued to write flowery love and goodness and happiness into the world's story, even though writing pink when I was filled with gray ink was difficult. In this prettier version of the story, I walked along springtime meadows, still seeing the flowers, and wondered if my husband had asked me to look at the snowflake before his death to make sure I could still see them? In this warmer form of my lifestory, I turned Stargust Original into an animal sanctuary for injured and abandoned animals, a refuge which kindred souls Hershel and Gladys tended, and I dedicated pages of Stargust Continued's story to a food pantry garden and Christmastown, a fantastic world where families stepped into a snow globe and saw actual reindeer (and moose). In this sweeter story, in Christmastown stood cabin-cozy Coleridge's Flowers, the Cupid of a sweet shoppe I had always wanted to nurture into being Cupid's Helper, a romantic place where falling in love was easy. In this melodic lifestory filled with music, at the survives-on-donations sweet shoppe, the "bratwurst," Ingrid, and her gentle giant brother, Mort, both unappreciated by Dariole, joined me, a collection of outcasts cast together to bring people sweets. Brad and Francine and other sweet-hearted Biskatine volunteers helped out in Christmastown. And musical Mr. Benny was always with me in Stargust Continued anytime I needed him, or he needed me, and he taught me to fly, and I promised, someday, with all the will in my heart, I would find the kind man's true love for him, since he had been responsible for bringing me my Sputty...

With my husband, my heart had been a hearth, but in the alternate version of my lifestory, the fire was out for so long, my heart gangrened. Frostbitten to the core, I turned *our* home into a tomb and *our* bed into a dwelling for crying. I squandered Stargust Continued—sentences,

673

paragraphs, chapters—on drowning myself in misery. I no longer *greeted* days but tried to avoid them by sleeping through them in dreamless voids. On my honeymoon, I had felt days were too short, but now days were too long; not every day was 24 hours, but some were much longer, dragged out by misery, even if clocks did not convey this. I had spent my youth dreaming of playing the *She* from Lord Byron's "She Walks in Beauty," and I had played her but too briefly for my dear Snowflake Physicist, but in this icy version of the story, I felt my heart change, felt it get cold and hard in its sheath of ice until it was ice throughout then decayed and foul, a heart whose love was no longer innocent. In this putrid form of my lifestory, walking amidst flowers whose beauty I could not see or smell, I wrote myself as The Frostbitten Widow, a bitter monster the world had always told me I should play, minus any hope for a poignant happy ending. Cloistered away from people, I condemned fantastical books I would have once loved like time travel stories. Love could not build a bridge between lovers separated by time, I cursed; if it could, I would have been back with my dear husband. *Romeo & Juliet!* Yes, they both died, but they died *together.* So, Shakespeare, there had been "a story of more woe." I became a curser of happy-ending love stories (The Frostbitten Widow saw *Romeo & Juliet's* ending as happy). As the headstone-gray pages of this tasteless lifestory, dying story, turned before my inner eyes, I was frightened. The pages kept getting grayer and colder with more overcast sentences like the tragic ones I had seen written in the lives of elderly people, mean lines that made them rain. As I got older in this noisy version of the story, people shouted and pelted "the monster" with more rocks: "Get off the road, old fool," honk honk honk. "Speed up, Lady!" they shouted at me, using the word "Lady" to mean "bitch," and the old-fashioned Lady Model was run off the modern road, but had nowhere to go, because the trailer had fallen apart and Stargust Continued was a reminder of a love that had not continued. So, the old Lady moved alone into a cold nursing home, a crumbly apartment held together with duct tape. After years of being pelted by rocks, in this ghastly form of lifestory, my appearance was that of someone who had suffered what felt—and looked—like thirteen billion years of misery, a misery as old as the very universe. "'Tis better to have loved and lost than never to have loved at all," and ooooh, how sweet the promise to the schoolgirl, but now the old bitter widow knew: such was not true, dear Tennyson. Losing love, I transformed into ice, exhausted of all light and warmth. Coleridge's Flower was only a dream. And I broke my promise to Moon-Moon—I wrote The End before the story's natural conclusion.

I slammed the cover, terrified by the future I had seen on the cold pages waiting to be written by choice in ink.

That freezing night, I had a dream about Sputnik. He was standing in front of the classroom. I was the only student, and I was so happy to see him again. He was not dressed like Professor Blagonravov but like the aviator, wearing his woodland colors and flight helmet but no goggles. I saw his beautiful eyes perfectly, just as I had seen them up close for the first time on the hayride. He looked so vivid, handsome and Brylcreemed, the way he had looked in life, but he did not have numbers tattooed on his arm, which I noticed because his sleeves were rolled up. "Ooh, Sput, you're okay!" But I could not leave my seat to rush over to hug him; I had a lesson to learn. I noticed pink snowflakes drawn on the chalkboard. Sputnik held up an eraser, the caramel-colored eraser I had used in algebra, about to wipe away the snowflakes, but I shouted, "Don't!" Then lesson learned, my molasses-haired aeronaut smiled as sweet as he had ever smiled, and he kneeled beside me, the way he had done on the first day of class to retrieve my fallen eraser, but he did not hand me the eraser this time—he handed me the snow globe I had given to him as a little girl. Light shined through old cloudy waters and I saw the angel inside.

I awoke with the same feeling I had experienced as a child after the Heavenly garden encounter—had that only been a dream? Whether I had truly visited with my dead husband or had received a message from my subconscious, I knew I had to pick up life's heavy pen and Write thus, for I did not want to play The Frostbitten Widow and spend the next fifty years in cold bitter gray gruel.

But I could not pretend to be happy either. I had to mourn. During a year of solid crying, experiencing every season and holiday without my husband, my beliefs sometimes boarded in blooming spring, when I remembered the garden, and sometimes in desolate winter, when I thought of Sputnik's death. Even though I could believe Gersh's untimely death had been some kind of test for me and him both, and I knew he had welcomed the opportunity to die for the woman he loved, and even though Sputnik and I had enjoyed many experiences too meaningful to be random and too miraculous to be coincidences, after my husband was murdered, my belief in a magical universe lost weight and felt as frail as it had when I had been taken away from Stargust as a child—how could something so cruel have been allowed to happen?

675

After the year of mourning, I finally chose to write the future with cream and sugar, but I did not know if I would ever recover the exclamation point of my life's story in devastation's aftermath. Believing the universe was magical was what had provided the exclamation point to "Write thus!"

How would I ever find an ingredient sweet enough in this bitter world to turn this iceblock into ice cream?

The answer came to me gently, inside myself: the ingredient is not of this world.

Autumn Ice Cream

T he New Year would ring in the anniversary of my heart

being a widow for fifty-two years.

Sputnik once said, "If you live long enough, you can see a once-in-a-lifetime-comet *twice*."

The comet that had lit our sky in 1965, on the evening when Sputnik had seen the snowflakes again, would be making another appearance this winter, and I wondered if I would be around to witness its second coming.

Many years earlier, Mr. Benny had built for me the sunshine cottage based on Sputnik's blueprints, but I preferred being in the old camper sometimes, around my memories of Sput, which warmed me even though the dying heater did not. At the Formica table where he had written our marriage contract, I looked out the morning window and saw three small crosses on Deer Hill, where my three friends (Mullybiski, Mr. Bunny, and Pythagoras) rested. The loss of Pythag and Mr. Bunny, like the deaths of Hershel and Gladys (who had become dear friends to me), had put icicles in my heart, but nothing had hurt as painfully as the death of my best friend Mullybiski, who I lost only one year after losing my husband. But Mr. Benny had comforted me with his blanket kind of kindness and warm humor, as always, a friendship we wrapped around our selves. I had always wanted to write a romantic lovestory but friendship lovestories were just as beautiful, just as light shined differently through ruby and diamond but equally lovely.

"I'll be joining you soon," I said to my friends, feeling my ink running thin. "Don't you worry," I soothed my seeing eye dog, Pumpkin, a friendly golden retriever whose sunshine fur I petted. "You'll be well taken care of when I leave. Our Stargust nation is citizened with those who love and respect animals."

I felt this character's The End was approaching after seventy-one chapters. My birth coincided with the blooming of flowers, and flowers wilted in winter. I was tired, a tired that could not be assuaged with a night's sleep, a tired that could only be satiated by eternal rest. Mr. Benny, in his ninety-ninth life chapter, had said I was much too young to be at the ending and what I was feeling was not impending death but ever-present lonesomeness.

Even though I had lost my reason for wanting to write this story at all (my soulmate), when I reviewed my lifestory, I was content I had still written passages I was proud of: helping Gladys train seeing eye dogs, which had granted me karma's payment of gaining a seeing eye dog companion when I had most needed the angel with paws; creating Christmastown that restored belief in Christmas magic in visitors; and starting the animal sanctuary, which I flew to Stargust often to visit; and nurturing the food pantry and the Cupid patisserie that offered free desserts, and love at first sight encounters, and the lesson to kids that generosity did still exist. I had tried to bring sunshine to the last gloomy days of the thieves, but Mr. Thief had only wondered if the silk roses I brought him in the hospital were "worth anything," and Mrs. Thief had seen my visit to her prison as cheap, but I had tried to warm them. Plus, I had once been a wife—some people had never been a character in a lovestory, not even for one blissful paragraph, so I had been fortunate to have starred in many sweet chapters of romance that I often read back.

But the story had been painful too—if I had ever awakened and there was no pain, I would have known I had stepped into someone else's life. I had chronic pain that doctors could not satisfactorily diagnose, because the pain's source would never be found in bloodwork and X-rays, which meant it did not exist, according to the doctors, regardless of what I was feeling. "You're just imagining pain," one had condescended. I had responded, "I'm imagining this pain the way you're imagining your coat is white. The coat is only white in your mind, due to the way your brain interprets the frequency of energy coming from the coat as white. Everything we see, feel, hear, taste is a product of our brain's imagination, and this pain is no more or less an imagining than we're solid when we're mostly empty space and energy. Don't think your smile of condescension changes the truth, because your ignorance is not trustworthy. I was married to a scientist. I know this world is an illusion fabricated by our senses. But as Einstein said, 'This is a persistent illusion,' and this pain is a painful one!"

I had also gone through breast cancer and all the IVs, tubes, and cuttings, but I had survived with Mr. Benny's help, although I had lost my "only pretty trait," my hair. And my chest was as flat as my back, where the female landscape had been tilled away by cancer (or by surgery, rather); the thick mass of scar tissue in place of breasts looked like a dirt mound reminder of the excavation of "the daisies" (as Sputnik had called them). My hair stolen by chemo and never given back, I dolled my dome in a blonde wig, Writing thus.

A year earlier, macular degeneration had stolen most of my sight. The world looked blurry as if viewed through water in a bottle, and beyond thirty feet, the world disappeared. Even within my sight, certain areas were erased by black voids that sometimes covered up people's faces and parts of the stars. What saddened me most was being unable to look clearly at my pictures of Sput and MullyB and Moon-Moon's meadow, but when I closed my eyes, I saw them, just like I could see my friends' crosses on the hill without my eyes, just like I would watch the twice-in-a-lifetime comet with a sense other than sight, if I survived long enough to do so.

Even though I had awakened this morning in a cheerful mood, thanks to a warm dream about Sputnik coming into the patisserie and telling me to meet him at the camper, I often felt the agony of guilt (for not having been able to save my husband). Plus, Mr. Benny was right—I was lonely. "Type R Loneliness," Mr. Benny had diagnosed, a type of lonely that could only be healed by romance, just like a Vitamin C deficiency could only be cured with Vitamin C, not Vitamin A or B or any other healthy vitamin. I was a Romantic dying from a romance deficiency.

Before I ran out of ink, I had to one) finish my thesis project, and two) before I wrote The End, I had to write The Beginning of the lovestory between Mr. Benny and Sammy. Then my story would be at its natural conclusion, and Moon-Moon would be proud of me for not writing The End even during all the suffering and sad chapters.

Although Sputnik had assumed Mr. Benny had no interest in romance, Sputnik had been unable to see the truth about his lonesome friend. Mr. Benny had been in love only once to a "cookie" named Zissy, who had survived a concentration camp. On a death march, cowardly Nazis had run away, scared of the encroaching Allies, and left a group of starved emaciated humans

680

by a barn in the middle of nowhere during icy winter. When Benny first saw Zissy, Zissy weighed sixty pounds and had not had a bath in two years. When Zissy first saw Benny approaching in bright morning sunlight, he thought Benny was God, literally, that he had died and God was reaching his hand out to him. No one had reached out to Zissy in kindness in years, so he no longer believed humans were capable of it, thus he saw the kindness giver as divine. Zissy and Benny had "it," magic, love at first moment, "the doll who turned some Glenn Miller on in my heart," and Benny was going to write the rest of his lifestory with Zissy, but Zissy died in the hospital. He had suffered and survived years in a Nazi prison only to be killed by a stomach illness on the day of his liberation. That was unfair. But like Frankl had advised, Benny saw meaning in the tragedy: as a reminder to never take love for granted, not even for a day.

I had met Sammy at school, and she now made pastries at Coleridge's Flowers. (I had lost my dear friends, the "bratwurst" Ingrid and gentle giant Mort, and regretted never having been able to play Cupid for either of them, but thankfully they had had each other through a lifetime). I had learned, from a science book, less sunlight was reaching Earth due to pollution in air; nowhere had that fact become more apparent to me, literally and metaphorically, than at Goldell University's windowless literature department, which would have been the most sunless polluted place on the planet if not for Sammy's sunshine.

Two years earlier, before macular degeneration had thieved landscapes from me, I had been the oldest person in Goldell's Writing Workshop, a non-degree-granting year-long program (from summer to summer) for anyone interested in crafting their writing. I had been accepted into the program because of a rather bitter story I had penned about Sputnik's death, a story which I had viewed as a cautionary tale. I had always wanted to write a book and had surmised the program could help motivate me before death took away my pen's ink. Since Goldell was ivy league, I had thought the university could get the book published, which their brochure had boasted they could do; plus, sometimes I had enjoyed walking by Professor Blagonravov's former office, and none of the students passing by the "old woman" in the hallway had ever imagined she had once made spicy love in office 309. Two nights a week, I had gone to class, sat at a round table with other students, and turned in writing assignments, which had gotten critiqued by teachers and students. And I had read other students' works to give my opinions about, which I had never felt comfortable doing, telling them how *I* would write *their* story, because doing so had been as conformity-upholding as telling them how to dress to match my tastes, or to match the tastes of literary trends. The writing "class" was called a "workshop" because stories were crafted like products to be sold, put together with the aid of market demographics, pushed through the assembly line, inspected first by worker bees (students training to be able to spot "defective" stories), and finally inspected by the factory, Goldell University. Goldell kept their products in line with the modern literary industry's specifications for sellable, and if not sellable, then "praiseworthy." Only stories that aligned with market trends and modern guidelines (evil "heroes," obscene violence, no emotions, no lessons, negativity beating positivity in the end and not as a cautionary tale) were pushed along the conveyor belt and out to stores; the rest were chucked in the trash. The program culminated in a thesis project that, if conformed to workshop standards, granted a student the "passed the program" certificate to affix to their writing like a "passed inspection" sticker.

When I was in high school, "thesis" had meant a story's point; in the writing program, "thesis" had meant a book or collection of stories, the final project; either way, thesis meant a "reason for being," a story's reason for being, or a writer's reason for being in writing at all.

At the university, I had been seen as "the cliché" old widow still wearing her wedding ring, still holding onto her husband's ashes, still clinging to the past and its traditions and all Sput's memories of The Snowflake Gal; at least my husband had imparted those memories to me, so those memoirs were not erased from the world completely yet, but soon this Lady would also be gone—would I take to the grave the last recollection of this world's Largest Snowflake?

That cold late-autumn morning, overlooking the crosses of my friends' graves on *Dear* Hill, I considered finally writing about The Snowflake Gal. I knew that story, the way Sputnik had intended it to be, would not have gone over well in the writing program, where one of the teachers had admitted she had read a love story, a pure love story, for "guilty pleasure"—how odd: feeling guilty for reading about love.

Well, the entire program had been odd, and I'd die with a guilty conscience if I didn't expose that workshop for what it was: a murderer of creativity, individuality, positivity, and femininity.

The writing workshop had been as utterly ridiculous as a soul workshop, a mess of strangers trying to craft an individual's soul based on their own tastes and on stats about market trends. Early on I had realized the writing program was just that—a program programming minds to think alike and pens to write alike. As Professor Blagonravov once taught, "Getting the grade 'A' means you provided the expected answers. It is impossible to get a good grade with innovative answers because tests are graded on known answers. School tests measure how aligned your ideas are with accepted ideas."

After reading aloud one of my short stories to be "workshopped," I had heard conflicting suggestions: "Make it funnier." "Make it sadder." "Take out the word 'charming,'" one nitpicker had advised, telling me to remove a trait from my personality to make it more appealing to his abhorrence of charm. This same student had scolded, "You can't write a character that girly. That's not realistic." I had responded, "But *I'm* that girly, so I can't write about myself because you think I'm unrealistic? Even if only a small percentage of the world is 'girly,' or romantic, does not the minority voice deserve to be heard?"

I had offered the workshoppers, "Should I write twelve different versions of *my* story to appease each of *your* preferences? Funnier for you but sadder for you. No, thank you, I won't do that. A story is not a shoe, not capable of coming in a size five for one reader, size ten for another, not capable of fitting the preferences of everyone, but only one for certain—the one who wrote it, as long as that one doesn't try to put on the wrong fit."

For those who claimed to despise censorship, many of the students and teachers upheld it fiercely, so long as what was being censored went against *their* ideas. What they could not accept was that the modern rebel was the Goody Goody, fighting to preach wholesomeness in a world that censored goodness (censored it by labeling goodness and "nice guys" as "corny," thus preventing goodness's message from achieving widespread popularity due to everyone being scared of being considered corny). Righteousness was thrown out as bad, whereas rancid was pushed through the product line quickly, so it could be consumed in mass quantity by the worst traits of humans: greed, violence, hatefulness, and fear.

The writing program released all sorts of pollutants into society through their stories promoting, not examining, but *promoting* violence and greed—robbing pages of peace, usually for the sake of profit. They were not writing Elie Wiesel's *Night* or Toni Morrison's *Beloved*, shining light on evil to prevent it from festering, but they were writing violence pornography, "sexy" serial killers and that sort of trash, and labeling that garbage "literature." Disturbingly, the program sought more "vector writers," a phrase I had borrowed from the life sciences: a vector writer, such as a vector organism (a mosquito), the carrier of something deadly. These vectors writers were carriers of negativity, infecting books with it, and spreading it globally.

The program had lessoned, "You write beautifully but that has to be trimmed" to fit in with modern literature as ornamental as flowerless hedge meant to convey the endless monotony of life incapable of blooming beauty. Yikes. I was supposed to trim my flowery writing to appease those incapable of seeing flowers as beautiful? In a society where the strongest substance on Earth was described as "mushy stuff," and "heartwarming" was an insult (as if warming someone's heart was a shameful thing to do), the Department of Literature had tried to make me hack the curly Qs off my romantic era script, because modern readers did not like that style of fancy writing. One boy had said Alfred Lord Tennyson's writing was "so old-fashioned and silly." The students of literature did not like Tennyson! "Better not be at all than not be noble," Tennyson had penned, yet they had labeled the poet "overrated." They had ridiculed his poetic line, "If I had a flower for every time I thought of you...I could walk through my garden forever" as corny drivel fit for a greeting card. But they had praised writers who said nothing with their writing but "I hope I win an award." Their criticism had only pushed me to write as fancily as possible as protest against those who would have workshopped so many classic books into unrecognizable nothings, or workshopped the stories out of existence completely, and changed the title of Tennessee Williams' *The Glass Menagerie* to *The Fragile Girl* to make it more mundane (a story they had labeled all-together too sentimental). As an assignment in "editing," the students had workshopped Thoreau's sublime "I do not need the police of meaningless labor to regulate me" to "I don't need anyone to tell me what to do for a living." They had "crafted" Shakespeare's "Love looks not with the eyes, but with the mind, And therefore is winged Cupid painted blind" to "Love isn't superficial," because "that says the same thing and is easier to read." Well, yes, Shakespeare could have said it that way, and Michelangelo could have painted stick figures on the ceiling of the Sistine Chapel, since the message would have been the same, but...ooh, well, I had not been able to get through to them, and even the Michelangelo analogy had been too embroidered for their tastes.

The students of the written word hated long sentences, long descriptions, and words; every story had to move at 1000 miles per hour with sentences short enough to fit on a "Status update." They loathed lengthy character descriptions; "guy, 20s, dumb" was sufficient enough details for them. Their preference for minimal character descriptions said something of their own characters: they did not care to truly get to know anyone at the soul level.

But for people who adhered to "absolute realism" in stories, mostly all of them used the standard "bell curve backbone" for stories. (I had learned the term "bell curve" from my mathematician.) The "bell curve" of rising action, climactic peak, then descending resolution (the curve of a bell structure), but that was not realistic for describing life's ups and downs, ups and downs, hills and valleys. For ones who claimed to be rebels, they had carved no new paths with their pens, too scared of getting so far away from literary standards, they would be shunned in awardless blue yonder.

Moon-Moon had once told me a parable from the East about Nasruddin, redone in her own style, as always. One day in the woods, Nasruddin came upon a bird, but he had never seen a bird, so he thought, "What a strange *squirrel*." The fool clipped the bird's wings to make it look more like the "normal" animal. The Goldell Writing Program was Nasruddin—clipping wings off stories to make them grounded in "reality."

Well, they could continue to mass produce particle board stories, let that assembly line junk pass as literature, but some of us wanted to keep hand carving our stories as ornately as possible.

The literature program had advised me to focus my thesis on a criminal "hero," a "sexy," "evil" story, destined to be a Hollywood film and "literary" classic. The teacher of "good writing" had wanted me to write about a man who would have shot my husband and to portray the creep as a complex "hero." The absurdity. My momma had taught that for a character *not* to change is a feat, especially when she has something worth holding onto. "Not letting the world change you is how you change the world." So, I had said defiantly to the teacher, "Sexy and evil should never be used as synonyms. I don't care if the two make profit when paired. I'll keep price tags off my morals and if that makes me destitute of cash, I'll still be rich in virtue." That defiance had made Goldell wish they had never accepted Little Goody Two-Shoes into their program.

The teachers of literature praised characters who had let go of their souls, characters like this: "She wore jewelry stolen from a dead woman. The last time she kissed her husband's gun-smoky fingertips was through the chain link at the jail cell." I had asked, "How complex is it to rot in a rotted environment?" To what end was the program trying to erase sweetness from stories?

The literary world wanted the anti-heroes who presented easier, if no, standards to achieve; stories that would not make readers feel a "preachy finger" was pointing at them. They "adored" *Killer Kal* movies about the "sexy" "complex" serial killer and advocated for the hero-ization of crooks in stories, where in the end, although unhappy, of course, crooks still made the "right" choice, which was completely unrealistic, nothing but a silly Hollywood tool used to make villains look "good," but producers kept "pushing the boundaries" of rightness to include even heinous crimes, and someday the "bad guy" would not even have to make the right choice in the end to be rooted on by the audience, for no one would have any sense of rightness anyway.

My constant questioning and "didactic" spiels had never been received well in a society where stories were no longer supposed to teach lessons; even children's books could not be "didactic," perchance a child should learn a standard to live by. I had read of a literary agent who sought "a serial killer series for middle-graders." Why? Because that had never been done and just think of all the money to be mined from it. One of the students had wanted to portray Attila the Hun in a positive light—Attila the Tyrant who had once said, "There, where I have passed, the grass will never grow gain." Why would anyone want to positively portray Attila? The student of literature had replied, "Because it has never been done." That flippancy was as dangerous as mixing two lethal chemicals just to see what would happen.

Why shouldn't we write about the nice guys, the good girls, the saints and angels, the decent parents whose good parenting helped children? Didn't they deserve attention in books too? Didn't they deserve a spotlight? The dad who told his daughter she was pretty, smart, and special, and she became a woman who had the great self-confidence of a girl whose dad had loved her, and she had a healthy view of men thanks to her good dad who showed her what a man can be—kind, admirable, courageous, faithful. Why only show in stories the outcome of a negative past but not the outcome of a positive one?

I understood how easy it was to be gloomy in this cold world, and as a Romantic I was definitely not against writing about lonesomeness and heartache, but I could not understand why teachers preached against the "dangers of sentimentality." What danger? We "budding" writers were to only focus on negative traits and be praised for curtailing compassion in our stories (or we could focus on making money by making stories violent and "sexy," another two words that should never be next to each other). I could not imagine how focusing continually on gloom would take away anyone's gloominess.

I realized these literatinazis, like the women who had picked on Moon-Moon for being "an angel," like the madman who had killed my husband for being in love, did not want to live up to any standard. Society wanted a standard of physical beauty, that was for certain, a standard impossible to attain by choice but only by chance (one was either born beautiful to society's eyes or not), but society did not want moral standards to accomplish—just too hard to do—and the Goldell literary world did not want any standard harder than particle board to achieve.

I had liked some of my classmates and teachers, thought them talented writers too. I had tried to get along with everyone, since I felt it imperative for humans to be able to get along with and respect those with differing opinions, even the Lemintads who subscribed to the idea "Endings are inherently sad, regardless of if they're happy or not."

One teacher had said to the class, "The first line sets the tone for the rest of the book, and the last line sets the tone for the rest of the reader's day."

I had agreed, "Yes, true, and the first line in my lifestory was about love."

One student had scoffed romances were unrealistic (the same student who had said "girly girls" were unrealistic). This same student had written a story set in a world where *dragons* existed. Magical was fine as long as the magic was wicked but not sweet. A writer could pen monsters without fear of ridicule but could not pen soulmates.

I had argued, "Every time writers say goodness is unrealistic, they perpetuate the idea that badness is the realistic nature of humans."

I had not made friends or allies in the literary world, or the world at large, but Hildegard and I were Writing thus.

Another student had praised a story for having no "sentimentality" and "degraded" another character by calling her "sweet." This student, herself, a religious girl, was sweet, yet she had been scared of letting niceness, and definitely morality, show through in her writing, and she had not even known why—she had never questioned why once but had just followed the university's "rubrics of literature" with absolute obedience, in hopes of gaining a pat on the back by the very people whose morals opposed her own. Goldell had felt quite pleased with itself in taking the soul from the virtuous student's writing and transforming her into one of the soulless. For the literatinazis were not just commercializing literature, they were guilty of the militarization of writing. They were creating soldiers, not writers, but soldiers obedient to the rules and trained to kill the enemy (anyone whose writing was different).

One young woman had openly admitted to being afraid of ridicule for writing "characters too nice."

All the adult students had once been children who had loved sugar, *The Little Prince* and *Frog and Toad,* but now saw "sweet" as an insult. Classmates had often described any sweet moment as "cliché," but sweetness was not cliché in their world; it was either non-existent, or a novelty, not cliché at all; they had just incorrectly used the word "cliché" to mean "corny." More and more scenes being labeled bathetic ("overly sentimental") reflected a growing emotionlessness in society that frightened my soul, and what frightened me even more was that very few others seemed frightened by the emotionlessness.

The students, so young, had already retired from believing life could be anything more than breathing through pain. I had confirmed this depressing fact at a store, of course, in the form of all things: a snow globe. Inside the globe had not been a romantic scene, but the phrase "f-ck you" spelled out. That was the world's message now and we were all supposed to buy it, sell it, and propagate it like the silly "life's a b-tch" slogan of the unimaginative.

I was convinced most young people had no interest in romance, just "hookups," that they preferred lyrics like "My body's fed up over you" to "My heart's under a streetlamp." Romantic comics were no longer made. Lady's fancy gloves were only worn as novelty costumes. Fine china was literally going extinct, since young people had no interest in fancy cups, just as they had no interest in fancy writing for pouring sweet cream tea. Every beautiful character, sentiment, and story from the past was treated as parody. Even "Sonnet 43" was parodied; "How I Love Thee" was uttered in commercials. A real love had inspired that sonnet by a woman who had felt unlovable except to one man; it had not been written for potato chips. Nothing was sacred. None of the modern stations played *our* songs. I missed Sputnik and his arm around me that said, "We're in this together."

Due to my desire to preserve Ladies and Knights, in a world where women were *fighting* for the "right" to be drafted for war, one male student had labeled me an "anti-feminist," thinking that would incite me to change my opinions for fear of going against modern currents. But I could see past dogma disguised as truth—drafting for war was a disastrous premise, one that had forced sweet Mr. Benny, at a young age, to hold a machine gun instead of a kite.

I had countered, "I am very pro-femininity, but much of modern feminism ignores the root of the word—feminine-ism—in our machismo-dominated war-obsessed society that won't be satisfied until all women are identical copies of men, in the name of 'equality' and 'femin'ism. I believe women, and men, have the right to be as masculine as they want to be—and as feminine. Picture all the young women trying on dresses at Macy's suddenly being plucked out of the store, shoved into combat suits, thrown onto the battlefield, perfume bottles taken out of their hands and replaced with machine guns. Does that sound like a smart military strategy? What about the women who want to be mothers? Are we going to replace a young woman's dream of holding a pacifier for holding a bazooka? In the way some men subscribe to a code of chivalry, some women adhere to a code of Ladyhood, which forbids her from engaging in violence. The government has no right to force a woman to give up her very womanhood, essence of her soul, no more than the government has the right to change someone's religious beliefs. If a woman wants to serve in the military that is her choice, but forcing certain women into battle is like forcing a bird to swim underwater—the task is completely outside their capabilities and at odds with their temperament. The task is outside many men's capabilities too, and/or in conflict with their conscience, and that's why men should not be drafted either—the military does not need anyone with scared-of-guns hands or an abhors-fighting heart on the battlefield. Not only is that cruel but it goes against military sense. Will children be drafted next 'in the name of equality'? Ooh yes, I'm letting the 'irrational woman' pathos fly free!"

I had stood up from my seat, not feeling like sitting down and submitting to be a student of lies.

691

"The truth is some women have no desire to engage in male-ego-derived combat, and the government should not be allowed to make a woman exchange her dress for armor, or her compassion for combativeness. If a war breaks out and women are drafted, it won't turn out like the movies—there will be much loss of female life. Unlike the aftermath of WW2 when men came home to wife and hearth and made a Babyboom, there won't be women to come home to."

I had looked around the round table, where everyone had removed the welcome mat of friendship for me, but Hildegard had to say thus.

"Why do we *want* to foster a world where everyone is forced to be a warrior? Do we want to kill chivalry? Call me old-fashioned—I'll take it as a compliment—but I yearn for the days when men wanted to protect women, not fight them. I was raised in a generation where boys were taught not to hit girls, not such a bad principle to uphold. Sure, over time, the more men fight women on the battlefield, the easier it will be for a man to kill a woman. Is that progress? Why would we want to create a world like that? The more movie scenes of men and women fist fighting that are shoved in front our eyes, the more we'll stop squinting at the sight of violence and accept it as normal behavior. Ensuring equality does not require making everyone identical, an impossible task anyway. I'm a feminist, yes—my heroes are great women like Elizabeth Stanton and Sojourner Truth, women that broke barriers—but that doesn't mean I support drafting women, or men, for war!"

"You're just an old-timer who suffers from internalized misogyny!" a male student had shouted, while standing up as if wanting to fist fight with me to uphold feminism.

"Because I value femininity? Because I love and respect my husband? No, that doesn't mean I'm harboring the belief of male superiority. But I see internalized misogyny all around me in this classroom, where females are being trained to write like men to gain respect. So many of our standard story structures and literary elements were derived by men and pertain to the male perspective. Even the classic 'conflict/resolution' is a very masculine, and capitalistic, way of storytelling: goals, battles, rising to the top of the food chain or money ladder or failing to do so. What about a story that focuses solely on a picnic? God forbid, no violence, no wars! And what about 'Chekhov's gun,' the idea that anything introduced in a story must have relevance later on. For example, if a writer mentions a pink doily on a breakfast table, that pink doily should have significance in the overall plot. It can't be used just for charm, setting, cuteness. God forbid, how girly! Ooh, do you think what I'm saying is sexist? You probably believe that all stars of cinema should be called 'actors,' because the term 'actress' is sexist—why shouldn't they all, men and women, be called actresses, not actors? You're the one who believes masculinity is superior, and your brand of pseudo-feminism is the one trying to erase femininity. You see misogyny in old advertisements of women all buttoned up, but I see misogyny in billboards and magazine covers, where women are half-naked to please men but pretending to claim their own sexual freedom. I see internalized misogyny in books and films by women and men who consider themselves feminists, in stories about girls wanting to be Knights, stories whose messages say, 'Of course, you girls really wanted to be like boys all along, warriors, because the girl roles, the peaceful princesses and fairies, are crummy, but you girls can now play all the roles once belonging to only boys. Doesn't that make you happy? Aren't you making progress?' But where is the reverse? Where is the heralding of the stories whose messages say, 'Boys can be princesses too?' Who is the champion of the girly girls and boys? I see internalized misogyny in the portrayal of fighting and guns as cool and superior to femininity and flowers, in the name of empowering women to be just as aggressive as men."

I had felt on an island in that moment, completely sequestered from mainland modernity.

"I grew up in the 40s and 50s, young man, so I experienced extreme chauvinism in a culture, where women were made to feel ashamed for being women—for reading 'silly women's magazines,' for liking romance, for being wives and not bread winners—and do you think that attitude has changed much? Still today, women are only congratulated when they take on predominantly male roles, but women still get no respect for being mothers and wives. In the modern world, if a woman dons a pair of boxing gloves, she's heralded as progressive, but if she has a tea party, she's labeled anti-feminist, and if she writes about war, she's a serious writer, but if she writes about love, she's *a woman*, ooh, the shame, to pen *women's fiction*."

The same student who had argued with me about internalized misogyny had decided on another angle of attack, claiming he did not lambaste romances because of their femininity but because of their "immaturity," and said I needed to "grow up," since my stories portrayed relationships at their apex, which was a "childish view of romance."

I had offered, "Modern books paint 'mature' relationships as bad relationships. Maturity means having a high level of skill in something, so if a relationship is bad, that is not a mature relationship. If a relationship is great, that is a mature relationship."

I had realized I did not need the program when my own rebuttal against a teacher's critique had dawned truth on me more than it had dawned on her, "Aside from teaching that a story is something told, like life is something lived, you have no right to tell me *how* a story should be told no more than how *my* life should be lived."

After hearing a student pitch a story that would portray a Nazi, who hunted Jews for sport, as a book's hero, and being told by a teacher "that sounds interesting," I had left the program, which had tried to program my heart to scoff at heartwarming ideals.

But I would still write my thesis—according to my own standards.

I had been blessed with one ally in class, a classmate who also wrote in pink, and I saw my romantic self reflected in Sammy, a young African American woman. I felt meeting her was the meaning behind my ever attending the writing program.

She was an antiquated gal, born a boy but more of a *she* than any she I knew, put together with lace doilies, an old-fashioned bespectacled wallflower. I had once thought the world accepting me as *She* was impossible, but I realized nonstandard Sammy had suffered an even more torturous time being recognized as *She*. The unintuitive could not see beyond Sammy's physicality to her feminine essence. Often ridiculed, she spent many moments inside with an old Victrola and Duke Ellington, because she liked solitude and love songs, not because she wanted to hide from the world. She was brave. And soft. Whereas I had done my early growing in a meadow, she had grown up in a city around concrete and brick, yet she had remained soft. She always wore what women once called a "smart" outfit—a thickly-knitted cardigan sweater, beige pants, beige flats, panty hose, a pale pink (or some other color) silk shirt with pearl buttons, and a simple necklace.

One night, walking home from a high school class through the flower garden, she had been attacked by her chemistry lab partner, a boy who had thought Sammy "liked him too much." With a scar on her face and a dozen more on her heart just for trying to love, she had decided to Write thus!

Before writing class, Sammy and I had often talked pastries and poetry. She once told me, "I've come to the conclusion no one on this planet, in this era, understands my heart. I'm candlelight. They're laser light." I had known exactly what she felt like in the unromantic classroom—she had felt like a Valetine's candy heart amongst SPAM.

In class, Sammy had said things like, "When a reader finishes any of my books, I want them to feel what they feel in their hearts listening to *Canon in D*." In her stories, she would not give morbid details; she described one character this way: "A deep love did not give birth to her. Hers was an unloved childhood. No more details need to be given because 'unloved' is horrific enough." And she ended her stories happily, such as, "He was a man, 'warts and all,' who became an angel through love." My heavens, that young Lady was a martyr for romance! She was using her one singular life to change, for the better, the lives of every person on this planet. My favorite of her quotes: "A heart doesn't look good in a business suit."

Through an open office door, I had once overheard a conversation about her thesis. The teacher, sounding like Mrs. Lemintad, had asked Sammy, "What's the purpose of this story?"

I had thought of *A Love Story Whose Soul Purpose is to Tell a Love Story*. That story was not meant to have dire conflicts, because the story wanted to show the peacefulness of love between Hoagy and Peridot, whose only conflict was trying to beat their world record for number of times to make love during the day, but the story's purpose had completely bypassed publishers and agents whose *hearts* never read books.

Rebelliously showing her strong feminine character, Sammy, too, suffered endlessly being pelted with rocks.

She was searching for the man who felt that her birth had been the greatest event in the universe, and she wanted that man to be ninety-nine-year-old Mr. Benny, just the kind of old-fashioned gent she dreamed of.

My good friend was also getting to his story's last pages, and I sensed he wanted his last sight to be Sammy, not a kite—the vision of her took him higher. But those two were so shy around each other. He would go into Coleridge's Flowers to order baklava, and he'd glance at her from the "snoop spot," known as the corner of the eye, and she'd get as bashful as if they were in a dressing room together, and her voice would get so soft and low anytime she said, "Yes, Mr. Benny." I had believed men treating women like Ladies died on the day the miniskirt was invented, but Mr. Benny's behavior around Sammy taught me otherwise. The town "weirdo" was an utter gentleman.

Now it was time for me to return Mr. Benny's kindness—he had played the part of Cupid for me and Sputnik, and I would play that role for him…but how?

That morning, as I procrastinated writing my thesis project and instead made hot tea, I talked to Sputnik in my heart. After his death, I had felt I needed to hold his urn to talk to him, but that had only reinforced my belief he was in the urn. I was proud of myself for having realized bad things, horrible cruel things, happened in the world's story, where everyone had free choice to write any sentence they wanted, but it was just that: a story. I had chosen to see my meeting with Sputnik after his death as real, a true encounter, proof of life after death, not just a dream; that was the otherworldly ingredient I had needed to turn ice into ice cream. After the year of mourning, I had started talking to him without his urn in my hand, the way I had talked to him in my mind before we had ever met in this story. I liked to keep him up to date on all the things he would have loved: Mars rovers, *Scooby Doo*, Big League Chew.

"Sput, I still deride polynomials, can't throw a spitball, despise ice cream, and haven't been able to get Mr. Benny a mate. What do you think about that, my love?"

Then…

At just this time, Mr. Benny came by, as he often did to check on Shom's widow. He placed his conductor's hat on the coat rack and I offered him breakfast. As excited as a little boy, he told me an ice cream truck—"a real genu-ine ice cream truck!"—would be coming to the Willows nursing home that afternoon. The ice cream man had wandered into the Hobby Hut on Friday, looking for a model boat, and asked if Benny wouldn't mind if he parked his truck and trailer outside the Hut, while he was in town for the next couple of weeks—"Don't mind a bit, kid!" Mr. Benny had promised to spread the word that the "treat truck" would be in Biskatine every Saturday for the remainder of autumn and at the Willows from one to two.

"An ice cream truck at a nursing home?" I asked.

Mr. Benny explained that kids and teenagers were in school during autumn afternoons, and on autumn Saturday afternoons, they had school social or sporting events to attend, or they played ice cream apps on their phones or something like that. But the Willows didn't have many social events, so the ice cream truck would stop there first. The truck would also make the rounds at the colleges and suburbs for any kids and adults not glued to a computer screen. (Many of the students in the Goldell writing program had been completely disconnected from nature. Searching "cloud" on the Internet returned results for computer data storage, not clouds in the sky, which made sense in a way, because one did not need to "look clouds up" on a computer, but just look up and see them.)

I thought only a fool sold ice cream, and ate it, in the northeast during autumn.

Would I like to join him for a treat? The coincidence of just thinking about how Sputnik had always told me he would get me to love ice cream someday then being invited for ice cream made me enthusiastically say, "I'd love to join you!"

"It's a date, kiddo. I'll pick you up in the Model T."

After breakfast, Mr. Benny went back to his hobby shop, and I bundled in coat and took a long cold walk on a well-worn path with Pumpkin through Stargust Continued. We strolled to the Cupid patisserie, where I casually told Sammy that Mr. Benny and I would be having ice cream at the Willows—the decision to be there too was up to her.

In the passenger seat of Mr. Benny's Model T, my heart felt like it was playing hopscotch, or jumping rope, or skipping, or any of those fun childhood pastimes, since this was not a drive to the bank or eye doctor or hospital—we were going to get ice cream. In the backseat rode Pumpkin, the golden retriever as happy-go-lucky as always.

The ice cream truck, Bashert, came like shoobie-shoobie doo-wop into hushed Willows Senior Living Apartments to dish autumn ice cream to autumn hearts. I could picture this hour, from one to two, becoming an unmissable hour, which would start with the rhythm of the ice cream truck gently pushing into stale wind, mining out a gush of breezy moans, and fluttering dried brittle leaves on Weepiest Willows and old Silver Maples, and the horn pouring The Cleftones or The Drifters or any of those groups who once sang in moonlight. The Sh-Boom and ice cream would gather aged faces to windows where they would shine like schoolgirls' fresh faces seeing their beaus drive up for a Saturday at the juke box soda shop. Then he would park deep up the driveway by unvisited Sugar Maples, where the gentle melody truck would showcase its baritone strength, vibrating crumbly pavement, so forcefully, surprisingly the old street would not break. Then the women would come out first with their coin purses, ooh just like schoolgirls yes, no need for a purse or a billfold, since every treat from the ice cream man could be bought with the change in a coin purse—"1950s prices," the truck tenderly assured. Then out would come the old boys wanting Bomb Pops and Sidewalk Sundaes and memories of Esther Williams in a bikini and teenaged years hanging out by the ice cream truck on the beach. Then, in the unmissable hour, there in chilly New England, every tenant of lonesomeness would find an imagined warm spot in the courtyard sun whose warmth had already retired for winter (the way it did in the northeast), even the ones whose mobility required a nurse and whose crankiness needed a warning label ("Stay back!"). Around dying trees and fruitflies or sitting alone in lonely wheelchairs with oxygen tank companions, every-one together would enjoy butter brickle and tutti frutti and cookie dough. *Lollipop Lollipop* would transform the air sweet and wide, during a breakout from the stuffy "red brick special" (a red brick square as inviting as prison, flat all around with flat windows, no balconies, no chance of escape, except in the event of a fire, but things never got that warm around there). Not all senior communities in town were docile, some were lively, and not all were as celibate as monasteries, some were "little

Peyton Places," where more bed hopping went on than in a rock star's tour bus, but not the Willows. Most residents of the Willows had gone more than seventy-five times around the sun in the 'round and 'round circle of heartache and loss, losing more things with each spin (eyesight, friends, savings) and having to start each new revolution without, without, without—what next? They were the abandoned "old folks," just like they had been the abandoned youths, those who had lost love, those who had never met love. They were sick, they were sad, they were outcasts, they were widows if not of love then of happiness and hope—they were all there amongst weepy trees to lose the last of their warmth to indifferent coldness, knowing their departure would not take the sugar out of anyone's day. So, what a treat, yes, when the ice cream truck would pull into decayed lives—a sweet event not to be missed. Yes, I could picture that memorable storybook scene. And the unmissable hour would end with the ice cream man slowly pulling away from all the smiles he had made, all around smiles.

The ice cream truck was painted in the colors of the taste of my first love (mint chocolate chip). It was decorated in decals of ice cream treats and cotton-candy pink bubble letters—"Fun in a Scoop!" With its horn billowing 1950s rock-n-roll, the truck parked on one of the rain wet crumbly driveways, amidst nine three-story red brick prisons stuck in dying ruddy grass and concrete. Despite my dreamy picture of ice cream Saturdays, I suspected in the world's story, this scene would be the case of the happy-looking ice cream truck, but once I got to the ordering window, I would encounter the ice cream man who would be as sweet as sauerkraut. Some grouchy Archie Bunker in a wifebeater. Like the grouch at the pawn shop who had called me an idiot for requesting the harp for free when I was a kid.

I did not plan to request any ice cream; I just wanted to stay in line with Mr. Benny and give him the chance to get gooeyeyed with Sammy, who had braved the opportunity to be there, so I waved her over to stand in line with us. We all joked about being kooks

700

getting ice cream in late autumn, as Ritchie Valens sang *La Bamba* over the horn.

The still flower in my chest fluttered, as Ritchie rolled the "r's" in "arriba," and my friends and I moved closer to Bashert's ordering window. Even I could read the signs "kosher" and "vegan options available."

Then my heart Lindy Hopped for the first time in over fifty years when I saw the ice cream maker was beautiful with a beauty I could see even if I had no eyes. The ice cream creator was a most handsome young Jewish fellow with picturesque pistachio-green eyes, an image I had not so much seen with my own failing eyes but with my soul.

I switched my focus from the retirement home to him on the lyric "I am not a sailor, I am a captain"…

The ice cream man had really gotten into the role, wearing the white sailor-style hat of an old-fashioned ice cream man. The paper hat sat atop a black kippah. His well-fit white T-shirt was tucked neatly into black dress pants and belt, and he looked like one of the boys from the malt shop era, those butterscotch boys whose smiles were sweet and bashful and cocky. His face also had interesting landmarks: the top of his right ear was slightly bent. His hair was almost a buzzcut; the Willow women who remembered USO dances must have fantasized he was a soldier come for a last dance with a Lady before shipping out. I wondered if his hair color was truly light brown, or only appeared light because sunlight soaked the short brush, the way sunlight could flood forests sparse of trees. Forests, I felt a gush in me, remembering those girlhood forests spent with him. His bare arms were the color of caramel ice cream, his forearms as tone as a saxophonist's forearms. His T-shirt with a V-neck cut was an open window to a glimpse of his dulce de leche chest, most certainly as warm as melty caramel sauce due to his strong young man's body working out a sweat amidst freezers, as his sweet hands gave the sweet fruits of his labor to the next in line for a scoop of kosher sugar. He was a dreamboat—

that had been the word in my day, which made sense: a dream sailing into one's life. This dream was named Orkney, which I could read from his large golden nametag. What an interesting name, cute too. It was also interesting that the young man in a kippah worked on Saturday, the Shabbat.

While Sammy made an order, the ice cream man gave me the same look as Sputnik had gifted me on the hayride: "A sweet blue-eyed girl" had approached the ordering window. Nonsense, I scolded my whimsical heart—wasn't believing *he* liked *me* too fantastical for even me? Your eyes are just bad, you old fool.

Come Go With Me, The Del-Vikings pleaded.

I had once believed finding someone who saw me as light would be a miracle, but continuing to see myself as light was the real miracle now that I no longer had Sputnik's adoring gaze and his tender touch to assure me of my beauty in a world where people turned away from the sight of me. Seeing my ragged self as light in front of this beautiful young man would be quite a challenge.

Mr. Benny began shooting the breeze with Orkney like they were old chums, talking about how the Hobby Hut had a model that looked similar to the ice cream truck. The two men got into a talk about cars, lusting for Corvettes, admiring something or other. I still knew nothing about cars.

With Pumpkin, I slinked off to the side, let Mr. Benny order, because I did not want to tolerate the pain of seeing a young man's face that sweet turn sour upon seeing mine, or hearing it in his voice. I knew Sputnik and Moon-Moon would be disappointed in my cowardice, so was I. My golden retriever friend kept barking as if purposely drawing the ice cream man's attention to us.

But time at the ice cream truck was not fruitless—Sammy and Mr. Benny did a lot of smiling at each other over tall ice cream cones (his chocolate, hers vanilla), and a lot of nibbling at conversation, a good prelude for any lovestory.

Sitting at a bench with my friends in the courtyard, while Pumpkin asked Sammy for just a small bite of vanilla ice cream please, I heard tenants of the Willows say "314" had died the previous night. "314" had never left their room. I knew nothing about 314, except they had not gotten to eat ice cream that afternoon, and that chilled me—they would never get a second chance to taste ice cream in this life. The next Saturday, I would order a scoop, the least I could do for Sputnik.

The whole week was more pleasant with something to look forward to—I could not wait to see the ice cream man again, even though he was young enough to be my grandson.

He had such warm eyes for an ice cream maker. "You can do more than a good description of beautiful eyes," I imagined hearing my writing advisor scold.

But, ooh, I adored his warm butterscotch smile, and his soft hair shades of streusel and pecan.

In the gazebo one pinkish dawn with a blanket wrapped around me, I went over everything I knew about him so far (thanks to others asking him questions):

Someone had asked his age.

"Twenty-eight," he had answered. "But telling someone how many times you've gone around the sun will give them no insight into you other than you're alive, subject to gravity, and rotating along with Earth. I don't let my age determine my interests or activities. Some twenty-eight-year-old men wouldn't dare watch a cartoon, but I watch them all the time, because I see no reason why traveling past the sun for the umpteenth time should take away my liking of Huckleberry Hound."

He was born after the Cold War and named after the South Orkney Islands in the Antarctic, where he was birthed, a land with no permanent inhabitants. I had learned that because a rude tenant had flat asked the young man, "What kind of name is Orkney?" I had hoped she would ask *why* were your parents in the Antarctic?

That was an intriguing backstory! But the reason for his being born close to the South Pole had not intrigued her, because she had only been interested in the way the young man's T-shirt clung to his chest, flat and strong as a surfboard.

In afternoon air scented with the cold sweet smell of ice cream, one customer, waiting for a dipped cone, had asked, "Do you own this truck?"

"He's too young to own anything but a bookbag," the rude woman had snapped.

"She's all mine." Ooh, his voice, especially saying "She's all mine"—lucky truck.

Johnny Cash's *Get Rhythm* had been rocking the truck's horn, and the ice cream man had really gotten into the song, tapping his hands flat against the ordering counter and singing along.

"Where do you live?" another tenant had asked.

"Somewhere new every season."

"You move somewhere new every season?"

"Yes, I travel with the seasons, because I want to see every place."

A wanderer!

"If you travel somewhere new every season, what are you doing here in Biskatine in *late* fall?"

The ice cream man had handed the customer a cone of cherries jubilee before answering, "I was north of here, at a convent of Protestant nuns, who really like ice cream, chocolate mudslide popular there, and the Lilies of the Field told me of this charming town, Biskatine, so here I am."

Ooh, I owed the sisters a blessing!

One afternoon, I asked Mr. Benny for a drive to the Hobby Hut, saying I wanted to see the new inventory of fancy dollhouses but truly I wanted to be around the camper, where the ice cream man lived. Parked outside the Hut, the quiet vintage trailer was red and white, quite recognizable attached to the mint-green ice cream truck.

"How does the ice cream stay cold?" I asked my friend, as we strolled arm in arm up the streetlamp sidewalk.

"See that thingamabob by the hitch, that's the propane generator."

A pennant flag of astronaut Snoopy was sticking up above the driver's door; an upside-down canoe was secured on the roof; a mountain bike was tacked on back; and the camper's tires and bumper were mud-crusted like an off-road vehicle.

"What's that on the antenna?" I asked.

"A round smiley face wearing a baseball cap."

My ailing eyes could not read the camper's numerous bumper stickers.

As if knowing I was curious about the bumper stickers, Mr. Benny offered, "That's a real weirdo there. Look at those stickers:

'Math Café Menu: Infinite Pi.'

'Math is confusing,' said 120% of people.'

'Population: 1.'

'I'd rather sail than sell.'

'Earth is my campground.'

'Boards cure boredom' with a drawing of a gameboard.

'I brake for rugelach and Loch Ness monsters.'

"Ain't that just weird?" Mr. Benny chuckled. "Kinda reminds you of someone, don't it?"

Enough so I felt warm even in chilly air.

The curtain on one of the camper's windows got pushed aside by a small, hairless, wrinkly pink cat, a Sphynx cat (my friend Ingrid had been a cat person who had told me much about cats). A pup, who looked like a mini wolf, joined his roommate at the window to watch the two nosy humans getting awfully close to the private camper all secretive in curtains.

"Arthur and Lancelot," Benny said.

"Are you kidding me?" I was overwhelmed by the coincidence.

"No, he told me their names, one early morning when he was on the sidewalk playing fetch with them."

"Playing fetch with a cat?"

Unfortunately, the ice cream man was out.

"He's a loner who hikes alone a lot," Mr. Benny explained. "I'm a nightbird, ya know, who stays in the hut at all hours, tinkerin' with trains, and I see him from the window, setting out early with bookbag and thermos, headed who knows where. I asked him one morning and he said, 'I want to meet some moose.' I told him to visit my friend's Christmastown, the snow globe world you created, enchanting in every season with good pastries to boot."

"When was this?"

"Sunday."

I remembered I had felt I should stroll Christmastown that day but had stubbornly stayed inside against my intuition's insistence.

"I see him wandering all over our streets like he's lookin' for something," Mr. Benny said, "and there ain't no moose in the city."

I could no longer stroll my storybook town without assistance, but I began strolling with Mr. Benny, saying I wanted to be out since the weather was so pleasant for autumn (felt pleasant to me). I strolled with Sammy too, perchance to bump into the wanderer.

Sammy had been there on Sunday when the ice cream man had come into the Cupid patisserie. He had seemed charmed by the sweet shoppe and ordered hot cocoa and butterscotch cookies "to go." Cookies I had baked that morning since I was still able to bake desserts. I regretted not having been there to offer him a poem with his pastry.

That week, I strolled Christmastown with Pumpkin, in case the ice cream creator came back for more desserts or to meet moose.

In the sunshine cottage the next Saturday, I rushed to start the day so as not to miss my moment with him. What tragedy: on the day opportunity knocks, not to be dressed. My ramshackle stomach could only tolerate one tasty food a day, and on this new day, by golly, it was going to be ice cream, finally. Beside my writing desk, where my laptop awaited my thesis to be dictated, I sifted through clothes in an old walnut armoire, scented in vanilla potpourri. Mostly pants and blouses inside, one pair of blue jeans; my body had lost its ability to make a dress pretty. I questioned, "Is that Writing thus?" So, on this day, I wore a dress, what Sputnik would have called my "orchid dress," the same blush/white color of the flower. I paired the dress with blush coat and sweet perfume. Maybe I should wear a necklace too? I pondered. Something beautiful enough to give his eyes something to focus on, to shine about, to play up the fantasy, to make it easier for him to pretend to be looking at beauty, since he was obviously a sweet fella who wanted to make everyone feel good (I had learned that the previous Saturday through his kind words to all). I chose not to wear a necklace. His eyes would have to be kind to my nonstandard face.

The afternoon was cold and pale, as Mr. Benny drove us to the Willows, where we walked side by side up to the long line beyond the ordering window. The bright ice cream truck glistened like a rainbow in gloom. "Butterscotch Nut" was the afternoon's special flavor, and if Sputty had cooked up something from beyond to give me a sign he could have done better than that. No, maybe not. That did seem like something his dry humor would have thought funny, but when I heard *Melt & Malt* over the ice cream truck's horn, my conviction that this whole experience was destined strengthened.

The rude woman, waiting for her rocky road, asked the ice cream maker, "Shouldn't you be in college? You can't make much money doing this. Why'd you get into this?"

The ice cream man leaned out the window and explained, while gently tapping the friendly menu on the truck's side, "This is why I got into this. Deciding on chocolate or cherry ice cream should be the toughest choice anyone should ever have to make on a Saturday afternoon. If I can make one worry free moment for a community, I will feel satisfied with the way I spent my day."

"That's some kinda destiny," an envious old man chuckled.

"Destiny is, mostly, the outcome of choice. I have chosen to use my days for making ice cream and for traveling in this cold truck to find the one Lady who will offer me a warm home."

He was searching for his Lady? I did not need ice cream in that moment to bring about goose bumps.

"You only work on Saturdays?" the old man chided, interested in finding out the boy's thoughts on work, not on romance.

"It's not work."

"You can't make much money on, what do you call it then? A hobby?"

"A duty. Ice cream makes people happy, that is the currency I get paid in, and enough coins to cover parking meters."

"What do you do with the rest of the days of the week?"

"I study, I learn, I tinker with boats and clarinets. Have you ever played clarinet to the open sea? Floating in starlight on *Rhapsody in Blue*. That's a pleasant way to use an hour. The lonely mermaids and Loch Ness monsters seem to like it."

One hour was not enough time in his interesting presence.

Mr. Benny, kind of cocky about hearing his song *Melt & Malt*, stood by a tree with his root beer float, so he could have a good view of Sammy, who was standing by a different tree with her hot fudge sundae. Smiles hop-skipped through the air separating them.

Nervously, holding a book of Elizabeth Barrett Browning's poems close, as if adding something pretty to my flat chest, I ordered an ice cream sandwich, but the beautiful ice cream maker said, "Oh, you do not want something prepackaged. Let me make something special for you. How about a Sonnet 43?" His smile, which I imagined took every breath away within his vicinity, asked, "Do you know what Sonnet 43 is?"

I answered by declaring aloud, "How do I love thee."

"You'll be counting the ways," the ice cream maker promised, "when you taste this."

I adored that he had mentioned Browning's poem, but he was selling ice cream to old people, who probably seemed old enough to him to have actually known Browning. Encountering my "monstrous" reflection in the ordering window, my returned insecurities concluded "special for me" had been said out of pity, or because the handsome young ice cream peddler knew the gray-haired women lined up were not there for butter pecan, and he wanted a generous tip, as generous as tips could be from retired folks living on limited income.

To test whether his sweet comment had come from a gigolo or a pity-er, I said, "I don't think I have enough in my coin purse for the homemade items."

"For you, Lovely, it's free." Pity! I reasoned if he was a gigolo selling flirtations to spinsters, he would not have offered the "ugly" widow anything free.

Again, I felt in my heart Sputnik and Moon-Moon would be disappointed in me, for being so skeptical of magic, for I was disappointed in myself.

"Hey, Snowflake, let's melt and malt" crooned the horn.

The ice cream man asked me to take a seat with my "large pretty dog," but all the benches were filled, so I stood by Mr. Benny at the tree, unfortunately too far away to hear the young man's conversations at the ice cream truck.

Even though being pitied felt better than being ridiculed, I did not want his pity, because I did not want him to see anything pitiful about my appearance.

When the ice cream man brought a dish of swirled chocolate and marshmallow to me, Mr. Benny chuckled, "She's anti-ice cream."

"She's about to become an ice cream addict," the ice cream man promised, and he was standing so close, I smelled his powdered doughnut scent. Even I could see he looked handsome in a teal-and-white bowling shirt tucked into caramel-brown pants.

I wondered if autumn ice cream would taste just as sweet as summertime ice cream. His pistachio-green eyes lay upon me while I found out the answer: "Sonnet 43," and its sweet lyrics, "I shall but love thee better after death," tasted like hot cocoa even in cold ice cream. Sputnik had been right—ice cream was heavenly!

"How did you know I simply adore hot cocoa and marshmallows?"

"I just had a sense you would *love thee*."

I smiled thanks, he smiled in return.

Mr. Benny patted the ice cream man's shoulder like they were old friends in cahoots to convert me to being an ice cream lover.

After the ice cream man wandered back to the truck, I asked, "Benny, did you tell him I like hot cocoa and marshmallows?"

Mr. Benny shook his head and said with his expression, "Kinda weird, ain't it?"

The whole experience felt like a scene my bobby socks girlhood self would have written in pink ink, and even I had a difficult time believing in its existence, because doubt bullied me just as much as it bullied everyone—the pink writing did not seem possible to write this story's The End, which my Wicked Stepmother warned would be gray (I had seen it written that way every time). Maybe those in the writing program had been correct. Maybe I was an old fool.

That week, I felt like an old fool, lying in bed in painful bones, amidst cold metallic walls in a moldy camper, staring at a long dead Knight, and holding an almost-eighty-years-old teddy bear for support, while planning what to say to the pistachio-eyed fellow but feeling too foolish to go through with it. I reasoned the ice cream seller was selling romantic fantasies to abandoned old hearts, and I was ready to buy one. For the rest of autumn, every Saturday, this handsome young ice cream fellow could be my beau (just for pretend). He'd be all the others' beau too, but ooh I'd still get the treat of his flirts, and yes, maybe I'd even flirt back. I had never been Primo Patsy at flirting, except with Sputnik, and even with him I had never been great at it. I wondered if flirting was like riding a bike, something you never forgot how to do? I was nervous to try, scared of the stumbles and scuffs, which hurt more on the heart than on the knees. But if I could brave taking the tasty opportunity, I could be his girl at the "malt shop." I could be his girl for the length of time it took Paul Anka to ask a gal to *Put Your Head on My Shoulder* and for the ice cream man to dish me a scoop. He and his green eyes would linger at the ordering window and his smile would suggest the last lyric of Pablo Neruda's "Love Poem XIV"—he wanted to do with me what springtime does to a cherry tree. Even the suggestion would do what springtime does to a cherry tree—bloom my face pink red. All he would really give, though, would be cherry ice cream. Ooh, yes, just a daydream, but I had not had a swoo-be swoo-be sweet one since I had lost my soul's mate. No one in line would complain about the ice cream man's lingering with me because everyone would get their chance to play the fantasy role of *his girl*. More delicious than butter brickle. He'd wink, he'd listen, he'd talk (if the customer wanted him to), he'd be gentle, he'd compliment, he might even let his fingertips touch mine when handing me a butterscotch sundae, while Elvis crooned from the horn *Love Me Tender*. But what price would I have to pay for the sweetness? The handsome young thing had probably sweet talked his way to every cent in many a lovesick fool's coin purse, but there was an even higher cost—the cost of having the heat turned off in my heart again. Not long ago, still deeply missing Sputnik, I had thought "Just hurry up, 'The End,' and get it over with," but now, I wanted extra pages. Just an autumn daydream with the ice cream man. I did not think I would ever again see springtime. But I would not get heart hurt, would not get another heart icicle, if I didn't take this too seriously, this fantasy, I assured myself.

The next chilly Saturday, I let the ice cream seller know I wanted to buy his sweet fantasy by flirtatiously ordering a "Sonnet 22," while handing him the book of Browning poems with that poem dog-eared.

Reading the romantic lyrics, he grinned and said, "Go wait by the tree, Lovely, and I will bring the poetic ice cream to you."

Earth Angel caressed the cold air.

By a sugar maple, he handed me a cone topped with soft ice cream the color of brown sugar, letting his bare fingertips linger against my gloved fingertips. Browning's verse "When our two souls stand up erect and strong" tasted like *molasses* and warmed me all over, the "coincidence"?

That night, lying alone in the marriage bed, I realized why I really felt foolish—because I wanted it to be real: his love. This was not just a crush, which I had known deep down all along. I had not cowered away that first ice cream day for fear of seeing his face turn soured upon glimpsing mine but for fear of his facial expression ruining my hope. Over fifty years earlier, during the same time of year, I had met my Sputnik. The ice cream man's eyes were green, but they had the same warmth as my husband's gray eyes. Sputnik had always been fascinated by *gilgul*, the concept of reincarnation in Judaism, and with him, I had felt convinced he and I had penned other stories together, where we had played various characters; one of our honeymoon nights, we had stayed up late thinking of all the different roles we would have liked to have played in history.

But was it not too late in this story for this romantic scene? Yet my seventy-one-year-old self felt about seventeen.

Pain stayed in the background while I thought of the ice cream man and his mint-chocolate-chip-colored ice cream truck.

I was disappointed in myself for being so skeptical and insecure, for letting doubt bully me into being a disbeliever of magic, but even though I had failed some tests, I would not be a failure as long as I bravely took the tests again.

That week, during Hanukkah, just when I was lighting the candles and accepting the burgeoning lovey-dovey mystical feelings, I heard town gossip that the ice cream man was a gigolo, who had been at nursing homes, fooling elderly folks out of money for his affection. I felt very hurt by this, my negative suspicions confirmed, my positive hope letdown.

Over breakfast, too upset to eat, I asked Mr. Benny about the rumors, and he said, "I don't think they're true. His camper's parked right outside my shop and I've never seen him with a woman. The kid's cocky, sure enough, but awkward too, not much for conversation, bashful, seems really unsure of himself around women. Don't think he's got too much self-esteem in the romance department. He collects Pez dispensers and gum wrappers. He's a nerd, or haven't you noticed?"

No, I had not noticed. To me, he was so beautiful, I assumed women flocked to him.

"He's got a crooked ear."

"Not *crooked*, adorably bent," I defended.

"Atta girl!" Mr. Benny, whose mother had been a "sideshow freak," patted my hand, telling me he appreciated my accepting nature. "There's no reason to try to hide your feelings from the old boy—I've known from the start how this is going to map out."

"What do you mean?"

"When that kid walked into the Hut, I said to myself, 'Shom has changed his duds, but that's Shom alright.' He's not a sourpuss this time around, but boy, hidy, he's still a nerd. Why do you think I asked you to join me for ice cream in the first place? I know you can't stand ice cream."

I had not admitted my feelings about the young man to anyone, for fear of being embarrassed (a seventy-one-year-old widow in love with a twenty-eight-year-old dreamboat), but Mr. Benny, as was his kind way, encouraged me to pursue love again even with someone "out of my league."

But tests were continual in this world of vices.

"Ooh, this is too...too...fantastical. Isn't it?"

"All the good lovestories are. Let it be. It's your story, kid. You going to let someone else write it?"

Instead of listening to my dear friend's opinion, my insecurities chose to listen to gossipers. The next Saturday, against Elvis's warning, *Don't Be Cruel*, I failed another test of my character by ordering "Sonnet Zero," while handing the cardigan-sweatered ice cream man my own poem: a bitter verse about a lonesome old Lady who loved a barista, ordered coffee from him every Saturday just to hear him call out her name when her order was ready and see what special latte art he would make for her, until the Saturday she feigned being unable to speak, to see if he would remember her name—and he did not. All he had ever wanted was a good tip.

After digesting that on an overcast afternoon, a holiday afternoon, the ice cream man walked over with a sour face to my bench and set down a cup of ice hard on the table.

Frankie Lymon seemed to be taunting me: *Why Do Fools Fall in Love?*

However, the afternoon was eventful for Mr. Benny. He and Sammy bonded over mutual destiny. There would be no winter for them this year. The lovebirds had already arrived in spring in autumn, and their days would keep getting warmer. My old friend winked at me, saying he thought the sentences would keep getting warmer for me too, but he didn't know I had spoiled my chance at starring in another lovestory.

That cold windy night (promising snow), I asked Mr. Benny to drive me to the vintage camper parked outside the Hobby Hut. After whistling some old ditty, my friend said, "I wasn't supposed to tell you this, or maybe I was, really, but the kid mills about in the Hobby Hut a lot and he's been asking about you, the shy doll always with me at the ice cream truck."

"Asking what?"

"Like 'Is she your wife?' And 'She doesn't go out much, does she? Never seen her around town.'"

"What did you tell him?"

"I told him you're a sweet old-fashioned Lady, a widow, who loved her husband with a love that broke world records, but your eyes have some problems seeing, but you once loved going out with your husband, who had been my best buddy."

"You didn't tell him anything else about me or Sput?" I asked like a skeptic asking her friends if they had supplied any personal information to a psychic that could be used to dupe her.

"I didn't tell him anything else, except your name."

Even though my distrust assumed the widow's purse was the gigolo's next target, the information about him asking about me gave me more courage to knock on his camper's door.

The opened door let out the song *We Belong Together* from the private curtained trailer. He seemed surprised to see me standing there, and I was flattered, his acting as if my entering his life was a great big surprise gift. He was eating from a half gallon drum of

715

chocolate chip ice cream and dressed like a young man from the 1930s in an old-fashioned letterman sweater as black as molasses with a brown 'B' emblemed center; his corduroy pants matched the sweater; and his socked feet were cute and vulnerable.

"Hi," he said.

"Hiii." Ooh, you old fool, I scolded myself.

Welcoming me inside, helping me up the steps, the ice cream man was warm and inviting, and I was delighted by his strong arms supporting me. He and Mr. Benny waved at each other, but my friend did not stick around—he wanted Orkney and me to have together time.

Since the trailer was not connected to electricity, it was lit by a few candles, which created the ambience of a Renaissance oil painting. I felt the loneliness in the room. The camper smelled like sugar in the woods, and its beechwood was the color of a canoe. The radio operated on battery, and a small propane heater kept the camper warm. A nautical motif decorated the room; a ship wheel was mounted on the wall. Arthur and Lancelot, cat and dog, were snuggled in a blanket on a plush mat. The door opened onto the tiny kitchen area with a window covered in a Major League Baseball logo curtain. An acoustic guitar leaned against the unsanitary counter, which was being used like a workbench strewn with glues and paints for crafting model boats; thankfully, his ice cream truck was immaculately clean, though. To the right were padded booths around a small shiny lacquered table, cluttered with heavy books, cookie boxes, and a half-dozen box of cake doughnuts. To the left was a bed warmed in flannels that looked like the nightsky with constellations visible, the "universe" topped with white and black checkered blanket, pulled down far past the pillows, revealing the messy sheets; a 7-foot-by-3-foot universe, just the right size to share cozily with him on a cold night. Above the bed was a breadbox-shaped window; on the sill sat a lighter and a lit menorah.

"Happy Hanukkah," I offered.

"And to you." He noticed my cross necklace. "Do you celebrate Hanukkah?"

"Yes, as a tribute to my late husband."

He smiled one of those smiles that could have made The Grinch's heart three times bigger.

"Please, have a seat," he offered and escorted me to the apple-red booths, only one booth capable of being sat in, the other piled with gizmos, whatnot, metal toolbox, and clarinet. Maybe he never did have company, at least not at the table.

I sat by the window overlooking Holly Lane and all its memories of the New Year when I lost my husband. On the windowsill above the table were a solar-powered calculator and framed photos that showcased he did not have many people in his life that were special to him.

"This is a nice table," I said, offering something sweet like offering pie to someone new in the neighborhood.

"Thanks, I made it."

"Ooh, wow, it's lovely." I ran my gloved hand across its shine.

"I made a boat with a similar look. At my parent's house on the lake. I gave it to them as a wedding anniversary gift. I figured thirty years together merited a dinghy."

"That's incredible. The gift and the thirty years of marriage."

After clearing the opposite booth of clutter, he took a seat.

"How do you survive in this camper without it being connected to even water?"

"There are these things on Earth called streams." Same dry humor. "Streams are good for bathing, drinking, so are these." He held up a bottle of water.

"But it's freezing outside."

"There's a grand little hot water stream I found."

"Ooh? All these years in Biskatine and I've never heard about it."

"Yeah, well, it's far north of here." A "secret" refuge he was sharing with me. "I could show you sometime, that is, if you want."

"I'd…love that."

I nodded toward the puffy letter patched on his letterman sweater. "What does the 'B' stand for?"

"I don't know." He laughed. "I found it at an antique store and thought it was neat."

"I think it's neat too."

"Weird minds think alike." He smiled to say he had meant that as a compliment. "I've been letting it stand for butterscotch."

"Is that your favorite?"

"You know the darndest thing: butterscotch makes me feel nostalgic, nostalgic for an era I never even lived in."

"The 1950s?"

"The 30s, 40s, 50s, the early 60s, I feel drawn to those time periods."

"I can tell by your choice in wardrobe and music."

The radio played *Only You* in this *Harold & Maude* scene.

"I don't believe they were always 'the good old days,' but I can't stop my attraction to those eras, and for whatever reason, butterscotch brings about the yearning for those days in me."

Why did you sit this one out for so long, Sput? I wanted to ask but instead I asked, "Mr. Benny told me you collect chewing gum wrappers—from those eras?"

To answer, he picked up an old candy tin from the floor, popped it open and revealed stacks of gum wrappers. "Here, look at this. Clove gum from World War 2."

"I remember chewing that as a child!"

He seemed touched by my interest in the gum wrapper collection—maybe no one else had taken interest in his interests before. So, we talked about retro chewing gum varieties for a while.

I nodded toward the clarinet. "You play?"

"Badly." He set the candy tin back on the floor.

"And you play guitar too?"

He went over to the guitar, brought it back to the booth and played some of *Come On, Let's Go*, loudly over the radio's music. I adored listening to his voice sing, "Oh, pretty baby."

"You're really good."

He laughed. "You're just being nice." He started to rest the guitar against the wall, but, "You really think so?"

"Very good."

"How about this?" He played Little Richard's *Rip It Up*.

I clapped and gave a standing ovation.

He stood and bowed before setting the guitar against the wall, and it was fun being silly like this with a fellow.

"So, what do I owe the privilege of your visiting me? I get it was not to ask me what the 'B' stands for or to hear me butcher a guitar."

I disliked ruining the playful mood to ask, "Why did you serve me a cup of ice?"

He held up his ice cream tub of chocolate chip. "Would you like some? You deserve some for listening to me sing. I'll go to the truck and make you a butterscotch sundae. It'll only take a minute."

He set the ice cream gallon on the table and got up from the booth, away from my question?

"You can stay here and get acquainted with Arthur and Lancelot." He slipped his socked feet into loafers. "I need to find each of them a Guinevere, but particularly Arthur, since he doesn't have any hair and needs a mate to keep him warm."

He left the camper but I didn't want to—I wanted to stay for the rest of my life and use my last pages to learn everything about him. I looked at his books on the table, which showcased the same interests Sputnik had enjoyed but new ones too like scuba diving and fairy tales.

My distrust warned, "Mr. Benny probably told him about *Melt & Malt*, and the gigolo's playing up to the songwriter's widow with all that butterscotch talk."

He brought me the butterscotch sundae and sat at the booth opposite me, while blowing warmth into his cold hands.

"Thank you for coming back," I said, "with this." I held up the scrumptious sundae, warm in its glass dish, thanks to the melted butterscotch.

"It was my pleasure." Such old-fashioned manners. But he had learned from Mr. Benny I was an old-fashioned Lady.

"I love this song," he said, hearing The Drifters' *Under the Boardwalk*. "I want my life to move with this same mellow melody."

"Me too."

Hands somewhat warmed, he went back to eating chocolate chip ice cream.

"Have you had dinner?" I asked.

He tapped the box of doughnuts: dinner. "I can make ice cream but that's the extent of my culinary capabilities. Doughnuts, cereal, good for breakfast and dinner."

"Don't you get offers for homecooked meals during your travels?"

"Not unless I visit my mom in Vermont."

"I could make you a homecooked meal one of these nights you're in town, the neighborly thing to do, my momma would have said."

"I won't stop you."

I wondered if he saw me as the grandmotherly type offering to make him a meal.

"In fact, I'll marry you if you make me butterscotch pie, not that that's a selling point for you to make the pie: an offer for marriage from a two-bit ice cream man."

"Ooh, is that the only requirement you have for wife, that she make butterscotch pie?"

"That and she has to like clarinet, played badly, or else she'll suffer listening to me fumble my way through *Moonglow* all the time. She has to inspire me to create new ice cream flavors too. Oh, and she has to be *the one*, know what I mean?"

My seventy-one-year-old heart was Lindy Hopping all over the place like a schoolgirl's heart around her first love.

With my ailing eyes, I looked at the framed pictures, searching for any photo of a girl who might be special in his life. He thought I was looking at the calculator and said, "That's my video games. I play calculator. She has to be okay with me staying up all night fiddling with equations too."

I wanted to caress his bent ear, let him know it was adorable, let him know he was beautiful.

"You remind me of my late husband."

"He fiddled with equations?"

"He was a mathematician."

"I am too. I just don't get paid for my insights." I knew he was not lying about that; he had not put all the math bumper stickers on his camper to trick me into believing he liked mathematics, and he did not have all Sput's interests and hobbies just to fool me into accepting he was my husband reincarnated.

I ate another bite of the sundae before asking again, "Can you not tell me why you rudely served me ice this afternoon?"

"Because that is what you served me." He took from his pants pocket my poem, "Sonnet Zero." "Correctly titled. It contributes zero feeling to my heart. I feel bad for serving you the cup of ice. I've worried all afternoon and night I'd never see you again. But my feelings were hurt. Boys' feelings get hurt too. I thought I had finally found a town where I would not be a stranger to everyone. It hurt that *you* portrayed me in your poem as a man who was only kind for tips. Do I seem like someone who cares much for money or material belongings?" He handed "Sonnet Zero" back to me. "Please, write me a sweeter, truer story, Lumi—see, I remembered your name. Your friend, Ben, told me. My mom once told me the recipe for a good life includes sugar."

Mr. Benny had been right, the young man was awkward, unskilled in conversation, and that drew me to him even more.

He pointed to a frame on the windowsill. His mom was a happy-looking woman, an Israeli American research scientist in the Antarctic. His Chicago American dad had been stationed at the weather center, a fact Orkney told me after I asked, "Who's that?" about all the people in a big family photo, taken during a Hanukkah dinner. These days, his "nerdy" dad, who no one had liked in school, was a beloved friendly neighborhood weatherman in Vermont, where his parents lived close to Mount Snow in a two-hundred-year-old renovated farmhouse.

He asked about my parents, and I told him some of my backstory, and there was excitement in our voices, in the air—ooh, to be in this Boy Meets Girl story again.

"What kind of science is your mother in?" I asked.

"Planetary science."

"Are you interested in that subject too?"

"Sure, I had a telescope pointed out the window all through childhood, and I'd often search for meteorites in the Antarctic. A part of me thinks it would be great to be a sailor in the stars, but I have this feeling what I'm looking for in this life is to be found here on Earth. How about you?"

"I've always been in love with the nightsky, and when I was a very young girl, I prayed to meet a sailor from the stars."

"Will a sailor from the South Pole do?"

I was so touched by his sweetness, I did not know how to respond.

"How do you spend your days?" he asked.

I told him about my life of writing, and with his gestures, he asked if I wanted to exchange a sample of butterscotch sundae for chocolate chip ice cream, and I was flattered by his willingness to eat off the same spoon as me.

My face still blushed, I looked at the picture frames again and picked one up to be able to see it. "Who's that?" I asked about a sunglassed fellow who looked quite handsome in a white Navy uniform.

"That's me. I only framed the picture because of the large hump shape in the water. I swear Nessie was out that day." He laughed but he was serious. "I always wanted to be a sailor but realized after signing over my life to the military, I wanted to sail where *I* wanted, not where the Navy wanted, and I didn't particularly like entering new places on a warship. I wanted to sail in on a little tranquil boat and find a hammock somewhere quiet, where I could wonder if I had finally found home. I detest guns. What was I doing in the military? Eh, sometimes we make mistakes. Can't erase them. But we can try to incorporate our mistakes in a meaningful way into a life that makes sense. I learned a lot about sailing from the Navy. I also learned I'd rather be the captain of my own ship than lieutenant on another's ship. After my 'tour of duty' was up, so to speak, I left the military but kept the haircut." He rubbed the top of his buzzed hair. "Easier to manage."

I felt comfortable enough with him to ask, "Where do you want to sail?"

He put on the ice cream man's "sailor" cap. "Everywhere to find my home. I don't think this camper is big enough for me, two dogs, and two cats, and all these books."

Was he after me or Stargust Continued? Mr. Benny had told him I owned the land and patisserie.

"But I wonder if others are right, if I'm just a fool, wasting my life making ice cream." He took off the hat, set it like a paper boat on the windowsill. "Shouldn't a man be doing something more with his days than dishing out tutti frutti?"

"I think it's beautiful and noble your going from town to town bringing sweetness to inhabitants of all ages. Plus, you're an interesting character in the world's story—the ice cream man."

"You said that with so much conviction it added pounds to my determination to continue making ice cream for a living."

"I'm glad because I would not want to be in a world without an ice cream man."

"Here was the grandest of ice cream makers," he said, while pointing out an elderly gentleman in the family photo. His grandfather in Israel had owned an ice cream parlor, one of Orkney's favorite places to visit as a boy, but a few years earlier, the parlor had been bombed. The young man had salvaged the recipes from the ruins and carried on his family's sweet legacy.

Sensing my gloomy thoughts, he said, "I must prefer playing the game set to difficult level. Listen, cold things happen, but I focus on the ice cream. I get a feeling you do too, so please, write me another sonnet, this one with the caramel of endings. I believe God likes stories, and love stories are God's favorite."

Before he could sweet talk me into melting, I boldly asked about the rumors.

"I guess some women can't believe a fellow would be nice to them without getting something in return," he said. "Do you really think I'm a *gigolo*?"

I asked why he brought ice cream to old folks.

"For one, when you get older, you rarely choose the conversation topic. You're so lonesome you'll listen to what anyone has to say, especially your children or grandchildren—you just want them around, and they can talk about anything. So, I listen. And I serve something sweet. For two, I've always been drawn to older women. A Lady whose hands look loveliest pouring tea. A Lady who has suffered much and needs to know her flat chest is pretty and that which beats inside her chest is prettiest of all." The tone of his voice was not one for talking to his grandma. His eyes landed on my scenery and strolled around long and soft. "Would you like to dance? I love this song."

In the Still of the Night, he reached out to my hand, alone on the table.

He took off my coat, telling me I no longer needed that for warmth this night, and he offered me an embrace. We twirled in the warm oil painting of a camper. I had no hair, no breasts, and a frostbitten face, but he held me like I was a supermodel.

"Why are you crying?" he asked, slowing the dance to a stop.

My face rested against his aftershave-scented neck, where he felt my tears cascading across his pulse, quickly beating, flattering me that my closeness raised his heartrate.

"Someday when you're my age and a beautiful young gal is holding you like you're the most precious gem in the universe, you'll understand why I'm crying."

"Lumi, we should stop pretending we don't recognize each other when we recognized our bond from glance one." With his warm

725

fingers, he wiped tears from my face. "Do you know what Bashert means? Destiny. Soulmate. Who I am seeking on my journeys from town to town."

"You're trying to steal my heart?"

"Steal it? No. *Accept* it. Trust me. Trust is a crucial ingredient for what we're trying to create."

"You'll have to forgive me for 'Sonnet Zero' and for being so skeptical, but it's hard to trust in a world of thieves."

But I did not want to sulk in distrust like The Frostbitten Widow. I did not want to fail this test, so I choose to write this line in my culminating lifestory:

"I do have a sweeter story to share with you, Orkney."

"I felt so."

We resumed our dance.

"Our first dance," he said. "What are you going to title that?"

"*Autumn Ice Cream.*"

"Do you know what you get for giving me your heart? My heart. It's not refurbished or anything. No one's ever wanted it. It's brand new for you to try out."

"I'll be gentle with your heart, young man, but you must know you'll suffer some heart frosts if you stay with me, because I'm somewhat older than you, and I'll be leaving the story a long time before you, and if you really have feelings for me, my departure will take some of your heart with me when I go."

"I'll worry about that in another forty years."

"Forty years! And I thought I was optimistic. You do know I'm almost three times your age, not quite but close? But if I do get *forty* more chapters, I'd like them to be written with you."

"Forty chapters of suffering my bad jazz."

"Forty chapters of you suffering as my seeing eye companion. You sure you want that?"

"I'll be as friendly and frisky and faithful as your golden retriever." He demonstrated the friskiness by whirling me around.

"You can't possibly be attracted to me."

"You can't possibly be attracted to me, but here it is—attraction—drawing us closer to this."

My lips met his softly, after waiting over half a century, a kiss so deep it reminded us we have souls.

In after-kiss wooziness, we sat in the booth, where he parted the window's curtain, so we could admire the scenery of our storybook town, as tinseled and cozy as ever in snowfall.

"God, I love snow," he said, ecstatic with life. "I'm not saying the Lord's name in vain; I'm telling God, I love snow, thanks for it."

I kissed his adorably bent ear before stepping out of the booth.

"Hey, you're already leaving me?"

Now it was time to confront my guilt. I sat back in the booth and gave my sweet boy a long warm hug. "I was just going to bake something for you."

"Chocolate croissants, strawberries, something romantic like that?"

"Be patient. You'll have to come over to Bashert to get your dessert, because I want you to feel how nice it feels to be served something sweet at the old-fashioned ice cream truck."

At Bashert's open window, I gave Ork my homemade treat, which answered the question he had waited many years for an answer to: "What does 'a heart whose love is innocent' taste like?"

Peppermint Kisses

T hen what happened?

The Snowflake Gal kept seeing the snowflakes.

And she kept dancing in the snowflakes.

And she kept tasting peppermint in snow. For the wind was cold but love's sweetness was mint in the coldness.

Although the goal of the Nazis' hatred was to erase her from the world's story, her goodest heart was not erased from literature, thanks to the one who loved her, Gershom, who kept her story inside him.

And when her time in the snow cycle came to transform, it wasn't long before she beheld her beloved Gershom again in the Stargust wheatfield, and they bonded again on an any-ol'-day hayride turned miraculous by their meeting. And they married, and on the honeymoon night when her soul's mate allowed his grayed heart to see the snowflakes again, on the night of the once-in-a-lifetime Christmas Hanukkah comet, she saw in his eyes that he knew who she was, that he had always known. And after Gershom's time came in the snow cycle to transform, the ice cream man who turned coldness into sweetness met his love again at the ice cream truck converted into a fairy tale carriage by love so good and powerful how could it not be viewed as magical? And her belief in happily ever after, as battered as it was by the pessimistic world, still gave the widow courage to pursue romance again. And the lovers viewed meaning in their departures as tests to their faith in reunion. Each other's existence upheld the exclamation point in their lifestory, their love the Holy Grail. And in renewing their wedding vows in their treasured forest, they made each other feel beautiful, forgiven, and wanted in the world's oft unwelcoming story. Their unbreakable bond fully brought forth the twinkles in their hearts on the night of the second-in-a-lifetime comet, when bitterness left bittersweet. And ooooh, every moment kept getting sweeter and sweeter, as they celebrated the holidays once more in Stargust Continued, where he polished her star to shine with Heavenly light to be able to write this very sentence confirming love's eternalness.

"Even though there is no such thing as a happy *ending*," Moon-Moon once taught, "the difference between a lovestory and every other story is a lovestory never has The End, just moments of 'to be continued.'"

After more glorious seasons with my love, writing more and more sweet chapters, when this life began to feel like the past, I, *She*, with blush-pink heart, knew the answer to my momma's question of how I would bring bunnies into the boy's life—I would *write* about the soft pretty wonders in a story, our lovestory in pink ink. I would suffer all the rocks skeptics throw, and someday, I will write another story, another lovestory, because those are the stories we Romantics like to write.

And, someday, when winter wilts the flowers again, I will walk an icy path with Root toward the last page of this book, knowing the Wicked Stepmother has the power to write The End for Cinderella by a fluke accident in ice, or by a madman waiting in the woodland to hunt, on the getaway from stealing a harp, but I will Write Thus! Hildegard and I, Champions of the Living Light. Walking beside the old moon, the way I had done as a child when I had walked onwards to see the snowflakes but had slipped into the icy pond and lost my face to frostbite, but onwards I will walk to our forest. I will open my husband's urn and release the Alaskan boy to the woodlands he cherished. And The Snowflake Gal will see snowflakes, not ashes, but snowflakes. Snowflakes blanketing mountains, mansions, and mobile homes equally, snowflakes all across the nightsky like stars, the biggest most beautiful snowflake of all, the one he created, until the snowflakes become warm, warmer, colorful flowers in springtime, in summertime. And in the warm sunshiny goodness, I will hear, "Sweetyheart," and I will run to his open heart, and to all those I love in their brightest forms, Moon-Moon waiting for her Lumi with a big momma bear hug, and pup Mullybiski, and my molasses-haired aeronaut, and Bubbe and Bow, and all our loved ones who were incapable of being erased...and it will not be a dream but an awakening to the truth: Coleridge's Flower from Heaven is real and planted inside each storyteller, who if they listen to intuition will feel it fluttering in love and love and love...ever after...truth unable to be stolen...the writer continues writing...as flowers continue to bloom in graveyards and death camps...

No one on Earth can say with certainty if a snowflake has a purpose, but I see one, yet I won't tell you what it is, because you must see purpose for yourself.

Ooh, yes, I want that to be my thesis—to make my real father proud.

To be continued...

Thank You

God, for strength and time to finish this story

My "Sputnik," for stars in the daytime sky, without whom this story could not have been written

The millions who were killed by Nazis, for reminding us never to forget your stories

My family, for support that affords me time to write

Joy, for being that and the greatest mother ever and an overall force of goodness in this world (all my love and gratitude is yours forever, "Budget")

Dad, for all those Dad tasks

My forever huckleberry friends, Mully and Biski, and MC, John, Grace, Pepper, Colby, both Mr. Trees, Chloe, Debby Moonbeam, Debby B., Tonia, Heather, Cameron, Buster, Gramps, Bud, Max, Spot, Tito, Tito Jr., "Cujo," Kenny, the Hampies, "Pancakes," T's, J, MOTF, and the old Moon, for friendship

Guardian angels (and the ones on Earth like Karen Morris, Karen Dickerson, and Teri Ann Ramey-Meeks), for help, healing, guidance, and encouragement

Walter, for starry nights, colas, and sweet caramels for the shy girl in the planetarium who did not believe any man would ever want to show her the stars, the girl who never said, "Thank you," so is saying so now (and I sometimes wonder about the waffles)

Heroes, for standards

Carl Sagan, for showing us all the stars like they were brand new

Eva Mozes Kor, for courage, inspiration, for telling your story and your mother's story, and for being a lighter of purpose for so many people (extra hugs and kisses for you)

Richard Bach, for Stormy & Strobe and reminding us all that stories don't need bad guys to be good

Viktor Frankl, for reminding us to always search for meaning

Everyone who writes kindness, sweetness, and romance into the world's story, for doing just that

Hot chocolate and other goodies, for being just that

The kind gentleman at the grocers, the sweet fella at the ice cream shoppe, the nice Lady in the cafeteria, and all the other "part-time angels" who smiled at me on days when I really needed to be smiled at and reminded I, too, could be liked, welcomed, and accepted on this planet

Anyone whose name my scattered brain forgot to mention but my heart will remember forever

Pi, for being built into this awe-inspiring universe and giving us all something to ponder in life's story

Romance comics, for being fun despite their superficiality and chauvinism

The reader, for reading this very long story to this last word

Illustrations

All illustrations in this book are in the public domain, except where noted.

Illustrations by chapter

Peppermint

1. Peppermint and chocolate candies.   Vintage recipe book.   c. 1903.

2. *My Love Story*.   No. 3.   Atlas Comics.   August 1956.

3. "I want someone different."   *Space Man*.   Dell Comics.   1962. Mixed with illustration from "My White Knight."   *Romantic Secrets*. Charlton Comics.   c. 1950s.

4. Spacecraft.   "Prisoners on Solar."   *Space Action*.   No. 1.   June 1952.

5. Knight and Lady.   "My White Knight."   *Romantic Secrets*.   Charlton Comics.   c. 1950s.

6. Pink carnation.   Pierre-Joseph Redouté.   c. 1830

7. Hospital illustration 1.   "I Couldn't Go Back to Him."   *All Romances*. No. 1.   A.A. Wyn, Inc.   August 1949.

8. Hospital illustration 2.   "I Couldn't Go Back to Him."   *All Romances*. No. 1.   A.A. Wyn, Inc.   August 1949.

9. Daydreaming.   "My White Knight."   *Romantic Secrets*.   Charlton Comics.   c. 1950s.

Apple & Cherry

1. Apples and bicycle.   Vintage recipe book.   c. Early 20th century.

2. Peter Rabbit.   *The Tale of Peter Rabbit*.   Written and illustrated by Beatrix Potter.   First edition.   Frederick Wayne & Co.   1902.

3. Chocolate pie.   Vintage recipe book.   c. Early 20th century.

4. Strawberries.   Vintage gardening catalogue.   c. Early 20th century.

5. Peter Rabbit.   *The Tale of Peter Rabbit*.   Written and illustrated by Beatrix Potter.   First edition.   Frederick Wayne & Co.   1902.

6. Little Goody Two-Shoes.   *The History of Little Goody Two-Shoes*. Author unknown.   John Newbery.   1765.

7. Knight.   *The Story of King Arthur and His Knights*.   Howard Pyle. First edition.   Charles Scribner's Sons.   1903.

8. Katherine Stinson.   Bain News Service, publisher.   c. 1910.

9. Root and Mullybiski and Write Thus pillow.   Rakesh Sharma. Copyright © 2021 the author.

10. *First Love*.   No. 48.   January 1948.

11. *Rocket Kelly*.   c. 1940s

12. *In the Meadow*.   Pierre-Auguste Renoir.   c. 1888-1892.

Mint Chocolate

1. Mint chocolate hearts.   *Chocolate and Cocoa and Homemade Candy Recipes*. Walter Baker and Co.   1911.

2. *Wanderer Above the Sea of Fog*.   Caspar David Friedrich.   c. 1818.

3. *All Romances*.   No. 1.   A.A. Wyn, Inc.   August 1949.

4. *Little Women*.   Written by Louisa May Alcott, illustrated by Frank Merrill.   1868.

5. Sojourner Truth.   1870.

6. Susan B. Anthony.   1890.

7. Ad.   A.A. Wyn, Inc.   August 1949.

8. *Science Leads the Way*.   A.C. Gilbert Company.   1959.

9. Elegant shoes.   Vintage clothing catalogue.   c. 1950s.

Hot Chocolate

1. Hot chocolate.   Vintage recipe book.   c. Early 20th century.

2. Hairdo.   Vintage romance comic.

3. Pastries.   *Balanced Daily Diet*.   Janet Hill Magazine.   1921.

4. "Perfect day for a picnic."   "My White Knight."   *Romantic Secrets*. Charlton Comics.   c. 1950s.

Molasses

1. *Love Journal*.   No. 24.   May 1954.

2. *Love at First Sight*.   David McKay Publications.   c. 1940s.

3. "Orchids from My Beloved."   *Boy Meets Girl*.   No. 1.   Lev Gleason Publications, Inc.   February 1950.

4. "Our analysis was correct."   *Cinderella Love*.   No. 27.   September 1955.

5. *Boy Meets Girl*.   No. 1.   Lev Gleason Publications, Inc.   February 1950.

6. *The Beyond*.   No. 27.   David McKay Publications.   September 1953.

7. "I Aimed Too High."   *Brides Romances*.   No. 15.   December 1955.

8. Fellow in fedora.   *All Romances*.   No. 1.   A.A. Wyn, Inc.   August 1949.

9. "Mysterious young god."   *All Romances*.   No. 1.   A.A. Wyn, Inc. August 1949.

10. Toolbox.   Rakesh Sharma.   Copyright © 2021 the author.

11. "Are You Really in Love?"   No. 1.   Lev Gleason Publications, Inc. February 1950.

12. Restless sleep.   "Honeymoon Spotlight."   *Boy Meets Girl*.   No. 1. Lev Gleason Publications, Inc.   February 1950.

13. "Oh, what will I do?"   *Boy Meets Girl*.   No. 3.   Lev Gleason Publications, Inc.   June 1950.

14. *Boy Meets Girl*.   No. 3.   Lev Gleason Publications, Inc.   June 1950.

15. *Love Romances*.   No. 61.   c. 1950s.

16. Woe is me.   Vintage romance comic.

17. On the phone (two illustrations).   Vintage romance comic.

18. Fellow on the phone.   "Orchids from My Beloved." *Boy Meets Girl.*   No. 1.   Lev Gleason Publications, Inc.   February 1950.

19. *Brides Romances.*   No. 20.   c. 1950s.

20. "He's much too nice for her."   "A Record-Breaking Affair." *Cinderella Love.*   No. 27.   September 1955.

21. "I'd better nip this in the bud."   "A Record-Breaking Affair." *Cinderella Love.*   No. 27.   September 1955.

Cream Cocoa

1. Cocoa cakes.   Vintage recipe book.   c. Early 20th century.

2. Lingering in bed.   "Sister Without Scruples." *All Romances.*   No. 1. A.A. Wyn, Inc.   August 1949.

3. Turtle doves.   *The Birds of America.*   John James Audubon.   c. 1827-1838.

4. Dress ad.   Vintage romance comic.

5. "You're just about the loveliest creature I've ever known."   "SOS - Love in Distress." *Love Journal.*   No. 24.   May 1954.

6. *Romantic Love.*   No. 10.   c. 1950s.

7. Hot fudge sundae.   Vintage recipe book.   c. Early 20th century.

Sweet Tea & Scones

1. Tea set.   Vintage recipe book.   c. Early 20th century.

2. Mr. Toad.   *The Wind in the Willows* by Kenneth Grahame.   1908.

Gingerbread & Candy Canes

1. Gingerbread camper.   Rakesh Sharma.   Copyright © 2021 the author.

Soft Apple Cider

1. "And their love was not infatuation." "Return to Romance." *Romantic Secrets*. No. 30. Dec. 1960.

2. Kiss in moonlight. "Return to Romance." *Romantic Secrets*. No. 30. Dec. 1960.

Cold Lager

1. Crying in bed. "Heartbreak on My Honeymoon." *Boy Meets Girl*. No. 1. Lev Gleason Publications, Inc. February 1950.

2. "Come in." "Heartbreak on My Honeymoon." *Boy Meets Girl*. No. 1. Lev Gleason Publications, Inc. February 1950.

Chocolate-Covered Cherry Cordials

1. Chocolate candies. Vintage recipe book. c. Early 20th century.

2. *Romantic Secrets*. No. 30. Dec. 1960.

Apricot Rugelach

1. Snuggly morning. "Honeymoon Spotlight." *Boy Meets Girl*. No. 1. Lev Gleason Publications, Inc. February 1950.

2. "This is the way it should be, darling." "Honeymoon Spotlight." *Boy Meets Girl*. No. 1. Lev Gleason Publications, Inc. February 1950.

3. Dancing. "Heartbreak on My Honeymoon." *Boy Meets Girl*. No. 1. Lev Gleason Publications, Inc. February 1950.

Snickerdoodles

1. "What a beautiful morning." "Perhaps to Dream." *Boy Meets Girl*. No. 3. Lev Gleason Publications, Inc. June 1950.

Strawberry Jelly Doughnuts

1. A break to kiss. Vintage romance comic. c. 1950s.

2. Grouch. Vintage romance comic. c. 1950s.

3. *Romantic Adventures.*   No. 76.   c. 1950s.

4. Sweet fella.   "Orchids from My Beloved."   *Boy Meets Girl.*   No. 1. Lev Gleason Publications, Inc.   February 1950.

5. Favorite pastime.   Vintage romance comic.   c. 1950s.

Pancakes & Syrup

1. Pancakes.   Vintage recipe book.   c. Early 20th century.

2. Hair brushing.   Vintage romance comic.   c. 1950s.

Fruitcake

1. Fruitcake.   Vintage recipe book.   c. Early 20th century.

Sorghum

1. Sorghum.   Vintage botanical book.   c. Early 20th century.

Milky Ways

1. "Winter never seemed so warm."   "Return to Romance."   *Romantic Secrets.*   No. 30.   Dec. 1960.

2. Doughnuts.   Vintage recipe book.   c. Early 20th century.

Icing

1. Buttercream cake.   Vintage recipe book.   c. Early 20th century.

2. Neapolitan ice cream.   Vintage recipe book.   c. Early 20th century.

Butterscotch

1. "I love you so much, darling."   *Romantic Secrets.*   No. 30.   Dec. 1960.

2. Butterscotch sundae.   Vintage recipe book.   c. Early 20th century.

3. Dancing in the New Year.   *Boy Meets Girl.*   No. 1.   Lev Gleason Publications, Inc.   February 1950.

4. Happy New Year! *Romantic Secrets*. No. 30. Dec. 1960.

Autumn Ice Cream

1. Sundae. Vintage recipe book. c. Early 20th century.

Peppermint Kisses

1. "The end?" Illustration retouched. "I'll Wait for You." *Boy Meets Girl*. No. 1. Lev Gleason Publications, Inc. February 1950.

Last illustration: *Cinderella Love*. No. 27. September 1955.

740

www.ingramcontent.com/pod-product-compliance
Lightning Source LLC
Chambersburg PA
CBHW050117030726
47505CB00007B/1911